INTO THE WOODS

INTO THE WOODS

WOODS

TALES FROM THE HOLLOWS AND BEYOND

KIM HARRISON

HARPER Voyager

An Imprint of HarperCollinsPublishers

Page 517 serves as a continuation of the copyright page.

INTO THE WOODS. Copyright © 2012 by Kim Harrison. All rights reserved. Printed in the United States of America. No part of this book may be used or reproduced in any manner whatsoever without written permission except in the case of brief quotations embodied in critical articles and reviews. For information, address HarperCollins Publishers, 195 Broadway, New York, NY 10007.

HarperCollins books may be purchased for educational, business, or sales promotional use. For information, please e-mail the Special Markets Department, at SPsales@harpercollins.com.

A hardcover edition of this book was published in 2012 by Harper Voyager, an imprint of HarperCollins Publishers.

FIRST HARPER VOYAGER PAPERBACK EDITION PUBLISHED 2013.

Designed by Shannon Plunkett

Library of Congress Cataloging-in-Publication Data has been applied for.

ISBN 978-0-06-219763-4

HB 07.20.2021

To the readers. This one is for you.

CONTENTS

THE HOLLOWS

BEYOND THE HOLLOWS

THE HOLLOWS

THE HOLLOWS

THE BESPELLED

Al is one of my more favorite characters in the Hollows. I never expected him to be anything other than the Big-Bad-Ugly—fun to hate, but nothing more. It was a surprise when Rachel began to understand him, and even more of a shock when Al responded not just by showing a softer side, but by lifting the veil on his past as well. "The Bespelled" was first published at the end of the mass market edition of The Outlaw Demon Wails, *and it shows Al in his earlier mind-set of use and abuse. But the appearance of the blue butterflies gives evidence that even before Al met Rachel, he was beginning to find himself lacking and was looking for more.*

Paperwork, Algaliarept thought in resignation as he blew gently upon the ledger book to dry the ink faster. *Ink that wasn't actually ink, paper that had never been wood*, he thought as he breathed deep for the cloying scent of blood. Though blood made a sublimely binding document, the nature of it tended to slow everything down. Even so, if he could pass this part of his job to a subordinate, he wouldn't. The knowledge of who owed him and what was worth a lot in the demon's world, and familiars were known for their loose tongues until you cut them out. It was a practice Algaliarept frowned upon. Most of his brethren were bloody plebeians. Removing a familiar's tongue completely ruined the nuances of their pleas for mercy.

Resettling himself at his small but elegantly carved desk, Algaliarept reached into a lidded stone box, dipping a tiny silver spoon for his Brimstone and letting the drug slowly melt on his tongue. The small tap of the spoon as he replaced it jolted through him like fire, and closing his eyes he breathed, pulling the air into him over the ashy blackness to bring a hundred faint smells to him as the Brimstone heightened his senses and took his mind into a higher state.

Paperwork has got to be the biggest pain in the ass, he thought as he hung for a moment in the mild euphoria. But as his eyes opened he gazed upon his opulent quarters—the walls draped with dark silk, vases painted with beautifully erotic bodies, richly shadowed corners with cushions and fragrant oil lamps, and underfoot, the rug showing a winding dragon devouring its smaller kin—Algaliarept knew he'd have it no other way. Everything about him would be missing if he worked for another.

The East was where the world's intelligence currently resided, and he quite liked the Asian people, even if they called him a dragon there, and expected him to breathe fire. Apart from the elves making a last stand in the mountains of Europe, Asia was the only real culture in the world right now—thanks to his efforts, mostly. One must create what another will covet.

Dipping his quill, Algaliarept bent to his work again, his brow tightening for no reason he could fathom. He was a dealer in flesh and seducer of souls, skilled in training people in the dark arts enough to make them marketable, then abducting them when they made a mistake in order to sell them to his peers into an extended lifetime of servitude. He was so good at it that he had achieved a status that rivaled the highest court members, reached on his own merits and owed to no one. Yet, as his quill scratched out the interest of a particularly long-running debt, he finally acknowledged the source of his growing feeling of dissatisfaction.

Where he'd once relished watching a potential familiar agonize over wanting more and thinking he was smart enough to evade the final outcome, now there was only an odd sensation of jealousy. Though doomed, the familiar was feeling *something*. Algaliarept, however, was feeling nothing. He'd lost the joy, and the chase had become too easy.

Another page tallied, and Algaliarept reached for a second spoonful of Brimstone while the red ink dried and turned black. As his silver spoon dipped, his moving reflection caught his attention and he hesitated, meeting his own gaze in the gilded mirror upon the desk. Tired, goat-slitted eyes stared back at him. They narrowed, and with a feeling of unhappiness, he watched himself let the black ash sift back into the box. If he wanted sensation, he should go out and take it, not sip it from dust. *Perhaps,* Algaliarept thought darkly as he touched his script to see if it was dry, *it was time to retire for a time.* Begin removing his name from the texts in reality to leave just enough for the occasional summoning instead of the numerous summons he fielded. He was weary of mediocre dealings and fast satisfaction that gave him nothing lasting. He wanted . . . more. Mood soured, he bent to his work. *This can't be all there is,* he thought as he tried to lose himself in the beauty of wants and needs, supply and demand.

Intent on his work, the soft tickling in his nose almost went unnoticed until he sneezed. His hand slammed down on the open Brimstone container, saving it. Shocked, he stared at his door, tasting the air and trying to decide where the sun had just fallen. Someone was summoning him. *Again,* he thought with a sigh, until he realized where it was likely coming from. *Europe?*

Algaliarept's gaze returned to the mirror, and his goat-slitted, red eyes glinted. A slow smile came over his creased face. Inside, a quiver of excitement coursed through him, more heady than Brimstone. It had to be Ceridwen. She was the only one who knew his name across that continent, the only one who could call him there. *Three months,* he thought, his excitement growing as he gazed into the mirror while his features became younger and more refined, taking on the strong jaw she was accustomed to. *I knew she couldn't resist.*

Humming a snippet of music that had never been penned, he shook out his sleeves, watching them turn from the casual silk kimono he appreciated into a stuffy European crushed green velvet coat. Lace appeared at his throat, and his hair slicked itself back. His ruddy complexion lightened, and white gloves appeared. He would be pleasing to her sight even if he thought the outfit ugly. Until she stopped three months ago without warning, Ceridwen Merriam Dulciate had summoned him every week for seven years. He was nothing if not patient, but the lapse did not bode well. That he was excited for the first time in as many weeks did not escape him, but Ceri was special. She was the most devious, intelligent, careful woman he had tried to snag in almost three hundred years, and he never knew what she was going to do.

Art, he realized suddenly. Ceri was art where everyone else was work. Was that where his dissatisfaction was coming from? Was it time to stop simply working and begin making art? But to do that, he needed the canvas before him. It was time to bring her home. If he could.

Standing, he sneezed again, more delicately this time. His thoughts went to a seldom-used curse and he winced, searching his mind until he remembered. "*Rosa flavus*," he whispered, shivering as the unusual curse shifted over him to leave a yellow rose in his grip. Damn his dame, this felt good. He'd bring her home this time. He was anxious to begin.

"Zoe!" he shouted, knowing the three-fingered man-whore would hear him. "I'm out! Take my calls!" And with no more thought, he allowed the summons to pull him from the splash of displaced time he existed in to reality.

He traveled by ley lines, the same force of nature that kept the drop of time he existed in from vanishing. The shock of the line melting him into a thought was a familiar ache, and it was with a sly confidence that he found himself drawn to a spot far up in the mountains of Europe. He never knew for sure where he was going until he got there, but this? Algaliarept smiled as the clean mountain air filled his lungs as he reformed, the stench of burnt amber that clung to him being replaced by the honest smell of horses and cultivated flowers. This was pleasant.

The hum of a binding circle grew oppressive, and Algaliarept found himself in a dusky garden surrounded by dark pines, the sky above them still holding the fading light of the sunset and fluttering blue butterflies. The circle holding him was defined by semi-precious stones inlaid in crushed gravel. Through the haze of energy trapping him came the sound of running water and birds. Music. A small orchestra. Something was badly off. And when his eyes went to the full moon rising above the fragrant pines, his smile faded in a wash of worry. *Is the bitch getting married?*

A soft clearing of a throat turned him around.

"Ceridwen," he said, allowing a sliver of his annoyance to color his words, then he hesitated. She was absolutely stunning in the puddle of nearby lamp light with blue butterflies flitting about her. "Ceri, you are exceptionally lovely." *Damn it to the two worlds colliding, she's getting married. Directly.* He had tarried too long. It was tonight, or never.

The slight, fair-haired woman before him modestly ran her hands over her clearly wedding garb, white and trimmed with her family's colors of maroon and gold. Her fair hair was piled atop her head but for a few strands artfully drawn down. She was pale and lithe, having wide green eyes and a narrow chin. If for no more than that, she would be unique among the predominantly Asian women populating the demon familiar market and bring a high price. But that wasn't why he'd courted her so carefully.

Though her eyes were cast down demurely, she knew she was beautiful, reveled in it, vainly believed it was why he was attentive and kind to her. He'd kept her oblivious to the real reason he stayed pliant to her summons and demands for knowledge when anyone else would have been met with anger and threats years ago for the audacity of being too clever to be caught and therefore was wasting his time. She carried the surname Dulciate. It was one of the most desired familiar names in the demon realm, though if the castle behind her was the level to which the elves had fallen to, there wasn't much left to take revenge upon. Even if she were ugly, he could make more from her then seven skilled familiars. And she was skilled, thanks to him—infuriatingly clever and careful. *Hopefully not careful enough*, he thought, his hands clenching in their white-gloved preciseness.

Behind her on the cropped grass, a round stone table was strewn with her golden tarot cards, clear evidence that she was upset. She knew he thought little of them, having spent summers striving to break her from their grip, failing even when he proved them false as she sought counsel from a power he didn't believe in. Rising beyond the garden was the gray-walled castle of her family. It was pitiful by the Asian standards he appreciated, but it was the pinnacle of society in this superstitious, cultural wasteland. Where he'd created a society in Asia with science, rivals had inundated Europe with superstition in their attempts to match his gains.

From the balcony walkway, clusters of overdressed women kept watch as the darkness took hold and the butterflies dwindled. As a member of the elven royal house, it was Ceridwen's right to summon demons, expected and encouraged until she took a husband. Tradition dictated that the ruling personage in waiting was to learn all they could of the arcane. It was just as expected that her station would grant her the privacy to do it wherever she wanted. So her fluttering ladies waited in the torchlight, holding Ceri's little dogs as they yapped furiously at him. They knew the danger, and it was a delicious irony that no one listened to them.

Looking closer, he gauged her aura to see if a rival had been poaching on his claim which could explain the three-month lapse. Ceridwen's aura, though, was as he had left it; the original bright blue marred by a light black coating of demon smut that was all his own.

Seeing the yellow rose in his hand, a heavy tear brimmed in her deep green eyes, unusual for the emotionally balanced woman. Her head bowed as it fell, but pride brought it up again immediately. Chin high, she looked behind her to her tarot cards, beginning to cry all the more. Her hands stayed stoically at her sides, fisted as she refused to wipe her tears away.

Hell and damnation, I'm too late, Algaliarept thought, taking an angry step forward only to stop short as the barrier she'd summoned him behind hummed a familiar, vicious warning. "Love, what's wrong?" he asked, pretending to be oblivious, though inside, he was scrambling. He had not labored seven years only to lose a Dulciate elf to marriage! "Why are you crying? I've told you not to look at the cards. They only lie."

Crestfallen, Ceri turned away, but her pale fingers straying to touch her tarot cards were still bare of gold, and Algaliarept felt a glimmer of hope. "I'm not your love," she said, voice quavering as she turned the lovers card face down. "And you're the liar."

"I've never lied to you," he said. Damn it, he was not going to lose her to some inane cards! Frustrated, Algaliarept nudged a booted toe at the circle's seam to feel her power repel him. Never had she made a mistake in its construction. It both infuriated him and kept him coming back, week after week, year after year, and now, because of it, he was going to lose her.

"I had to tell you good-bye," she continued as if he hadn't spoken, pleading as she fingered a gold-edged card. "They told me not too, that with the responsibility of marriage, I must sever all ties to the arcane."

Agitated, he gripped his rose until a thorn pierced his glove and the pain stifled his fidgeting. "Good-bye, my love?" He had to make her control lapse—if only for an instant.

"I'm not your love," she whispered, but her gaze was upon the cards. There were no others like them, having been painted by a second-rate Italian painter who had attempted to put the royal family within the artwork. It hadn't pleased him to find out Ceri was on the death card, being pulled away by a demon.

"Ceri, you *are* my unrequited love," he said earnestly, testing the strength of her circle until the stench of burning leather from his shoes drove him back. "Tell me you've not wed. Not yet." He knew she wasn't, but to make her say the words would make her think.

"No." It was a thin whisper, and the young woman sniffed, holding a hand out for a tiny blue butterfly seeking warmth in the fading day. He'd seen them only once before in this profusion, and it was likely the wedding had been planned around the beautiful, fragile creatures. But butterflies like carrion as much as flowers, battlefields as much as gardens.

Algaliarept looked at the yellow rose in his grip, his thoughts lifting and falling as the music rose high in celebration. Fast. He had to work fast. "Why do you hurt me?" he said, squeezing his hand until a drop of blood fell upon it, turning the entire rose a bright scarlet. "You summon me only to spurn me?" He dropped the rose, and she blanched, eyes rising to his bloodied glove. "To say good-bye?" he accused, allowing his anger to color his voice. "Do our seven years mean nothing to you? The skills I've taught you, the music, ideas that we shared from across the sea? It all means nothing? Was I just your demon, your pet? Nothing more?"

Distressed, Ceridwen faced him, the butterfly forgotten. "Talk not to me of love. They are naught but pretty words to trap me," she whispered, but under her misery was a frantic need he had yet to figure out. There was more here than she was saying. Could she be unhappy about the marriage? Was this the key to making her control lapse?

"As you trapped me!" he exclaimed, jerking his hand back when he intentionally burned himself on the barrier between them. Excitement was a pulse when she reached out, concern for him showing briefly. "Ceridwen," he pleaded, breath coming faster, "I watched you grow from a shy, skittish colt to a rightfully proud woman, fiery and poised to take responsibility for your people. I was there when all others grew distant, jealous of your skills. I didn't expect to grow fond of you. Have I not been a gentleman? Have I not bent to your every whim?"

Green eyes deep with misery met his. "You have. Because you're caught in my circle."

"I would regardless!" he said violently, then looked to the darkening sky as if seeking words, though what he was going to say he'd said to untold others. This time, though, he meant them. "Ceri, you are so rare, and you don't even know it. You are so beyond anyone here because of what I've shared with you. The man who waits for you . . . He cannot meet your intellectual needs. When I hear your summons, my heart leaps, and I come directly, a willing slave."

"I know."

It was a faint affirmation, and Algaliarept's pulse raced. This was it. This was the way to her downfall. She didn't desire her husband. "And now you'll abandon me," he whispered.

"No," she protested, but they both knew tradition dictated otherwise.

"You're going to wed," he stated, and she shook her head, desperate as her tiny feet tapped the flagstones, coming closer in her need to deny it.

"That I'm wed doesn't mean I won't summon you. Our talks can continue."

Feigning dejection, he turned his back on her, all but oblivious to the manicured gardens going dark and damp. "You will abandon me," he said, chin high as he probed the circle to find it still perfect. Though he was a demon and could crush an army with a single word, such was the strength of a summons that a simple circle could bind him. He had to upset her enough such that she would make a mistake and he could break it. Until then, nothing but sound and air could get through.

Taking a ragged breath, he dropped his head, his hands still laced behind him. "You will begin with all good intentions," he said, his voice flat. "But you'll summon me into underground rooms where no one can see, and our time together once open and celebrated will become brief snatches circled by guilt instead of precious stones. Soon you will call me less and less, shame dictating that your heart be ruled over by your head, your responsibilities." He took a breath, turning his tone thin. "Let me go. I can't bear seeing what we shared abandoned bit by bit. Make of my heart a clean death."

The clatter of the gravel sliding beneath her shoes sparked through him like lightning, and he grit his teeth to hide his anticipation. One tiny stone, knocked out of place, would do it. "I would not do that," she protested as she faced him, a gray shadow against the dark vegetation.

Refusing to meet her gaze because he knew it would hurt her, he looked at the moon, seeing a few lone butterflies daring the dark to find a mate. Crickets chirped as the music from the castle dissolved into polite applause. "Marry him if you will," he said stoically. "I'll forever come if you call, but I'll be but a broken shadow. You can command my body, but you cannot command my heart." He looked at her now, finding she was clutching a golden card to her chest, hiding it. "Do you love him?" he asked bluntly, already knowing the answer in her frantic expression.

She said nothing as torchlight shined upon her tears.

"Does he make your heart beat fast?" Algaliarept demanded, a shudder running through him when her eyes closed in pain. "Can he make you laugh? Has he ever brought new thoughts to you, as I have? I've never touched you, but I've seen you tremble in desire . . . for me."

He nudged at the circle with a booted toe, jerking back at the zing of power. Though her face wore her anguish, her circle still held strong, even when her chest heaved, and her grip on her dress dropped, leaving creases in the otherwise perfect fall of fabric.

"Don't hurt me like this, Algaliarept," she whispered. "I only wanted to say good-bye."

"It's you who hurt me," he stated, forcefully where before he had always been demure. "I'm forever young, and now you'll make me watch you grow old, watch your beauty fade and your skills tarnish as you shackle yourself to a loveless marriage and a cold bed."

"It is the way of things," she breathed, but the fear in the back of her eyes strengthened as she touched her own face.

Her fondness for the mirror had always been her downfall, and he felt a surge of renewed excitement. "I will mourn your beauty when you could have been young forever," he said, looking for a crack in her resolve. "I would've forever been your slave." Faking depression, he slumped his perfect posture. "Only in the ever-after does time stand still and beauty and love last forever. But, as you say, it's the way of things."

"Gally, don't speak so," she pleaded, and he tensed when she used the nickname she'd chosen for him. But his lips parted in shock when she reached for him only to drop her hand mere inches from the barrier between them. His breath came in with a shudder, and his eyes widened. Had he been cracking the nut the wrong way? He had been trying to rattle her, make her lose her resolve so he could find a crack in her circle and break it, even knowing that her will would likely remain absolute even when her world was crashing down about her. She would not let her circle weaken, but what if she would take it down voluntarily? Ceri was of royal blood, a Dulciate. Generations of crown-sanctified temptation had created women who would not make a mistake of power. *But she might make a mistake of the heart.*

And the instant he realized why he had failed these seven years, her gaze went past him to the palace, lit up and replete with joy. Her eyes closed, and panic hit him as he saw everything fall apart. *Shit, she was going to walk.*

"Ceri, I would love you forever," he blurted, not faking his distress. *Not now. Not now when he'd found her weakness!*

"Gally, no," she sobbed as the tears fell and tiny blue butterflies rose about her.

"Don't call me again!" he demanded, the words coming from him without thought or plan. "Go to your cold bed. Die old and ugly! I would make you wise beyond all on earth, keep you beautiful, teach you things that the scholars and learned men have not even dreamed of. I will survive alone, untouched, my heart becoming cold where you showed me love. Better that I had never met you." He looked at her as a sob broke from her. "I was happy as I was."

"Forgive me," she choked out, hunched in heartache. "You were never just my demon."

"It's done," he said, making a hitch in his voice. "It's not as if I ever thought you would trust me, but to show me heaven only to give it to another man? I can't bear it."

"Gally—"

He raised a hand and her voice broke in a sob. "That's three times you've said my name," he said, crushing the now red rose beneath his foot. "Let me go, or trust me. Take down the wall so I may at least have the memory of your touch to console me as I weep in hell for having lost you, or simply walk away. I care not. I'm already broken."

Expression held at an anguished pain, he turned his back on her again, shifting his shoulders as if trying to find a new way to stand. Behind him, he heard a single sob, and then nothing as she held her breath. There was no scuffing of slippers as she ran away and no lessening of the circle imprisoning him, so he knew she was still there. His pulse quickened, and he forced his breathing to be shallow. He was romancing the most clever, most resolute bitch he'd ever taught a curse to, and he loved her. Or rather, he loved not knowing what she would do next, the complexity of her thoughts that he had yet to figure out—an irresistible jewel in a world where he had everything.

"Do you love him?" he asked, adding the last brushstrokes to his masterpiece.

"No," she whispered.

His hands quivered as adrenaline spiked through him, but he held perfectly still. He would've given a lot to know which card she held crushed in her grip. "Do you love me?" he asked, shocked to realize he'd never used those particular words to seduce a familiar before.

The silence was long, but from behind him came a soft, "Yes. God help me."

Algaliarept closed his eyes. His breath shook in him, hid excitement racing through him like a living ley line, burning. Would she drop her circle? He didn't know. And when a light touch landed on his hand, he jumped, looking down to find a blue butterfly slowly fanning its wings against him.

A butterfly? he thought in shock, and then he realized. She had broken the summoning circle, and he'd never even felt it go down. *Oh God*, he thought, a surge of what was almost ecstasy making his knees nearly buckle as he turned, finding her standing before him, nervous and hopeful all at the same time. She had let him in. Never had he taken anyone like this. It was like nothing he'd ever felt before, debilitating.

"Ceri," he breathed, seeing her without the shimmer of her power between them. Her eyes were beautiful, her skin holding a olive tint he'd never noticed before. And her face . . . She was crying, and he reached out, not believing when he ran a white-gloved hand under her eye to make her smile at him uncertainly. It was a smile of hope and fear.

She should be afraid.

"Gally?" she said hesitantly.

"Do you really love me?" he asked her as the butterflies swarmed, drawn by the scent of burnt amber, and she nodded, gazing at him as tears slipped down and she hesitantly folded herself into his arms.

"Then you are one stupid bitch."

Gasping, she flung her head up. Pushing from him, she tried to escape, but it was too late. Silently laughing, Algaliarept wrapped his arm around her neck, grabbing her hair with his free hand and pulling her across the garden to the nearest ley line. "Let me go!" she screamed, and gathering herself, she shouted, *"celero inanio!"* sobbing as she flung the entire force of the nearest ley line at him.

With a quick thought, Algaliarept deflected the burning curse, chuckling as flickers of light blossomed to show where the blue butterflies burned before they hit the dew-wet grass. In his grasp, Ceri hesitated her struggles, aghast that he had turned her magic into killing something she loved. "Do that again, and I'll burn anything that comes round that corner," he encouraged, winding his fist in her hair until she began hitting him with her tiny fists.

"You lied! You lied to me!" she raged.

"I did nothing of the kind," he said, holding her close and dragging her out of the circle so that the people now running toward her screams wouldn't be able to trap him easily. "I'm going to keep you forever young and teach you everything I know, just as I promised." She was panting, her struggle hesitating as she waited for the help that wouldn't be able to free her. Closing his eyes, he smelled her hair. "And I'm going to love you," he whispered into her ear as she began to pray to an uncaring god he'd teach her not to believe in. "I'm going to love you within an inch of your life, then love you some more."

Anticipation high, he reached for her inner thigh. The instant his fingers touched her, she screamed, fighting to be free. A fierce smile came over him and his blood pounded in his loins. This was going to be everything he wanted. A distraction for as long as he cared to make it last.

"Let me jump you to my bed so we may begin your tutelage," he said as the bobbing torches came closer.

"No!" she cried out, wiggling as her hair came undone to fall about her face. She looked so much more fetching, her color high and rage making her eyes sparkle.

"Wrong answer," he said, flooding her with the force of the line.

Her eyes widened, her small lips opening to show perfect teeth. Gasping, she bit her lip, trying not to scream. Almost she passed out, and he let up the instant she started to go limp. That she wouldn't scream made him smile. She'd scream before it was over, and finding her breaking point would be . . . exquisite.

"I'm giving you everything you want," he breathed in her ear when she could think again, hanging in his grasp as she panted. "Everything and more, Ceri. Let me take you." He could knock her out and take her by force, but if she gave in entirely to him . . . it would be beyond anything he'd ever accomplished.

The bobbing torches turned the corner, little dogs yapping in over-dressed women's arms.

"Stop! For the love of God, stop!" she shouted, and Algaliarept felt a deep surge of satisfaction. Destroying her will would fulfill his every need.

A young man in white and gold pushed past the women, stumbling to a stop, shock in his perfect face. A wailing outcry rose from the nobles behind him, and several turned and ran.

Ceri's bridegroom was perfect, Algaliarept decided bitterly as he held her tighter. The man before him now complimented her in every way, slim, fair—everything Algaliarept was not. And then Algaliarept smiled—she had shunned elven perfection to be with him.

The man's lips parted in horror as Algaliarept's fingers entwined deeper in her hair, jerking her head up to expose the long length of her neck to him. And still Ceri stared at her bridegroom, color in her cheeks as her lungs heaved. Turning, the prince called for magicians.

At the sight of his back, Ceri's hand opened and the card she held fell to the earth. Something in Algaliarept sparked when the devil card fell to the manicured grass. The bent gold glinted in the torch light, but it was easy to see the beautiful maiden being dragged off by an ugly, red-skinned demon. "Take me," she whispered as three magicians stumbled into the clearing, frightened but determined. "I don't want to grow old. You are my demon."

With her acquiescence, it was done. Seven years of labor culminated in one satisfied laugh that made the young man in white pale. But he didn't move to save her.

"You don't deserve her," Algaliarept said, and then, as the magicians moved, he shifted his thoughts to leave. The yapping dogs, the wailing women, everything vanished into the clean blackness of thought. And as they traveled the lines back to the drop of time that had been flung from space itself, Algaliarept touched her soul, ran his fingers through her aura and felt her squirm. She had wanted it. Even with her denials and screams, she wanted it. Wanted him. She was his little blue butterfly, seeking out carrion.

Don't cry, Ceri, he thought, knowing she heard him when her mind seemed to quiver.

He was going to keep this one for himself. Turn the Dulciate elf into a showcase of his talents. No one had ever come willingly, before. He was an artist, and destroying her as he made her into what he wanted, would be his finest masterpiece.

Until I find someone with a little more skill, that is, he thought, knowing that wasn't likely to happen for, oh, probably another thousand years.

TWO GHOSTS FOR SISTER RACHEL

Two Ghosts for Sister Rachel *first appeared in the anthology* Holidays Are Hell. *Family was becoming more important to Rachel at about this time in the series, and dropping back to when she was still living at home and working for her hard-won independence gave me a chance to show where Rachel developed not only her stamina but also her refusal to give up hope in the face of low odds. I thought it was important for the reader to see the Rachel beyond the tough, capable, and get-back-up kind of girl I usually focused on, the one who came from the fragile, weak, and death-row childhood. It makes her choices easier to understand.*

 ONE

I stuck the end of the pencil between my teeth, brushing the eraser specks off the paper as I considered how best to answer the employment application. WHAT SKILLS CAN YOU BRING TO INDERLAND SECURITY THAT ARE CLEARLY UNIQUE TO YOU?

Sparkling wit? I thought, twining my foot around the kitchen chair and feeling stupid. *A smile? The desire to smear the pavement with bad guys?*

Sighing, I tucked my hair behind my ear and slumped. My eyes shifted to the clock above the sink as it ticked minutes into hours. I wasn't going to waste my life. Eighteen was too young to be accepted into the I.S. intern program without a parent's signature, but if I put my application in now, it would sit at the top of the stack until I was old enough, according to the guidance counselor. Like the recruiter had said, there was nothing wrong with going into the I.S. right out of college if you knew that's what you wanted to do. The fast track.

The faint sound of the front door opening brought my heart to my throat. I glanced at the sunset-gloomed window. Jamming the application under the stacked napkins, I shouted, "Hi, Mom! I thought you weren't going to be back until eight!"

Damn it, how was I supposed to finish this thing if she kept coming back?

But my alarm shifted to elation when a high falsetto voice responded, "It's eight in Buenos Aires, dear. Be a dove and find my rubbers for me? It's snowing."

"Robbie?" I stood so fast the chair nearly fell over. Heart pounding, I darted out of the kitchen and into the green hallway. There at the end, in a windbreaker and shaking snow from himself, was my brother Robbie. His narrow height came close to brushing the top of the door, and his shock of red hair caught the glow from the porch light. Slush-wet Dockers showed from under his jeans, totally inappropriate for the weather. On the porch behind him, a cabbie set down two suitcases.

"Hey!" I exclaimed, bringing his head up to show his green eyes glinting mischievously. "You were supposed to be on the vamp flight. Why didn't you call? I would've come to get you."

Robbie shoved a wad of money at the driver. Door still gaping behind him, he opened his arms, and I landed against him, my face hitting his upper chest instead of his middle like it had when we had said goodbye. His arms went around me, and I breathed in the scent of old Brimstone from the dives he worked in. The tears pricked, and I held my breath so I wouldn't cry. It had been over four and a half years. Inconsiderate snot had been at the West Coast all this time, leaving me to cope with Mom. But he'd come home this year for the solstice, and I sniffed back everything and smiled up at him.

"Hey, Firefly," he said, using our dad's pet name for me and grinning as he measured where my hair had grown to. "You got tall. And wow, hair down to your waist? What are you doing, going for the world's record?"

He looked content and happy, and I dropped back a step, suddenly uncomfortable. "Yeah, well, it's been almost five years," I accused. Behind him, the cab drove away, headlamps dim from the snow and moving slowly.

Robbie sighed. "Don't start," he begged. "I get enough of that from Mom. You going to let me in?" He glanced behind him at the snow. "It is cold out here."

"Wimp," I said, then grabbed one of the suitcases. "Ever hear about that magical thing called a coat?"

He snorted his opinion, hefting the last of the luggage and following me in. The door shut, and I headed down the second, longer hallway to his room, eager to get him inside and part of our small family again. "I'm glad you came," I said, feeling my pulse race from the suitcase's weight. I hadn't been in the hospital in years, but fatigue still came fast. "Mom's going to skin you when she gets back."

"Yeah, well I wanted to talk to you alone first."

Flipping the light switch with an elbow, I lugged his suitcase into his old room, glad I'd vacuumed already. Blowing out my exhaustion, I turned with my arms crossed over my chest to hide my heavy breathing. "About what?"

Robbie wasn't listening. He had taken off his jacket to show a sharp-looking pinstripe shirt with a tie. Smiling, he spun in a slow circle. "It looks exactly the same."

I shrugged. "You know Mom."

His eyes landed on mine. "How is she?"

I looked at the floor. "Same. You want some coffee?"

With an easy motion, he swung the suitcase I had dragged in up onto the bed. "Don't tell me you drink coffee."

Half my mouth curved up into a smile. "Sweat of the gods," I quipped, coming close when he unzipped a front pocket and pulled out a clearly expensive bag of coffee. If the bland, environmentally conscious packaging hadn't told me what was in it, the heavenly scent of ground beans would have. "How did you get *that* through customs intact?" I said, and he smiled.

"I checked it."

His arm landed across my shoulders, and together we navigated the narrow hallway to the kitchen. Robbie was eight years older than me, a sullen babysitter who had become an overly protective brother, who had then vanished four-plus years ago when I needed him the most, fleeing the pain of our dad's death. I had hated him for a long time, envious that he could run when I was left to deal with Mom. But then I found out he'd been paying for Mom's psychiatrist. Plus some of my hospital bills. We all helped the way we could. And it wasn't like he could make that kind of money here in Cincinnati.

Robbie slowed as we entered the kitchen, silent as he took in the changes. Gone was the cabinet with its hanging herbs, the rack of dog-eared spell books, the ceramic spoons, and copper spell pots. It looked like a normal kitchen, which was abnormal for Mom.

"When did this happen?" he asked, rocking into motion and heading for the coffeemaker. It looked like a shrine with its creamer, sugar, special spoons, and three varieties of grounds in special little boxes.

I sat at the table and scuffed my feet. *Since Dad died,* I thought, but didn't say it. I didn't need to.

The silence stretched uncomfortably. I'd like to say Robbie looked like my dad, but apart from his height and his spare frame, there wasn't much of Dad about him. The red hair and green eyes we shared came from Mom. The earth magic skill I dabbled in came from Mom, too. Robbie was better at ley line magic. Dad had been topnotch at that, having worked in the Arcane Division of the Inderland Security, the I.S. for short.

Guilt hit me, and I glanced at the application peeking out from under the napkins.

"So," Robbie drawled as he threw out the old grounds and rinsed the carafe. "You want to go to Fountain Square for the solstice? I haven't seen the circle close in years."

I fought to keep the disappointment from my face—he had been trying to get tickets to the Takata concert. Crap. "Sure," I said, smiling. "We'll have to dig up a coat for you, though."

"Maybe you're right," he said as he scooped out four tablespoons, glanced at me and then dumped the last one back in the bag. "You want to go to the concert instead?"

I jerked straight in the chair. "You got them!" I squealed, and he grinned.

"Yup," he said, tapping his chest and reaching into a pocket. But then his long face went worried. I held my breath until he pulled a set of tickets from a back pocket, teasing me.

"Booger," I said, falling back into the chair.

"Brat," he shot back.

But I was in too good a mood to care. God, I was going to be listening to Takata when the seasons shifted. How cool was that? Anticipation made my foot jiggle, and I looked at the phone. I had to call Julie. She would die. She would die right on the spot.

"How did your classes go?" Robbie said suddenly. His back was to me as he got the coffeemaker going, and I flushed. Why was that always the second thing out of their mouth, right after how tall you've gotten? "You graduated, right?" he added, turning.

"Duh." I scuffed my feet and tucked a strand of hair behind my ear. I'd graduated, but admitting I'd flunked every ley line class I had taken wasn't anything I wanted to do.

"Got a job yet?"

My eyes flicked to the application. "I'm working on it." Living at home while going to college hadn't been my idea, but until I could afford rent, I was kind of stuck here, two-year degree or not.

Smiling with an irritating understanding, Robbie slid into the chair across from me, his long legs reaching the other side and his thin hands splayed out. "Where's The Bat? I didn't see it in the drive."

Oh . . . crap. Scrambling up, I headed for the coffeemaker. "Wow, that smells good," I said, fumbling for two mugs. "What is that, espresso?" Like I could tell? But I had to say something.

Robbie knew me better than I knew myself, having practically raised me. It had been hard to find a babysitter willing to take care of an infant prone to frequently collapsing and needing shots to get her lungs moving again. I could feel his eyes on me, and I turned, arms over my chest as I leaned back against the counter.

"Rachel . . ." he said, then his face went panicked. "You got your license, didn't you? Oh my God. You wrecked it. You wrecked my car!"

"I didn't wreck it," I said defensively, playing with the tips of my hair. "And it was my car. You gave it to me."

"Was?" he yelped, jerking straight. "Rache, what did you do?"

"I sold it," I admitted, flushing.

"You what!"

"I sold it." Turning my back on him, I carefully pulled the carafe off the hot plate and poured out two cups. Sure, it smelled great, but I bet it tasted as bad as the stuff Mom bought.

"Rachel, it was a classic!"

"Which is why I got enough from it to get my black belt," I said, and he slumped back, exasperated.

"Look," I said, setting a cup beside him and sitting down. "I couldn't drive it, and Mom can't keep a regular job long enough to get a month's worth of pay. It was just taking up room."

"I can't believe you sold my car." He was staring at me, long face aghast. "For what? To be able to dance like Jackie Chan?"

My lips pressed together. "I was mad at you, okay?" I exclaimed, and his eyes widened. "You walked out of here after Dad's funeral and didn't come back. I was left trying to keep Mom together. And then everyone at school found out and started pushing me around. I like feeling strong, okay? A car I couldn't drive wasn't doing it, but the gym was. I needed the money to get my belt, so I sold it!"

He looked at me, guilt shining in the back of his eyes.

"You, ah, want to see what I can do?" I asked hesitantly.

Robbie's breath came in fast, and he shook himself. "No," he said, gaze on the table. "You did the right thing. I wasn't here to protect you. It was my fault."

"Robbie . . ." I whined. "It's not anybody's fault. I don't want to be protected. I'm a lot stronger now. I can protect myself. Actually . . ." I looked at the application, my fingers cold as I reached for it. I knew he wouldn't approve, but if I could get him on my side, we might be able to convince Mom—and then I wouldn't have to wait. "Actually, I'd like to do more than that."

He said nothing as I pulled the paper out like a guilty secret and shoved it across the table. My knees went weak, and I felt the hints of lightheadedness take over. God, how could I ever hope to be a runner if I didn't have enough nerve to bring it up with my brother?

The sound of the paper rasping on the table as he picked it up seemed loud. The furnace clicked on, and the draft shifted my hair as I watched his gaze travel over the paper. Slowly his expression changed as he realized what it was. His eyes hit mine, and his jaw clenched. "No."

He went to crumple the paper, and I snatched it away. "I'm going to do this."

"The I.S.?" Robbie said loudly. "Are you crazy? That's what killed Dad!"

"It is not. I was there. He said so. Where were you?"

Feeling the hit, he shifted to the back of the chair. "That's not fair."

"Neither is telling me I can't do something simply because it scares you," I accused.

His brow furrowed, and I grabbed my cup of coffee, sliding it between us. "Is this why you're so hell bent on those karate classes?" he asked bitterly.

"It's not karate," I said. "And yes, it puts me ahead of everyone else. With my two-year degree, I can be a full runner in four years. Four years, Robbie!"

"I don't believe this." Robbie crossed his arms over his chest. "Mom is actually letting you do this?"

I stayed silent, ticked.

Robbie made a derisive noise from deep in his chest. "She doesn't know," he accused, and I brought my gaze up. My vision was blurring, but by God, I wasn't going to wipe my eyes.

"Rachel," he coaxed, seeing me teetering in frustration. "Did you even read the contract? They have you forever. No way out. You're not even twenty yet, and you're throwing your life away!"

"I am not!" I shouted, my voice trembling. "What else am I good for? I'll never be as good as Mom at earth magic. I've tried flipping burgers and selling shoes, and I hated it. I hate it!" I almost screamed.

Robbie stared, clearly taken aback. "Then I'll help you get a real degree. All you need is the right classes."

My jaw clenched. "I *took* the right classes, and I *have* a real degree," I said, angry. "This is what I want to do."

"Running around in the dark arresting criminals? Rachel, be honest. You will never have the stamina." And then his expression blanked. "You're doing this because of Dad."

"No," I said sullenly, but my eyes had dropped, and it was obvious that was part of it.

Robbie sighed. He leaned to take my hand across the table, and I jerked out of his reach. "Rachel," he said softly. "If Dad was here, he'd tell you the same thing. Don't do it."

"If Dad was here, he'd drive me to the I.S. office himself," I said. "Dad believed in what he did with his life. He didn't let danger stop him; he just prepared for it better."

"Then why did he let himself get killed?" Robbie said, an old pain in his pinched eyes. "He'd tell you to expand on your earth witch degree and find something safe."

"Safe!" I barked, shifting back. *Damn it, now I'd never convince Mom.* I needed her signature on the application, or I'd have to wait until I was nineteen. That meant I'd be twenty-three before I was actually making money at it. I loved my mom, but I had to get out of this house. "If Dad was here, he'd let me," I muttered, sullen.

"You think so?" Robbie shot back.

"I know so."

It was silent apart from my foot tapping the chair leg and the ticking of the clock. I folded up the application and snapped it down between us like an accusation. Reaching for my coffee, I took a swig, trying not to grimace at the taste. I don't care how good it smelled, it tasted awful. I couldn't believe people actually enjoyed drinking this stuff.

Robbie stood, startling me as the chair scraped and bumped over the linoleum. "Where are you going?" I asked. *Not home for five minutes, and we were arguing already.*

"To get something," he said, and walked out. I could hear him talking under his breath, and the harsh sound of a zipper as he opened his suitcase. His bedroom door slammed shut and the familiar stomp of his feet in the hall as he came back was loud.

I knew I was wearing that same unhappy, ugly look he had when he dropped a heavy book on the table in front of me. "Happy solstice," he said, slumping into his chair.

I waited, not knowing what to say. "What is it?"

"A book," he said shortly. "Open it."

I scooted closer and tucked my hair behind an ear. It was as big as a dictionary, but the pages were thick, not thin. The stark brightness told me it was new, but the charms in them . . . I'd never even heard of them.

"That's an eight-hundred-level textbook from the university in Portland," he said, voice harsh. "Now that you have your two-year degree, I wanted to ask if you would come out with me to take classes."

My head came up. He wanted me to go out to the West Coast with him?

"Mom, too," he added, and then his expression shifted to pleading. "Look at those spells, Rachel. Look what you can do if you apply yourself and invest some time. If you go into the I.S., you won't ever be able to do charms like that. Is that what you want?"

Lips parted, I looked at the pages. I was okay with earth magic, but these looked really hard. "Robbie, I—"

My words cut off and I stared at the page. "Oh wow," I breathed, looking at the charm.

"See," Robbie coaxed, his voice eager. "Look at that stuff. It's yours if you want it. All you have to do is work for it."

"No, look!" I said, shoving the book across the table and standing to follow it around. "See? There's a charm to summon the wrongfully dead. I can ask Dad. I can ask Dad what he thinks I should do."

Robbie's mouth dropped open. "Let me see that," he said, bending over the book. "Holy shit," he breathed, long fingers trembling. "You're right." He was wearing a smile when he pulled his gaze from the pages. "Tell you what," he said, leaning back with a look I recognized, the one he used to wear when he was getting me into trouble. "You do this spell to summon Dad, and ask him. If it works, you do what he says."

My pulse quickened. "You said it was an eight-hundred-level spell."

"Yeah? So what?"

I thought for a minute. "And if he says I should join the I.S.?"

"I'll sign the application myself. Mom gave me your guardianship right after Dad died."

I couldn't seem to get enough air. It was a way out. "And if I can't do it? What then?"

"Then you come out to Portland with me and get your master's so you can do every single charm in that book. But you have to do the spell yourself. Front to back. Start to finish."

I took a deep breath and looked at it. At least it wasn't in Latin. How hard could it be?

"Deal," I said, sticking my hand out.

"Deal," he echoed. And we shook on it.

 TWO

Squinting, I crouched to put my gaze level with the graduated cylinder, knees aching with a familiar fatigue as I measured out three cc's of white wine. It was this year's pressings, but I didn't think that mattered as long as the grapes had been grown here in Cincinnati, in effect carrying the essence of the land my dad had lived and died on.

My mom's light laughter from the other room pulled my attention away at a critical moment, and the wine sloshed too high. She was cloistered in the living room with Robbie under the impression that I was making a last-minute solstice gift and the kitchen was totally off limits. Which meant I was trying to figure out this crappy spell without Robbie's help. See, this was why I wanted to be a runner. I'd be so damn good, I could afford to buy my spells.

I grimaced as I straightened and looked at the too-full cylinder. Glancing at the hallway, I brought it to my lips and downed a sip. The alcohol burned like my conscience, but when the liquid settled, it was right where it was supposed to be.

Satisfied, I dumped it into Mom's crucible. She had gone over it with a fine-grit sandpaper earlier this afternoon to remove all traces of previous spells, as if dunking it in salt water wasn't enough. She had been thrilled when I asked to use her old equipment, and it had been a trial getting everything I needed amid her overenthusiastic, wanting-to-help interference. Even now, I could hear her excitement for my interest in her area of expertise, her crisp voice louder than usual and with a lilt I hadn't heard in a long time. Though Robbie being home might account for that all on its own.

I leaned over the textbook and read the notes at the bottom of the page. WINE AND HOLY DUST ARE INVARIABLY THE BUILDING BLOCKS OF CHOICE TO GIVE SPIRITS SUBSTANCE. Scratching the bridge of my nose, I glanced at the clock. This was taking forever, but I'd do anything to talk to my dad again, even if the spell only lasted until daybreak.

It was getting close to eleven. Robbie and I would have to leave soon to get a good spot at Fountain Square for the closing of the circle. My mom thought Robbie was taking me to the Takata concert, but we needed a whopping big jolt of energy to supplement the charm's invocation, and though we could find that at the concert, the organization of several hundred witches focused on closing the circle at Fountain Square at midnight would be safer to tap into.

I had really wanted to go to the concert, and sighing for the lost chance, I reached to snip a holly leaf off the centerpiece. It would give the spell a measure of protection. Apparently I was going to open a door, and holly would insure my dad's essence wouldn't track anything bad in on the soles of his feet.

Nervousness made my hands shake. I had to do this right. And I had to do it without Mom knowing. If she saw Dad's ghost, it would tear her up—send her back to the mess she was in almost five years ago. Seeing Dad was going to be hard enough on me. I wasn't even sure by the description of "desired results" how substantial a ghost he'd be. If we both couldn't see him, Robbie would never believe that I'd done it right.

Standing at the table, I used my mom's silver snips to cut the holly leaf into small segments before brushing them into the wine. My fingers were still shaking, but I knew it was nerves; I hadn't done enough to get tired, low fatigue threshold or not. Steadying the crucible with one hand, I ground the holly leaves with all my weight behind it. The lemon juice and yew mix I had measured out earlier threatened to spill as I rocked the table, and I moved it to a nearby counter.

Lemon juice was used to help get the spirit's attention and shock it awake. The yew would help me communicate with it. The charm wouldn't work on every ghost—just those unrestful souls. But my dad couldn't be resting comfortably. Not after the way he died.

My focus blurred, and I ground the pestle into the mortar as the heartache resurfaced. I concentrated on Robbie's voice as he talked to my mom about how nice the weather was in Portland, almost unheard over some solstice TV cartoon about Jack Frost. He didn't sound anything like my dad, but it was nice to hear his words balanced against Mom's again.

"How long has Rachel been drinking coffee?" he asked, making my mom laugh.

Two years, I thought, my arm getting tired and my pulse quickening as I worked. *Crap, no wonder my mom quit making her own charms.*

"Since you called to say you were coming," my mom said, unaware it was my drink of choice at school as I struggled to fit in with the older students. "She is trying to be so grown up."

This last was almost sighed, and I frowned.

"I didn't like her in those college classes," she continued, unaware that I could hear her. "I suppose it's my own fault for letting her jump ahead like that. Making her sit at home while she was ill and watch TV all day wasn't going to happen, and if she knew the work, what harm was there in letting her skip a semester here or there?"

Brow furrowed, I puffed a strand of hair out of my face and frowned. I had been in and out of the hospital so often the first four years of public school that I was basically homeschooled. Good idea on paper, but when you come back after being absent for three months and make the mistake of showing how much you know, the playground becomes a torture field.

Robbie made a rude noise. "I think it's good for her."

"Oh, I never said it wasn't," my mom was quick to say. "I didn't like her with all those damned older men is all."

I sighed, used to my mom's mouth. It was worse than mine, which sucked when she caught me swearing.

"Men?" Robbie's voice had a laugh in it. "They're not that much older than her. Rachel can take care of herself. She's a good girl. Besides, she's still living at home, right?"

I blew a strand of my hair out of the mix, feeling a tug when one caught under the pestle. My arm was hurting, and I wondered if I could stop yet. The leaves were a gritty green haze at the bottom. The TV went loud when a commercial came on, and I almost missed my mother chiding him. "You think I'd let her live in the dorms? She gets more tired than she lets on. She still isn't altogether well yet. She's just better at hiding it."

My shoulder was aching, but after that, I wasn't going to stop until I was done. I was fine. I was better than fine. Hell, I'd even started jogging, though I threw up the first time I'd run the zoo. All those hills. Everybody throws up the first time.

But there was a reason there were very few pictures of me before my twelfth birthday, and it didn't have anything to do with the lack of film.

Exhaling, I set the pestle down and shook my arm. It hurt all the way up, and deciding the holly was pulped enough, I stretched for the envelope of roots I'd scraped off my mom's ivy plant earlier. The tiny little roots had come from the stems, not from under the ground, and the book said they acted as a binding agent to pull the lingering essence of a person together.

My head came up when the TV shut off, but it was only one of them turning on the stereo. Jingle Bells done jazz. One of my dad's standbys.

"Look, it's snowing again," Robbie said softly, and I glanced at the kitchen window, a black square with stark white flakes showing where the light penetrated. "I miss that."

"You know there's always a room here for you."

Head bowed over the mortar as I worked, I cringed at the forlorn sound of her voice. The spell had a pleasant wine-and-chlorophyll scent, and I tossed my hair out of the way.

"Mom . . ." Robbie coaxed. "You know I can't. Everyone's on the coast."

"It was just a thought," she said tartly. "Shut up and have a cookie."

My knees were starting to ache, and knowing if I didn't sit down they'd give way in about thirty seconds, I sank into a chair. Ignoring my shaking fingers, I pulled my mom's set of balances out of a dusty box. I wiped the pans with a soft rag, then recalibrated it to zero.

The wine mixture needed dust to give the ghost something to build its temporary body around, kind of like a snow cloud needs dust to make snowflakes. I had to go by weight since dust was too hard to measure any other way. Robbie had collected some from under the pews at a church while out shopping for a coat, so I knew it was fresh and potent.

My breath made the scales shift, so I held it as I carefully tapped the envelope. The dust, the wine, and the holly would give the ghost substance, but it would be the other half with the lemon juice that would actually summon him. Yew—which was apparently basic stuff when it came to communing with the dead, the ivy—to bind it, an identifying agent—which varied from spell to spell, and of course my blood to kindle the spell, would combine to draw the spirit in and bind it to the smoke created when the spell invoked. There wasn't anything that could make the situation permanent, but it'd last the night. Lots of time to ask him a question. *Lots of time to ask him why.*

Guilt and worry made my hand jerk, and I shook too much dust from the envelope. *Please say I should join the I.S.,* I thought as I alternately blew on the pile of dust and held my breath until the scales read what they should.

Moving carefully to prevent a draft, I got the tiny copper spell pot with the lemon juice and carefully shook the dust into it. I breathed easier when the gray turned black and sank.

The box of utensils scraped across the Formica table, and I dug around until I found a glass stirring rod. It was almost done, but my pleased smile faltered when Robbie asked, "Have you given any thought to coming out with me? You and Rachel both?"

I froze, heart pounding. *What in hell? We had a deal!*

"No," she said, a soft regret in her voice, and I stirred the dust in with a clockwise motion, paying more attention to the living room than to what I was doing.

"Dad's been gone a long time," Robbie pleaded. "You need to start living again."

"Moving to Portland would change nothing." It was quick and decisive. When she used that tone, there was no reasoning with her. "Rachel needs to be here," she added. "This is her home. This is where her friends are. I'm not going to uproot her. Not when she's finally starting to feel comfortable with herself."

I made an ugly face and set the stirring rod aside. I didn't have many friends. I'd been too sick to make them when younger. The girls at the community college treated me like a child, and after the guys found out I was jail bait, they left me alone too. Maybe moving wasn't a bad idea. I could tell everyone I was twenty-one. Though with my flat chest, they'd never believe it.

"I can get her into the university," Robbie said, his voice coaxing. I'd heard him wield it before to get both of us out of trouble, and it usually worked. "I've got a great two-room apartment, and once she's a resident, I can pay her tuition. She needs to get into the sun more."

We had a deal, Robbie, I thought, staring at the empty hallway. He was trying to work an end around. It wasn't going to work. I was going to do this spell right, and he was going to sign that paper, and then I was going to join the I.S.

"No," my mom said. "Besides, if Rachel wants to pursue her studies, Cincinnati has an excellent earth magic program." There was a telling hesitation. "But thank you.

"Did she tell you she's taking martial arts?" she said to change the subject, and I smiled at the pride in her voice. The lemon half was done, and I reached for the mortar with the wine and holly mix.

"She got her black belt not long ago," my mom continued as I stood to grind it up a little bit more, puffing over it. "I wanted her to tell you, but—"

"She sold The Bat to pay for it," Robbie finished glumly, and I grinned. "Yeah, she told me. Mom, Rachel doesn't need to know how to fight. She is not strong. She never will be, and letting her go on thinking she can do everything is only setting her up for a fall."

I froze, feeling like I'd been slapped.

"Rachel can do anything," my mom said hotly.

"That's not what I mean, Mom . . ." he pleaded. "I know she can, but why is she so fixated on all these physical activities when she could be the top witch in her field if she simply put the time in? She's good, Mom," he coaxed. "She's in there right now doing a complicated charm, and she's not batting an eye over it. That's raw talent. You can't learn that."

Anger warred with pride at his words on my skill. My mom was silent, and I let my frustration fuel the grinding motions.

"All I'm saying," he continued, "is maybe you could get her to ease up on trying to be super girl, and point out how some guys like smart chicks wearing glasses as much as others like kick-ass ones in boots."

"The reason Rachel works so hard to prove she's not weak is because she is," my mom said, making my stomach hurt all the more. "She sees it as a fault, and I'm not going to tell her to stop striving to overcome it. Challenge is how she defines herself. It was how she survived. Now shut up and eat another damned cookie. We get along just fine here."

My throat was tight, and I let go of the pestle, only now realizing my fingers had cramped up on it. I had worked so hard to get my freaking black belt so the I.S. couldn't wash me out on the physical test. Sure, it had taken me almost twice as long as everyone else, and yeah, I still spent ten minutes at the back of the gym flat on my back recovering after every class, but I did everything everyone else did, and with more power and skill than most.

Wiping an angry tear away, I used the stirring rod to scrape every last bit off the pestle. Damn it. I hated it when Robbie made me cry. He was good at it. 'Course, he was good at making me laugh, too. But my shoulders were aching beyond belief, and a slow lethargy was taking hold of my knees once more. I had to sit down again. Disgusted with myself, I sank into a chair, elbow on the table, my hair making a curtain between me and the rest of the world. I wasn't that much stronger now than when they kicked me out of the Make-A-Wish camp. I was just getting better at feeling it coming on and covering it up. *And I wanted to be a runner?*

Miserable, I held my arm against the ache, both inside and out. But the spell was done apart from the three drops of witch blood, and those wouldn't be added until we were at the square. Mom and Robbie had lowered their voices, the cadence telling me they were arguing. Pulling

34   KIM HARRISON

a second dusty box to me, I rummaged for a stoppered bottle to put the potion in.

The purple one didn't feel right, and I finally settled on the black one with the ground glass stopper. I wiped the dust from it with a dishtowel, and dumped the wine mix in, surprised when I found that the holly and the ivy bits went smoothly without leaving any behind. The lemon half was next, and my fingers were actually on the copper pot before I remembered I hadn't mixed in the identifying agent.

"Stupid witch," I muttered, thinking I must want to go to the West Coast and bang my head against the scholarly walls. The spell wouldn't work without something to identify the spirit you were summoning. It was the only ingredient not named. It was up to the person stirring it to decide. The suggested items were cremation dust, hair . . . hell, even fingernails would do, as gross as that was. I hadn't had the chance this afternoon to get into the attic where Dad's stuff was boxed up, so the only thing I'd been able to find of his was his old pocket watch on my mom's dresser.

I glanced at the archway to the hall and listened to the soft talk between Mom and Robbie. Talking about me, probably, and probably nothing I wanted to hear. Nervous, I slipped the antique silver watch out of my pocket. I looked at the hall again, and wincing, I used my mom's scissors to scrape a bit of grime-coated silver from the back. It left a shiny patch, and I rubbed my finger over it to try to dull the new brightness.

God, she'd kill me if she knew what I was doing. But I really wanted to talk to my dad, even if it was just a jumbled mess of my memories given temporary life.

My mother laughed, and in a sudden rush, I dumped the shavings in. The soft curlings sank to the bottom, where they sat and did nothing. Maybe it was the thought that counted.

I gave the potion another quick stir, tapped the glass rod off, and poured the mess into the glass-stoppered bottle with the wine. It was done.

Excited, I jammed the bottle and a finger stick into my pocket. The book said if I did it right, it would spontaneously boil when I invoked it in the red and gray stone bowl I'd found in the bottom of a box. The spirit would form from the smoke. *This had to work. It had to.*

My stomach quivered as I looked over the electric-lit kitchen. Most of the mess was from me rummaging through mom's boxes of spelling supplies. The dirty mortar, graduated cylinder, plant snips, and bits of discarded plants looked good strewn around—right somehow. This was how the kitchen used to look; my mom stirring spells and dinner on the same stove, having fits when Robbie would pretend to eat out of what was clearly a spell pot. Mom had some great earth magic stuff. It was a shame she didn't use it anymore apart from helping me with my Halloween costume, her tools banished to sit beside Dad's ley line stuff in the attic.

I dunked the few dishes I had used in the small vat of salt water to purge any remnants of my spell, setting them in the sink to wash later. This had to work. I was not going to the coast. I was going to join the I.S. and get a real job. All I had to do was this one lousy spell. Dad would tell me I could go. I knew it.

THREE

The temporary lights of Fountain Square turned the falling snow a stark, pretty white. I watched it swirl as I sat on the rim of the huge planter and thumped my heels while I waited for Robbie to return with hot chocolate. It was noisy with several thousand people, witches mostly, and a few humans who were good with ley lines or just curious. They spilled into the closed-off streets where vendors sold warmth charms, trinkets, and food. The scent of chili and funnel cakes made my stomach pinch. I didn't like the pressing crowd, but with the fridge-sized rock that the planter sported at my back, I found a measure of calm.

It was only fifteen minutes till midnight, and I was antsy. That was when the lucky seven witches chosen by lot would join hands and close the circle etched out before the fountain. The longer they held it, the more prosperous the following year was forecast to be. My name was in the hat, along with Robbie's, and I didn't know what would happen if one of us was drawn. It would have looked suspicious if we hadn't added our names when we passed through the spell checker to get into the square.

I had known about the spell checker, of course. But I'd never tried to sneak a charm in before and had forgotten about it. Apparently a lot of people tried to take advantage of the organized yet unfocused energy that was generated by having so many witches together. My charm was uninvoked, undetectable unless they searched my pockets. Not like the ley line witch ahead of me who I had watched in horror while security wrestled him to the ground. It was harder to smuggle in all the paraphernalia a ley line spell needed. All I had was a small stoppered bottle and a palm-sized stone with a hollowed-out indentation.

My heels thumped faster, and in a surge of tension, I wedged my legs under me and stood above the crowd. Toes cold despite my boots, I brushed the snow from the ivy that grew in the small space between the rock and the edge of the planter. I searched the crowd for Robbie, my foot tapping to Marilyn Manson's "White Christmas." He had set up on the far stage. The crowd over there was kind of scary.

Fidgeting, my gaze drifted to the only calm spot in the mess: the circle right in front of the fountain. Some guy with CITY EVENT blazoned on his orange vest darted across the cordoned-off area, but most of the security simply stood to form a living barrier. One caught my eye, and I sat back down. You weren't supposed to be on the planters.

"Take a flier?" a man said, his voice dulled from repetition. He was the only person facing away from the circle as he moved through the crowd, and I had prepared my no-thanks speech before he had even gotten close. But then I saw his "Have you seen me?" button and changed my mind. I'd take a stinking flier.

"Thanks," I said, holding out my gloved hand even before he could ask.

"Bless you," he said softly, the snow-damp paper having the weight of cloth as I took it.

He turned away, numb from the desperate reason for his search. "Take a flier?" he said again, moving off with a ponderous pace.

Depressed, I looked at the picture. The missing girl was pretty, her straight hair hanging free past her shoulders. Sarah Martin. Human. Eleven years old. Last seen wearing a pink coat and jeans. Might have a set of white ice skates. Blond hair and blue eyes.

I shoved the flier into a pocket and took a deep breath. Being pretty shouldn't make you a target. If they didn't find her tonight, she probably wouldn't be alive if and when they did. I wasn't the only one using the power of the solstice to work strong magic, and it made me sick.

A familiar figure captured my attention, and I smiled at Robbie in his new long coat. He had a hesitant, stop-and-go motion through the crowd as he tried not to bump anyone with the hot drinks. Besides the new coat, he now sported a thick wool hat, scarf, and a pair of matching mittens that my mom had made for him for the solstice. He was still in his thin shoes, though, and his face was red with cold.

"Thanks," I said when Robbie shuffled to a halt and handed me a paper and wax cup.

"Good *God* it's cold out here," he said, setting his cup beside me on the planter and jamming his mittened hands into his armpits.

I scooted closer to him, jostled by some guy. "You've been gone too long. Wimp."

"Brat."

A man in an orange security vest drifted past, the way opening for him like magic. I busied myself with my drink, not looking at him as the warm milk and chocolate slid down. The bottle of potion felt heavy in my pocket, like a guilty secret. "I forgot tapping into the communal will was illegal," I whispered.

Robbie guffawed, taking the top off his drink and eyeing me with his bird-bright eyes brilliant green in the strong electric lights that made the square bright as noon. "You want to go home?" he taunted. "Come to Portland with me right now? It's freaking warmer."

He was getting me in trouble, but that's what he did. He usually got me out of it, too. Usually. "I want to talk to Dad," I said, wiggling my toes to feel how cold they were.

"All right then." He sipped his drink, turning to shield me from a gust of snow and wind that sent the crowd into loud exclamations. "Are you ready?"

I eyed him in surprise. "I thought we'd find a nearby alley or something."

"The closer, the better. The more energy you can suck in, the longer the magic will last."

There was that, but a noise of disbelief came from me. "You really think no one's going to notice a ghost taking shape?" It suddenly hit me I was stirring a white charm in a banned area to get into the I.S. *This will look really good on my employment essay.*

Robbie gazed over the shorter people to the nearby circle. "I think you'll be all right. He's not going to be that substantial. And that's assuming you do it right," he added, teasing.

"Shut up," I said dryly, and I would've bobbed him but that he was drinking his hot chocolate.

Marilyn Manson finished his . . . really odd version of "Rudolph the Red-Nosed Reindeer" and the people surrounding the stage screamed for more.

"They're drawing names," Robbie said, watching the circle instead of the stage.

Excitement slithered through me, and as the crowd pressed closer, I levered myself back up onto the planter wall. No one would make me leave now for standing on it. Robbie moved so I could steady myself against his shoulder, and from the new vantage point, I watched the last of the names pulled from the informal cardboard box. I held my breath, both wanting to hear my name blared from the loudspeaker and dreading it.

Another man with a city event vest put his head together with an official-looking woman with white earmuffs. The two spoke for a moment, her head bobbing. Then she took the wad of names and strode to the stage where Marilyn was blowing kisses and showing off his legs in black tights. The crowd turned like schooling fish, the noise growing as a path parted for her.

"Can you see?" Robbie asked, and I nodded, bumping my knee against his back.

A wave of expectation grew to make my fingertips tingle. With my back to that huge rock and high above everyone, I had a great view, and I watched the woman stand at the stage and peer up at the band. Someone extended a hand to help her make the jump to the plywood. A laugh rippled out when she made the leap, and the woman was clearly flustered when she tugged her coat straight and turned to face the crowd. Marilyn handed her a mike, giving her a word or two before the straitlaced woman edged to the middle of the stage.

"I'm going to read the names now," she said simply, and the square filled with noise. She glanced shyly behind her to the band when the drummer added to it.

Robbie tugged at my coat and I missed the first name—but it wasn't me. "You should start now," he said as he peered up, his cheeks red and his eyes eager.

Adrenaline spiked through me to pull me straight, and my gloved hand touched the outside of my pocket. "Now?"

"At least set it up while everyone is looking at the stage," he added, and I nodded.

He turned back around and applauded the next person. Here, on our side of the square, there were already two people standing in the middle of the circle, flushed and excited as they showed their IDs to security. I glanced at the people nearest to me, heart pounding. Actually, Robbie had picked a really good spot. There was a narrow space between that big rock and the edge of the planter. No one else could get too close, and with Robbie in front of me, no one would see what I was doing.

The snow seemed to swirl faster. My breath left me in little white puffs as I dropped the egg-shaped red and white stone to the ground and nudged it into place. The shallow dip in it would hold a potion-sized amount of liquid. It was one of my mom's more expensive—and rare—spelling utensils, and I'd be grounded for a year if she knew I had it.

The last name was read, and the crowd seemed to collectively sigh. Disappointment quickly turned to anticipation again as the last lucky few made their way to the circle to sign their name in the event book and become part of Cincinnati's history. I jumped when the big electric lights shining on the square went out. Expected, but still it got me. The tiny, distant lights from the surrounding buildings seemed to shine down like organized stars.

Tension grew, and while the noise redoubled, I dropped to a crouch before the stone and pulled my gloves off, jamming them into a deep pocket. I had to do this right. Not only so Robbie would get me into the I.S., but I didn't want to go to the West Coast and leave my mom alone. Robbie wouldn't be so mean, would he?

But when he frowned over his shoulder, I didn't know.

My fingers were slow with cold, and in the new darkness, I twisted the ground-glass stopper out, gave the bottle a swirl, then dumped the potion. It silently settled, ripples disappearing markedly fast. I couldn't risk standing up and possibly kicking snow into it, so I could only guess by the amount of noise that the seven lucky people were now in place.

"Hurry up!" Robbie hissed, glancing back at me.

I jammed the empty bottle in a pocket and fumbled for the finger stick. The snap of the plastic breaking to reveal the tiny blade seemed to echo to my bones, though it was unheard over the noise of the crowd.

Then they went silent. The sudden hush brought my heart into my throat. They had started the invocation. I had moments. Nothing more. It was in Latin—a blessing for the following year—and as most of the people bowed their heads, I jabbed my index finger.

My fingers were so cold, it registered as a dull throb. Holding my breath, I massaged it, willing the three drops to hurry. One, two, and then the third fell, staining the wine as it fell through the thinner liquid.

I watched, breathing in the heady scent of redwood now emanating from it. Robbie turned, eyes wide, and I felt my heart jump. I had done it right. It wouldn't smell like that if I hadn't.

"You did it!" he said, and we both gasped when the clear liquid flashed a soft red, my blood jumping through the medium, mixing it all on its own.

Behind us, a collective sound of awe rose, soft and powerful. I glanced up. Past Robbie, a bubble of power swam up from the earth. It was huge by circle standards, the shimmering field of ever-after arching to a close far above the fountain it spread before. In the distance, the faint resonating of Cincinnati's cathedral chimes swelled into existence as the nearby bells began ringing from the magic's vibration, not the bells' clappers.

We were outside the circle. Everyone was. It glittered like an opal; the multiple auras of the seven people gave it shifting bands of blues, greens, and golds. A flash of red and black glittered sporadically, red evidence of human suffering that made us stronger, and black for the bad we knowingly did—the choice we all had. It was breathtaking, and I stared at it, crouched in the snow, surrounded by hundreds, but feeling alone for the wonder I felt. The hair on the back of my neck pricked. I couldn't see the collective power rolling back and forth between the buildings—washing, gaining strength—but I could feel it.

My eyes went to Robbie's. They were huge. He wasn't watching the stone crucible. Mouth working, he pointed a mittened hand behind me.

I jerked from my crouch to a stand and pressed my back to the stone. The liquid in the depression was almost gone, sifting upward in a golden-sheened mist, and I held a hand to my mouth. It was person-shaped. The mist clearly had a man's shape, with wide shoulders and a masculine build. It was hunched in what looked like pain, and I had a panicked thought that maybe I was hurting my dad.

From behind us, a shout exploded from a thousand throats. I gasped, eyes jerking over my brother's head to the crowd. From the far stage, the drummer beat the edge of his set four times to signal the start of the all-night party, and the band ripped into music. People screamed in delight, and I felt dizzy. The sound battered me, and I steadied myself against the stone.

"Blame it all to the devil," a shaky, frightened voice said behind me. "It's Hell. It's Hell before she falls. Holy blame fire!"

I jerked, eyes wide, pressing deeper into the stone behind me. A man was standing between Robbie and me—a small man in the snow, barefoot with curly black hair, a small beard, wide shoulders . . . and absolutely nothing on him. "You're not my dad," I said, feeling my heart beat too fast.

"Well, there's one reason to sing to the angels, then, isn't there?" he said, shivering violently and trying to cover himself. And then a woman screamed.

FOUR

S treaker!" the woman shouted, her arm thick in its parka, pointing.

Heads turned, and I panicked. There were more gasps and a lot of cheers. Robbie jumped onto the planter beside me and shrugged out of his coat.

"My God, Rachel!" he said, the scintillating glow from the set circle illuminating his shock. "It worked!"

The small man was cowering, and he jumped at a distant boom of sound. They were shooting off fireworks at the river, and the crowd responded when a mushroom of gold and red exploded, peeking from around one of the buildings. Fear was thick on him, and he stared at the sparkles, lost and utterly bewildered.

"Here. Put this on," Robbie was saying. He looked funny in just his hat, scarf, and mittens, and the man jumped, startled when Robbie draped his coat over him.

Still silent, the man turned his back on me, tucking his arms into the sleeves and closing the coat with a relieved quickness. Another firework exploded, and he looked up, mouth agape at the green glow reflected off the nearby buildings.

Robbie's expression was tight with worry. "Shit, shit, shit," he muttered, "I never should have done this. Rachel, can't you do a damned spell wrong once in a while?"

My heart dropped to my middle, and I couldn't breathe. Our bet. Damn it. This wasn't Dad. I'd done something wrong. The man hunched before me in bare feet and my brother's new coat wasn't my dad.

"I speculated hell was hot . . ." he said, shivering. "This is c-cold."

"It didn't work," I whispered, and he fixed his vivid blue eyes on me, looking like a startled animal. My breath caught. He was lost and afraid. Another distant boom broke our gaze as he looked to the snowy skies.

From nearby came a shrill, "Him. That's him right over there!"

Spinning, I found the woman who had screamed earlier. Security was with her, and they were both looking this way.

"It's an outrage to all decent folks!" she said loudly in a huff.

My eyes went to my brother's. Crap. Now what?

Robbie jumped off the planter. "We have to go."

The small man was scanning the crowd, a look of wonder replacing his fear. At my feet, Robbie grabbed my mom's stone crucible and jammed it in his pocket. "Sorry everyone!" he said with a forced cheerfulness. "Cousin Bob. What an ass. Did it on a dare. Ha, ha! You won, Bob. Dinner is on me."

I got off the planter, but the man—the ghost, maybe—was staring at the buildings. "This fearsome catastrophe isn't hell," he whispered, and then his attention dropped to me. "You're not a demon."

His accent sounded thick, like an old TV show, and I wondered how long this guy had been dead.

Robbie reached up and grabbed his wrist, pulling. "It's going to be hell if we don't get out of here! Come on!"

The man lurched off the planter. All three of us stumbled on the slick stone, knocking into people wearing heavy winter coats and having red faces. "Sorry!" Robbie exclaimed, all of us in a confused knot as he refused to let go of my wrist.

I squinted as the wind sent a gust of snow at me. "What did I do wrong?" I said, too short to see where we were going. The fireworks were still going off, and people in the square had started singing.

"Me, me, me," Robbie cajoled, shoving the ghost ahead of us. "Why is it always about you, Rachel? Can you move it a little faster? You want to end up at the I.S. waiting for Mom to pick you up?"

For an instant, I froze. *Oh, God. Mom.* She couldn't find out.

"Hurry up! Let's go!" I shouted, pushing on the man's back. He stumbled, and I jerked my hands from him, the sight of his bare feet in the snow a shocking reminder of where he had come from. *Holy crap, what have I done?*

We found the blocked-off street with an abrupt suddenness. The smell of food grew heavy as the crowd thinned. My lungs were hurting, and I yanked on Robbie's sleeve.

His face was tight in bother as he turned to me, but then he nodded and stopped when he saw me gasping. "Are you okay?" he asked, and I bobbed my head, trying to catch my breath.

"I think they quit following," I said, but it was more of a prayer than a true thought.

Next to me, the man bent double. A groan of pain came from him, and I lurched backward when he started in with the dry heaves. The people nearby began drifting away with ugly looks. "Too much partying," someone muttered in disgust.

"Poor uncle Bob," Robbie said loudly, patting his back gingerly, and the man shoved him away, still coughing.

"Don't touch me," he panted, and Robbie retreated to stand beside me where we watched his hunched figure gasp in the falling snow. Behind us, the party continued at the square. Slowly he got control of himself and straightened, carefully arranging his borrowed coat and reaching for a nonexistent hat. His face was almost too young for his short beard. He had no wrinkles but those from stress. Silently he took us in as he struggled to keep his lungs moving, his bright blue eyes going from one of us to the other.

"Robbie, we have to get out of here," I whispered, tugging on his sleeve. He looked frozen in his thin shirt with only his mittens, hat, and scarf between him and the snow.

Robbie got in front of me to block the man's intent gaze. "I'm really sorry. We didn't mean to . . . do whatever we did." He glanced at the square, arms wrapped around himself and shivering. "This wasn't supposed to happen. You'll go back when the sun comes up."

Still the man said nothing, and I looked at his bare feet.

Over the noise came an aggressive, "Hey! You!"

My breath hissed in. Robbie turned to look, and even the man seemed alarmed.

"We need a cab," my brother said, grabbing my arm and pushing the man forward.

I twisted out of his grip and headed the other way. "We won't get a cab five blocks from here. We need a bus." Robbie stared blankly at me, and I yelled in exasperation, "The main depot is just over there! They can't close it off. Come on!"

"Stop!" a man's voice shouted, and we bolted. Well, Robbie and I bolted. The guy between us was kind of shoved along.

We dodged around the people with little kids already leaving, headed for the bus stop. It took up an entire block length, buses leaving from downtown for all corners of Cincy and the Hollows across the river. No one seemed to notice the small man's feet were bare or that Robbie was drastically underdressed. Song and laughter were rampant.

"There," Robbie panted, pointing to a bus just leaving for Norwood.

"Wait! Wait for us!" I yelled, waving, and the driver stopped.

The door opened and we piled in, my boots slipping on the slick rubber. Robbie had shoved the man up the stairs ahead of me, falling back when the driver had a hissy about the fare. I stood a step down and fumed while Robbie fished around in his wallet. Finally he was out of my way, and I ran my bus pass through the machine.

"Hey," the driver said, nodding to the back of the otherwise empty bus. "If he blows chunks, I'm fining you. I got your bus pass number, missy. Don't think I won't."

My heart seemed to lodge in my throat. Robbie and I both turned. The man was sitting alone beside a center pole, clutching it with both hands as the bus jerked into motion. His bare feet looked odd against the dirty, slush-coated rubber, and his knees were spread wide for balance to show his bare calves.

"Uh," Robbie said, making motions for me to move back. "He's okay."

"He'd better be," the driver grumbled, watching us in the big mirror.

Every block put us farther from the square, closer to home. "Please," I said, trying not to look desperate. "We're just trying to help him get home. It's the solstice."

The driver's hard expression softened. He took one hand off the wheel to rummage out of sight beside him. With a soft plastic rustle, he handed me a shopping bag. "Here," he said. "If he throws up, have him do it in there."

My breath slipped from me in relief. "Thank you."

Shoving the bag into a pocket, I exchanged a worried look with Robbie. Together we turned to the back of the bus. Pace slow, we cautiously approached the man as the city lights grew dim and the bus lights more obvious. Thankfully we were the only people on it, probably due to our destination being what was traditionally a human neighborhood, and they left the streets to us Inderlanders on the solstice.

The man's eyes darted between us as Robbie and I sat down facing him. I licked my lips and scooted closer to my brother. He was cold, shivering, but I didn't think he was going to ask for his coat back. "Robbie, I'm scared," I whispered, and the small man blinked.

Robbie took his mittens off and gripped my hand. "It's okay." His inhale was slow, and then louder, he said, "Excuse me, sir?"

The man held up a hand as if asking for a moment. "My apologies," he said breathily. "What year might this be?"

My brother glanced at me, and I blurted, "It's nineteen ninety-nine. It's the solstice."

The man's vivid blue eyes darted to the buildings, now more of a skyline since we weren't right among them anymore. He had beautiful, beautiful blue eyes, and long lashes I would have given a bra size for. If I had any to spare, that is.

"This is Cincinnati?" he said softly, gaze darting from one building to the next.

"Yes," I said, then jerked my hand out of Robbie's when he gave me a squeeze to be quiet. "What?" I hissed at him. "You think I should lie? He just wants to know where he is."

The man coughed, cutting my brother's anger short. "I expect I'm most sorry," he said, taking one hand off the pole. "I've no need for breathing but to speak, and to make a body accept that is a powerful trial."

Surprised, I simply waited while he took a slow, controlled breath.

"I'm Pierce," he said, his accent shifting to a more formal sound. "I have no doubt that you're not my final verdict, but are in truth . . ." He glanced at the driver. Lips hardly moving, he mouthed, "You're a practitioner of the arts. A master witch, sir."

The man wasn't breathing. I was watching him closely, and the man wasn't breathing. "Robbie," I said urgently, tugging on his arm. "He's dead. He's a ghost."

My brother made a nervous guffaw, crossing his legs to help keep his body heat with him. We were right over the heater, but it was still cold. "That's what you were trying to do, wasn't it, Firefly?" he said.

"Yes, but he's so real!" I said, hushed. "I didn't expect anything but a whisper or a feeling. Not a naked man in the snow. And certainly not him!"

Pierce flushed. His eyes met mine, and I bit back my next words, stunned by the depth of his bewilderment. The bus shifted forward as the driver braked to pick someone up, and he almost fell out of his seat, grabbing the pole with white hands to save himself.

"You drew me from purgatory," he said, confusion pouring from him even as he warily watched the people file on and find their seats. His face went panicked, and then he swallowed, forcing his emotions down. "I suspected I was going to hell. I suspected my penance for my failure was concluded, and I was going to hell. I'll allow it looks like hell at first observance, though not broken and lacking a smell of burnt amber." He looked out the window. "No horses," he said softly, then his eyebrows rose inquiringly. "And you bricked over the canal, nasty swill hole it was. Are the engines powered then by steam?"

Beside me, Robbie grinned. "He sure uses a lot of words to say anything."

"Shut up," I muttered. I thought he was elegant.

"This isn't hell," Pierce said, and, as if exhausted, he dropped his head to show me the top of his loose black curls. His relief made my stomach clench and burn.

I looked away, uncomfortable. Thoughts of my deal with Robbie came back. I didn't know if he would think this was a success or not. I did bring a ghost back, but it wasn't Dad. And without Dad saying yes to the I.S., Robbie would probably take it as a no. Worried, I looked up at Robbie and said, "I did the spell right."

My brother shifted, as if preparing for an argument. My eyebrows pulled together, and I glared at him. "I don't care if it summoned the wrong ghost, I did the freaking spell right!"

Pierce looked positively terrified as he alternated his attention between us and the new people calmly getting on and finding their seats. I was guessing it wasn't the volume of my voice, but what I was saying. Being a witch in public was a big no-no that could get you killed before nineteen sixty-six, and he had clearly died before then.

Robbie frowned in annoyance. "The deal was you'd summon Dad," he said, and I gritted my teeth.

"The deal was I would do the spell right, and if I didn't, I would come out to Portland with you. Well, look," I said, pointing. "There's a ghost. You just try to tell me he isn't there."

"All right, all right," Robbie said, slouching. "You stirred the spell properly, but we still don't know what Dad would want, so I'm not going to sign that paper."

"You son of a—"

"Rachel!" he said, interrupting me. "Don't you get it? This is why I want you to come out with me and finish your schooling." He gestured at Pierce as if he was a thing, not a person. "You did an eight-hundred-level summoning spell without batting an eye. You could be anything you want. Why are you going to waste yourself in the I.S.?"

"The I.S. isn't a waste," I said, while Pierce shifted uncomfortably. "Are you saying Dad's life was a waste, you dumb pile of crap?"

Pierce stared at me, and I flushed. Robbie's face was severe, and he looked straight ahead, ticked. The bus was moving again, and I sat in a sullen silence. I knew I was heaping more abuse on Robbie than he deserved. But I had wanted to talk to my dad, and now that chance was gone. I should've known I wouldn't be able to do it right. And as much as I hated myself for it, the tears started to well.

Pierce cleared his throat. Embarrassed, I wiped my eyes and sniffed.

"You were attempting to summon your father," he said softly, making nervous glances at the people whispering over Pierce's bare feet and Robbie's lack of a coat. "On the solstice. And it was I whom your magic touched?"

I nodded fast, struggling to keep from bawling my fool head off. I missed him. I had really thought I could do it.

"I apologize," Pierce said so sincerely that I looked up. "You might should celebrate, mistress witch. You stirred the spell proper, or I expect

I'd not be here. That I appeared in his stead means he has gone to his reward and is at peace."

Selfishly, I'd been wishing that Dad had missed me so much that he would have lingered, and I sniffed again, staring at the blur of holiday lights passing. I was a bad daughter.

"Please don't weep," he said, and I started when he leaned forward and took my hand. "You're so wan, it's most enough to break my heart, mistress witch."

"I only wanted to see him," I said, pitching my voice low so it wouldn't break.

Pierce's hands were cold. There was no warmth to him. But his fingers held mine firmly, their roughness stark next to my unworked, skinny hands. I felt a small lift through me, as if I was tapping a line, and my eyes rose to his.

"Why . . ." he said, his vivid eyes fixed on mine. "You're a grown woman. But so small."

My tears quit from surprise. "I'm eighteen," I said, affronted, then pulled my hand away. "How long have you been dead?"

"Eighteen," he murmured. I felt a growing sense of unease as the small man leaned back, glancing at Robbie with what looked like embarrassment.

"My apologies," he said formally. "I meant no disrespect to your intended."

"Intended!" Robbie barked, and I made a rude sound, sliding down from my brother. The people who had just gotten on looked up, surprised. "She's not my girlfriend. She's my sister." Then Robbie's expression shifted. "Stay away from my sister."

I felt the beginnings of a smile come over my face. Honestly, Pierce was a ghost and too old for me even if he was alive. At least twenty-four, I'd guess from the look at him. All of him.

I flushed as I recalled his short stature, firmly muscled and lean, like a small horse used to hard labor. Glancing up, I was embarrassed to see Pierce as red as I felt, carefully holding his coat closed.

"If the year is nineteen ninety-nine, I've made a die of it for nearly a hundred and forty-seven years," he said to the floor.

Poor man, I thought in pity. Everyone he knew was probably gone or so old they wouldn't remember him. "How did you die?" I asked, curious.

Pierce's gaze met mine, and I shivered at the intensity. "I'm a witch, as much as you," he whispered, though Robbie and I had been shouting about spells for the last five minutes. But before the Turn, being labeled a witch could get you killed.

"You were caught?" I said, scooting to the edge of the bus seat as we swung onto a slick, steep road, captivated by his air of secrecy. "Before the Turn? What did they do to you?"

Pierce tilted his head to give himself a dangerous air. "A murder most powerful. I'd have no mind to tell you if you're of a frail constitution, but I was bricked into the ground while breath still moved in my lungs. Buried alive with an angelic guard ready to smite me down should I dare to emerge."

"You were murdered!" I said, feeling a quiver of fear.

Robbie chuckled, and I thwacked his knee. "Shut up," I said, then winced at Pierce's aghast look. If he'd been dead for a hundred and forty years, I'd probably just cursed like a sailor.

"Sorry," I said, then braced myself when the bus swayed to a stop. More people filed on, the last being an angry, unhappy woman with more of those fliers. She talked to the bus driver for a moment, and he grumbled something before waving her on and letting the air out of the brakes. Leaning back, he shut his eyes as the woman taped a laminated flier to the floor in the aisle, and two more to the ceiling.

"Take a flier," she demanded as she worked her way to the back of the bus. "Sarah's been missing for two days. She's a sweet little girl. Have you seen her?"

Only on every TV station, I thought as I shook my head and accepted the purple paper. I glanced down as she handed one to Robbie and Pierce. The picture was different from the last one. The glow of birthday candles was in the foreground and a pile of presents in the back, blurry and out of focus. Sarah was smiling, full of life, and the thought of her alone, lost in the snow, was only slightly more tolerable than the thought of what someone sick enough to steal her might be using her for.

I couldn't look anymore. The woman had gotten off through the back door to hit the next bus, and I jammed the flier in my pocket with the first one as the bus lurched into traffic.

"I know who has her," Pierce said, his hushed, excited voice pulling my attention to him. The lights of oncoming traffic shone on him, lighting his fervent, kind of scary expression.

"Driver!" he shouted, standing, and I pressed into the seat, alarmed. "Stop the carriage!"

Everyone looked at us, most of them laughing. "Sit down!" Robbie gave him a gentle shove, and Pierce fell back, coat flying open for a second. "You're going to get us kicked off."

"I know where she's been taken!" he exclaimed, and I glanced at the passengers, worried. The driver, though, already thought he was drunk, and everyone else was snickering about the peep show.

"Lower your voice," Robbie said, shifting to sit beside him. "People will think you're crazy."

Pierce visibly caught his next words and closed his coat tighter. "He has her," he said, shaking the paper at Robbie. "The man, that . . . beast that murdered me to death. The very creature I was charged to bring to midnight justice. He's taken another."

I could tell my eyes were round, but Robbie wasn't impressed. "It's been almost two hundred years."

"Which means little to the blood-lusting, foul spawn from hell," Pierce said, and my breath caught. Vampire. He was talking about a vampire. A dead one. Crap, if a vampire had her, then she was really in trouble.

"You were trying to tag a vampire?" I said, awed. "You must be good!" Even the I.S. didn't send witches after vampires.

Pierce's expression blanked and he looked away. "Not good enough, I allow. I was there on my own hook with the belief that pride and moral outrage would sustain me. The spawn has an unholy mind for young girls, which I expect he satisfied without reprisal for decades until he abducted a girl of high standing and her parents engaged my . . . midnight services."

Robbie scoffed, but I stared. Figuring out what Pierce was saying was fascinating.

Seeing Robbie's disinterest, Pierce focused on me. "This child," he said, looking at the paper, "is the image of his preferred prey. I confronted him with his culpability, but he is as clever as a Philadelphian lawyer, and to pile on the agony, he informed the constables of my liability and claimed knowledge of the signs."

Pierce's eyes dropped, and I felt a twinge of fear for the history I'd missed by a mere generation. Liability was a mixed-company term for witch—when being one could get you killed. I suspected spawn was pre-Turn for vampire. Midnight services was probably code for detective or possibly an early Inderlander cop. Philadelphian lawyer was self-explanatory.

"Truly I was a witch," he said softly, "and I could say no different. The girl he murdered directly to protect his name. That it was so fast was a grace, her fair white body found in solstice snow and wept over. She could no more speak to save me than a stick. That I showed signs of liability about my person and belongs made my words of no account. They rowed me up Salt River all night for their enjoyment until being buried alive in blasphemed ground was a blessing. This," he said, shaking the paper, "is the same black spawn. He has taken another child, and if I don't stop him, he will foul her soul by sunrise. To stand idle would be an outrage against all nature."

I stared at him, impressed. "Wow."

Robbie crossed his arms over his chest. "Kind of poetic, isn't he?"

Pierce frowned, looking at Robbie with a dark expression.

"I think he's telling the truth," I said, trying to help, but the small man looked even more affronted.

"What would I gain from a falsehood?" he said. "This is the same sweet innocence looking at me from my memory. That damned spawn survived where I didn't, but being dead myself, mayhap I can serve justice now. I expect I have only to sunup. The charm will be spent by then, and I'll return to purgatory. If I can save her, perhaps I can save my soul."

He stopped, blinking in sudden consternation at his own words, and Robbie muttered something I didn't catch.

"I need to study on it," Pierce said softly as he looked out the windows at the tall buildings. "Spawn are reluctant to shift their strongholds. I've a mind that he is yet at his same diggings. A true fortress, apart in the surrounding hills, alone and secluded."

Apart in the hills, alone and secluded was probably now high in property taxes and crowded, right in the middle of a subdivision. "I have a map at home," I said.

Pierce smiled, his entire face lighting up as he held onto the pole. The gleam in his eyes had become one of anticipation, and I found myself wanting to help him until the ends of the earth if I could see his thanks reflected in them again. No one had ever needed my help before.

Ever.

"Whoa, wait up," Robbie said, turning to face both of us. "If you know this vampire and think you know where he is, fine. But we should go to the I.S. and let them take care of it."

I took a fast breath, excited. "Yes! The I.S.!"

Pierce's enthusiasm faltered. "The I.S.?"

Robbie looked out the window, probably trying to place where we were. "Inderland Security," he said, pulling the cord to get the driver to stop. "They police the Inderlanders, not humans. Witches, Weres, vampires, and whatever." His look slid to me and became somewhat wry. "My sister wants to work for them when she grows up."

I flushed, embarrassed, but if I couldn't admit it to a ghost, maybe I shouldn't even try.

Pierce's free hand scratched at his beard in what I hoped was simply a reflexive action. "That was what my midnight profession was," he said, "but it wasn't called such. The I.S."

The bus swayed and squeaked to a stop. Pierce didn't move, holding tight to the pole as Robbie and I stood before the bus had halted. I waited for Pierce, letting him walk between Robbie and me as we got off.

The cold hit me anew, and I squinted into the snowy night as the bus left. "You want to wait for a bus going back into town?" I said, and Robbie shook his head, already on his cell phone.

"I'm calling a cab," he said, looking frozen clear through.

"Good idea," I said, cold despite my coat, mittens, and fuzzy hat.

"We need to go to the mall," Robbie said, "and I don't want to waste a lot of time."

"The mall?" I blurted as we dropped back deeper into the Plexiglas shelter. "What for?" Then I winced. "You need a new coat."

Phone to his ear and his face red from cold, Robbie nodded. "That, and it's going to be hard enough getting the I.S. to believe we're not nuts coming in with a naked man in a coat."

Pierce looked mystified. "The mall?"

I nodded, wondering if he'd let me pick out his clothes. "The mall."

 FIVE

Bored, I sat in the comfy brown fabric chair beside Pierce and shifted my knee back and forth. The mall had been a success, but Robbie had pushed us from store to store inexcusably fast, getting us in and out and to the I.S. in about two hours. Pierce was now respectably dressed in jeans and a dark green shirt that looked great against his dark hair and blue eyes. He still had on Robbie's coat, and I swear, he had almost cried when he was able to shift up a half size of boot with the ease of simply pulling another pair off the rack.

But for the last hour, we had been sitting on the third-floor reception area doing nothing. Well, Pierce and I were doing nothing. Robbie, at least, was being taken seriously. I could see him down the open walkway at a desk with a tired-looking officer. As I watched, Robbie took off his new, expensive leather jacket and draped it over his lap in a show of irritation.

Pierce hadn't said much at the mall, spending a good five minutes trying to locate the source of the mood music until he got brave enough to ask. I made sure we passed an electric outlet on the way to get him some underwear. The food court had amazed him more than the electric lights, though he wouldn't try the blue slurry I begged off Robbie. The kiddy rides made him smile, then he stared in astonishment when I told him it wasn't magic but the same thing that made the lights work. That was nothing compared to when he saw a saleslady in a short skirt. Becoming beet red, he turned and walked out, his head tilted conspiratorially to Robbie's for a quiet, hushed conversation. All I caught was a muttered, "bare limbs?"

but Robbie made sure we went past Valeria's Crypt so he could see the same thing in lace. Men.

Pierce's silence deepened after finding an entire building devoted to Inderland law enforcement, but even I was impressed with the I.S. tower. The entryway was a fabulous three floors high, looking more like the lobby of a five-star hotel than a cop shop. Pierce and I had a great view of the lower floors from where we sat. It was obvious that the designers had used the techniques of cathedral builders to impart awe and a feeling of insignificant smallness.

Low lights on the first floor created dark shadows that set off the occasional burst of light. Acoustically, the space was a sinkhole, making what would be a loud chatter into a soft murmur. The air carried the faint scent of vampire, and I wrinkled my nose wondering if that was what was bothering Pierce, or if it was that we were three stories up.

A minor disturbance pulled our attention to the street-level entrance as two people, witches, I guess, brought in a third. The man was still fighting them, his arms securely behind his back and fastened with a zip-strip of charmed silver. It looked barbaric, but bringing in a violent ley line witch was impossible unless they were properly restrained. Sure, there were ways to prevent magic from being invoked in a building, but then half the officers would be helpless, too.

Pierce watched until the witch was shoved into an elevator, then he turned to me. His expressive eyes were pinched when he asked, "How long have humans known about us, and how did we survive giving them the knowledge?"

I bobbed my head, remembering Pierce's shock when two witches started flirting in the mall, throwing minor spells at each other. "We've been out of the closet for about forty years."

His lips parted. "Out of the closet . . ."

A grin came over my face. "Sorry. We came clean . . . uh . . . we told them we existed after a virus hiding in tomatoes—a sort of a plague—started killing humans. It dropped their numbers by about a quarter. They were going to find out about us anyway because we weren't dying."

Pierce watched my moving foot and smiled with half his face. "I've always been of the mind that tomatoes were the fruit of the devil," he said. Then he brought his gaze to mine and gestured to take in the entire building. "This happened in four decades?"

I shrugged, twisting my boot toe into the tight-looped carpet. "I didn't say it was easy."

Crossing his knees, he rubbed his beard as if noticing not many men had them. Though very quiet since our shopping trip, he had clearly been taking everything in, processing it. Even his words, few as they had been, were starting to sound . . . less odd.

"Your brother," he said, gesturing at him with his chin, "said you want to devote your life to this?"

I smiled somewhat sheepishly. "The I.S. Yes." A sudden worry pulled my brows together. "Why? You think I shouldn't?"

"No," he rushed. "A daughter's wish to follow in her parent's occupation is proper."

Startled he knew my dad had worked for the I.S., I caught my breath until I remembered our conversation in the bus. "Oh. You heard that."

He ducked his head. "Yes, mistress witch. And who am I to tell you the profession of protecting the helpless is too dangerous? I live for it."

I felt a quiver of connection, that he might really understand. Pierce, though, gave me a wry look. "Lived for it," he amended sourly.

Used to arguing about my chosen profession, I lifted my chin. "I'm stronger every year," I said as if he had protested. "I mean, markedly stronger."

"You suffered an illness?" Pierce asked, seemingly genuinely concerned.

I nodded, and then feeling some honesty was due, added, "I still am sick, sort of. But I'm doing much better. Everyone says so. I have more stamina all the time. I attend classes to keep from slipping back, and I haven't been in the hospital for about four years. I should have died, so I really don't have any cause to complain, but I want to do this, damn it. They can't keep me out because of my health. I got a black belt and everything."

I stopped, realizing not only was I babbling to the first understanding person I'd found, but I was swearing, too. "Sorry," I said, twisting my foot again. "That's probably gutter talk for you."

Pierce made a soft sound, neither accusing nor affirming. He was look-ing at my middle in a soft puzzlement. "You're passionate," he finally said, and I smiled in relief. I knew he would be gone by sunrise, but I didn't want to alienate him. I liked him, even if he was a ghost. *Oh God, I was* not *crushing on him.*

"I'm in the medical books, you know," I said, trying to get his mind off my bad mouth. "The only survivor of Rosewood syndrome."

He started, turning from where he had been watching Robbie argue with his interviewer. "You . . . Rosewood? You survived? I lost two sisters and a brother to that, passed before they were three months. Are you sure that's what ailed you?"

I smiled because there was no pain in him. The hurt, apparently, was old. "That's what it was. Is. Modern medicine I suppose, or all the herbal remedies they gave me at that Make-A-Wish camp for dying kids. I was there for three years until they kicked me out when I quit dying so fast."

The wonder was stark in his gaze as he settled back as if not believing it. "You're a wonder, mistress witch."

I scoffed and ran my fingernails to bump over the chair's fabric. "I'm not really a witch yet. I haven't gotten my license. You can call me Rachel."

Pierce's subtle fidgeting ceased and I looked up to find him staring. In sudden understanding, I warmed. Crap, giving him my first name might be extremely intimate. He certainly didn't seem to know how to react.

Embarrassed, I focused on Robbie. "I, uh, am sorry for bringing you from your rest," I said. "I was trying to call my dad. See, I had this bet with Robbie. I said Dad, my father, would want me to put my application in to the I.S., and Robbie said if he were still alive, he'd want me to get a higher degree in my earth witch studies. So Robbie challenged me to call him and ask. If I could do it, I promised I'd do what Dad said; if not, I'd go with Robbie and go to school for four more years. I didn't figure on him being at peace. I suppose I should be glad," I said, feeling guilty. "But I really wanted to talk to him."

"Miss Rachel," Pierce said, and my head came up when he took my hand. "Don't weep for your father. I expect he's at rest, watching you and wishing you happiness."

"You don't know that," I said contrarily, pulling away. "You're stuck in purgatory."

But instead of taking that as a brush-off, he nodded as if he liked it.

"You do know the intent behind your brother's challenge was to prove to you how skilled you are at earth magic, so you will follow that path?"

My mouth dropped open and I looked at Robbie. "The dirtbag," I whispered. "Well, I'm not doing it," I said while Pierce puzzled over the modern phrase. "We don't know if my dad would have approved or not, so the deal is off. I'm not going to Portland. I'm going to stay here with my mother and become the best damned runner since my dad."

Crap, I'm swearing again, I thought, then gave Pierce an apologetic smile. "What do you think I should do?"

The small man leaned forward, startling me with his intensity. "I believe," he said, inches away, "that if you don't follow your passions, you die slowly."

He was holding my hand again. A slow quiver built in me, and I pulled my hand away before I shivered outright. The office chatter seemed to grow loud, and Pierce resettled himself.

"My apologies," he said, clearly not sorry at all. "I've overstepped my boundaries."

Yeah, like I don't want you to? "It's okay," I said, boldly meeting his gaze. "I've held hands with guys before." *And kissed them. I wonder what it's like to kiss a ghost?* God, he had a beard. It would probably be all prickly and nasty. But maybe it was soft?

Yanking my thoughts back where they belonged, I looked down the open walkway to Robbie. He was clearly upset as he talked to the man, his arms moving in sharp angry motions. "I wonder what they're saying," I murmured.

Pierce still had that devilish look, but I liked it.

"Let me see if I can commune with the ever-after," he said. "I've a mind to speak a charm to hear them, though it's wicked to do so." But almost immediately his enthusiasm faltered. "I can't find a line," he said, touching his beard as if nervous. "Being a spectre, one might think it would be easier, not forbidden."

Well, nuts to that. I want to know what Robbie is saying. In a spontane-ous motion, I grabbed Pierce's wrist. My focus blurred as I searched for the nearest ley line, finding the university's glowing in my thoughts: a dusky red ribbon of power all witches could tap into regardless of where their talents lay.

Reaching out a thought, I connected to it. Warmth spilled into me in a slow trickle, running to my chi and making my skin tingle. Forcing my vision to focus, I looked at Pierce. My pleased smile faded. Crap, I'd done it again. The small man was staring at me as if I had just taken off all my clothes and was dancing naked on the desks.

"So you can do the spell . . ." I said in a small voice, and took a breath as if only now remembering how to breathe. "Didn't you share lines in your time?"

"Not often," he said, setting a hand atop mine so I wouldn't let go. "But I'm not there anymore. Thank you. Let me . . . do the spell."

He steadied himself, and while I felt like a whore on the corner, he flicked a nervous gaze at me with his beautiful, deep blue eyes. "Well?" I prompted.

"I'm not of a mind to hurt you," he admitted.

"Then don't pull so much," I said, glancing at Robbie. *God, did he think I was a child?*

"Um, yes," he stammered, and I shifted my shoulders when I felt a soft draw through me.

"You're fine," I encouraged, and he pulled more until my hair was floating from static. Intrigued, I watched Pierce close his eyes as if trying to remember something. His lips moved and I heard the faintest hint of Latin, dark and alien sounding. His free hand sketched a quick figure, and then my ears popped.

"A moment," he said, his hand atop mine tightening to keep me from breaking the link.

My gaze shot to Robbie. "Oh, wow," I breathed as his voice came clear, as if I was listening to a phone.

"Wow. Yes," Pierce repeated, smiling from behind his beard, and we turned to listen.

"But I know he took her," Robbie said forcefully, his lips moving in time with the spoken words. "Can't you just get a car out there or something?"

The I.S. officer he was with had his back to us, but I could see he was typing. "Mr. Morgan. I assure you we're giving the matter our full attention."

"Are you?" my brother said. "She'll be dead by sunup if you don't do something. He's done this before. He just made the mistake of taking someone who would be noticed this time."

The man in his wrinkled suit clicked a window on his computer closed. One hand on the mouse, he gave my brother a long look. "And you know this how?"

Robbie said nothing, and I looked at the entryway floor when the vampire turned to see Pierce and me.

"Mr. Morgan," the man said, his voice thick with dismissal. "I've taken twelve statements like yours over the past three hours. We're working on them in turn, but you can understand we can't devote all our manpower to one missing child who is angry she isn't getting what she wants for Christmas and has run away to her daddy."

"I'm not a crank," Robbie said tightly. "My father used to work in the Arcane Division, and I know real from fake. This isn't a joke."

I breathed easier when the vampire focused on my brother again. "Monty Morgan?" he said, and I nodded even as Robbie did.

Pierce's grip on my hand twitched when the vampire stood. The ghost's expression of concern surprised me.

"Wait here," the officer said. "I'll be right back."

Pleased, I smiled at Pierce. "See?" I said, feeling like we were getting somewhere.

But Pierce's brow was creased in a deep worry. "Spawn," he muttered, and while I held his one hand, he made a small gesture with the other. I stifled a jump when the energy he was pulling off the line through me shifted. His lips pressed tight, he pointed to the I.S. officer, now bending to speak to another, clearly higher-up, officer.

"Sir, do you have a minute?" Robbie's interviewer said, his voice clear.

I couldn't see the new man's face, but his tone was bothered as he brought his attention up from his paperwork and said, "What?"

"It's the missing girl," the first officer said, fingers moving nervously behind his back.

I caught a glimpse of the supervisor's face when he turned to Robbie. It was smooth and nice looking despite his expression of annoyance. Young. "So?" he said.

Shifting his feet, the older man bent closer. "He knows things not released to the press."

The vampire went back to his paperwork, the pencil skating across the form too fast for a human. "So?" he said again.

"So he's one of Morgan's kids."

I felt a stir of satisfaction when the officer set his pencil down. "Who?"

"The witch in Arcane," Robbie's interviewer prompted. "Died about four years ago?"

But my pride shifted to a stark fear when the vampire looked at Robbie, his pupils swelling to black. Crap, I could see it from here. He was vamping out. But why?

"Morgan's boy?" he murmured, interested, and my pulse quickened. Something was wrong. I could almost taste it. "I thought he was out of state."

Pierce let go of my wrist and I jumped when the connection between us broke. My chi was suddenly overfull, and I forced most of the energy back into the ley line. I didn't let go of the line completely, ready for anything.

"I expect we should leave," the small man said, eyes darting over the three floors to linger on the building's main entrance.

I rubbed my wrist to get rid of the remaining tingles. "What's wrong?"

Pierce eased to the front of the chair and held his coat closed. "It's been my experience that instinct, not what you've been taught, is the clearest indicator of direction. They have a mind that your brother is involved with the girl's abduction and is finding reason to beg clemency by cooperating. We need to pull foot."

"Wait up," I said when he rose and drew me to a stand. "What about Robbie?"

As if having heard me, my brother met my gaze. His face was ashen. Behind him, the two vampires were headed his way. Clearly frightened, he mouthed, "Go!"

"Your brother won't come to any hurt," Pierce said, and I fell into motion when he gripped my elbow and started us toward the wide stairway. "They will give him Jesse until sure of his innocence, but by that time, the sun will be risen. Blame it all, I should have been of a state to fix his flint myself."

I had no idea what he was saying, but Pierce had us on the steps before the first shout. My head whipped around, and I stumbled. Two brutish men were heading our way, and with a little gasp, I pushed Pierce down faster. A chime rang through the air, and my skin prickled. "Lock down!" someone shouted.

"Damnation," Pierce swore, but our feet were still moving, and we had passed the second floor without trouble. My pulse was too fast, and my lungs hurt, but I wouldn't slow down. We wouldn't be caught because of me. Apart from the two guys following us and the uniformed woman standing in front of the doors with her arms crossed over her chest, everyone seemed content to watch. Actually, they were moving back, making room. *Swell.*

"Mistress witch," Pierce said, his tone terse as we neared the ground floor, my steps barely keeping up with his. "I'd respectfully ask that I might commune a line through you." He glanced at me, shocking me again with how blue his eyes were. "To help make our escape. If there were another way, I would use it."

I slid my hand into his, gripping it firmly. "Pull on a line." He shot a bewildered look at me and I shouted, "Commune with the ever-after!"

My breath hissed in as he did, and I squeezed his hand to tell him it was okay. Power burned like ice as we found the first floor, and I felt my tongue tingle. Pierce gathered himself, and with a shout, a head-sized sphere of ever-after enveloped his free hand.

That came through me, I thought in wonder, even as we continued to head for the doors.

Pierce threw the ball. The witch waiting for us yelped and dove for the floor. Green power edged in red and black hit the glass doors, spreading out like slime. A boom shook the air and almost sent me falling. Glass pushed outward in a silent cascade.

"Are you well, Miss Rachel?" Pierce said earnestly when my ears recovered.

I looked up as he steadied me with his grip tight on my elbow. For an instant we stood, focused on each other, linked by way of the line and our need to escape. My inner ear pulsed from the blast. Behind me, shouts started to make sense. Past the shattered doors came the sound of traffic and the crisp cold of a winter night. The witch on the floor looked up from around her fallen hair, shocked. "Wow," I said, and Pierce's concern eased.

Satisfied I had my balance, he let go of my elbow but kept our fingers entwined. "Allow me, mistress witch," he said gallantly, escorting me through the broken glass.

"Hey! Stop!" someone called. My pulse raced, and knowing my mom was going to "give me Jesse" when she found out, I nevertheless stepped elegantly over the jagged remnants of the door and onto the salted sidewalk.

"A moment," Pierce said, turning, and I felt another strong pull through me when he ran two fingers across both the lintel and threshold of the wide doors and a green sheet of ever-after swam up from the frozen slush sidewalk to seal everyone inside. "Now we may depart," he said exuberantly, the light shining out from the I.S. offices showing his good mood. "Perhaps a carriage is in order," he said, whistling as if he had grown up in Cincy, but he had watched Robbie do the same thing. "I fear we should make an unpleasant haste. The ward won't last long. And we must stay holding hands until then."

I grinned. When he was excited, he didn't stop to think what he was saying and was charmingly elegant. "Maybe we should walk a few blocks so they don't know what cab we take?" I suggested. "Otherwise they'll just radio ahead."

Pierce's brow creased, and he waved away the cab that had pulled up. "Like the music from the boxes?" he said, and I nodded. It was close enough.

"Then we walk," he said. With a last wave to the angry I.S. officers behind the green-tinted sheet of ever-after, he tightened his grip on my fingers, and we strode down the sidewalk.

My pulse was fast and I felt breathless. I'd never done anything like this before, and I felt alive. For the first time in my freaking life, I felt alive—the adrenaline making me light and airy and my steps long and sure. The snow drifted down peacefully, and I wished that I could do this forever—walk with a man's hand in mine, happy and pleasantly warm with this alive feeling running through me. He wasn't much taller than me, and our steps were closely matched.

I glanced behind us at the retreating I.S. building, then shyly at Pierce, but his attention was on the buildings and storefront displays. I eyed the colored lights and the happy people walking in the snow with last-minute solstice and Christmas shoppers finding a final, perfect gift.

"No beggars," he whispered.

"Well, a few," I said, abruptly seeing the street in an entirely different way. "But they're probably at the square, partying."

Pierce pulled our joined fingers up, mine almost blue from the cold. "I can't keep communing with—ah, pulling a line through you," he said softly. "I'm not one born in the woods to be afraid of an owl, yet to save that child with only my fists I expect is a fool's errand. Do you know . . ." He hesitated, attention flicking from a truck slushing past and back to me. "Do you know a witchy woman or man I might procure ley line charms from?"

"Oh!" I said brightly, determined to keep up with him though my chest was starting to hurt. Of course he'd need something, seeing as he couldn't tap a line himself. "The university's bookstore has an entire floor of ley line stuff. I'm sure they'll have something."

"Magic studies? In the university?" he asked, and I nodded, my free arm swinging. But a frown creased his brow, and leaning to me, he whispered, "I would prefer a smaller shop if you know of it. I don't have even a stick to barter with or a . . . card of credit," he added hesitantly, as if knowing he hadn't gotten the words in the right order.

My eyes widened. "I don't have much money either. Cab fare, is all."

Pierce took a deep breath and exhaled. "No matter. I will suitably impress upon the proprietor my desperate need." His chin rose and a defiant gleam entered his eyes as we continued forward. "I will beg. If they are honorable, they will help."

Beg, eh? I thought, fully believing he would get down on his knees before the night manager at the university bookstore, who would promptly throw him out, not pleased to be working on the solstice. "I've a better idea," I said, praying my mom would go for it. My dad's stuff was in the attic. I knew my mom wouldn't be happy, but the worst thing she could do was say no. Edging us to the curb, I searched for a cab. "I'll take you home," I said, leaning into the street in the universal language of cabbies. "You can look over my dad's old ley line stuff. He worked for the I.S. He probably has something."

Pierce drew me back from the curb, and I blinked at him, surprised. His expression was pinched as he stood in the puddle of streetlight and falling snow, elegant in his long coat and shiny new boots. "Miss Rachel, no. I'm not of a mind to endanger you anymore. I'll escort you home, then go alone to the university. If there are learned men there, they will assist me."

I winced, imagining all Pierce would find right now would be half-drunk students and solstice parties. "Good God, Pierce," I said, when a passing cab saw us standing there and did a U-bangy. "I'm the one that got you involved. Lighten up."

"But—" he said, and I twined my fingers more surely into his as the cab pulled up.

"I'm involved. You're not getting rid of me, so get used to it."

Pierce's grip tightened on mine, and then he relaxed. "Thank you," he said, and in those two words, I saw how lost he was. He had until sunrise to save both the girl and his soul, and I was the only one who could get him through this nightmare that I lived in.

SIX

The cabbie drove away from my house slowly, the sound of his car muffled from the piled snow. In the Hollows there would be bonfire parties and neighborhood howls, but here, on my street, it was quiet. Pierce's steps were almost silent next to mine as we left prints on the walk to the porch. It had stopped snowing, and I looked up at the red-bottomed clouds through the cold, black branches of the maple tree I had planted for my dad upon his death. My throat closed and I touched the tree in passing. I was glad he was at rest, but it would have been nice to have had him back again as solid as Pierce was—even if just for the night.

Pierce hung back as I went up the three cement steps and twisted the knob to no avail. "My mom must be out," I said, swinging my bag around to look for my keys. The porch light was on, and her prints showed where she had gone to the garage and not come back. Maybe some last-minute shopping? Maybe down to the I.S. tower to pick up Robbie? I had a bad feeling it was the latter.

"This is a very beautiful house," Pierce said, facing the neighborhood and the bright lights and snowmen keeping guard.

"Thanks," I said as I dug in my jeans pocket for my house key. "Most witches live in the Hollows across the river in Kentucky, but my mom wanted to live here." Finding my keys, I looked up to see a faint bewilderment in his gaze. "Both she and my dad were in high school during the Turn, and I think she likes passively making trouble when she can get away with it—like living in a predominantly human neighborhood."

"As is the mother, so the daughter?" he said dryly.

My key was warm, and I slipped it into the lock. "If you like."

Only now did Pierce come up the steps, giving the street a last look before he did.

"Mom?" I called when I opened the door, but I knew from the dull glow of light in the hall coming from the kitchen that the house was empty. Glancing at Pierce on the threshold, I smiled. "Come on in."

Pierce looked at the gray slush on his boots. "I'm not of a mind to soil your rugs."

"So stomp your feet," I said, taking his arm and pulling him in. "Shut the door before you let all the heat out."

The shadow of the closing door prompted me to flick on the hallway light, and Pierce squinted at it. I hated the green color my mom had painted the hallway and living room. Pictures covered the passage to the kitchen: pictures of me and Robbie, slices of our lives.

I glanced back at Pierce, who was still staring at the light but clearly making an effort to not say anything. I hid a smile and wondered how much longer his efforts to not look impressed would win out over his curiosity.

"You have so many rugs," he finally said, following suit as I stomped my feet.

"Thanks," I said, and I shuffled out of my coat.

His eyes finally hit the walls, and he reached out. "And photographs. In color."

"You've seen pictures?" I asked, surprised, and he nodded.

"I've had my picture taken," he said proudly, then reached out. "This is you? It's beautiful," he said in awe. "The expression the artist captured is breathtaking. None of God's landscapes has ever looked so beautiful."

I gazed at the picture he was touching in reverence and then away with mixed feelings. It was a close-up of my face among the fall leaves, my eyes as green and vivid as all creation, my hair bringing out all the shades of autumn clustered about. I had just come back from a stint at the hospital and you could see that I was ill by my pale complexion and thin face. But my smile made it truly beautiful, my smile I had given to my dad as the shutter snapped, thanking him for the joy we had found in the simple pleasure of the day.

"My dad took it," I said, looking away. "Come in the kitchen," I said, wiping my eye when I noticed it was damp. *I was supposed to die before him, not the other way around.*

"I don't know how long my mom will be out," I said loudly, hearing his steps behind mine. "But if we can get what we need and leave, it will be all the better. Forgiveness being easier to get than permission . . ."

Pierce entered slowly, hesitating by the laminated table and taking in the ticking clock, the cold stove, and the double-pan sink as I dropped my coat and bag onto my chair. "You and your mother are alone?" he asked.

Surprised at the amount of wonder in his voice, I hesitated. "Yes. Robbie is visiting from the West Coast, but he goes back next week."

His deep blue eyes came back from the ceiling. "California?"

"Oregon."

Pierce looked again at the cold stove, undoubtedly guessing its use from the pot of solstice cranberry tea on it, now scrummed over and cold. "Your mother should be commended for raising you alone."

If he only knew how often it was the other way around. "She should, shouldn't she," I said, going to the coffeemaker and peeking into the filter to find unused grounds. "You want some coffee?"

Taking off his coat, Pierce draped it carefully over a chair. He checked his nonexistent tie, then moved his arms experimentally as if taking in how warm it was. "I'm of a mind, yes, but does our limited time allow for it?"

I flipped a switch and the coffeemaker started. I kind of liked his extra words. It made him sound classy. "Yup. You want to help me with the attic?"

Without waiting for an answer, I went down the other hallway to the rest of the house, Pierce right behind me. "That's the bathroom there," I said as we passed it. "My room is at the end of the hallway, and my mom's is across from it. Robbie has the front room, though it's more of a storage room, now."

"And the servants are in the attic?" he asked as I halted under the pull-down stairs.

"Servants?" I asked, gaping at him. "We don't have any servants."

Pierce looked as surprised as I felt. "But the rugs, the photos, the warmth of your home and its furnishings . . ."

His words trailed off as his hands spread wide in question, and I flushed when I got it. "Pierce," I said, embarrassed. "I'm totally middle class. The closest I've ever come to having a servant is winning a bet and having Robbie clean my room for a month."

The man's jaw dropped. "This is middle class?"

I nodded, stretching up for the pull cord and putting my weight on it. "Most of the city is." The trapdoor barely moved, and my arms gave out. It snapped shut with a bang, and I dropped back down on my heels, disgusted.

Pierce smoothly took the cord and stepped under the door. He wasn't much taller, but he had more muscle. "I can do it," I said, but my arms were trembling, and I backed up while he swung the ladder down like it was nothing. But then again, it was.

Pierce looked up into the inky blackness spilling cool air down onto us, jumping when I flicked on the light.

"Sorry," I said, taking advantage of his surprise by pushing past him and up onto the ladder. "I'll be right back," I said, enjoying the cooler air up here smelling of wood and dusty boxes. The shush of a passing car from outside sounded odd and close. Arms wrapped around me, I looked over the past boxed up and piled haphazardly about, like memories in a person's brain. It was only a matter of knowing where a thought was and dusting it off.

My eyes lit upon the stack of carefully labeled tomato boxes that had my stuffed animals. A faint smile came over my face, and I stepped over the Halloween decorations to touch a dusty lid. I must have had about two hundred of them, all collected during my stints in and out of the hospital. I had counted them my friends, many taking on the names and personalities of my real friends who never made it out of the hospital that one last time. I knew my mom wanted them gone, but I couldn't throw them away, and as soon as I got my own place, I'd take them with me.

I lifted the first one and set it aside to find the box hiding under them. It was my dad's, tucked away lest my mom throw it out in a fit of melancholy. Some of his best stuff. I dug my fingernails into the little flaps to get a grip, grunting when it proved heavier than I thought. *God, what had I put in here, anyway?*

"Allow me," came Pierce's voice from my elbow, and I spun.

"Holy crap!" I exclaimed, then covered my mouth, feeling myself go red. "I'm sorry. I didn't know you were up here."

Pierce's shock at my language melted into almost laughter. "My apologies," he said, and I shifted to let him to lift the box with enviable ease.

"I like attics. They're as peaceful as God's church. Alone and apart, but a body can hear everything. The past stacked up like forgotten memories, but with a small effort, brought down and enjoyed again."

I listened to the cold night and smiled. "I know exactly what you mean."

Watching my footing, I followed him to the stairway. He took the box from me and gestured that I should go before him, and, flattered at the chivalry, I did. My shoulders eased as the warmth of the house slipped over me, and I stood aside when Pierce lightly descended. He handed me the box to fold the ladder back up, but he hesitated at the bare bulb, still glowing in the attic. Without glancing at me for permission, he carefully pushed the light switch down.

Of course the light went out. A delighted smile came over him, and much to his credit, he didn't play with the switch but shoved the collapsible ladder closed and back into the ceiling. I watched his eyes travel over the lines of it as he did, as if memorizing how it worked.

"Thank you," I said as I went before him, back into the kitchen with the box.

The coffeemaker was gurgling its last, and Pierce looked at it, undoubtedly figuring out what it was from the rich scent that had filled the kitchen. "If that doesn't cap the climax," he said, almost missing the table as he took the box from me and set it down. "It made itself."

"I'll get you some," I said as I hustled to the cupboard. It smelled great as I poured out two cups and I handed him one, our fingers touching. He smiled, and something tightened in my chest. *God, I am not falling for him. He's dead.* But he did have a nice, mischievous smile.

"I hope I'm not making a mistake drinking this," he said. "How real am I?"

I shrugged, and he took a sip, eyeing me over the rim to make my breath catch. God, he had beautiful eyes.

His eyebrows shot up, and jerking, he started to violently cough.

"Oh, golly," I said, remembering not to swear as I took the cup from him before it could spill. "I'm sorry. You can't drink, huh?"

"Strong," he gasped, his blue eyes vivid as they watered. "Really strong."

I set his cup down and took a sip of mine. My mouth tried to pucker up, and I forced myself to swallow. Crap, my mom had filled the filter, and the coffee was strong enough to kill a cat. "Don't drink that," I said, taking his cup and mine to the sink. "It's terrible."

"No, it's fine."

I froze as he caught my hand. I turned, feeling his light but certain grip. A slow quiver rose through me, and I stifled it before it could show as a tremor. I was suddenly very aware that we were here alone. Anything could happen—and as the moment hung, his silence and almost-words ready to be whispered that he was having thoughts, too—I nearly wished it would. He was different. Strong but unsure. Capable but lost. He knew I had been ill, and he didn't baby me. I liked him. A lot, maybe. And he needed my help. No one had *ever* needed my help before. No one. Especially someone as capable and strong as him.

"It's undrinkable," I said when I found my voice, and he took his cup from me.

"If you made it, it's divine," he said, smiling like the devil himself, and I felt my heart thump even as I knew he was bullshitting me.

His fingers left mine, and my presence of mind returned. I wasn't a fainting debutante to fall for a line like that, but still, to have a man drink nasty coffee to impress me was way flattering. My eyebrows rose, and I wondered how far he would go. I had half a thought to let him drink the nasty stuff.

"Why thank you, Pierce," I said, smiling. "You are a true gentleman."

I turned to open the box, looking over my shoulder in time to see him staring into his mug with a melancholy sigh. Ten to one he was going to spill it, but there was an entire pot to refill his cup with.

The dust made my nose tickle as I unfolded the flaps. A slow smile spread over me as I looked at the stash and saw my dad everywhere. He'd made many of his own ley line charms for work, and being home sick most of the time, some of my earliest memories were of him and me at the table while the sun set and he prepped for a night on the street apprehending bad guys. I had my crayons, he had his chalk, and while I colored pixies and fairies, he'd sketch pentagrams, spill wax in ley line figures, and burn all sorts of concoctions to make Mom wave her hands and complain about the smell, secretly proud of him.

Smiling distantly, I ran a hand over my hair, remembering how it would snarl up from the forces that leaked from his magic as he explained a bit of lore while he worked, his eyes bright and eager for me to understand.

The soft scrape of Pierce setting his cup down by the box jerked me from my memories, and my focus sharpened. "Is there anything here you can use?" I asked, pushing it closer to him as we stood over it. "I'm more of an earth witch. Or I will be, when I get my license."

"Miss Rachel," he said lightly, his attention on the box's contents as his calloused fingers poked around, "only a witch of some repute can summon those at unrest, and only those of unsurpassed skill I expect can furnish them a body." A faint smile crossed his eyes. "Even one as transient as this one."

Embarrassed, I shrugged one shoulder. "It wasn't all me. Most of the energy came from the collective emotions of everyone at the square."

"And whose idea was it to work the charm at the square?" he said, taking out a handful of metallic disks and pins and discarding them into an untidy pile.

I thought back. It had been mine to go to the concert and use the emotion to help strengthen the curse, but Robbie's to use the square's instead. "Robbie's, I guess."

Pierce held a charm up to the light. "Ah," he said in satisfaction. "This I can use."

I looked at the thick silver washer with its pin running through it. Apart from a few ley line inscriptions lightly etched on it, the charm looked like the ones he'd set aside. "What is it?"

The man's smile grew positively devilish. "This likely bit of magic is a noisy lock picker," he said, then set it beside his cup of coffee.

"Noisy?"

Pierce was again rummaging. "It makes an almighty force to jolt the door from its hinges," he said lightly.

"Oh." I peered into the box with more interest and held the flaps out of his way. It was like looking into a box of chocolates, not knowing which ones were good until you took a bite.

A pleased sound escaped Pierce, and he held up another charm, his fingertip running over the symbols etched into it. "This one senses powerful magic. Perhaps it's still working?"

His gaze on the charm, he pulled the pin. The empty interior of the washer-like charm started to glow a harsh red. Pierce seemed surprised, then he laughed. "Land sakes, I'm a fool. You hold it," he said, handing it over.

I took it, bemused when Pierce backed up, nearly into the hall.

A faint cramping seemed to make my palm twitch, and the harsh red faded to a rosy pink. I glanced at the box of ley line stuff, and Pierce shook his head, coming back and taking it from me. Again it glowed brilliantly.

"It's functioning perfectly," he said, and the spell went dark when he put the pin back in place. "I've no mind to guess how effective it will be if it's glowing like that from me," and he set it gently on the table.

My lips parted, and I looked at him, and then the charms on the table. "You're triggering it? I thought it was the spells."

Pierce laughed, but it was nice. "I'm a spectre, walking the earth with a body that is a faint step from being real. I expect that qualifies as strong magic."

Flustered, I shrugged, and he put his attention back in the box.

"This one is for calling familiars," he said, dropping it onto the table with the discards. "This one for avoiding people who are searching for you. Oh, this is odd," he said, holding one up. "A charm to give a body a hunched back? That has to be a misspelling."

I took it from him, making sure our fingers touched. Yeah, he was dead, but I wasn't. "No, it's right," I said. "It's from a costume. My dad used to dress up on Halloween."

"Halloween?" Pierce asked, and I nodded, lost in a memory.

"For trick-or-treat. I'd be the mad scientist, and he'd be my assistant. We would go up and down the halls of the hospital . . ." My emotions gave a heavy-hearted lurch, and I swallowed down a lump. "We'd hit the nurse's desk in the children's ward, and then the old people's rooms."

I didn't want to talk about it, and my fingers set it down, sliding away with a slow sadness. It seemed Pierce understood, since he was silent for a moment, then said, "You look the picture of health, Miss Rachel. A fair, spirited, young woman."

Grimacing, I picked up the charm and dropped it back into the box. "Yeah, well, try telling my brother that."

Again he was silent, and I wondered what his nineteenth-century morals were making of me and my stubborn determination. He said I was spirited, but I didn't think that was necessarily a good thing back then.

"This is one I'd like to take if I might," Pierce said as he held up a rather large, palm-sized metallic amulet. "It detects people within a small space."

"Cool," I said, taking it from him and pulling the pin. "Does it work?"

Again, that cramping set my hand to feeling tingly and odd. The entire middle of the amulet went opaque, two dots showing in the middle. Us, apparently. "Still works," I said, replacing the pin and handing it to him. "You may as well have it. I've got no use for it."

"Thank you," he said, dropping it into his pocket with the noisy lock picker. "And this one? It also creates a distraction."

I grinned. "Another boom spell?"

"Boom?" he said, then nodded, getting it. "Yes, a boom spell. They are powerful effective. I have the understanding to set one unaided, but I need to commune with the ever-after to do it. This one will suffice."

I had a feeling that most of the spells he was putting in his pocket were ones he knew how to do unaided. I mean, he'd blown the doors in the I.S. tower, and then set a ward over them. I hadn't minded his using me to draw off the line. Which made the next step of wanting to go with him easy. I mean, I could really help him, not just this tour-guide stuff.

"Pierce," I said, fingering the charm to make a hunchback.

The man's attention was in the box, but he seemed to know where my thoughts lay as his next words were, "There is no need for you to accompany me, Miss Rachel. It has nothing to do with your health, and everything to do with me resolving this on my own." He pulled out a charm. "This is a likely one, as well."

Momentarily distracted, I leaned until our shoulders touched. "What is it?"

Pierce slid down a few inches to put space between us. "It allows a body to listen upon a conversation in a room set apart."

My eyebrows rose. "So that's how they always knew what I was up to."

He laughed, the masculine rolling sound seeming to soak into the corners of the kitchen like water into the dry sand bed of a stream. The house had been so empty of it, and hearing it again was painful as our lack was laid bare.

"Your father was a rascal," Pierce said, not aware I had been struck to the core and was trying to blink back the unexpected tears.

"You say that like it's a bad thing," I quipped. *Why is this hitting me so hard?* I thought, blaming it upon my recent hope to talk to him again.

"Oh look," I said, my hand diving in to pull out a familiar spell. "What's this doing in here? This is my mom's."

Pierce took it from me, our fingers touching a shade too long, but his eyes never flicked to me. "It's a ley line charm to set a circle, but unlike the ungodly rare earth magic equivalent, you need to connect to a line to use it."

"My mother is terrible at ley line magic," I said conversationally as Pierce collected all the discards and dumped them in, my mom's included. "My dad used to make all her circles for her. She used to set this when she still made his earth magic charms for him."

I saw him stiffen when I reached back in the box, took out my mom's amulet, and placed it around my neck. "I can tap a line. It will work for me."

"No," he said, facing me. "You aren't coming. I've forbidden it."

My breath came out in a scoff. "You forbid it?" I said, tilting my head up. "Look, Pierce," I said, hand going to my hip. "You can't forbid me anything. I do what I want."

"I have forbidden you from accompanying me," he said as if that settled it. "I'm thankful for what you have done, and that you're letting me borrow your father's spells shows how gracious and honorable your spirit is. Now prove it and stay home as you should."

"You little chauvinistic pig!" I exclaimed, feeling my pulse race and my knees start to go weak. Trying to hide it, I crossed my arms over my chest and leaned against the counter. "I can help you, and you know it. Just how are you going to get there, Mr. Man From The Past? Walk it? In the snow? It's got to be at least fifteen miles."

Pierce didn't seem to be fazed by my temper, which ticked me off all the more. He calmly shrugged into his long coat and folded the box closed. "May I still take these?" he asked, eyebrows high.

"I said you could," I snapped. "And I'm coming too."

"Thank you," he said, dropping the last into a pocket. "I will try my best to return your father's belongs to you, but it's unlikely."

He turned to go, me tight behind him. "You can't just walk out of here," I said, my legs shaking from fatigue. Damn it, I hated being like this. "You don't know where you're going."

"I know where he was before. It's unlikely he's moved."

We were in the hall, and I nearly ran into Pierce when he stopped short at the door, eyeing the handle. "You're going to walk?" I said in disbelief.

He opened the door and took a deep breath of dry, chill air. "I've a mind to, yes."

The cold hit me, and I held my crossed arms close now for warmth. "The world is different, Pierce. We're out, and it's harder to find just one of us now."

That seemed to give him pause. "I will find him," he said, and he stepped out onto the snowy stoop. "I have to. My soul and the girl's both depend upon it."

"You won't find them before the sun comes up," I called after him. *God, what is it with men and their pride?*

"Then I expect I should run."

Then I expect I should run, I mocked in my thoughts, then came out on the stoop. "Pierce," I said, and he turned. There was a whisper of hidden heat in his eyes, shocking the words right out of my head. I blinked at him, stunned that it was there and directed at me. He wasn't amused at my temper. He wasn't bothered by it. He respected it, even as he told me no.

"Thank you, Miss Rachel," he said, and I stumbled back, my eyes darting from his for an instant when my heel hit the frame of the open door. "I can't endanger you any further."

He leaned in, and I froze. My heart pounded. I found my hands against his chest, but I didn't push him away.

"You are fiery and bold," he whispered in my ear, and I shivered. "Like a fey filly who knows her own thoughts and won't be broke but by her will. I don't have a mind to be delicate about it. If I did, I would court you long and lovingly, living for the hour when I would earn your trust and your attentions. I have but this night, so my words must be bold at the risk of offending you and being handed the mitten."

"You didn't," I said, not knowing what my gloves had to do with it. Tension had me stiff, but inside I was a quivering mix of anticipation. "I'd give anything if you'd kiss me," I said. "I mean," I said when he tilted his head to look at me, his eyes wide in shock, "I've kissed guys before. It's like a handshake these days," I lied, just wanting to know what his lips on mine would feel like. "Almost required if you're leaving."

He hesitated, and my shoulders slumped when his fingers began slipping away.

"Ah, the devil take it," he said suddenly, then rocked back. Before I knew what he was doing, he curved an arm around my back, setting his free hand against the doorframe by my head. He leaned in, and as I took a startled breath, his lips found mine.

A small noise escaped me, and my eyes flew wide. I stood there on my porch in the cold and electric light, and let him kiss me, too shocked to do anything else. His lips were cool, but they warmed against me, and his beard was soft. His hand at my back kept me to him, protective and aggressive all at the same time. It sent a tingling jolt to dive to my middle, settling low and insistent.

"Pierce!" I mumbled, nearly driven to distraction by the sudden passion, but when he threatened to pull away, I wrapped my arms hesitantly about his waist. Hell, I had been kissed before, but they were bad kissers, all groping hands and sloppy tongues. This was . . . exquisite, and it plucked a chord in me that had never been touched.

He felt it when my desire rebounded into him, and with a soft sound that held both his want and restraint, he pulled away. Our lips parted, and I stared at him, shaken to my core. Damn, he was a good kisser.

"You are a most remarkable woman," he said. "I thank you humbly for the chance you have gifted me to redeem my sins."

Redeem sins. Yeah.

I stood there like an idiot as he took the stairs with a purposeful gait until he reached the shoveled walk. Unhesitating, he turned to the left and picked up the pace to run.

Damn . . .

I swallowed, trying to shake it off. Arms going around myself, I glanced up and down the quiet, snow-hushed street to see if anyone was watching. No one was, but I imagined Pierce had looked before he pinned me to the door like that . . . and kissed me senseless.

"Damn," I whispered, then took a deep breath to feel the cold slip in to replace the warmth. He certainly knew what he was doing. Not only had he gotten me to stay, but I wasn't angry with him at all. Must be a charm.

Charm. Yeah, he was charming all right. *Like that changed anything?*

Pulse fast, I went inside. I flicked off the coffeemaker, and then seeing the dusty box sitting there like a red flag waving in the breeze, I scribbled a quick note for my mom, telling her Robbie was at the I.S. and that I had fled with someone I had met at the square who knew who had taken Sarah. I had the car and was going to help him. I'd be back about sunrise.

I looked at it, then added, LOVE YOU—RACHEL.

I shivered as I stuffed an arm into a coat sleeve. I was going to help a ghost rescue a missing child from a vampire. God! A dead vamp, probably.

"This is what you want to do for a living," I muttered as I snatched up a set of keys, my fingers trembling. "If you can't do it now, you may as well go to the coast with your brother."

No way. I felt alive, my heart pounding, and my emotions high. It was a great sensation, and it stayed with me all the way out to the garage. A spring in my step, I yanked the garage door up and into the ceiling with a satisfying quickness. I usually had to have my mom do it.

As I strode to the driver's side, my fingers traced the smooth lines of the beat-up Volkswagen bug I had bought with what had been left over from selling The Bat. It ran most of the time. I got in, feeling how stiff the vinyl seats were from the cold. The temperature had been dropping steadily now that the snow had stopped, and I was freezing.

"Please start . . ." I begged, then patted the steering wheel when it sputtered to life. "Tell me I can't come?" I whispered, turning to look behind me as I backed out with a tinny putt-putt of a sound. Okay, I didn't have a real license yet, but who was going to give me a ticket on the solstice? Scrooge?

Still riding the high, I putted down the street, lights on and scanning the sidewalk. I found him two blocks down. He was still running, but he was in the street now, probably after finding too many of our neighbors hadn't shoveled their walks. I rolled my window down and pulled up alongside of him. He glanced at me, then stopped with a look of ambivalence.

I grinned. "Sorry for ruining your farewell speech. I really liked it. You want a ride?"

"You can drive," he said, his eyes tracing the car's odd shape.

"Of course I can." It was cold, and I flicked the heat on. The almost-warm air shifted my hair, and I saw him look at the drifting strands, making me wonder what it would feel like if he ran his fingers through it.

He stood in the freezing night, not a puff of breath showing as he stood to look charming in his indecision. "It's powerfully difficult to run and not try to breathe at the same time," he finally said. "Do you know the streets to the east hills?"

I nodded, and my grin grew that much wider. His head down dejectedly, he came around the front, the lights flashing bright as they hit him. I stifled my smile when he fumbled for the latch, finally figuring it out and getting in. He settled himself as I accelerated slowly.

"You will stay in the carriage when we get there," he grumbled, stomping the snow from his boots, and I just smirked.

Yeah. Right.

SEVEN

F aint on the cold air was the singing of Christmas carolers, obvious now that I'd turned the car off. My car door thumped shut, the sound muffed from the mounds of snow the plows had thrown up, and I breathed slowly, pulling the crisp night deep into me. Above, the stars looked especially sharp from the dry air. It had gotten cold, ice-cracking cold. The faint breeze seemed to go right through my coat. It was about four in the morning. Only Inderlanders and crazy humans were up this time of night, which was fine by me.

Pierce's door shut a moment behind mine, and I smiled at him over the car. He didn't smile back, his brow furrowed in an expression of coming nastiness. While he paced around to my side, I leaned against the cold metal and gazed at the house we had parked across from.

We were way up in the hills in the better part of town where the well-to-do had lived ever since inclined-plane railways had made it easy to make it up the steep slopes. The house in question was older than that, making it remote and lonely in Pierce's time. It was a monster of a structure, clearly added to and rebuilt along with the times, with multiple stories, turrets, and a wraparound porch of smooth river rocks: old money, big trees, and a fantastic view of Cincinnati. Bright Christmas decorations were everywhere, flashing in an eerie silent display.

The sound of Pierce's shoes crunching on the frozen slush jolted me into motion, and I pushed off the car and headed to the wide porch.

"I would request you retire into the carriage and wait," he said from beside me.

I kept my eyes forward as we crossed the street. "It's called a car, and you can request all you want, but it's not going to happen."

We reached the shoveled sidewalk and Pierce grabbed my wrist. I jerked to a stop, startled at the strength he was using.

"Forgive me, Miss Rachel," he said, lips pressed thin and tight. "You're full of grit, but I simply will not be able to live with myself if harm comes to you because of me."

My own anger stirred. "Then it's a good thing you're not alive, huh?"

Shaking his head, he started to tug me back to the car. "I'm sorry for using my advantage to force you. Truly I am."

Here comes the him-hoisting-me-over-his-shoulder bit, with me kicking and screaming as he locks me in my own car? Not going to happen. "Let go," I threatened as he pulled me a step. "I mean it, Pierce. Let go, or you're going to be in a world of hurt." But he didn't.

Glad now I didn't have on mittens, I yanked him to a stop, spun my wrist with a loop-de-loop motion into a modified acrobat twin-hold on his palm, stepped under his arm, and flipped him into a snowbank.

He hit it with a puff of snow, staring up at me in surprise. "Land sakes, how did you do that?" he stammered, eyes wide in the low street light.

I stood over him with my hands on my hips, utterly satisfied. "Try to lock me in the car again, and I'll show you."

Pierce started to get up, and I reached to help him. Making a grunt, he accepted, rising to brush the snow from his long coat with sharp, bothered motions.

"I'm going in there," I said, nodding at the house.

"Miss Rachel," he started, and I took a step forward, getting into his face.

"This is what I want to do with my life," I said. "I have a circle amulet. I'm not helpless. And you can't stop me."

Shifting on his feet, he started to look annoyed. "Rachel, I'm schooled for this."

"And you still ended up dead," I shot back.

"That's my very argument. A body can see it's too dangerous." I made a face, and he took both my hands in his, adding sincerely, "I know you're of a mind to help. You're a brave, courageous woman, but you mustn't kick. This vampire is several hundred years dead, and you are eighteen. Consider it logically."

I rather liked his fingers in mine, but I pulled away, not wanting him to make me into putty. Again. "Logically?" I said, starting to get cold. "Yes, let's look at this logically. Training or not, you don't have anything but a few trinkets to help you if you can't tap a line. You don't have a chance to rescue that girl without me, and you know it."

He hesitated, and I surged ahead at the worried slant to his eyes. "Tell me you don't need me," I said, pointing. "That being able to tap a line isn't going to make the difference between saving her or not. Tell me that."

Pierce's gaze went to our feet, then rose. "I can't," he said firmly.

"Then I'm coming with you."

Again I started for the door. Pierce walked a step behind, slow and ponderous. "Now I have to watch for you, too," I heard him mutter, but I didn't care. I was going.

I slowed to slip my hand into his. He started, and I tapped a line. Energy flowed coolly into me to make my hair start to float around the edges of my hat, and I gave his fingers a squeeze. "It's going to be all right," I said firmly, and I shivered when he pulled a thin trace of power into himself.

We were almost up to the wide porch with its stylized Christmas tree when I realized his intent was to storm the front. "Uh, shouldn't we go in the back door or something?" I asked, and he smiled.

"You've listened to too many adventure tales. They never expect the front door."

"Still," I said as he knocked briskly.

"The front door," he said, glancing askance at me and tugging his coat straight. "They undoubtedly have made note of our presence, and it looks foolish to be caught skulking behind the trash bins."

I jumped at the rattle of the doorknob. A surge of adrenaline, and my pulse quickened. I stood wide-eyed beside Pierce as the door opened to show Sarah, standing alone and beautiful in an elegant dress of old lace. Her face was pale, but her look of fear set one of my worries to rest. She hadn't been bitten and bound yet.

Pierce saw her, and he smiled. "And sometimes, it's that easy."

Sarah's mouth opened. "It's a trap!" she shrilled, still standing there. "Help me!"

With a thump, my heart tripped into overdrive. I stumbled back when two men in black came from around the doorframe. One yanked Sarah inside. The other reached past the threshold, and before I could find the breath to scream, jerked us over the threshold.

Now I shrieked, finding myself skating across the hardwood floor to slide into the wall in a crumpled heap.

A loud "Ow!" pulled my head up, and I found Pierce askew on the stairway leading to the upper floors. I got to my feet, tense and hunched. Sarah was gone, but I could hear her crying. Her sobs grew fainter, but never disappeared. A door slammed.

Pierce rose and tossed his black hair out of his eyes. His lips were pressed together, and he seemed mad at himself more than anything else. The remaining man, a vampire by the glint of fang and telltale grace, was fronting him. I stumbled to stand against the wall, and he focused on me.

"Don't touch me," I said, feeling a faint pull from his charisma and a lot of fear.

Pierce touched his lip, surprise widening his eyes when his hand came away red with blood. "Inform your master I wish to parlay," he said, his words almost laughably formal. "We have a small gentleman-matter standing between us."

"Where's the girl?" I blurted, thinking I could hear her under my feet somewhere.

The vampire between us and the door smiled, chilling me. "I'd be more worried about your own neck, little witch," he said to me, but looking at Pierce, clearly the greater threat.

"Christopher!" Pierce shouted, and I felt a wash of dizziness. "Come out of your hole, you disgusting spawn. We have a matter of early interment to discuss!"

The vampire moved. I pressed against the wall as he took a too-fast step to Pierce and smacked him.

"Pierce!" I shouted as the small man fell backwards into the stairs again. "Leave him alone!" I shouted at the vampire.

Standing at the foot of the stairs, the vampire smiled. "Do you have a mommy, little girl? Will she cry for you?"

Fear slid down my spine, pushing out the fatigue and the dizziness. I stood, alive for what seemed like the first time. Too bad it was about to end. Right when it was getting good.

"Pay me mind, not her," said Pierce, picking himself up again.

The vampire took one step to me, and Pierce pulled a charm from his pocket. I had an instant to prepare, and then he pulled the pin.

The front hallway shook in a *boom* of sound. I cowered as the chandelier swayed, and the windows in the door blew out. Falling into a ball, I crouched in the corner where the wall met the stairway, feeling my ears throb.

Someone touched my shoulder. Panic gave me strength. Wide-eyed, I turned to strike, stopping at the soft pull of ley line running through me.

Pierce.

Exhaling in a wash of relief, I found him close and worried. He crouched beside me and fingered another amulet. "Grit your teeth, and close your eyes," he said. "Forgive me if it's too much."

I nodded. Hunching down, I tried to become one with the floor. My breath caught as a silver-lined ribbon of ever-after iced through me to leave the taste of tinfoil in my veins. The soft presence of Pierce's body covered mine, sheltering me.

A second boom of sound pulsed over us, and in a visible cloud, the scent of dust and broken wood rose. Coughing, I looked up as Pierce slipped his hand in mind and helped me stand. The vampire was out cold against the wall beside the door. But even more startling was the four-foot-wide hole in the floor between us.

Pierce peered into my eyes, striking me silent with how concerned he was. "Are you well? Did I hurt you?"

I shook my head. "There's a hole in the floor."

Pierce pulled me to it. "I'll catch you."

I held my breath as he nonchalantly stepped off the edge of the floor and dropped from sight. From across the room came a soft groan, and the vampire moved.

Pulse hammering, I sat on the floor and dangled my feet. "Here I come!" I warned him, then dropped.

I stifled a shriek, but it came out as a yelp when he caught me and we fell in a tangle of arms and legs. We were in a lower living room with soft carpet and lighting, and expensive paintings on the walls. An entertainment center stood in one corner. There were two doors, one beside us, the other across the room.

"You're heavier than you look," Pierce puffed, and I scrambled off of him.

"Yeah, well, you're a lousy catch." I glanced up at the hole in the floor, then back to the TVs. There were a couple of them, and my lips parted when I recognized a black and white shot of my little car looking funny out there against the expensive estates. Closer to the house was the imprint in the drift where Pierce hit. It made me glad we'd come in the front.

A frightened whimper caught my attention. Together Pierce and I looked to a far corner dusky with a soft light. My hope withered to nothing as I saw Sarah in the grip of a small man dressed in casual sophistication. His silk-clad arm was wrapped around her, covering her mouth. Tears marked her face, and she was terrified.

"Gordian Pierce," the vampire said in a soft, almost feminine voice. "You should have stayed dead."

I pressed back into Pierce, then realizing it made me look afraid, I rocked forward. I was still holding his hand. I was telling myself it was so he could do his magic, but the real reason was I was as scared as Sarah.

"You haven't changed," Pierce said, a new accent coloring his words. "Still the same Nancy boy forcing your putrid self on little girls, I see."

Sarah made a heartbreaking sound, and the vampire, Christopher, I guess, stiffened. His knuckles went white where he pressed his hand over her mouth. "I saw you in the ground," he said bitterly. "You shouldn't be here."

Pierce's hand clenched on mine in a bitter anger. "Your first mistake was putting me in blasphemed ground," he said shortly. "It left me in a mind to return. Eliminating your filth of existence is worth postponing heaven for."

Christopher's chin rose, and a snarl curved his lips up. I knew he was several hundred years old, but he looked thirty. Witch magic at its finest.

"Good," he said, shoving the girl to a nearby couch, where she collapsed to sob. "I'll enjoy hearing your screams again between the beautiful thumps of dirt hitting your casket."

I felt a chill, imagining it. Pierce's hand on mine went damp with sweat. Mine probably.

"You foul bastard," Pierce said, his voice shaking. "I will not leave without the girl."

Intuition and the shifting of light pulled my attention to the hole in the ceiling. "Look out!" I cried, pulling Pierce and myself back when the two vampires from the front door dropped down. Pierce's free hand started making gestures behind his back, and my pulse raced to make me light-headed. Smiling like death, they started to advance.

"No!" their master shouted, and they hesitated. "Let them stand." He flicked his eyes to the one who had carried Sarah down here earlier. "You, man the outside grounds," he said, then turned a disparaging look at the other. "You mind the stairs. From outside. I don't want to be disturbed."

He turned to Pierce and me, and I thought I heard the small man beside me mutter a curse. "I enjoy trespassers," the vampire said. "The law is going to see you dead again, Pierce. All you have brought to me is more terror to lap up. What a timely gift. Thank you."

He nodded curtly at the two vampires, and they slipped away, one through the door and stair behind us, the other jumping straight up through the hole in the floor. Sarah was still crying, and the twin clicks of two doors shutting were ominous. Great. I think it was about to get ugly.

"Believe me," Pierce whispered, his hand giving mine a quick squeeze.

I flicked a look at him, then back to the vampire. "What?"

Pierce angled to get in front of me. "He's going to kill me, but I'm already dead. Trust me. As soon as he thinks I'm dead, I'll move against him. Get the girl out. Please."

I didn't want to leave him here. I wouldn't! "Pierce . . ."

But his fingers slipped from mine.

A jolt of line energy burst in me as I took the entire line myself. Pierce had been siphoning off of me, and I hadn't even known it. Stumbling back, I barely saw Pierce jump away from me, shouting curses at the vampire.

Lips curled to show his teeth, Christopher went to meet him.

"Pierce, no!" I shouted from where I had fallen to one knee, transfixed when they met. The man didn't have a chance. My heart pounded in fear as they grappled, the vampire finding his neck and sinking his teeth.

Pierce's groan struck through me, and I almost panicked. "This can't be happening," I whispered. "This can't be happening!"

I jumped when the girl darted across the room, a white shadow fleeing.

She clutched at me, her tear-streaked face pleading up at me. "Get me out," she whispered, as if afraid he would hear. "Please, get me out!"

I looked at Pierce, slack in the vampire's grip. The animal hung over him, sickening me.

"Help me!" she sobbed, trying to drag me to the door, but I knew what was behind it.

Jaw clenched, I pried her grip off my arm and shoved her behind me. "Give me a minute," I muttered. My heart was pounding too fast, and my knees were going weak. Striding to the nearest wall, I lugged a picture from it, staggering at its unexpected weight.

"Get off him!" I shouted, dropping it on the vampire.

Glass cracked and it slid off his back. Snarling, the vampire let Pierce fall, turning with a look on his face to send a ribbon of fear-laced adrenaline through me. Slowly I backed up. Maybe I should've taken my chances with the vampire behind door number one.

His mouth red with Pierce's blood, the vampire started for me, hunched and looking as if he was in pain. "Stupid, foolish witch," he said, wiping his mouth and then licking the blood from his hand. "Your species will thank me for taking you out before you can breed. The too smart and the too stupid are all culled first. I don't know which one you are."

"Stay back," I said, hand raised as I almost tripped on the rug.

From behind me the girl gasped. My gaze darted to Pierce as he moved. Hope surged, and sensing it, the vampire turned around.

"How many times do I have to kill you?" he snarled when Pierce pulled himself upright, and with a dark grimace, tugged his coat straight. His neck was clean. Not a mark on it.

I didn't understand. I had seen blood. But had it been real? He was a freaking ghost!

"Once was enough, and I expect it will be your undoing, God willing," the man said raggedly, and my breath came in with a hiss when a ball of green ever-after swirled into existence between his two hands. He flung it at the vampire. The vampire lunged sideways, and the green, red, and black mass smacked into the wall, harmless.

My short-lived hope vanished, and I looked at Pierce across the living room. I knew it had been everything he had stored in his chi. He had gambled everything on that one throw. There was nothing left. He was helpless unless he could reach me and refill his chi. And there was a vampire between us.

Christopher seemed to know it, and he started to laugh. "I may not be able to kill a ghost," he said in perverted glee. "But I can still tear your fucking head off."

I backed to the door with the girl. Nothing left. Pierce had nothing left but those stupid ley line charms of my dad. I felt my expression go slack in thought. The ley line charms . . .

My hand went up to grip the charm around my neck. It would make a circle only I could break. Sarah and I would be safe, but Pierce . . .

Pierce saw my hand, trembling as it gripped the spell. "Use it, Rachel," he said, falling into a crouch. "Invoke the amulet!"

I tried to swallow, failing. I pulled the charm from around my neck, the chain catching my hair and tugging free. The vampire lunged to catch Pierce. He cried out in pain.

"Hey, prissy face!" I shouted, voice trembling. "You're a pathetic excuse of a bat, you know that? Can't get your fangs wet without a glass of milk? Come and get me. He doesn't have any blood in him."

The vampire turned and hissed, and my stomach did a flip-flop. *Shit.*

"Rachel, no!" Pierce cried, but the vampire tossed him into a wall like a rude book. I winced when he hit and slid down to stare at me in fear.

"Trust me," I mouthed, and he scrambled up. But he was too far away, and he knew it.

Pulse hammering, I fell into a crouch and beckoned the vampire to me. "You're nothing but a sorry-assed, hide-in-the-ground child molester," I taunted, and the vampire went almost choleric.

"I'm going to kill you slow," he said, advancing slowly.

"Great," I said, estimating the distance between us. "But first, catch this!"

His hands flew up as I pulled the pin and threw the amulet. It thumped into the vampire's grip, and he sneered at me. I smiled back, and as smooth and pure as water, a wash of gold-tinted ever-after flowed up and around him, trapping him.

"No!" the vampire screamed, throwing the amulet, but it was too late.

My eyes widened and I fell back in shocked awe as the vampire seemed to devolve into a raving lunatic, hammering at the barrier between us, almost spitting in frustration. Howling like a mad thing, he threw himself against it, over and over. And it held.

Shaking, I leaned against the back of a couch. "Stupid ass," I muttered.

"Miss Rachel!" Pierce cried out, and I blinked when he grabbed me, spinning me to face him. His hands heavy on my shoulders, he looked me up and down, his blue eyes searching me. "Are you well?"

I blinked again at him. The adrenaline was wearing off, and I was feeling woozy. "Sure. Yes. I think so."

The girl screamed, and a vampire dropped into the room through the hole in the ceiling. From behind the other door, the thumping of feet said the other was coming, too, drawn by Christopher's furious shouts.

Pierce took me in a brief, surprising hug. "You're grit, Rachel. Pure grit," he said, rocking me back. "But you should have used it to save yourself and the girl. All they have to do is throw you into the bubble, and it will fall."

"Nonsense," I said, hearing my words slur. "Just pull some more power from me and blast them back to hell."

His eyes widened, and he held me upright as the door behind us opened to show the second vampire. The girl was at our feet, sobbing. I might have joined her, but I had a feeling I was going to pass out soon, anyway. Damn it, I hated this. I was just kidding myself that I could do this for a living.

I pushed from Pierce, unsteady as I put my hands on my hips and looked from one vampire to the other. I felt like I was drunk. Faint through the broken ceiling came the wail of sirens. "You all better go," I said boldly, sounding like John Wayne to my ears. "Or my friend here will blast you all to hell. He can do it. Can't you?"

But Pierce was watching the monitors with the strength of hope in his grip as he held me upright. I wavered as the two vampires exchanged a knowing look. The master vampire trapped in the circle hesitated in his tantrum, going white-faced when his two servants gave him a short, nervous bow.

"Don't leave me!" the master vampire shouted, hammering on the invisible barrier. "I will hunt you down and take your last blood, then kill you again!"

I smirked, muscles going slack. Pierce caught me with a little grunt. On the monitor were several I.S. cruisers, a news van, and, Lord help me, my mother in her Buick. Robbie got out first, having to be restrained from storming the house on his own. "That's the I.S.," I said, my words running into each other in a soft, slow drawl. "I left my mother a note. She's probably got half the force behind her." Blinking, I struggled to focus on the two vampires. "Don't mess with my mom. She'll kick your . . . ass."

The two vampires looked at each other, and as their master howled, they levered themselves back out through the ceiling. There was a faint thump of feet overhead—and they were gone.

"I think I'm going to pass out," I said, breathless, and Pierce eased me to the carpet. My head lolled, and the edges of my sight grayed. "I'm sorry," I started to babble, feeling light and airy. "I shouldn't have come down here. I'm no good at this."

"You are exceptional at this." Pierce held my hand and fanned me with a magazine. "But please, Miss Rachel, don't pass out. Stay with me. At least a little longer. If you succumb, your circle might fall."

"That's not good," I mumbled, struggling to keep my eyes open, but damn it, I had overtaxed my body and it was shutting down. When the adrenaline had flowed, it had been fantastic. I had been alive and strong. I felt normal. Now all that was left was the ash of a spent fire. And it was starting to rain.

"Rachel?"

It was close, and I pulled my eyes open to find Pierce had cradled my head in his lap. "Okay," I breathed. "Are you okay?"

"Yes," he said, and I smiled, snuggling in so I could hear his heartbeat. Maybe it was mine. "Stay with me," he said. "Just a few minutes more. They're almost here."

Distantly I heard the sound of thumping feet overhead and loud voices. The heater clicked on, and the warm breeze made my hair tickle my face. Pierce brushed it off me, and I opened my eyes, smiling up at him blissfully.

"Holy shit!" a deep voice said. "There's a hole in the floor."

The girl revealed us with a little sob. Standing under the hole she peered up, screaming, "Get me out of here! Someone get me out of here!"

"My God, it's the girl!" another man said. "Damn, he was telling the truth."

"Just a little longer, Miss Rachel," Pierce whispered, and I closed my eyes again. But an icing of fear slid through me, almost waking me up when my mom's voice cut through the babble, high-pitched and determined.

"Of course Robbie was telling the truth. You smart-assed agents think you're so clever your crap doesn't stink, but you couldn't spell your way out of a paper bag."

"That's my mom," I whispered, and Pierce's grip on me tightened.

"Rachel?" she called, her voice getting louder, then, "Get your sorry ass out of my way. Rachel! Are you down there? My God, she circled a vampire. Look what my daughter did! She got him. She got him for you, you lazy bastards. Ignore my kids when they come to you, huh? I bet the news crew would like that. You either drop the charges on my kids, or I'm going out there and give them what they want."

I smiled, but I couldn't open my eyes. "Hi, Mom," I whispered, my breath slipping past my lips. And then to Pierce, I added, "Don't mind my mother. She's a little nuts."

He chuckled, raising my head and rocking me. "I expect a body would have to be to raise you properly."

I wanted to laugh, but I couldn't, so I just smiled. There was the brush of wind against me as people moved about us. Someone had finally gotten Sarah out of here, and the sound of two-way radios and excited chatter had replaced her blubbering. "I'm sorry," I said, feeling like I'd failed them. "Someone needs to circle him. I'm passing out."

"Rest," Pierce whispered. "They have him. Let your circle down, Miss Rachel. I've got you."

I could hear a faint call for an ambulance and oxygen, and I had a fading thought that I was going to spend the last half of my solstice in the hospital, but we had done it.

And with that, I let go of the line and let oblivion take me, satisfied to the depths of my soul.

EIGHT

They say when you're ten, you think your parents know everything. At sixteen, you're convinced they know nothing at all. By thirty, if you haven't figured out they really did know what they were doing, then you're still sixteen. After watching my mom work the I.S. like a fish on a line, I was suitably impressed that she knew everything in the freaking world.

Smiling, I tugged the wool blanket tighter around me and scooted my folding chair closer to the small fire Robbie had started in the backyard. My mom was beside me, pointedly between my brother and me as we toasted marshmallows and waited for sunrise. I hadn't been outside very long, and my breath steamed in the steadily brightening day. It was a few hours past my normal bedtime, but that's not why my arms shook and my breath was slow. Damn, I was tired.

I'd fully expected to wake up in the hospital or ambulance, and was surprised when I had come to in the back of my mom's car, still at the crime site. Wrapped in an I.S. blanket, I had stumbled out looking for Pierce to find myself in a media circus. Robbie and I had stood in the shadows and watched in awe as my mother worked a system I hadn't even known existed. Through her deadly serious threats disguised as scatter-brained fussing, she not only managed to get the charges against me for willful destruction of private property dropped, but got them to agree that I didn't have anything to do with their doors being blown out, much less fleeing their custody with an unknown person. The I.S. personnel were more than happy to give my mom whatever she wanted if she would keep her voice down, seeing as three news crews were within shouting distance.

Apparently the vampire I'd helped bring in had a history of such kidnappings, but because of his clout, he'd been getting away with it for years. I hated to go along with the shush work, but I didn't want a record, either. So as long as my mother, Robbie, myself, and the girl kept quiet—her parents being placated with enough money to put Sarah through the university and therapy of her choice—the vampire would be charged with kidnapping, not the stiffer crime of underage enticement.

It didn't bother me as much as I'd thought it would. He was still going to jail, and if vampire justice was like any other kind, he'd probably wake up one night with a wooden spoon jammed through his heart. Vampires didn't like pedophiles any more than the next guy.

So Robbie's and my trip to the I.S. had been dulled to an anonymous tip, making the I.S. out to be the heroes. Whatever. Along with the notoriety went any charges they might file against me. Mom had grounded me, though. God, I was nearly nineteen and grounded. What was up with that?

Of Pierce, there had been no sign. No one remembered seeing him apart from my mom.

A sigh shifted my shoulders, coming out as a thin mist catching the pink light of the nearing sunrise.

"Rachel," my mom said, reaching to tug the blanket closed around my neck, "that's the third sigh in as many minutes. I'm sure he will be back."

I grimaced that she knew where my thoughts were, then searched the sky and the strips of clouds throwing back the sun in bands of pink. I'd known he'd be gone by sunrise, but I wished I'd had the chance to say goodbye. "No," I said, bobbing my marshmallow in and out of the flame. "He won't. But that's okay."

My mom gave me a sideways hug. "He looked like he really cared. Who was he?" she asked, and a hint of alarm slipped through me. "I didn't want to ask in front of the I.S. because he rushed off as if he didn't want to be noticed." She huffed, taking my stick with the now-burning marshmallow. "I don't blame him," she muttered as she blew the little fire out. "They would have probably tried to pin the entire kidnapping on him. I don't like vampires. Always shoving their nastiness under a rug or onto someone else's plate."

Fingers gingerly taking the burnt marshmallow off, she smiled, her eyes brilliant in the clear light. In witch years, she wasn't that much older than me, always dressing down to make herself match the other moms in the neighborhood. But the morning light always showed how young she really was.

"So was he someone from school?" she prodded, a small smile dying to come out.

I gestured for her to eat the sticky black mass if she wanted it, and while she was occupied, I glanced nervously at Robbie. He was ignoring me. "Just a guy I met at the square," I offered.

My mother huffed again. "And that's another thing, missy," she said, but it was Robbie who got the thwack of the back of her hand on his shoulder. "You said you were going to the concert."

Robbie shot me a black look. "Aw, Mom, I had to scalp the tickets to get your solstice gift."

It was a lie, but she accepted it, making happy-mom sounds and giving him a marshmallowy kiss on his cheek.

"That's where we met Pierce," I said to give some truth to the story. "If we hadn't helped him, no one would."

"You did the right thing," my mom said firmly. "If I toast you a marshmallow, will you eat it, honey?"

I shook my head, wondering if she knew exactly *how* we had made his acquaintance. Probably, seeing as by the time I got into the kitchen, all evidence of my spelling had been boxed up and was back in the attic.

Robbie took the stick and put a new marshmallow over the fire. He liked them so light brown it was almost not worth doing. "So, I imagine your little adventure has cured you of wanting to go into the I.S.?" he asked, and my head jerked up.

Shocked he would bring it up in front of Mom, I stared at him from across her suddenly still figure. "No."

Silent, my mom eased back into her chair and out of the way of the coming argument.

"Look at you," my brother said after a cautious glance at our mom. "You passed out. You can't do it."

"That's enough, Robbie," Mom said, and I flicked my gaze at her, surprised at her support. But Robbie turned in his seat to face her. "Mom, we have to look at it logically. She can't do it, and you letting her believe she can only makes it worse."

I stared at him, feeling like I'd been kicked. Seeing me floundering, Robbie shifted awkwardly. "Rachel is a damn fine witch," he said, suddenly nervous. "She stirred a level eight hundred earth magic arcane spell. Mom, do you know how hard those are? I couldn't do it! If she goes into the I.S., it's going to be a waste. Besides, they won't take her if she passes out at the end of a run."

It had been an arcane spell? He hadn't told me that. Surprise kept my mouth shut, but it was that damned fatigue that kept me in my seat and not pummeling him into the snow. He'd told her. He never said he wouldn't, but it was an unwritten rule, and he had just broken it.

"You put a level eight hundred arcane spell in front of her?" my mom said crisply, and I paled, remembering her equipment used without her knowledge.

Robbie looked away, and I was glad I wasn't under her angry expression. "I can get her into a great school," he said to the ground. "The I.S. won't accept her, and to keep encouraging her is cruel."

Cruel? I thought, tears starting to blur my vision. Cruel is throwing my hopes in the dirt. Cruel is giving me a challenge, and when I meet it, telling me I lose because I fell down after it was done.

But he was right. It did matter that I had fainted. Worse yet, the I.S. knew it. They would never let me pass the physical now. I was weak and frail. A weak prissy face.

I sniffed loudly, and my mom glanced at me before turning back to my brother. "Robbie, can I have a word with you?"

"Mom—"

"Now." Her tone was sharp, brooking no complaint. "Get in the house."

"Yes, ma'am." Pissed, he stood, dropped his marshmallow and stick into the fire, and stomped inside. I jumped when the screen door slammed.

Sighing heavily, my mom took the stick out of the fire and rose. I didn't look at her when she handed the marshmallow to me. It was all out now, and I couldn't even pretend I had the ability to do what I wanted, do what made my blood pound and made me feel alive.

"I'll be right back," she said, giving my shoulder a squeeze. "I was saving these for the sunrise, but I want you to open them now—before the day begins."

Her thin but strong hands drew from her coat pocket a card and small present, which she set into my lap.

"Happy solstice, sweetheart," she said, and a single tear slipped down my cheek as she followed Robbie into the house. I wiped the cold trail away, heartbroken. It just wasn't fair. I had done it. I had summoned a ghost, though not Dad. I had helped save that little girl's life. So why was mine in the crapper?

Setting Robbie's marshmallow to burn, I took off my mittens and ran a cold finger under the seal of the card. Eyes welling, I opened it up to find my I.S. application, signed by my mother. Blinking furiously, I shoved it back in the envelope. I had permission, but it didn't mean anything anymore.

"And what are you?" I said to the box miserably. "A set of cuffs I'll never get to use?" It was about the right size.

I stared at the brightening pink clouds and held my breath. Exhaling, the fog from my lungs seemed to mirror my mood, foggy and dismal. Setting the envelope aside, I opened the box. The tears got worse when I saw what was in it. Cradled in the black tissue paper was Dad's watch.

Miserable, I glanced back at the silent house. She knew what spell I had done. She knew everything; otherwise why give me the watch?

Missing him all the more, I clenched Dad's watch in my hand and stared at the fire, almost rocking in heartache. Maybe things would have been different if he had shown up. I was glad he was at peace and the spell wouldn't work on him, but damn it, my chest seemed to have a gaping hole in it now.

A warm sensation slipped through me, and startled, I sniffed back my tears and sent my eyes to follow a small noise to the side yard. A pair of hands was gripping the top of the wooden fence, and as I wiped my face, a small man in a long coat vaulted over it. Pierce.

"Oh, hi," I said, wiping my face in the hopes he couldn't tell I'd been crying. "I thought you were gone." I dried my hand on my blanket and folded my hands in my lap, hiding my dad's watch and my misery all at the same time.

Pierce looked at the house as he approached, boots leaving masculine prints in the snow. "After seeing your mother at that spawn's house, I had a mind to heed the better part of valor."

A faint smile brought my lips curving upward despite myself. "She scares you?"

"Like a snake to a horse," he said, shuddering dramatically.

He glanced at the house again and sat down in Robbie's spot. I said nothing, noting the distance.

"I couldn't find your home," he said, watching the fire, not me. "The drivers of the public carriages . . . ah . . . buses, won't be moved by pity, and it took me a space to figure the Yellow Book."

I sniffed, feeling better with him beside me. "Yellow Pages."

Nodding, he looked at the still-burning wad of Robbie's marshmallow. "Yes, Yellow Pages. A man of color took pity on me and drove me to your neighborhood."

I turned to him, aghast, but then remembered he was over a hundred years dead. "It's polite to call them black now. Or African-American," I corrected, and he nodded.

"They are all free men?"

"There was a big fight about it," I said, and he nodded, eyes pinched in deep thought.

I didn't know what to say, and finally Pierce turned to me. "Why are you so melancholy, Miss Rachel? We did it. My soul is avenged and the girl is safe. I'm sure that when the sun rises, I will go to my reward." A nervous look settled in the back of his eyes. "Be it good or bad," he added.

"It will be good," I said hurriedly, my hands gripping the watch as if I could squeeze some happiness out of it. "I'm thrilled for you, and I know you will land on the good side of things. Promise."

"You don't look thrilled," he muttered, and I scraped up a smile.

"I am. Really I am," I said. "It's just that—It's just that I tried to be who I wanted to be, and I—" My throat closed, as if by admitting it aloud, there was no way it could happen. "I can't do it," I whispered. Fighting the tears, I watched the fire, forcing my breathing to stay even and slow.

"Yes, you can . . ." Pierce protested, and I shook my head to make my hair fly around.

"No, I can't. I passed out. If you hadn't been there, I would have passed out, and he would have gotten away, and it would have been all for nothing."

"Oh, Rachel . . ." Pierce slid to my mother's chair. His arms went around me and he gave me a sideways hug. Giving up my pretense, I turned into him to make it a real hug, burying my face in his coat. I took a shaky breath, smelling the scent of coal dust and shoe polish. He had a real smell, but then, I'd heard most ghosts did.

"It's not bravery you lack," he said, his words shifting the hair on the top of my head. "That's the most important part. The rest is incidental. Real strength is knowing you can live with your failure. That sometimes you can't get there in time and that your lack might mean someone dies. It was cleverness that captured the vampire, not brute strength. Besides, the strength will come."

It sounded so easy. I wanted to believe him. I wanted to believe him so bad, it made my chest hurt. "Will it?" I said as I pulled back to see his own eyes damp with tears. "I used to think so, but I'm so damned weak. Look at me," I said derisively. "Wrapped up like a baby, my knees going shaky when I get up to turn the TV channel. I'm stupid to think the I.S. would want me. I should give it up and go out to Portland to be an earth witch, set up a spell shop and . . ." My eyes started to well again. *Damn it!* "And sell charms to warlocks," I finished, kicking a snow clod into the fire.

Pierce shook his head. "That's the most dang fool idea I've heard since having ears to hear with again, and I expect I've seen and heard a few fool things since you woke me up. If I might could talk to the dead, I'd ask your father, and I know what he would say."

His language was slipping again; he must be upset. I looked up from where my kicked snow had melted, dampening out the fire to show a patch of wood. "You can't know that," I said sullenly. "You've never even met him."

Still he smiled, his blue eyes catching the brightening light. "I don't need to. I expect a man who raised a young lady with such fire in her would have only one answer. Do what your heart tells you."

A frown pressed my lips together. "I'm too weak," I said, as if that was all there was to it. "Nothing is going to change. Nothing."

I didn't want to talk about it anymore. My hands were cold, and I dropped the watch in my lap to put my mittens back on.

"Hey!" Pierce said, seeing it. "That's mine!"

My mouth dropped open, but in a moment, I looked at him in understanding. "No wonder the charm didn't work. It's your watch?" I hesitated. "Before it was my dad's? Maybe I can try again," I said. But he was shaking his head, clearly wanting to touch it.

"No," he said. "You're his daughter, and your blood that kindled the charm is a closer bond than a bit of metal and fancy. If he had been in a position to come, he would have." An eager light was in his eyes, and, licking his lips, he asked, "May I?"

Silently I handed it over.

Pierce's smile was so beautiful that it almost hurt to see it. "It's mine," he said, then quickly amended. "Pardon me. I meant that it once had been. I expect it was sold to pay for the stone they used to keep me from rising up to avenge my wrongful death. See here?" he said, pointing out a dent. "I did this falling into a post to avoid a nasty-tempered nag of a horse."

I leaned to look, finding a small comfort in his history.

"I wonder if my sweetheart's silhouette is still in it," he said, turning it over. My eyebrows rose when he wedged a ragged fingernail into a tiny crack and whispered a word of Latin. The back hinged open, and a folded paper fluttered to the ground.

"That's not it," he said with a sigh, and I picked it up, handing it to him.

"What is it?" I asked, and he shrugged, handing me my dad's watch to unfold the off-white scrap of paper. But then my heart seemed to stop when the scent of my dad's pipe lifted through my memory, rising from the paper itself.

Pierce didn't see my expression, and he squinted at the words. "My little Firefly," he said, and tears sprang into my eyes as I realized who had written them. "I write this on the evening of our day in the leaves as you sleep. You're still a child, but today, I saw the woman-to-be in you—" Pierce's words cut off, and he brought his gaze to my swimming eyes. "This is for you," he said, extending it. His expression looked tragic as he shared my heartache.

"Read it to me," I said, catching a sob. "Please."

Pierce shifted awkwardly, then began again. "Today I saw the woman-to-be in you, and you are beautiful. My heart breaks that circumstance will probably keep me from seeing you reach your full strength, but I'm proud of your courage, and I stand in awe at the heights you will achieve when your strength builds to match your spirit."

I held my breath to keep from crying, but my head started to hurt and a hot tear slipped down.

"Don't be afraid to trust your abilities," he said, voice softening. "You're stronger than you think. Never forget how to live life fully and with courage, and never forget that I love you." Pierce drew the paper from his nose and set it in my lap. "It's signed 'Dad'."

I sniffed, smiling up at Pierce as I wiped my eyes. "Thank you."

"Little Firefly?" he questioned, trying to distract me from my heartache.

"It was the hair, I think," I said, bringing the paper to my nose and breathing deeply the faded scent of pipe smoke. "Thank you, Pierce," I said, giving his hand a soft squeeze. "I never would have found his note if it hadn't been for you."

The young man smiled, running a hand over my hair to push it out of my eyes. "It isn't anything I did a'purpose."

Maybe, I mused, smiling brokenly at him, the spell to bring my dad into existence had worked after all—the only way it could, his love bending the rules of nature and magic to bring me a message from beyond his grave. My dad was proud of me. *He was proud of me and knew I could be strong.* That was all I had ever wanted, and I took a gulp of air.

I was going to start crying again, and, searching for a distraction, I turned to find my mom's gift. "My mom signed my application," I said, fumbling with the envelope beside me with a sudden resolve. "I'm going to do it, Pierce. My dad said to trust in my abilities, and I'm going to do it. I'm going to join the I.S."

But when I turned back to him with my signed application, he was gone.

My breath caught. Wide-eyed, I looked to the east to see the first flash of red-gold through the black branches. From across the city came the tolling of bells, celebrating the new day. The sun was up. He was gone.

"Pierce?" I said softly as the paper in my grip slowly drooped. Not believing it, I stared at where he had been. His footprints were still there, and I could still smell coal dust and shoe polish, but I was alone.

A gust of wind blew on the fire, and a wave of heat shifted my hair from my eyes. It was warm against me, comforting, like the touch of a hand against my cheek in farewell. He was gone, just like that.

I looked at my dad's watch and held it tight. I was going to get better. My stamina was going to improve. My mom believed in me. My dad did, too. Fingers shaking, I folded up the paper and snapped the watch shut around it, holding it tight until the metal warmed.

Taking a deep breath, I sent my gaze deep into the purity of the morning sky. The solstice was over, but everything else? Everything else was just beginning.

UNDEAD IN THE GARDEN OF GOOD AND EVIL

When I first began writing the Hollows, there were very few strong female vampire characters making it into print, and when I realized how large a role Ivy was going to play, I decided I needed to develop the social structure of the Hollows vampires from the female point of view. The novella Undead in the Garden of Good and Evil *was the perfect chance for me to try out a few of my ideas. I learned a lot, not only about the Hollows vampires—both living and dead—but also about Ivy. The depth of her mental abuse is touched upon here, and it is also here that it's easiest to see why she stays with Rachel, who is both her crutch and her saving grace.* Undead in the Garden of Good and Evil *was first published in the anthology* Dates from Hell.

 ## ONE

Phone cradled between her shoulder and ear, Ivy Tamwood scooped another chunk of chili up with her fries, leaning over the patterned wax paper so it wouldn't drip onto her desk. Kisten was bitching about something or other, and she wasn't listening, knowing he could go on for half her lunch break before winding down. The guy was nice to wake up to in the afternoon, and a delight to play with before the sun came up, but he talked too much.

Which is why I put up with him, she mused, running her tongue across the inside of her teeth before swallowing. Her world had gone too quickly from alive to silent on that flight back home from California. *My God, was it seven years now?* It had been unusual to foster a high-blood living vampire child into a sympathetic camarilla, taking her from home and family for her last two years of high school, but Piscary, the master vampire her family looked to, had become too intense in his interest in her before she developed the mental tools to deal with it, and her parents had intervened at some cost, probably saving her sanity.

I could keep Freud in Havana cigars all by my lonesome, Ivy thought, taking another bite of carbs and protein. Twenty-three ought to be far enough away from that scared sixteen-year-old on the sun-drenched tarmac to forget, but even now, after multiple blood and bed partners, a six-year degree in social sciences, and landing an excellent job where she could use her degree, she found her confidence was still tied to the very things that screwed her up.

She missed Skimmer and her reminder that life was more than waiting for it to end so she could get started living. And while Kisten was nothing like her high school roommate, he had filled the gap nicely these last few years.

Smiling wickedly, Ivy gazed through the plate-glass wall that looked out on the floor of open offices. Weight shifting, she crossed her legs at her knees and leaned farther across her desk, imagining just what gap she'd like Kisten to fill next.

"Damn vampire pheromones," she breathed, and pulled herself straight, not liking where her thoughts took her when she spent too much time in the lower levels of the Inderland Security tower. Working the homicide division of the I.S. got her a real office instead of a desk in the middle of the floor with the peons, but there were too many vamps—both living and undead—down here for the air circulation to handle.

Kisten's tirade about prank phone calls ended abruptly. "What do vamp pheromones have to do with humans attacking my pizza delivery crew?" he asked in a lousy British accent. It was his newest preoccupation, and one she hoped he'd tire of soon.

Rolling her chair closer to her desk, Ivy took a swig of her imported bottled water, eyes askance on the boss's closed door across the large room. "Nothing. You want me to pick up anything on the way home? I might be able to wing out of here early. Art's in the office, which means someone died and I have to go to work. Bet you first bite he's going to want to cut my lunch short"—she took another sip—"and I'm going to take it off the end of my day."

"No," Kisten said. "Danny is doing the shopping today."

One of the perks of living atop a restaurant, she thought, as Kisten started in on a shopping list she didn't care about. Pulling her plate of fries off her desk, she set them on her lap, being careful to not spill anything on her leather pants. The boss's door opened, catching her eye when Art came out, shaking hands with Mrs. Pendleton. He'd been in there a full half hour. There was a stapled pack of paper in his hands, and Ivy's pulse quickened. She'd been sitting on her ass going over Art's unsolved homicides for too long. The man had no business being in homicide. Dead did not equal smart.

Unless being smart was in manipulating us into giving the undead our blood. Ivy forced herself to keep eating, thinking the undead targeted their living vampire kin more out of jealousy than maintaining good human relations, as was claimed. Having been born with the vampire virus embedded into her genome, Ivy enjoyed a measure of the undeads' strengths without the drawbacks of light fatality and pain from religious artifacts. Though not in line with Art's abilities, her hearing and strength were beyond a human's, and her sense of smell was tuned to the softer flavors of sweat and pheromones. The undeads' need for blood had been muted from a biological necessity to a bloodlust that imparted a high like no other when sated . . . addictive when mixed with sex.

Her gaze went unbidden to Art, and he smiled from across the wide floor as if knowing her thoughts, his steady advance never shifting and the packet of paper in his hand moving like a banner of intent. Appetite gone, she swiveled her chair to put her back to the room. "Hey, Kist," she said, interrupting his comments about Danny's recent poor choice of mushrooms, "change of plans. By the amount of paperwork, it's one of Art's cleanup runs. I won't be home till sunup."

"Again?"

"Again?" she mocked, fiddling with a colored pen until she realized it telegraphed her mood and set it down with a sharp tap. "God, Kisten. You make it sound like it's every night."

Kisten sighed. "Leave the paperwork for tomorrow, love. I don't know why you bust your ass so hard. You're not moving up until you let Artie the Smarty go down on you."

"Is that so," she said, feeling her face warm and the chili on her tongue go flat. Tossing her plate to her desk, she forced herself to remain reclining with her booted feet spread wide when what she wanted to do was hit someone. Martial arts meditation had kept her out of civil court until now; self-control was how she defined herself.

"You knew the system when you hired in," he coaxed, and Ivy tugged the sleeves to her skintight black pullover from her elbows to her wrists to hide her faint scars. She could feel Art crossing the room, and adrenaline tickled the pit of her stomach. *It was a run*, she told herself, but she knew Art was the reason for the stir in her, not the chance to get out of the office.

"Why do you think I wanted to work with Piscary instead of the I.S.?" Kisten was saying, words she had heard too many times before. "Give him what he wants. I don't care." He laughed. "Hell, it might be nice having you come home wanting to watch a movie instead of ready to drain me."

Reaching to her desk, she finished her water, wiping the corner of her mouth with a careful pinky. She had known the politics—hell, she had grown up in them—but that didn't mean she had to like the society she was forced to work within. She had watched it end her mother's life, watched it now eat her father away, killing him little by little. It was the only path open to her. And she was good at it. Very good at it. That's what bothered her the most.

She stiffened when Art fixed his brown eyes to the back of her neck. Undead vamps had been looking at her since she had turned fourteen; she knew the feeling. "I thought you stuck with Piscary because of his dental plan," she said sarcastically. "His dentals in your neck."

"Ha, ha. Very funny," Kisten said, his good humor doing nothing to ease her agitation.

"I like what I do," she said, putting a hand up against the knock on her open door. She didn't turn, smelling the stimulating, erotic scent of undead vampire in her doorway. "I'm damn good at it," she added to remind Art she was the reason they had pulled his murder-solved ratio up the last six months. "At least I'm not delivering pizzas for a living."

"Ivy, that's not fair."

It was a low blow, but Art was watching her, and that would unnerve anyone. After six months of working with her, he had picked up on all her idiosyncrasies, learning by reading her pulse and breathing patterns exactly what would set her rush flowing. He had been using the information to his advantage lately, making her life hell. It wasn't that he wasn't attractive—God, they all were—but he had been working the same desk for over thirty years. His lack of ambition didn't make her eager to jump his jugular, and being coaxed into something by way of her instincts when her thoughts said no left a bad taste in her mouth.

Even worse, she had realized after the first time she had come home hungering for blood and finding Piscary waiting for her that the master vampire had probably arranged the partnership knowing she'd resist—and Art would insist—the end result being she'd be hungry for a little decompression when she got home. The sad thing was she wasn't sure if she was resisting Art because she didn't like him or because she got off on the anticipation of not knowing if it would be Piscary, Kisten, or both that she'd be calming herself with.

But her weakness was no reason to bark at Kisten. "Sorry," she said into the hurt silence.

Kisten's voice was soft, forgiving, since he knew Art was playing hard on her. "You gotta go, love?" he asked in that lame accent. *Who was he trying to be, anyway?*

"Yeah." Kisten was silent, and she added, "See you tonight," that curious tightening in her throat and the need to physically touch someone settling more firmly inside her. It was the first stage of a full-blown bloodlust, and whether it stemmed from Kisten or Art didn't matter. Art would be the one trying to capitalize on it.

"Bye," Kisten replied tightly, and the phone clicked off. He said it didn't bother him, but he was alive as she was, with the same emotions and jealousy they all had. That he was so understanding of the choices she had to make made it even worse. She often felt they were like children in a warped family where love had been perverted by sex, and the easiest way to survive was to submit. Her invisible manacles had been created by her very cells and hardened by manipulation. And she didn't know if she would remove them if she could.

Ivy watched her pale fingers as she set the phone down. Not a tremor showed. Not a hint of her rising agitation. That was how she kept them away—placid, quiet, no emotion—a skill learned while working summers at Pizza Piscary's. She had learned it so well that only Skimmer knew who she really wanted to be, though she loved Kisten enough to show him glimpses.

Carefully removing all emotion from her face, she swiveled her chair, boot tips trailing along the faded carpet. Art was standing to take up half her doorway, with a packet of stapled paper in his long fingers. Clearly they had a run. By the amount of paperwork, it couldn't be pressing. Probably cleanup from before she became his partner and started following behind him with her dust broom and pan.

"I'm eating," she said, as if it wasn't obvious. "Can it wait a friggin' ten minutes?"

The dead vampire—at least fifty years her senior on paper, her contemporary by appearances—inclined his head in a practiced motion to convey a sly sophistication mixed with a healthy dose of sex appeal. Soft black curls fell to frame his brown eyes, holding her attention. His small, boyish features and his tight ass made him look like a member of a boy band. He had the same amount of personality, too, unless he made an effort. But God, he smelled good, his aroma mixing with hers to set in play a series of chemical reactions that whipped her blood and sexual libido high. "I'll wait," he said, smiling.

Oh joy. He'd wait. Art's practiced voice sent a trail of anticipation down her back to settle at the base of her spine. Damn it all to hell, he was hungry. Or maybe he was bored. He'd wait. He'd been waiting six months, learning the best way to manipulate her. And she knew she'd more than enjoy herself if she let him.

Bloodlust in living vampires was tied to their sex drive, an evolutionary adaptation helping ensure an undead vampire would have a willing blood supply to keep him or her sane. Being "bidden for blood" imparted a sexual high; the older and more experienced the vampire, the better the rush, the ultimate, of course, being blood-bidden by a powerful undead undead.

Art had been dead for four decades, having passed the tricky thirty-year ceiling where most undead vampires failed to keep themselves mentally intact and walked into the sun. Why Art was still working was a mystery. He must need the money since he certainly wasn't good at his job.

The vampire breathed deeply as he stood on her threshold, pulling in her mood the way she inhaled a rare fragrance. Sensing her rising agitation, Art rocked into motion, rounding her desk and easing himself down in her leather office chair in the corner. Her face blanked as her pulse quickened. Art was the only person to ever sit there. Most people respected her attempts to avoid office friendships—if her sharp sarcasm and outright ignoring them weren't enough. But then, Art didn't like her for her personality but for the reputation he had yet to get a taste of.

Eyes on her immaculate desk, Ivy exhaled. He was dead, and she was alive. They were both vampires driven by blood: she sexually, he for survival. A match made in heaven—or hell.

Art reclined, smiling, with his long legs crossed and an ankle on one knee, managing to look powerful and relaxed at the same time. He brushed his hair back, trailing his fingers suggestively across his face kept at a clean-shaven tidiness as he tried to blend in with the younger crowd who would be more receptive to what he offered.

A shiver of anticipation rose through her. It didn't make any difference that it came from Art pumping the air full of pheromones rather than true interest. The desire to satiate herself was as much a part of her as breathing. Inescapable. *Why not get it over with? The gossip was because she was resisting, not because it was expected.* And that was why he sat there in his expensive slacks and shirt with his two-hundred-dollar shoes and that confident bad-boy smile. The dead could afford to be patient.

"Tying off some of your loose ends?" she said dryly, glancing at the packet of papers and leaning back. She wanted to cross her arms over her chest, but instead put her boot heels up on the corner of her desk. *Confident. She was in control of herself and her desires.* Art could turn her into a pliant supplicant if he bespelled her, but that was cheating, and he would lose more than face, he'd lose the respect of every vamp in the tower. He had to bid for her blood. Playing on her bloodlust was expected, but bespelling her would piss Piscary off. She wasn't a human to be taken advantage of and the paperwork "adjusted." She was the last living Tamwood vampire, and that demanded respect, especially from him.

"Homicide," he said, his teeth a white flash against his dark skin that hadn't seen the sun in decades. "We can get there before the photographer if you're done with your . . . lunch."

She allowed a sliver of her surprise to show. A homicide wouldn't come with that much information. Not anymore. She had pulled their solved ratio high enough that they were often among the first on the scene. Which meant they'd get an address, not a file. As her eyes returned to the papers he had set over his crotch, he moved them so she was looking right where he wanted her to. Irritation flickered over her. Her eyes rose to meet his gaze, and his smile widened to show a glimpse of teasing fang.

"This?" he said, standing in a graceful motion too fast for a human. "This is your six-month evaluation. Ready to go? It's clear across the bridge in the Hollows."

Ivy stood, part habit and part worry. Her work had been textbook exemplary. Art didn't want her moving up the ladder and out from under him, but the worst scenario would be a reprimand, and she hadn't done anything to warrant that. Actually the worst would be that he'd give her a shitty review and she'd be stuck here another six months.

Her job in homicide was a short stop on the way to where she belonged in upper management, where her mother had been and where Piscary wanted her to be. She had expected to be on this floor for six months, maybe a year, working with Art until her honed skills pulled her into the Arcane Division, and then to management, and finally a lower-basement office. Thank God her money and schooling let her skip the grunt position of runner. Runners were the lowest in the I.S. tower, the cops on the corner giving traffic tickets. Starting there would have put her back a good five years.

Confident and suave, Art brushed by her, his hand trailing across the upper part of her back in a professional show of familiarity that no one could find fault with as he guided her out of her office. "Let's take my car," he said, plucking her purse and coat from behind her door and giving them to her. A jingle of metal pulled her hand up in anticipation, and she caught his keys as he dropped them into her waiting palm. "You drive."

Ivy said nothing, her faint bloodlust evaporating in concern. That he was pleased with her evaluation meant she wouldn't be. Arms swinging as if unconcerned, she walked beside him to the elevators, finding herself in the unusual position of meeting the faces of the few people eating at their desks. She hadn't made friends, so instead of sympathy, she found a mocking satisfaction.

Her tension rose, and she kept her breathing to a measured pace to force her pulse to slow. Whatever Art had scrawled on her evaluation was going to keep her here—her family name and money had pulled her as far as they could. Unless she played office politics, this was where she was going to stay. *With Art? The luscious-smelling, drop-dead gorgeous, but lackluster Art?*

"Well, screw that," she whispered, feeling her blood rise to her skin and her mind shift into overdrive. That was not going to happen. She would work so well and so hard that Piscary would talk to Mrs. Pendleton and get her out of here and where she belonged.

"That's the idea," Art murmured, hearing only her words, not her thoughts. But Piscary wasn't going to help her. The bastard was enjoying the side benefits of her coming home frustrated and hungry from Art's attempts at seducing her blood. If she couldn't handle this alone, then she deserved the humiliation of picking up after Art the rest of her life.

They halted at the twin sets of elevators in the wide hallway. Ivy stood with her hip cocked, frustrated and listening to the soft conversation filtering in from the nearby offices. Art *was* attractive—more so given the pheromones, God help her—but she didn't respect him, and letting her instincts rule her conscious thought, even to move ahead, sounded like failure to her.

Leaning closer than necessary, Art pushed the UP button. His scent rolled over her, and while fighting the pure pleasure, she watched his eyes go to the heavy clock above the doors to check that the sun was down. She could feel his confidence that the sun would rise with him getting his way, and it pissed her off.

Her booted foot tapped, and her image in the double silver doors did the same. Behind her, Art's reflection watched her with a knowing slant to his pretty-boy features. *He was an ass. A sexy, powerful, conceited, ass.* Because of who she was, it was assumed that she would rise in status by way of her blood, not her skills or knowledge. It was how business was done if you were a vampire. Always had been. Always would be. There were papers to sign and legalities to observe when a vamp set his or her sights on anyone other than another vampire, but having been born into it, she fell under rules older than human or Inderland law. That she had been conditioned to enjoy giving her blood to another left her feeling like a whore if it ended with her being alone. And she knew it would with Art.

As her mother had said, the only way out was to give them what they wanted, to sell herself and keep selling until she reached the top where no one would have a claim on her. If she did this, she would be promoted out from under Art and someone a little smarter and more depraved would be her new partner. Everyone would want a taste of her on her way up. God, she might as well break off her fangs and become an unclaimed shadow. But she had grown up with Piscary and found that the more powerful and older the vampire, the more subtle the manipulation, until it could be confused with love.

Taking a slow breath, she touched the ponytail she had put her hair in this afternoon, pulling the band out and shaking the black waist-length hair free. It and her brown eyes were from her mother. Her six-foot height and pale skin she got from her father. Accenting her Asian heritage was an oval face, heart-shaped mouth, thin eyebrows, and a leggy body toned by martial arts. No piercings apart from her ears and a belly button ring Skimmer had sweet-talked her into while high on Brimstone after finals, kept as a reminder. *Twenty-three, and already tired of life.*

Art was gazing at her reflection beside his, and his eyes flashed black when she melted her posture from annoyed to sultry. God, she hated this . . . but she was going to enjoy it, too. *What the hell was wrong with her?*

Pulling away from Art, she set her back casually against the wall and put one foot behind her, balancing it on a toe as they waited for the lift. "You're a fool if you think I'm going to let an evaluation keep me in this crappy job," she said, not caring if the people in earshot heard. They probably had a pool going as to where and when he'd break her skin.

Art moved with an affected slowness, eyes pupil-black. He knew he had her; this was foreplay. Her eyes closed when he placed the flat of his arm beside her head, leaning to whisper in her ear, "I like you following behind me, tying off my loose ends. Picking up my slack. Doing my—paperwork."

He smelled like leaf ash, dusky and thick, and the scent went right to the primitive part of her brain and flicked a switch. Her breath caught, then came fast. She hesitated, then with a feeling of self-loathing she knew would fade and return like the sun, she breathed deeply, bringing his scent deep inside, coating her dislike for him with the sweet promise of blood ecstasy, silencing her desire to avoid him with the quick, bitter lust for blood. She knew what she was doing. She knew she would enjoy it. Sometimes, she wondered why she agonized over it. Kisten didn't.

Letting his keys drop to the carpet with her coat and purse, she curled an arm around his neck and pulled him close, an inviting sound lifting through her, realigning her thoughts, shutting down her reasoning to protect her sanity. "What do you want to change my evaluation?"

She sensed more than saw his smile widen as she leaned forward. His earlobe was warm when she put her lips on it, sucking with just a hint of pressure from her teeth. He slid his fingers along her collarbone to rest atop her shoulder, easing his fingers under her shirt. Eyes closing at the growing warmth, her muscles tensed. He exhaled against her, a soft promise to bring her to life with an exquisite need, then satisfy it savagely.

The elevator dinged and slid open, but neither of them moved. Art breathed deeply when the doors closed, an almost subliminal growl that touched the pit of her soul. "Your paperwork is above reproach," he said, his fingers moving to grip the back of her neck.

A jolt of blood-passion lit through her. Without thought, she jerked him forward into her, spinning them until Art's back hit the wall where hers had been. Breath fast, she met his hunger-laced eyes with her own. She felt her jaw tighten and knew her eyes had dilated. *Why had she put this off?*

It was going to be glorious. What did she care if she respected him? Like he respected her? Like any of them did?

"And my investigative skills are phenomenal," she said, maneuvering a long leg between his and hooking her foot behind his shoe, tugging until their hips touched. Adrenaline zinged, promising more.

Art smiled, showing his longer canines that death had given him. Hers were short by comparison, but they were more than sharp enough to get the job done. Undead vamps loved them. She likened it to how a sexual pervert loved children. "True," he said, "but your interpersonal skills suck." His smile widened. "More accurately, you don't."

Ivy chuckled low, deep, and honestly. "I do my job, Artie."

The vampire pushed from the elevator, and together they found the opposite wall. Ivy's jaw clenched as he tried to physically manipulate her, making her feel as if she was moving on animal instinct. She had been putting this off so long that it might last all night if she let it.

"This isn't about your job," Art said, his fingers tracing the trails he wanted his lips to follow, but there was a strict policy against bloodletting in the tower. She could tease and flirt, drive him crazy, let him drive her to the brink, but no blood. Until later.

"It's about putting your time in," he continued, and Ivy shivered when his lips touched her neck. *God help her, he'd found an old scar.* Pulse hard and fast, she pushed him away and around again so he was between her and the wall. He let her do it.

"I am putting my time in." Ivy put a hand to his shoulder and shoved him back. He hit the wall with a thump, black eyes glinting from behind his black curls. "What is my evaluation going to say, Mr. Artie?" She leaned into his neck, taking a fold of skin between her lips and tugging. Her eyes closed, and as her own bloodlust pulsed through her, she forgot that they were standing in the elevator hallway, deep underground, amid the hum of circulation fans and electric-lit black.

Art rode the feeling she knew she was instilling in him, letting it grow. He had been dead long enough to have gained the restraint to string the foreplay out to their limits. "You're argumentative, closed, and refuse to work in a team environment," he said, his voice husky.

"Oh . . ." She pouted, gripping the hair at the base of his scalp hard enough to hurt. "I'm not bad, Mr. Artie. I'm a good little girl . . . when properly motivated."

Her voice had an artful lilt, playful yet domineering, and he responded with a low sound. The bound heat in it hit her, and her fingers released. She had found his limit.

He moved so quickly, she sensed more than saw the motion. His hand abruptly covered hers, forcing her fingers back among the black ringlets at his neck and making them close about them again. "Your evaluation is subjective," he said, his eyes stopping her breath as time balanced. "I decide if you're promoted. Piscary said you'd be a worthwhile hunt, pull me up in the I.S. hierarchy as you resisted, but that you'd give in and I'd have a better job *and* a taste of you."

At that, Ivy paused, jealousy clouding her. Art was conceited enough to believe Piscary was giving her to him when the truth was Piscary was using Art to manipulate her. It was a compliment in a backward way, and she despised herself for loving Piscary all the more, craving the master vampire's attention and favor even as she hated him for it.

"I am giving in," she said, anger joining her bloodlust. It was a potent mix most vamps craved. And here she was, giving it to him. The only thing they liked more was the taste of fear.

But Art's domineering smile surprised her. "No," he admonished, using his undead strength to force her back to the elevators. Her back hit hard, and she inhaled to catch her breath. "It's not that easy anymore," he said. "Six months ago, you could have gotten away with a nip and a new scar I could brag about, but not now. I want to know why Piscary indulges you beyond belief the way he does. I want everything, Ivy. I want your blood *and* your body. Or you don't move from that shitty little office without dragging me with you."

Fear, unusual and shocking, trickled through her and gripped her heart. Art sensed it, and he sucked in air. "God yes," he moaned, his fingers jerking in a spasm. "Give this to me . . ."

Ivy felt her face go cold, and she tried to push Art off her, failing. Blood she could give, but her blood and body both? She had flirted with insanity the year Piscary had called her to him, breaking her, lifting her to glorious heights of passion her young body could scarcely contain before dropping her soul to the basest of levels to pay for it, to make her kneel for more and do anything to please him. She knew it had been a studied manipulation, one practiced on her mother, and her grandmother, and her great-grandmother before that until he was so good at it that the victim wept for the abuse. But that didn't stop her from wanting it.

True to his word, she got as good as she gave. And she almost killed herself from the highs and lows as Piscary carefully built within her an addiction to the euphoria of sharing blood, warping it, mixing it with her need for love and her craving for acceptance. He had molded her into a savagely passionate blood partner, rich in the exotic tastes that evolve in mixing the deeper emotions of love and guilt with something that, at its basest, was a savage act. That he had done it only to make her blood sweeter didn't matter. It was who she was, and a guilty part of herself gloried in the abandonment she allowed herself there that she denied herself everywhere else.

She had survived by creating the lie that sharing blood was meaningless unless mixed with sex, whereupon it became a way to show someone you loved him or her. She knew that the two were so mixed up in her mind she couldn't separate them, but she had always been in a position to choose who she would share herself with, avoiding the realization that her sanity hung on a lie. But now?

Her eyes fixed on Art's black orbs, taking in his mocking satisfaction and checked bloodlust. He would be an exquisite rush, both beautiful and skilled. He would let her burn, make her weep for his pull upon her, and in return she would give him everything he craved to find and more—and she would wake alone and used, not cradled among sheltering arms that forgave her for her warped needs, even if that forgiveness was born in yet more manipulation.

Jaw clenching, she shoved Art away and moved to get her back from the wall. He fell back a step, surprised.

She did not want to do this. She had protected herself with the lie that blood was just blood, and had been prepared for the mental pain of whoring that much of herself. But Art wanted to mix blood with her body. It would touch too closely to the truth to keep the lie that held her intact. She couldn't do it.

Art's lust shifted to anger, an emotion that crossed into death where compassion couldn't. "Why don't you like me?" he questioned bitterly, jerking her to him. "I'm not enough?"

Ivy's pulse hammered as they stood before the elevators, and she cursed herself for her lack of control. *He was enough. He was more than enough to satisfy her hunger, but she had a soul to satisfy, too.* "You have no ambition," she whispered, instincts pulling her into his warmth even as her mind screamed no. Art's jaw trembled, and his heady scent sang through her, starting a war within her. *What if she couldn't find a way past this?* She had always been able to avoid a test between her instinct and willpower by walking away, but here that wasn't an option.

"Then you aren't looking deep enough." Art gripped her shoulder until it hurt. "Either I get a taste of why Piscary indulges you, or you take me up with you, promotion by promotion. I don't care, Ivy girl."

"Don't call me that," she said, fear mixing with the sexual heat he was pulling from her. Piscary called her that, the bastard. If she gave in, it would start her on the fast track at work but kill what kept her sane. And if she held to her lie and refused, Art had her doing his dirty work.

Art's smile became domineering as he saw her realize the trap. That Piscary had probably arranged the situation to test her resolve only made her love the master vampire more. She was warped. She was warped and lost.

But her very familiarity with the system she had been born into would save her. As she stilled her panic, her mind started to work, and a wicked smile curled the corner of her lips. "You forgot something, Art," she said, tension falling from her as she faked passivity and hung in his grip. "If you break *my* skin without *my* permission, Piscary will have you staked."

All she had to do was best her hunger. She could do that.

He gripped her tighter, his fingers pressing into her neck where the visible scars of Piscary's claim had been hidden with surgery. The scars were gone, but the potent mix of neuron stimulators and receptor mutagens remained. Piscary had claimed her, sensitized her entire body so that only he could make it resonate to past passions with just his thoughts and pheromones, but she still felt a spike of desire dive to her groin at the thought of Art's teeth sinking cleanly into her. She had to get away from him before her bloodlust took over.

"You knew that, didn't you?" she mocked, her skin tingling.

"You'll enjoy it," he breathed, and the tingles spun into heat. "When I'm done with you, you'll beg for more. Why would you care who bit who first?"

"Because I like to say no," she said, finding it difficult to keep from running her fingernail hard down his neck to bring him alive with desire. She could do it. She knew exactly how exhilarating the feeling of domination and utter control over a monster like him would feel. Her fear was gone, and without it, the bloodlust returned all the harder. "You take my blood without my acquiescence, and I'll get you bumped down to runner," she said. "You can coerce, you can threaten, you can slice your wrist and bleed on my lips, but if you take my blood without me saying yes, then you—lose." She leaned forward until her lips were almost touching his. "And I win," she finished, pulse fast and aching for him to run his hand against her skin.

He pushed her away. Ivy caught her balance easily, laughing.

"Piscary said you'd resist," he said, his eyes black and tension making his posture both threatening and attractive.

God, the things she could do with this one, she thought in spite of herself. "Piscary is right," she said, cocking her hip and running her hand provocatively down it. "You're in over your head, Art. I like saying no, and I'm going to drive you into taking me without my permission, and then?" She smiled, coming close and curling her arms about his neck and playing with the tips of his curly hair.

Eyes black with hunger, Art smiled, taking her fingers in hers and kissing the tips. The hint of teeth against her skin brought a shiver through her, and her fingers trembled in his grip. "Good," he said, voice husky. "The next six months are going to be pure hell."

Instinct rose and gathered. Licking her lips, she pushed him from her. "You've no idea."

He retreated to the wall beside the elevator. With a friendly ding, the elevator door opened as he bumped the call button. He stepped into the elevator, still wearing that shit-grin. "Coming?" he mocked, looking too damn good to resist in the back of the elevator.

Feeling the pull, she swooped for his keys beside her purse. Her pulse was faster than she liked, and she felt wire-tight from hunger thrumming through her. *Damn it, it was only nine. How was she going to get to the end of her shift without taking advantage of the mail boy?*

"I'm taking my cycle," she said, throwing his keys at him. "I'll meet you there. Better put your caps on. I want out of this crappy job, and I'd say you've got a week. You won't be able to resist once I put my mind to it."

Art laughed, ducking his head. "I'm older than you think, Ivy. You'll be begging me to sink my teeth by Friday."

The door closed and the elevator rose to the parking garage. Ivy felt her eyes return to normal as the circulation fans pulled away the pheromones they had both been giving off. One week, and she'd be out from under him. One week, and she'd be moving to where she belonged.

"One week, and I'll have that bastard taking advantage of me," she whispered, wondering if at the end of it, she would be counted the winner.

 ## TWO

I went an entire two weeks saying no to Piscary, once, Ivy thought as she idled into the apartment complex's parking lot on her cycle's momentum. Art didn't have a shit's chance in a Cincy sewer.

Feeling a flush of confidence, she parked her bike under a streetlight so the assembled I.S. officers could get a good look. It was a Nightwing X–31, one of the few things she had splurged on after getting her job at the I.S. and a paycheck that wasn't tied to Piscary or her mother. When she rode it, she was free. She wasn't looking forward to winter.

Engine rumbling under her provocatively, Ivy took in the multispecies-capability ambulance and the two I.S. cruisers, their lights flashing amber and blue on the faces of gawking neighbors. The U.S. health system had begun catering to mixed species shortly after the Turn, a natural step since only the health care providers who were Inderlanders in hiding survived the T4–Angel virus. But law enforcement had split, and after thirty-six years, would stay that way.

The FIB, or human-run Federal Inderland Bureau, wasn't here yet. Art wasn't here yet, either. She wondered who had called the homicide in. The man in the back of the I.S. cruiser in pajama bottoms and handcuffs? The excited neighbor in curlers talking to an I.S. officer?

Art wasn't the only thing missing, and she scanned the lot for the absent I.S.'s evidence collection van. They wouldn't show until Inderland involvement was confirmed, and while many humans lived across the river to take advantage of the lower taxes in the Hollows, to think that this was strictly a human matter was a stretch.

The man in the car was in custody. If he had been an Inderlander, he'd be in the tower by now. It seemed they had a human suspect and were waiting for the FIB to collect him. She'd probably find the crime scene almost pristine, with only the people removed to help preserve it.

"Idiot human," she muttered, her foot coming down to balance her weight as she shut off her cycle and slid the key into the shallow pocket of her leather pants to leave the skull key chain dangling. She knew what she'd find in his apartment. His wife or girlfriend dead over something stupid like sex or money. Humans didn't know where true rage stemmed from.

Fixing her face into a bland expression to hide her disgust, she removed her helmet and took a deep breath of the night air, feeling the humidity of the unseen river settle deep in her lungs. The man in the back of the cruiser was yelling, trying to get her attention.

"I didn't mean to hurt her!" he cried, muffled through the glass. "It wasn't me. I love Ellie. I love Ellie! You gotta believe me!"

Ivy got off her cycle. Clipping her ID to her short leather jacket, she took a moment to collect herself, concentrating on the damp night. The man's fear, not his girlfriend's blood he was smearing on the windows, pulled a faint rise of bloodlust into existence. His face was scratched, and the welts were bleeding. The man was terrified. Locking him in the cruiser until the FIB picked him up was for his own safety.

Her boot heels making a slow, seductive cadence to draw attention, Ivy walked to the front door and the pool of light that held two officers. Spotting a familiar face, Ivy let some of the tension slip from her and her arms swing free. "Hi, Rat," she said, halting on the apartment complex's six-by-eight common porch. "Haven't you died yet?"

"It's not for lack of trying," the older vamp said, his wrinkles deepening as he smiled. "Where's Art?"

"Biting himself," she said, and his partner, a slight woman, laughed. The living vamp looked right out of high school, but Ivy knew it was a witch charm that kept her that way. The woman was pushing fifty, but the disguise was tax deductible since she used her looks to pacify those who needed . . . pacifying. Ivy nodded warily to her, and got the same in return.

The faint scent of blood coming from the hallway sifted through her brain. It wasn't much, but after Art's play for her, her senses were running in overdrive. "Is the body still in there?" she asked, thinking the situation could be useful. Art hadn't been up long and his resistance would be lower. With a little planning, she might tip him into making a mistake tonight, and she stifled a shudder of anticipation for what that actually meant.

Rat shrugged, eyeing her speculatively. "Body's in the ambulance. You okay?"

His teeth sinking deep into her, the salt of his dusty blood on her tongue, the rush of adrenaline as he drew from her what made her alive . . . "I'm fine," she said. "Vampire?" she questioned, since they usually left bodies for the morgue unless there was a chance it might decide it was well enough to get up.

Rat's expressive face went hard. "No." His voice was soft, and she took a pair of slip-on booties that his partner extended to her. "Witch. Pretty, too. But since her staked-excuse of a husband was encouraged to ignore his rights and confessed to beating her up and strangling her, they moved her out. He's a paint job, Ivy. Only good for draining and painting the walls."

Ivy frowned, not following his gaze to the man shouting in the cruiser. *They moved her?*

Rat saw her annoyance and added, "Shit, Ivy. He confessed. We got pictures. There's nothing here."

"There's nothing here when I say there's nothing here," she said, stiffening when the recognizable rumble of Art's late-model Jaguar came through the damp night. Damn it, she had wanted to be in there first.

Ivy's exposed skin tingled, and she felt a wash of self-disgust. God help her, she was going to use a crime scene to get Art off her back. Someone had died, and she was going to use that to seduce Art into biting her against her will. How depraved could she be? But it was an old feeling, quickly repressed like all the other ugly things in her life.

Handing her purse to Rat, she got a packet of evidence bags and wax pencil in return. "I want the collection van here," she said, not caring that Rat had just told her to collect any evidence she thought pertinent herself. "I want the place vacuumed as soon as I'm out. And I want you to stop doing my job."

"Sorry, Ivy." Rat grinned. "Hey, there's a poll started about you and Art—"

Ivy stepped forward, coiled arm extending. Rat blocked it, grabbing her wrist and pulling her off balance and into him. She fell into his chest, his weight twice hers. His partner snicked. Ivy had known the strike would never land, but it had burned off a little frustration.

"You know," Rat breathed, the scent of his partner's blood fresh on his breath from an earlier tryst, "you really shouldn't wear those high-heeled boots. They make your balance suck."

Ivy twisted and broke from him. "I hear they hurt more when I crotch-kick bastards like you," she said, the fading adrenaline making her head hurt. "Who else has been in there?" she asked, thinking a room stinking of fear would be just the thing to tip Art into a mistake. He was currently standing by the cruiser, looking at the human and letting his blood-ardor grow. *Idiot.*

Rat was rubbing his lower neck in invitation. God, it had started already. By sunup, they'd all think she was in the market to build up the IOUs necessary to reach the lower basement and she'd be mobbed. Imagining the coming innuendos, suggestions, and unwanted offers, Ivy stifled a sigh. *Like the pheromones weren't bad enough already?* Maybe she should start a rumor she had an STD.

"The ambulance crew," the vampire was saying. "Tia and me to get him out. He was crying over her as usual. A neighbor called it in as a domestic disturbance. Third one this month, but when it got quiet, she got scared and made the call."

Frowning, Ivy took a last breath of clean night air, and stepped into the hall. Not too many people to confuse things, and Rat knew not to touch anything. The room would be as clean as could be expected. And *she* wasn't going to sully it.

The tang of blood strengthened, and after slipping on the blue booties, she bent to duck under the tape across the open door. She stopped inside, taking in someone else's life: low ceilings, matted carpet, old drapes, new couch, big but cheap TV, even cheaper stereo, and hundreds of CDs. There were self-framed pictures of people on the walls and arranged on the pressboard entertainment shelves. The feminine touches were spotty, like paint splatters. The victim hadn't lived here very long.

Ivy breathed deeply, tasting the anger left in the air, invisible signposts that would fade with the sun. Blue booties scuffing, she followed the scent of blood to the bathroom. A red handprint gripped the rim of the toilet, and there were several smears on the tub and curtain. Someone had cut his scalp on the tub. The pink bulb gave an unreal cast, and Ivy shut off the exhaust fan with the end of her wax pencil, making a mental note to tell Rat that she had.

The soft hum stopped. In the new silence, she heard the soft conversation and laugh track of a sitcom coming from a nearby apartment. Art's satisfied voice filtered in from the hallway, and Ivy's blood pressure rose. Rat had said the man had strangled his wife. She'd seen worse. And though he hadn't said where they found the body, an almost palpable anger flowed over the bedroom's doorjamb, broken about the latch with newly painted-over cracks.

Ivy touched the hidden damage with a finger. The bedroom had the same mix of careless bachelor and young woman trying to decorate with little money to spend. Cheap frilly pillows, pink lace draped over ugly lampshades, dust thick on the metal blinds that were never opened. No blood but for smears, and they were likely the suspect's. Pretty clothes in pink and white were strewn on the bed and floor, and the closet was empty. She had tried to leave. A black TV was in the corner, the remote broken on the floor under a dent in the wall smelling of plaster. On the carpet was Rat's card and a Polaroid of the woman, askew on the floor by the bed.

Forcing her jaw to unclench, Ivy pulled the air deep into her, reading the room as if the last few hours of emotion had painted the air in watercolors. Any vampire could.

The man in the car had hurt the woman, terrified her, beat her up, and her magic hadn't stopped him. She had died here, and the heady scents of her fear and his anger started a disturbing and not entirely unwelcome bloodlust in Ivy's gut. Her fingertips ached, and her throat seemed to swell.

The sound of Art's scuffing steps cut painfully through her wide-open senses. A thrill of adrenaline built and vanished. Eyes half lidded, she turned, finding a seductive tilt to her hips. Art's eyes were almost fully dilated. Clearly the fear of the man outside and its echo still vibrating through the room were tugging on his instincts. Maybe this was why he continued to work homicide. Pretty man couldn't get his fangs wet without a little help, maybe?

"Ivy," he said, his voice sending that same shiver through her, and she felt a dropping sensation that said her eyes were dilating. "I make the call for the evidence van, not you."

Posture shifting, Ivy stepped to keep him from getting between her and the door. "You were busy jacking off on the suspect's fear," she said lightly. She moved as if to leave, knowing if she played the coy victim it would trigger his bloodlust. As expected, Art's pupils went wider, blacker. She felt his presence rise up behind her, almost as if pushing her into him. He was pulling an aura, not a real one, but simply strengthening his vampiric presence.

Art snatched her arm, domineering and possessive. Teasing, she feigned to draw away until his grip tightened. "I call the van," he said, voice dangerous.

"What's the matter, Art?" she said languorously, pulling her wrist and his hand gripping it to her upper chest. "Don't like a woman who thinks?" Sexual tension lanced through her. Enjoying it, she put a knuckle between her lips, letting it go with a soft kiss and a skimming of teeth. Piscary had made her who she was, and despite his experience, Art didn't have a chance.

"You think I'm going to lose it over a fear-laced room and a pair of black eyes?" he said, looking good in his Italian suit and smelling deliciously of wool, ash, and himself.

"Oh, I'm just getting started." With her free hand, she took Art's fingers off her wrist. He didn't stop her. Smiling, she ran her tongue across her teeth, hiding them even as they flashed. The fear in the room flowed through her, inciting instincts older than the pyramids, screaming unhindered through her younger body. She stiffened at the potent rush of blood rising to her skin. She expected it, riding and enjoying it. It wasn't the scent of blood, it was the fear. *She could handle this. She controlled her bloodlust; her bloodlust didn't control her.*

And when she felt that curious drop of pressure in her face as her eyes dilated fully, she turned to Art, her paper-clad boots spread wide as she stood in the middle of the room stinking of sex and blood and fear, lips parted as she exhaled provocatively. A tremble lifted through her, settling in her groin to tell her what could follow if she let it. She wouldn't give him her blood willingly, and that he might forcibly take it was unexpectedly turning her on.

"Mmmm, it smells good in here," she said, the adrenaline high scouring through her because *she* was in control. She was in control of this monster who could kill her with a backhanded slap, who could rip out her throat and end her life, who could make her powerless under him—and who couldn't touch her blood until she allowed him, bound by tradition and unwritten law. And if he tried, she'd have his ass and a better job both.

Pulse fast, she took a step closer. He wanted her—he was so ready, his shoulders were rock hard and his hands were fists to keep from reaching for her. His inner struggle was showing on his face, and he wasn't breathing anymore. There was a reason Piscary indulged her. This was part of it, but Art would never taste it all.

"Can't have . . . this," she said, her hand sliding up from her inner thigh, fingers spread wide as they crossed her middle to her chest until they lay provocatively to hide her neck. She felt her pulse lift and fall against them, stirring herself as much as Art. Her eyes were on the vampire before her. He would be savagely magnificent. She exhaled, imagining his teeth sinking into her, reminding her she was alive with the promise of death in his lips.

Almost . . . it might be worth letting him have his way.

Art read her thought in the very air. In a flash of motion too fast for her to follow, he moved. Ivy gasped, her core pulsing with fear. He jerked her to him. His hand gripped the back of her neck, the other twisted her arm painfully behind her. He hesitated as he caught himself, his eyes black and pained with the control needed to stop. She laughed, low and husky.

"Can't have this," she taunted, wishing he would take it as she lolled her head back to expose the length of her neck. *Oh God. If only he would . . .* she thought, a faint tickling in her thoughts warning her a war had started between her hunger and will.

"Give it to me," Art managed, his voice strained, and she smiled as he started to weaken. "Give this to me . . ."

"No," she breathed. Her pulse lifted under his hand, and her eyes closed. Her body demanded she say yes, she wanted to say yes. *Why*, she thought, hunger driving through her as she found his hard shoulders, *why didn't she say yes? Such a small thing . . . And he was so deliciously beautiful, even if he didn't stir her soul.*

Art sensed her falter, a low growl rising up through him. He pressed her to him, almost supporting her weight. With a new resolve, he nuzzled the base of her neck.

Ivy sucked in her air, clutching him closer. Fire. This was fire, burning promises from her neck to her groin.

"Give this to me," he demanded, his lips brushing the words against her skin. His hand slipped farther, edging between her coat and shirt, cupping her breast. "Everything . . ." he breathed, his exhalation filling her, making her whole.

In a breathless wave, instinct rose, crushing her will. *No!* she panicked even as her body writhed for it. It would turn her into a whore, break her will and crack the lie that kept her sane. But with a frightened jolt, Ivy realized her lips had parted to say yes.

Reality flashed through her, and with a surge of fear, she kneed him in the crotch.

Art let go, falling to kneel before her, his hands covering himself. Not waiting, she fell back a step and snapped a front kick to his jaw. His head rocked back and he hit the floor beside the bed. "You stupid bitch," he gasped.

"Ass," she panted, trembling as her body rebelled at the sudden shift of passions. She stood above him, fighting the desire to fall on him, sink her teeth into him while he knelt helpless before her. Damn it, she had to get out of this room. Two unrequited plays for her blood in one night was pushing it.

Slowly Art lost his hunched position and started to chuckle. Ivy felt her face flame. "Get off the floor," she snapped, backing up. "They haven't vacuumed yet."

Still laughing, Art rolled onto his side. "This is going to be one hell of a week," he said, then hesitated, eyes on the carpet just beyond the bedspread knocked askew. "Give me a collection bag," he said, reaching into his back pocket.

Bloodlust still ringing in her, Ivy came forward, pulled by his intent tone. "What is it?"

"Give me a bag," he repeated, his expensive suit clashing with the ugly carpet.

She hesitated, then scooped up the bags from where they had fallen. Checking the time, Ivy jotted down the date and location before handing it to Art. Still on the floor, Art reached under the bed and rolled something shiny into the light with a pen from his pocket. With an eerie quickness, he flicked it into the bag and stood. The growing brown rim about his pupils said he was in control, and smiling to show his teeth, he lifted the bag to the light.

Seeing his confidence, Ivy felt a flash of despair. It had been a game to him. He had never been in danger of losing his restraint. *Shit*, she thought, the first fingers of doubt she could do this slithering about her heart.

But then she saw what he held, and her worry turned to understanding—and then true concern. "A banshee tear?" she asked, recognizing the tear-shaped black crystal.

Suddenly the words of the distraught man in the car had a new meaning. *I didn't mean to hurt her. It wasn't me.* Pity came from nowhere, making the slice of low-income misery surrounding her all the more distasteful. He probably *had* loved her. It had been a banshee, feeding him rage until he killed his wife, whereupon the banshee wallowed in her death energy.

It was still murder, but the man had been a tool, not the perpetrator. The murderer was at large somewhere in Cincinnati, with the alibi of time and distance making it hard to link her to the crime. That's why the tear had been left as a conduit. The banshee had targeted the couple, followed them home, left a tear when they were out, and when sparks flew, added to the man's rage until he truly wasn't capable of resisting. It wasn't an excuse; it was murder by magic—a magic older than vampires. Perhaps older than witches or demons.

Art shook the bag to make the black jewel glitter before letting his arm drop. "We have every banshee on record. We'll run the tear through the computer and get the bitch."

Ivy nodded, feeling her pupils contract. The I.S. kept close tabs on the small population of banshees, and if one was feeding indiscriminately in Cincinnati, they could expect more deaths before they caught her.

"Now, where were we," Art said, slipping an arm about her waist.

"Bastard," Ivy said, elbowing him in the gut and stepping away. But the strike never landed, and she schooled her face to no emotion when he chuckled at her a good eight feet back. God, he made her feel like a child. "Why don't you go home after the sun comes up," she snarled.

"You offering to tuck me in?"

"Go to hell."

From the hallway came the sounds of soft conversation. The collection van was here. Art breathed deep, bringing the scents of the room into him. His eyes closed and his thin lips curled upward as he exhaled, apparently happy with what he sensed. Ivy didn't need to breathe to know that the room stank of her fear now, mixing with the dead woman's until it was impossible to tell them apart.

"See you back at the tower, Ivy."

Not if I stake you first, she thought, wondering if calling in sick tomorrow was worth the harassment she'd get the next day. She could say she'd been to the doctor about her case of STD—tell everyone she got it from Art.

Art sauntered out of the room, one hand in his pocket, the other dropping the banshee tear onto the entering officer's clipboard. The werewolf's eyes widened, but then he looked up, eyes watering. "Whoa!" he said, nose wrinkling. "What have you two been doing in here?"

"Nothing." Ivy felt cold and small in her leather pants and short coat as she stood in the center of the room and listened to Art say good-bye to Rat and Tia. She forced her hands from her neck to prove it was unmarked.

"Doesn't smell like nothing," the man scoffed. "Smells like someone—"

Ivy glared at him as his words cut off. Adrenaline pulsed, this time from worry. She had contaminated a crime scene with her fear, but the man's eyes held pity, not disgust.

"Are you okay?" he asked softly, his clipboard held to himself as he obviously guessed what had happened. There was too much fear in here for just one person, even a murdered one.

"Fine," she said shortly. Psychic fear levels weren't recorded unless a banshee was involved. That she hadn't known one was, wasn't an excuse. She'd get reprimanded at the least, worse if Art wanted to blackmail her. And he would. Damn it, could she make this any easier for him? Flushed, she scooped up the rest of the collection bags and gave them to the Were.

"I don't know how you can work with the dead ones," the man said, trying to catch her eyes, but Ivy wouldn't let him. "Hell, they scare my tail over my balls just looking at me."

"I said, I'm fine," she muttered. "I want it vacuumed, dusted, and photographed. Don't bother with a fear level profile. I contaminated it." She could keep quiet about it, but she'd rather suffer an earned reprimand than Art's blackmail. "Keep the tear from the press," she added, glancing at it, small and innocuous on his clipboard. "The last thing we need is the city in a panic, calling us every time a high schooler cries over her boyfriend."

The man nodded. His stubble was thick, and stifling the thought of how it would feel to rake her fingers and then her teeth over it, Ivy strode from the room, fleeing the stink of the dead woman's fear. She didn't like how it smelled exactly like her own.

Ivy passed quickly through the living room and into the hallway, trying not to breathe. She should have planned this, not made a fool of herself by acting on impulse. Because of her assumptions, Art had her by the short hairs. Avoiding him the rest of her day was going to be impossible. Maybe she could spend it researching banshees. The files were stored in the upper levels. Art might follow her, but the Inderlander ratio would be slanted to witch and Were, not only reducing the pheromone levels, but also making it easier to pull out early since the entire tower above ground emptied at midnight with their three to twelve shift. Only the belowground offices maintained the variable sunset to sunrise schedule.

Wine, she thought, forcing herself to look confident and casual when she emerged on the stoop and found the lights of a news crew already illuminating the parking lot. She'd pick up two bottles on the way home so Kisten would be drunk enough not to care if she hurt him.

 THREE

Even with her intentions to leave at midnight, the sun was up by the time Ivy was idling her bike through the Hollows's rush-hour traffic, winding her way to the waterfront and the spacious apartment she and Kisten shared above Piscary's restaurant. That she worked for the force that policed the underground he controlled wasn't surprising or unintentional, but prudent planning. Though not on the payroll, Piscary ran the I.S. through a complicated system of favors. He still had to obey the laws—or at least not get caught breaking them lest he get hauled in like anyone else. It reminded Ivy of what Camelot had probably really been like.

Her mother had worked in the top of the I.S. hierarchy until she died, and Ivy knew that was where she and Piscary wanted Ivy to be. Piscary dealt in gambling and protection—on paper, both legal ways to make his money—and the master vampire had more finesse than to put her where she'd have to choose between doing what he wanted and what her job required. The corruption was that bad.

Or that good, Ivy thought, checking to see that the guy behind her was watching before she slowed and turned left into the restaurant's parking lot. If it hadn't been for the threat of Piscary coming down on aggressive vampires in backstreet justice, the I.S. wouldn't be able to cope. She was sure that was why most people, including the FIB, looked the other way. The I.S. was corrupt, but the people actually in charge of the city did a good job keeping it civilized.

Ivy slowed her bike by the door to the kitchen and cut the engine, scanning the empty lot. It was Wednesday, and whereas any other day of the week the restaurant would be emptying out of the last stragglers, today it was deserted. Piscary liked a day of rest. At least she wouldn't have to dodge the waitstaff and their questions as to why her eyes were half dilated. She needed either a long bubble bath before bed, or Kisten, or both.

The breeze off the nearby river was cool and carried the scent of oil and gas. Taking a breath to clear her mind, she pushed the service door open with the wheel of her bike. It didn't even have a lock to let the produce trucks make their deliveries at all hours. No one would steal from Piscary. For all appearances he obeyed the law, but somehow, you'd find yourself dead anyway.

Purse and twin wine bottles in hand, she left her bike beside the crates of tomatoes and mushrooms and took the cement steps to the kitchen two at a time. She passed the dark counters and cold ovens without seeing them. The faint odor of rising yeast mixed with the lingering odors of the vampires who worked here, and she felt herself relax, her boots making a soft cadence on the tiled floor. The scent brought to memory thoughts of her summers working in the kitchen and, when old enough, on the floor as a waitress. She hadn't been innocent, but then the ugliness had been lost in the glare of the thrill. Now it just made her tired.

Her pulse quickened when she passed the thick door that led to the elevator and Piscary's underground apartments. The thought that he would meet her with soothing hands and calculated sympathy was enough to bring her blood to the surface, but her irritation that he was manipulating her kept her moving into the bar. He wouldn't call her to him, knowing it would cause her more mental anguish to come begging to him when she could take no more, desperate for the reassurance that he still loved her.

It was comfortingly silent in the restaurant proper, and the low ceilings and dim atmosphere seemed to follow her into the closed-party rooms in the back. A wide stairway behind a door led to the private second floor. Her hand traced the wall for balance as she rose up the wide, black-wood stairs, eager to find Kisten and an understanding ear that wasn't attached to a manipulating mind.

She and Kisten lived in the converted apartment that took up the entire top floor of the old shipping warehouse. Ivy liked the openness, arbitrarily dividing it into spaces with folding screens and strategically placed furniture. The windows were spacious and smeared on the outside with the dirt and grime of forty years. Piscary didn't like being that exposed, and this granted the two of them a measure of security.

Wine bottles clinking, Ivy set them on the table at the top of the stairs, thinking she and Kisten were like two abused children, craving the attention of the very person who had warped them, loving him out of desperation. It was an old thought, one that had lost its sting long ago.

Shuffling off her coat, she set it and her purse by the wine. "Kist?" she called, her voice filling the silence. "I'm home." She picked the bottles back up and frowned. Maybe she should have gotten three.

There was no answer, and as she headed back toward the kitchen to chill the wine, the scent of blood shivered through her like an electrical current. It wasn't Kisten's.

Her feet stopped, and she breathed deeply. Her head swiveled to the corner where the deliverymen had put her baby grand last week. It had dented her finances more than the bike, but the sound of it in this emptiness made her forget everything until the echoes faded.

"Kist?"

She heard him take a breath, but didn't see him. Her face blanked and every muscle tightened as she paced to the couches arranged about her piano. The dirty sunshine pooling in glinted on the black sheen of the wood, and she found him there, kneeling on the white Persian rug between the couch and the piano, a girl in tight jeans, a black lacy shirt, and a worn leather coat sprawled before him.

Kisten lifted his head, an unusual panic in his blue eyes. "I didn't do it," he said, his bloodied hands hovering over the corpse.

Shit. Dropping the bottles on the couch, Ivy swung into motion, moving to kneel before them. Habit made her check for a pulse, but it was obvious by her pallor and the gentle mauling on her neck that the petite blonde was dead despite her warmth.

"I didn't do it," Kisten said again, shifting his trim, pretty-boy body back a few inches. His hands, strong and muscular, were shaking, the tops of his fingernails red with a light sheen. Ivy looked from them to his face, seeing the fear in his almost delicate features that he hid behind a reddish blond beard. A smear of blood was on his forehead behind his brown bangs, and she stifled an urge to kiss it away that both disgusted and intrigued her. *This is not who I wanted to be.*

"I didn't do it, Ivy!" he exclaimed at her continued silence, and she reached over the girl and brushed his too-long bangs back. The gentle swelling of black in his gaze made her breath catch. God, he was beautiful when he was agitated.

"I know you didn't," she said, and Kisten's wide shoulders relaxed, making her wonder if that was why he was upset. It wasn't that he had to take care of Piscary's mistake, but that Ivy might think he had killed her. And somewhere in there, she found that he loved her.

The pretty woman was Piscary's favorite body type with long fair hair and an angular face. She probably had blue eyes. *Shit, shit, and more shit.* Mind calculating how to minimize the damage, she asked, "How long has she been dead?"

"Minutes. No more than that." Kisten's resonant voice dropped to a more familiar pitch. "I was trying to find out where she was staying and get her cleaned up, but she died right here on the couch. Piscary . . ." He met her eyes, reaching up to tug on a twin pair of diamond-stud earrings. "Piscary told me to take care of it."

Ivy shifted her weight to her feet, easing back to sit on the edge of the nearby couch. It wasn't like Kisten to panic like this. He was Piscary's scion, the person the undead vampire had tapped to manage the bar, do his daylight work, and clean up his mistakes. Mistakes that were usually four foot eleven, blond, and a hundred pounds. Damn it all to hell. Piscary hadn't slipped like this since she had left to finish high school on the West Coast.

"Did she sign the release papers?" she asked.

"Do you think I'd be this upset if she had?" Kisten arranged the small woman's hair as if it would help. God, she looked fourteen, though Ivy knew she'd be closer to twenty.

Ivy's lips pressed together and she sighed. So much for getting any sleep this morning. "Get the plastic wrap from the piano out of the recycling bin," she said in decision, and Kisten rose, tugging the tails of his silk shirt down over the tops of his jeans. "We open in eight hours for the early Inderland crowd, and I don't want the place smelling like dead girl."

Kisten rocked into motion, headed for the stairs. "Move faster, unless you want to have the carpet steam cleaned!" Ivy called, and she heard him jump to the floor from midway down.

Tired, Ivy looked at the woman's abandoned purse on the couch, too emotionally exhausted to figure out how she should feel. Kisten was Piscary's scion, but it was Ivy who did most of the thinking in a pinch. It wasn't that Kisten was stupid—far from it—but he was used to having her take over. Expected it. Liked it.

Wondering if Piscary had killed the girl on purpose to force Kisten to take responsibility, Ivy stood with her hands on her hips, her eyes going to the filthy windows and the river hazy in the morning sun. It sounded just like the manipulative bastard. If Ivy had succumbed to Art, she would have spent the morning at his place—not only obediently taking the next step to the management position Piscary wanted for her, but forcing Kisten to handle this alone. That things hadn't gone the way he planned probably delighted Piscary; he took pride in her defiance, anticipating a more delicious fall when she could fight no longer.

Warped, ruined, ugly, she thought, watching the tourist paddleboats steam as they stoked their boilers. Was there any time she hadn't been?

The sliding sound of plastic brought her around, and with no wasted motion or eye contact, she and Kisten rolled the woman onto it before her bowels released. Crossing her arms over her like an Egyptian mummy, they wrapped her tightly. Ivy watched her hands, not the plastic-blurred face of the woman, trying to divorce herself from what they were doing as they passed the duct tape Kisten had brought around her like lights on a Christmas tree.

Only when she had been transformed from a person to an object did Kisten exhale, slow and long. Ivy would cry for her later. Then cry for herself. But only when no one could hear.

"Refrigerator," Ivy said, and Kisten balked. Ivy looked at him as she stood bent over the corpse with her hands already under the woman's shoulders. "Just until we decide what to do. Danny will be here in four hours to start the dough and press the pasta. We don't have time to ditch the body *and* clean up."

Kisten's eyes went to the blood-smeared rug. He lifted a foot and winced at the tacky brown smear on it, tracked downstairs and back again. "Yeah," he said, his fake British accent gone, then took the long bundle entirely from Ivy and hoisted it over his shoulder.

Ivy couldn't help but feel proud of him for catching his breath so quickly. He was only twenty-three, having taken on Piscary's scion position at the age of seventeen when Ivy's mother had accidentally died five years ago and abdicated the position. Piscary was active in his control of Cincinnati, and Kisten had little more to do than tidy up after the master vamp and keep him happy. Stifling her tinge of jealousy that Kisten had the coveted position was easy.

Piscary's savage tutorial had made her old before she had begun to live. She wouldn't think about what she was doing until it was over. Kisten hadn't yet learned the trick and lived every moment as it happened, instead of over and over in his mind as she did. It made him slower to react, more . . . human. And she loved him for it.

"Is there a car to get rid of?" she asked, already on damage control. She hadn't noticed one in the parking lot, but she hadn't been looking.

"No." Kisten headed downstairs with her following, his vampire strength handling the weight without stress. "She came in with Piscary right around midnight."

"Off the street?" she asked in disbelief, glad the restaurant had been closed.

"No. The bus station. Apparently she's an old friend."

Ivy glanced at the woman over his shoulder. She was only twenty at the most. How old a friend could she be? Piscary didn't like children, despite her size. It was looking more and more likely Piscary *had* orchestrated this to help Kisten stand on his own. Not only planned it, but built in the net of the woman's cryptic origins in case Kisten should fall. The master vamp hadn't counted on Ivy catching him first, and she felt a pang of what she would call love for Kisten—if she knew she could feel the emotion without tainting it with the desire for blood.

Ivy caught sight of Kisten's grimace when she moved to open the door to the kitchen. "Piscary killed her on purpose," he said, adjusting the woman's weight on his shoulder, and Ivy nodded, not wanting to tell him about her own part in the lesson.

Tucking a fabric napkin from the waiting stack into her waistband, she yanked up the handle of the walk-in refrigerator and slid a box with her foot to prop it open. Kisten was right behind her, and in the odd combination of moist coldness Piscary insisted his cheese be kept at, she moved a side of lamb thawing out for Friday's buffet, insulating her hands with the napkin to prevent heat marks from making it obvious someone had moved it.

Behind the hanging slab was a long low bed of boxes, and Kisten laid the woman there, covering the blur of human features with a tablecloth. Ivy had the fleeting memory of seeing a similar bundle there once before. She and Kisten had been ten and playing hide-and-seek while their parents finished their wine and conversation. Piscary had told them she was someone from a fairy tale and to play in the abandoned upstairs. Seemed like they were still playing upstairs, but now the games were more convoluted and less under their control.

Kisten met her eyes, their deep blue full of recollection. "Sleeping Beauty," he said, and Ivy nodded. That was what they had called the corpse. Feeling like a little girl hiding a broken dish, she moved the slab of lamb back to partially hide the body.

Cold from more than the temperature, she followed him out, kicking the box out of the way and leaning against the door when it shut. Her eyes went to the time clock by the door. "I'll get the living room and stairs if you take the elevator," she said, not wanting to chance running into Piscary. He wouldn't be angry with her for helping Kisten. No, he'd be so amused she had put off Art again that he would invite her into his bed, and she would quiver inside and go to him, forgetting all about Kisten and what she had been doing. God, she hated herself.

Kisten reached for the mop and she added, "Use a new mop head, then put the old one back on when you're done. We're going to have to burn it along with the rug."

"Right," he said, his jaw flushing as it clenched. While Kisten filled a bucket, Ivy made a fresh batch of the spray they wiped the restaurant tables down with. Diluted, it removed the residual vamp pheromones, but at full strength, it would break down the blood enzymes that most cleaning detergents left behind. Maybe it was a little overkill, but she was a careful girl.

It would be unlikely to have the woman traced here, but it wasn't so much for eliminating her presence from a snooping I.S. or FIB agent as it was avoiding having the restaurant smell like blood other than hers and Kisten's. That might lead to questions concerning whether the restaurant's mixed public license, or MPL, had been violated. Ivy didn't think her explanation that, no, no one had been bitten on the premises—Piscary had drained a woman in his private apartments—and therefore the MPL was intact, would go over well. From the amount of aggravation Piscary had endured to get his MPL reinstated the last time some fool Were high on Brimstone had drawn blood, she thought he'd prefer a trial and jail to losing his MPL again. But the real reason Ivy was being so thorough was that she didn't want her apartment smelling like anyone but her and Kisten.

Her thoughts brought her gaze back to him. He looked nice with his head bowed over the bucket, his light bangs shifting in the water droplets being flung up as it filled.

Clearly unaware of her scrutiny, he turned the water off. "I am such an ass," he said, watching the ripples settle.

"That's what I like about you," she said, worried she might have made him feel inadequate by taking over.

"I am." He didn't look at her, hands clenching the rim of the plastic bucket. "I froze. I was so damn worried about what you were going to say when you came home and found me with a dead girl, I couldn't think."

Finding a compliment in there, she smiled, digging through a drawer to get a new mop head. "I knew you didn't kill her. She had Piscary all over her."

"Damn it, Ivy!" Kisten exclaimed, lashing the flat of his hand out to hit the spigot, and there was a crack of metal. "I should be better than this! I'm his fucking scion!"

Ivy's shoulders dropped. Sliding the drawer shut, she went to him and put her hands on his shoulders. They were hard with tension, and he did nothing to acknowledge her touch. Tugging into him, she pressed her cheek against his back, smelling the lingering fear on him, and the woman's blood. Eyes closing, she felt her bloodlust assert itself. Death and blood didn't turn on a vampire. Fear and the chance to *take* blood did. There was a difference.

Her hands eased around his front, fingers slipping past the buttons to find his abs. Only now did Kist bow his head, softening into her touch. Her teeth were inches from an old scar she had given him. The intoxicating smell of their scents mixing hit her, and she swallowed. The headiest lure of all. Her chest pressed into him as she breathed deep, intentionally bringing his scent into her, luring fingers of sexual excitement to stir along her spine. "Don't worry about it," she said, her voice low.

"You'd be a better scion then I am," he said bitterly. "Why did he pick me?"

She didn't think this was about which one of them was his scion but his stress looking for an outlet. Giving in to her urge, she lifted onto her toes to reach his ear. "Because you like people more than I do," she said. "Because you're better at talking to them, getting them to do what you want and having them think it was their idea. I just scare people."

He turned, slowly so he would stay in her arms. "I run a bar," he said, eyes downcast. "You work for the I.S. You tell me which is more valuable."

Ivy's arms slipped to his waist, pressing him back into the edge of the sink. "I'm sorry for the pizza delivery crap," she said, meaning it. "You aren't running a bar, you're learning Cincinnati, what moves who, and who will do anything for whom. Me?" Her attention went to the wisp of hair showing at the V of his shirt. "I'm learning how to kiss ass and suck neck."

His gaze hard with self-recrimination, Kisten shook his head. "Piscary dropped a dead girl in my lap, and I sat over her and wrung my hands. You walked in and things happened. What about the next time when it's something important and I fuck it up?"

Running her hands up the smooth expanse of silk to his shoulders, she closed her eyes at the deliciously erotic sensation growing in her. Guilt mixed with it. She was ugly. All she had wanted to do was console Kisten, but the very act of comforting him was turning her on.

The thought of Art and what had almost happened hit her. Between one breath and the next, the muscles where her jaw hinged tightened and her eyes dilated. *Shit. May as well give in.* Feeling like a whore, she opened her eyes and fixed them on Kisten's. His were as black as her own, and a spike of anticipation dove to her middle. *Warped and twisted. Both of them. Was there any way to show she cared other than this?*

"You'll handle it," she whispered, wanting to feel her lips pulling on something, anything. The soft skin under his chin glistened from the thrown-up mist, begging her to taste it. "I save your ass. You save mine," she said. It was all she had to offer.

"Promise?" he said, sounding lost. Apparently it was enough.

The lure was too much, and she pulled herself closer to put her lips softly against the base of his neck, letting his pulse rise and fall teasingly under her. She felt as if she was dying: screaming because they needed each other to survive Piscary, pulse racing in what was going to follow, and despairing that the two were connected.

"I promise," she whispered. Eyes closed, she raked her teeth over skin but didn't pierce as her fingers lifted through the clean softness of his hair.

Kisten's breath came fast, and with one arm he picked her up and set her on the counter, forcing his way between her knees. She felt her gaze go sultry when his hands went behind her hips, edging over the top of her pants. "You're hungry," he said, a dangerous lilt to his voice.

"I'm past hungry," she said, twining her hands behind his neck as if bound. Her voice was demanding, but in truth she was helpless before him. It was the bane of the vampire that the strongest was the most in need. And Kisten knew the games they played as well as she did. Her thoughts flitted to Sleeping Beauty in the refrigerator, and she shoved away the loathing that she wanted to feel Kisten's blood fill her not ten minutes after a woman had died in their apartment. The self-disgust she would deal with later. She was eminently proficient at denying it existed.

"Art bothering you again?" he said, his almost delicate features sly as he slipped a hand under her shirt. The firm warmth of his fingers was like a spike through her.

"Still . . ." she said, stifling a tremor to entice the feeling to grow.

His free hand traced across her shoulder and her collarbone to slide up the opposite length of her neck. "I'll have to write a letter and thank him," he said.

Eyes flashing open, Ivy yanked him to her, wrapping her legs around him, imprisoning him against her. His hands were gone from her waist, leaving only a cool warmth. "He wants my blood and my body," Ivy said, feeling her lust for Kisten mix with her disgust for Art. "He's getting nothing. I'm going to drive him into taking my blood against my will."

Kisten's breath was against her neck, and his hands were at the small of her back. "What's that going to get you?"

A smile, unseen and evil, spread across her as she looked over his shoulder to the empty kitchen. "Satisfaction," she breathed, feeling herself weaken. "He promotes me out from under him to keep my mouth shut or he becomes the laughingstock of the entire tower." But she didn't know if she could do it anymore. He was stronger than she had given him credit.

"That's my girl," Kisten said, and she sucked in her breath when he bent his head, his teeth gently working an old scar to send a delicious dart of anticipation through her. "You're *such* a political animal. Remind me never to cross stakes with you."

Breathless, she couldn't answer. The thought of having to deal with the contaminated scene flitted past, and was gone.

"You'll need practice saying no," Kisten murmured.

"Mmmm." Eyes open, she found herself moving against him as his hands pulled her closer. His head dropped, and her hands splayed across his back curled so her fingers dug into him. Kisten's lips played with the base of her neck, moving ever lower.

"Could you say no if he did this?" Kisten whispered, grazing his teeth along her bare skin while his hands under her shirt traced a path to her breast.

The two feelings were joined in her mind, and it felt as if it was his teeth on her breast. "Yes . . ." she breathed, exhilarated. He worked the hem of her shirt, and she gripped the hair at the base of his skull, wanting more.

"What if he made good on his promise?" he asked, dropping his head, and she froze at the wash of a silver feeling cascading to her groin when he set his teeth where his fingers had been. It was too much to not respond.

Pulse racing, she jerked his head up. It could have hurt, but Kisten knew it was coming and moved with her. She never hurt him. Not intentionally.

Lips parted, she tightened her legs around him until she nearly left the counter. And though she buried her face against his neck, breathed in his scent, and mouthed his old scars, she didn't break his skin. The self-denial was more than an exquisite torture, more than an ingrained tradition. It was survival.

The truth was that she was very nearly beyond thought, and only patterns of engraved behavior kept her from sinking her teeth, filling herself with what made him alive. She lusted to feel for that glorious instant total power over another and thus prove she was alive, but until he said so, she would starve for it. It was a game, but a deadly serious one that prevented mistakes made in a moment of passion. The undead had their own games, breaking the rules when they thought they could get away with it. But living vampires held tight to them, knowing it might be the difference in surviving a blood encounter or not.

And Kisten knew it, enjoying his temporary mastery over her. She was the dominant of the two, but unable to satisfy her craving until he let her, and in turn he was helpless to satisfy himself until she agreed. His masculine hands pushed her mouth from his neck, forcing his own lips against her jugular, rising and falling beneath him. Her head flung to the ceiling, she wondered who would surrender and ask first. The unknowing sparked through her, and feeling it, a growl lifted from her.

Dropping her head, she found his earlobe, the metallic diamond taste sharp on her tongue. "Give this to me," she breathed, succumbing, uncaring that her need was stronger than his.

"Take it," he groaned, submitting to their twin desires faster than he usually did.

Panting in relief, she pulled him closer, and in the shock of him meeting her, she carefully sank her teeth into him.

Shuddering, Kisten clutched her closer, lifting her off the counter.

She pulled on him, hungry, almost panicked that someone would stop them. Blessed relief washed through her at the sharp taste. Their scents mixed in her brain, and his blood washed into her, making them one, rubbing out the void that loving Piscary and meeting his demands continually carved into her. His warmth filled her mouth, and she swallowed, sending it deeper into her, desperately trying to drown her soul somehow.

Kisten's breath against her was fast, and she knew the exquisite sensations she instilled in him, the vamp saliva invoking an ecstasy so close to sex it didn't matter. His fingers trembled as they traced her lines and reached for the hem of her shirt, but she knew there wasn't time. She was going to climax before they could work themselves much more.

Breathless and savage from the sensations of power and bloodlust, she pulled back from him, running her tongue quickly over her teeth. She met his eyes, pupil-black. He saw her teetering.

"Take it," she breathed, desperate to give him what he needed, craved. It wouldn't make amends for the savagery of the act, but it was the only way she could find peace with herself.

Kisten didn't wait. A guttural sound coming from him, he leaned in. Sensation jerked through her, the instant of heady pain mutated almost immediately into an equal pleasure, the vampire saliva turning the sting of his fangs into the fire of passion.

"Oh God," she moaned. Kisten heard, and he dug harder, going far beyond what he usually did. She gasped at the twin sensations of his teeth on her neck and his fingernails on her breast. Body moving with his, she pulled his hand from where he gripped the back of her neck and found his wrist. She couldn't . . . bear it. She needed everything. Everything at once.

His mouth pulled on her, and with elation filling her, she bit down, slicing into old scars.

Kisten shook, his grip faltering as sexual and blood rapture filled them both. He pulled away from the counter, and her legs tightened around his waist.

She heard in his breathing that he was going to reach fulfillment, and content that they would end this with both of them satisfied, she abandoned all thought. Everything was gone, leaving only the need to fill herself with him, and she took everything he gave her, not caring he was doing the same. Together they could find peace. Together they could survive.

Ivy's grip tightened, and she sank her teeth deeper. Kisten responded, a low rumble rising up through him. It sparked a primitive part of her, and fear, instinctive and unstoppable, jumped through her. Kisten felt it, gripping her aggressively.

She cried out, and with the pain shifting to spikes of pleasure, she climaxed, her pulse a wild thrum under Kisten's hand, and in his mouth, and through him. He tensed, and with a last groan, his lips left her as he found the exquisite mental orgasm brought on by satiating the hunger and blood.

No wonder she was screwed up, she thought, even as her body shook and rebelled at the rapturous assault. *Evil or wrong didn't matter. She couldn't resist something that felt so damn good.*

"Kist," she panted when the last flickers faded and she realized she still had her legs wrapped around him, her forehead against his shoulder and her body trying to figure out what had happened. "Are you okay?"

"Hell yes," he said, his breathing haggard. "God, I love you, woman."

As his arms tightened around her, an emotion she seldom felt good about filled her. She loved him more than she would admit, but it was pointless to plan for a future that was already mapped out.

Slowly he settled her back on the counter, his muscles starting to shake.

The rim of blue about his pupils was returning, and his lips, still reddened from her blood, parted and his eyebrows rose. "Ivy, you're crying."

She blinked, shocked to find she was. "No, I'm not," she asserted, swinging her leg up and around to get him out from between them. Her muscles protested, not ready to move yet.

"Yes, you are," he insisted, grabbing a cloth napkin and pressing it to his wrist, and then his neck. The small punctures were already closing, the vampire saliva working to stimulate repair and fight possible infection.

Turning away, she slipped from the counter, almost stumbling in her need to hide her emotions. But Kisten grabbed her upper arm and turned her back.

"What is it?" he said, and then his eyes widened. "Shit, I hurt you."

She almost laughed, choking it back. "No," she admitted, then closed her eyes, trying to find the words. They were there, but she couldn't say them. She loved Kisten, but why did the only way she could show him involve blood? Had Piscary completely killed in her how to comfort someone she loved without it turning into a savage act? Love should be gentle and tender, not bestial and self-serving.

She couldn't remember the last time she had slept with someone without blood. She didn't think she had since Piscary first turned his attentions fully to her, warping her until any emotion of caring, love, or devotion stimulated a bloodlust that seemed pointless to resist. She had carefully built the lie to protect herself that blood was blood and sex-and-blood was a way to show she loved someone, but she didn't know how much longer she could believe it. Blood and love had become so intertwined in her that she didn't think she *could* separate them. And if she had to admit that sharing blood was how she expressed her love, then she'd have to admit she was a whore every time she let someone sink his or her teeth into her on her way to the top. *Was that why she was forcing Art into taking her against her will? She had to submit to rape in order to keep herself sane?*

Kisten's eyes roved the kitchen, and she saw his nose widen as he took in their scent. They'd endure a ribbing from the entire staff for having "relieved their vampiric pressures" in the kitchen, but it would cover up the smell of the corpse, at least. "What is it then?" he asked.

Anyone else would have been pushed aside and ignored, but Kisten put up with too much of her crap. "All I wanted to do was comfort you," she said, dropping her head to hide behind the curtain of her hair. "And it turned into blood."

Making a soft sigh, Kisten took her in a slow, careful embrace. A shiver lifted through her when he gently kissed away the last of the blood from her neck. He knew it was so sensitive as to almost hurt and would be for a few more minutes. "Hell, Ivy," he whispered, his voice telling her he knew what she was not saying. "If you were trying to comfort me, you did a bang-up job."

He didn't move, and instead of pulling away, she stayed, allowing herself to accept his touch. "It's what I needed, too," he added, the smell of their scents mingling inciting a deep contentment instead of a dire need now that the hunger had been satisfied.

She nodded, believing him though she still felt ashamed. *But why is that the only way I know how to be?*

 FOUR

Ivy swiveled her chair, rolling the banshee tear safe in its plastic bag between her fingers and wondering if it was magic or science that enabled a banshee to draw enough emotional energy through the gem to kill someone. Science, she was willing to believe. A science so elaborate and detailed that it looked like magic. Resonating alpha waves or something, like cell phones or radio transmissions. The files hadn't been clear.

The office chatter coming in her open door was light because of the ungodly hour. She was working today on the upper-tower schedule, having a three-thirty afternoon appointment to talk to a banshee who had helped the I.S. in the past. That it would get her out of here at midnight was a plus, but it was still damn early.

Mood souring, Ivy leaned back in her chair and listened to the quiet, the usual noises sounding out of place because of their sparseness. The office atmosphere had changed, the glances she caught directed at her having gone from bitter to sympathetic. She didn't know how to react. Apparently the word had gone out that Art had made a real play for her blood, causing her not only to contaminate a crime scene but also to almost succumb. And whereas she could have taken comfort in the show of sympathy, she felt only a resentful bitterness that she was the object of pity. How in the hell was she going to get rid of Art if she couldn't say no to him? It was a matter of pride, now.

Ivy's eyes lifted to the humming wall clock. Art was tucked underground, and knowing he wouldn't be coming in for several hours gave her a measure of peace. She'd like to stake the bastard. *Maybe that's what Piscary wanted her to do?*

Over the ambient office noise of keyboards and gossip, she heard her name spoken in a soft, unfamiliar voice. Focusing, Ivy listened to someone else give directions to her office. Ivy set the tear beside her pencil cup with its colored markers, turning to her door when the light was eclipsed.

Her breath to say hello hesitated as she evaluated the woman, forgetting to invite her in. She'd never met a banshee before, and Ivy wondered if they all had that disturbing demeanor or if it was just Mia Harbor.

She was wearing a dramatic calf-length dress made of strips of sky blue fabric. It would have looked like rags if the fabric wasn't silk. The cuffs of the long sleeves ran to drape over her fingertips, and it fit her slight figure perfectly. Her severely short hair was black, cut into downward spikes and iced with gold, completely contrary to her pale complexion and meadowy attire but somehow harmonizing perfectly. Dark sunglasses hid her eyes. Small, petite, and agelessly attractive, she made Ivy feel tall and gawky as she stood in her doorway, the expression on her delicate features shifting from question to a tired acceptance.

Ivy realized she was staring. Immediately she stood, hand extended. "Ms. Harbor," she said. "Please come in. I'm Officer Tamwood."

She moved forward, her dress furling about her calves. Her hand was cool, with a smooth strength, and Ivy let go as soon as it was polite. The confidence of her grip caused Ivy to place her somewhere in her sixties, but she looked twenty. *Witch charm,* Ivy wondered, *or natural longevity?*

"Please call me Mia," the woman said, sitting in Art's chair when Ivy indicated it.

"Mia," Ivy repeated, sinking back down behind her desk. She considered asking the woman to call her by her first name, but didn't, and Mia settled herself with a stiff formality.

Unusually uncomfortable, Ivy leafed through the report to hide her nervousness. Banshees were dangerous entities, able to draw enough energy from people to kill them, much like a psychic vampire. They didn't need to kill to survive, able to exist on the natural sloughing off of emotion from the people around them. But that didn't mean they wouldn't gorge themselves if they thought they could get away with it. She had never had the chance to talk to one before. They were a dying species as public awareness grew about this innocent-looking but highly dangerous Inderlander race.

Like black widow spiders, they generally killed their mate after becoming pregnant. Ivy didn't think it was intentional; their human husbands simply lost their vitality and died. There had never been much of a population of them anyway—every child born was female, and the magic needed to conceive outside one's species made things difficult.

"I make you nervous," Mia said, sounding pleased.

Ivy glanced at her and then back to the papers. Giving up trying to maintain her stoic demeanor, she leaned back in her chair, setting her hands in her lap.

"I won't be *taking* any emotion from you, Officer Tamwood," Mia said. "I don't need to. You're throwing off enough nervous energy and conflicted thoughts to sate me for a week."

Oh joy, Ivy thought sourly. She took pride in suppressing her emotions, and that Mia not only felt them but was sopping them up like gravy wasn't a pleasant thought.

"Why am I here?" Mia asked, pale hands holding her tiny blue-beaded purse on her lap.

Ivy gathered herself. "Ms. Harbor," she said formally, seeing Mia grimace when Ivy made an effort to calm herself. "I'd like to thank you for coming to see me. I have a few questions that the I.S. would be most grateful if you can help me with."

A sigh came from Mia, chilling Ivy—it sounded like the eerie moan of a lost soul. "Which one of my sisters killed someone?" she asked, looking at the tear in its evidence bag.

Ivy's prepared speech vanished. Relieved to be able to sidestep the formalities, she leaned forward, the flat of her forearms on the desk. "We're looking for Jacqueline."

Mia held out a hand for the tear, and Ivy pushed it closer. The woman let go of her purse and took the bag, slipping a white nail under the seal.

"Hey!" Ivy exclaimed, standing.

Mia froze, looking at Ivy over her sunglasses.

Breath catching, Ivy stopped her vamp-fast reach for the evidence bag and rocked back. The woman's eyes were the shockingly pale blue of a near albino, but it was the aching emptiness that halted Ivy. Unmoving, her heart pounded at the raw hunger they contained, chained by an iron-laced restraint. The woman was holding a hunger whose depths Ivy had only tasted. But Ivy had learned enough about restraint to see the signs that her control was absolute: her lack of emotional expression, the stiffness with which she held herself, the soft preciseness of her breathing, the careful motions she made as if she would lose control if she moved too fast and broke through the envelope of her aura and will.

Shocked and awed by what the woman confidently contained, Ivy humbly sat back down.

A smile quirked Mia's face. The snap of the seal breaking was loud, but Ivy didn't stop her, even when she shook the tear into her palm and delicately touched it briefly to her tongue. "You found this at the crime scene?" she asked, and when Ivy nodded she added, "This tear is not functioning." Ivy took a breath to protest, and Mia interrupted, "You found this in a room stinking of fear. If it had been working, every wisp of emotion would have been gone."

Surprised, Ivy struggled to keep her emotions close. That the room reeked of fear when she entered hadn't made it to her report. Since she had contaminated it, it seemed pointless. That might have been a mistake, but amending her report to include it would look questionable.

Mia dropped the tear back into the bag. "It wasn't Jacqueline who killed. It wasn't any of my sisters. I'm sorry, but I can't help you, Officer Tamwood."

Ivy's pulse quickened. Thinking Mia was protecting her kin, she said,

"The man admits to killing the victim, but doesn't know why he did. Our theory is Jacqueline left the tear knowing there was the chance domestic violence would cover her crime. Please, Mia. If we don't find Jacqueline, an innocent man will be sentenced for murdering his wife."

The crackle of the broken seal was loud, and Ivy wondered what the black crystal tasted like. "A tear older than a week won't function as a conduit for emotions," Mia said. "And while that tear is Jacqueline's"—she tossed the bag to the desk—"it is at least three years old."

Wondering how she was going to explain why the original seal was broken, Ivy frowned. This had been a waste of time. Just as well she hadn't told Art about it. "And you know that how, ma'am?" she said, frustrated. "You can't date tears."

From behind her black glasses, Mia smiled to show her teeth, her canines a shade longer than a human's. "I know it's at least that old because I killed Jacqueline three years ago."

Smooth and unhurried, Ivy rose and shut the door. The hum of a copier cut off, and Ivy returned to her desk in the new silence, trying to maintain her blank expression. She watched the woman, reading nothing in her calm. Silently she waited for an explanation.

"We are not a well-liked group of people," Mia said bluntly. "Jacqueline had become careless, falling back on old traditions of murdering people to absorb their death energy instead of taking the paltry ambient emotions that Inderland law grants us."

"So you killed her." Ivy allowed herself a deep breath. This woman was scaring the shit out of her with her casual admission of so heinous an act.

Mia nodded, the hem of her dress seeming to shift by itself in the still air. "We police ourselves so the rest of Inderland won't." She smiled. "You understand."

Thinking of Piscary, Ivy dropped her eyes.

"We aren't substantially different from each other," the woman said lightly. "Vampires steal psychic energy, too. You're just clumsy about it, having to take blood with it as a carrier."

Head moving slowly in acceptance, Ivy quashed her feelings of guilt. Generally only vampires knew that a portion of a person's aura went with the blood, but a banshee would, seeing as that's what they took themselves. A more pure form of predation that stripped the soul and made it easy to break it from the body. A person could replace a substantial amount, but take too much aura too quickly, and the body dies. Ivy had always thought banshees were higher on the evolutionary ladder, but perhaps not, seeing as vampires used the visible signs of blood loss to gauge when to stop. "It's not the same," Ivy protested. "No one dies when we feed."

"They do if you feed too heavily."

Ivy's thoughts lighted on the body in Piscary's refrigerator. "Yes, but when a vampire feeds, they give as much emotion as they get."

And though Mia didn't move, Ivy stiffened when the slight woman seemed to gather the shadows in the room, wrapping them about herself. "Only living vampires with a soul give as well as take," she said. "And that's why you suffer, Ivy."

Her voice, low and mocking, shocked Ivy at the use of her given name.

"You could still find beauty amid the ugliness, if you were strong enough," Mia continued. "But you're afraid."

Ivy's stomach clenched and her skin went cold. It was too close to what she had been searching for, even as she denied it existed. "You can't find love in taking blood," she asserted, determined to not get upset and unwittingly feed this . . . woman. "Love is beautiful, and blood is savagely satisfying an ugly need."

"And you don't need love?"

"That's not what I'm saying." Ivy felt unreal, and she gripped the edge of her desk. "Blood isn't a way to show you love." Ivy's voice was soft, but inside she was screaming. She was so screwed up that she couldn't comfort a friend without tainting it with her lust for blood. To mix her need for love and her need for blood corrupted love and made it vile. Her desire to keep the two separate was so close to her, so vulnerable, that she almost choked when Mia shook her head.

"That's not who you want to be," she taunted. "I see it. It pours from you like tears. You lie to yourself, saying that blood and love are separate. You lie saying sanity exists in calling them two things instead of one. Only by accepting that can you rise above what your body demands of you, to live true to who you want to be . . . with someone you love, and who is strong enough to survive loving you back."

Shocked, Ivy froze. This slight woman sitting before her was pulling from Ivy her most desperate, hidden desires, throwing them out for everyone to see. She wanted to control the bloodlust . . . but it felt so damn good to let it control her. And if she called it love, then she had been whoring herself half her life.

As she stared at Mia's knowing smile, memories filled her: memories of Piscary's touch, his praise, of his taking everything from her and saying it was proof of her devotion and love, and her flush of acceptance, of finding worth in being everything he wanted. It was as raw as if it happened last night, not almost a decade ago. Years of indulgence followed, as she found that the more dominating she was, the more satisfaction she craved and the less she found. It was a cruel slipknot that sent her begging for Piscary to give her a feeling of worth. And though she never found it, he had turned the pain sweet.

Now this woman who could sip misery from another as easy as breathing wanted her to accept that the dichotomy that had saved her sanity was a hollow truth? That she could find beauty in her cravings by calling it love?

"It is not love," she said, feeling as if she couldn't breathe.

"Then why do you resist Art?" she accused, a hint of a smile on her face and one eyebrow raised tauntingly. "The entire floor is thinking about it. You know it's more than a casual act. It's a way to show your love, and to give that to Art would mean you were a demimonde; no—a whore. A filthy, perverted slut selling herself for a moment of carnal pleasure and professional advancement."

It was so close to what she had been thinking herself that Ivy clenched her jaw, glad the office door was closed. She felt her eyes dilate, but the memory of Mia's leashed hunger kept her sitting. She knew that Mia was provoking her, inciting her anger so she could lap it up. It was what banshees did. That they often used truth to do so made it worse. "You can't express love in taking blood," Ivy said, her voice low and vehement.

"Why not?"

Why not? It sounded so simple. "Because I can't say no to blood," Ivy said bitterly. "I need it. I crave it. I *want* to satisfy it, damn it."

Mia laughed. "You stupid, whiny little girl. You want to satisfy it because it's tied to your need for love. It's too late for me. I can't find beauty in satisfying my needs since anyone a banshee loves dies. You can, and to see you so selfish makes me want to slap you. You are a coward," she accused. "Too frightened to find the beauty in your needs because to do so would admit that you were wrong. That you have been fooling yourself for most of your life, lying that it has no importance so you can indulge yourself. You are a whore, Ivy. And you know it. Stop deluding yourself that you aren't."

Ivy felt her eyes flash entirely to black, pulled by anger. "You need to leave," she said, muscles so tense, it took all her restraint to keep from striking the banshee.

Mia stood. She was alive and vibrant, her smooth face flushed and beautiful—an accusing angel, hard and uncaring. "You can live above your fate," she mocked. "*You* can be who you want to be. So Piscary warped you. So he broke you and remade you to be a pliant source of emotion-rich blood. It's up to you to either accept or deny it."

"You think I like being like this?" Ivy said, standing when her frustration spilled over. "That I like anyone with long teeth able to take advantage of me? This is what I was born into—there's no way out. It's too late! Too many people expect me to be the way I am, too many people force me to be the way they want me to be." The truth was coming out, pissing her off.

Mia's lips were parted and her face was flushed. Her eyes were lost behind her sunglasses, and the gold in her short black hair caught the light. "That is the excuse of a lazy, frightened coward," she said, and Ivy tensed, ready to tell her to shut up but for the memory of the leashed hunger in her eyes. "Admit you were wrong. Admit you are ugly and a whore. Then don't be that way anymore."

"But it feels too good!" Ivy shouted, not caring if the floor heard her.

Mia trembled, her entire body shuddering. Breath fast, she reached for the back of her chair. When she brought her gaze up from behind her sunglasses, Ivy realized that the air was as pure and pristine as if the argument hadn't happened. Pulse fast, Ivy breathed deeply, finding only the hint of Mia's perfume and the softest trace of her sweat. *Damn. The bitch was good.*

"I never said it would be easy," Mia said softly, and Ivy wondered exactly what the hell had just happened. "The hunger will always be there, like a thorn. Every day will be worse than the previous until you think you won't be able to exist another moment, but then you'll see the filth in your eyes trying to get out—and if you're strong, you'll find the will to put it off another day. And for another day, you will be who you want to be. Unless you're a coward."

The humming of the wall clock grew loud in the new silence, almost deep enough to hear Mia's heartbeat, and Ivy stood behind her desk, not liking the feelings mixing in her. "I'm not a coward," Ivy finally said.

"No, you're not," Mia admitted, subdued and quiet. Satiated.

"And I am not weak of will," Ivy added, louder.

Mia inhaled slowly, her pale fingers tightening on her purse. "Yes, you are." Ivy's eyes narrowed, and Mia's mien shifted again. "Forgive me for asking," she said, sounding both embarrassed and nervous, "but would you consider living together?"

Ivy's gut tightened. "Get out."

Mia swallowed, taking off her sunglasses to show her pale blue eyes, her pupils carrying a familiar swelling of black that made her look vulnerable. "I can make it worth your while," she said, her eyes running over Ivy as if she was a past lover and moistening her lips. "My blood for your emotion? I can satisfy everything you need, Ivy, and more. And you could kindle a child in me with the pain you carry."

"Get—out."

Head bowing, Mia nodded and moved to the door.

"I am not weak of will," Ivy repeated, shame joining her anger when Mia crossed the small office. Mia opened the door, hesitating to turn and look at her.

"No," she said, a gentle sadness in her ageless features. "You aren't. But you do need practice." Dress furling, the woman left, the click, click of her heels silencing the entire floor, the fluorescent lights catching the highlights in her hair.

Angry, Ivy lurched to the door, slamming it shut and falling back into her chair. "I am not weak of will," she said aloud, as if hearing it would make it so. But the idea she might be wiggled in between thought and reason, and it was too easy to doubt herself.

Her boot heels went up onto her desk, ankles crossed. She didn't want to think about what Mia had said—or what she offered. Eyes closed, Ivy took a breath to relax, forcing her body to do as she told it. She hadn't liked Mia using her, but that's what they did. It was Ivy's own fault for arguing with her.

Again, Ivy inhaled, slower to make her shoulders ease. She could ignore everything but what she wanted to focus on if she tried—she spent a great deal of her life that way. It made her quick to anger, depressed her appetite, and caused her to be overly sensitive, but it kept her sane.

Ivy's eyes opened in the silence, falling upon the tear. As inescapable as shadows, her mind fastened on it, desperately seeking a distraction. Disgust lifted through her at the torn bag. *How was she going to explain the broken seal to Art?*

Leaning forward, she felt her muscles stretch as she pulled the bag closer, and in a surge of self-indulgence, shook the tear into her palm. A moment of hesitation, and she touched it to her tongue. She felt nothing, tasted nothing. With a guilty motion, she dropped it back in and pressed the seal shut, tossing it to her desk.

The tear was three years old, found in a room stinking of fear. A banshee hadn't been responsible. The man had murdered his wife with a plan already in place to shift the blame. Where had he gotten a tear? A tear three years old, no less?

Three years. That was a long time to plan your wife's murder. Especially when they had been married only eight months, according to Mr. Demere's file. *Long-term planning.*

Ivy leaned forward in a spike of adrenaline and fingered the bag. Vampires planned that long. Jacqueline had a record. Only a vampire who worked for the I.S. would be in a position to know she was dead, unable to clear her name. And only an I.S. employee would have access to a tear swiped from the old-evidence vault. A tear no one would miss.

"Holy shit," Ivy softly swore. This went to the top.

Dropping the tear, Ivy reached for the phone. Art would crap his coffin when he found out. But then a thought struck her, and she hesitated, the buzz of the open line a harsh whine.

The apartment had been full of fear—anger and fear that should have been soaked up by the tear but wasn't—fear that Art had covered up with her own emotions.

The buzz of the phone line turned to beeping, and she set the phone back in the cradle, the acidic taste of betrayal filling her thoughts. Art had used her to muddle the psychic levels in the room. The guy from the collection van had commented on it when he had come in, blaming it on her after he saw the banshee tear, not knowing she had only added to what was already there. No one documented psychic levels unless a banshee was involved, and they hadn't known until after she contaminated the scene. "After Art stole and planted the tear," she muttered aloud. Art, who was so dense he couldn't find his pretty fangs in someone's ass.

Plucking a pen from her pencil cup, she tapped it on the desk, wanting to write everything down but resisting lest it come back to bite her. *Maybe not so dense after all.* "Motive . . ." she breathed, enjoying the adrenaline rush and feeling as if it cleansed her somehow. Why would Art help plan and cover up a murder? What would he get out of it? Being undead, Art was moved only by survival and his need for blood.

Blood? she thought. Had the suspect promised to be Art's blood shadow in exchange for the opportunity to murder his wife? *Didn't sound right.*

Her lips curled upward and she smiled. Money. Art's rise in the I.S. had stopped when he died and was no longer a potential source of blood. Without the currency of blood for bribes, he couldn't rise in the vampiric hierarchy. He was existing on the interest from his postdeath funds, but by law he couldn't touch the principal. If the suspect gave Art a portion of his wife's insurance money, it might be enough to move Art up a step. That the undead vampire had openly admitted he wasn't adverse to using Ivy to pull him up in the ranks only solidified her belief that he was having money problems. Undead vampires didn't work harder than they had to. That Art was working at all said something.

Pen clicking open and shut so fast it almost hummed, Ivy tried to remember if she had ever heard that Art had died untimely. He'd been working the same desk over thirty years.

Jerking in sudden decision, she dropped the pen and pulled out the Yellow Pages, looking for the biggest insurance ad that wasn't connected to one of Cincinnati's older vamp families. She would call them all if she had to. Pulse quickening, she dialed, using the suspect's social security number to find out his next payment wouldn't be due until the fifteenth. It was for a hefty amount, and she impatiently kept hitting the star button until the machine had a cyber coronary and dumped her into a real person's phone.

"Were Insurance," a polite voice answered.

Ivy sat straighter. "This is Officer Tamwood," she said, "and I'm checking on the records of a Mr. and Mrs. Demere? Could you tell me if they upped their life insurance recently?"

There was a moment of silence. "You're from the I.S.?" Before Ivy could answer, the woman continued primly. "I'm sorry, Officer Tamwood. We can't give out information without a warrant."

Ivy smiled wickedly. "That's fine, ma'am. My partner and I will be there with your little piece of paper as soon as the sun goes down. We're kind of in a hurry, so he might skip breakfast to get there before you close."

"Uh . . ." the voice came back, and Ivy felt her eyes dilate at the fear it held. "No need. I'm always glad to help out the I.S. Let me pull up the policy in question."

Ivy tucked the phone between her ear and her shoulder, picking at her nails and trying to get her eyes to contract.

"Here it is!" the woman gushed nervously. "Mr. and Mrs. Demere took out a modest policy covering each of them shortly after getting married . . ." The woman's voice trailed off, sounding puzzled. "It was increased about four months ago. Just a minute."

Ivy swung her feet to the floor and reached for a pen.

"Okay," the woman said when she returned. "I see why. Mrs. Demere finished getting her degree. She was going to become the major breadwinner, and they wanted to take advantage of the lower payment schedule before her next birthday. It has a payout of a half million." The woman chuckled. "Someone was a little enthusiastic. A data entry degree won't get her a good enough job to warrant that kind of insurance."

A zing of adrenaline went through Ivy, and the pen snapped. "Damn it!" she swore as ink stained her hand and dripped to the desk.

"Ma'am?" the woman questioned, a new wariness to her voice.

Staring at the blue ink on her hand, Ivy said, "Nothing. My pen just broke." She dropped it in the trash, and using her foot, she opened a lower drawer and snatched up a tissue. "It might be in your company's best interest to misfile any claim for a few weeks," she said as she wiped her fingers. "Could you give me a call when someone tries to process it?"

"Thank you, Officer Tamwood," the insurance officer said cheerfully over the sound of a pencil scratching. "Thank you very much. I've got your number on my screen, and I'll do just that."

Embarrassed, Ivy hung up. Still trying to get the worst of the ink off her, she felt a stirring of excitement. It wasn't in any report that the tear wasn't functioning. This had possibilities. But she couldn't go to the basement with her suspicions; if Art had promised someone down there a cut of money, her suspicions would go nowhere and she'd look like a whiny bitch trying to get out of giving Art his due blood. That she was doing just that didn't bother her as much as she thought it would.

Balling up the inkstained tissue, Ivy reached again for the phone. Kisten. Kisten could help her on this. Maybe they could have lunch together.

 FIVE

The muted sounds of the last patrons being ushered out the door vibrated through the oak timbers of the floorboards, and Ivy relaxed in it, finding more peace there than she'd like to admit. Extending her long legs out under the piano, she picked up her melted milkshake and sipped through the straw as she planned Art's downfall. Before her on the closed lid were written-out plans of contingencies, neatly arranged on the black varnished wood. Below her, Piscary's living patrons stumbled home in the coming dawn. The undead ones had left a good hour ago. The scent of tomato paste, sausage, pasta, and the death-by-chocolate dessert someone had ordered to go drifted up through the cracks.

The light coming in the expansive windows was thin, and Ivy looked from her pages set in neat piles and stretched her laced fingers to the distant ceiling. She was usually in bed this time of day—waiting for Kisten to finish closing up and slide in behind her with a soft nibble somewhere. More often than not, it turned into a breathless circle of give and take that left them content in each other's arms as they fell asleep with the morning sun warming their skin.

Focus blurring, Ivy plucking at the itchy fabric of her lace shirt, her thoughts returning to Mia. Banshees were known for inciting trouble, often hiring themselves in to a productive company and putting old friends at each other's throats with a few well-placed words of truth, whereupon they would sit back and lap up the emotion while everything fell apart. That they usually did this with the truth made it worse. She loved Kisten, but to call it love when she took his blood? That was savage need. There could be no love there. Eyes dropping to the papers surrounding her, she pushed at them as if pushing away her thoughts, bringing her hand up to slide a finger between her neck and the collar of itchy lace.

Ivy felt like a vamp wannabe, dressed in tight jeans and a black stretchy shirt with a high collar of peekaboo lace and an open, low neckline. A pair of flat sandals finished the look. It wasn't what she would have picked out for framing her partner for homicide, but it was close to what Sleeping Beauty had on.

She had been here at the piano for hours, having called in sick after meeting Kisten for lunch, blaming it on bad sushi. Kisten wasn't convinced putting Art in jail by dumping Piscary's mistake in his apartment was a good way to get promoted, but Ivy liked its inescapable justice. Going to the I.S. would gain her nothing but their irritation for interfering. True, Mr. Demere wouldn't be going to jail for murdering his wife, but that didn't mean he was going to walk away from it. She'd take care of him later when he thought he had escaped unscathed.

It surprised her that she was enjoying herself. She liked her job at the

I.S., working backward from where someone else's plan went wrong to catch stupid people making stupid decisions. But plotting her own action to snare someone in her own net was more satisfying. She was headed for management, but she'd never stopped to ask herself if it was something she wanted.

And so after she had discussed it with Kisten, he had reluctantly bought her car for cash, and she had gone shopping with the untraceable money. She had felt ignorant at the first charm outlet she had gone into, but the man had become gratifyingly helpful once she showed him the money.

Fingers cold from her melted shake, Ivy set the wet glass on a coaster and reached for the sleep amulet safe in its silk bag. She had wanted a potion she could get Art to drink or splash on him, but the witch refused to sell it to her, claiming it was too dangerous for a novice. He had sold her an amulet that would do the same thing, though, and she felt the outlines of the redwood disk on its cord carefully through the bag, satisfied it would work. The man had cautioned her three times to be sure there was someone there to take it off her or she'd sleep for two days before the charm spontaneously broke for safety reasons.

A second, metallic amulet would give her the illusion of blond hair and take off about eight inches of height, making her closer to the size and look of Sleeping Beauty. She didn't know how witches in the I.S. managed to make any money, seeing as the two charms had cost as much as her car, and she wondered if the witch had upped the price because she was a vampire.

She had been sitting here writing out contingencies for nearly two hours, and she was growing stiff. The I.S. tower had cleared out by now, and Art was home. He had called her cell phone shortly after sunset, feeling her out as to what she was doing avoiding him, and with her charms literally in her hand, she had agreed to a date with him. Sunup. His place.

Agitated, Ivy clicked her pen open and shut, imagining he had probably spent his time in the office talking himself up big as to his plans for tonight. Her eyes fell on the purple stains in her cuticles from breaking her pen earlier, and she set it down.

A creak on the stairway brought her heart into her throat. She hadn't told Piscary what she was doing, and only he or Kisten would be coming up. But then her eyes went to the windows and she berated herself. Piscary would never come up here so close to sunrise.

Determined to keep her back to the stairs, she hid her unease behind turning off the table lamp and shuffling her papers, but she didn't think Kisten was fooled—he was grinning from behind his reddish blond beard when she looked up. Eyebrows rising, she sent her gaze across his shiny dress shoes, up his pinstripe suit, and to the tie he had loosened.

"Who are you trying to be?" she asked sharply, rarely seeing him in a suit, much less a tie.

"Sorry, love," he said, using that British accent. "Didn't mean to startle you."

He bent to slip a hand around her waist and give her a soft tug, but she ignored him, pretending to study her papers. "I don't like your accent," she said, releasing some of her tension in a bad mood. She smelled someone on him, and it made things worse. "And you didn't startle me. I smelled you and some tart halfway up the stairs. Who was it? That little blond that's been coming in here every payday to make black eyes at you? She's early. It's only Thursday."

Fingers sliding from her, Kisten edged a step away. Eyes down, he picked up a paper. "Ivy . . ."

It was low and coaxing, and her jaw clenched. "I'm doing this."

"Ivy, he's an undead." With a soft sound, he sat beside her on the piano bench. "If you make a mistake . . . They're so damn strong. When they get angry, they don't even pretend to remember pity."

They both knew that all too well. Her pulse quickened, but she kept her face impassive. "I won't make a mistake," she said, scratching a notation on her paper.

Kisten took the pen from her and set it atop her papers. "All you have is a few witch charms and the element of surprise. If he has any idea that you might betray him, he's going knock you out and drain you. And no one will say anything if you went down there looking to tag him. Even Piscary."

Ivy pulled her fingers from his as if unconcerned. "He won't kill me. If he does, I'll sue his ass for unlawful termination."

Clearly unhappy, Kisten opened the piano. The light made shadows on him, throwing his faint scars into sharp relief. "I don't want you to get hurt," he said, spreading his fingers to hit almost an entire octave, but he made no sound. "And I don't want you dead. You won't be any fun that way."

Her eye twitched, and she forced it to stop with pure will. If things went right, Art would be really pissed. If things went wrong, Art would be really pissed and in a position to hurt her. "I don't want to die, either," she admitted, tucking her feet under the bench.

Kisten struck a chord, modifying it into a minor that sounded wrong. As the echoes lifted through the brightening room, she cursed herself for being so addicted to blood that it was such an overriding factor in her life. Mia had said all it took was practice to say no. Ivy had always scorned living vampires who abstained from blood, thinking they were betraying everything they were. Now she found herself wondering if this was why they did it.

The eerie chord ended when Kisten lifted his foot from the pedal and reached for the blue silk pouch.

"Careful," Ivy warned, gripping his wrist. "It's already invoked and will drop you quicker than tequila."

Dark eyebrows high, Kisten said, "This?" and she let go. "What does it do?"

Hiding her nervousness, Ivy bent back over her paper. "It gets Art off my neck." He held it from the drawstring like it was a rat. Clearly he didn't like witch magic either. "It's harmless," she said, giving up on her last-minute planning, "Just bring Sleeping Beauty when you get my call."

Kisten leaned backward, touching the front pocket of his slacks. "I've got my phone. It's on vibrate. Call me. Call me a lot."

Ivy allowed herself a smile. Setting the pen aside, she stood, gingerly wedging the amulet safe in its bag into a pocket. Kisten turned on the bench to keep her in view, and she tucked a placebo vial of saltwater down her bustier-enhanced cleavage. The man at the charm outlet had insisted she take the vial since it could do double-duty as a quick way to permanently break the sleep charm if she spilled it on the amulet. The cool spot it made caused her to shift her shoulders until the glass warmed. Kisten was wearing a shit-grin when she brought her head up. "How do I look?" she asked, posing.

Smiling, he drew her to him. "Mmmm, dressed to kill, baby," he said, his breath warming her midriff since he was still sitting on the piano bench. "I like the shirt."

"Do you?" Eyes closing, she let the mingling of his scent with hers stir her bloodlust. Her hands ran aggressively through his hair, and when his fingers traced the outlines of her buttocks and his lips moved just under her breast, she wondered if finding love in blood might be worth the shame of having lied to herself, of letting others tell her who she was, and letting them make her into this ugly thing. Feeling the rise of indecision, she pulled away. "I've got to go."

Kisten's face was creased in worry, and as he ran a hand through his hair to straighten it, she found herself wanting to arrange his tie. Or better yet, rip it off him. "I'm going to change, then I'll be right behind you," he said. "Your wine is downstairs on the counter."

"Thanks." She hefted her duffel bag with its change of clothes and hesitated. She wanted to ask him if he thought it was possible to find love in sharing blood, but shame stopped her. Sandals loud on the hardwood floor, she walked to the stairs, feeling as if she might never walk this floor again. Or that if she did, she'd be changed beyond recognition.

"Burn those papers for me?" she called, and got an "Already ahead of you" in return.

The restaurant had emptied of patrons, and the soft chatter of the waitstaff was pleasant as she passed the bar. Music was cranked in the kitchen over the sounds of the oversized dishes being hand washed, and everyone was enjoying the span between Piscary becoming unavailable and quitting time. Like children left home alone, they laughed and teased. Ivy liked this time the best, often lying in bed and listening, never telling anyone she could hear. Why the hell couldn't she join in? Why was everything so damn complicated for her?

Grabbing a bottle of Piscary's cheapest wine in passing, she gave a high-five to the pizza delivery guy coming in the receiving dock/garage as she went out. She couldn't help but notice that the kitchen atmosphere was radically different from the one she found in the I.S. tower. The office held pity; the kitchen was sly anticipation.

Shortly after opening this afternoon, the entire staff knew there was a body in the refrigerator. They also knew Kisten was in a good mood. And with her change in her work patterns, they knew she was up to something. Maybe Kisten had it right.

The wine went into the duffel bag, which she then strapped to the back of her cycle. Swinging onto it, she started it up, eyes closing at the power beneath her as she put her helmet on. Waving to the second delivery guy pulling in, she idled into the rush hour traffic. It would soon slack off as humans took over Cincinnati, calling it theirs alone until noon when the early-rising Inderlanders began stirring.

Ivy felt insulated in her helmet, the wind tugging at her hair a familiar sensation. She was alive, free, the smooth movement of the earth turning under her instilling a peace she couldn't readily find. Wishing she could just get on the interstate and go, she sighed. It would never happen. Her need for blood would follow her, and without Piscary providing protection as her master, she would be taken by the first undead vampire she ran into. There was no way out. There never had been. Mia's invitation surfaced, and Ivy tasted it in her thoughts, trying it on before dismissing it as a slow, pleasant way to suicide.

The sun was rising as she crossed the bridge into Cincinnati. She was late. Art would be either pissed or still glowing from the men's-club talk of the day. The thought that she was a whore flitted through her before she quashed it. She wasn't going to sell herself to move up the corporate ladder. She could resist Art long enough to knock him out, and then she'd nail his ass to the wall and use it to make a new ladder.

Pulse quickening, she took a sharp right, weaving in and out of traffic until she reached Fountain Square. The plaza was empty, and she found a parking spot near the front of the belowground garage. Nervousness crept into her as she shut off her cycle. A moment with a small mirror and a red lipstick, and she was ready. Leaving her helmet on the seat, she fumbled for her duffel bag and headed to the rectangle of light with more confidence than she felt. There was no reason for her anxiety. She'd planned sufficiently.

A furtive glance to make sure no one was watching, and she found the charmed silver that would change her appearance. She pulled the tiny pin out of the watch-sized amulet to invoke the disguise, tossed the pin aside, and laced the metallic amulet over her head. This one didn't need to touch her skin, just be on her person. The witch had said it worked using her own aura's energy, but she really hadn't cared beyond what she needed to make it function properly.

An eerie feeling rippled over her, and Ivy shuddered, her sandals grinding the street grit. It wouldn't make her look like Sleeping Beauty—that was illegal, she had been primly told—but with the clothing, hair, and attitude, it would be close enough.

She squinted in the brighter light when she came out onto the sidewalk and headed for the bus stop. Witch magic was powerful shit, and she wondered if no one realized the potential it had, or if no one cared, seeing as witches didn't try to govern anything but themselves, quietly going about their business of blending with humanity.

The bus was pulling up as she got there—precisely as she had timed it—and she was the third one on, dropping a token in before finding a seat and putting her duffel bag to prevent someone from sitting beside her. She had a swipe card, but using a token would add to her anonymity.

Jostled, she watched the city pass, the professional buildings giving way to tall thin homes with dirt yards the size of a Buick. Her clenched jaw eased when the yards got nicer and the paint jobs fresher as the house numbers rose. By the time she reached Art's block, the salt-rusted, dented vehicles had been replaced by late-model, expensive cars. She watched Art's house pass, waiting two blocks before signaling the driver she wanted off. It wasn't a regular stop, but he pulled over, letting irate humans on their way to work pass him as she said, "Thank you" in a soft voice and disembarked.

She was walking before the door shut behind her. Free arm swinging, she hit her heels hard to attract attention. Warming, she shortened her pace to accommodate her smaller look. The clip-clack, clip-clack cadence was unnatural, and she dropped her head as if not wanting to be seen when she heard a car start.

At Art's house, she hesitated, pretending to check an address. It was smaller than she expected, though well-maintained. Her parents had a modest mansion built with railroad money earned by her great-grandfather, the elaborate underground apartments added after her great-grandmother had attracted Piscary's attention. Art couldn't have much of a bedroom; the footprint for the two-story house was only fifty-by-thirty.

Swinging her duffel bag to her front, she took the stairs with a series of prissy steps. Thirty years ago, the house would have been low high-class, and it was obvious why Art needed the money. His interest income when he died had been sufficient to keep him at low high-class—of the seventies. Inflation was moving him down in the socioeconomic ladder. He needed something to pull himself up before he slid into poverty over the next hundred years.

There was a note on the door. Smirking, she pulled it from the screen and let it fall to the bushes for the forensics team to find. "Late, am I?" she muttered, wondering if he had the front miked. Pitching her voice high, she called, "Art, I brought wine. Can I come in?"

There was no answer, so she opened the door and entered a modest living room. The curtains were drawn and a light was on for her. She wandered into the spotless kitchen with a dry sink. Again there were leather curtains, hidden behind a lightweight white fabric to disguise them. Leather curtains couldn't protect an undead vamp from the sun, but boarding up the windows was against the city ordinances. Another note on an interior door invited her down.

Her lip curled, and she started to wish she had arranged this during night hours so she didn't have to play this disgusting game. Crumpling the note, she dropped it on the faded linoleum. She took off the charmed silver amulet, shivering when something pulled through her aura. Her hair lost its corn yellow hue, and she hung the amulet on the knob so Kisten would know where she was.

Knocking, she opened the door to find a downward leading stair and music. She wanted to be annoyed, but he'd done his research and it was something she liked—midnight jazz. A patch of cream carpet met her, glowing under soft lights. Gripping her duffel bag, she called, "Art?"

"Shut the door," he snarled from somewhere out of sight. "The sun is up."

Ivy took three steps down and shut the door, noting it was as thick as coffin wood and reinforced with steel with a metal crossbar to lock it. There was a clock stuck to its back, along with a page from the almanac, a calendar, and a mirror. Her mother had something similar.

Again Ivy wanted to belittle him, but it looked professional and businesslike. No pictures of sunsets or graveyards. The only notation on the calendar about her was "date with Ivy." No exclamation points, no hearts, no "hubba-hubba." *Thank God.*

She touched her pocket for the sleep amulet and looked down her cleavage for the fake potion. Relying on witch magic made her nervous. She didn't like it. Didn't understand it. She had had no idea witch magic was so versatile, much less so powerful. They had a nice little secret here, and they protected it the same way vampires protected their strengths: by having them out in the open and shackled by laws that meant nothing when push came to shove.

Sandals loud on the wooden steps, she descended, watching Art's shadow approach the landing. The faint scent of bleach intruded, growing stronger as she reached the floor. She kept her face impassive when she found him, glad he was still wearing his usual work clothes. If he had been in a Hugh Hefner robe and holding a glass of vodka, she would have screamed.

Ignoring him watching her, she looked over his belowground apartments. They were plush and comfortable, with low ceilings. It was an old house, and the city had strict guidelines about how much dirt you could pull out from under your dwelling. They were in what was obviously the living room, a wood-paneled hallway probably leading to a traditional bedroom. Her eyes went to the lit gas fireplace, and she felt her eyebrows rise.

"It dries the air out," he said. "You don't think I'm going to romance you, do you?"

Relieved, she dropped her duffel bag by the couch. Hand on her hip, she swung her hair, glad it was back to its usual black. "Art, I'm here for one thing, and after I'm done, I'm cleaning up and leaving. Romance would ruin my entire image of you, so why don't we just get it over with?"

Art's eyes flashed to black. "Okay."

It was fast. He moved, reaching out and yanking her to him. Instinct got an arm between them as he pulled her to his chest. Her pulse pounded, and she stared when he hesitated, her naked fear striking a chord with him. It was a drug to him, and she knew he paused so as to prolong it. She cursed herself when her own bloodlust rose, heady and unstoppable. She didn't want this. She could say no. Her will was stronger than her instincts.

But her jaw tightened, and he smiled to show his teeth when she felt her eyes dilate against her will. Lips parting, she exhaled into it. The savage desire to force her needs on him vibrated through every nerve. Mia was wrong. There could be no love here, no tenderness. And when Art forced her closer and ran his teeth gently across her neck, she found herself tense with anticipation even as she tried to bring it under control. *Concentrate, Ivy,* she thought, her pulse quickening in her conflicting feelings. She was here to nail his coffin, not be nailed.

He knew she wouldn't say yes to him until he pulled her to the brink where bloodlust made her choices. And even as she thought no, she gripped his shoulder, poised as he ran his hand down her hips and eased to the inside of her thighs, searching. A rumbling growl came from him, shivering through her. His hands became possessive, demanding. And she willed the feeling to grow, even when self-loathing filled her.

How had it come on so fast? she thought. Had she been wanting this all along, teasing herself? Or was Mia right in that she had refused Art because giving in would prove she knew she could find love in the ugliness, but was too cowardly to fight for it?

Art carefully hooked a tooth into the lace of her collar and tore it, the sound of the ripping fabric cutting through her. His teeth grazed her, promising, and she lost all thought but how to get him to sink them, to fill her with glorious feeling proving she was alive and could feel joy, even if she paid for it with her self-respect.

Art didn't speak as he stood, holding her against him, the demanding pressure in his lips, his fingers, his very breathing, waking every nerve in her. He hadn't bespelled her; he hadn't needed to. She was willing to be everything he wanted, and a tiny part of her screamed, drowned out by her need to give to him and to feel in return, even though she knew it was false.

His fingers rose from his grip upon her waist, tracing upward with a firm insistence until they found her chin and tilted her head. "Give this to me," he whispered, his fingers among her hair. "This is mine. Give it . . . to me."

It was haggard, almost torn by the need in him that her tortured willingness had sparked. The thought that she was buying empty emotion rose like bubbles to pop against the top of her mind. Mia had said she could live above the bloodlust. Mia didn't know shit, didn't know the exquisite pleasure of this. She wanted his blood, and he wanted hers. What difference did it make how she would feel in the morning? Tomorrow she could be dead and it wouldn't matter.

And then she remembered the leashed hunger Mia contained and counted it stronger than her own. She remembered the scorn in Mia's voice, calling her a whiny little girl who could have everything if she had the courage to live up to her greater need for love. Even if she did have to taint it with bloodlust.

Ivy's heart pounded as she tried to find the will to pull away, but the lure of what he could fill her with was too strong. She couldn't. It was ingrained too deeply. It was what she was. But she wanted more, damn it. She wanted to escape the ugliness of what she really was.

As she struggled with herself, she found Art's mouth with her own, drawing his lips from her neck and putting them on hers. The salty electric taste of blood filled her, but it wasn't hers. Art had cut his own lip, sending her into a dizzy lust for the rest of him.

Gasping, she pushed away. *It would stop here.*

She fell back, fingers fumbling for the vial. Eyes black, Art gripped her wrist, the tiny glass bottle exposed. Ivy flushed hot as she stood, her arm stretched between them.

Hunched from the pain of breaking from her, Art wiped his mouth of his blood. He let go of her, and she stumbled back. In Art's hand was the vial.

"What's this?" he asked, wary but amused when he unscrewed the top and sniffed at it.

"Nothing," she said, truly afraid even as her body ached at the interruption.

He sucked in her fear, his eyes going blacker and his smile more predatory. "Really."

Panicking that he would drop it and come at her again, she fumbled in her pocket, bringing out the real charm, invoked but quiescent in its silk pouch.

Art's eyes went to it, and before he could think, she jumped at him. Arm moving in a quick arc, Art flung the contents of the vial at her. Heavy droplets, warm from her body, struck her like shocks from a whip. Adrenaline pounding to make her head hurt, she forced her muscles to go slack. She collapsed as if she'd run into a wall, falling to where he had been standing a second earlier. The carpet burned her cheek, and she exhaled as if passing out.

From across the room, she heard him shift his feet against the carpet, trying to figure out what had happened. She forced her breathing to slow, feigning unconsciousness. It had to work. If not, she had only an instant to escape.

"I knew you'd try something," Art said, going to the wet bar and pouring himself something. The undead didn't need to drink, but it would cleanse his cut lip. "Not as clever as Piscary said you'd be," he said amid the heavy clink of a bottle against glass. "Did you really think I wouldn't have you followed on your shopping?"

Ivy clenched her stomach muscles when a dress shoe edged under her and flipped her over. Forcing herself to remain flaccid, she kept her eyes lightly shut as her back hit the carpet. He might bite her anyway, but fear and desire tainted the blood with delicious compounds, and he'd rather have her awake. Heart pounding, she loosened her fingers and let the pouch slip from them. Curiosity could put the cat in the bag when force could not.

"I'm forty-two years dead," he said bitterly. "You don't survive that long if you're stupid." There was a slight hesitation, and then, "And what the hell was this supposed to do?"

Ivy heard him pick up the silk pouch and shake the amulet into his hand. She tensed, springing to her feet as he exhaled. He was still standing, his eyes losing their focus when she shot her hand out, curling his slack fingers around the amulet before it could slip from him.

With a sigh, he collapsed, and she went down with him, desperate to keep the amulet in his grip. They hit the carpet together, her arm wedged painfully under her.

"You can survive that long if you're stupid *and* lucky," she said. "And your luck's run out, Artie."

Slowly Ivy shifted her legs under her into a more comfortable position, her hand still gripped around Art's fingers. Hooking her foot in the handle of her duffel bag by the couch, she dragged it closer. With one hand, she opened it to pull out a plastic-coated metallic zip-strip the I.S. used to bind ley line witches to keep them from escaping by jumping to a ley line. Art couldn't use ley line magic, but the strip would hold the amulet to him. At the sound of the plastic ratcheting against itself to pinch the amulet between his palm and the strip, she relaxed.

Exhaling, she got to her feet. Drawing her foot back, she kicked him. Hard. "Bastard," she said, wiping his spit off her neck. Limping, she went to the stereo and clicked it off. She'd never be able to listen to "Skylark" again. She rummaged in her duffel bag, and upon finding her phone, headed for the stairs. Three steps from the top, and she had enough bars. She hit speed-dial one, struggling to listen and take off her disgusting shirt simultaneously.

"Ivy?" came Kisten's voice, and she pinched the phone between her shoulder and her ear.

"He's down. Bring her in," she said.

Without waiting for an answer, she ended the call, adrenaline making her jumpy. Shaking, she stripped off her clothes and slipped into her leather pants and a stretch-knit shirt, wiping her neck free of Art's scent with a disposable towelette that then went into the contractor garbage bag she shook out with the sharp crack of thick plastic. She considered the lacy shirt for an instant, then dropped it in, too. Her sandals went into her duffel bag.

Barefoot, she crouched by Art. Lifting his lips from his gums, she sucked up blood and saliva with a disposable eyedropper, putting a good quarter inch into the empty saltwater vial. Done, she opened the wine, sat on the raised hearth, and with the hissing flames warming her back, took a long pull. It was bitter, and she grimaced, taking another drink, smaller this time. Anything to get rid of the lingering taste of Art's blood in her mouth.

Toes digging into the carpet, she looked at Art, out cold and helpless. Witch magic had done it. God, they could be a serious threat in Inderland politics if they put their mind to it.

The sound of feet upstairs brought her straight, and she set the bottle aside. It was Kisten, thumping down the stairs with a large cardboard box in his arms. Ivy looked, then looked again. He had changed into an institutional gray jumpsuit, but that wasn't it.

"You're wearing the charm," she said, and he flushed from under his new blond bangs. He was shorter, too, and she didn't like it.

"I always wanted to know what I'd look like blond," he said. "And it will help with the repairman image." Grunting, he set down the box with Sleeping Beauty in it. "God almighty," he swore as he stretched his back and looked at Art with the amulet strapped to his palm. "It smells like a cheap hotel down here, all blood and bleach. Did he wing you?"

"No." Ivy handed him the bottle, unwilling to admit how close Art had come.

Kisten's Adam's apple bobbed as he drank, and he exhaled loudly as he lowered the bottle. His eyes were bright and his smile was wide. *Just one big joke to Kisten*, Ivy thought, depressed. She had acted just in time. If she hadn't dropped Art, she would have said yes to him—even when she hadn't wanted to. Mia was right. She needed more practice.

"Where do you want to put her?" Kisten said cheerfully.

A shrug lifted her shoulders. "The bathtub?"

Clearly enjoying himself, he lifted the box and headed into the paneled hallway. "Holy Christ!" he shouted, faint from the wall between them. "Have you seen his bathroom?"

Tired, Ivy rose from the hearth, trying not to look at Art sprawled on the floor. "No."

"I'm going to put her in the hot tub."

"He's got a hot tub?" That would explain the scent of chlorine, and Ivy went to see, her eyebrows rising at the small tub flush with the floor. Kisten had turned it on, and though it wasn't warm yet, tiny bubbles swirled in the artificial current. Putting Sleeping Beauty in that was going to make a mess, but it would help remove any traces of Piscary and blur that she had been stuck in the refrigerator for a day. Not to mention a dripping wet corpse was harder to get rid of than a dry one. Art wasn't smart enough to manage it before the I.S. knocked on his door.

Kisten had gone respectfully silent, and keeping the woman in the box, they worked at getting her out of the plastic and duct tape. Jaw clenched, Ivy worked her out of her clothes, handing them to Kisten one by one to be sprayed with the de-enzyme solution from the bar to remove Piscary's scent. The bottle was heavy as it hit Ivy's palm, and with Kisten's help, they sprayed her down as well, taking extra care with the open wounds.

Disturbed, she met Kisten's eyes in the silence, and together they slipped Sleeping Beauty into the water, wedging the corpse between an edge and the railing. While Kisten tidied, Ivy went back for the wine and a glass.

Carefully keeping her prints off it, Ivy pressed Sleeping Beauty's hand around the glass several times before adding a few lip prints. She dribbled some wine into the woman's mouth, then the glass, which she set at arm's length. There wouldn't be any in her stomach, and there wouldn't be any of her blood in Art's system either, but it was a game of perception, not absolutes. Besides, all she needed to do was eliminate any evidence of Piscary.

Kisten had the vial of Art's spit, and crouching by the tub, she took a sterile swab and ran it through the woman's open wounds. Finished, she stood, and together they looked down at her.

"She had a nice smile," Kisten finally said, gaze flicking to Ivy. "You okay with this?"

"No, I'm not okay with this," Ivy said, feeling empty. "But she's dead, isn't she. We can't hurt her anymore."

Kisten hesitated, then grabbed the box and maneuvered his way out.

Ivy picked up the heavy-duty shears he had left and tucked them behind her waistband. Looking at the woman, she crouched to brush the long hair from the corpse's closed eyes. An impulsive "thank you," slipped from Ivy's lips, and, flustered, she stood.

Sickened, she backed out of the room. This was ugly. She was ugly. The things she did were ugly, and she didn't want to do them anymore. Her stomach was cramping when she found Kisten standing above Art, and she forced herself to look tall and unbothered. The broken-down box and plastic wrap were already in the trash bag, along with everything else. "You sure you don't want me to move him upstairs?" he asked. "They might call it a suicide."

Ivy shook her head, checking the bottom of the woman's shoes and setting them by the stairway. "Everyone's going to know what I did, but as long as there is no easy evidence, they'll let it go as me thinking outside the box. No one likes him anyway. But if I kill him, they'll have to do a more thorough investigation."

It was perfect in so many ways. Art would be cited for Piscary's homicide and end up in jail. She would get to write her own six-month review. No one would mess with her for a while, not wanting a dead body showing up in their bathroom. She was a force not to be taken lightly. The thought didn't make her as happy as she thought it would.

Kisten seemed to notice, since he touched her arm to bring her eyes to his. She blinked at the color of his hair and the fact that he was shorter than she, even if it was an illusion. It was a damn good illusion. "You did all right," he said. "Piscary will be impressed."

She hid her face by leaning to scoop up the duct tape. That Piscary would be proud of her lacked the expected thrill, too. For a moment, only the sound of the tape being unwound and wrapped about Art's wrists and ankles rose over the hiss of the propane fireplace. The tape wouldn't stop him, but all they needed was to get to the stairs.

"Ready?" Ivy asked when she tossed the tape into her duffel bag and took out her boots.

Kisten turned from his last-minute wipe down of fingerprints. "All set."

UNDEAD IN THE GARDEN OF GOOD AND EVIL   173

As she sat on the hearth and laced her boots, Ivy looked over the room. The scent of chlorine was growing stronger as the water warmed, hiding the odor of dead girl. She wanted a moment with Art. Why the hell not? She'd earned a little gloating. Let him know she caught him covering up a murder. "Wait for me in the van," she said. "I'll be right there."

Kisten grinned, clearly not surprised. "Two minutes," he said. "Any longer than that, and you're playing with him."

She snorted, giving him a swat on the ass as he started up the stairs with her duffel bag and the trash. His blond hair caught the light, and she watched until he vanished in a flash of morning sun. Still she waited until the faint sound of the van starting up met her before she turned Art's hand palm up and cut the strip with the shears. Tucking them behind her waistband, she stepped back and teased the amulet off his hand and into its little bag.

For a panicked moment she thought she had killed him, but her fear must have scented the air since Art jerked, his eyes black when they focused on her. He tried to move, his attention going to the duct tape about his wrists and ankles. Chuckling, he wedged himself into an upright position against the couch, and Ivy's face burned.

"Piscary thinks so much of you," he said condescendingly. "He needs to wipe the sand from his eyes and see you as the little girl you are, playing with boys too big for her."

He tensed his arms, and Ivy forced herself to stay relaxed. But the tape held and she bent at the waist to look him in the eyes. "You okay?"

"This isn't winning you any friends, but yes, I'm okay."

Satisfied she hadn't hurt him, she rose and plucked up the wine bottle and gave it another pull, the heat of the fire warming her legs. "You've been a bad boy, Art," she said, hip cocked.

He ran his eyes over her, going still when he realized she was wearing her usual leather and spandex. His face abruptly lost its emotion. "Why is my hot tub going? What day is this? Who was here?"

Again he pulled against the tape, starting a rip. Ivy set the bottle down and moved closer, sending her wine breath over him to shift his silky black curls. It didn't matter if her presence was placed here. The entire I.S. tower knew where she was this morning. "I'm not happy," she said. "I came over here to make good on our arrangement, and I find another girl down here?"

Art shifted his shoulders, arms bulging. "What the hell did you do, Ivy?"

Smiling, she leaned over him. "It's not what I did, Artie. It's what I found. You need to be more careful with your cookies. You're leaving crumbs all over your house."

"This isn't funny," he snarled, and Ivy moved to the stairway.

"No, it isn't," she said, knowing that the tape would last as long as his ignorance. "You have a dead girl in your hot tub, Artie, and I'm out of here. The deal is off. I don't need your approval to move into the Arcane Division. You're going to jail." Adrenaline struck through her when she turned her back and her foot touched the lowest stair. The door was open and ambient sunlight was leaking in. He couldn't put one foot on them without risking death. She almost hoped he would.

"Ivy!" Art exclaimed, and she turned at the sound of ripping tape.

Pulse pounding, she hesitated. She was safe. It was done. "You made one mistake, Art," she said, taking in his anger. "You shouldn't have tried to use me to cover up that witch's murder," she said, and the color drained from him. "That pissed me off." Giving him a bunny-eared "kiss-kiss" she turned and took the stairs with a slow, taunting pace.

"This isn't going to work, Ivy!" he shouted, and her pulse leaped at the sound of the tape ripping, but she had reached the top and it was *far* too late. She smiled as she emerged into his kitchen. He was stuck down there with that corpse until the sun went down. If he called in help to get it out, it would damn him faster. An anonymous tip from a concerned neighbor was going to bring someone knocking on his door within thirty minutes. "No hard feelings, Art," she said. "Strictly business." She went to shut the door so he wouldn't get light sick, hesitating. "Really," she added, closing the door on his scream of outrage.

Scooping up her duffel bag from where Kisten had left it, she sauntered out the front door and down the steep walk to the street. Kisten was waiting, and she slipped into the passenger-side seat, throwing her bag into the back. She imagined the fury belowground, glad she could walk away. It didn't matter if anyone saw her leave. She was supposed to be here.

"Two minutes on the nose," Kisten said, leaning over to give her a kiss. He was still wearing her disguise amulet, and she caught him looking at himself and his hair. "Are you okay, love?" he asked, hitting his new accent hard and fussing with his bangs.

Rolling down the window, she put her arm on the sill as he drove away and the sun hit her. The memory of being unable to say no to Art resounded in her, and the lure of the bloodlust. Saying no had been impossible, but she had stopped him—and herself. It had been hard, but she felt good in a melancholy way. It wasn't the glorious shock of ecstasy, but more like a sunbeam, unnoticed when you first find it, but its warmth growing until you felt . . . good.

"I'm all right," she said, squinting from the morning sun. "I like who I am today."

 SIX

Ivy dropped the empty box on her desk and sat before it, swiveling her chair back and forth until someone walked past her open door. Adopting a more businesslike mien, she looked over her office. Her eyebrows rose, and she plucked her favorite pen from the cup and then tossed the empty box into the hall. The thump silenced the gossip, and she smirked. They could have everything. All she wanted was her favorite pen. Well, and a pair of thicker leather pants. And an updated map of the city. A computer would be helpful, but they wouldn't let her take the one she'd been using. Some really comfortable boots. Sunglasses—mirror sunglasses.

A soft knuckle-knock at her open door brought her head around, and she smiled without showing her teeth. "Rat," she said companionably. "Come to see me off?"

The large officer eased into her office, a manila folder in his hand. "I won the pool," he said, ducking his head. "I've got your, ah, transfer papers. How you doing?"

"Depends." She leaned across her desk, biting her finger coyly. "What's the word on the street?"

He laughed. "You're bad. No one will be looking at you for a while." Brow pinching, he came in another step. "You sure you don't want to work Arcane? It's not too late."

Ivy's pulse quickened at the lure of bloodlust she knew she couldn't resist. "I don't want to work in the Arcane anymore," she said, eyes lowered. "I need to get out from underground. Spend some time in the sun."

The officer slumped, the folder before him like a fig leaf. "You're ticking them off with this rebellious shit. This isn't Piscary's camarilla, it's a business. They had a late meeting about you this morning in the lowest floor."

Fear slid through her, quickly stifled. "They can't fire me. There was no evidence that I had anything to do with that girl in Art's tub."

"No. You're clear. And remind me to stay on your good side." He grinned, but it faded fast. "You did contaminate that crime scene, and they're almost ignoring that. You should lay low for a while, do what they want you to do. You have your entire life and afterlife ahead of you. Don't screw it up your first six months here."

Ivy grimaced, flicking her attention past him to the outer offices. "They're already blaming my demotion on my—lapse. They can't punish me twice for the same thing." The reality was she was being demoted because she refused to move up to the Arcane. That was fine by her.

"Publicly," he said, making her agitated. "What happens behind closed doors is something else. You're making a mistake," he insisted. "They can use your talents down there."

"Don't you mean a new infusion?" Rat winced, and she held up a hand and leaned back into her chair, well aware it put her in a position of power with him standing. "Whatever. I won't be manipulated, Rat. I'd rather take a pay cut and go where I don't have to worry about it for a while."

"If only it was that easy." Rat dropped the folder on her desk as if it meant something. "Ah, I thought you'd like to see your new partner's file."

In a smooth, alarmed motion, Ivy sat up. "Whoa. Put your caps on. I agreed to move upstairs, but no one said anything about a partner."

Rat shrugged, his wide shoulders bunching his uniform. "They can't give you a pay cut, so you're pulling double duty chaperoning a newbie for a year. Intern with two years of social science and three years pulling familiars out of trees. Management wants her under someone with a more, ah, textbook technique before they instate her as a runner, so she's all yours, Ivy. Don't let her get you killed. We like you ju-u-u-ust the way you are."

The last was said with dripping sarcasm, and her face hot, Ivy pushed the folder away. "She's not even a full runner? I've worked too hard for my degree to be a babysitter. No way."

Rat chuckled and pushed it back with a single, thick-knuckled finger. "Yes way. Unless you want to move down to Arcane where you belong."

Ivy almost growled. She hated her mother. She hated Piscary. *No, she hated their control over her.* Slowly she pulled the folder to her and opened it. "Oh my God," she breathed as she looked at the picture, thinking it couldn't get any worse. "A witch? They partnered me with a witch? Whose bright-ass idea was *that*?"

Rat laughed, pulling Ivy's eyes from her "partner's" picture. Slumping back, she tried not to frown. Though it was clearly meant to be a punishment, this might not be a bad thing. A witch wouldn't be after her blood, and the relief of not having to fight that would be enough to compensate for the extra work that having such a weak partner would engender. *A witch? They were laughing at her. The entire tower was laughing at her.*

"You said management doesn't want her on her own. What's wrong with her?" she asked and Rat took her shoulder in a thick hand and drew her reluctantly to her feet.

"Nothing," he said, grinning. "She's impulsive is all. It's a match made in heaven, Ivy. You'll be best friends before the week is out: going shopping, eating chocolate, catching chick-flicks after work. You'll love it! Trust me."

Ivy realized she was clenching her jaw, and she forced her teeth apart before she gave herself a headache. Her partner was a flake. She was partnered with a girly-girl flake who wanted to be a runner. This was going to be pure hell. Rat laughed, and seeing no other option, Ivy dragged the folder to her, tucked it under her arm, and headed for the door with Rat, leaving her old office and its comforting walls behind for an open office with pressboard walls and bad coffee.

It was only for a year. How bad could it be?

DIRTY MAGIC

Banshees were once far less known and rarely popularized paranormal figures. Up until I wrote "Dirty Magic" (first published in Hotter Than Hell*), I had only a vague idea that they cried inconsolably when someone was going to die, sort of an early warning system in the hills of Ireland, and I tried to keep that kernel in mind while developing my idea of a Hollows banshee. Tears as a way to store psychic energy and death by way of aura depletion turned banshees from passive warnings to apex predators, making them much more interesting. For those in the know, the banshee is one of the most feared Inderlanders whose takes often go undetected or simply ignored. Mia had enough to say that she made the jump to the series as the major antagonist in* Black Magic Sanction.

Mia walked down the damp, rain-deserted sidewalk, her seventy-five-dollar heels clicking faintly from fatigue on the wet cement. She was tired, but she could still maintain her elegant, upright posture if she moved slowly. Her dress-length overcoat and matching umbrella of midnight blue kept her dry, and it was rainy enough that she didn't need to wear her sunglasses to protect her pale, nearly albino eyes.

With a small toss of her head, she shifted her black hair, cut short as she liked it. Traffic was light, but she didn't want to risk being splashed, so she shifted closer to the classy, well-maintained narrow buildings that lined the street. The paper sack of groceries on her hip wasn't heavy, but her daughter's needs were telling. It wasn't the usual fatigue brought on by an energetic newborn. Holly was the first banshee born in Cincinnati in over forty years, and if Mia couldn't keep her in an emotion-rich environment, the child took what she needed from her mother. It wasn't as if Holly could draw upon her father for her emotional needs. Not now anyway.

Frowning, Mia brushed her hair from her eyes and wondered if having a child at this particular time had been a good idea. But when Remus—psychopath, murderer, and gentle lover—had fallen into her lap by way of a bungled rape attempt, the chance to use his anger and frustration to engender a child in her had been too great. A smile curved Mia's delicate mouth up. Remus had quickly learned the difference between his unreasonable rage at the world and her true hunger, becoming pliant and gentle. Respectful. The perfect husband, the model father.

And at the thought of Holly, happy, inquisitive Holly, so pretty and soft, looking like a younger, mirror image of her mother, babbling innocently as she sat on her mother's lap and basked in the love for her, Mia knew she'd have it no other way. She would do anything for her daughter. As her mother had done for her.

The soft whoosh of a passing car brought Mia's head up, and she blinked at the rain heavy on her eyelashes despite the umbrella. It was cool and damp, and she was weary. Seeing a rain-abandoned table outside a cafe, she slowed, brushing once at the wrought-iron chair before sitting with her groceries on her lap and trusting her coat to keep her dry. The awning helped shield the rain and she closed her umbrella. She was just a casually sophisticated young woman waiting for a cab that would never come.

People passed, and slowly her pulse eased and her fatigue lessoned as she soaked in the emotions of the pedestrians, taking in flashes of feeling like water eddying around a rock in a streambed. It was all the law would allow now, this passive sipping of emotions. If she fed well, people noticed.

Mia straightened when a couple arguing over whether they should have taken a cab walked by, sensation rolling over her like a sunbeam. Almost she rose to fall into step behind them, to linger and drink it in, but she didn't, and the warmth faded as the couple continued on.

One might think that a predator existing on emotions might have an easy life living in a city that measured its population in the hundreds of thousands, but since humanity had learned banshees were not the stuff of story but living among them, humans had armed themselves with knowledge, and their numbers had dwindled.

The image of a mysterious weeping woman foretelling death had given way to the reality of a sophisticated predator: a predator who could feed well upon office arguments started between co-workers with a careful word or two, gorge upon the death-energy a person released when dying, but barely survive upon the ambient emotions around her that the law allowed.

As in most fairy tales, there was a kernel of truth in the myth of a banshee's tears. Created to serve as a conduit of emotions, they let a banshee feed from a safe distance or simply store the emotion for later consumption. For though banshees were predators thriving on death, they were also fragile. Much like a rattlesnake, they left their poison, then sat back to feed in safety while others fought, loved, or killed each other. Psychic vampires was what the psychology texts called them, a definition that Mia could not find fault with.

Her subconscious had brought her down this street for a reason, and as she fingered the tarnished coin draped around her neck on a tattered purple ribbon, her gaze traveled to the apartment building across from her, rising up through the misty rain, all the way to the topmost floor. The light was on, golden and hazy in the afternoon's rain. Tom was in. But Tom was always in now. He was too tired to go to work. Not like when she first met him.

Nervous, Mia spun the wedding ring on her finger. Tom hadn't given it to her. Tom hadn't given Mia her beautiful daughter either. Remus had. There had been so much raw anger in him that she could have used it to create two children. But Remus could no longer give Holly the emotion she needed.

Glancing at the window hazy with rain, Mia hesitated. She had to be so careful never to permanently harm anyone. There were old ways to track her down and new, excruciating techniques to punish a species that lived on the emotions of another. Mia was a good girl, and now she had a daughter to think of.

I shouldn't be doing this, Mia thought in worry. *It's too soon.* Someone might see her. Someone might remember she'd been here. But she was tired, and the thought of Tom holding her, filling her with the strength of his love, was too strong a pull. He loved her. He loved her even knowing that she was why he was ill. He loved her knowing she was a banshee and unable to keep from stripping his emotions and strength from him. She needed to feel his arms around her, for just a moment.

With a soft quiver of anticipation to set her skin tingling, Mia stood, gathered her grocery bag onto her hip, and pushed herself into motion. Not bothering with the umbrella, she crossed the street with a false confidence, pacing to the unattended common door with a single-minded intensity, looking neither left nor right, praying no one would notice her.

Fear a dim substitute for strength, she pulled the glass door open and slipped inside. In the small space where the mailboxes were, she lifted her chin and ran a hand over her wet hair, feeling more sure now that she was off the street and out from so many potential eyes. The shiny front of the mailboxes threw back a blurry image—color mostly: dark hair, pale skin, and an almost-black coat.

Leaving the umbrella in a corner, she ascended the stairs so as to keep the cameras in the elevator from getting a good look at her. The open stairway taking up the middle of the building wasn't monitored, and anyone looking out here would only notice an usually petite woman with a bag of groceries, cold from the rain. Worry someone might actually see her trickled back, and her pace quickened, gaining strength as she rose instead of fatigue.

Around her was the flow of life, slipping under the doors and into the hallway like the scent of baking bread or someone's too-strong cologne. It eddied about her feet and puddled on the stairs, and she waded through it like surf, able to see the energy the people living behind the doors sloughed off, kicking up anger here, and frustration there, her pace slowing to take in the softer, harder-to-find emotions of love, a mere whisper lingering outside a door like perfume.

She paused, pretending to be tired outside a door where the soft sounds of music and laughter were a muted hush. Love and desire carried the headiest amount of energy, but they were hard to find, not because they were scarce, but because people directed the emotions to a specific person, holding the feeling close to themselves as if knowing how powerful they were. Love seldom ventured past a person's aura unless it flowed into another. Not like the wild bitterness of anger, which people threw away from them like the refuse it was.

Mia closed her eyes, swallowing up the ambient love the couple had left in the hall as they had fumbled for their keys. It had only been a few hours ago, and though it bolstered her, it caused her pain. It had been too long since she had felt the full, unshielded warmth of another's aura. She was tired of filling herself on garbage and stolen wisps of love.

With a sudden resolve, she took off her ring. Slipping it into a pocket, she guiltily patted it to see if it made a telltale shape against her coat. Head high, she continued up until she reached the top floor.

Tom's door was unadorned, and with her pulse fast in tension, she tapped softly, hoping he heard. She didn't want a neighbor remembering a knock in the hall. Tom had promised her he wouldn't tell anyone he knew a banshee, afraid they would see him failing and convince him to never see her again. She shouldn't be here this soon, but the memory of his love was like the scent of flowers, begging to be inhaled and irresistible.

The door opened with a quickness that sent her back a step, and she stared at Tom, her eyes wide and her breath held. He looked good. Better than the last time she'd seen him, the lines of fatigue only lightly etching his mid-thirties face. Standing tall, he had once had a beautifully vigorous, if slight, body, but since meeting her in the grocery store a year ago, nearly all the substance had been stripped away to leave him looking as if he was recovering from a long illness. His short brown hair was clean but untidy from his shower, and he wore jeans and a comfortable flannel top against the damp chill.

Seeing her, he smiled, pleasure coming over his long, somewhat sallow face. His skin was pale from a lack of sun, and his muscles had lost their tone months ago. His fingers, long enough to facilitate a high amount of proficiency with his instrument, looked thin as he reached to pull her into a hug.

Mia felt his arms go around her and almost walked away. Breathing in his initial delight, she realized it was too soon. She should not be here, even if she *was* pining for him. Someone might have seen her, and he hadn't recovered fully from her last visit. But she was so tired, and even a wisp of his love would renew her.

"I saw you on the sidewalk," Tom said as he felt her shoulders tense and his hands dropped from her. "I'm glad you came up. It's been lonely here by myself. Come on in. Just for a moment."

Her pulse raced, and she stepped into his apartment with a guilty quickness. "I can't stay," she said, her voice high. "Tom, I promised I'd only stop by to say hi, and then I have to go."

She sounded frantic even to herself, and she bit her lower lip, wishing things were otherwise. The click of the door closing mixed with the soft sound of talk radio. The warmth of his apartment soaked into her, and she felt herself relax at the emotion-rich air his apartment had. He'd been practicing his music, and that always filled his rooms with life. It was what had attracted her to him in the first place, as he had strolled past the grapes, trailing joy like the wisps of the symphony he'd been humming. Slowly her jaw unclenched, and the worry and guilt slid into nothing. She couldn't help herself. This was what she was.

"Let me take those," he said, reaching for her groceries, and she let him, following him soundlessly down the short hall to the kitchen as she untied her coat. The kitchen opened to the living room where Tom usually practiced his music now that he was too tired to make the trip to the university's hall. Down the corridor at the back was the single bedroom and bath. Everything was tidy and clean, done in soothing tones of brown and taupe. The furnishings were simple and clearly masculine, and Mia loved the contrast from her own home, filled with the primary-colored clutter and untidy life of a new baby.

"I won't stay long," she said, noting his thin, trembling hands. "I was passing by, and . . . I missed you."

"Oh, Mia," he said, his deep voice swirling over her like his aura was as he took her in his arms. "I know how the rain depresses you."

Depresses her wasn't exactly it. It depressed everyone else, and in turn, lowered the amount of ambient emotion they gave off. She was hungry, and she lowered her gaze before he saw the rising need in their pale blue depths.

"I missed you, too," she whispered, eyes closing in bliss as his love soaked into her, his arms gentling her to him, forgiving her for what she did to him, knowing she had no choice. The scent of his soap was sharp, and she drew away when she heard his pulse quicken. She was pulling his strength from him as she soaked in his aura, rich with emotion. That was why he was weak. A person could replace a surprising amount of their aura, but take too much too fast, and the person died when their soul was left bare to the world and unprotected.

"I'm sorry," she said, blinking to keep her emotions in check. "I shouldn't have come."

"I'm fine," he said, smiling wearily down at her.

"Fine?" she said bitterly as she pulled away. "Look at you. Look what I did to you. I hardly walked in the door, and you're shaking already."

"Mia."

"No!" she exclaimed, pushing him away when he tried to hold her. "I hate who I am. I can't love anyone. Damn it, Tom, this isn't fair!"

"Shhhh," he soothed, and this time, Mia let him take her in his embrace, laying her head against his chest as he swayed her gently as if she was a child. "Mia, I don't mind giving my strength to you. It comes back."

Mia couldn't breathe from the wave of pure love rolling off of him, carrying the delicate beauty of wind chimes tinkling forgotten in the sun. His love was so heady, so sweet. But she shouldn't take it. She had to resist. If she could keep from drinking it in, it would eventually flow back into him, keeping him strong and untouched.

"But not fast enough," she mumbled into his flannel shirt, hardening herself to his emotion if not his words. "I came back too soon. You're not well. I should go."

But his arms didn't release her. "Please stay," he whispered. "Just a little while? I want to see you smile."

She pulled back, gazing into his earnest eyes. It was too soon, but she would make it be okay. She could do this. "I'll make you coffee," she said as if in concession, and he let her go.

"I'd like that. Thank you."

Motions unsure, Mia took off her overcoat and slipped off her shoes. Barefoot and in a soft dress of pale blue and gray, she busied herself in the kitchen, taking a moment to arrange her hair in the reflection in the microwave. Guilt stared back at her, with a rising black of hunger in her pale eyes. The pierced coin on the purple ribbon about her neck dangled like a guilty accusation, and her pale fingers held it for a moment as she thought. She would not take anything more from this man. She could do this. She had wanted to find love, and she had. It was worth the risk.

Tom's sigh as he sat at the table between the kitchen and the living room was weary but happy. Past the tasteful furniture and his scattered music was a large plate-glass window overlooking the street. The drapes were open, but the rain was like a sheet, gray and soothing to create a soft, hidden world.

Her silk dress was a gentle hush as Mia sat two empty cups on the table. She watched Tom's long fingers curve about his, though the cup was dry and cold. Concerned, she sat beside him and took his hand in her own, drawing his attention to her. Behind them, the coffeemaker warmed. "How are you doing?"

He smiled at the worry in her voice. "Better now that you're here."

Mia smiled back, unable to keep from soaking in his love like a sponge. Overcome by the purity of it, she dropped her gaze, only to have them fall upon the coin. Her mood tarnished.

"Work going okay?" she asked, hoping he would practice, but Tom gave her hand an apologetic squeeze in a gentle refusal. When he played, he expended a huge amount of emotion when he became lost in his music, as if tapping into the universe still ringing from its creation. If she were here to soak it up, it would leave him weak for days. If she wasn't, the expended emotion would linger in his rooms, bathing his soul in what was akin to an extended aura. Not exactly feng shui, but more of a lingering footprint of emotion that could alter moods even days later.

It was what had attracted her to him from the first.

"Work's going great," he said, leaning back and away to look at the coffeepot. "There's a concert next month, and it looks like I'll be ready."

As long as you don't take my strength, Mia could almost hear him finish in his mind.

"I'm sorry," she breathed, starting to lose her upright posture and her eyes beginning to swim as they looked at his instrument propped lovingly in a corner. She could feel a puddle of intensity on the couch from earlier this morning, and she hardened herself to ignore it. If she went to sit in it, it would warm her like a sunbeam.

"I don't mean to take so much from you," she said. A single tear slipped down, and Tom moved his chair to hers. His long arms enfolded her, and her pulse raced from the love swirling through her aura, seeping into her despite her trying to stop it.

"Mia," he crooned, and she held her breath, stiff and resolved to not take it, but it was hard. So hard.

"Don't cry," he soothed. "I know you can't help it. It must be hell to be a banshee."

"Everyone I love dies," she said bitterly into the soft depth of his shirt as the guilt of three hundred years of existence rose anew. "I can't come back here. I'm making you ill. I have to leave and never come back."

With an abrupt motion, she broke from him. She stood, panic an unusual showing on her usually collected, proud face. *What if he told her to leave?* Tom stood with her, and as she reached for her coat, he pulled her back.

"Mia," he said, giving her a little shake. "Mia, wait!"

Head lowered, she stopped, allowing his fear to coat her in a soothing sheen like fragrant lemon oil, and she felt her hunger jealously claim it. It was bitter after the exquisite airy lightness of love, but she took it. Stronger in body and resolve, she pulled her head up to see him through a haze of unshed tears.

"You are so beautiful," he said, wiping a tear away with a thumb. "We will find a way to make this work. I recover faster every time."

He didn't, and Mia dropped her gaze at the wishful lie.

"There has to be a way," he said, holding her close.

Head tucked under his chin, Mia felt a quiver start in the deepest part of her soul. *Again. It was going to happen again.* She had to be strong. Need would not rule her. "There is . . ." she said, her hand creeping up between them to hold the coin about her neck.

Tom pushed her back, his long face showing his shock. "There's a way? Why didn't you tell me before?"

"Because . . . because it won't work," she said, not wanting to deal with a false hope. "It's too cruel. It's a lie. If it doesn't work, you might die."

"Mia." His grip on her upper arms pinched. "Tell me!"

In a quandary, she refused to look at him. From the living room, the talk radio turned to a classical guitar, the intensity rising with her tension. "I have a wish . . ." she breathed, hand clenched about the pierced coin on its purple ribbon. It was how wishes were stored, and she had had it for years.

Braver now for having admitted it, she looked up, feeling his excitement roll off of him in a wave. It washed into her, and she forced herself to keep from taking it. The room grew richer with subtle shades of want and desire, purple and green, shifting about her feet like silk.

"Where . . . where did you get it? Are you sure it's real?"

Mia nodded miserably, opening her hand and showing him. "I got it from a vampire. I don't know why she gave it to me, except perhaps that I shamed her into trying to become who she wanted to be. But that was years ago. I was so bad that day, making her angry so that I could drink in her guilt. I shamed her, but I shamed myself more for telling her I couldn't love anyone without killing them, giving her my pain in return for her strength. Perhaps she wanted to thank me. Or perhaps she pitied me and wanted to give me the chance . . . to find love myself."

Steadying herself, Mia took a breath, refusing to let his hope warm her like the sun. She wouldn't take any more. She had to be strong. "I've had it all this time," she finished faintly.

Together they looked at it, small and innocuous in her palm.

"You waited?" he said in wonder, taking it up and running his fingertips over the detailed relief engraved on it. "Why?"

Mia blinked to keep from crying as she gazed up at him. "I wanted to fall in love first," she said, almost bewildered he didn't understand.

Tom's expression turned to one of pure, honest love, and Mia choked, muscles trembling from the effort to keep from taking it in. He gathered her to him, and she shook in the effort. Thinking it was tears, Tom shushed her, making things worse. It was almost too much, and Mia forced herself to stay, feeling the emotions in the room build and grow like a sheltering fog. It was like spreading a feast before a starving man, and she held back by her will alone. She would take no more from Tom.

"Use your wish," he said, and hope leapt in her. "Use it so we can be together."

"I'm afraid," she said, trembling. "Wishes don't always come true. Some things you simply can't have. If it doesn't work, then I not only lose you, but I lose my hope to ever have anyone." Vision swimming, she gazed at him. "I can't live without hope. It's all I have when I'm alone."

But Tom was shaking his head as if she was a child. "This is love, Mia," he said, both their hands holding the coin between them. "All things are possible. It's a wish. It has to work! You have to have faith."

A single tear slipped from Mia to make a cold trail down to her chin.

"Make the wish," he said, drying her cheek. "Wish that I can love you."

"What if it doesn't work?" she whispered, feeling the weight of the emotions in the room pressing on her skin in a deepening tingle.

His eyes full of his love for her, he timorously smiled with a raw hope. "What if it does?"

"Tom—" she protested, and he leaned over the space between them and covered her mouth with his.

Fear flashed through her, and she tried to pull back. It was too much. She wouldn't be able to stop herself. If he gave so freely, she had no way to stop it, and he would die!

But his lips were so soft on hers, and her breath caught at the depth of his feeling, his love, all for her, as encompassing and dark as a moonless night. *I was right,* she thought as she curved her arms around his neck and stretched to reach him. She couldn't stop herself, not when he was trying to give his love to her, and she soaked in the strength he had put in his kiss, almost crying at the sensation filling her. It was going to happen again. There was nothing that could stop it.

Tom broke their kiss, and she stumbled back, afraid.

"Please," he said, shaking from the energy he had given to her. "For us. I want to love you," he pleaded. "All of you in every way."

Mia leaned against the cheerful yellow wall of the kitchen, her pulse fast and her chin high. This was the best she had felt in weeks. She could take on the world, do anything. To have this every day would be the fulfillment of her deepest wish. Humans were so ignorant, taking for granted what they received from each other, never knowing the energy they passed between themselves. But the only reason she could see it was because it was what she needed to survive. She could drain the love from Tom like scooping water from a well, but it would kill him.

"I'm afraid," she whispered, though she stood powerful and strong.

Trembling, he stepped forward and took her hands. "Me too. I want you to be happy. Make the wish."

Mia's eyes filled, but they didn't spill over. "I wish," she said, her voice shaking, "that this man be protected from the pull of a banshee, that love will protect him and keep him safe, that no harm should come to him through my love for him." She held her breath, forcing herself to keep from taking even a wisp of emotion as a single tear fell to splash on their fingers, joined about the wish.

For a moment, they did nothing, waiting. The guitar on the radio changed to a full orchestra, and Tom looked at her, wide-eyed with his hope radiating to fill the room. Mia almost swooned at the effort to leave it untouched, to keep him strong. "Did it work?" he asked.

A lump in her throat, Mia steadied herself. "Kiss me?"

She tilted her head up as Tom leaned in, his long hands holding her shoulders. Dropping the coin to fall between them, she tentatively put her hands about his waist, unsure at how they felt there. She had never kissed him back. With a gentle sigh, Tom met her lips, and Mia went dizzy from the will needed to keep from soaking him in.

A wall, she thought, strengthening her own aura to keep them separate, gradually making it opaque, and then solid. She thickened her aura so that nothing could penetrate, nothing would come to her. He would fill the room with his love, and if she left it there, he would remain strong. His emotion would wash against her like water on a beach, and like a wave, it would ebb back to the ocean, undiminished.

And though it left her shaking in hunger, it worked.

Hope replaced her aching need in a rush, and somehow Tom felt it. Perhaps having been pulled upon so often by a banshee he had become sensitive to the emotions in a room. Perhaps because of his love for music he could read them easier. Whatever the reason, he knew she was taking nothing from him even as they shared their first passionate kiss.

Breaking from her, he stammered breathlessly, "Mia, I think it worked."

She smiled at him, a real one, and tamped down her excitement lest it break her control. "Do you?"

In answer, he pulled her to him, and with a tenderness born in the fragile beginnings of love, he cupped her face and kissed her again. Mia felt his lips on hers, but walled herself off, not allowing any of his emotion to stir her, even as his hands left her face and began to search, his beautiful long fingers tentatively seeking her skin beneath the shoulder of her dress. It had been in his eyes a long time and Mia welcomed it, even as she struggled to stay passive, to withhold her instincts to drive him into a deeper state of vulnerability. She wanted this. She wanted this so badly.

"Be careful . . ." she whispered, her heart pounding as his one hand found the buttons of the back of her dress, and she gasped at the wave of heat that his fingers, slipping the buttons free with a soft pop, made along her spine.

"I love you," he said, his voice husky and standing too close to see his face. "You can't hurt me. It worked, Mia. I can feel it. It worked."

He gently slid her dress from her shoulders, and the patterned silk fell softly to her waist to leave her shivering in the chill of the kitchen. She looked deeply at him, seeing her hope reflected in his eyes, feeling it pool about them like a heady wine. A tremble took her, but if it was from the new coolness on her skin or the effort she was exerting to let his love continue to build in the room, she didn't know. Maybe she didn't care.

He believed, and that was enough to soothe her fear.

She closed her eyes, and with that as an invitation, Tom pulled her to the living room. He sat on the edge of the couch amid the pooled emotion of his music, bringing her bare middle to his face as she stood before him, breathing her scent, his hands at her back. Her hands were among his hair, holding him there so he knew his touch was welcome.

"Mia," he whispered, and at the sensation of his words on her skin, she threw her head back to the ceiling. Desire cascaded from him, and she caught her breath, wire-tight as she refused to taste its strength, made doubly hard as it was directed to her. Her hands clenched once, and mistaking it for desire, he brought her to sit atop one knee.

He nestled his head between her small breasts, holding her to him with one arm as he nuzzled her, promising more. A wave of sexual heat hit Mia, and dizzy with her conflicting emotions, a slip of his need cracked the barrier she had made of her aura. Groaning, she went limp, basking in the depth of it. He responded by taking her in his mouth, pulling, tugging, not aware that she was growing tense with a hunger older than his religion.

"Tom, stop," she breathed, but he didn't. It was too late. He was filling the room with his desire. It would be up to her to keep from killing him outright, to take everything he was giving her. She could do this. It would end well.

His breath grew heavy, falling into a deliberate pace. Mouth never leaving her, he fumbled with the rest of her dress. It slipped to the floor at her feet when she leaned into him, pushing him back into the couch. Shifting his weight, he moved her, settling her light weight into the cushions and holding himself above her.

He pulled back, strong and dangerous with the heat of his emotions falling from his hands to warm her. She gazed at him in a bewildered haze, struggling to keep even the smallest bit from getting through to her again. She loved seeing him like this, strong and alive, and she reached up to undo the buttons of his shirt.

It was a bold move for her, for despite her confidence, she had little experience with men. Usually they were dead by this point.

Tom's smile grew gentle as he saw her fingers tremble, and as she got the last of the buttons free, he worked his pants from himself, easing down beside her. The rain was a hush against the glass, insulating them from the world.

Softer, more gently now as if knowing how rare this was, Tom caressed her middle with all the skill of a musician pulling a gentle note into life. She sighed, feeling his touch crack her aura. Everywhere his fingers alighted, every stroke he made, melted through the barrier she had made to give her jolts of his passion and desire, filing her with an almost never-tasted depth of feeling.

She moaned, and he lowered his head to take her breast again. A flash of need struck through her, and blood pounding, her hands darted into his hair, pressing him into her. Spurred on, he became aggressive. The pinch of teeth was like knives in her, slicing through her defenses to lay her bare to his lust. There was no love anymore. This was raw, animal hunger, and she relished it even as she strove to mend the tears in her aura he was making. She had to keep from taking it all. She shouldn't take anything. Even this little bit would show.

But his weight atop her was delicious, and the heat from his body drove everything else out. Mia shifted under him, tracing her hands down his back, feeling the muscle and bone, running lower as his mouth broke from her to rise and find her lips.

Her need quickened, and panting from effort, she met his eyes once, reading her desperation in her reflection in her gaze. And then he kissed her.

Once more he broke through her aura, and she moaned, clutching him and arching her back as he drove his tongue into her with an animalistic fervor. Wave after wave of strength flooded her. She simply couldn't shield herself from this intimate contact that reached far past her aura and into her soul. She was alive, alive and scintillating. But she was taking too much, and she felt it in his faltering heartbeat.

"No," she whispered, groaning in despair. "Tom, stop."

He wouldn't, sending a pulse of heat through her when his hands grew stronger on her, demanding. Fear that she couldn't do this, fear she couldn't wall herself from him and it would all be for naught, was a sharp goad, and with a sudden realization, she knew what she had to do.

Desperate to regain control and keep from draining him of his life force, she took his face in her hands and turned his mouth to hers. Panting from a desperate need, she held him to her, and forced a kiss. Again, his desire broke through her aura, flooding her with an almost unbearable emotion, but this time, she pushed her own desire into him—redoubled.

He gasped, his entire body shaking as it rested atop her.

Mia felt the heat of tears under her closed lids. It was hard, so hard to push what he had given her back into him. It went against every instinct she had, but clearly he felt it, and his kiss and his hands upon her grew rough, savage. He hadn't several centuries to learn how to control such an influx of power and strength as she had.

His grip upon her waist hurt, and she did nothing as he forced her legs apart. She wanted this. Exalting in the savage response she could invoke, she gave him more, feeling it leave her in a scintillating sensation of sparkles.

A guttural sound came from him, and Mia gasped in an exquisite pain as he entered her, pushing to fill all of her in one move. She groaned, arching into him, wanting this. Wanting it so badly that she gave him even more of herself.

Wave after wave of emotion drenched her, running off her to pool in the room as if to drown her in lust. He moved against her, dominating and aggressive. Every motion was like knives in her aura, breaking it, destroying what she had built to protect him. But she gave back more than she took, and he grew wilder, more demanding. He forgot all as he sweated above her, and she moaned with every breath, feeling an end coming, the wait an exquisite pain.

And in a sudden pulse, it broke upon them. A twisted groan eased from him, and he clenched her to him as wave after wave of ecstasy fell on them. Mia's barrier shattered. Gasping, she clutched at him, feeling his entire soul empty into her as she reached fulfillment, her body wracked with tremors as they hung unmoving in a haze of bliss.

Emotion shook the room in silent thunder only she could feel, and she almost passed out, taking breath after heaving breath until the sensation gave a final pulse and vanished.

"Tom," she panted, feeling his breath in her hair as he lay atop her, too spent to move. "Tom, are you okay?"

He didn't answer, and she pushed on his shoulder. "Tom?"

"I love you, Mia," he whispered, and he sighed, his full weight coming to rest against her.

"Tom!" she exclaimed, shoving him to the back of the couch and wiggling out from under him. The air felt thick, like sunshine pooled at the bottom of a valley, eddying about her feet with the heaviness of honey. She hadn't kept any of the emotion from the room. It was all here, cloying and thick, making her dizzy with a repressed need. But Tom . . .

Clutching her discarded dress, she stared as his aura went wispy and thin. An unbearable brightness began to emanate from him, and seeing it, a single tear trickled from her. Her hand trembling, she reached to touch him, shaking at the taste of his aura. It was fading, spreading out, becoming silver and thin to fill the room with unseen sparkles. Any other banshee would take it, gorge on the last life energy and dance in exaltation—but she didn't. Mia walled herself off, and a tear slipped down as she watched his life fill the room in a bright, ever so bright, light.

"Tom . . ." she whispered, weary even as her body still sang with the ecstasy he had filled her with. She had seen this before. He was dead. He was dead, and there was nothing that would bring him back. In that single moment of fulfillment, his emotion-rich aura had washed over her, laying his soul bare. She hadn't taken it, and it lay pooled about her feet to rise like a slow fog shifting from gold to purple. But she hadn't given him anything back, either, not like a human would have, protecting his soul until he gathered it back unto himself again.

Mia fell to her knees before him, still touching his shoulder warm with the last of his life. Misery twisted her delicate features, and then a sob broke free, harsh and pain-filled. It was followed by another, and she knelt beside him, her hand trembling as she gripped the wish that had caused his death. The tears falling into her lap turned from salt water to black crystal, the mark of a banshee's pain, and they fell soundlessly as she wept.

The glow from Tom's soul filled the room, and she closed her eyes, the light too painful for her pale eyes. The doors were shut, the windows locked, and though his soul was gone, the energy of his death lingered.

And Mia cried. She had killed him, sure as if she had driven a knife into his lungs. Sob after sob filled the apartment, her crystalline tears soaking up the energy of the room until the brightness dimmed to a memory, and then, even that vanished and the air was pure. The love was gone, the fear, the comfort, everything was gone, as if no one had loved, lived, and died sheltered by these walls. She kept none of his energy for herself. It had been hard, but to take it into herself had never been her intention.

Slowly, Mia's tears abated until her breathing steadied and her breath no longer came in racking gasps. The tears falling from her had eased from black to gray and were now perfectly clear, reflecting the dim sun from the ended rain. The emotions of the room were condensed and pooled in them. There would be nothing to link her to the death of this man, nothing to indicate that he had died in anything other than peaceful sleep.

Tom's body lay facedown on the couch, an arm trailing to brush the floor. Not looking at him, Mia slowly got dressed, drained and tired. She looked once at the wish about her neck, then left it to hang. The tears she gathered like photos of lost children, love and pain mixed in equal parts. If she didn't, someone would find them, recognize them, and she would be pulled in for questioning. The law knew what a banshee was capable of, and she would not allow herself to be jailed for this.

Fingers slow and clumsy, Mia felt the back of her dress to be sure the buttons were done up properly. The coffeepot was steaming, and she carefully put her empty cup away in the cupboard before unplugging the pot and setting his filled cup on the coffee table beside him. She turned the music down, and guilt prompted her to drape an afghan over him as if he was sleeping. His clothes went into the hamper.

Silent, she stood above him in her coat. "Goodbye, Tom," she whispered before gathering her groceries and quietly leaving.

Fatigue hit her anew when she found the sidewalk. The rain had stopped, and the sun was peeking past the heavy clouds. Fumbling, Mia put her sunglasses on. Traffic hissed wetly, and she breathed deep when a couple passed her, hotly discussing the amount of the tip one of them had left. It was a sour taste after Tom's love, and she let it eddy behind her unsipped.

She glanced at her watch and picked up the pace. Digging in a pocket, she found her wedding ring and put it back on. With a shamed slowness, her fingers slipped back into the pocket, running through Tom's life force, pooled and condensed.

Delicate features pulling into a grimace, Mia took out a handful of tears, slipping the lightest one between her lips and sucking guiltily on it. His strength poured into her, and her pace quickened, heels clicking smartly against the concrete shining with the new sun.

Stupid man, she thought as she waved and jogged to catch the bus. The wish did work. Well, perhaps it would be more fair to say it *had* worked. It had worked very well when she met Remus—savage, angry Remus whose psychotic rage had been strong enough to bring Holly into existence. The love had come later, until now, she, Holly, and Remus were a real family. Like any family on the street, and Mia was proud of it.

Holly was the first banshee child to know her father, plying him with innocent love and devotion. It had been watching father and daughter that Mia learned it was possible to force emotion back into a person, lulling them into thinking they were safe while making themselves more vulnerable. The child had, in her innocence, returned to her species all the cunning and power human laws had taken from them, and for that alone Holly was going to be revered among her own. Once she learned how to walk and talk, that is.

Breathless, Mia smiled at the bus driver as she just made it to the door, fumbling for her bus pass. Tom, dead in his apartment, was hardly a glimmer of memory as she settled beside a young man smelling of cologne and shedding lust Mia knew to be from a new girlfriend. Easing back, she soaked it in, sated.

Her lids fluttered as they rumbled over the railroad tracks, and she looked at her watch, mildly concerned. Remus would likely throw a bloody-hell tantrum that she was running late, being unable to go to work until she got home to watch Holly. But they would both enjoy her kissing him into a calm state, and he'd get over it.

Besides, little Holly was hungry, and it wasn't as if *he* could do the shopping.

THE BRIDGES
OF EDEN PARK

The death of Kisten was not just a shock to the readers, it was also one to me. He didn't actually find his end until the editorial rewrite of For a Few Demons More, *when I realized that Kisten's role was destined to become a dead end. I couldn't stand to see his character wither and die, so I made a clean end of it. "The Bridges of Eden Park" was my way to say good-bye, and was added to the mass market edition.*

I still miss Kisten.

"You have duck sauce on your face," Kisten said, smiling as he leaned into me to kiss it away.

"Kisten!" Flustered, I drew back. I wasn't a prude, but we were standing atop the footbridge at Eden park, and there was an old couple sitting across the shallow lake watching, as if we were on display.

"What . . ." he complained, contenting himself with wiping it away with his finger and making me roll my eyes when he suggestively licked it off.

A quiver rose through me, halfheartedly suppressed. Squinting from the sun, I tossed my head to the ancient-looking pair. "I'm not going to end up with my picture in the *Cincinnati Gazette* again. My mom gets that, you know."

Kisten turned to look, leaning against the bridge's cement railing with his blond eyebrows high in speculation. The wind coming up from the distant river ruffled his blond-dyed hair, and when he smiled with half his face, he looked heart-stopping. God, what was it with vampires? When they were dead, they were attractive, but when there was a soul still attached . . . Damn!

"They don't look like the paparazzi," Kisten said as he turned back, giving me a slip of fang to think about. "I say we give them something to watch."

I was tempted, man was I tempted, but the memory of my picture under the what-not-to-wear-to-a-stakeout headline made me a wiser woman. I still didn't know who had taken it, and when I found out, I was going to put slugs in his or her glove box. Making a huff of negation, I angled too close for him to do anything, shifting my body into his and sending my arm about his waist. I rolled the bag of takeout down and handed it to him as a substitute for nibbling on my earlobe. He sighed at the mild rebuke, knowing it was a temporary stalemate. I'd pay him back after work.

Breakfast with Kisten could mean anything from fast food in his car to a three-course meal at the Carew Tower restaurant. Today it was Chinese at Eden park at noon. I didn't mind. With him managing the affairs of his imprisoned master vampire and me trying to maintain my independent runner firm, our time together was often taken in snatches. It had been my suggestion to eat here, seeing as I wanted to go to the nearby conservatory to pilfer some of the orchid pollen for a charm, and if Kisten was with me, no one would say boo if I was caught.

Orchid pollen, I thought, snuggling into the security of Kisten's arm over my shoulders as we leaned over the railing to look eight feet down into the fast moving water. I didn't think orchids even *had* pollen. But it was either I take my tiny makeup brush to the nearby conservatory or one of the local home improvement stores.

The water bubbling under the bridge into the large catch pond was soothing, and feeling Kisten relax against me, I sighed happily and breathed in the vampire incense he was unconsciously giving off. The rich, almost subliminal scent mixed with the sunshine and wind to give a sensation of quiet intensity. I trusted Kisten implicitly to not push his advantage as a vampire, but the potential was heady. Playing with fire, but it felt so good. Besides, as a witch, I wasn't without my own "evolutionary adaptations."

A faint smile quirked my lips. It was full summer, the sun was high, the wind was cool, and because I didn't have a job today, all I had to do was find orchid pollen. Nothing could possibly ruin my mood of contentment.

The soft hum of Kiṣten's phone vibrated through me, and I stiffened.

Well, that came pretty damn close.

Kisten shifted, and my jaw clenched. "You're not going to take that, are you?" I complained, then dropped with my arms over my chest when he edged out of my grip. "I never take calls when we're out."

His smile showed a glint of small fang. He wouldn't get the extended versions until he was really dead, but just that little glimpse started a quiver in my middle. Crap on toast, I couldn't stay mad at the man.

"You're not trying to run the city," he said as he pulled the tiny phone from a pocket and squinted at the screen.

"Run the city . . ." I put my elbows on the railing and looked away to give him some privacy. "You're not running the city; you're running a nightclub."

"In this case, it's the same thing." Kisten made a small sound of concern as he looked at the number. "It's my sister. You mind if I take a call from my sister?"

I straightened in surprise. I hadn't even known he had a sister. "Sure," I said. "I'll get us an ice cream."

"Don't leave. She probably just wants a number." Kisten set the takeout on the railing and opened the phone. "Hi, Chrissie," he said, and then his brow furrowed. "Where are you?"

My good mood hesitated, then worsened when Kisten peered past me at the distant road beyond the open space where people walked their dogs and flew kites.

"Shit," he swore softly, his eyes pinching in concern. "Why didn't you go to Piscary's?" His lips pressed tight, and he put a hand to his head. "For Christ's sake, Chrissie, what do you think I can do?"

He paused to listen, and the incense coming from him grew strong, taking on a sharper scent, aggressive. His eyes, too, were going black in anger as his pupils dilated. "Is he okay?" he asked softly. "No, you did okay. I'm at the bridge. Can you see me?"

Now I was really concerned, and I followed Kisten's gaze across the open park. There was a young woman in a short business dress in heels trudging over the grass with a towheaded little boy in tow. She had a phone to her ear. *Kisten's sister?* The woman was yelling, her pace quickening as she looked over her shoulder. I could almost hear her. The little boy holding her hand had to move fast to keep up, but if he was Kisten's nephew, he was a living vampire and could probably run faster than me, even if he did look about six.

"I see you," Kisten said, tension making his muscles hard. "I'll talk to you in a minute." My pulse fast when he closed the phone and turned to me. "You need to go home."

Surprised, I dropped back a step. "If your sister is in trouble, I can help. It's what I do for a living. What's the problem?"

He hesitated as if to demand I leave, then exhaled. His fingers trembled when he took my upper arm and leaned close, but his gaze never left the edges of the park. His sister was still out of earshot, even for a vampire, but he leaned in close. "Short version," he said. "Seven years ago, my sister had a fling with a vampire out of Piscary's camarilla. Nine months later, she has a little boy, finds out Sean's married, comes home, and life goes on with the addition of a car seat in the back. A few months ago, the bastard's shadow junkie wife gets herself killed, which leaves Sean married but without a living heir, so he sues my sister to get custody."

I turned to glance at the pair of them. The little boy was in a school uniform, and he looked tired, head down as he lagged behind. "What an ass," I said, and Kisten bobbed his head in agreement.

"It gets better. He's got no right to the boy because it's been six years, but because Piscary is in jail, Sean thinks he can force the issue by way of possession. He just tried to snatch Audric from the schoolyard."

Aghast, I looked past Kisten to the little boy. "Holy crap! Is he okay?"

Kisten smirked and turned to the end of the bridge as his sister approached, her heels clicking as they found the paved path. "He's fine, but my sister is ready to rip someone's head off."

"I'll bet."

"She called the club and they told her where I was. I know they're following her." Kisten's hands clenched and released. "I hope they're following her."

He was itching for a fight. I'd seen this before. Kisten wasn't an especially big man, but he had a vampiric strength that he liked to use, and thanks to his occasional bouncer work, he knew how to use it.

"Kisten," I urged, not wanting to spend my afternoon in the emergency room, "all we need to do is convince him that Piscary in jail does not make his vampires easy pickings."

His eyes when they met mine were black, and though his emotion wasn't directed at me, I felt a slither of fear-laced anticipation tighten every muscle. "That's exactly what I intend to do," he said in a flat voice.

I took a breath to protest, but the sharp click-clack of heels and the soft hiss of scuffing sneakers sounded against the cement footbridge. Kisten's sister was in her early thirties, maybe. She must have had Audric young, but most living vampires did in case of premature death. The few lines in her face were from stress and anger. Dressed in a trendy business suit, she gave the impression of a pissed CEO, dragging her unfortunate offspring along on a day-with-mommy-at-work excursion, powerful and harried all at the same time.

"Damn it, Chrissie," Kisten said as he gave her a hug. "I told you that Sean was scum."

The family resemblance was uncanny, save that she didn't dye her hair, letting the long, dark waves curl gently around her face. Anger was a dark sheen in her eyes, the pupils so large they looked black in the sun. She didn't let go of the little boy's hand as she embraced Kisten, her lips brushing his cheek for an instant. I could smell a whiff of citrus scented perfume.

"I love you, too," she said dryly as she dropped back. Her eyes flicked to me, then back to Kisten. "Thanks for helping me. They aren't far behind."

Her voice was strong, but I could hear fear in it, not for herself, but for her child. She looked at me again, and I stuck my hand out.

"I'm Rachel," I said, seeing as Kisten wasn't going to introduce us. "Kisten's girlfriend."

Her grip was tight and preoccupied. "Nice to meet you. You're a witch, aren't you?"

I nodded, not surprised she could tell. Vampires had better noses than just about any non-human species, apart from pixies. "Yup."

Kisten ruffled the little boy's hair and said, "Rachel has her own running firm with Ivy."

The woman actually blinked, and a thin rim of blue appeared around her pupil. "You live with Ivy? In that church? It is a true pleasure to meet you."

Her smile became a whole lot more . . . accepting, as if she was taking me serious now. Not as in "I want to take a bite out of you," but as an equal. It was a nice feeling—one I didn't get much.

Seeing that we weren't going to be at each other's throats—literally—Kisten dropped down on his knee to Audric's height. "Hey, Squirt. How you doing?"

The little boy looked up. There were tear marks on his cheeks, wiped away and probably vigorously denied. "Hi, Uncle Kisten," he said softly as he rubbed his arm where a handprint showed. "I don't feel so good."

Kisten rose with the youngster on his hip, and it surprised me how right he looked there. "I'm sorry," he said as he made a little hop to settle him. "Your mom and I are going to take care of that right now." He turned to me. "This is Ms. Rachel. Rachel, this is Audric."

I smiled, thinking he looked like Kisten. "Hi, Audric."

The boy turned away to hide his face in Kisten's neck.

"Audric," Kisten admonished in a very adult voice. "This is a very handsome woman. She's too old for you, but don't be shy. Her name is Rachel."

Chrissie put a hand to her hip. "Kisten . . ."

But Audric turned and gazed at me with big, beautiful blue eyes. His past tears made his eyelashes long and beautiful. "Hi, Ms. Rachel," he said, and I knew he was going to break hearts when he got older. Vampires make beautiful children, products of centuries of careful breeding by their long-lived masters who enjoy beauty and have the time to play with bloodlines like master artists play with pigments.

"That's better," Kisten said, and my gut twisted at the thought that Kisten was as much a product of Piscary's breeding as this child. "Never be afraid of beautiful women."

"Kisten..." Chrissie said again, her tone carrying a lot more impatience.

Kisten looked across the park, a hint of worry in his eyes. "There's always time to be polite," he said as he picked up the takeout and turned to the parking lot and my car. I didn't know how we were all going to fit. My car didn't really have a back seat.

But we stopped when the distinctive sound of a van door sliding open scraped through the peaceful afternoon. Beside my little convertible, five people were getting out of a white panel van. They were all dressed in suits and wore shades. Living vampires, and not from Cincinnati. Their stance of brash confidence screamed of being on someone else's ground but not giving a crap about it.

I turned the other way to find five men closing in from over the grassy knoll. "Too late," I whispered as the three of us came to a clustered halt on the highpoint of the wide footbridge.

Audric's eyes were huge, but he was silent. His mother took him from Kisten, managing his weight easily. "Don't start a fight," she said, fear in her voice.

Kisten turned to her. "How do you propose I keep him from taking Audric then?"

Think, Rachel, think. "Sharps?" I called out, wondering if the resident bridge troll I'd befriended when I worked for the I.S. might still be here. He'd help even if it was sunny—as long as the I.S. hadn't chased him out again. But there was no answering wispy gurgle or whoosh of water. We were on our own against ten living vampires. *Fair fight,* I thought, warming to the task, then realized I was standing over water. Damn it, I couldn't tap a ley line to do a line charm, and all my earth charms were in the car.

"Stop right there," Kisten said, hands extended both ways. His posture was hunched and he looked like a predator with his eager, black eyes. I felt the adrenaline dump into me, and I stepped from Chrissie to give myself room to move. I didn't have my charms, but I still had my fists and feet. *This is so not good. I have to get off this bridge.*

A thin man in a business suit pushed to the front of the group that had come over the grass. It had to be Audric's dad from the blond hair and facial structure. "That's my boy," he said simply, pointing to show he was wearing too many rings. "He comes with me."

Good, I thought. *No monologue. Right to it. I had things I had to do today.*

Audric shivered, and his mother gripped him tighter. Kisten let his arms drop now that both groups had halted at the ends of the bridge. "I'm his uncle," he said softly, his voice making the sensation of ice down my spine. "If you think you can take him, try."

Sean looked past us to the five vamps from the van. I moved my fingers as if I was starting a ley line charm, and he pressed his lips together, recognizing it.

"You feel lucky?" Kisten added, almost laughing.

This wasn't good. This was *so* not good. We were standing here on a bluff. Me being beaten up was one thing, but that kid could not be taken. Worried, I sidled closer to Kisten. "Kisten?" I hedged. "Tell me you ate your Wheaties today."

He glanced at me then back to Sean. "Relax. I already hit 911 on my phone. Set a circle and we'll wait them out until the I.S. gets here."

"I'm over water, Kisten," I said pointedly. "I can't."

There was the slightest tick to his eye, but he didn't move otherwise. "Oh," he said without moving his lips. "We have a problem then."

Chrissie's eyes were black again as she shifted closer, and sensing a new weakness, the group from the van took a collective step forward.

"Delay them," I said. "He thinks I can tap a ley line, or he'd be on us by now. Maybe we can get off the bridge."

Kisten's sister took a deep breath. Her face was pale as she saw her world teetering. I was getting the distinct impression she would die twice before giving Audric up. But she was a Phelps, and she was thinking. "He's mine," she said loudly. "I never would have slept with you if I knew you were married, you lying bastard."

Sean copped an attitude, with all the anger and hurt he had never let go. "Chrissie—"

"You never wanted him!" she screamed, and I wondered if the old couple had left. "Get the hell out of Cincy before you wake up dead!"

"Lovely as ever, little bitch."

I stiffened, but Kisten stepped between us, his phenomenal people skills, a mix of charm and vampire charisma, coming to the forefront. "And I'm a low-life Romeo," he said, self-deprecatingly. "Sean, it's not going to happen. Leave under your own power, or limping. I don't care."

Sean stepped forward, and Kisten raised a warning hand. "Put one foot on this bridge, and it will get ugly," he promised, and Sean stopped from the force of his words alone. "You and Chrissie need to talk."

"Kisten!" his sister complained, and I watched both groups of vampires relax at the apparent mutiny among the enemy. The thing was, it was all contrived.

"You screwed up, Chrissie!" Kisten shouted, but his lips were quirking in a faint smile only we three could see. "Talk to him. Find out what he wants."

Get one of us the hell off this bridge, I thought to myself.

"He wants my baby!" she said, clutching Audric.

"Well, it's his boy."

"He abandoned us!" she shrieked, and I risked a look to see that the old couple on the bench was still there.

"You left him, which is why he's here with his balls in his hands, begging."

Sean stiffened, and seeing he was pushing it, Kisten eased back. "Give the guy a break," he added. "Talk to him."

Chrissie was one hell of an actress, but still my heart was pounding when she looked at the scum backed by his ten guys. "What do you want, Sean?" she asked. "Joint custody?"

He laughed. "Sure. Joint custody," he said, telling me if he touched the boy, he would be gone forever.

"You just want him because your hickey-sucker died," she said bitterly. "Go to hell."

The men from the van inched closer. "Can we please get off this bridge?" I muttered.

Kisten eyed them, then nodded almost imperceptibly. "Sean, get back. We're coming off the bridge to talk."

We took a step forward, then froze at the sight of three weapon muzzles pointing at us. *Oh, how nice. Vampires with guns.*

"Stay there," Sean said. "You and the witch don't move. Chrissie and the boy, come here."

My eyebrows rose. *Right . . .* Just how stupid did he think we were? But if he wanted me to stay where I was, he had figured out I was at least partially helpless here. Crap.

Chrissie looked pained, and Kisten reached out to take Audric. "Just talk to him, sis," he said softly. "The I.S. is bound to show up eventually."

God, what I would give for my backup right now.

Audric went easily into Kisten's arms, and I wondered at the complete trust the boy had, coupled with his instinctive understanding of how deep into the shit we all were. He was terrified, but there were no tears, just trust that we would die for him. Well, Kisten and Chrissie might. Dead was dead for me, so I was going to be a little more careful.

"Audric stays," Kisten said as Chrissie walked slowly toward her ex, and Sean grinned.

"Can't blame me for trying," he said.

Can't blame me for wanting to jam my elbow into your nose, I thought, my knees starting to shake from the accumulated adrenaline.

Chrissie got to the end of the bridge and waited for them to back off a good eight feet before walking between them. I didn't feel any less secure standing here with only Kisten. Chrissie didn't know how to fight, so her help would have been chancy at best.

Kisten jiggled Audric as his mother moved a small distance away and started to talk under the trees. My tension eased into a ready state, and I started to notice what was going on outside of the narrow space around us. The park was empty but for those two old people on the bench. The wind was just as fresh and the sun just as bright, but the fear in that little boy was enough to chill the strongest soul.

The vampires from the van had dropped back, and I watched them close to make sure no one slid under the bridge to take us from surprise. That they might was probably why Sean agreed to this . . . parley.

"How you holding up, Sport?" Kisten said as he sat Audric on the wide cement railing.

The boy blinked several times, and took a deep breath, relaxing as he intentionally took in the pheromones Kisten was giving off. "I'm scared," he admitted when he could.

"That's okay." Kisten laid a hand on his shoulder. "This is scary shit. But your mom is smart. She takes good care of you, right?"

He nodded.

"Good." Kisten looked over at his sister, violently arguing with Sean. "She loves you very much. Never forget that. No matter what happens."

It sounded like final advice, and that had me worried. There was a good chance the I.S. wouldn't respond, especially if Piscary had arranged the abduction himself, either to bring Chrissie in line or to cement relations with the outside camarilla of vampires. In that case, we were really on our own.

Audric squinted in the sun up at me, then Kisten. "Are you and Ms. Rachel going to get married?" he asked from nowhere.

My mouth dropped open, and Kisten started. "Ah, not today, Sport. Maybe someday."

Oh God. I'd forgotten kids were like that, and I warmed.

"Do you kiss her?" the boy asked.

Kisten grinned as his hand fell from Audric's shoulder. "Every chance I get."

Audric thought about that for a moment as he picked at a bit of mortar and dropped it into the water for the bridge troll to eat. "Mommy says if you love someone, and you like kissing them, and they don't ever, ever hurt you, you should marry them."

If only it was that simple.

Audric squinted up at me, and I panicked, not knowing what had come into that little brain and was now going to come out his mouth. "Do you hurt Uncle Kisten?" he asked.

I opened my mouth to answer—it was a disturbing question for anyone but a vampire child—but Kisten beat me to it. "Only my heart, Audric," he said. "Ms. Rachel is like the sun. See her sparkling there with the wind in her hair and fire in her eyes? You can't catch the sun. You can only feel its touch on your face. And if you get too much of it, it burns you."

It had been nice until the end, and I made a sour face.

"Maybe you should kiss her in the dark," was Audric's next thought, and I smiled.

"That's a good idea," Kisten said as he handed him the bag of cold takeout. "Why don't you feed the ducks."

It was a good distraction, but that frightened, brave little boy kept an eye on his mother the entire time he coaxed the ducks in. He was wise beyond his six years, and I wondered what his life had been like so far, protected by his mother, shielded from a master vampire's view. Seeing. Knowing. Helpless.

I watched Kisten break apart the folded bit of bland pastry for him, knowing that their bond went deeper than uncle and nephew. They were the same, only at different places, and seeing them together, the sun glinting on their hair and their thoughts on their future as they calmly fed the ducks, I felt sick.

Kisten felt my misery, and he turned. Seeing my expression, he murmured a few words to Audric and left him with a handful of fried bread.

"The sun, eh?" I said as he stood beside me.

Kisten brushed by that, telling me how worried he was. "Sharps isn't here, is he?"

I shook my head, watching Audric feed the ducks as his future hung in the balance of the next few minutes. "He looks a lot like you," I offered.

Kisten's brow smoothed to make him beautiful. "He's got the Phelps eyes."

"And his dad's hair," I added.

Wincing, Kisten ran a hand through his own dyed strands. "And his mother's smarts. God, I hate it when this happens. It's hard to keep the beautiful children from them."

He meant a master vampire, not Sean. And my face went cold as I finally understood what was going on. That's why Sean had taken an interest. Not for him, but for his master. Audric was going to be a present. A freaking gift. "He's six years old!" I hissed, clutching my arms around my middle.

His eyes on his feet, Kisten nodded. "That's why he had an affair with Chrissie. He wanted a pretty child to offer his master other than his own."

Frantic, I shifted, frustrated and helpless. This was not going to happen. It wasn't!

"A pretty child?" I exclaimed, then dropped my voice. Audric was scared enough.

Kisten pulled his gaze up. I could see an old fear, shame, maybe, deep in his thoughts. "A master vampire won't touch a child," he said, "but they do like to find them early so as to have a say in their upbringing. Make sure they take the right classes, make the right friends." Kisten threw a chunk of fried bread at a duck and it splashed short.

Generally make them powerless while giving them the trappings of importance, I thought. It was Kisten all over, and the first real glimmer of his past was scaring me shitless.

"Kisten, I'm sorry," I said as I reached to touch his arm.

He was smiling with old pain as he met my gaze. "Don't be. I love my life."

But still . . . there was regret.

"I have a good life," he said, his gaze pinched as it landed on Audric, seemingly oblivious but taking it all in. "I have a lot of opportunities that I otherwise wouldn't."

"And yet you're fighting to keep Audric away from them."

Kisten's jaw clenched, then relaxed. "Audric is smart," he said softly. "He doesn't need a master vampire to open doors for him. He's better than that." He threw another piece of bread, landing it far farther than I could throw and making the ducks work for it. "He's the son I'm never going to have, and I don't want him to go through the hell I did."

Stomach queasy, I trailed my hand down his arm and slipped my fingers into his. No children. Because of Piscary. Piscary wanted a child from Kisten to further his plans, and saying no was Kisten's last bastion of defiance, one small way to say that he didn't belong to Piscary—even if he did.

For all the power and privilege Piscary gave Kisten, it came with a cost that his children might be called on to pay. And Kisten didn't want Audric to pay it. Feeling ill, I gave Kisten's hand a squeeze. "I'm sorry," I whispered.

"I'm happy. Shut the hell up, Rachel," he said, his fingers gentle in mine.

Audric turned to us, out of fried bread to feed the ducks. Kisten opened the bag for the rest, and together we went forward while the adults argued. The sun was warm, and for a moment, we could laugh and pretend that the world was an innocent place where the only thing we needed to worry about was if feeding ducks bread softened with duck sauce was a mild form of cannibalism.

Maybe that was one of the reasons Kisten worked so hard to keep it going between us, I thought, laughing as a duck went completely under water to pop up somewhere else. There would never be any children between Kisten and me. Any child would be adopted or engendered from a one-night-stand with a witch, and free of Piscary's attentions. Seeing Audric beside Kisten, beautiful in the sun and their easy companionship born from knowing they both shared the same curse of great power granted borne in great degradation. Sacrifice. Kisten would sacrifice all for his nephew—anything to prevent him from living the hell he endured. It was touching, beautiful, and tragic all at the same time, and I was almost in tears for lost chances and histories that could not be fixed.

Chrissie's shout of pain lanced through us, and adrenaline surged painfully. Kisten scooped Audric up before I even turned, and I stared aghast at Sean pinching Chrissie's arm as he held her against a tree.

"Damn him," Kisten swore, and I suddenly found Audric in my arms. Kisten had abandoned us.

"No weapons!" Sean shouted. "He's no good dead!"

That was just sick. I sucked in my breath and slid Audric down to stand behind me. "Audric," I said as suddenly every vampire was moving with a slow pace of a predator angling for an ambush. "Do everything I say as fast as you can. Kisten trusts me. I can't help you unless you trust me too."

His little hand in mine brought a surge of strength and defiance I could only guess came from a maternal source. One I never knew I had. But it felt damn good, and I'd use it.

There would be, I thought as I scanned the park, backing up until we found the waist-high railing. Kisten was fighting them off his sister, and the two of them, clearly the bigger threat, were pulling half the vampires away from Audric and me. Five vampires on a bridge, I might be able to handle. I had to be able to handle, at least long enough to get to land where I could tap a line and do some bad-ass witchy stuff. Kisten had pulled half the threat away, not abandoned us.

Audric was between me and the railing, and falling into a fighting stance, I lifted my chin. It was all the invitation the first vamp needed.

He came at me, hands reaching. If not for my sparring with Ivy, I'd never have had a chance. I extended my hands for him to grab, and when he did, I shoved my right arm under his, taking his left arm with it. In one smooth motion, I dove under his extended arm, turned, and snapped his elbows against each other. There was a sickening crack, and part of me wondered that it had even worked as I moved to finish the move. And as the vampire howled in pain, I used his own momentum to flip him over the railing and into the shallow water.

The splash rose up the eight feet. Audric was clutching the railing, peering through the openings with awe and surprise. Below him in six inches of water, the vampire tried to get up without using his arms. Pain showed in every motion as he staggered to the shore. The van started, and I spun to make sure Audric was with me.

"Wow," I whispered, rubbing my sore wrists, "it worked." I'd never had the chance to use that particular move with the strength of adrenaline behind me, and I was impressed. And a little scared. But there were two now coming at me together. I couldn't match two. It had been luck I had bested one. I needed something at my back besides a stone railing.

Pulse pounding, I scanned the park. Nothing. Just the bridge we were on. *Just the bridge* . . . "Jump off the bridge, Audric!" I shouted when an idea came to me. "Land on that bastard. Then tuck-in under the bridge. Wait for me."

I heard his scramble up and over, watched his progress by following the eyes of the vampires left, listened and smiled at the pained huff of sound coming from the man he landed on.

"You two get the van started," the front vamp said, then touched his companion's shoulder. "You're with me."

The two vampires rushed me. Gasping, I flung myself over the railing, palms scraping on the cement. I landed on the vampire already down there, and he screamed in agony. "Sorry," I panted, then rolled off him. Twin splashes of sound told me the two vampires had followed me. Water soaked me, and heavy with it, I staggered up.

"Audric!" I shouted, then lunged to the small shadow hiding under the bridge. "Good boy," I said, pushing him behind me until his back was against the upward curving side of the bridge. He was shaking, and I vowed they wouldn't touch him. Not if I had breath in me.

Kisten was shouting from somewhere, and over that was the faint wail of a siren. The vampires facing me here heard it too. They exchanged looks and grinned to show their fangs.

"Get my boy!" Sean yelled from the top of the bridge, and the two men with their feet in the water attacked.

"Oh, hell no!" I shouted, hitting the first one in the gut, but the second one had me.

Agony flamed in my arm as it was twisted backward, and someone's breath was in my ear. "Got you now, witchy," that same someone said.

Feet almost off the rocky streambed, I hung in his grip, teeth clenched and straining. Before me, Audric fought like a child as the other vampire tucked him under his arm. *This is not going to happen.*

"Let me down!" I demanded, and the one holding me laughed. Right until I slammed my head back into his teeth.

Screaming, he threw me away from him. I hit the shore hard, my right palm catching most of the impact on a smooth rock. Pain flared to my skull. They were laughing. Audric was yelling in fear. Slowly I got up and turned around, one foot in the water, the other on the shore. Throwing me away had been a big mistake. Huge. Up to now, I was just a woman with a good roundhouse. Now I was a woman with a good roundhouse and a hell of a lot of magic.

"Idiot," I said, smiling grimly, and then I tapped the nearest ley line.

I was almost standing in it, which was good since it was hardly a line at all, weak from the manmade lake running right over it. I yanked on the line, demanding more, and the power surged as if the distant ends curled in on themselves, condensing. My fingertips tingled, and if my hair weren't sopping wet, it would be floating from static. Something must have showed in my eyes because the one holding Audric paled. The sirens were getting closer, but they were not close enough.

"You first," I said, pointing. "Put him down or—"

He didn't listen. I heard a van door open and someone shouting to hurry up. They both went for it.

"*Consimilis calefacio!*" I shouted, and a wave of steam rose up between them and the bank when a bathtub size portion of water flashed to boiling. I staggered at the draw of energy through me needed to do it, but they halted, shocked and surprised. Pushing myself up, I screamed, "Drop the kid, or I'll turn your balls into apple dumplings!"

That they listened to, though I didn't know the charm to heat living tissue. That would be a black curse, and despite what the papers said I was still a white witch. Audric cried out when they dropped him and he fell into the cool water that had replaced the evaporation. The vampires ran like bunnies on fire, up the steep embankment and out of my line of sight. The van peeled out with a scattering of stones, and I heard the wailing of an I.S. cruiser tear through the lot following it. Another followed close behind, and the distinctive sound of an I.S. radio added to the din.

"Audric!" Chrissie screamed, the heartrending sound tearing through me. She thought she had lost him. "Kisten, they have my baby. They have my little boy!"

I stumbled into the water toward Audric. Immediately my connection to the line, weak at best, dropped. Along with it went my strength. It was over. That fast, it was done. Smiling, I held my hand out to Audric, stunned and staring at me with wide eyes. "Come on, Audric," I said, holding my hand out.

Audric's gaze went to the bridge overhead. "Look out!" he cried, and I jumped back, pulse jerking. Sean hit the shallow water in a belly flop right where I had been. Groaning, he levered himself up. Blood spurted from his nose and made a red stream. Gasping, I looked to see Kisten above me at the railing, smiling.

"Thanks," I said, shaking from the adrenaline spike, and he grinned wider.

"I've got your back, Rachel," he said. "Never forget that. I knew where you were the entire time." His eyes went to Audric. "Come on, Sport. Your mom's about ready to have a cow."

I held my hand out to the little boy. Audric looked at it for a moment, then smiled. The soft feel of his fingers in mine was better than a letter of thanks from the head of the I.S. tower. He was going to be okay. They wouldn't be back. The I.S. had showed, meaning we were under the grace of Piscary and were protected. Well, at least Chrissie and Audric were. I doubt very much that Piscary would let the I.S. save my butt, seeing as I was the one who put him in jail.

I pulled Audric up in a splash of water, and together we slogged our unsteady way to the opposite shore. "We're down here!" I shouted, and Chrissie's cry of joy was enough to bring tears to my eyes.

"Audric!" she exclaimed, sliding down the embankment and pulling him to her. His hand slipped from mine, and I felt an unexpected feeling of loss. I stood alone as she held him close, crying and rocking him as if he was back from the dead. On the bridge were two uniformed I.S. agents, weapons pointed at Sean.

The vampire pulled himself up out of the water, disgust in his every motion. Water dripped from him as he wiped the blood from his nose with a wet handkerchief, then he let it drop to float dramatically away into the deeper water. He glanced up at the officers, and waved bitterly to acknowledge their demand to get out of the water with his hands on the back of his head. Another officer waited at the shore, and the sound of the vamp-proof cuffs ratcheting close never sounded better.

"It's a sad day when a master vampire uses a witch to keep his children safe," Sean snarled as he was led away, and my gaze shot to Kisten, still at the apex of the bridge. *Sean thought I worked for Piscary?*

I laughed, and the wary slant to Sean's eyes grew deeper, more threatening.

Chrissie was making a very loud statement to the officer before her, using lots of adjectives and clutching Audric to her so tight that the little boy was squirming with little complaints. I slogged to the embankment, bone tired. Kisten was there, and he helped me up until I was leaning against the bridge support. I gingerly felt my arm for the bruise that was bound to show. So much for a quiet breakfast at the park.

"I never thought I'd be happy to see the I.S.," I said as I dug my soggy ID out of a back pocket and flashed it at them. Satisfied, they moved off to give me space to collect myself before I made a statement. "Thanks for getting that last one."

Kisten put an arm around me, soggy clothes and all. "I told you, Rachel," he said in my ear to start a warm spot in me. "I've got your back. Nothing alive will ever hurt you if I have breath in me. And nothing dead will hurt you if I don't."

He leaned in to give me a kiss, and this time, I let him, my lips moving against his to turn it into a spine-tingling, stomach quivering kiss that delved deep and set my pulse racing.

The old couple on the bench gave a cheer, and I broke from him, embarrassed. One of them had a camera phone, and I looked away when it flashed.

"Crap," I muttered, then thought, *the hell with it.* I could feel Kisten press against me through my wet clothes. Eyes closing, I wrapped my arms about his neck and kissed him again, deeper.

"Apple dumplings?" he murmured when the kiss broke, buzzing my ear with his lips to make the tingles his kiss started flash anew, and I smiled.

"They're really good for breakfast," I said, and with his arm over my shoulder, we hobbled back to my car.

LEY LINE DRIFTER

Ley Line Drifter *was first published in the anthology* Unbound. *I had been playing with the idea of dryads for years and thought that it was time to see how the Hollows could shape the concept of tree spirits. Though trees abound in Cincinnati, the idea of using a statue as a prison caught my interest, and from there the usually passive, feminine image of a tree spirit evolved into more of a savage, innocent Amazon.*

This was also a chance to see the world from Jenks's eye, something I'd wanted to do for a long time. Throwing Bis into the mix was the icing on the cake. Rachel still doesn't know how her smallest spell pot got dented, and she probably never will.

 ONE

The dim gloom was heavy in the lower level of Jenks's stump, only the high ceiling of the cavernous great room still holding the fading haze of the setting sun. Working by the glow of his dragonflylike wings, Jenks hovered in the wide archway leading to the storerooms, feet dangling and shoulders aching as he smoothed a nick from the lintel. The smell of last year's garden drifted up past him: musty dandelion fluff, dried jasmine blossoms, and the last of the sweet clover used for their beds. Matalina was a traditionalist and didn't like the foam he'd cut from a sofa he'd found at the curb last fall.

The rasping of his lathe against the living oak only accentuated the absence of his kids; the quiet was both odd and comforting after a winter spent in his human-size partner's church. Shifting his lower wings to push the glowing, silver pixy dust upward to light his work, Jenks ran a hand across the wood to gauge the new, decorative curve. A slow smile spread across his face.

"Tink's panties, she'll never know," he whispered, pleased. The gouge his daughter had made while chasing her brother was now rubbed out. All that was needed was to smooth it, and his beautiful and oh-so-clever wife would never know. Or at least she'd never say anything.

Satisfied, Jenks tilted his wings and darted to his tools. He would've asked his daughter to fix the archway, but it took cold metal, and at five Jolivia didn't yet have the finesse to handle toxic metal. Spilling more dust to light his well-used tools, he chose an emery board, swiped from Rachel's bathroom.

Late March, he thought as he returned to his work, the sparse sawdust mixing with his own pixy dust as he worked in the silence and chill. Late March, and they still hadn't moved back into the garden from Rachel's desk, on loan for the winter. The days were warm enough, and the nights would be fine with the main hearth lit. Cincinnati's pixies were long out of hibernation, and if they didn't move into the garden soon, someone might try to claim it. Just yesterday his kids had chased off three fairy scouts lurking about the far graveyard wall.

Breath held against the oak dust, Jenks wondered how many children he would lose this fall to romance and how it would affect the garden's security. Not much now, with only eight children nearing the age of leaving. Next year, though, eleven more would join them, with no newlings to replace them.

A burst of anxious motion from his wings lit a larger circle to show the winter-abandoned cushions about the main central hearth, but it wasn't until a sudden commotion at the ground-floor tunnel entrance that he spilled enough dust to light the edges to show the shelves, cupboards, and hooks built right into the living walls of the stump. "If there's no snapped wings or bones sticking out, I don't want to hear about it!" he shouted, his mood brightening as he recognized his children's voices.

"Papa. Papa!" Jerrimatt, one of his youngest sons, shouted in excitement as he darted in, trailing silver dust. "We caught an intruder at the street wall! He wouldn't leave, even when we scared him! He said he wanted to talk to you. He's a poacher, I bet, and I saw him first!"

Jenks rose, alarmed. "You didn't kill him, did you?"

"Naww," the suddenly dejected boy said as he tossed his blond hair in a credible mimicry of his dad. "I know the rules. He had red on."

Exhaling, Jenks let his feet touch the ground as, in a noisy mob, Jack, Jhem, Jumoke, and Jixy pushed a fifth pixy wing-stumbling into the room.

"He was on the fence," Jixy said, roughly shoving the stranger again to make his wings hum, and she touched her wooden sword, ready to smack him if he made to fly. She was the eldest in the group, and she took her seniority seriously.

"He was looking at our flower beds," Jumoke added. The dark-haired pixy's scowl made him look fiercer than usual, adding to his unusual dark coloring.

"And he was lurking!" Jack exclaimed. If there was trouble, Jack would be in it.

The five were on sentry detail this evening, and Jenks set the emery board aside, eyeing his own sword of pixy steel nearby. He would rather have it on his hip, but this was his home, damn it. He shouldn't need to wear it inside. Yet here he was with a strange pixy in his main room.

Jerrimatt, all of three years old, was flitting like a firefly on Brimstone. Reaching up, Jenks caught his foot and dragged him down. "He is wearing red," Jenks reminded him, glad they hadn't drawn blood from the hapless pixy, wide-eyed and scared. "He gets passage."

"He doesn't want passage," Jerrimatt protested, and Jixy nodded. "He was just sitting there! He says he wants to talk to you."

"Plotting," Jixy added suspiciously. "Hiding behind a color of truce. He's pixy trash." She threatened to smack him, stopping only when Jenks sent his wings clattering in disapproval.

The intruder stood with his feet meekly on the floor, his wings closed against his back, and glancing uneasily at Jumoke. His red hat of truce was in his hands, fingers going around and around the brim. "I wasn't plotting," he said indignantly. "I have my own garden." Again, his gaze landed on Jumoke in question, and Jenks felt a prick of anger.

"Then why are you looking at ours?" Jhem demanded, oblivious to the intruder's prejudice against Jumoke's dark hair and eyes. But when Jhem went to push him, Jenks buzzed a warning again. Eyes down, Jhem dropped back. His children were wonderful, but it was hard to teach restraint when quick sword-point justice was the only reason they survived.

At a loss, Jenks extended a hand to the ruffled pixy as his children watched sullenly. The pixy buck before him looked about twelve or thirteen, old enough to be on his own and trying to start a family, married by the clean and repaired state of his clothes. He was healthy and well-winged, though they were now blue with the lack of circulation and pressed against his back in submission. The unfamiliar sword in Jumoke's grip led Jenks to believe the intruder's claim to having a garden was likely not an exaggeration, even if it was fairy steel, not pixy. The young buck wasn't poaching. So what did he want?

Jenks's own suspicions rose. "Why are you here?" he asked, his focus sliding again to his own sword, set carelessly next to his tools. "And what's your name?"

"Vincet," the pixy said immediately, his eyes roving over the sunset gray ceiling. "You live in a castle!" he breathed as his wings rose slightly. "Where is everyone?"

Vincet, Jenks thought, wary even as he straightened with pride at Vincet's words concerning his home. A six-letter name, and out on his own with cold steel. Pixies born early into a family had short names, those born later, the longest. Vincet was the fifth brood of newlings in his family to survive to naming. That he had a blade and a long name to his credit meant that his birth clan was strong. It was the children born late in a pixy's life that suffered the most when their parents died and the clan fell apart. Most children with names longer than eight letters never made it. Jerrimatt, though . . . Jenks's smile grew fond as he looked at the blond youngster scowling fiercely at Vincet. Jerrimatt, his birth brother, and both his birth sisters would survive. Matalina was stronger now that she wasn't having children anymore. One or two more seasons, and all her children would survive her. It was what she prayed for.

Not knowing why he trusted Vincet, Jenks gestured for his children to relax, and they began shoving one another. The earth's chill soaked into Jenks now that he wasn't moving, and he wished he'd started a fire.

"I heard you investigate things," Vincet blurted, his wings lifting slightly as the kids ringing him drifted a few paces back. "I'm not poaching! I need your help."

"You want Rachel or Ivy." Jenks rose up to show him the way into the church. "Rachel is out," he said, glad now he hadn't accompanied her on her shopping trip as she searched for some obscure text her demonic teacher wanted. She'd be in the ever-after tomorrow for her weekly teaching stint with the demon, and of course she'd waited until the last moment to find the book. "But Ivy is here."

"No!" Vincet exclaimed, his wings blurring but his feet solidly on the poker-chip floor, rightfully worried about Jenks's kids. "I want *your* help, not some lunker's. I don't have anything they'd want, and I pay my debts. They'll tell me to move. And I can't. I want you."

His kids stopped their incessant shoving, and Jenks's feet touched the cold floor. *A job?* he thought, excitement zinging through him. *For me? Alone?*

"Will you help me?" Vincet asked, the dust from him turning a clear silver as he regained his courage and his wings shivered to try and warm himself. "My newlings are in danger. My wife. My three children. I don't dare move now. It's too late. We'll lose the newlings. Maybe the children, too. There's nowhere to go!"

Newlings, Jenks thought, his focus blurring. A newborn pixy's life was so chancy that they weren't given names or considered children until they proved able to survive. To bury a newling wasn't considered as bad as burying a child. Though that was a lie. He and Matalina had lost their entire birthing the year they moved into the church, and Matalina hadn't had any more since, thanks to his wish for sterility. It had probably extended Mattie's life, but he missed the soft sounds newlings made and the pleasure he took in thinking up names as they grasped his finger and demanded another day of life. Newlings, hell. They were children, every one precious.

Jenks's gaze landed squarely on Vincet, assessing him. Thirteen, with a lifetime of responsibility on him already. Jenks's own short span had never bothered him—a fast childhood giving way to grief and heartache—until he'd seen the other side, the long adolescence and even longer life of the lunkers around them. It was so unfair. He'd listen.

And if he was listening, then he should probably make Vincet feel at home. As Rachel did when people knocked on her door, afraid and helpless.

A flush of uncertainty made his wings hum. "We're entertaining," he told his kids with a firmness he'd dredged up from somewhere, and they looked at one another, wings drooping and at a loss. Pixies didn't tolerate another on their land unless marriage was being discussed, much less invite him into their diggings.

Smiling, Jenks gestured for Vincet to sit on the winter-musty cushions, trying to remember what he'd seen Rachel do when interviewing clients. "Um, give me his sword, and get me a pot of honey," he said, and Jerrimatt gasped.

"H-honey . . ." the youngster stammered, and Jenks took the wooden-handled blade from Jhan. The fairy steel was evidence of a past battle won, probably before Vincet had left home.

"Tink's burned her cookies, go!" Jenks exclaimed, waving at them. "Vincet wants my help. I don't think he's going to run me through. Give your dad an ounce of credit, will you?"

His cursing was familiar, and knowing everything was okay, they dove for the main tunnel, chattering like mad.

"I brought you all up," he shouted after them, conscious of Vincet watching him. "You don't think I know a guest from a thief?" he added, but they were gone, the sound of their wings and fast speech fading as they vanished up the tunnel. It grew darker as their dust settled and went out. Chilled, Jenks vibrated his wings for both warmth and light.

Making a huff, Jenks handed the pixy his sword, thinking he'd never done anything like *that* before. Vincet took it, seeming as unsure as Jenks was. Asking for help was in neither of their traditions. Change came hard to pixies when adherence to rigid customs was what kept them alive. But for Jenks, change had always been the curse that kept him going.

Jenks darted to a second, smaller hearth at the outskirts of the room for the box that held kindling. Insurance wouldn't allow a fire inside the church, and the kit had never made it inside. *And if I'm interviewing a client*, he thought, worried he might not make a good impression, *it should be by more than the glow of my dust.* The interview should be given the honor of the main hearth in the center of the room.

Vincet slid his sword away, his wings shivering for warmth as he looked at the ceilings.

"Um, you want to sit down?" Jenks said again as he returned with the kindling, and Vincet gingerly lowered himself to the edge of the cushion beside the dark fire pit. Though never starting outright war, poaching was a plague upon pixy society. Even being used to bending the rules, Jenks felt a territorial surge when Vincet's eyes scanned the dim room.

"I heard you lived in a castle of oak," Vincet said, clearly in awe. "Where is everyone?"

Watching him, Jenks struck the rocks together, whispering the words to honor the pixies who first stole a live flame and to ask for a prosperous season. Matalina should be at his side as he started the season's first flame, and he felt a pang of worry, wondering if it was wrong to do this without her.

"Right now we're living in the church," he said as an ember caught the charred linen, glowing as he added bits of fluff. "We're going to move out this week." *I hope.*

Vincet's wings stilled. "You live inside. With . . . lunkers?"

Smiling, Jenks began placing small sticks. With an instinctive shift of the muscles at the base of his wings, he modified the dust he was laying down to make it more flammable. It caught immediately, and stray bits floated up like motes of stars. "For the winter so we don't have to hibernate. I've seen snow," he said proudly. "It burns, almost, and turns your fingers blue."

Perhaps I could turn one of the storage rooms into an office? he thought as he set the first of the larger sticks on the flames and rose from his knees. But the thought of Matalina's eyes, pained as strangers violated their home repeatedly, made him wince. She was a grand woman, saying nothing when his fairy-dusted schemes burned in his brain. Better to ask Rachel to bury a flowerpot upside down in the garden beside the gate at the edge of the property. Hang a sign out or something. If he was going to help Cincinnati's pixies, he should be prepared.

"I need your help," Vincet said again, and Jenks's dust rivaled the firelight.

"We don't hire ourselves out for territory disputes," Jenks said, not knowing what else the pixy buck could want.

"I'd not ask," Vincet said, clearly affronted as his wings slipped a yellow dust. "If I can't hold a piece of ground, I don't deserve to garden it. My claim is strong. My wife and I have land, three terrified children from last year, and six newlings. I had seven yesterday."

Though the young pixy's voice was even, his smooth, childlike face clenched in heartache. Seeing his pain, Jenks settled back, impressed that this was his second season as a father, and he had managed to raise three children already. It had taken him and Matalina two seasons to get their first newlings past the winter, and no newlings at all had survived that third winter. "I'm sorry," he said. "Food is hard at this time of year."

Vincet had his head bowed, mourning. "It's not the food. We have enough, and both Noel and I would gladly go hungry to feed our children. It's the statue." His head came up, and Jenks felt a stab of concern at Vincet's haunted expression. "You've got to help me—you work with a witch. It's magic. It's driving my daughter mad in her sleep, and last night, when I kept her awake, it killed one of my newlings."

Jenks's wings angled to catch the heat from the fire, and a sudden surge of warmth drove out the chill that had taken him. *A statue?* Leaning forward, Jenks wished he had a clipboard or a pencil like Ivy always had when she interviewed clients. He didn't know what to say, but a pen always made Ivy look like she knew what she was doing. "A statue?" he prompted, and Vincet bobbed his head, his blond hair going everywhere.

"That's how we got the garden," he said, his words faster now that Jenks was listening. "It's in a park. The flower beds abandoned. No sign of pixy or fairy. We didn't know why. Last year, we held a spot of ground in the hills, but lunkers cut it down, built a house, and didn't put in any flowers or trees to replace what they destroyed. I barely got my family out alive when the dozers came. Noel—that's my wife—was near her time. She couldn't fly much. The park was empty. We didn't know the ground was cursed. I thought it was goddess-sent, and now my children . . . The newlings . . . They're dying in their sleep, burning up!"

Jenks crossed his knees, trying to look unaffected by Vincet's outburst, but in reality, he was worried. Rachel always got as much information as she could before saying yes or no. He didn't know what difference it made, but he asked, "What park are you in?"

Vincet licked his lips. "I don't know. I've not heard anyone say the name of the place yet. I'll take you there. It's by a long set of steps in the middle of a grassy place. It was perfect. We took the flower beds, dug out a small room under the roots of a dogwood. Noel brought to life seven newlings. We were even thinking of naming them. Then Vi, my daughter, began sleepflying."

Frowning, Jenks shivered his wings for some light as he sat across the fire from him. "Sleepflying? She'll outgrow it. One of my sons spent a summer waking up in the garden more than his bed." Jenks smiled. There was always some question if Jumoke had been sleepflying, or simply looking for solitude. His middle-brood son endured a lot of good-natured ribbing from his elder siblings due to his brown hair and hazel eyes, rare to the point of shame among pixies.

Vincet made a rude huff, the dust from his wings turning black. "Did your son scream in pain as his wings smoldered while he beat at a statue? Did his aura become sickly, and pale? My daughter isn't sleepflying, she's being attacked. I can't wake her up until the moon passes its zenith. Even if I bend her wing backward. It's been happening every night now that the moon is nearly full."

Vincet's face went riven with grief, and his head dropped. "Last night I kept her awake, and the statue attacked a newling. Noel held him as he died, unable to breathe, he was screaming so. It was . . ." The young pixy's wings drooped, and he wiped his eyes, black dust slipping from his fingers when the tear dried. "I couldn't wake him. We tried and tried, but he just kept screaming as his wings turned to powder and his dust burned inside him."

Horrified, Jenks shifted on his cushion, not knowing what to say. Vincet's child had burned alive?

Vincet met his eyes, begging without saying a word. "Noel is afraid to let the newlings sleep," he whispered, his hands wringing and his wings still as he sat on Jenks's winter-musty cushion. "My children are terrified of the dark. A pixy shouldn't be afraid of the dark. It's where we belong, under the sun and moon."

Jenks's paternal instincts tugged on him. Vincet wasn't much older than Jax—his eldest now on his own. If he hadn't seen Vincet's fear, he would have said the pixy buck was dust-struck. Taking a stick as thick as his arm, Jenks knelt to put it on the fire, dusting it heavily to help it catch. "I don't see how a statue can cause children to go wandering," he said hesitantly, "much less set their dust on fire. Are you sure that's the cause? Maybe it's a mold or a fungus."

Vincet's dust turned a muddy shade of red as it pooled about his boots. "It's not a mold or fungus!" he exclaimed, and Jenks eyed his sword. "It's the statue! Nothing grows on it. It's cursed! And why would her aura shift like that? Something is in her!"

Jenks's wings hummed as he drew back from the hearth. Making a statue come to life to torment pixies didn't sound like witch magic, but there were other things that hadn't come out of the closet when the pixies, vampires, and witches had—things that would cause humans to raze the forests and plow the abandoned smaller towns into dust if they knew. But a statue? And why would a statue want to destroy itself? Unless . . . something *was* trapped in it?

"Have you felt anything?" he asked, and Vincet glanced at the dark tunnel behind him.

"No." He shifted uncomfortably, looking at his sword. "Neither has Noel. I've nothing to give you but my sword, but I'd gladly hand it over to you if you'll help us. I'm lost. I can defend my land from fairies, hummers, crows, and rats, but I can't see what is killing my children. Please, Jenks. I've come such a long way. Will you help me?"

Embarrassed, Jenks looked at the young man's sword as Vincet held it out to him, his face riven with helplessness. "I won't take another man's steel," Jenks said gruffly, and the young pixy went terrified.

"I have nothing else . . ." he said, the tip of the sword falling to rest on his knees.

"Now, I wouldn't say that," Jenks said, and Vincet's wings filled the room with the sound of a thousand bees and the glow of the sun. "You have two hands. Can you make a dragonfly hut out of a flowerpot?"

Vincet's hope turned to disgust. "I'll not take charity," he said, standing up with his sword in a tight grip. "And I'm not stupid. You have a castle and a large family. You can make a dragonfly hut yourself."

"No!" Jenks said, standing up after him. "I want an office on the edge of the property, on the street side of the wall that divides the garden from the road. Can you build me that? Under the lilac? And paint me a sign if I give you the letters for it? It's not garden work, and I can't ask my children to make me an office. My wife would pluck my wings!"

Vincet hesitated. His eyes shut in a slow blink, and when they opened, hope shone again. "I can do that."

Smiling, Jenks wondered if Jax had made half as honorable a man. The dust-caked idiot had run off, poorly trained, with a thief. Jenks's last words to him had been harsh, and it bothered him, for once a child left the garden, he was gone forever. Usually. But Jenks's kids were changing that tradition, too. "I'll take a look," Jenks said. "Me and my partner, Bis," he added in a sudden thought. Rachel never went on a run without backup. He should take someone, too. "If I can help you, then you'll build me an office out of a flowerpot."

Looking up at him, Vincet nodded, relief a golden dust slipping from him. "Thank you," he said, sliding his sword away with a firm intent. "Can you come now?"

Jenks looked askance at the ceiling to estimate the light. The sun was down by the looks of it, and Bis would be awake. "Absolutely. But, ah, I have to let my wife know where I'm going."

Vincet sighed knowingly, and together they flew up the short passage to the sun, leaving the fire to go out by itself.

PIXY SITUATIONS, INQUIRE HERE, Jenks thought as he guided Vincet to the garden wall to sit with Jumoke while he talked with Matalina. What harm could ever come of that?

 TWO

Hands on his hips to maintain his balance, Jenks shifted his wing angle to keep his position as the night wind gusted against him. Before him, the distant evening traffic was a background hum to the loud TVs, radios, and phone conversations beating on his ears in the dark, coming from the brightly lit townhouses across the street. Behind him were the soft sounds of a wooded park. The noise from the nearby city was almost intolerable, but the small garden space with its two statues and profusion of flowers in the middle of the city was worth the noise pollution. The barrage was likely reduced to low thumps and rumbles underground where Vincet had begun to make a home for his young family.

His middle was empty, and as he waited for Vincet to return from telling Noel they were back, Jenks fumbled in a waist pack for a sticky wad of nectar, honey, and peanut butter. His human partners were clueless, but if he didn't eat every few hours, he'd suffer. What Rachel and Ivy didn't know wouldn't hurt them.

"That's the statue, eh?" he said when Vincet rejoined him and they both came to rest on the back of a nearby bench. It was across the sidewalk from Vincet's flower beds, and staying off the greenery made both of them happier—even if he had been invited and was wearing his red bandanna like a belt. He hesitated, and then thinking it might be required as part of his new "helping" role, he offered Vincet a sweetball. He'd never given food to anyone outside his family before. It felt odd, and Vincet blinked at him, clearly shocked at the offer.

"No, thank you," he said, looking confused. "Um. Yes, that's the statue." Vincet pointed at the closest statue, and Jenks slipped the second sweetball away. "It won't attack until the moon is higher," Vincet added, more at ease now that the food was put away. Wings shivering, he glanced up at the moon, a day shy of full. "It attacks at midnight, not the lunkers' clocked midnight, but the real midmoon when it's at its zenith."

Jenks's attention dropped to the twin statues spaced about ten feet apart, surrounded by new annuals and low shrubs. Both had a Greek look about them, with a classic beauty of smooth lines and draping robes. The older statue was black in places from pollution, making it almost more beautiful. Carved ringlets of hair pulled back and braided framed a young-looking face, almost innocent in her expression. Her stone robes did little to hide her admittedly shapely legs from her thighs down. There was a flaccid water sack on her belt, and her fingers were wrapped about the butt of a sword, pushing into the pedestal at her toe.

The second statue was of a young man with smooth, almost feminine features. An empty ankle sheath was on one bare leg not covered by his stone robe. He was lithe, thin, with a hint of wild threat in his chiseled expression. The sign between them, framed by newly planted, honey-smelling alyssum, said that both statues had been donated by the Kalamack Foundation to commemorate Cincinnati gaining city status in 1819, but only the statue of the woman looked old. The other was a pearly white as if brand-new. Or freshly scrubbed, maybe.

A distant argument over burned rice became audible from over the grass between the garden and the nearby townhouses. Tink's tampons, humans were noisy. It was as if they didn't have a place in the natural order anymore, so they made as much noise as they could to prove they were alive. His garden and graveyard stretching an entire block within the suburbs, now made his by human law and a deed, was a blessing he'd come to take for granted. Rachel and Ivy never seemed to make much noise. 'Course, they slept a lot, and Ivy was a vampire, if living. She never made much noise to begin with.

"Did you clean it?" he asked Vincet, and the young pixy shook his head, looking scared.

"No. It was like that when we got here. Vi wakes as if in a trance, mindless as she hits the base of the statue until the burning brings her down. Then she screams until the moon shifts from the top of the sky and the statue lets her go."

Jenks scratched the base of his wings, puzzled. Though he didn't move from the back of the bench, his wings sent a glitter of dust over them. Holy crap, he had to pee again.

Vincet pulled his frightened gaze from the white stone glinting in the light of a nearby streetlamp. "I'd fight if I could. I'd die defending my children if I could see it. Is it a ghost?"

"Maybe." Pulling his hands from his hips, Jenks crossed his arms. It was a bad habit he'd gotten from Rachel, and he immediately put his fists back on his hips where they belonged.

A sudden noise in the trees above them caught them unawares, and while Jenks remained standing on the back of the bench, Vincet darted away, clearly surprised. It was Bis, returning from his circuit of the park under Jenks's direction. Jenks was used to giving orders, but not while on a run, and he nervously hoped he was doing this right.

With a soft hush of sliding leather and the scent of iron, the cat-size gargoyle landed on the back of the bench, his long claws scrabbling for purchase. Bis could cling to a vertical slab of stone with no problem, slip through a crack a bat would balk at, but trying to balance on the thin back of the slatted bench was more than he could manage. With an ungraceful hop, he landed on the concrete sidewalk between the bench and the statues.

"Nothing larger than an opossum near here," the gray, smooth-skinned kid said, his ears pricked to make the white fur lining them stick out. He had another tuft on the tip of his lionlike tail, but apart from that, his pebbly patterned skin was smooth, able to change color to match what was around him and creep Jenks out. He had a serious face that looked something like a pug's, shoved in and ugly, but Jenks's kids loved him. And his cat, Rex, was enamored of the church's newest renter. Jenks sighed. Once the feline found out Bis could kick out the BTUs when he wanted to, adoration was a foregone conclusion.

Bis was too young to be on his own, and after having been kicked off the basilica for spitting on people, he'd found his way to the church, slipping Jenks's sentry lines like a ghost. Bis slept all day like a proverbial stone, and he paid his rent by watching the grounds during the four hours around midnight when Jenks preferred to sleep. He ate pigeons. Feathers and all. Jenks was working on changing that. At least the feathers part. He was working on getting Bis to wear some clothes, too. Not that anything showed, but if Bis was wearing something, Jenks might catch him sneaking around on the ceiling. As it was, all he ever saw was claw marks.

"Thanks, Bis," Jenks said, standing straighter and trying to look like he was in charge. "You grew up around stone. What's your take on the statue? Is it haunted?"

It might have been a jest if anyone else had said it, but both of them knew there were such things as ghosts. Rachel's latest catastrophe, Pierce, was proof of that, but he had been completely unnoticed when bound to his tombstone. Only when it had cracked had Pierce escaped to harass them. Get a body. Become demon-snagged. Confuse Rachel into a love/hate relationship. Something was wrong with the girl. But now that he thought about it, maybe that's why Vincet's daughter was trying to break the statue. *Tink's a Disney whore*, not *another ghost*.

The gargoyle flicked his whiplike tail in a shrug. His powerful haunches bunched, and Vincet darted back with a flash of pixy dust when Bis landed atop the statue in question, his skin lightening to match the marble perfectly. Looking like part of the statue itself, he scraped a claw down a fold of chiseled hair. Bis brought it to his nose, sniffing, then tasting. "High-quality granite," he said, his voice both high and rumbling. "From Argentina. It was first worked hundreds of years ago, but it's only been here for a hundred and twenty."

Impressed, Jenks raised his eyebrows. "You got all that from tasting it?"

Smirking to show his black teeth, the kid pointed a claw to a second sign. "Just the high-quality part. There's a plaque."

Vincet sighed, and Jenks's wings went red.

Wheezing his version of laugher, the gargoyle hopped to the spot of light on the sidewalk. "Seriously, something is wrong. Both statues are on the ley line running through the park. No one puts two statues on a ley lines. It pins it down and weird stuff happens."

"There's a line?" Jenks asked, seeing Vincet looking understandably lost. "Where?"

Bis pointed at nothing Jenks could see, cocking his ugly, bald head first one way, then the other as he focused on the flower beds. "Lines don't move, but they shift like the tide under the moon—unless they're pinned down. Something is absorbing energy from the line—right between the statues where it's not moving."

"It's the statue," Vincet said, glancing at the shadowed hole beside the dogwood tree where his family lived. "It comes alive when the moon is high and the pull is the strongest. It's possessing my daughter!"

"I don't think it's the statue," Jenks murmured, hands on his hips again. "I think it's something trapped in it." Puzzled, he stared at nothing. His partner Rachel was a witch. She could see ley lines, pull energy off them, and use it to do magic. Bis could see ley lines, too, which made Jenks doubly glad he'd brought Bis with him. "You can see it, huh?" Jenks asked.

"It's more like hear it," Bis said, his big red eyes blinking apologetically.

"It's almost time," Vincet said, clearly scared as he glanced up at the nearly full moon with his fingers on the hilt of his sword. "See? As soon as the moon hits that branch, it will attack Vi. Jenks, I can't move my family. We'll lose the newlings. It will break Noel's heart."

"That's why we're here," he said, putting a hand on Vincet's shoulder, thinking it felt odd to give comfort to a pixy not of his kin. The pixy buck looked too young for this much grief, his smooth features creased in a pain that most lunkers didn't feel until they were thirty or forty, but pixies lived only twenty years if they were lucky. "I won't let any of your children die tonight," he added.

Bis cleared his throat as he scraped his claws on the sidewalk, silently pointing out the danger in making promises that he couldn't guarantee. Vincet's wings drooped, and Jenks took his hand from his shoulder. "Maybe I should go to sleep," Jenks said softly. "If you kept all your children awake, it would have no choice but to attack me."

"Too late." Bis made a shuffling hop to land on the bench's seat, wings spread slightly to look ominous. "The resonance of the line just shifted."

"Sweet mother of Tink," Vincet whispered, wings flashing red as he looked at his front door. "It's coming. I have to wake them!"

"Wait!" Jenks flew after him and caught his arm. Their wings almost tangled, and Vincet yanked out of his grip.

"They'll die!" he said angrily.

"Wake the newlings." Jenks's hand dropped to the butt of his sword. "Let the children sleep. I'm sorry, but they'll survive. I'll protect Vi as if she was my own."

Vincet looked torn, not wanting to trust another man with his children's lives. Panicked, he turned to a secluded knoll and the freshly turned earth of his newling's grave, still glowing faintly from the dust of tears. "I can't . . ."

"Vincet, I have fifty-four kids," Jenks coaxed. "I can keep your child alive. You asked me to help. I have to talk to whatever is trapped in that statue. Please. Bring her to me."

Hesitating, Vincet's wings hummed like a thousand bees in the dark.

"I promise," Jenks said, only now understanding why Rachel made stupid vows she knew she might not be able to keep. "*Let me help you.*"

Vincet's wings turned a sickly blue. "I have no choice," he said, and trailing a gray sparkle of dust to light the dew-wet plants, he flew to his home and disappeared under the earth.

Watching him, Jenks started to swear with one-word sentences. What if he couldn't do this? He was a stupid-ass to have promised that. He was as bad as Rachel. Angry, he fingered the butt of his sword and glared at the statue. Bis edged closer, his eyes never leaving the cold stone glinting in the moon and lamplight. "What if I'm making a mistake?" Jenks asked.

"You aren't," the gargoyle said, then stiffened, his glowing eyes widening as he pointed a knobby finger at the statue. "Look at that!"

"Holy crap, what is it doing?" Jenks exclaimed, the heartache of a child's death gone as the moonlight seeping through the branches brushed the statue, seeming to make it glow. *No,* he thought as a gust of wind pushed him back. The stone really *was* glowing, like it had a second skin. It wasn't the moonlight!

"Are you seeing what I'm seeing?" Jenks said, dropping to land beside Bis on the bench.

"Yeah." The kid sounded scared. "Something's trapped in that stone, and it's still alive. Jenks, that's not a ghost. This isn't right. Look, I've got goose bumps!"

Not looking at Bis's gray, proffered arm, Jenks muttered, "Yeah, me too."

Across the street, three TVs exploded into the same laugh track. The glow about the statue deepened, becoming darker, less like a moonbeam and more like a shadow. It stretched, pulling away to maintain the same shape as the statue, looking like a soul trying to slip free.

"Fewmets!" Bis barked, and with a ping of energy Jenks felt press against his wings, the shadow separated from the statue and vanished. "Did you see that? Did you freaking see that!" Bis yelled, wingtips shaking.

"It's gone!" Jenks said, unable to stop a shudder.

The bench shook as Bis hopped to the sidewalk and tucked under the slatted wood. "Not gone, loose," he said from underneath, worrying Jenks even more. "Hell's bells, I can hear it. It sounds like bird feathers sliding against each other, or scales. No, tree branches and bones."

Uneasy, Jenks slipped through the slats of the bench to alight beside Bis on the sidewalk where the heat of the day still lingered, watching the same empty air that the gargoyle was staring at. A thin lament rose from the small hummock of Vincet's home. The sound hit Jenks and twisted, and he wasn't surprised when the glow about the door brightened, and in a glittering yellow pixy dust, Vincet emerged with a small child in his arms.

She was in a white nightgown, her fair hair down and tousled. Two wide-eyed children clung to the door, a matronly silhouette beside them, crying and unable to leave the newlings.

The memory of the past night's torment was on Vincet when he joined them under the bench. "It's Vi," he said, grief-stricken. "Please, you said you'd help."

Jenks awkwardly took another man's child, feeling how light she was, stifling a shudder when the girl's unnatural, silver-tinted aura hit him. A piercing wail came from her throat, too anguished to be uttered by someone so young. Bis's ears pinned to his skull, and Jenks shifted his grip, binding her swinging arms and tightening his hold on her.

"Please make it stop," Vincet said, touching his daughter's face to wipe her dusty tears.

Though it went against his instincts, Jenks brought the girl to his shoulder. Like a switch, the child's wailing shifted to an eerie silence. Bis hissed and backed up, the scent of iron sifting over them as his claws scraped the sidewalk until he found the earth.

Jenks shivered. Not knowing what he'd find, he pulled the child from his shoulder and held her at arm's length.

At the shift of her weight, the child opened her eyes. They were black, with silvery pupils—like the sky and the moon—and her weird-ass aura.

"Trees," whispered Vi, clearly not Vi at all. Her voice was wispy, like wind in branches. "This cold stone is killing me."

Bis hissed as he clung to a tree like a misshapen squirrel, black teeth bared and tail switching. Vincet stood helpless, wings drooped and silent tears falling from him to dry into a black, glittery dust. He reached out, and Vi screamed wildly, "I have to get out!"

Jenks held her with her bare feet dangling. It wasn't Vincet's daughter speaking. Under the hatred streaming from Vi's eyes was a pinched brow and a fevered panting. Whatever gripped Vi was drawing the ley line through her. That's why she burned.

"Something is wrong with it," Bis hissed, half hidden by the tree. "The statue is sucking up the line like it's feeding off it, and I can hear it going right into her."

"Who are you?" Jenks whispered.

The young girl's eyes rolled to the moon. "Free me, Rhenoranian!" she begged it. "I beg you! Have I not suffered enough!"

Rhenoranian? Jenks's wings blurred into motion. It sounded like a demon's name. His hands holding Vi were warm from her heat, and he gently set her down, catching her shoulders as she swayed, oblivious to him. "What are you?" he asked, changing his demand as he knelt before her. "You're hurting the girl. Maybe I can help, but you're hurting Vi."

Vi's eyes tore from the moon as if seeing him for the first time. "You can hear me?" she whispered as her wings smoldered, limp against her back. Eyes focusing on Jenks, Vincet, and Bis, Vi seemed to shake herself. "Gracious Rhenoranian! You are wise and forgiving!"

Jenks rocked backward when Vi flung herself at him, her little arms encircling his knees. Bis hissed at the sudden movement, and even Vincet dropped back.

"Please, help me," she babbled, her long hair tangled as she gazed up at Jenks. "I'll do anything you ask. I'm trapped in that statue—a moon-touched nymph put me there, jealous of my attentions to her sisters. Rhenoranian sent you. I know he did. I've waited so long. Break the statue. Quick, before she comes back! She's going to come back! Please!" Vi begged.

Vincet watched wide-eyed as Jenks disentangled himself, pushing her off him and making her stand up. His hands warmed where they touched her shoulders, and he jerked away. "You're burning the child," he said. "Stop, and maybe I can help."

Anger flashed in the girl's face, then vanished. "There's no time. Break the statue!"

"You are *killing* my daughter!" Vincet shouted. "You already killed my son!"

Vi's eyes went wide. Taking a deep breath, she glanced at the second statue of the woman. His jailer, probably, and likely dead and gone. Nymphs had vanished during the Industrial Revolution, long before the Turn, brought down by pollution. "I'm sorry," she panted, but the edges of Vi's wings were starting to smolder. "I didn't know I was hurting anyone. I . . . I can't help it. It's Rhenoranian's blood. It keeps me alive, but it burns. I've been burning forever."

Rhenoranian's blood? Did he mean the ley line?

Behind them, Bis hissed. "Jenks?" he questioned. "I don't like this. It's eating the line. That's wrong like three different ways."

"Of course it's wrong! That's why it burns!" Vi shouted, then went silent, frustrated. "Break the statue and let me out, and I'll never bother the child again."

Eyes narrowing in suspicion, Jenks clattered his wings in acknowledgment to Bis. It sounded almost like a threat. Let it out or else. But the line energy running through Vi was making her tremble, and the higher the moon got, the worse it became. Soon, she would be screaming in pain, if Vincet was right, and his chance to talk to it would be gone.

"Tell me what you are," he said, grasping her wrist and bring her attention to him, but when Vi looked at him, Jenks let go, not liking what lay in the depths of her eyes.

"I'm Sylvan, a dryad," Vi said. "The nymph imprisoned me unfairly. Punishing me for my attentions to her sisters. She believes she's a goddess. Completely touched, but the demons didn't stop her. Why do you hesitate? Break my statue. Let me out!"

Jenks blinked, surprised. A dryad? In a city? Between him and the statue, Bis dropped to the grass, clearly amazed as well. "You're supposed to live in trees," Jenks said. "What are you doing in a statue?"

Twitching in pain, the child looked at Bis then back to Jenks, assessing almost. "I told you, the nymph put me there. She's touched in the head. But I survived. I learned to live on the energy right from a ley line instead of that filtered from a living tree. Though every moment I exist as if burning in Hell itself, I can survive in dead stone. I beg you, break my statue. Free me!" Vi's eyes went to her father with no recognition. "I promise I'll leave you pixies in peace. Forgive me for the agony upon the child. I cannot help it."

Still, Jenks hesitated as he looked at Vi, the hope in her flushed face too deep for her years. Something wasn't right.

Jenks pinned his wings when the wind gusted. He looked up, the scent of honey and gold tickling a memory he'd never had. Vi's eyes widened. "Too late!" she shrieked. Darting to Vincet, she kicked his shin. The pixy yelped, dropping his sword to grasp his leg. Even as Jenks flung himself into the air, Vi snatched the sword up, running, not flying, to the statue. Her nightclothes furled behind her like a ghost, and, screaming, she swung the blade at the stone. With a ping, the fairy steel broke. Using the broken hilt like a dagger, she beat at it, trying to chip the stone away.

"Jenks!" Bis shouted, and Jenks turned, bewildered but not alarmed. Until he saw what the gargoyle was pointing at.

A robed, barefoot woman stood in the middle of the sidewalk, heart-shaped face aghast as she stared at the hush of cars at the edge of the park. Lungs heaving as if in pain, she put a hand to her chest and looked at the distant buildings, their lights twinkling brighter than the stars. A sword was in her grip, and she appeared exactly like the second statue, even down to the braid her black ringlets were arranged in, shining in the light as if oiled. And her aura was *shiny*?

"It's her!" Bis shouted, bringing the woman's gaze to them.

"Who dares defile my sacred grove to free Sylvan?" she intoned, robe furling as she gestured to Bis. "Is it you?" Her arm dropped, and she peered at him in the dark. "What are you?" she asked. "A new demon dog? Come into the light."

"Let me go!" shrieked Vi, struggling now in Vincet's arms. "Let me *go*!"

Jenks darted to help Vincet, and still she fought them, her skin red and hot to the touch. At his nod, Bis awkwardly went to stand in the middle of the sidewalk between them.

"I'm a gargoyle, not a dog," he said, fidgeting like the teenager he was. "Who are you?"

The woman spun a slow circle, dismissing him. "Someone tried to free Sylvan, woke me from my rest. Did you see who it was, honorable . . . ah . . . gargoyle?"

"It was me," Jenks said, grunting when Vi's foot escaped his grip and kicked him. "What's it to you?" Turning to Vincet, he screwed his face up. "I gotta go talk to her. Can you hold her alone?"

Vincet nodded, and together they got the girl facedown on the mani-cured grass as she howled. Looking miserable, the young father sat on her, wincing as her screams grew violent.

Satisfied, Jenks rose up into the air to the woman's level, frowning when he saw her amusement in her steely eyes. They were silver, like the moon, and just as warm. "A pixy?" she said, laughing. "Leave my sacred grove, little sprite. Return to it, and you will die. Your children will die. I will hunt you down and destroy the very earth you ever walked upon. Go."

Fists on his hips, Jenks sifted a red dust that made it all the way to the sidewalk. "Sprite? Did you just call me a sprite, Little Miss Shiny Aura? What did you do? Eat a roll of tinfoil?"

Claws scraping, Bis edged closer, his white-tufted ears pinned to his head in submission. "Jenks," he hissed, not taking his eyes off the woman. "We should go. She's doing something weird with the line."

But Jenks flitted almost to her nose. She smelled like violet sunshine, and the gold pin holding her robe shut sparkled. "Did you just threaten me, little prissy pants?" he shot out.

Her nostrils flared, and her hand gripped her sword tighter. "You mock me? I am Daryl, and you are warned!"

Jenks snickered, his own hand on the butt of his sword. "I think if you think I'm going to fly away and let you keep some helpless dryad forever imprisoned, burning in a ley line, you got your toga too tight, babe."

Mouth open, she put a hand to her chest. "You . . . you defy me?" she said, wheezing slightly, clearly not doing well. "Do you know who I am!"

Glancing at Bis, who was silently looking up at him, pleading with him to be nice, he said, "You look asthmatic, is what you look like. Forget your inhaler at the temple?"

"I am Daryl!" she stated, then coughed. "Goddess of the woods. I've learned of steel and leather to defend my sisters, and you are . . . warned!" Turning away, she struggled to breathe.

"See, she's touched!" Vi yelled from under Vincet. Struggling, the little girl got an arm free. "Go crying to your demon, Daryl! You're a concubine! A minor nymph with delusions of goddesshood!"

Jenks's eyes widened as the woman's coughing suddenly ceased. Head turning to the base of Sylvan's statue, she straightened. A murderous look was on her, and Jenks felt a moment of panic. "Get out of that pixy, Sylvan," she intoned. "Now!"

Straining, the little girl gestured rudely. *"Ay gamisou!"* she yelled defiantly.

Jenks had no idea what she had said, but he filed it away for future use when the woman staggered back, clearly appalled.

"Jenks!" Bis whispered from under him. "Let's go!"

"I promised to help!" Jenks said, fascinated at the color the woman was turning in her outrage. "And I'm not going to leave Sylvan stuck in a statue by some nymph!"

Daryl's attention flicked to Jenks and Bis, then back to Vi. "I will not allow you to hurt another, Sylvan!" she said loudly, gesturing.

Bis reached up, wings spread as he half jumped to snag Jenks from the air and pull him down. Bis's warmth hit him as Jenks cowered in his hand while a wave of nothing he could see passed over them, pressing against his wings and driving the blood out. His wings collapsed for an instant, then rebounded on his next heartbeat.

Vi screamed, the sound reaching deep into Jenks and driving him to wiggle from Bis's fingers. His head poked free, and he saw Vincet spring into the air with his daughter. Her dust had taken on a deathly shade of black, bursting into a white-hot glow as it fell from her. Again Vi's scream tore the silence of the night as Daryl clenched her fist, her face savage with bloodlust.

"She's killing her!" Vincet shouted, terrified. "Jenks, she's killing my daughter!"

"Get her away from the line!" the gargoyle cried out as he stood his ground. "I can see the energy flowing into her. You have to get Vi out of the line!"

Jenks's lips parted. Cursing himself as a fool, he darted to Vincet, snatching the pain-racked child to him and throwing himself straight up. The line. The entire garden was in the line between the statues! Get her far enough away, and the connection would break!

Vi fought him as his ears popped painfully, thumping her fists into his chest and squirming until she suddenly went terrifyingly limp. "Vi!" Jenks shouted, scrambling to catch her as she threatened to slip from him, a good forty feet up. Her skin was hot, and her face was pale in the glow of his own dust. But a profound peace was on her face, and as he held her far above the dark city, fear struck him deep. The silver tint to her aura was gone.

"Vi," he whispered, jiggling her as the night cocooned them. "Vi, wake up. It's over." Oh God. Had he failed her? Was she dying? Killed by his own shortsightedness? Another man's child dead in his arms because of his failing?

Vi's lips parted, sucking in air like it was water. Her eyes flashed open, green and full of terror in the light of the moon.

"Tink save you, you're okay," he whispered, his eyes filling with tears. She was herself. Sylvan was no longer in her thoughts. That terror of a woman no longer burned her.

With a frightened whimper, Vi threw herself at him, her thin arms cold as they wrapped around his neck. "Don't let him hurt me," she begged as she cried, her little body shaking. "Please, don't let the statue hurt me anymore!"

A clear, healthy glow enveloped them as Jenks held her close, his hand against the back of her head as he whispered it was over, that she was okay, and he was taking her to her papa. He promised her that the statue wouldn't hurt her again and that Uncle Jenks would take care of everything. Foolish promises, but he couldn't stop himself.

Uncle Jenks, he thought, wondering why the term had fallen into his mind but feeling it was right. But below them, Daryl waited on the dark sidewalk. And Jenks—was pissed.

Jaw clenching, he descended more slowly than he wanted in order to give her younger ears a chance to adjust. Vincet met them halfway down, his wings clattering and dusting in fear until he saw Vi's tears. With a cry of joy, the grateful man took his daughter. Vi's sobs only strengthened his resolve.

"Get your family to ground and stay there," Jenks said grimly.

"I can help," Vincet said, even as Vi clung desperately to him.

"I know you can. I'll take the field, you take the hearth," he said, falling back on the battle practices of driving off invading fairies. One always stayed in earth to defend the hearth—to the end if it came to that.

Vincet looked as if he was going to protest, then probably remembering his sword was broken at the base of the statue, he nodded, darting away with Vi to vanish beneath the dogwood.

Free, and anger burning in his wings, Jenks drew his sword and dropped to where Bis was clinging to Sylvan's statue, hissing at Daryl as she stood in a spot of light with a satisfied smile.

"What the hell is wrong with you!" Jenks shouted, darting to a stop inches from the woman to make her jerk back. "You could have killed her! She's only a year old!"

Daryl's thin eyebrows rose. "A pixy?" she said haughtily, then stifled a cough. "Take your complaint to what demon will listen to you. Sylvan is in that statue, and there he will stay!"

"I'll take my complaint to you!" Jenks shouted, poking his sword at her nose.

The woman shrieked, robes furling as she swung her fist to miss him completely. "You cut me! You filthy little mouse!"

Jenks darted back, only to dive in again to slice another cut under her eye. "I'm letting Sylvan go if only to piss you off! You look like a sorority sister in hell week with that discount sheet around you! What is that, a one-fifty thread count? My three-year-old can weave better than that."

Clasping a hand over her eye, the woman shrieked, her voice echoing in the darkness. "I'll destroy you for that!" she cried, spinning to keep Jenks in front of her.

"Jenks?" Bis said loudly, half hiding behind Sylvan's statue. "Maybe we should leave the goddess alone."

"Goddess!" Jenks pulled up a safe eight feet into the air. His sword glinted red in the lamplight, and his wings hummed. Cocky, he dropped back down. "She's no goddess. She's a whiny. Little. Girl."

Angry at the woman's lack of respect, Jenks slashed at her robes with each word.

"Uh, Jenks?" Bis warbled his creased face bunched in worry as she screeched.

"Get out of here!" Jenks yelled at her like she was a stray dog. "Go find a museum or something. That's where you belong! Tell them Jenks sent you."

Panting, the woman came to a halt, staring up at him. Her face was red, and determination was equally mixed with anger. A car door slammed in the distance. Someone had heard her and was coming across the wide expanse of lawn. Oblivious, the woman jumped straight up at him with a fierce yell.

"Holy crap!" Jenks exclaimed, darting up. But the woman had sprung to her statue, scattering Bis and using it to make another leap for him. "Whoa! Lady. Chill out!" Jenks shouted as he darted to the nearby tree. Immediately he realized his mistake when Daryl leapt into the branches, following him.

"I am a *goddess*!" she screamed, her sword thunking into the branches as he dodged her. "You will die, pixy! Your name will be forgotten. Anyone who aligns themselves with Sylvan is a shade still walking!"

Maybe he went too far, Jenks wondered as her blade got closer with each swing, but before he could retreat, his wings unexpectedly froze. He had a glimpse of Daryl blowing at him with her lips pursed, and then he plummeted, falling through the leaves to the cement below.

"No!" Jenks exclaimed as the smacking of leaves against his back ceased and he dropped into free fall. A yelp escaped him when long, thin, gray fingers caught him, pulling him closer to the ashy scent of iron and dry stone. Above, Daryl scrambled to reach the ground.

"Bis!" Jenks said, dazed as he looked up to the gargoyle's red eyes. "Good God. We have to get out of here!"

"Yeah, that's what I've been telling you," Bis said dryly.

In the distance, the sound of car doors slamming and the revving of an engine told him whoever it was, was now leaving. Bis landed again on Sylvan's statue, shaking in fear. Carefully testing his wings, Jenks took to the air. Daryl was again on the sidewalk, her steely eyes watching them both in evaluation.

"You okay?" Bis said as his claws scratched the statue's forehead.

"Yeah," he said, stretching his shoulders and wondering if there was a remaining stiffness. "We have to get this bitch away from the garden before she hurts someone."

"How?"

Bis was trembling, his eyes wide and whirling. Grinning, Jenks rose farther up into the air. "I'll get her to follow me," he said to the gargoyle, then turned to the woman. "Hey, bright eyes! What's your problem with Sylvan? Did the dude bump uglies with one of your girlfriends?"

Jenks shifted his hips back and forth to make sure she knew what he was talking about, and Daryl's eyes narrowed. With no warning, she came at him silently, her robes furling in the wind from her passage.

Adrenaline pushing him, Jenks darted into the green field, leading her away. The city was nearby. He'd get her among the buildings, then ditch her. The cops would pick her up for disturbing the peace. Inderland Security would love bringing in a thought-to-be-extinct species of Inderlander with a goddess complex, but that was their job.

Laughing, Jenks sped across the grass, dark and black with the night. A ripple of wind shifted under his wings, and he looked down. An eerie keening dove down upon him, and in a surge of panic, he found himself tossed in a sudden whirlwind.

His sense of direction vanished. Tumbling, the wind beat at him, almost a living force bending his wings and tearing his breath from his lungs. Starved for air and out of control, he fell out of the sky and slammed into the ground. The wind collapsed on him, bringing him to his knees. Eyes shut, he held his wings to his back, one hand gripping his sword, the other clenched upon the grass to keep him from spinning away.

Just as suddenly as it came upon him, the wind broke into a thousand pieces of shrill voice and vanished. Dazed, he looked up, still kneeling.

Daryl was standing over him, her silver eyes gleaming like a cat's in the dark. Wheezing from the pollution, she raised her foot. "You are rude, and you will die."

"Oh, shit . . ." Jenks whispered.

A dark gray streak slammed into her chest, and, stumbling, Daryl fell back.

"Bis!" Jenks exclaimed as the gargoyle swung back around, plucking him from the ground and holding him close. "Tink loves a duck, you're a great backup!"

"You can't fly," Bis said breathlessly. "You're too light. Let's get out of here!"

"'Kay," Jenks said, grateful but feeling somewhat sheepish. This was the kind of spot he was always getting Rachel out of. He didn't like being carried, but if the woman could whistle up the wind, then he'd be better off with Bis. The moon had shifted, and Vincet and his family would be okay for another day. If the garden was sacred, Daryl wouldn't be likely to tear it apart.

Behind them came an infuriated shriek, and Jenks cringed when the roar of the wind came again. Wiggling, he inched himself up to look over Bis's shoulder, not liking the dips and swerves Bis was putting into his flight. Squinting, he looked behind him expecting to see a frustrated women standing alone, but the grass was empty. Satisfaction filled him. Until he saw the black, boiling cloud bearing down on them, rolling over the grass to leave it untouched.

"Holy shit!" he exclaimed, seeing a tiny white figure at the center. "Bis, she's flying! The freaky bitch is flying!"

Bis's smooth wing beats faltered. Glancing back, he gulped. "She's riding a ley line. Jenks, I don't know how she's doing it or what she is!"

Pointing at them with her sword, the woman clenched her teeth and grinned, clearly eager for battle. Her oiled ringlets lay flat, and her robe plastered to her like a second skin. The chugging of heavy air reverberated off the nearby buildings, but the trees were utterly still.

"Go!" shrilled Jenks, smacking Bis's shoulder. "Go to ground!"

The heat off the street was a wave as they left the park. Town homes gave way to buildings, flashing past and reduced to blurs. Cars were moments of light and noise, and still she came on, leaving the sound of horns and folding metal in her wake. Glass shattered, and Jenks hunched into Bis's protection, a new terror filling him as he realized that to take to the air now would be his death. Bis's flight grew sickeningly erratic among the buildings, and Jenks looked behind him.

They weren't going to make it.

"Down!" he screamed, voice lost in the shrieking wind. "Go to ground, Bis!"

Twisting wildly, Bis brought his wings in close, diving for a gutter drain.

"Oh-h-h-h-h no-o-o-o!" Jenks exclaimed, ducking his head.

Wings back, winging furiously in the sudden dark, Bis hit the wall with a grunt, sliding down to land in a sludge of water and goo. Putrid muck splashed up, coating Jenks in cold. Shaking his head, he lay on Bis and tried to figure out what happened.

I'm in a hole, he realized, his pulse hammering hard enough to shake him. *I'm alive.*

Above him, the wind shrieked, sounding like a woman screaming in battle. Bis shifted underneath him, and Jenks put a finger to his own lips when the gargoyle's eyes opened. Together they listened to the destruction as glass shattered and heavy things hit the earth. Slowly the roaring wind faded to leave the frightened calls of people and the growing sounds of sirens.

Shaking, Bis began to wheeze in laughter. "Pigeon poop. That was close," he said, sitting up slowly until Jenks took to the air.

Jenks's flash of anger at Bis's mirth dissolved as he realized they were okay and they would both live to see the sun rise. "Watch this! I'll get her to follow me, Bis!" he said, shaking his wings until a sludgy dust spilled from him to light the hole.

Bis stood shin-deep in the muck, his skin shifting toward pink as he upped his body temp. Appreciating the warmth, Jenks moved to his shoulder and tried to wipe the muck off his clothes. Matalina wouldn't be happy, and he enviously watched the mud dry and flake off Bis.

"Think she's gone?" Bis asked as he gazed up to the rectangle of brighter dark.

Jenks darted to the opening and the fresher air to hover with his head in the opening. Hands on his hips, he whistled long and low. "She tore up the street," he said loudly, looking up at the broken streetlights. "Power's out. Cops are coming. Let's get out of here."

The scrabbling of claws made him shiver, and he made the quick flight to the sidewalk when Bis slid out like an octopus. Bis shook his wings and sniffed at his armpits, then turned black to remain unnoticed. The sirens were coming closer, seeming to pull the distraught people together.

Frowning, Bis somberly clicked his nails in a rhythm that Jenks recognized as Mozart as he took in the tossed cars and broken windows. Fingers shaking, Jenks wedged a sweetball out of his belt pack and sucked on it, replenishing his sugar level before he started to burn muscle.

"Do you think all nymphs were like that?" Jenks asked, glad the muck hadn't gotten to his snack.

"Beats me."

With a push of his wings, Bis was airborne. Jenks joined him, shifting to fly above him where they could still talk. The night air felt heavy and warm, unusually muggy as they flew straight down the street and to the park. Only a small section of the city was without power, and it looked like the park was untouched.

"Maybe we should check on Vincet," Jenks said, and the gargoyle sighed, turning back to the cooler grass to check, but Jenks was already thinking about tomorrow. He had promised to help Vincet, and he would—even if it was a dryad trapped in a statue by a warrior nymph.

He had to help these people, and he had to do so before midnight tomorrow.

 THREE

Even from inside the desk, Jenks could hear Cincinnati waking up across the river. Under the faint radio playing three houses down, the deep thumps of distant industry were like a heartbeat only pixies and fairies could hear. The hum of a thousand cars reminded him of the beehive he'd tormented when he was a child and living in the wild stretches between the surviving cities. It wasn't a bad life, living in the city—if you could find food.

Worried, he sat in his favorite chair, thinking as his family lived life around him. The doll furniture he reclined in had been purchased last year at a yard sale for a nickel, but after stripping it down, reupholstering it with spider silk, and stuffing it with down from the cottonwood at the corner, he thought it was nicer than anything he'd seen in any store Rachel had taken him in. Nicer than Trent Kalamack's furniture, even. Distant, he rubbed his thumb over the ivy pattern that Matalina had woven into the fabric. She was a master at her craft, especially now.

A faint sifting of dust slipped from him to puddle under the chair, but his glow was almost lost in the shaft of light slipping in through the crack of the rolltop desk. The massive oak desk with its nooks and crannies had been their home for the winter, but after Matalina had perched herself on the steeple last night to wait for his return, she'd breathed in the season and decided it was time to move. So move they did.

The voices of his daughters raised in chatter were hardly noticed, as was the bawdy poem four of his elder sons were shouting as they cheerfully grabbed the corners of the long table made of Popsicle sticks and headed for the too-narrow crack.

Matalina's voice rose in direction, and the rolltop rose just enough. It wasn't until Matalina sent the rest of them out to scout for a nest of wasps to steal sentries from that it grew quiet. All his children had lived through the winter. It was a day of celebration, but the weight of responsibility was on him.

Responsibility wasn't new to him, but he was surprised to feel it—seeing as it was coming from an unexpected source. He'd always felt bad for pixies not as well off as he, but that was as far as it had ever gone. A part of him wanted to tell Vincet that he chose badly and he'd have to move, newlings or not. But Vi clinging helplessly to him had gone through Jenks like fire, and the smell of the newlings on Vincet kept him sitting where he was, thinking.

Jax had been his first newling he'd managed to keep alive through the winter. Jih, his eldest daughter, had survived in Matalina's arms that same season. Scarcely nine years old, Jih had moved across the street alone to start a garden, and Jax left to follow in his father's footsteps by partnering with a thief instead of devoting himself to a family and the earth.

Jenks had never wanted more than to tend a spot of ground, but four years ago, forced by a late spring and suffering newlings, he'd shamefully taken a part-time job as backup for Inderland Security, finding that he not only enjoyed it, but was good at it. Working for the man had eventually evolved into a partnership with Rachel and Ivy, and now he was on the streets more than in the garden. Turning his back on his first independent job wasn't going to happen. Blowing up the statue wouldn't be the hard part—it would be getting around Daryl to do it.

A nymph and a dryad, he thought sourly as he sucked on a sweetball in the quiet. Why couldn't it be something he knew something about? Nymphs had vanished during the Industrial Revolution, and the dryads had been decimated by deforestation shortly after that. There was even a conspiracy theory that the dryads had been responsible for the plague that had wiped out a big chunk of humanity forty years ago. If so, it had sort of worked. The forests were returning, and eighty-year-old trees were again becoming common. Nymphs, though, were still missing. Sleeping, maybe?

And what about Daryl, anyway? A deluded nymph, Sylvan had said. A goddess, Daryl claimed. There were no gods or goddesses. Never had been, but there were documented histories of Inderlanders taking advantage of humans, posing as deities. He frowned. Her eyes were downright creepy, and he hadn't liked demons being mentioned, either.

Jenks started, jerking when his chair moved. The breeze of four pairs of dragonfly wings blew the red dust of surprise from him, and he looked up to find four of his boys trying to move his chair with him in it. They were all grinning at him, looking alike despite Jumoke's dark hair and eyes, in matching pants and tunics that Matalina had stitched.

"Enough!" Matalina called out in a mock anger, her feet in a shaft of light, a dusting rag in her hands, and a flush to her cheeks. "Leave your papa alone. There's the girls' things to be moved if you need something to do."

"Sorry, Papa!" Jack said cheerfully, dropping his corner to make the chair thump. Jenks's feet flew up, and his wing bent back under him. "Didn't see you there."

"Dust a little," Jaul said, tangling his wings with Jack's, and Jack dusted heavily, shifting as he pushed him away. "The fairies will think you're dead," he finished, sneezing.

"Come and carry you away," Jumoke added, his wings lower in pitch than everyone else's. It made him different, along with his dusky coloring, and Jenks worried, not liking how Vincet had looked at him as if he were ill or deformed.

Jake just grinned, his wings glittering as he hovered in the background. Apart from Jumoke, they were the eldest in the garden now, as fresh-faced and innocent as they should be, strong and able to use a sword to kill an intruder twice their size. He loved them, but it was likely this would be the last spring they'd help the family move. Jack, especially, would probably find wanderlust on him this fall and leave.

"Go do what your mother said," he grumped, grabbing four sweetballs from the bowl beside him and throwing them to each boy in turn. "And keep your sugar level up! You're no good to me laid flat out in a field."

"Thanks, Papa!" they chorused, cheeks bulging. It kept them quiet, too.

Matalina came closer, smiling fondly as she shooed them out. "Go on. After the girls' room, find the big pots and fill them. Check for cracks. I'm soaking spider sacks tomorrow for the silk. They've been in the cool room all winter. If we're not careful, we're going to have a hatching. I'm not going to make your clothes out of moonbeams, you know."

"Naked in the garden is okay with me," Jumoke mumbled, and Matalina swatted him.

"Out!"

"Remember what happened the last year?" Jaul said, his words muffled from the sweetball as they headed for opening.

"Webs everywhere!" Jack said, laughing.

"Yeah, well you're the one that moved the sacks into the sun," Jumoke said, and they were gone, the dust from them settling in a glowing puddle to slowly fade.

"How else was I going to win the bet as to when they were going to hatch?" came faintly from outside the desk, and Jenks chuckled. It had been an unholy mess.

Slowly their voices vanished, and Jenks watched Matalina's expression, gauging her mood as she smiled. Wings stilling, she walked across the varnished oak wood to settle next to him, their wings tangling as she snuggled in against him. Slowly their mingling dust shifted to the same contented gold.

"I can't wait to get back into the garden," she said, gazing at the pile of laundry across the room. "I'll admit I don't like moving day, but I'll not set myself to sleep like that again with the fear of guessing who might not wake up with me in the spring." Reaching to the bowl, she deftly twisted a sweetball into two parts and handed him half. "You're quiet. What's got your updraft cold this morning?"

"Nothing." Setting his half of the sweet back in the bowl, he draped his arm over her shoulder, moving his thumb gently against her arm. Remembering the smell of the newlings, he dropped his gaze to her flat belly, not swelling with life for more than a year now. His wish for sterility might have extended her life—but had it also made her last years empty?

Setting her sweetball aside as well, Matalina shifted from him, pulling out of his reach to sit facing him. "Is it the pixy that you and Bis went into Cincinnati to help? I'm proud of you for that. The children enjoy watching the garden when you're gone. They feel important, and they'll be all the more prepared when they've a garden of their own."

A garden of their own, he thought. His children were leaving. Vincet's children were so young. His entire adult life was before him. "Mattie, do you ever wish for newlings?" he asked.

Her eyes fell from his, and her breath seemed to catch as she stared at the piles of clothes.

Fear struck Jenks at her silence, and he sat up to take her hands in his. "Tink's tears. I'm sorry," he blurted. "I thought you didn't want any more. You said . . . We talked about it . . ."

Smiling to look even more beautiful, Matalina placed a fingertip to his lips. "Hush," she breathed, leaning her head forward to touch his as her finger dropped away. "Jenks, love, of course I miss newlings. Every time Jrixibell or any of the last children do something for the first time, I think that I'll never see the joy of that discovery on another child's face, but I don't want any more children who won't survive a day after me."

Worried, he shifted closer, his hands tightening on hers. "Mattie, about that," he started, but she shook her head, and the dust falling from her took on a red tinge.

"No," she said firmly. "We've been over this. I won't take that curse so I can have another twenty years of life. I'm going to step from the wheel happy when I reach the end, knowing all my children will survive my passing. No other pixy woman can say that. It's a gift, Jenks, and I thank you for it."

Beautiful and smiling, she leaned forward to kiss him, but he would have none of it. Anger joining his frustration, he pulled away. *Why won't she even listen?* Ever since he'd taken that curse to get lunker-size for a week, his flagging endurance had returned full force. It had fixed his mangled foot and erased the fairy steel scar that had pained him during thunderstorms. It was as if he was brand-new. And Mattie wasn't.

"Mattie, please," he began, but as every other time, she smiled and shook her head.

"I love my life. I love you. And if you keep buzzing me about it, I'm going to put fairy scales in your nectar. Now tell me how you're going to help the Vincet family."

He took a breath, and she raised her eyebrows, daring him.

Jenks's shoulders slumped and his wings stilled to lie submissively against his back. Later. He'd convince her later. Pixies died only in the fall or winter. He had all summer.

"I need to destroy a statue," he said, seeing the clean wood around him and imagining the dirt walls Vincet was living between, then remembering the flower boxes he and Mattie had raised most of their children among. He was lucky, but the harder he worked, the luckier he got.

"Oh, good," she said distantly. "I know how you like to blow things up."

His mood eased, and he shifted her closer to feel her warmth. Pixies had known how to make explosives long before anyone else. All it took was a little time in the kitchen. *And a hell of a lot of nitrogen*, he thought. "By tonight," he added, bringing himself back to the present, "to help free a dryad."

"Really?" Eyeing him suspiciously, Matalina popped her half of the sweetball into her mouth. "I 'ought 'ay were cut 'own in the great deforestation of the eighteen hundreds. 'Ave they emigrated in from Europe?"

"I don't know," he admitted. "But this one is trapped in a statue, existing on energy right off a ley line instead of sipping it filtered from a tree. He's been slipping into Vincet's children's minds when they sleep, trying to get them to break his statue." He wasn't going to tell her the dryad had accidentally killed one. It was too awful to think about.

Matalina stood, rising on a burst of energy to dust the ceiling. "A city-living dryad?" she murmured, cleaning wood that would lay unseen for months if Rachel continued her pattern and avoided her desk even after they vacated it. "Tink loves a duck, what will they think of next?"

Jenks reclined to see if he could see up her dress. "Blowing it up isn't the problem. See, there's this nymph," he said, smiling when he caught a glimpse of a slim thigh.

She looked down at him, her disbelief clear. Seeing where his eyes were, she twitched her skirt and shifted, eyes scrunched in delight even as she huffed in annoyance. "A nymph? I thought they were extinct."

"Maybe they're just hiding," he said. "This one said something about waking up. She was having a hard time breathing through the pollution." *Until she came after us.*

Flitting to the opening in the desk, Matalina shook her rag with a crack. "Hmmm."

"She's got this goddess . . . warrior vibe," he said when Matalina returned to the ceiling. "Mattie, the woman is scary. I think if I get the dryad free, the nymph will follow him and leave Vincet in peace."

Again Matalina made that same doubt-filled sound, not looking at him as she dusted.

"Freeing the dryad is the only way I can help Vincet," Jenks said, not knowing if Matalina was unsure about Sylvan or the nymph. "He's only been on his own for a year, and he has three children and passel of newlings. He's done so well."

Matalina turned at the almost jealous tone in his words, the pride and love in her expression obvious. "You were nine, love, when you found me," she said as she dropped to him, her wings a clear silver as they hummed. "Coming from the country with burrs in your hair and not even a scrap of red to call your own. Don't compare yourself to Vincet."

He smiled, but still . . . "It took me two years to be able to provide enough for Jax and Jih to survive," he said, reaching up to take her hand and draw her to him.

His wife sat beside him, perched on the very edge of the couch with her hands holding his. "Times were harder. I'm proud of you, Jenks. None has done better. None."

Jenks scanned the nearly empty desk, the sounds of his children playing filtering in over the radio talking about the freak tornado that had hit the outskirts of Cincinnati last night. Not wanting to accept her words, he pulled her to sit on his lap, tugging her close and resting his chin on her shoulder and breathing in the clean smell of her hair. He could have done better. He could have given up the garden and gone to work for the I.S. years sooner. But he hadn't known.

"You need to help this family," she said, interrupting his thoughts. "I don't understand why you do some of the things you do, but this . . . This I understand."

"I can't do it alone," he said, grimacing as he remembered Daryl controlling the wind, taking the very element he lived in and turning it against him.

"Wasn't Bis a help?" she asked, sounding bewildered.

Jenks started, not realizing what his words had sounded like. "He was the perfect backup," he said, his words slow as he remembered almost being squished, and then Bis's frantic flight in the streets. "He's no fighter, but he yanked my butt out of the fire twice." Smiling, Jenks thought he couldn't count how many times he'd done the same for Rachel. "I'd ask Rachel to help," he said, "but she won't be home until tomorrow."

Still on his lap, Matalina reached for Jenks's half of sweetball and put it in his mouth. "Then ask Ivy," she said as he shifted it around. "She'll help you."

"Ivy?" he said, his voice muffled. "It's my job, not hers."

Collapsing against him in irritation, Matalina huffed. "The vampire is always asking *you* to help *her,*" she said severely. "I don't begrudge it. It's your job! But don't be so slow-winged that you won't ask for help in return. It would be more stupid than a fairy's third birthday party for Vincet to lose a newling because you were too proud to ask Ivy to be a distraction."

Jenks thought about that, lifting Matalina to a more comfortable position on his lap. "You think I should ask her?" he asked.

Matalina shifted to give him a moot look.

"I'll ask her," he said, feeling the beginnings of excitement. "And maybe have Jumoke come out with me, too. The boy needs something other than his good looks."

Matalina made a small sound of agreement, knowing as much as he did that his dark hair and eyes would make finding a wife almost impossible.

Grinning, Jenks pushed them both into the air. She squealed as their wings clattered together, and a real smile, carefree and delighted, was on her as he spun her to him, hanging midair in the closed rolltop desk. "I'll teach Jumoke a trade so he has something to bring to the marriage pot beside cold pixy steel and a smart mind," he said, delighting in her smile. "I can teach him everything I know. It won't be like Jax. I'll make sure he knows why he's doing it, not just how. And with Ivy distracting the nymph, I'll blow up the dryad's statue. I already know how to make the explosive. I just need a whopping big amount of it."

Matalina pulled from him, holding his hands for a moment as she looked at him in pride. "Go save them, Jenks. I'll be in the garden when you get back. Bring me a good story."

Jenks drew her close, their dust and wings mingling as he kissed her soundly. "Thank you, love," he said. "You always make things seem so simple. I don't know what I'd do without you."

"You'll get along just fine," she whispered, but he was gone, already having zipped through the crack in the rolltop desk. Smile fading, Matalina looked over the empty desk. Picking up the discarded fabric, she followed him out.

FOUR

The shouts of his kids came loud through the church's kitchen window, their high-pitched voices clear in the moisture-heavy air as they played hide-and-seek in the early dark. The boys, especially, had been glad to get out of the desk and into their admittedly more-cramped-than-a-troll's-armpit quarters in the oak stump. More cramped, but vastly more suited to a winged person smaller than a Barbie doll.

A parental smile threatened Jenks's attempt at a businesslike attitude as he stood on the spigot before the window and cleared his throat. Jumoke's apprenticeship had begun, and Jenks was trying to impress on him the sensitivity needed in mixing up some pixy pow. It wouldn't be napalm, which pixies had first used to get rid of weeds—then fairies when it was discovered to their delight that it would go boom under the right conditions. And it wouldn't be C4, C3, or any other human explosive. It would be something completely different, thanks to the dual properties of stability and ignition that pixy dust contained.

"That's it, Papa?" Jumoke said doubtfully as he penciled in the last of the ingredients on one of Ivy's sticky notes. Unlike most of Cincinnati's pixies, Jenks's family could read. It was a skill Jenks taught himself shortly after reaching the city, then used it to claim a section of worthless land before the proposed flower boxes existing on a set of blueprints went in.

"That's it," he said, gazing at his son's hair. It looked especially dark in the fluorescent light. For the first time, he saw it as perhaps an asset. It wouldn't catch the sun as his own hair did, a decided advantage in sneaking around. Perhaps Jumoke was the reigning hide-and-seek champion for a reason.

Bis, newly awake and doing his sullen gargoyle thing atop the fridge, rustled his wings in disbelief. "There is no way that soap, fertilizer, lighter fluid, and pixy dust is going to blow that statue up. It's solid rock!"

"Wanna bet a week's worth of sentry duty?" Jenks asked. "I use it all the time. A pixy handful will blow surveillance lines and fry motherboards, QED. We're just going to need a lot more." Rising up, he eyed the rack of spelling equipment hanging over the center island counter. "Can you get that pot down for me?"

Jumoke made a small noise, and Bis's pebbly gray skin went black. "Rachel's spell pot?" the gargoyle squeaked in apparent fear.

Hands on his hips, Jenks hummed his wings faster. "The little one, yes. Jumoke, go see if you can find Ivy's lighter fluid out by the grill. We need more propellant than we have dust."

The young pixy darted out into the hallway, and Jenks frowned at the worried tint to his son's aura now. Tink's titties, he could use Rachel's spelling equipment. The woman wouldn't mind. Hell, she'd never even know.

Ears pinned to his ugly skull, Bis hopped the short distance from the fridge to the center island counter, jumping up with his wings spread to pluck the small copper pot. It would hold about a cup of liquid and was Rachel's favorite-size spell pot. She had two of them.

"Can I have the other one, too, please?" Jenks said dryly, and the kid's tail wrapped around his feet, his ears going flatter. "I can't touch anything but copper," he complained. "And if I use the plastic ones, they'll smell funny. Will you grow a pair and get the bowl?" he said, darting upward and smacking it to make it ping.

"Don't blame me if Rachel yells at you for using her spell pots," Bis muttered as he plucked it from the overhead rack and set it rocking next to the first. The draft from his wings blew Jenks back when Bis hopped to Ivy's chair at the big farmhouse kitchen table, pulling first the phone book, then *Vixen's Guide to Gathering Guys and Gals* down and onto the seat. The guide was the larger of the two.

"Don't blame me if Ivy de-wings you for using her computer," Jenks shot back as Bis settled onto the stack of books and shook the mouse to wake the computer up. One day he was going to get caught, and then there'd be Tink to pay. Tugging a bowl to the middle of the counter, Jenks felt a moment of guilt. "Rachel will never know. What's the problem here?"

Bis looked up from the keyboard. His thin fingers were curved so his nails touched the keys, and he snapped off Ivy's password without looking. "You didn't ask her."

"Yeah, like you said pretty-please for Ivy's password," he said, and Bis flushed dark black. Smug, Jenks pulled the recipe closer and wondered how he was going to size up the amounts. "I'll polish the stinkin' bowls when I'm done," he muttered, and Bis smirked. "I'm not afraid of Rachel!" he said, hands on his hips.

"And I'm not afraid of Ivy."

They both jumped at the hum of dragonfly wings, but it was Jumoke. "It's metal," he said, his expression going confused when he saw the panicked look on their faces. "What did I do?"

"I thought you were your mother," Jenks said, and Jumoke's wings turned a bright red as he drifted backward, giggling. It didn't seem right to be teaching a six-year-old how to make explosives. The giggling didn't help. But now was the time to start teaching him, not two weeks before he left the garden like he had Jax. There was a moral philosophy that went along with the power a pixy could wield, and he wouldn't make the same mistake with Jumoke as he had with Jax.

Bis stood, stretching his wings until the tips touched over his head. "I'll help," he said, and the two flew out into the hall and then the back living room. The cat door squeaked, and Jenks sighed, glancing at the clock. He'd already called Ivy, but she wouldn't be home for a couple more hours. The three of them would have to make a whopping amount of explosive before she got home; he didn't want Ivy to know he could make this stuff. Word would get out, and then Inderland Security would start drafting them into service. Pixies liked where they were, on the fringes and ignored . . . mostly.

Jenks drifted down until his feet hit the polished stainless steel, harmless through his boots. The squeak of the cat door brought him back to reality, and he pretended to be estimating the depth of the bowl when Bis and Jumoke flew in with the reek of petroleum.

"Because their horns don't work," Bis said. "Get it? Because their horns don't work?"

The thunk of the tin can hitting the counter was loud, and Jenks's hair shifted in the gust from Bis's wings. "Jumoke, what do you think. A cup?" Jenks asked, measuring the bowl off at his shoulder and pacing around the perimeter.

"I don't get it," Jumoke said, and after landing inside one of the bowls, he added, "A cup and a third to the brim?"

"You know, their horns?" The gargoyle reached up and touched the tiny nubs where his would be when he grew up.

"Bis, I don't get it!" Jumoke said, clearly embarrassed. "Dad, what's next?"

Jenks smiled, pleased. A cup and a third. Jumoke had it right. Jenks looked up to find Bis and Jumoke watching him eagerly. Teaching an adolescent pixy and teenage gargoyle how to make explosives might not be such a good idea. But hell, he'd learned when he was five.

"Mmmm, Ivory soap," he said. "Ivy has a stash of it—"

"In Rachel's bathroom under the sink," Jumoke finished, already in the air. "Got it."

Bis was a moment behind, his wind-noisy takeoff making the bowls rock.

"Just one bottle ought to do it!" Jenks shouted after them. "We're blowing up a statue, not a bridge." The Turn take it, they were *far* too eager to learn this.

When the sound of their rummaging became muffled, he braced himself against the copper bowl and pushed it to the can of lighter fluid. Taking to the air, he tapped the can with his sword point, moving down until he heard a sound he liked. Marking the spot with his eyes, he darted back, aimed his sword, and flew at it.

With a stifled yell for strength, he jammed his sword into the canister. The hard pixy steel went right through. His elder children had fairy steel, taken from invaders testing their strength. Jenks's blade was stronger, and the thin sheet of metal was nothing. Grinning as he imagined it was an invading fairy he had just pierced, Jenks put his foot on can for support and pulled the sword out, darting back to avoid the sudden stream flowing out and arching into the bowl . . . just as he had planned.

Wiping his sword on the rag over the sink, Jenks listened to the changing sound to estimate how full the bowl was getting. Little splashes spotted the counter, and he dropped to the floor, slipping into the cupboards by way of the open space at the footboard.

It was a weird world of wooden supports and domesticity behind the cupboards, and using his arms as much as his wings, he maneuvered himself to the kitchen's catch-all drawer. Vaulting into the shallow space, Jenks hunched over, vibrating his wings to create some light as he moved to the front, dodging dead batteries and mangled twist ties until he found the spool of plumber's putty. The trip out was faster, and eyeing Bis and Jumoke standing on the counter and panicking about the rising level of lighter fluid, he expertly plugged the hole.

"More than one way to empty a can," he said, vertigo taking him when the flow stopped and the fumes hit him hard. "Don't get too close, Jumoke. I swear, this is the worst part."

"It stinks like a fairy's funeral pyre," the boy said, plugging his nose and backing up.

Standing on the counter beside his son, Bis looked huge. There was a bottle of soap in his grip, and the gargoyle easily wedged the top open. Jenks could have done it, but it would have been a lot harder. "How much?" Bis asked, poised to squirt it out.

Still reeling, Jenks covered his eyes, now streaming a silver dust as his tears hit the air and tuned dry. "Put it in the empty bowl. I'll say when."

"Rachel's spell bowl?" Bis said, hesitating.

"It's soap!" Jenks barked, rubbing his eyes and staggering until Jumoke grabbed his shoulder. Holy crap, it was nasty stuff until it all got mixed together.

The squirt bottle made a rude sound as it emptied, and feeling better, Jenks peeked over the edge to see how much they had. "That's good," he said, and Bis capped the bottle by smacking the tip on the counter. "Jumoke, see the proportion to the lighter fluid? Now all we need is the nitrogen and the pixy dust. Lots of nitrogen to make the boom intense."

"Fertilizer," Jumoke said. "In the shed?" he asked, and when Jenks nodded, Jumoke rose up. "I'll check."

In an instant, he was gone. Glancing out the night-darkened window, Jenks watched Jumoke's arrow-straight path, the sifting dust falling to make a gold shadow of where he'd been. His siblings called out for him to join them, but Jumoke never even looked.

Pleased, Jenks turned to find Bis trying to get the fridge open by wedging a long claw between the seals. It felt good to be teaching someone his skills. Tink knew that Jax had been a disappointment, but Jumoke was genuinely interested. He already knew how to read.

Leaning against the bowl of soap, Jenks scratched the base of his wings, watching Bis hang from a fridge shelf with one hand and pull out a tinfoil-covered leftover with the other. His claws scrabbled on the linoleum when he dropped, and Jenks wasn't surprised when Bis shook the leftover lasagna into the trash under the sink and ate the tinfoil instead.

The rasping sound of teeth on metal made him shudder. Black dust sifted from him, and seeing it, Bis shrugged, crawling back up onto his elevated seat before Ivy's computer. "A gargoyle doesn't live on pigeon alone," he said, and Jenks winced.

Pushing off into the air, Jenks rose into the hanging utensils for his own snack. There was a pouch of sweets for the kids in the smallest ladle. Rachel never used it. Opening it, he popped one of the nectar and pollen balls into his mouth, then grabbed another for Jumoke. The kid had a lot to learn about maintaining his sugar level. Unless he was snacking in the garden. How long did it take to look through the shed, anyway?

Angling his wings, Jenks dropped to the dark windowsill and pocketed the second sweet. Hands on his hips, he stared out into the dark garden and watched the bands of colored light sift from the oak tree. Jumoke wasn't among them. The individual trails of dust slipping down were as pixy-specific as voices, and he knew them all. There'd been no new patterns to learn in years.

No more newlings, he thought, more melancholy than he thought he'd be. He'd done it to save Mattie's life, and it had seemed to have worked. A healthy pixy woman gave birth to more sons than daughters by almost two to one. The size of the brood, too, was telling, which was why only two children were born that first season, none the next, then eight, eleven, ten, twelve . . . then seven—four of them girls. That was the year he panicked, going to work for Inderland Security. Matalina had borne only three children the year he'd met Rachel, two of them girls. None had survived to naming. His wish for sterility had saved her life. Another birth of newlings might have killed her.

What he hadn't anticipated was with the absence of newlings, both he and Matalina had time to spare on other things. He'd gone from side jobs to a full-time career outside the garden, gaining enough money to buy the church and the security that went with it. Matalina had been able to help their eldest daughter take land before taking a spouse, something that only pixy bucks traditionally managed. Not to mention Matalina pursuing her desire to learn how to read, and then teaching the rest of the children—all impossible if caring for a set of newlings. Children were precious, each one a hope for the future. How could they be detrimental?

Frowning, Jenks tried to figure it out, failing. Perhaps he wasn't old enough yet, because it didn't make sense to him. Maybe Mattie could help him. She was the smart one. As soon he got her to take the Tink-damned curse, he'd rest easier. They'd live in the garden for another twenty years, then, watching their children grow, take their places . . .

The sharp taps of Bis on the keyboard stopped, and the gargoyle ruffled his wings. "Listen to this," he said, his high, gravelly voice pulling Jenks's attention from the window. "'Dryads declined with the deforestation, and many ghosts have been blamed on them as they learned to live in statues placed on ley lines.'"

Jenks flitted close, thinking he looked nothing like Ivy. "Kind of like pixies adapting to city gardens. Humans. Learn to live with them, or die trying."

Bis blinked his red eyes at him. "We've always lived with humans. I can't imagine living in the woods. What would I eat? Iron ore and sparrows?"

Ignoring his sarcasm, Jenks moved closer to the screen. Now that he thought about it, gargoyles were dependent on people. The picture of the dryad on the monitor was his size, and he tapped it. "Look at that. It looks like the statues in the park, doesn't it?" He turned, starting when he found Bis unexpectedly inches from him. *Holy crap, didn't the kid breathe?*

"Yeah . . ." Bis said softly, not noticing he had jumped.

Trying to cover his surprise, Jenks walked across the keyboard to the "down" arrow, scrolling for the rest of the article. "'Because they declined before the Turn,'" he read aloud, proud that he could, "'little is written about them without the trappings of fairy tale, but it's commonly accepted that they live as long as the tree they frequent does, perhaps even hundreds of years. Though generally thought of as meek and gentle, Grimm has placed them several times in the position of wildly savage.'"

Chuckling, Jenks put his hands on his hips. "Yeah," he said as Jumoke flew in trailing a disappointed green dust. "And the freak had kids shoving witches into ovens, too." Scraping his wings for his son's attention, he tossed Jumoke the pollen ball.

Catching it, his son tucked it away, saying, "It's not there. I think Rachel used it."

"Crap on toast," Jenks swore, using one of Rachel's favorites, but pleased that Jumoke had indeed been tapping off his sugar level. The kid had a head on his shoulders. "She did. I remember now. She put it around the azaleas this spring." Frustrated, he rose up as his wing speed increased. "I hate it when people use stuff and don't replace it. How am I supposed to make a bomb without nitrogen?"

Bis brought up a serious-looking black screen and started deleting evidence of Web sites and searches. "How about mothballs?" he asked, and Jenks laughed.

"You've been watching TV again. No, mothballs and pixy dust don't mix. Besides, that would make something more like napalm, and we want inward destruction, not outward devastation. Vincet wouldn't thank me for destroying his garden." Jenks frowned. Ammonia, maybe, but Ivy didn't keep that on hand like she did the soap and lighter fluid. "We want a nice simple pop, and for that, we want fertilizer."

"How much?"

Jenks looked at Bis as he pushed back from the table, wondering what Ivy would say if she knew the gargoyle had been using her computer. Silent, Jenks pointed to a bowl hanging from the overhead rack.

Bis's pushed-in face smiled as he flew to the rack, his wings sending the loose papers on the table flying. Jumoke took flight, yelling that Bis was as dumb as a downdraft, but Jenks squinted through it, not moving as the gargoyle dropped to the counter with the larger bowl.

"We've got lots of nitrogen at the basilica," Bis said, grinning at him through the settling papers. "I'll ask my dad about nymphs and dryads, too."

Alarmed, Jenks clattered his wings. "Hey, this is a run, not a job," he called, and Bis hesitated, flipping in midair to cling to the archway to the hall with the bowl dangling from a hind foot. "You can't steal it from the gardener shed."

Bis made his wheezing laugh, looking evil as he hung upside down with the white tuft of his tail twitching. "No problem. They can't give this stuff away. Thirty minutes." Instead of dropping to fly out, he slithered up to the hall ceiling, going nearly invisible as he shifted his skin tone to match the shadows. Only the glint of the copper bowl gave him away. That, and the faint scrabbling of claws. Jenks would be really worried about the scratches on the ceiling if he didn't know where they came from. The ceiling, the walls, the window ledges . . . He had to get Bis to start wearing some clothes. A bandanna or something.

Stifling a shudder, Jenks turned back to Jumoke, seeing him pale and wide-eyed. "It gives me the creeps when he does that skin thing," the small pixy said, and Jenks nodded.

"Me too. But we need to figure out how to mix this stuff up in one batch before he comes back or we'll be here all night. I know Vincet's going to keep his kids up, and Sylvan might burn another one of his newlings. And carefully!" he added when Jumoke tipped the bowl with the lighter fluid to look in it. "The last thing I need is Ivy coming home and finding fire trucks at the curb. She'd have hairy canaries coming out her, ah, ear."

At his shoulder, peering in at the lighter fluid, Jumoke shook his head. "Women."

That one word jerked Jenks's attention up, and his own smile grew to match Jumoke's. Pride filled him. Jax hadn't been like this. He wasn't making a mistake teaching Jumoke his skills. This was going to work, and his son would have a unique talent, one that would help him find a wife, and then all his children could have their happy-ever-after.

Jenks clapped him across the shoulders. "Can't live with them, can't die without them," he said, beaming with pride. This was not a mistake. Not a mistake at all.

FIVE

Pigeon poop?" Vincet exclaimed, aghast as he hovered with his three children clustered behind him, clearly frightened of the sight of Ivy reclining on the nearby bench. "You're going to save my family with pigeon poop!"

"Pigeon poop," Jenks affirmed, concentrating on the silvery goop in the bowl Bis was holding steady. The moon was up, making it easy to see Vincet's horror as he dug his hand into the softly glowing mess. Taking another oozing wad back to the statue, he slapped it onto the smooth stone with the rest. "That and pixy dust!" he said cheerfully, trying not to think about it as he wiped his hands off on a fold of stone. He'd never be able to handle a mixture of lighter fluid, soap, and nitrogen like this without the pixy dust to act as a stabilizer. It was the dust that made it go boom so spectacularly, too.

"That's disgusting!" Vincet said softly, and Bis, holding the bowl, rolled his eyes.

"Tell me about it," the gargoyle said. His voice was stoic, but Jenks could tell he was almost laughing. The white tufts of fur in his ears were trembling.

Ivy, too, smirked. The living vampire had driven them out here on her cycle—Bis on the gas tank and grinning into the air like a dog—but now she looked bored, lying back on the bench with her knees bent to gaze up into the branches of the tree. It was obvious that she'd been at someone earlier tonight; her color was high, her motions edging into a vampire-quick speed, and her obvious languorous sultriness, which she tried to hide from Rachel, poured from the slightly Asian-looking woman in a flood of release. Even Vincet had noticed, wisely not saying anything when the leather-clad woman had strode up to Daryl's statue, hip cocked as she pronounced she could take the nymph—if she had the brass to show up.

Right now, though, Ivy looked more inclined to seduce the next being on two legs she encountered, not fight them, her long straight hair falling almost to the cement as she lay on the bench, and a sated smile on her placid face. No wonder Ivy satisfied her blood urges during Rachel's weekly absences. Seeing Ivy like this might blow everything to hell. An emotionally constipated Ivy was a safe Ivy.

"This would go faster if someone would help me," Jenks said, eyeing the goop remaining when he flew down for another handful.

In a smooth motion, Ivy sat up and swung her boots to the cement to stand. "I'm going to do a perimeter," she said, heels silent on the sidewalk as she headed out. "And don't put that bowl in my cycle bag. Got it?" she shouted over her shoulder.

Jumoke landed atop Bis's head and fell into wide-footed stance that would allow him the best balance if the wind should gust. "Mom made me promise not to touch it," the kid said, clearly proud of his new red belt.

"I'm holding the bowl," Bis said quickly, eyes darting.

Vincet took his daughter's hand, pretending he needed to watch her.

"Chicken shits," Jenks muttered, scooping out a handful and throwing it at the statue. It hit with a splat, and Ivy, somewhere in the dark, gasped, swearing at him.

At that, Bis grinned to look like a nightmare. "Pigeon shits," he said cheerfully, and Jenks smeared another glowing handful on Sylvan's statue's nose.

The chiseled face looked as if it could see him and knew what he was doing. "It's not *that* bad," Jenks muttered, but his nose was wrinkling at the stink. It seemed to be sticking to him even if the modified plastique wasn't. His gaze dropped to Rachel's bowl, glinting in the lamplight, and his wings hummed faster. Ivy wouldn't tell Rachel, would she?

Hovering backward, he looked over his work, almost putting his hands on his hips before stopping at the last moment. If he'd done it right, it'd shatter at the base and out toward the walkway. Sylvan would be free. Jenks's gaze shifted to the small opening under the dogwood that was Vincet's home. It was too close for his liking.

"Jumoke," Jenks said tersely, and the young pixy rose on a glittering column of sparkles. "Set down a layer of flammable dust on the plastique. I have to get this crap off of me."

"You bet, Dad," he said enthusiastically, zipping to the statue. Jenks had put a heavy layer of dust in the mix already, but a top dusting would flash it all into flame faster than any petroleum product made from dead dinosaur.

Bis was stretching his neck to get away from the smell, holding the bowl and being more dramatic than Jrixibell pretending to have a sore wing so she wouldn't have to eat her pollen. He'd used only about half of what he had made. Maybe he should blow both statues up. That would piss off Daryl.

"You got a problem?" Jenks asked, and Bis shook his head, breath held.

"No," Bis said, his thick lips barely moving. "You done with this?"

"For now," he said, and Bis shoved the bowl under the bench, then scuttled to the middle of the sidewalk, gasping dramatically when he stopped in the puddle of lamplight.

Frowning, Jenks wiped his hands off on his red bandanna, then wondered what he was going to do with it. He couldn't put the symbolic flag of good intent back around his waist. Not only did it stink, but taking it back to Matalina to wash wasn't an option. Glancing at Vincet, he dropped it into the bowl. If Vincet had a problem with it, he could just suck Tink's toes.

Just off the sidewalk beside Sylvan's statue, Vincet was on one knee, trying to get his kids to go inside. The triplets were clearly unhappy about being told to go to ground. Vincet was just as reluctant to leave Jenks alone to take them there. Even now, he was eyeing the bow and quiver that Jenks had brought with him to ignite the explosive.

Give me a break, Jenks thought dryly. Like he'd take the man's garden? Frowning, he reached for his bow peeking from the small bag beside the dung-filled copper pot. Vincet stiffened when Jenks put the quiver over his shoulders and strung the bow. Maybe he shouldn't have gotten rid of his red bandanna.

"Go inside," Vincet said tersely to his children, but they only clung to him tighter.

"Papa? I'm scared," Vi said, her eyes riveted to the crap-smeared statue.

Irritation flashed over Vincet, and taking her hands, the young father faked a smile for his eldest and only daughter. "Go wait with your mother so Jenks can fix this," he said. "I can't leave another man alone in my garden with a bow, Vi. Even Jenks. It isn't right."

"But Uncle Jenks won't touch the flowers," she whined. "Papa, please come with us. Don't let the ghost out. Please!"

Smiling, Jenks gestured for Jumoke, who was bored and flying up and down like a yo-yo. They had time before the moon hit its zenith point. Daryl wouldn't appear until Sylvan did, and hopefully the statue would be demolished before then. Jenks had to give Jumoke something to do. That darting up and down was irritating.

"Come here," he said as he brought out from the bag a pot the size of two fists. "I want you to hold on to the coal pot," he said, handing it to the excited pixy.

"Got it," he said, wings clattering, and Jenks reached up, snagging his foot when he started to flit away.

"Keep it lit, Jumoke," he said, yanking him back down so hard Jumoke lost his balance and had to scramble to find it again. "Give it sips of air, nothing more. If it goes out from too much or too little air, I'm going to have to ask Ivy for a light, and that would be embarrassing."

"Uh, guys?" Bis interrupted, claws scraping as he slid to a stop beside them.

"Just a minute, Bis," Jenks said, turning back to Jumoke. "When I ask, take the top off, okay? Not before. The coal won't last long given full air." His voice was severe, but Jumoke was holding the small pot with the right amount of care now, and Jenks was satisfied.

"Go wait with your mother!" Vincet shouted across the way, and his two boys darted away to leave a heavy dust trail. But Vi . . . Vi didn't look so good.

"Jenks?" Bis said, clawed feet shifting, but Jenks's attention was riveted to Vi. Her dust didn't look right, and as he watched, her eyes rolled back and her wings collapsed. And her aura—went silver.

Shit.

"Vi!" Vincet shouted, scooping up the girl as she fell into convulsions. "The dryad's taking her!" he exclaimed, eyes wide in horror as he held his daughter. "She wasn't even asleep! Blow it up! Blow it up now!"

"Sorry," Bis said, ears pinned as he looked sheepish. "I tried to tell you."

Feeling betrayed, Jenks looked at the moon. It wasn't anywhere near its zenith! Reaching behind him, he fumbled for one of his arrows tied with dandelion fluff at the tip. Wings clattering, he turned to Jumoke, finding him . . . gone.

"What the hell?" he stammered, rising up to scan the area, but there wasn't a single twinkle of dust anywhere. He was gone! "Jumoke!"

Vincet flew to him with Vi in his arms, his wings clattering and desperation falling from him like the dust he was shedding. "He's hurting her!" Vincet shouted, Vi's skin red and her dust white-hot. "Blow it up! Free him!"

"I can't! Jumoke has the firepot!" Jenks hovered, poised and scanning. Bis waited on the sidewalk, tail lashing, but Jumoke was gone. Ivy was gone. By the dogwood, Noel was a faint glow gathering the two boys and pulling them underground. They were safe. *Where the hell is Jumoke!*

"Jumoke!" Jenks shouted, exasperated, and Bis took to the air with two heavy wing beats to find him. They didn't have time for this, but as Jenks started off in the other direction, he jerked to a halt in midair. Something smelled like honey and sun-warmed gold.

Tink's dildo, the warrior woman was back.

"You will not!" echoed a vehement voice off the nearby townhouses, and there she was, standing on the sidewalk beside her statue, her bare feet spread wide and her robes shifting. Her expression was frantic, and upon seeing the bow in his hands, she flung her hand out.

"Look out!" Bis shouted, leaping for him.

A blast of honey-smelling air hit them. Tumbling into the air, Jenks felt his heart pound, but he fought with his instinct, folding his wings against him and tightening into a ball as he flew out of control. Holy crap, he was heading right for the trees!

"Gotcha!" came Bis's faint exhalation, and the wind shifted as the gargoyle caught him, pulling him close.

Jenks's eyes opened to see the world dip and swoop. In Bis's other hand were Vincet and Vi. Vincet looked terrified, but Vi's expression held a shocking amount of hatred. It was Sylvan. That's why Daryl had appeared! The stupid dryad. Couldn't he have waited a few more minutes?

With a sharp drop and a wrench that hurt Jenks's neck, Bis dropped to the ground beside the sidewalk next to a large rock. The wind died. Daryl was coughing with her hand to her chest, shaking as she tried to catch her breath in the pollution-stained air.

Jenks unwedged himself from Bis's grip and flitted down to feel small beside him. Taking to the air was too chancy, and he could hit the statue from here.

"Why didn't you shoot it!" Vincet yelled at him, angry as he struggled with Vi, they, too, firmly on the earth.

Where the hell is Jumoke! Jenks thought, still not sure what end was up yet.

"I warned you," Daryl wheezed, pulling herself straight again. She wiped her mouth, then hesitated, shocked at the sheen of blood glinting in the lamplight. Gathering her resolve, she hid it, shouting, "You will *die* before I allow Sylvan to perpetrate his abuse on another!"

"You're a whiny little nymph!" Vi shouted as she struggled to be free. "The gods are dead, and actors play their rules! You're alone! Give up! The world's too ugly for your kind!"

"That's the trouble with you dryads. You talk too much," Daryl said. Eyes narrowed, she raised her sword. The nearby light flickered and went out. The one behind it went black, too, and like dominos, the townhouses across the park went dark. A distant chorus of complaint rose, joined by the beeping of smoke detectors.

Bis shifted his wings, his back to the rock. "I got a bad feeling about this!" he squeaked.

"Hey! Golden girl!" Ivy shouted from behind them, and Jenks rose up, wings flashing red when he saw the silver dusting of Jumoke with her. "Pick on someone your own size!" she added as she strode forward, boots clacking aggressively.

"Dad!" Jumoke exclaimed as he darted to him.

"Where have you been?" Jenks shouted, his relief coming out as anger. "We can't blow up the statue without that pot!"

Jumoke's wings drooped as he landed beside him, pot hugged to his middle. "I'm sorry. I was getting Ivy. I saw Daryl, and I just . . ." The boy's face screwed up. "I'm sorry, Dad. I shouldn't have left."

"Blow it up!" Vincet exclaimed, jerking when Vi got her arm free and smacked his face. He caught her wrist, and Sylvan howled. The white-hot dust spilling from Vi was turning the moss black, burned.

"Let me out!" she said, her childlike voice sounding wrong. "Before that bitch stops you!"

"Ivy's in the way," Jenks said tightly. Giving both Jumoke and Vincet a look to stay grounded, Jenks darted after her, coming to a halt at her shoulder as his partner stopped eight feet back from Daryl. The spicy scent of vampire spun through him, seeming to shift his own dust a darker tint. Ivy was pissed. Hell, even her aura was sparkling.

Seeing them together, Daryl dropped her sword, flushed as she looked at Ivy's tight clothes and anger. "You're aligned with the pixy? Who are you? A goddess?"

"Ooo! Ooo!" Jenks said, looping the bow over his shoulder so he could have both hands free for his own sword. "I've heard this one before. Just say yes, Ivy."

Ivy was eyeing Daryl with the same evaluation. "Worse," she said softly, and Jenks shuddered. "I'm heir to madness. Vessel of perversion. Your nightmare should you cross me."

Daryl's chin lifted, trembling. "Indeed. We might be sisters then, for I'm the same."

Ivy hunched slightly, eyeing the woman almost hungrily. "You hurt my friends." A long hand went out, beckoning. Her lips drew back in a horrible smile, and she let her small but sharp canines show. "Can you hurt me?"

The nymph blinked as the moonlight hit them, then she tightened her sword grip.

The air seemed to hesitate, and when Bis's nails scraped, Ivy jerked, jumping at her.

Jenks shot straight up, yelling, "Get her away from the statue so I can blow it up!"

"You can't!" Daryl cried out, moving impossibly fast as she dodged out of Ivy's attack. Her sword was swinging toward Ivy's back, and Jenks yelled a warning.

Ivy dropped. Daryl's sword point missed, but just. Rolling backward, Ivy tried to knock Daryl down, but the nymph jumped straight up. Ivy was standing when she landed, and the two women hesitated, looking at each other in surprise and what might be respect.

"Blow it up, Jenks!" Ivy called out. "I'll get out of the way!"

Jenks's mouth dropped open. Holy shit. Ivy didn't know if she could take her or not.

Darting back to the rock for protection, he sheathed his sword and pulled an arrow from his quiver. "Everyone get behind the rock!" he shouted. "Jumoke, the firepot!"

Leathery wings shaking, Bis scrambled behind the rock. Vincet fought his child as he dragged her to safety, the freedom-hungry dryad screaming. Vi was only a year old. Her tiny body couldn't take this. She was dusting heavily, glowing like a demon as the energy of the ley line ran through her. Vincet's own tears turned to dust as he fought to keep her from attacking Daryl—but he looked up at Jenks with hope.

"Here, Dad!" Jumoke shouted, taking off the lid. The scraping of the lid was loud, and Jenks buried the tip of the arrow in it. Immediately the wad of dandelion fluff ignited. *Matalina was the real archer*, he thought as he took aim and the arrow arched away. Fortunately, all he had do to was hit the statue. "Fire in the hold!" he shouted. "Everyone down!"

"No!" Daryl screamed, stretching her hand out. A flash of wind came at him, and he went tumbling backward, but a pained cry echoed, and the force immediately died.

When he found air again under his wings, his arrow was lost and the statue untouched. Daryl was writhing on the cement, downed by Ivy in the instant the nymph lost her concentration. Ivy herself looked winded, holding her arm where the nymph's sword had scored on her.

"Rhenoranian, help me!" Daryl said, coughing as she got to her knees, undeterred.

Expression pinched, Ivy strode forward, but Daryl groaned, kneeling as she shoved the air at her with both hands.

"Watch out!" Bis cried as Ivy was flung back to land in the flower bed beside Sylvan's statue as if having been pulled by a string. Frustrated, Jenks lowered his next arrow, not yet lit.

"Let me be your strength, Rhenoranian!" Daryl said, staggering to her feet. "Let me be your vessel!" She turned to Jenks, and his wings went cold. "Let me be your vengeance!"

Worried, Jenks darted up, then down. He couldn't see the ley line she was pulling on, but the force of it made his wings tingle. Daryl pointed at him with a new confidence, and then Ivy's scream echoed against the dark windows across the street. Motions blurring, the battle began again. Twelve feet up, Jenks watched, useless bow in hand and knowing he wouldn't be able to shoot until Ivy downed the nymph. Daryl kept pushing Ivy back to the statue.

Moving faster than seemed possible, Daryl ducked Ivy's crescent kick, only to fall when Ivy continued the spin and knocked her feet out from under her.

The nymph hit the ground, coughing. Ivy jumped into the air, elbow poised and clearly ready to slam it into Daryl's throat as she fell to hit the dirt beside her.

Daryl saw it coming and pulled her sword up to protect her throat. Ivy screamed, knowing she couldn't move enough to avoid being cut. The blade nicked Daryl's face, too, upon impact, but it protected her throat. Ivy was hurt more.

The small success seemed to galvanize the nymph, who staggered to her feet when Ivy rolled away holding her numb elbow. Swinging her blade in a wide arc, she waited—grimacing.

Like a mad thing, Ivy rushed her, plowing her foot right into her solar plexus between the gaps of the blade.

Daryl bent, and Ivy lashed out with a front kick, snapping the nymph's head back.

And still the woman wouldn't go down, falling back as she tried to find her breath.

"Now, Jenks!" Ivy called out, and Jenks dropped down to the rock and the firepot.

One hand to her middle, Daryl groaned, staggering to a stand. "Help me, Rhenoranian!" she screamed, shaking hand outstretched.

The wind came from everywhere. The black roared. It beat at the trees. Jenks tumbled, fighting it.

"Stop!" Ivy shouted, and when Jenks squinted, he saw she had yanked the nymph up and was pinning her to the tree across from her statue. "Stop, or I will fucking kill you!"

"Let me go, or I will pierce your liver," the nymph said, her teeth gritted.

"Oh, shit," Jenks whispered, seeing the glint of metal at Ivy's side.

Screaming down from the hills, the wind circled them like wolves. A small spot of stillness grew, surrounded by a wall of gray and black fury. The lights of Cincinnati vanished as if behind water. Even the ever-present thumps of industry were gone, overpowered by the chugging of the wind.

But here, in Daryl's sacred grove, the moon shone down in perfect stillness.

Jenks glanced to Jumoke peeping up from behind the rock as the torn leaves drifted down, gesturing for him to stay. Vi had stopped struggling. Her breath rasped like oven air, and her wings were starting to smolder by the acrid smell now pinching his nose.

Ivy still pinned Daryl to the tree, her arm against her throat. One in white, one in black, one in silk, the other in leather, both unmoving apart from their lungs heaving.

Slowly Jenks started to drop toward the firepot.

"Why do you stand against me?" Daryl whispered. "It's honor that gives your limbs the strength to best me." She took a careful breath. "It glows in you, and you hurt from it."

Ivy flinched when Daryl touched her jaw. "I'm not hurt," she said quickly.

"Sylvan went against the gods' law," the nymph was saying, her cracked lip starting to bleed. "Taught himself to exist in cold stone, then used the knowledge not to live, but to kill for enjoyment. Why do you free him? I don't understand."

"She lies!" Vi shouted, elbowing Vincet. "She's touched! Break the statue! Now!"

Sylvan was in jail? Not imprisoned by a jealous lover? Jenks hesitated, his wings going cold as Vincet struggled to hold her wildly struggling body. Had they had almost let him free? A murderer?

"The demons imprisoned him in stone," Daryl said, her fingers opening. The sword dropped to the grass, and Ivy flinched. "His heart remains as cold, even now when the fire of the demon's blood burns through him. I begged for the honor to guard him as it was my sisters he murdered. I fought for the right, learned to kill, to be heartless, only to fail here when it counts. If you free Sylvan, kill me as well, for I'm too cowardly to live when honorable people give such filth freedom."

Around them, the wind died to let the clamor from the townhouses and city beat upon them once more. The lights were on again, and people were talking loudly. "You're not a coward," Ivy said softly, and Daryl's eyes met hers, widening at something only the nymph could see.

Abruptly Ivy let go of her and stepped back, frightened. Holding her arms to herself, she looked for Jenks, now hovering right over the rock, Jumoke below him with the firepot. "We need to reassess this," she said, white-faced.

"No!" Vi exclaimed, exploding into motion and hitting her father right between the legs.

"Ooooh," Jenks said with a wince, then yelped when she scrambled up the rock as if she didn't have wings, snatching his bow and yanking an arrow from his quiver.

"Jumoke!" Bis shouted as the little girl jumped at the boy, screaming wildly. Jenks's son took to the air, frightened, but she crashed right into him. The coal pot hit the grass. The lid popped off and coals scattered, flashing orange with the new breath of air.

Screaming in victory, Vi ran for them, burying the tip of an arrow against one. It flared to life even as she pulled the bow back, arrow notched.

"Get her!" Jenks shouted as he tackled her about the knees.

He hit her hard, and they slid across the grass, his arms scraping. Taking a breath, he looked up to see the flaming arrow was arching true to its target.

"Drop!" he shouted, trying to cover Vi from the coming blast. Panic iced his wings as he saw Jumoke still hovering in midair, shocked into immobility. He'd never reach him in time.

Then Bis raised his hand, cupping it before him.

The night turned white and orange, and an explosion pulsed against his ears and echoed up through the ground into him. Hunching down, Jenks tried to bury himself in the grass, feeling the blast push the blood from his wings for an instant. Jumoke fell to the ground in front of him.

"Why didn't you drop!" Jenks shouted, his own voice sounding muffled from his stunned ears as he got off Vi and went to his son, bewildered on the ground. "Jumoke, are you okay?"

Panicking, he pulled his son up. Frantic, he felt Jumoke's face, then ran his hands down his wings, looking for tears. Jumoke yelped, wiggling to get out from under Jenks's hands.

"Oh, that was everlastingly cool," the boy said, grinning from under his dark hair.

Jenks smacked his shoulder in relief. He was okay. "What's wrong with you!" he shouted, glad his hearing was coming back. "I told you to drop!"

Bis's thick skin on his brow was furrowed in worry, but Jenks didn't think it was from the cut he was looking at on the back of his hand. In the distance, a car alarm was going off. "Um, Jenks?" he said in question.

A quick glance told him Vincet was okay. Vi was in his arms looking stunned but herself. Sylvan no longer possessed her, which meant he was probably free. Great, just freaking great. He only wanted to help, and he freed a murderer. Rachel and Ivy were not going to be happy.

Ivy.

Alarmed, Jenks darted up. Chunks of marble the size of apples and melons littered the sidewalk. A few pieces were embedded in the tree that Ivy had pinned Daryl against, and the scent of cracked rock pervaded. Vincet's home and Daryl's statue looked untouched. But no Ivy. No Daryl, either.

"Ivy!" Jenks shouted, realizing he was about to fall from exhaustion. Damn it, he'd let his sugar drop. Immediately he found a sweetball in his pocket and sucked on it. The sugar hit him fast, and his wings sped up. Across the street, people were starting to come out of their homes, aiming flashlights at the park. They had to get out of here.

"Ivy!" he shouted again. "You okay?"

Bis poked his head up from behind the rock, his ears pricked as he looked at the tree, and Jenks wasn't surprised when Daryl stumbled out from behind it. Ivy levered herself up from the ground, having found a dip to take shelter in. They both picked their way carefully to the sidewalk, taking in the damage with a numb acceptance.

"He's free," Daryl whispered, her smooth features bunching in distress.

A crack of noise made them all jump. It was the snap of breaking stone, and the sharp sound echoed off the town homes across the street. As they watched, a huge slab of broken rock slid from Sylvan's statue, falling to crush the flowers.

"I didn't do it, Papa!" Jumoke exclaimed, eyes wide as he darted close. "It wasn't me!"

"It was me," a new voice said, sly and wispy.

Startled, Jenks turned in the air even as Daryl caught her breath only to start coughing. Ivy held her back from attacking him, but her lips were pressed in anger. A thin figure was standing in the moonlight, his feet on the moss beside the dogwood tree. It looked like Sylvan's statue. Moving as if it might be hurt, the shadowy figure edged out into the moonlight, drawing back as one bare foot touched the concrete. It was Sylvan. It had to be.

"You lied to me," Jenks said, loosening his sword.

"I'm free!" the dryad exclaimed, and he leaped lightly onto the concrete, exuberant as his robes furled.

The glow of Vincet's dust was a sickly yellow as he hovered beside Jenks, his broken sword in hand. The dryad probably didn't know it, but it was a real threat.

"Is Vi okay?" Jenks asked, and Vincet nodded.

"But I fear we have let loose a demon."

"You are trash, Sylvan!" Daryl shouted, sagging in Ivy's arms as she wheezed. "I will not rest until you are *dead*!"

Sylvan stopped his twirling. Looking at Jenks as if seeing him for the first time, the dryad smiled, his gaze alighting briefly on Vincet, Jumoke, and finally Bis, all fronting him. "Daryl is a crazy bitch," he said softly, pulling himself to a dignified stance. "I didn't lie." Glancing at the people coming across the park from the town homes, he added, almost as an afterthought, "Not much, anyway."

"Now!" Ivy shouted, springing into action. Jenks darted forward, sword in hand.

"No, wait!" Bis exclaimed, but Ivy was already pinwheeling to a stop. The spot of air where Sylvan had been, was gone.

"Where did he go!" Ivy asked, turning back to them.

Bis shook himself, resetting his wings as he looked at the people coming closer. "Into the line," he said, clearly unnerved. His ears were pinned and his tail was lashed about his feet. "He shouldn't be able to do that," he added, meeting Jenks's gaze.

Daryl slumped on the bench to look totally undignified and out of character. "It's why he was imprisoned in stone," she said, pushing a chip of his statue off to clatter on the cement. "Now I'll never find him."

Jenks stifled a shiver as he met Ivy's eyes. Tink's contractual hell, he'd made a big mistake. "Let's get out of here," he said. "We can worry about Sylvan later."

"Right behind you." Bis flew to their satchel, ducking behind Daryl's robes and coming out with it and the grimy, dented bowl. A bobbing flashlight across the grass caught his eyes, and they glowed red. Seeing it, someone called out. More lights angled their way.

"Jenks, I'm taking Daryl to the hospital," Ivy said. "Can you get home from here okay?"

Jenks looked at Daryl, struggling to breathe, and he nodded. "See you there."

Daryl was complaining she wasn't going to go to the butchers and leechers when Vincet dropped down to him. "Thank you, Jenks," he said, his expression solemn in the dim light. "You saved my family."

Wincing, Jenks looked to Vincet's front door where his wife and sons were silhouetted in the warm glow of a fire. "You're welcome. I don't think Sylvan will be back."

"Tomorrow," Vincet said, shaking his hand. "I'll come tomorrow. Thank you. I can't ever do enough."

Jenks managed a smile as he thought of Vi. She'd be fine, now. "Just be nice to some pixy buck who needs it," he said. "And build me an office."

Vincet's head was bobbing as he drifted back, but it was clear he wanted to return to his home. "Yes. Anything. Tomorrow."

"Tomorrow," Jenks agreed, then darted up when a flashlight found him, bathing him in a bright white light. "Sorry about the mess!" he shouted.

Vincet went one way, Ivy and Daryl another, and in an instant, even their dust was gone. He waited until he heard the soft sound of Ivy's muffled engine before he turned his back on the demolished grove and rose higher. Like a switch, the sounds of chaos went faint and the air turned chill. An uncomfortable mix of success and failure took him. And as Jenks quickly caught up to Jumoke and the slower-flying gargoyle winging his way back across the Ohio River, he had a bad feeling that this was far from over.

SIX

Hands on his hips, Jenks hovered a good five inches above the damp moss, newly transplanted from somewhere half across the Hollows. He gazed in satisfaction at the freshly scrubbed, upside-down flowerpot buried halfway into the soft soil. The sun was high, but here, under the shelter of an overgrown lilac, it was cool. It had taken almost a week working the four hours before the sun rose, but Vincet had finally called his office done.

While Jenks's children watched, Vincet had chipped out a door in the upside-down flowerpot, built a hearth, and laid a circle of stone that said "welcome" in pixy culture. Seeds had been planted from Vincet's own stash, and Jenks wasn't sure how he felt about another man putting plants into his own soil. How was he to know what was going to come up?

Watching Vincet had been a good lesson to his own kids, who up to now had only seen their parents work, and when Jenks rubbed his wings together to signal the all-clear, his children swarmed down in a wave of silk and noise. The babble grew high, and he fled, darting to where Matalina was on the wall with Jrixibell, again refusing to eat her pollen, having stuffed herself with nectar. He hadn't a clue where she was getting it. The little girl probably had a stash of flowers somewhere that even her mother didn't know about.

"Go!" the woman relented as the little girl whined, her wings down in a pitiful display. "But you're going to eat twice as much tonight!"

"Thank you, Mama!" she chimed out, and Jenks watched for birds until she reached her brothers and sisters, already buzzing in and out of his new office.

Happy, Jenks settled himself beside Matalina, thinking she was beautiful out here in the dappled sun. She handed him a sweetball, and he took it, pulling her close to make her giggle. "I'd rather have you," he said, stealing a kiss.

"Jenks," she fussed, clearly liking the attention. "I'm pleased it ended well."

A flash of guilt darkened his wings. "Yeah, as long as Sylvan doesn't come back and Rachel doesn't find out," he said, gaze going to his kids as they doused Jumoke in pollen from an early dandelion, temporally turning him blond until he shook himself.

"You're such the worrier," Matalina teased. "Let the future take care of itself. Vincet's family is safe, and Jumoke is considering a career outside the garden. I'm proud of you."

He turned to her, his guilt easing. "You think it will be okay?" he said, and she leaned in, putting her arms around his neck and her forehead against his.

"I'm sure of it. That dryad is long gone. No need to worry."

Jenks sighed, feeling a knot untying, but still . . . "How do you like the office?" he asked, trying to change the subject. "I'll get a little bell and they can ring it. I don't think anyone will come, anyway."

Matalina smiled as a shaft of light found her face. "They'll come, Jenks. Just you wait."

The sound of one of their children wailing drifted to them, and together they sighed.

"Not today, though," Jenks said, giving her a kiss before he took to the air, his hands leaving hers reluctantly. "Today, I belong entirely to you."

And, happy, he rose up, scanning his garden, assessing in an instant what had happened and darting down to make things right.

It was what he did. It was what he always did. And it was what he would always do.

MILLION-DOLLAR BABY

I like to tell people that I wrote Pale Demon *to answer the question about whether anything was possible between Rachel and Trent, but when I got done with it, I found a new question had popped up. What happened between Trent and Jenks when they went off on their elf quest? It seemed the readers wanted to know as well, so here's the answer, the fallout from which has peppered the last few Hollows novels.*

 ONE

Vertigo threatened, not at the sensation of disconnection spilling down through his core, but from the abrupt feel of stone under his soft-soled shoes after the nothingness of line travel. Tightening his gut muscles, Trent caught his balance as the organized chaos of the King Street train station materialized around him as if, well . . . like magic, not the well-balanced act of scientific shifting of realities that it was. Calling it magic was convenient.

The twangy echo of announced departures mixed with a myriad of conversations and one child demanding that he wanted his book *no-o-o-ow!* Even at five thirty in the morning, it was busy. *And somewhat . . . smelly,* he thought, shivering at the final ribbons of power sliding off him to vanish like water into sand, or in this case, creation energy slipping through the molecule-thin cracks in the colorful mosaic now under him. The station had the distinctive tang of old mold growing on marble as a faint backdrop.

Seattle never seemed to dry out. He didn't know how Ellasbeth tolerated it. Perhaps her nose was stuck so far up in the air that she didn't notice.

"Hey, you moss wipe! We haven't said good-bye yet!" A high voice shrilled inches from his ear. Wincing, Trent glanced past the pixy's fit-fully moving wings to the attractive shadow of five-foot-eight inches of bothersome redhead vanishing from his elbow. Rachel Morgan was gone—never having fully materialized. Just as well. Her surreptitious ogling made him self-conscious. Then again, she'd never seen him in skintight spandex before.

"Seems she has pressing business elsewhere." Smiling faintly, Trent looked down at the elaborate compass rose the demon Algaliarept had dropped them on, then squinted up to the marvelously tooled ceiling. He would sooner suffer great loss than owe a demon a favor, but since Rachel was paying for the jump, he'd take it: eight hundred miles between San Francisco to Seattle in a blink of an eye. Technically speaking, owing Rachel a favor was the same thing as owing a demon, not that she truly understood that—yet.

Head coming down in a flash of guilt, Trent moved off the compass rose and into the flow of people. Rachel would never understand there was only one way to save her life *and* keep her out of the ever-after. But what did it matter, really? She didn't have to like him. He didn't like the decisions he made, either.

"I'm becoming my father," he whispered, an unexpected flash of anger coloring his thoughts. Just how much was he going to be asked to sacrifice for his people? His morals? His integrity? Even so, he was ready to give it, and watching Ellasbeth selfishly walk away from her responsibility had more than angered him. It wasn't her selfishness that kept him awake at night, though—it was his undeniable envy of her cowardly decision to walk. He did not like the person he needed to be to pull his people back from the brink of extinction.

The faint hum of Jenks's wings faded as the pixy came to an unfelt landing on his shoulder. Rachel's business partner and backup was on loan to him for the duration. "Dude, look at those ceilings," the pixy said, then snickered. "Hey, I, ah, get the whole thief outfit thing you were going for, but you'd be more inconspicuous in a suit. I'll be right back. The Withons would be more stupid than a winter-born pixy to not have a man here. I'll ferret him out."

Trent took a breath to tell him not to bother, but the pixy was gone, his dragonfly-like wings glinting in the faint light coming in the high round windows. "A man in a suit is exactly who they're looking for," he muttered. Pace stiff, he angled to a billboard advertising the latest computer system where his black tights and shirt would be less conspicuous. The specially tailored guise was perfect. In the right setting, he would look like a cyclist, a diver, or a thief, though what he was after was worth far more than a bauble or money.

His eye twitched, and Trent rubbed his chin. There was a high probability that thieving from the Withons' family estate would cost him his life, but his people wouldn't listen to him if he didn't. Trent's eyes closed in a long, soul-searching blink. If he survived, his species would survive—but he might damn his soul in the process. Perhaps it would be better to die.

High above him, the clock tower chimed the half hour. It had begun. Trent stifled a pang of angst, scanning the station as he walked. Reaching the wall, he leaned back against the billboard. His stomach began to knot. Before him, people in suits with briefcases and families in jeans with pull-behind suitcases crisscrossed in tired distraction. Attendants with little hats instead of winged pins directed people, and they seemed to smile more than their airplane counterparts. Jenks was right. He didn't fit in. Where the hell was his contact? His window was small, his timetable tight. The stress of hitting the mark on a short-note was not unfamiliar, but this was the first time his life depended upon it.

But then a slim man in tight-fitting racing spandex came in the King Street entrance, a biking helmet under one arm, a package under the other—right on time. Exhaling, Trent pushed off from the billboard, taking a longer, circular route that would keep him out of the main floor space. True, he was wearing black tights while surrounded by suits and casual clothes, but in a moment, no one would see him at all.

He heard Jenks before he saw him. "We got trouble," the pixy said, hovering backward as Trent continued to walk. "Sniper on the balcony.

Don't look up!" he shouted when Trent's head shifted. "He spotted you already. You keep going on this line, and he'll have a good shot in about twenty paces. I told you you were a sore thumb."

"Thank you." The words came out of his mouth with a terse quickness, and he made a quick right through an open archway and into the men's room. Tall ceilings and inlaid floors did little to disguise the room's purpose even if the doors on the stalls were mahogany. The attendant with his jar of breath mints, cologne, and wolfsbane never looked up as Trent washed his hands as he thought. Most of his thief tools were in the package with the man in the bike suit.

Looking up, he was startled by the sight of Jenks sitting on his shoulder. *If I have a pixy, I should use him.* "My contact is in the bike suit at the west entrance," he said, his lips barely moving as his eyes met Jenks's through the mirror.

Immediately the pixy brightened, a bright silver dust slipping from him to pool in the sink to look like mercury floating on the running water. "The biker? What are we doing, anyway? Stealing your grandma's wedding ring back?"

Trent stifled a surge of pique. He wasn't used to being questioned, especially by someone who was four inches tall. "I can't move forward until that sniper is gone." He turned the water off and shook his hands. "Is he coming in or waiting for me to come out?"

"I'll check."

The attendant, an older man with a mustache and a uniform that looked vaguely like a train conductor's, watched Jenks fly out, his eyes widening. Coming closer, Trent wrangled his belt pack open. Most of what he needed was in that package under the courier's arm, but money went a long way. Giving the man a twenty, he said, "Can I borrow this?" as he pointed at the glass jar of packaged mints. It looked like an old-fashioned caboose lantern and was heavy enough to do some damage.

"Sure, governor." The man fingered the bill as Jenks darted back in, the green dust sifting from him telling Trent all he needed to know.

"He's coming," the pixy said breathlessly. Trent, his heart pounding, hefted the glass container and moved to stand right beside the archway. "What can I do?" Jenks asked.

"Stay out of the way." Trent took a breath, reaching out to tap a line in case he needed it. Energy tasting of fish and cracked rock seeped into him, making the tips of his hair float. The Goddess help him, but the lines were awful in the earthquake-prone West Coast. No wonder his parents had never returned.

Teeth clenched at the uncomfortable sensation, Trent lifted the jar high, listening to the soft scuff of fine leather on stone, hardly audible over the calling of another train's numbers. The attendant's eyes widened.

"No, wait!" Jenks shouted, but Trent was already swinging at the brown shadow passing through the marble archway.

The impact reverberated up Trent's arms. His hands went numb, and the jar of mints hit the tile floor, shattering. Panic shocked through him as the round-faced man in a suit turned to look at him, his eyes rolling up into the back of his head as he collapsed.

Damn it, it is the wrong man!

"It's the wrong man, cookie farts!" Jenks exclaimed, his wings clattering. "Did I say now? Did I! Tink's little pink dildo, save me from amateurs!"

Trent stared at the man on the floor, his legs twisted under his briefcase. Now what?

"Behind you!" Jenks shrilled, and he spun, heart pounding as a man in jeans and a too-large coat came in. His eyes flicked to the man on the floor, then Trent. In a smooth, unhurried motion, he reached behind the fold of his coat.

Adrenaline was a slap. Grabbing the attendant's metal chair, Trent swung it around and up, knocking the man's arm aside. Snarling, the assassin watched his pistol arc through the air to clatter into a distant corner, but Trent was still moving, dancing forward over the fallen businessman. The chair landed squarely on four feet, and Trent used it to lever himself up, teeth clenched as he smashed his feet into the assassin's chest.

Arms flailing, the man fell back, grunting as he hit the marble wall, his head meeting it with a dull *thwap*.

Trent followed the man down, hand aching with power and ready to stun him into submission with a blast of ley line energy.

"Whoa, whoa, whoa, Mr. Kung Fu!" Jenks shouted, silver sparkles dusting. "I think you got him!"

His fisted hands sprang open, and Trent let go of the line. Shaky, he pulled himself to his full height, staring down at the assassin as the twin feelings of elation and revulsion flowed through him. *I am not my father*, he thought as he lifted the man's eyelids to see that they both dilated properly. But it was hard to argue with the thrill coursing through him as the man slumped at his feet, bleeding from his nose.

Jenks whistled long and loudly, as Trent, his hands shaking, moved the chair back where it belonged. The attendant was wide-eyed, his mints scattered and the two men at his feet. The distinctive odor of sea and rock that all West Coast elves had was growing stronger. Sort of surfer meets sandbar, with a bit of red wine thrown in to keep it happy.

"What the hell did you do that for?" the attendant mumbled, edging back as Trent searched the downed man's pockets. "Is he a mugger?" he added as Trent tossed the cartridge of bullets into the trash and slid the two-way radio into his belt pack. "You want me to get security?"

Shaking his head, Trent stood, and dipping into his belt pack, he handed the man five one-hundred-dollar bills. "The first man fell into your table, breaking the jar, and the second tripped on him," Trent said, and the man took them. "What a shame."

The man's alarm evolved into pleasure as he turned the bills over as if never having seen one before. "Yes, sir, they did," he said loudly, pulling his arthritic back more erect. "You have a nice day, now. Mind your step. Those mints are slippery!"

Relieved, Trent gave him a sharp nod and sidestepped the next man coming in. Ignoring the cry of "What happened?," Trent exited, breathing in the cooler air of the huge lobby. One down, a hundred to go. From behind him, the attendant was already deep into his story, enthusiastically explaining what had happened and telling the man to watch his step until he got the mints swept.

The clatter of pixy wings brought Trent's hand up, and he almost smacked Jenks, mistaking the sound as an attack.

"It's only me, moss wipe," Jenks grumbled, easily evading him and coming to a halt on his shoulder. "You're kind of jumpy, you know that? Nice going. You could have avoided most of it if you would've listened to me."

"I'll do better next time," Trent grumped, relieved when he saw that his contact was still waiting.

"If you don't, you're going to be dead," Jenks grumbled back. "And another thing," he said as he preceded to run down a list of do's and don'ts.

Ignoring him, Trent started for his contact, his feet finding a familiar, confident pace. He wove gracefully around the people who dismissed him, noting the ones who made eye contact and slid out of his way. His stomach was knotted, and he had to work hard for a casual expression. It was an odd feeling, being on his own after a lifetime spent with someone generally within earshot. His billions would be of little help today. If he failed, the Withons would kill him and stuff him in a sea grotto, but what had him worried was what would happen if he succeeded.

"Are you even listening to me?" Jenks said, tugging at the hair behind Trent's ear, and Trent frowned.

"Yes, of course. I appreciate you being here, and I'll let you know when I need your help," he said, nodding to the bike courier as he closed the gap.

"Tink's panties, I don't know why I'm helping you. You are such a snot."

Trent came to a halt, silently shrugging into the dull green zip-up jacket the man was handing him, then taking the bike helmet, and finally the package. A knot of tension eased as he slipped the small one-by-two-by-four box under his arm. Maybe he could do this.

"You're not listening to me," Jenks complained as he darted from Trent's shoulder, his hands on his hips and his disgust obvious. The irate but tiny man took a breath, then hesitated. "Hey, you guys look a lot alike," he said, and the bike courier smiled silently as he gave Trent a pair of sunglasses and, without a word, tossed his short, almost white hair back and strode for the doors leading out to the loading area.

"Pretty close." The soft sound of feet sliding pulled Trent's eyes back to the bathroom, and he stiffened, turning halfway around as the would-be sniper staggered out, a hand holding a wad of brown paper to his nose. From the loudspeaker came a final boarding call. The assassin spotted the slim shape of a man in black spandex slip through the doors to the platform, and he staggered into a run, his hand slapping his coat where his two-way had been.

"Pretty slick, you mean," Jenks added, seeming to have forgiven Trent as he put the sunglasses on his nose and headed out the King Street entrance. "That's good planning right there."

"I have the luxury of time." The temperature shifted, becoming warmer, damper as Trent went through the first set of twin doors. Traffic passed, and people intent on getting where they wanted to be. Just as expected, no one noticed him in his courier uniform, and he zipped his dull green jacket up against the possible rain. Risking a look back through the milky windows, he saw the sniper just make the train. Another knot eased, and then he tensed right back up again. He had hardly started. A sleek bike leaned against a nearby rack, chained with a familiar lock, and he strode to it.

"But you're as sloppy as Rachel," Jenks said loudly, his dust blown away by a traffic-born gust. "Money will get you only so far, and then I'm going to have to work my wings off keeping you alive. Especially if you don't unplug your sphincters and tell me what you're doing."

Setting down the box, Trent crouched beside the bike and looked up at Jenks perched on the bike's rearview mirror. "Unplug my . . . Excuse me?"

Hands on his hips, Jenks lifted his wings in a pixy's version of a shrug. "Keep thinking I'm fluff, and I'll kill you myself. I work best when I know what the general theme is." He tracked a passing man. "Quen at least took me *seriously*. Let me do my *job*."

The lock clicked open, and Trent stood, tossing it to the side, unneeded. It would be better if the rain would hold off for an hour or so, but what were the chances of that?

"I can do more than look pretty here!" Jenks shouted, darting back off the bike as Trent fit the package in the saddlebag and swung his leg over.

"I could have made sure that you beaned the right guy," Jenks continued as Trent took his round fabric cap from his belt pack and lined his bike helmet with it. "Saved you five minutes right there. Did you know the camera sweeps are only once every three minutes? You could have been invisible, but nooooo! Ignore the pixy! No dust off my ass, but if you aren't alive to help Rachel tomorrow, I'll be pissed."

"It was a negligible risk." Trent fastened his helmet under his chin, not needing to adjust the straps. "By the time someone looks at the tapes, it will be too late."

"You were lucky!" Jenks shouted, loud enough to make a passerby glance up, mildly curious at seeing a pixy arguing with a courier. "You could be dead on the tile right now, leaving Rachel up crap creek without her Kalamack life preserver." The pixy darted close, and Trent refused to back up as a silver dust tickled his nose. "We need to get one thing straight, cookie fart," Jenks said, poking his nose with the tip of his sword. "Either you include me, or you don't. Tell me now so I can catch the next train south and maybe get there in time to save her ass. I'm not here for you, not here for your elf quest, and not for whatever bauble we're stealing back from your old girlfriend. I'm here to keep you alive so you can help Rachel."

Squinting at the pixy, Trent sat where he was, wanting to move but forced to deal with this first. Having to explain himself was almost as bad as someone telling him no without options. But he'd been accused of being too hard to work with before, and learning the knack of seeming to include others in his decision making even when he wasn't would be good in the long run. Or so Quen said.

"Well?" the pixy snarled, and Trent quashed a sudden feeling of angst.

"It's not a ring we are stealing. It's my child."

Jenks choked, dropping three inches before finding the wind beneath his wings. Embarrassed, Trent pushed the bike in motion, checking behind him before taking the low curb and entering into traffic. He could hear pixy wings, but he kept his eyes forward, an increasingly familiar feeling of repressed unease seeping into him as his legs took on the stress of a hill. He shifted the gears and stood up on the pedals, the bike swaying from side to side with his weight. He should have worked harder to keep Ellasbeth happy, but by God, the woman was bitter, vindictive, and so smart that she couldn't get a joke.

"Child?" Jenks said, flying backward two feet in front of him. "You mean like a baby?" He checked behind him and rose up as Trent went around a parked car. "You and Ellasbeth, right?" he asked as he dropped back down. "Eewww . . ."

Trent kept pedaling, his breathing quickening. This had been a mistake.

"He'd be what, five months?" Jenks asked from behind him, drafting. "The marriage Rachel broke up was to make an honest woman out of her? Damn!"

"She's three months," Trent said, recalling the baby sites he'd been lurking on. She wouldn't even be sitting up yet, just learning how push up on her palms and possibly reach for things. "The marriage was to solidify the East and West Coast clans divided by the Turn. Lucy is the physical show of that, and whoever raises her will chart the next thirty years until she can do it herself. Ellasbeth would keep us hiding, and to survive the resurgence of our numbers, we must have the strong feeling of community that coming out of the closet would give us."

The pixy whistled, and Trent sat down as the hill crested, easily coasting with traffic. Worry furrowed his brow. He'd been raised by nannies and paid caretakers. His mother and father had been loving but distant figures. He wanted to be more than that to his daughter.

"Lucy?" Jenks said, not breathing hard at all as he caught up. "You named her Lucy? The elven golden child is named Lucy?"

Trent squinted at the pixy, the wind pulling Jenks's dust away almost as fast as it fell from his wings. "It's a family name," he said coolly. Ellasbeth's family name. He would've named her something grander. Lucinda, Lucianna, or Lucile, perhaps. *What am I going to do with a baby?*

Again the pixy laughed, and Trent made a quick right turn, Jenks's chiming voice going faint as he missed it. "Oh. My. God!" Jenks said as he caught up, landing on the bar between the handles and folding his wings to avoid wind damage. "Rachel is going to crap her panties when she finds out you're a daddy! Trent, you dog!"

They were getting close to the waterfront, the traffic easing slightly in the largely tourist area. The bike hummed up through him, and he turned sharply to avoid a cobbled street. Jenks wasn't laughing nearly as much as he thought he would. "You can understand why I didn't tell her," he muttered, and Jenks lost his mirth.

"No, not really." One hand holding his wings tight to his body, Jenks turned to look behind him at their forward progress. "Rachel makes enough mistakes in one week to fill a twenty-yard dump truck."

"Lucy wasn't a mistake," Trent said hotly.

They were among the darker shade of large buildings, and Trent watched Jenks shiver. "Sorry, sorry," he said, holding up a hand in protest. "You don't give Rachel enough credit. She won't think twice about it." He hesitated, looking up at the towers. "Once it sinks in. You really have a kid? For realsies?"

There was an unexpected relief at Jenks's reaction, and it bothered him. What did he care what a pixy thought—even if that pixy had Rachel's ear?

Distracted, he adjusted the rearview mirror attached to the handlebars, and Jenks cleared his throat. "No one is following you," he said, taking to the air as they paused at a stop sign for five eager tourists to cross. "Why do you think I've been sitting with my back to the wind?"

"Thank you." Trent pushed himself back into motion, and Jenks landed next to his ear. The streets were all downhill, and Trent was starting to see other cyclists with logos and colorful patterns on their tights. His pulse hammered, responding to his tension, not the road.

"But you gotta tell me what the plan is," Jenks prompted. "I get the black-jumpsuit-biker thing. It was a good idea. Beaning the next guy through the bathroom doorway wasn't. What are you going to do? Pose as a delivery guy? I bet I could find a better way in."

Trent nodded to an unknown biker across the street in colorful racing spandex. He was at least five inches shorter and twenty pounds lighter than Trent. "I've got a way," he said cagily.

"What the hell is it!" Jenks almost exploded, and Trent winced as his words seemed to go right through his head. "God, Trent, I'm trying to help you, and you act as if I'm looking to screw you over. How about a little trust!"

He trusted people. He trusted quite a few, and quite a few had "screwed him over" as Jenks put it. The difference was that when people betrayed him, sometimes other people died. And then other people thought it was his fault. He was tired of it. Everything he had was at risk for the next four hours. Quen said he was not his father, but he was doing the same damning things. *How can a child love a murderer?* The Goddess help him, they had to come out of the closet if only so he could stop killing people.

Frustrated, Trent pulled into a tiny alley. Jenks darted from his shoulder as the bike pivoted in a tight circle to face the opening. His eyes came up to find Jenks waiting, hands on his hips, a frown on his face . . . and hope in his eyes as he hovered. It was the last that did it, and Trent took a deep breath. It was almost harder to trust Rachel's partners than it was to trust her.

"Well?" Jenks prompted as three bikers whizzed by the mouth of the alley.

Propping the bike against a wall, Trent removed the saddlebag, setting the box with his equipment aside before throwing the empty bag into a Dumpster. "There's a bike race at Pike Place Market," Trent said, and Jenks waved a hand in a tiny circle as if to say get on with it. "The course runs to within half a mile of the Withons' front door, a quarter mile off from a secondary entrance that will be lightly guarded, if at all."

Wings humming, Jenks watched Trent tear open the box and stuff its contents in his belt pack. There wasn't much: a short utility knife, two hundred yards of thin prototype cord with a fastener clip, harness, baby sling, collapsed float, tire repair kit, wad of explosive gum and fuse wire, a pen flashlight, lighter, and a handful of elven sleep charms. Earth magic wasn't reliable this close to the ocean, but bringing the charms had seemed prudent even if it took several to work.

"They'll be watching the race," Jenks said, hovering with his feet inches over the emptying box, and Trent nodded.

"I expect the Withons will have a few men in it, as do I." A flash of easily repressed anxiety passed through him as he looked at his wad of money, then the unexpected two-way radio. Grimacing, he threw the money away. *Now it fit.* "A quarter mile off the course there's a secondary entrance to the Withons' house—an escape tunnel used by monks. The Withon estate is a converted monastery on the edge of a cliff overlooking the ocean."

Jenks's dust shifted from gold to red. "No shit!"

Trent smiled, shocked at how much it lightened his mood. Maybe this was how Rachel survived being someone she didn't want to be. "No shit. I think Mr. Withon has delusions of being the Count of Monte Cristo. They know about the tunnel, but it will likely have the lightest guard and is the best way in. It starts in a cliff and ends in the main kitchen."

Jenks nodded in thought, his dragonfly-like wings dusting heavily. "That gets us in. How do we get out with a three-month-old? They make a lot of noise, you know. And you can't stuff them in your coat and run, though that's probably what Rachel would do."

Again smiling, Trent flicked a look past the mouth of the alley to a rider skimming past, looking as sleek and athletic as one of his thoroughbreds, one hand on the handlebars and halfway turned to look behind him. "I need a west-facing window," he said. A west-facing window within a narrow parameter of time, but no need to tell Jenks that. Either he would make it, or he wouldn't.

Snorting, Jenks landed on the handlebars, turning sideways to look at himself in the tiny rearview mirror and shift his sword. "I didn't know elves had wings. You gonna fly out?"

Silent, Trent tossed the empty box into the trash and got on the bike. "I'm more worried about finding the nursery without . . . alerting anyone," he said, catching himself before voicing his real fear. He wasn't afraid to kill—he was afraid that it was becoming too easy. "They know I'm coming. There will be guards." Frowning, he pushed the bike into motion, and he rolled smoothly back into the street. *What if they had a decoy?*

"I can help with the guards."

Jenks was flying beside him, easily keeping up as they followed a pair of riders to the start of the bike race. When Trent said nothing, the pixy's dust shifted to a mustard yellow. "I can!" he said belligerently. "I can kill people your size if they aren't using magic. I could kill you, with half a day to plan it."

"Okay."

It might not have been the right thing to say, but Trent didn't care if he insulted him. He'd only accepted his help to shut him up and maybe get Rachel to trust him a little. But instead of bristling in anger, the pixy snorted, his dust a bright silver stream behind him. "Your disbelief amuses me," Jenks said dryly. "But if you keep ignoring me, I'm going to stab you in your ear. Nothing permanent, but you'll lose some hearing from the scar tissue."

Pulse fast from his exertions, Trent chuckled, only to find Jenks laughing with him. This might not be so bad if the pixy understood his dry sense of humor. "I have a boat to pick us up, but it has a narrow window," he said, leaning as he took a wide curve.

Jenks's wings shifted pitch as he kept up. "You're going down on that fish line you stuffed in your pack?" he said, his disbelief obvious. Trent could understand why. It didn't look like it could support a cat, much less him and a . . . baby. The Goddess help him, what was he going to do with a baby? He hadn't planned on raising a child this soon, and certainly not alone, but now that he had one, he wanted to do it right.

The way suddenly opened up into a wide courtyard of people, bullhorns, colored banners, and flags. Damping an unexpected surge of alarm, Trent slowed. "Well?" he said as they cruised into the starting area. "Is there anything you can add to my plan?"

Jenks landed on his shoulder, surprising him. "Trent, I've decided I'm going to help you get your kid," he said, and Trent blinked, the bike continuing forward on momentum. "Not just so you can help Rachel, but for you. Getting your kid back is important."

"Thank you," he whispered, wondering what it meant to have the unconditional support of a pixy.

"I'll let you know if something strikes me," Jenks said casually. Trent stifled a shiver when the pixy's fitfully moving wings tickled the side of his neck. "Stealing babies," the pixy said with a laugh. "I can't wait to tell Rachel."

Rachel. What was she going to say when he walked in with a baby? he wondered as he found a curb and brought the bike to a rest among the milling throng of bikes. Laugh at him? Tell him he should have kept his weasel in its cage? True, Lucy hadn't been expected, but now that she existed, he wanted to be a part of her life, not just because of who she was going to become, but because of a nameless feeling pulling him across the city.

He had a daughter, and his daughter needed him.

TWO

Trent breathed in and out in time with his pedaling, the ache in his chest beginning to hurt more than his legs as he held his head down and drafted off the bike ahead of him. *My God, would the Weres ever shut up?* he thought, tilting his head to watch the pack of three men and one woman, clearly a team from a local radio station by the looks of their colorful spandex and logo-plastered water bottles. They were more than a third of the way into the race, and they hadn't stopped talking the entire way as they pushed through the peloton and left most of the riders behind, their natural endurance putting them ahead of all but the most conditioned humans.

He had joined them early because anyone talking so much couldn't be planning an attack, and he'd stuck with them because they were going faster than most everyone else. Now, after an hour of their chatter of killer hills, salt blocks, carbing up, and butt butter, he was wishing he'd found someone else.

The road before him snaked around a wide turn as it began another slow rise up, and after a quick glance at his handlebar-mounted GPS, he wondered if he should start dropping back to put distance between him and the radio team before he slipped off the marked route and into the national forest they were biking through.

He glanced behind him; there was no one visible between him and the last curve, almost a half mile back. Head lifting, he began to slow, watching the last biker pull away, talking, still talking. Weres were undoubtedly the chattiest of all Inderlanders, their mouths going nonstop whenever they did anything even remotely physical. One of his best horse whisperers had been a Were, and the woman had never shut up, not even in bed.

Slowly the Weres pulled ahead as the sun-dappled road wound along the top of a ridge overlooking the sound. To the left, the land fell away quickly to the surf. To the right, scrubby trees and brush of the forest made a slow incline up. The five-foot-wide path was paved, clearly made for bike travel, and his thin street tires hummed under him. He'd been cruising at a good speed, but after an hour, the pace was starting to tell. *Save some energy for later*, he mused, backing off even more. What waited for him at the Withon compound was not encouraging.

The sound of Jenks's wings cut through his worrisome musings, and the pixy landed on the GPS, his dust making the liquid crystal screen blank out. "There are two guys back there being very careful to stay just behind every curve," he said, his wings flat to his back as the wind pulled at them. "They smell like elves and have that same straw-yellow hair as Ellasbeth. If you drop from the pack now, they're going to catch you alone. They've been taking out everyone who catches up with them. The guy in the blue is popping their tires."

Frowning, Trent tucked his chin to lessen the wind. Magic users. No surprise there. "How long until we reach the turnoff?" he asked, looking up to see that the team of Weres wasn't as far ahead of him as he had thought they'd be.

Jenks looked down at the GPS, head cocked when he realized his dust blanked the screen. "Ah, about a half mile. The turnoff is at the bottom of the next hill. It runs through a patch of thistles, so watch it."

The thistles hadn't been on his intel, and grateful, he silently thanked Rachel for insisting he include Jenks. He had thought it had been unusual that no one had caught up to them—Ellasbeth's men conveniently eliminating witnesses. His agreement with the Withon family concerning the theft of Lucy was not necessarily legal, but it was binding.

"Thank you," he whispered, knowing Jenks heard him when his dust shifted color. "I'd rather take them out in the woods than on the road." Standing up on his pedals, Trent started to power up the hill, his legs protesting until they rallied to the demand. Jenks darted off, and the GPS/MPH indicator gave a hiccup and returned to life. Swinging to the left, Trent began overtaking the complaining Weres. They'd likely shave minutes off their time if they'd quit talking.

"You want me to take them out before you get to the turnoff?" Jenks asked, his dust streaming out behind him as he easily kept up, and Trent eyed him.

"Can you?" he said, starting to breathe hard.

Jenks shrugged, and the Were they were currently passing almost fell off his bike, staring at the pixy. "Not if they're magic users, but I can slow them down to give you a few more seconds to get on the turnoff."

Trent nodded, not speaking as they passed another Were. "Don't endanger yourself more than what's prudent," he wheezed. One more Were to go, and then he'd be free of them.

A burst of gold dust sifted from the pixy, lost in the cool breeze rising up from the ocean. "Check!" he said cheerfully. He hesitated a moment as if he was going to say something more, then shifted direction and was gone.

Still standing on the pedals, Trent forced himself up the hill, his legs protesting and his chest on fire. The last Were fell behind him when she halted at the top of the hill, stopping to look back down the hill and shout encouraging words to her teammates. Ellasbeth's house/castle/monastery was visible in the ocean mist ahead of him as he rounded the curve and started down. It looked cold even from this distance, the edifice jutting out past the trees and bracken. There was ocean between him and it, the road falling down and to the right before it rose and swung high again to pass within a stone's throw of the front gate. It was here, though, where he'd break from the race.

The wind buffeted him as he took the curving road into the shade, his hammering pulse easing. Ellasbeth's home held his attention. It still looked like a monastery, one that had not sheltered happy monks growing vegetables and glorying God, but rather those bitterly hiding from the world. It was forbidding, so close to the sea that earth magic would not be a sure thing, and so near a fault line that ley line magic would be difficult unless having grown up among the fractured feel of the lines here. He couldn't help but think he was rescuing his daughter, imprisoned in a castle, shut off from the world but for what her caretakers thought was appropriate.

The hum of the tires buzzed up into him, and in an instant, the heat of the sun vanished as he cruised under the shade of the trees, eclipsing his view of the monastery. At the bottom was a patch of thistle. A walking path bisected it, the left-hand way going down the cliff to the rocky beach, the right rising up into the primeval forest. Trent glanced at his GPS. This had to be it.

Downshifting and braking hard, he came to a halt.

The sound of the wind stopped, and his face warmed even as he shivered in the shade of ancient trees. He glanced back, seeing no one on the road, but the top of the hill was hidden behind a curve. Sweat broke out on him. Legs protesting, Trent swung a foot over, and hoisting his sixteen-pound racing bike onto a shoulder, he strode to the right, trying not to disturb the thistles as he found the narrow dirt path.

A faint shout brought his head up. Deep under the trees, he looked back to see a lone rider speeding down the hill; behind him, the three Weres were shouting curses and howling at him. The sun caught a haze of dust, and he smiled and faded back into the woods. One rider now, not two. He could see why Rachel relied on the pixy.

Pulse hammering, he pulled the GPS from the handlebars and tucked it under his armpit as he threw the racing bike into the bracken and out of sight of the path. His helmet was next, his spelling cap now tucked into his pocket. The fronds waved and settled to hide the gleaming black frame. The lone rider knew where he was going, but no need to advertise it. Satisfied, Trent turned and ran down the dirt-packed path. Immediately his legs cramped up, and he grit his teeth, running through it until his clumsy, awkward motion smoothed out into a mile-eating lope he could keep up for hours.

A bird called in the distance, and a woodpecker sounded. His breaths in and out eased as more familiar muscles took over. Running, he could do. The sun came and went on his shoulders, and the sound of the ocean vanished under the hushed sighing of the wind in the trees.

He almost wished he had bowed to Ellasbeth's demand and abandoned his business dealings in the Midwest if only to claim a chunk of this peace. But then his heart hardened. Cincinnati might not be rich in wild spaces, the forests that once covered her hewn down and burned in the furnaces that had fueled her industrial revolution, the multitude of species she'd once boasted trampled into extinction under her droves of pigs and then people who flocked to the new city and a society built on human values. But for all her loud, brash exuberance, Cincinnati had welcomed his mother and father when they'd fled those who had promised to protect them. Cincinnati offered them shelter, meager, humble, but honest. And his mother, Trent remembered, had loved the fields more than the woods.

An image of his mother sitting in the sun with a horse cropping behind her rose up from his forgotten memories, shocking him. She was laughing with him, a daisy brushing her lips before touching it to his forehead fondly. Trent gasped, stumbling as his feet misplaced themselves. Recovering, he continued on with a panicked pace. He remembered his mother so rarely, and he grasped the image of her smiling at him, the sun blinding on her white dress, the grass as green as her eyes, sealing the memory away so he'd never forget it again. His mother had loved the fields, so far from the sea that she had forgotten its lure.

"Hey, Trent!"

The mental image of his mother vanished at Jenks's voice. Stifling his annoyance, he squinted up at the pixy. "One left?" he panted as he ran. *My mother was of the field*, he thought, vowing to share his love of horses with Lucy. Girls loved horses. That was one thing they could share. Maybe he could do this.

"Yep," Jenks said proudly. "One rode right off the cliff swatting at a bug. That would be me. He gashed his leg open on a rock and will be lucky to make it up to the main road and the rescue car. That would be pure dumb luck. The other guy in the blue tights is still on your trail. He took one of the Were's bikes when I crashed his. You've about five minutes ahead. He's trying to bike in. Stupid ass. You were smart ditching yours. He's banged his bahoogies twice already."

Coming to a halt to read the GPS, Trent smacked the mosquito biting his elbow and squinted at the sun-faded map. The system was flashing, having an electronic hissy because he'd gone off the race route, but that the walking trail wasn't on record was a good thing. *The stream has to be close.* Tucking the GPS away, he squinted up at the cliff rising to his left.

"You going to try to lose him in the woods?" Jenks said as Trent started forward at a slower pace, hoping to catch his breath so he'd have something when push came to shove.

"No. I can't outrun him. I need a good place for an ambush," Trent said absently. He looked up, startled to find Jenks hovering backward as he walked forward, staring at him in what appeared to be apprehension. "Ah, thank you, Jenks. I appreciate you taking care of the one man. My chances have improved dramatically."

Jenks squinted at him, then frowned. "Sure. What can I do to help with this last one? He uses magic like it's his first language. The broken lines here don't bother him at all."

Concerned, Trent felt the bumps in his belt pack. He had only three sleepy-time potions he wanted to keep for the compound. Everything else he had was ley line based and potentially lethal—and with the fractured state of the ley lines this close to the faults, it wouldn't be a fast implementation. He'd need a distraction if he was to even have a chance. He didn't want to end up trapping himself in a bubble of protection and lose because he ran out of time, pinned down by one of the Withons' guards until they came for him and then killed him as a trespasser. *I am so weary of ultimate resolutions . . .*

"I've got an idea," he said as he jogged through a stand of young trees, ducking some of the larger branches as he moved through them. "Is he still on his bike?"

"Tink loves a duck, you're improvising. I'll go check," Jenks said dryly, and he darted back down the way they had come.

Heart thumping, Trent continued to run up the path before slipping off it and doubling back amid the short grass and ferns. Cursing the insects he stirred up, he worked back to the thicket of young trees. Being careful not to crush more vegetation than necessary, he pulled a sapling back like a bow, ready to smack the next thing that came down the path. It was hard to see, and he tucked his sunglasses aside, squinting as his eyes adjusted.

A mosquito landed on his arm, then another. Three found the tiny slip of skin showing between his black biking tights and his socks. Slowly the forest reclaimed the silence, and the sound of insects and wind became obvious. Grimacing, Trent reached out his awareness and tapped a line.

Silver-flecked energy tasting of green and broken rock flowed into him, heady but intermittent. The "amperage" was adequate, but the flow was erratic and might cause a breakage in his charm that the wise practitioner could exploit. If his familiar had been closer, he could have drawn a clean line through him, but the auratic bond between him and his horse didn't work past the curve of the earth.

The soft hum of Jenks's wings grew loud, and Trent winced as the pixy stopped dead in the path in a spot of sun, right where the tree was going to swing. His wings blurred to invisibility and the sun caught his silver dust to make him a primordial vision—until the pixy swore, darting sideways when a blue jay dove at him. A blue feather drifted down, and the jay screamed.

"Jenks!" Trent whispered, thinking Rachel would joyfully kill him if he came back without the pixy. She'd never believe he was taken by a blue jay.

Brightening, Jenks darted over. "Tink blasted birds," he said loudly as he stabbed the mosquitoes on Trent's arm with his sword and they exploded in little drops of blood. "There are *obviously* no pixies around here."

Trent continued to gather the energy to him, hoping that by holding it in his chi, he might give it some semblance of order. He held his breath, listening for the sound of a bike, unable to hear over the low hum of Jenks's wings. "Will you settle somewhere?" he asked, and the pixy alighted on the bent-back tree. "Not there!" he hissed, but it was too late. The soft rattle of a street bike pretending to be a dirt cycle became obvious. In a flash of sun, a man in blue riding tights shimmied up the path, the man standing on the pedals to make progress.

Eyes flicking over the man's thick legs and wide shoulders, Trent grimaced. He was stocky for an elf, and his straw-blond hair poking from under his helmet and his heavy build said he had a large portion of human in him. He'd been behind Trent at the start of the race, and he had thought it odd that someone so athletic would put himself in the middle of the start instead of the front where he could break from the casual racers sooner and have a better time.

If Trent was lucky, the man would have enough human in him to slow his magic down, a prospect that seemed unlikely when the man looked up and met his eyes. Intelligence glittered, followed by anticipation of dealing out pain, then alarm as he saw the bent tree and realized what was about to happen.

"Now!" Jenks shouted, and Trent let go of the tree.

The bent branch sprang forward, Jenks rising up so it moved harmlessly under him, sighing with its passage. Dirt sprayed as the man skidded to a halt, turning sideways to avoid a full strike, but unbalanced, he fell. Heart pounding, Trent launched himself at the man still disentangling himself from the bike.

The thump of impact rocked them both, the man pinned under his bike dazed but reactive. Reaching out, Trent grasped the man's arm, ignoring the pinch of pain in his foot.

"*Ta na veno!*" Trent shouted, gasping as the words triggered a memory flash and line energy jagged through him. The twenty minutes it took to prepare the wild-magic charm unrolled in his mind faster than thought itself, reliving it in an instant and harnessing the energy now flowing through his hands. He had to touch the man for it to work. The charm could not puncture the assassin's aura on his own. Wild magic needed every ounce of direction he could muster.

Trent's eyes widened as he felt the spell peel from his soul like new skin. It raced through his body, following his neural pathways, condensing, becoming more powerful the farther it got from his chi and the fewer pathways it had to take. It would explode like a bomb once it reached the man under him, acting like mental shrapnel to burn the assassin's own neural network to render his magic useless and put them on equal footing.

"Son of a bitch!" the man shouted, and with a grunt, he shoved his bike up. Trent's grip on the man was torn away, and in a panic he scrambled for anything as his magic crested, hesitated, and then not finding anything to fall into, collapsed back into Trent.

Agony arched through him. His jaw clenched as his muscles violently contracted. He fell back, his head hitting the soft earth and his breath whooshing out. His heart spasmed once, fighting to find a rhythm as the charm exploded. He couldn't think as images of the people he knew, alive or dead, flashed like strobes in his thoughts as the magic randomly jolted the neurons in his brain, burning through him, shredding his aura . . . leaving him helpless.

Someone was groaning, and he bit his tongue when he realized it was him.

"Not bad," the man said, and Trent blearily looked up at the metallic thump of the straw-blond man shoving the bike off himself and standing. "I don't know that one. Your witch is right, though. You should leave the magic to those who know what they're doing."

Idiot, Trent thought, his chest hurting as he clenched at the dirt, trying to put the world back together, but he couldn't even stand up. Nothing was responding. His charm had backfired right at him. He had nothing, no magic, no weapons. Nothing.

"Damn, you made me break my bike," the man said, bending over his knees, clearly trying to catch his breath. "That really pisses me off."

"Sorry," Trent managed. "I was aiming for your face. I don't suppose you'd be willing to just leave?"

The man looked up from his leg, bleeding and caked with dirt and bark, and shook his head. Grimacing, he unclipped his bike helmet and took it off. "Get up. Ellasbeth wants to talk to you before she peels your skin off and drops you into the ocean."

Trent held up a finger for a moment. With a muffled groan, he got a leg under him, and from there, got to a kneel. Panting, he squinted in the sun at the man. Things were starting to work again, and his resolve strengthened. He didn't have his magic. Big deal. He wasn't helpless. "You're going to have to kill me," he rasped, meaning it.

The big man shook his head. "I get paid more if you're alive. We can do broken and bleeding, though."

The sound of the knife pulling from a sheath was chilling, the cold steel hissing softly before the last *ting* of release. It glinted in the dappled shade, and seeing it, Trent went still. His eyes flicked everywhere, and he tensed, even as he settled himself deeper into the mold and earth, becoming one with it, easing his seared thoughts until nothing remained but the knife and the man wielding it. *Not again. Restraint. Show some Goddess-blessed restraint. I am not an animal.*

"Hey! Dewdrop!" Jenks shrilled as the man moved toward Trent, knife bared, and Trent's air sucked in as the pixy dove down.

"Jenks!" Trent shouted as the man moved faster than Trent would have believed was possible, knocking Jenks aside. The pixy screamed a curse as he spiraled into the bracken.

The man grabbed Trent's shirt front, the smell of him cascading through Trent: sweat, anger, testosterone, satisfaction. It plinked through him like little drops of fire, igniting his anger. He was a Kalamack. This was the space he defended, the companion he protected. He would prevail.

The knife arched toward him. Trent watched it, still rising to meet it from his kneel. Leaning sideways, he grabbed the man's free hand, yanking him off balance and stepping behind him. Dancing almost, he struck at the man's grip on the knife, hitting the nerve complex perfectly and swiveling his wrist to catch the knife as it fell.

The man's eyes widened, but it was too late, and with a spinning grace, Trent tossed the knife to shift its grip, and smoothly ran it under the man's ear, falling back six feet as the man's heart pounded once with no restriction . . . and his life's blood surged free.

"Holy Tinker's damn!" Jenks exclaimed.

The large man before him clamped his hands to his neck, bright crimson blood coating them in his second heartbeat.

Damn it, Trent thought, grimacing as the man gaped at him, and with a third heartbeat, his body was depleted of enough blood to maintain the pressure to feed his mind. Disgusted with himself, Trent tossed the knife to land before the kneeling man. A fourth heartbeat, and he fell forward to hide it.

"You . . ." Jenks stammered from a fallen log, his wing bent and leaking dust. "Tink loves a duck, you're good!" But Trent was anything but pleased. He'd done it again. What the hell was he turning into? Maybe Rachel was right.

"Hey!" Jenks said as he jumped from the log, and Trent put a finger to his lips, his brow furrowing as he realized too late it was covered in blood. Frowning, he patted the man down, searching his pockets until he found a two-way radio.

"Target . . . —nated," he said, pitching his voice low and breaking his words to simulate a bad connection. "Hurt and requ— pick up at—. Coordi—," he finished, then dropped it, using his foot to smash the radio until the back came off and the radio broke into three pieces. Jaw clenched, he stomped on it a few more times just for the hell of it. Adrenaline surged through him, ugly but exhilarating. *I do not enjoy this.* But the feeling of perfect grace and movement—finding an absolute end to the dance—had left him with a calm that was only now dissipating.

His hands were sticky: avoiding Jenks's eyes, he found a wipe in his belt pack and cleaned his fingers. The flies were starting to gather already, and Trent backed into the shade, sitting on the low log beside the pixy, and listened to the wind in the trees as he found himself.

Damn it all to the Turn and back, he hadn't wanted to kill the man. Okay, he had, but not like this. The more he tried to not be his father, the more he became him. The man was dead, and he didn't care, didn't wish it were otherwise but for a mild feeling of having failed to find a better way.

"That was slick!" Jenks said as he clambered up beside him, his wings moving fitfully. "I don't know what I'm more impressed with, that you just bought yourself an hour, or . . . that."

Trent stared into space beyond the body in the patch of sun. Why didn't he feel anything? Had he become the task of keeping his species alive so deeply that his own soul had been swallowed up by it? Was it too late?

"Rachel is right," Jenks said, his voice holding both encouragement and unexpected understanding. "You *are* a murdering bastard. If you were small enough, I'd bang knuckles with you. Hell, if you were small enough, I'd put you on my own lines."

Trent's breath slipped from him in a sigh as he thought of Rachel. Why did the woman hold him to such a narrow line of behavior? It wasn't like the people she lived with didn't end lives when the need demanded it. She knew it, and yet if he killed someone to save his life, she labeled him a failure. *Maybe it's because I label myself as one*, he thought, then grimaced at the pixy, blinking at the expression of pity and understanding on Jenks's face. He had to get better at magic—killing people was starting to wear on him.

"You okay?" the pixy asked, his mood serious, and Trent nodded, his breath hissing in as he tried to touch a line and found himself burned.

"Mostly," he said as he stood, knees shaking. They had to get moving. The Withons might have a helicopter.

"You leaving him here? It's a lot of evidence."

Trent looked back at the body, knowing the knife with his fingerprints was somewhere under him, not to mention his prints on the bike and the man, and his footprints. Jenks stood, waiting. The pixy's nonchalance should have soothed him, but it only bracketed his own realization that something in him was on the verge of dying. Rachel suffered every time she was remotely responsible for anyone's death. She agonized over it, tortured herself until she found the knowledge that made her strong enough that ultimate force could be avoided. He just kept killing people until it had gotten easy.

"We leave him here," Trent said softly. "This is an arranged madness. There will be no inquiry, no backlash killing." His gaze landed on Jenks. The pixy hadn't flown since being hit, and silver dust was still leaking from him. "Can you fly?"

Jenks rose up, his wings unusually noisy. "Some, but it hurts like hell. Can I ride for a while? We got what, another half mile?"

Trent nodded, and Jenks landed on his shoulder, making him shiver as something seemed to sift down through him like Jenks's dust. Still shaken, he turned and started up the path, his pace slower. He could have done something else. Maybe cut his hamstrings and tied him to a tree. Knocked him out. Used one of those sleepy-time charms he had tucked away. It wouldn't last long this close to the ocean, but it would have been enough to slip away. *Anything* other than letting his reactions get the best of him. He'd slit the man's Goddess-blessed throat.

The cool shadow of the trees took him as he stepped off the path and struck out to the north, and Trent stomped ahead without breaking a single twig, crushing a solitary stem. Head down, he unconsciously wove between the trees, taking the path of least resistance as Jenks became quieter and quieter. "Ah, are you sure you're okay?" Jenks said, and Trent jerked, having forgotten he was with him. "Your aura looks like it took a hit."

Trent slapped at a mosquito, then rubbed another one out of existence. "It did." He'd forgotten pixies could see auras all the time. His now damaged aura was a direct result of burning his neural net and was probably why Jenks's dust was making his skin tingle. "I can't tap a line."

Jenks's high-pitched noise went right through Trent's head. "Wait up. You just lost your magic? All of it? And we're still headed for the fortress of doom?"

Trent craned his neck to look at the sheer cliff face facing them. He couldn't see the monastery from this angle, but the opening to the monk escape was close. *Where's the creek?* "Yes. Everything that is not invoked and in my belt pack is out. I'm going to have to improvise."

Jenks was silent. The birds had found them, and jays screamed at them from the canopy until they were out of their territory. "This just got a lot more complicated," the pixy said, and Trent paused to listen for the sound of water.

"Rachel catches offenders without magic," Trent said. But Rachel knew what she was doing. And when she didn't, she could improvise on the fly, coming up with options that left a lot of collateral damage but usually only hurt herself, not the people around her. It was one of the things he would never admit that he admired about her. The more he tried not to be his father, the more he saw his father's face in the mirror.

"Yeah," Jenks said, and Trent continued along the base of the cliff. "But Rachel is a professional," he said, making Trent wince. "You, on the other hand, are a well-prepared, wealthy elf with too much time on his hands and a grudge for having been stood up at the altar. And you just became less well-prepared, cookie maker."

Steeling his face into a bland mask, Trent trudged forward, slipping through the sunlit shadows without stirring a leaf. "You can stay here if you want. It will take me a couple of hours to get to a phone and send someone for you."

"Whoa, whoa, whoa! I said I was with you, and I am. I just don't want you to go in with a damaged battle plan. Rachel does that, and it drives me batty."

Somewhat reassured, Trent's pace smoothed. "My plan will work without magic. I'll just have to be more aggressive." Again his mood darkened, and both he and the pixy went silent as he remembered the man's shock and surprise in the sun. It had been fast, but not fast enough. What the hell was wrong with him, and how could someone like him take care of a baby? How could Lucy ever love him?

Angry, Trent pushed at a branch, almost snapping it.

"You sure you're okay?" Jenks asked.

"Fine." Trent took a slow breath as he stopped, listening again. "There should be a stream here. We need to get on the other side of it. The tunnel is halfway up a cliff at its base."

"No." Jenks persisted, his wings clattering as he made the short flight to a leafless lower branch and sat in a drop of sun that made it through the canopy. "What's eating at you? I know you don't care about that man you just offed except that you wish you'd done something less permanent."

Startled, Trent dropped his gaze from the cliff top. "Excuse me?"

Jenks reached back to run a hand over his damaged wing, reminding Trent of a tiny cat. "You're distracted. It's making you slow, not to mention my job twice as hard. Spill it. You need all your focus if you're going to survive this, and by Tink's panties, you are going to survive it. Rachel needs your help."

Trent held his breath, trying to decide what to say. The faint sound of water came faint on the wind as it gusted, and he leaned into motion. "Nothing is bothering me."

The harsh sound of Jenks's wings made him squint, and the pixy landed on his shoulder to find his balance by gripping his ear. "Damn it, you did it again," the pixy grumbled.

"Did what?"

"You lied to me," Jenks said, and Trent frowned. "Pixies can tell when people lie. That's why Rachel and I get along so well."

Trent tried to see him as he stepped over a moss-covered log, but he was too close. "Rachel doesn't lie?"

"Oh, hell, she lies all the time, but she knows it. You're lying to yourself, not just me. What gives, Trent? Let's have it now so we can get on with our lives, short as they might be."

The smugness in Jenks's voice scraped over Trent's frayed nerves. The last person who had pointed out his flaws like this had found himself down the camp's well for three days. "It's none of your business," he said with a false lightness, not wanting to admit to a pixy that he was worried he was turning into a psychopath to save his species. How could anyone, much less a little girl, love that? His daughter deserved the best, and his soul felt like it was dying. "Can you hear water running?"

Jenks was silent for a long moment, then he said, "Yep. You're headed right for it."

The earth fell away in front of him, and he slowed as the scent and sound of running water rose up like a balm. Cautioning Jenks to hold on, Trent slid down the mossy, rocky side, his thoughts churning. He hadn't expected children for another twenty years. Ellasbeth, at least, had had nine months to realign her thinking. He had had three.

A branch he had his foot propped against gave way, and he slid, effortlessly catching himself on a rock. Money didn't make a child happy, only spoiled. And if he was going to raise a child, he wanted to do it right— without relying on Ceri. All he had was the distance his father had shown him and brief snatches of motherly affections taken in glimpses, hardly remembered. He didn't want Lucy to grow up feeling alone, surrounded by everything and having nothing.

Trent's final lurch brought him before the small stream, and he stood straight, assessing both the best way to get across it as well as the sunny ridge high above him on the other side. His hands were scraped, and he wiped them on his dirty and torn biking outfit. The thought of raising this child was only slightly less terrifying than the thought of losing her forever.

"You're not worried about getting your daughter, you're worried about what happens afterward," Jenks said suddenly, and Trent's jaw clenched. Head up, he reached for an overhanging branch and went hand over hand, feet swinging above the rushing cold water.

"You're worried you won't be good enough," Jenks said, darting off when Trent swung wildly and jumped for the bank.

Looking at his scraped, bleeding hands, Trent muttered, "Hardly."

"Liar." Jenks stood on a bare branch, his hands on his hips and a smile quirking his expression. "You don't think she's going to love you, and it's killing you."

"I have no doubt that I'm good enough," Trent said, then lowered his voice. "If I wasn't, I wouldn't be risking my life to acquire her."

The pixy laughed at him, sifting a bright silver dust. "I'm not talking about being good enough to get in and out of the Withons' compound with her. You're scared about what you are going to do with a little girl, Mr. Most

Eligible Bachelor Multibillionaire with More Money and Resources Than a Small City."

It was too close to the truth for him to admit, and Trent tilted his head to see where the top of the cliff and the sky met, almost straight up. "I have people to care for her already lined up," he said, stifling the rising feeling of inadequacy. He didn't have one person interviewed, one inquiry made. He wanted to raise this child himself, as he wished he had been. "Can you fly yet? I think the opening is above the ledge."

Jenks darted in front of him, his wings loud but clearly functioning again. "Wet nurses and nannies," he scoffed, looping before him like a courting hummingbird. "You want to raise her yourself, and you're afraid you're not going to be a good dad. That you won't know how to take care of her, that you might *break* her."

His brow furrowed, and Trent forced it smooth. He was never going to work with pixies again. His father had been right to ban them from the grounds. "Will you fly up there and check? The opening is about four by four and will have a small ledge before it."

Jenks's looping stopped, and he hovered right in front of him, looking both young and wise, honest and angry. "Let me tell you something, Kalamack," he said as the sparkles sifted from him. "There is no way that you can be more scared than I was with Matalina pregnant and us living in a flower box that didn't have enough dirt to keep out the heat, much less hibernate through. I was ten years old and a family on the way."

Trent didn't flinch, already knowing about Jenks's life. "Lucy will be well cared for," he said shortly, and he reached for a handhold. He'd simply climb up. The opening was said to be very close to the waterfall.

"That's not why you're scared," Jenks said as he flew in front of him, landing on the best handholds before Trent moved to them. "You're scared that she's not going to like you, that you're going to do something wrong and she's going to hate you."

Stretching for a handhold, Trent met his eyes, hesitating as he found understanding had replaced Jenks's biting, sarcastic accusations. He had slit a man's throat and left him. He didn't have a moment's regret for it other than he should have found a better way. Something was wrong with him. How could a child love someone who takes the life of another and doesn't care?

Trent took a breath to speak, changed his mind, and reached for the next crack. The sound of Jenks's wings mixed with the chattering water, and slowly Trent inched up into the light.

"You got nothing to worry about, cookie maker."

Stretched along the rock face, Trent squinted up. Jenks's silhouette was lost in the sun's glare until the wind shifted a bough and shade covered them again.

"I can guarantee it," Jenks said as their eyes met. "The second that you see her, you will fall in love. You will do anything for her, anything at all, and she will know it and love you back. That's all kids want to know—that you love them."

He tried to say something, anything, but the glare of the sun struck him, catching the words in his throat.

"And you will," Jenks said, his voice coming as if from the sunbeam. "You can't help it. It's built in. It doesn't matter that you weren't there for the first three months of her life. She's been waiting for you, and you're going to fall in love. Take it from someone who held his first five children as they died in his arms."

Trent swallowed hard, blinking the sun from his eyes. "I'm sorry," he said, his voice low so it wouldn't crack. His legs were trembling, and his hands ached. The top of the cliff was close, and he lifted himself another foot, straining.

Jenks moved to the shade, his head down and his wings slumped. "I didn't tell you for your pity. Fairy farts, I don't know why I even brought it up. I'll see where the tunnel is."

The wind from his wings shifted Trent's hair to tickle his face. Wondering, Trent watched him dart away, pixy dust making a brilliant sunbeam. Why indeed?

uscles straining, Trent levered himself up onto the wide ledge. His leg scraped the cliff face, and his arms began to tremble under his weight. Exhaling heavily, he twisted to sit with his back against the rock, legs dangling over the edge, his eyes closed against the sun, the cool breeze eddying from the mouth of the tunnel beside him. Fatigue pulled at him, a fatigue that was from more than biking thirty miles and climbing halfway up a cliff, from more than killing a man he hadn't wanted to. He couldn't remember the last time he slept. Catnaps in the back of the car were a poor substitute. It was about eight in the morning, but his body was still on East Coast time and he was ready to nap.

The dull throb in his leg stirred him, and he opened his eyes, bending forward over his pulled-up knees to run a hand over the smooth fabric of his riding clothes. His tights were torn, and he'd made a mess of them, the original shine now scraped and dulled.

"Tink's panties, I'm tired," Jenks said, and Trent flicked his eyes to the pixy perched on a rock near the edge, his wings moving slow enough that he could watch their lazy motions and the dust spilling from them. "What do you do to keep awake?" Jenks said, half to himself as he dug in his belt pack and shoved a wad of what was probably nectar and pollen into his mouth. "Me, I 'eep eatin'," the pixy said around a sticky mouthful. "I'd offer 'ou un', but you're oo big."

A sudden hunger pinched at Trent's middle, and he reached for his own belt pack. "That's okay. I've got something," he said as the crackle of shiny paper caught the sun and sent blinding flashes against the cliff side as he ripped open the packaging. Neither of them said anything as they ate, and the sticky sweet, almost musty tasting chewy bar of energy and free radicals disappeared in five easy bites.

An unexpected feeling of camaraderie stole through him as he sat in the sun and crumpled the packaging up. He didn't think it stemmed from Jenks's easy acceptance of the elves' unusual crepuscular lifestyle of being most active at dusk and dawn. Pixies were the same, napping the four hours around noon and midnight. It wasn't often he spent time with someone who was comfortable enough with him to not have to keep up a running conversation. Jenks talked a lot, but only when he had something to say.

A stray thought drifted through Trent, and he surreptitiously watched Jenks finishing his own meal, wondering if perhaps pixies had once been elven pets thousands of years ago. But as his eyes flicked to the sword at Jenks's belt, he decided it was more likely they had served as guards in exchange for the land to safely raise a family, much as Rachel and he seemed to do. Smiling, he tucked his blowing hair behind his ears. They had lost so much history.

His arms had quit trembling, and still silent, he spun to his feet and turned his back on the heat of the day, peering into the low-ceilinged tunnel smelling of damp and wet rock. "Ready?"

"Just a sec." Jenks's wings hummed as he lifted off. "I gotta pee."

Nodding, Trent took several hunched steps into the darkness, fumbling for the penlight in his belt pack as his sunstruck eyes struggled to adapt. He clicked it on and played it over the rough-hewn ceiling inches over his head. Something smelled off, and he couldn't put his finger on it. Not like an animal had taken up residence, but . . . crickets. Dead crickets?

He took several more steps, the chill deepening about him. The walls had been chiseled to a bumpy smoothness, and the floor even more so. The way sloped upward as expected, going only a few feet until it turned and his light struck on bare rock. The dampness from the nearby waterfall made him wrinkle his nose. That there was no guard struck him as suspicious, and he breathed deeper for the scent of elves, finding nothing but that thick, cloying scent of crickets.

"Crap on toast, where's the guards?" Jenks said as he hummed in, his silver dust a temporary sunbeam pooling on the floor. "I don't smell any sign of anyone being here. Ever."

Trent took another step forward, his thoughts on their timetable. Finding the sharp turn, Trent played the light over the ceiling and floor, nose wrinkling. It smelled worse.

Jenks darted ahead past Trent's penlight. Suddenly he pulled up short and drew his sword, sputtering as he waved it about. "Spiderwebs," he said in disgust, and Trent stiffened.

Spiderwebs? "Jenks. Get back here!"

A good fifteen feet down the passage, Jenks hovered in the middle of the tunnel, a bewildered expression on his face. "It's a web," he said. "A real one, at that. Not sticky silk."

Beady eyes stared at him from beyond Jenks, never blinking. Trent fumbled for the radio he'd taken from the man in the bathroom.

"Hey!" Jenks shouted, darting up as Trent threw it past him. As the radio hit the wall and fell, a palm-sized spider, furry and arms wiggling, fell with it. "Holy shit!" the pixy exclaimed, darting back to him as three more spiders scuttled out from the shadows, descending upon their injured companion to rip him into unequal pieces. "What the Tink-blasted hell are those?"

Stifling a shudder, Trent panned his light over the ceiling. "Poisonous. Hold on a sec." Tucking the penlight under an arm, he unzipped another pocket in his belt pack. He tore open the small package, and steam began to rise as chemicals in the outer package mixed and generated heat. The scent of beef stew mixed with the smell of dead crickets to make his stomach turn, and he tossed the bag to slop against the floor.

It's probably the motion they respond to, rather than the smell of the food, he thought as a dozen spiders of all sizes converged, fighting as they each claimed a portion and retreated to the shadows.

"That is uglier than a shit sandwich," Jenks said, not having moved from his shoulder.

"We haven't seen the matriarch," Trent cautioned, not moving as a spider the size of a salad plate crept out of the darkness, moving slowly as it came to sit on the largest hunk of meat. Shaking his head in disgust, Trent started to edge around them, Jenks pressed close to his neck. He'd never thought he'd ever see them, especially not an entire self-sustaining colony.

"I hope you brought more din-din than that," Jenks said as they passed the last one, and Trent breathed easier, shuddering as he turned his back and paced forward, his light swinging in a predictable arch: floor, walls, ceiling.

"They have a very narrow temperature and light preference," Trent said softly, realizing why there were no guards at this end of the tunnel. "A few more feet in, and we'll be fine. I hate to say it, but they're a genetically modified spider that my father came up with before he moved out east. It was his doctoral thesis." And then a modified virus destroyed the world, and genetic research was outlawed. Trent's thoughts shifted back to the spiders; he began to see a sliver of wisdom in it.

"Nice," Jenks said sarcastically, still on his shoulder. "Hey, you don't have any of these in your garden, do you?"

"They must survive on whatever stumbles in," he said, ignoring Jenks's question. "That's why no animal scat or guards. It smells better now, don't you think?"

Jenks's wings hummed to make a draft on Trent's neck, but he didn't fly away. "You, ah, don't have any of these, right?" he asked again, and Trent only smiled. Leave the pixy guessing.

A bright dust spilled down Trent's front, and seeing no more webs, Jenks took to the air, his wings doing as much as Trent's light to illuminate the tunnel. "Okay, killer spiders. Check. What do you have for the guards at the other end?"

Frowning, Trent checked his watch. Maybe he should chance running some of this. He could use a warm-up. "I've got a doppelgänger glamour," he said, ducking a low spot. *Which might be harder than anticipated if I can't tap a line.*

Jenks sighed so heavily that Trent could hear him. "Pixy pus, Trent. Why are you doing this?" he said, gesturing to include the narrowing tunnel. "You're risking your life, everything you and your family worked for. Couldn't you and Ellasbeth have come to some sort of joint custody thing instead of Elven Death Quest 2000?" The pixy shivered, a shade of green briefly joining the silver sparkles sifting down to show where they'd been. "Not that I'm not having a fun time here and all with the spiders."

Trent's smile faded, and he pushed himself into a faster pace, hunched as he fought both the rising incline and the lowering ceiling. "Ellasbeth didn't tell me Lucy existed, even after her birth. I found out through a mutual 'friend.' "

It had been Lee, and the anger he'd felt at the time rushed back, as bright and shiny as the day he'd found out.

"You sure she's yours?" the pixy said dryly, and Trent eyed him. "Sorry. Okay, you're bitter. I get that, but what are you going to do if we get in there, and she's holding the baby? You're not going to kill her. Right?"

As Trent tightened his grip on the light, his thoughts went to the sleep charms in his pack. "Of course not," he said, but it took longer than it should for the words to pass his lips. "Lucy is my child as much as hers, and Ellasbeth won't share. Believe me, I tried." A chunk of harder rock made a curtain of pink and red, and he slipped around it, having to turn sideways. "It's not just Lucy, it's the voice of the people that Ellasbeth won't let go of."

The tunnel past the rock curtain was smoother, and he picked up the pace, the light bobbing wildly. "You lost me," Jenks said, a stable spot of light flying beside him.

The weight of the cliff pressed down on his thoughts more than he had anticipated. "Lucy is the first elf born without the demon curse destroying her genetic integrity. I would've given the cure freely, obviously, but Ellasbeth stole it, hoping that I'd not know about Lucy until it was too late." Again the bitterness rose, thick and choking, and he carefully pushed it to the back of his mind to brood over later. Anger would cause him to make mistakes. He could be angry after it was over. "As the first elf born free of the demon curse, she represents our future. Whoever has custody of her will be listened to, and things need to change if we are going to survive the resurgence of our numbers."

Jenks frowned, his brow furrowed. "How can more babies be dangerous? I don't get it."

"Neither does Ellasbeth," he muttered, then took a breath to collect his thoughts as he jogged uphill. "No one likes a minority suddenly becoming prosperous. Especially the vampires," he said softly, and Jenks's dust shifted to a startled gold. "The more elves are born, the more obvious it will become what we are. Without a public species awareness, we will be divided and not survive the increased attention our rising numbers will bring." *That, and they needed the endangered species protection laws to keep the vampires from picking them off one by one as they had done to the banshees.* "If Lucy remains with the Withons, nothing will change and we will die even as we are poised to recover. Besides," he muttered, checking his watch, "if we come out of the closet, I won't have to kill so many people."

For a moment, Jenks was silent, then he said, "*You* could just come out."

Trent nodded wearily, recalling the hours he'd argued this with Quen. "I could on a personal basis, yes, and I intend to, but no one will follow me unless . . ." Steps slowing, Trent aimed the flashlight deep into the rising tunnel. "I need to prove myself," he said, embarrassed. "Not to myself, but everyone else. Everything I've done is on the coattails of my father."

Jenks's wings were almost silent, and the pixy landed on his shoulder, clearly cold. "Elf quest. Right. I got that part. You have to steal a child before you can have one."

Trent shifted his head as he jogged forward, trying to see the pixy, failing. "No. That's not it. You pixies have your own right of passage. If you can't make it on your own, you die."

"Yeah," Jenks said matter-of-factly, "but that's because if we don't, it's because we're stupid and shouldn't pass on our genes."

A quick glance at his watch, and worry spiked through him, pushing him back into a faster pace. "Or unlucky. Stealing children is a tradition that once kept our species alive, rightfully abandoned when my father found a way to arrest the degradation of our genome. I'm not proud of it, but traditions die hard, and stealing an infant, especially a royal infant with extended protection, will prove to the remaining elves that I will see us all through the next hundred years or so." He slowed, feeling the ground start to level out. There were cobbles worked into patches, and the ceiling was higher. Almost he could walk upright. They were close, and his fingers tingled. "It's an assurance that my decisions will be made to benefit everyone else before myself, that I'll risk my safety for the health of our species as a whole."

The image of the man dying in the woods flashed before him. And how considerate was it to tear Lucy from her mother and grandmother? He liked Mrs. Withon. Liked her a lot.

A flush of guilt warmed him, and he slowed to a walk, breathing hard and legs aching from the angle of climb. What the hell was he doing here, forced to rob a cradle in order to see his own child?

"Even if you have to kill someone to do it," Jenks said as if reading his thoughts.

Grimacing, he checked his watch again. Jenks was right. The agreement he had entered into had forced him to use ultimate resolutions. Perhaps he should grow up and call it what it really was—murder. He could've worked harder to arrange a joint custody, but he'd been angry with Ellasbeth. She hadn't been thinking responsibly, either, and it was hard not to fight when both people feel betrayed. He needed to learn the art of setting his personal feelings aside. This could have been avoided. Somehow.

Jenks's wings hesitated, and Trent watched as the pixy dropped several feet, his dust seeming to flicker as he caught himself and rose back up again. "Listen!" he said in excitement, eyebrows arched high in the dim light. "Do you smell that? I'll be right back."

Trent took a breath to stop him, but Jenks had darted off, and Trent changed his motion, stopping altogether and breathing deeply, ears straining. Nothing. But pixies were said to have the best senses in Inderland.

The air felt warmer, and figuring they'd found the end, he slipped a finger into his belt pack, finding his spelling ribbon and looping it around his neck, tucking it behind his collar and shirt. His cap was next, and he reached out to touch his consciousness to the nearest ley line, wincing as the energy flowed and his head felt as if it had been clamped in a vise.

"Bless it back to the Turn," he whispered, easing his hold on the slightly greasy feeling line tasting of broken rock and lightening until his headache eased. He could do the doppelgänger charm. Fast magic was out, but invoking the spell in his pocket was a definite possibility, even if it did hurt like hell.

Relief cascaded over him, strong enough to make him feel foolish. Face reddening, he looked down at the cap and ribbon in his tight grip. He didn't know if he believed in the Goddess his magic called on, even if he had seen what had to be her touch in his magic, felt her laugh at his clumsy attempts to achieve the impossible. There in the dark, buried by broken mountains and surrounded by shattered lines of power, he closed his eyes, desperate.

Let me do this without killing anyone, he prayed, ribbon and cap in his hand. *Give me the speed and surety in action to be merciful in deed. Give this to me, and I will . . .* He hesitated, feeling within him a gathering of foreign will, a great eye among thousands turning to him in speculation and consideration. He didn't know if it was real or imagined as his heart pounded, but he knew that despite what Quen said, the means did not justify the ends. If he won his daughter through a careless disregard of life, he would become what he most hated. Taking life was not damning; taking it carelessly and without respect was.

Trent swallowed hard, his pulse hammering. *Give me strength today, and I will strive to find within me the person who can be both*, he thought, not sure what he meant, but it felt right—as if his promise to not give up on his foolish attempt to be two things was enough of a sacrifice—or amusement—for the trickster goddess his ancestors had both worshipped and called upon for their magic.

Breath shaking as he exhaled, Trent opened his eyes, fingers trembling faintly as he looped the ribbon behind his neck and fixed the cap on his head. Something felt different, even if it was his imagination. Embarrassed again, he turned his penlight off and slipped it in his pocket. Again he touched the top of his head to reassure himself his cap was on, then strained to hear the slightest sound. His heart beat loud in his ears, and just when he had decided Jenks was in trouble, the pixy returned, his glow and wing clatter breaking the silent dark with the abruptness of a shot. A surprising relief spilled through Trent, and he steeled his expression.

"No guard," Jenks said, pulling up short as he realized the light was out. "But they don't need one with the setup they have. It's slicker than snot on a frog." His attention flicked to Trent's cap and ribbon. "You can do your magic now?"

"More or less," Trent hedged.

"Huh," Jenks snorted. "In my experience in working with you lunkers, more or less means I work more 'cause you're less than up to it."

"I'm fine." Frowning, Trent started forward.

"Which means F'ed in extreme," Jenks said, but he was laughing, making the sound of wind chimes in the pixy dust lit dark. "Seriously, just how heavily will you be leaning on me?"

Annoyance flashed through Trent. Sensing it, Jenks slowed and his wing hum dropped in pitch. Trent stopped, wanting to explain but lacking the words. Jenks wasn't a babysitter, which was the feeling Trent always had gotten from Quen. He'd proven to be an admirable help, dependable, resourceful, and best of all, not trying to change his plan but work within it. He was stupendous at his job, and it was obvious why Rachel put her trust in the pixy before anyone else.

But trust came hard to him as well, and old guards fall slowly. Continuing to withhold information from Jenks in order to preserve a feeling of independence wasn't only useless, but made him look bad. Shoulders slumping, he dropped his head. Jenks was waiting for him when he looked up.

"You're right," he said, and Jenks's dust flashed. "Ley line magic is going to hurt, but I can invoke the doppelgänger charm and possibly manage a burst of defensive magic in a pinch. Making a protective circle is out, seeing as my connection will be flimsy at best."

His dust sifting down brightening, Jenks nodded, his lack of a smart-ass comment clearly stating that he knew something had changed—and that he appreciated it. "Ten feet ahead is a wooden door with a narrow airhole to feed the fire with," Jenks said, his voice stronger somehow. "There's no lock. Once you're through, you've got a three-by-three shaft with a ladder older than my grandmum's underwear which leads to a tiny space behind the fireplace. You go through a slit, and you're *in* the fireplace. It's going, by the way. Big-ass fire made out of maple and oak. Are your tights fire retardant?"

Trent winced. "To a certain point," he said hesitantly, and Jenks smirked.

"I'll dust the fire down for you," he offered, and again Trent was ashamed at how he had been thinking of Jenks as a tool, not an equal member. "They probably think the fire is enough of a guard since the kitchen is empty. There's lots of people passing in the hall." He hesitated as Trent adjusted his cap. "We're still good to go, right?"

Adrenaline zinged through him, and he thought of his promise, vowing to see it through. Then he thought of his private jet waiting on the tarmac. He wanted this to be over and he and Lucy on it in the worst way. "Yes. Thank you for the layout. It's far better than what I had."

Jenks's wings hit a higher pitch, and he darted toward the door like a glowing hummingbird. Trent followed, waving his dust aside and taking care not to disturb the tiny chunks of plaster since they were deep within the fortress and who knew what the Withons had listening. The escape tunnel was extremely clever. If it needed to be used, it'd be an easy matter to slip past a banked fire, then build the fire high to disguise the opening. By the time the fire had died down and someone thought to even look for the escape tunnel, the fleeing monks would be miles away. That's not how they would be escaping, though.

The glow of Jenks's light dipped once and then held steady, and Trent winced as the tiny door materialized in his glow: three feet tall and two wide, with an elaborately carved latticework to allow for the passage of air. Jenks was sitting on the lintel and dangling his legs, his falling dust being pulled through the airholes. Crouching before it, Trent touched the wood to find it was warm. The fireplace was indeed in use.

"The latch is a lever on top of the frame," Jenks said, rising up to show him. "It's stuck, but you could probably get it."

Trent's fingers searched, and his eyes met Jenks's when he felt the smooth warmth of iron snuggled into the door frame. If you didn't know it was there, it would have been impossible to find. Together they smiled, and the adrenaline thumped through him in time with his heart. His thoughts darted back to his promise. Maybe he could do this without leaving death behind him. Maybe with a pixy's help he could do what needed to be done, and not kill anyone.

"Give me a sec to see if there's anyone in the kitchen," Jenks said as he took to the air. "The fire is going to flair when you open the door." It went dark as he darted through the latticework, and Trent nodded, even though the pixy was gone. Almost immediately he was back, giving him a glowing thumbs-up through the latticework.

Exhaling his tension, Trent worked the latch and slipped through. An unexpected billow of smoke eddied down the shaft, quickly dissipating as the natural flow of air was reestablished when he shut the door. Eyes smarting, he stood in the narrow shaft, looking up at the soft glow of fire-light and the sound and smell of burning wood.

"Hurry, before anyone comes back!" Jenks prompted from the top of the ladder, and Trent tentatively put his weight on the lowest rung. The oak felt old, but it was the rope holding it together that he was concerned about; holding his breath, he edged himself upward, trying not to shake or stress the bindings more than he had to.

The heat grew with ever step. He was sweating by the time he reached the top and clambered into a narrow four-by-two room, solid rock on all sides, ceiling, and floor—except for the narrow one-foot slit that led to the back of the fireplace. An orange glow of heat poured through it, and Trent tried to breathe shallowly as Jenks sat on the top rung of the ladder and basked.

"I got this," he said as his wings hummed into invisibility and he lazed into the air. "I'll shout when it's safe. Don't dawdle. It doesn't last long."

Dawdle? Trent thought, pulling his hand back from the wall when he touched it and found it hot. He liked the warmth, but this was like a sauna turned death trap.

The orange glow on the walls dimmed, and he moved to the slit, shoulders stiffening. "Now!" Jenks's voice came faintly.

"God help me, I'm trusting a pixy with my life," he whispered, then plunged through, his back scraping. He stopped, shocked as he ran into the heat as if it was a wall. No wonder they hadn't put a guard here. His toes were almost *in* the fire, the firebox not as large as the one in his great room, but large enough to put his desk into—and seemingly every inch of it was near the ignition point. The coals glowed dully, and the blackened wood smoldered under Jenks's dust. On the far side of him, flames flickered still. Beyond the hearth was an industrial-looking kitchen with several cooking stations, bright lights, stone walls, and very high ceilings with ventilation slits among the waist-thick support beams.

"Move your lily white elf ass!" Jenks shouted from the nearest stainless steel counter, and Trent jolted into motion.

Hair lifting from the draft, Trent lurched over the chunks of smoldering wood, smelling his shoes start to melt. Grimacing, he leaped out of the firebox, landing on the raised hearth made of natural stone. Behind him, the fire whooshed upward, Jenks's dust spent.

"Jenks, that is as impressive as anything I've ever seen," he whispered, dumbfounded and grateful as he watched the three-foot-high flames, feeling as if he had been baptized by fire. But then both his and Jenks's heads came up at the noise in the hall—military steps and a woman's voice raised in complaint.

"Crap on toast," he muttered, then blinked, wondering when—on the coast-to-coast excursion he'd been on with Rachel—that he'd picked that up.

"Let's go, cookie maker," Jenks shrilled, but leaning against the counter, Trent pulled his melted shoes off and tossed them back into the fire. "Come on!" the pixy shouted, and Trent ran a hand over his ash prints on the hearth, then wildly looked for something to hide behind. There was nothing, and plucking a pan that had to weigh at least fifteen pounds from a rack, he made a dash for the only door to the place, his sock feet slipping on the smooth slate.

"No, here!" Jenks exclaimed as he hovered before an industrial-looking freezer door.

Trent skidded to a stop. "You're kidding."

"It's a pantry!" Jenks said, hovering as he made a "get-in" gesture. "A root cellar. Come on! I wouldn't make you hide in a Tink's frozen titties freezer."

He ran, bringing the pan with him. Heart pounding, he yanked the locking pin out and slipped inside, not looking in the tiny, thick window first. Breathless, he eased the door shut as the voices became loud. Jenks hummed in satisfaction as Trent leaned against the wall and closed his eyes, relishing the cool damp of the clearly temperature controlled room. Damn, that had been close.

"Sorry, I should have told you about the pantry earlier," Jenks said, hovering so that just his head was showing through the window, in effect, an invisible watcher.

"You think?" Trent said sarcastically. How Rachel did this for a living was beyond him. To be honest, though, she didn't break into millionaires' estates very often—unless you counted the times she'd broken into his.

The smell of mushrooms pulled his eyes open, and as the woman's muffled voice complained of the elaborate precautions this last week, he looked over the racks of roots and tubers, baskets of apples, and bottles of wine—and row upon row of jars of organic baby food.

Trent looked at his watch, panicking. He'd planned to get her at her late-morning feeding, and now he was standing in the very place that they were going to be coming into!

"She's not old enough for creamed peas yet," Jenks said dryly, not turning from his spying at the window. "Chillax, dude. I wouldn't point you to a bad hiding spot."

Chillax? Trent thought as his emotion soured into disgust, not liking that the pixy could read him so well. *Had he told him to chillax?*

"We got three people in the kitchen," he said, then waved Trent off with a rude clattering noise when he leaned to the window to see. "You can hear the woman. She's about Rachel's age, I think. You all look alike to me unless you have wrinkles. Man, that girl doesn't stop complaining. She looks athletic, though. Definitely not your average nanny. She'll take you out if the other two don't. Guns, uniforms, attitudes." Jenks looked at him, grinning. "Should be fun."

The knot in his gut eased, then tightened right back up. It had been a miracle to have gotten here in time. It would take another to find Lucy and escape. *Twenty minutes*, he thought, glancing at his watch. It would be over in twenty minutes. *Give me the strength to succeed, and I will die trying to be the man my father wasn't.* It was frightening because he believed it. He had to.

"Okay, we're down to one guard," Jenks said, still hovering at the window, gazing out as if it was TV. "The big guy went back into the hall. I think the woman told him to leave. Dude, that is one bitchy nanny."

Trent fingered his doppelgänger charm, tucking it into the sleeve of his biking suit for quick retrieval. He had to have more control, less anger. More control led to less damage, less need to kill anyone. The pantry had a lock. Once he knocked the guard out, he could shove him in here and be done with it. The woman would go down under the sleep charms. He only needed ten minutes to finish this, a lifetime in the art of child abduction.

Taking a breath, Trent reached for the handle.

"What do you need for your glamour?" Jenks said as he turned, still hovering before the window. "Hair? Rachel always needs hair."

Lips parting, Trent hesitated. "Ah, yes," he stammered, then glanced through the window to see the woman with her back to him, warming up a bottle on the stove. "I was going to get it when I down the man."

Jenks's dust turned gold, and the pixy raised one eyebrow, his head cocked and his hands on his hips. "And then what? Convince the woman you knocking him out was a bad dream? Wait here. I can get you a hair."

Trent carefully opened the door a crack, and Jenks slipped out, immediately darting up to the tall ceiling.

"—driving me batty," the woman was saying, the pitch of her voice making her in her late twenties and having a brain in her head. She was indeed athletic looking as she stood before the industrial stove with her hands on her hips and watched the thermometer, appearing as if she would know as many ways as Quen to take out someone. "Dust the lightbulbs, Megan," she said in a nasally falsetto. "I can smell the dust burning. Adjust the temperature of the room, will you, Megan? The baby feels warm. Megan, fetch my laptop. I need to check my portfolio and see if I have enough to buy that island I've been wanting." The woman snorted, cranking the gas higher until it nearly ran up the sides of the warming pot. "I am *not* her personal slave. I am *a nanny*, and she needs to leave me the *fuck alone*!"

Trent bit his lip, trying not to laugh as the man with her was. He had overheard similar complaints from his staff until Ellasbeth had had enough and left—taking his unborn child with him.

His smile faded, and he turned his attention to the guard as Jenks dropped straight down and plucked a hair from his shoulder, continuing to fall to the floor where he skimmed above the slate and under the open, stainless steel counters on wheels. The man never even heard him.

Trent's heart beat twice, and Jenks slid into the pantry before a silver-lined streak of dust.

"You'd better hurry," the pixy said, his eyes bright and eager as he dropped the hair into Trent's waiting grasp. "That milk is almost at the right temp."

Trent flicked the tiny vial of prepared charm open with his thumb, the soft pop of the plastic making him jump. Carefully he angled the short black hair into it, resealed the vial, and shook it.

"You're not going to drink that, are you?" Jenks said as he landed on a jar of mashed sweet potato, his wings stilling as he gave Trent a dubious look.

"No, thank God." Touching his hat for reassurance, Trent closed his eyes to mumble the traditional ancient elf plea, then hesitated. Exhaling, he dropped his head, feeling unsure. He had called upon the gods they no longer believed in hundreds of times, but now . . . to do so casually felt . . . risky. *I am here*, he thought simply. *Judge my actions sound.*

Teeth clenched against the expected pain, he tapped the line, wincing. His eyes were still shut, and he heard Jenks take wing. Panting, he finished the incantation that actually made the spell work, the vial tight in his grip. He opened his eyes, finding Jenks watching.

"You don't look different," the pixy said, and Trent nodded, moving creakily as he popped the top of the vial again. He was still connected to the line, and moving hurt.

"It's invoked," he breathed. "Just not implemented." As Jenks checked the window, Trent dabbed some of the potion on his hat, then moistened the entirety of the ribbon before replacing it around his neck.

I do this for my child. I do this for me, he thought, and the tingle of the line seemed to settle through his aura. Faint in the back of his mind, he thought he heard a satisfied chuckle. It was done. Finished, he dropped the line, sagging in relief as his headache vanished.

"Hey, she's pouring it into a bottle," Jenks said from the window, then he whistled, catching sight of him. "Holy toad pee in a bucket!" he exclaimed, darting up and down as he took in the changes. "You even look like you're wearing his clothes! That's slicker than—"

"Snot on a frog, yes," Trent interrupted him, grinning at his apparent success. He didn't look any different to himself, but clearly it had worked. He was going to pay for this later with a string of bad luck. He knew it, even with his promise to suffer and dance for the amusement of the ancient elf gods. The last time he'd used wild magic this heavily, he'd ended up freeing an insane demon. Too bad he was going to have to do it again tomorrow.

Jenks met him, grin for grin. "Okay, I'm impressed. It's a good thing that there're no pixies on the premises. You might look like Harold, but your aura is off." And without another word, he put both feet against a baby food jar and shoved it off the counter.

Horrified, Trent jumped, adrenaline pounding through him as he stared aghast at the laughing pixy. "What the hell are you doing!" he said with a hiss, glancing at the window. The door only muffled sound; it did not cut it off.

Wings a blur, Jenks gazed out the tiny window. "I'm helping! The guy is coming. Hit him, and walk out. It doesn't get any easier than that, cookie maker."

Realizing he was right, Trent flung himself to stand beside the door, snatching up the pan he had brought in with him. My God, he was down to beaning people with kitchen pans, but it probably wouldn't kill him. Containment. Minimalization of effect. Palms sweaty, he adjusted his grip on the heavy pan. He might not need the charms for the woman at all. Jenks was thinking better than he was.

"It's probably a rat," the woman was saying as the door cracked open and Trent tensed. Maybe he should have used the sleep potion instead. This was going to make some noise.

"Hi there!" Jenks said cheerfully, and the man peering in through the door looked up, his eyes widening. His mouth opened, and Trent reached to yank the man inside.

Feet stumbling, the man spun, but Trent was already swinging, and the pan met his forehead with a clang. His eyes rolled, but he wasn't out, and Trent struggled to hit him again as the man blocked it, falling to the floor stunned but fighting.

"Harold?" the woman called, and Trent got a grip on him, clamping his arm around his neck in a sleeper hold.

"Tell her it's a rat and to stay out," he whispered, and the man grunted.

"Tell her, or I'm going to stab your eyes out," Jenks added, hovering before the suddenly frightened man.

"Ah, it's a rat!" the man warbled, his terrified eyes fixed to Jenks's bared sword. "D-Don't come in! I've got it cornered. I'll be out in a sec."

"Don't count on it," Jenks whispered, grinning evilly.

"No kidding?" the woman said, and Trent tightened his grip. The man choked, his fingers digging into Trent's arm as he fought for air, crashing into the shelves and sending jars of baby food that would never get eaten shattering against the floor. Jenks darted to the ceiling, and Trent hung on, feeling as if he was breaking an unruly horse as the man flung them into the walls, produce, everything . . . until he slowly lost consciousness and stopped moving.

At the window, Jenks motioned for him to hurry up. Trent let go, shoved the man off him, and stood. Shaking, he brushed at the baby food and potato dust. "Got it," he said, trying to match the man's voice, then snatched the guard's hat off the floor. Jenks tucked in under it as he put it on his head, sliding in between Trent's own cap and the bigger hat from Harold. Trying to catch his breath, Trent looked down at the slumped man. A flash of memory of the forest intruded: sunshine, birdsong, blood upon the fern. His fingers twitched, reaching for the knife.

Please don't lead me astray, he thought, agonizing over his decision. It would be easy. It would be sure. To leave him as he was might lead to his own death. To trust an ancient elf goddess was inane! She wasn't real! The only real thing here was if he was caught, he would die and his species would fight another thousand-year-war only to die with him.

But then his hand closed into a fist. He needed to hope that miracles could happen; otherwise he would lose all chance that he could find a way to be who he wanted, who his daughter needed.

"Did you get it?" the woman called, and Trent reached for the pan on the floor, ignoring Jenks's questioning hum.

As Jenks hovered uncertainly, Trent hit the guard once more for good measure, the reverberation echoing all the way up his arm to his spine. "Yes, ma'am," he mumbled. Tossing the pan to the floor, he staggered out.

Time to get his daughter and get out of here.

FOUR

T he young woman stood with her back to the counter, a warmed bottle in her hand and her arms crossed over her chest. "Well," she said sourly. "Did you get it?"

Heart pounding, he smiled his best sheepish expression and nodded. His voice wasn't disguised. He'd heard Harold speak; he knew he couldn't match it.

"That's what I thought," she said, pushing herself up with a slow wariness. "I'm not cleaning that up. Let's go. Ms. Tight-ass is probably itching to leave. That woman is driving me crazy." She was headed for the door, and Trent adjusted his hat to cover his ears, wincing when Jenks swore at him. "You don't wake up a baby to eat," the woman complained, arms swinging casually. "And then Tight-ass wonders why she won't go to sleep. You can't set a baby's schedule; you work around hers!"

His knees were quivering as he got to the heavy doors, opening one for her. He wanted to blame it on the exertion of thirty miles on a bike, half a mile in the cliff tunnel . . . and all of it when he should be sleeping, but he knew it was excitement and fear. *His daughter.*

"Thank you, Harold," the woman said, hesitating briefly before she went out into the hall.

"Mmmm," he muttered, dropping his head as her eyes ran from the top of his borrowed cap to his bare feet, hopefully covered by his glamour. A spike of tension snaked through him when, for an instant, he thought she could see beyond it, but then she turned away, hips swaying as she went into the hall.

He exhaled heavily as he followed her, hearing it mirrored by Jenks sandwiched between his cap and the guard's borrowed hat. A soft clearing of his throat pulled his gaze up to the four guards waiting for them, pistols on one hip, ley line charms on another. "Assume the position, Megan," the shortest man said, a hand on the butt of his pistol, a half smile on his face.

"Shove it. You know it's me," the woman, Megan apparently, said, her smart-ass attitude doing more than anything else to ease Trent's pounding heart. "If you try to frisk me one more time, I'm going to pull your balls off and make Princess-Cries-A-Lot a rattle."

Megan turned on a heel, shocking Trent as she looped her arm in his. "Besides, they caught the guy, right?" she said, jauntily walking them down the tiled, whitewashed hall.

The men jumped to follow, two hustling to get in front of them, two behind. The ceilings were low and made of darkly varnished timbers. Painted stone walls threw back the echo of the men's boots and the soft scuffing of Megan's shoes. There were no windows, but wall sconces illuminated everything in a soft, comfortable glow between the closed doors made of thick wood, varnished as dark as the ceiling.

"I'll be glad after tomorrow," Megan chatted as they walked, and Trent wondered if Harold and Megan had a little thing going as she squeezed his arm and smiled up at him. "This is insane. Guards in the hallways and escorts everywhere . . . I really appreciate you being my assigned guard. I hate picking work buddies."

Trent shrugged, trying to hide that he was feeling the first hints of a cold sweat breaking out. He'd never seen so many elves together before, even at his own botched wedding. His jaw was clenched, and he forced himself to relax as Megan gave him a sidelong glance at his continued silence. They were all West Coast elves with their straw-yellow hair smelling faintly of salt. His father had always taken time to remove that particular human tag when tweaking damaged genomes, wanting to preserve what he could of their true beginnings. There were lots of special camps scattered around the United States tending to the elves' stagnant population, and though the mechanisms and techniques to repair the demon-wrought damage came from his father, the artistry varied, especially west of the Mississippi.

Megan kept up a running commentary as the hallways widened, branched, and began to take on the feel of home and comfort, the occasional chair and table set at the increasingly numerous windows that opened up to ocean views. The walls were three feet thick, with wide billowing drapes moving in the free-flowing wind coming in through spell-protected windows. He could hear Jenks muttering, memorizing the layout as he peered through the grommet holes in Harold's hat. Trent was starting to think that they might actually be able to do this without killing anyone else when they made a sharp series of turns and found the nursery door. At least, Trent assumed it was the nursery. What other room would have six men guarding it?

All six men came to a threatening attention as his group approached, and Megan's chatter cut off. "Hired help," Jenks whispered. "Mercenaries. This is your dragon, elf man."

Worry pinched his brow as he estimated the damage he was going to have to do to get past them with a baby in arms if there wasn't a window in the nursery. Smoothing it away, Trent cleared his throat, pulling his arm from Megan as they came to an uneasy halt. He tried not to look at the featureless door. His child was beyond it. He would find a way.

"Identification?" the one closest to the door barked, and Trent's back stiffened. *Blast it all to hell* . . .

Megan sighed, her lips tight as she pulled a card from around her neck and offered it to the man, her motions slowly belligerent, an ugly squint to her eye. Saying nothing, the man ran a scanner over it, handing it back when it beeped.

Trent's pulse quickened. His badge was still in the kitchen around Harold's neck, presumably. There were ten men and one woman within earshot, probably more within thirty seconds from this spot. He had only his questionable sleep potions, and who knew who was behind that door with his child. He was not going to start his parenthood by killing his daughter's mother if Ellasbeth was there. The Goddess, if there was one, was laughing at him.

"Harold?"

He felt Jenks shift under his cap; clearing his throat in a negative sound, Trent shuffled forward, feeling his pants as if looking for it.

"Oh God," Megan moaned, standing with her hip cocked. "Please don't tell me you dropped your pass? I bet you lost it in the kitchen killing that rat."

"Rat?" The man with the portable scanner met Megan's eyes, then Trent's. Eyebrows high, he reached for the two-way on his belt.

It was getting out of control, and Trent tensed. "Ah-a-a-a," he muttered, talking more to Jenks than the man with the scanner. He couldn't take this many people down, even with Jenks's help. He might be able to escape, but he wasn't leaving without his daughter. He could go back and get the pass. Maybe duck out of sight and send Jenks. He was faster.

He met the man's eyes, trying to look sheepish. Putting a hand in the air as if asking for him to wait, he started to back up. The man with the scanner frowned, his eyes flicking behind Trent as if telling the guards to stop him. Trent's fingertips began to tingle even as he forced his shoulders to slump, trying to look harmless. The man before him was the biggest threat. He would go down first. If he could get his pistol, he might be able to take three more down before the rest reacted. Perhaps not. They seemed immune to violence, even Megan.

The click of the door opening shocked through him, and his attention jerked to the nursery along with everyone else's. Around him, the guards pulled themselves together as if for a superior they had no respect for—reluctantly and with sour glances. A sliver of stone floor and white walls showed beyond the door, and then it was eclipsed as Ellasbeth strode through, looking more frazzled and tired than he'd ever seen her.

Trent shifted to a halt, his bare feet silent on the cold floors. His expression carefully blank, he studied her, this woman who had promised they would bring the elves back to greatness together, then stole both the technology and his child that would bring it about. His hands were clenched, and he opened them. Megan was watching him.

Ellasbeth's yellow hair was pulled back into a ponytail, something he'd never seen before. It made her look younger, more vulnerable, and with her height and natural athleticism, he was reminded of the professional women's volleyball team he'd once met. She had a degree in nuclear transplantation, but she looked more like a student than the professor she was. No makeup marked her, and she looked better for it, even if her green eyes were tired and droopy. It was nearing noon, a time when elves would be napping if they had a choice, but he thought her tired look was due more to the stresses of having a new baby than lack of sleep.

She was wearing cream-colored pants and a matching suit coat as if it were a casual Friday—like she would ever unknot her emotions enough to partake in one. If her expression was even halfway pleasant, he might feel guilty for what he was about to do, but only anger filled him—anger at her lack of understanding, anger at her inability to see beyond her immediate self, anger she had embarrassed him in front of Cincinnati's elite by walking out on him at their wedding, giving him an ultimatum that he had no immediate control over, anger at himself that he was jealous she was doing what she wanted, not sacrificing all for the betterment of their species.

Trent fought to keep his anger out of his eyes as he dropped his gaze to her tiny feet, wrapped in an elaborate silk and bamboo fabric instead of shoes. It was all the rage, from what he understood, something to make the feet look even smaller, but he didn't understand the appeal. *Swallow the anger*, he thought. *It won't help you now.*

"Ixnay on the at-ray," Megan whispered from the side of her mouth as the tired woman beckoned the man with the scanner to her. "I've got a day off tomorrow, and I'm not spending it hunting for vermin!"

"Good, you're here," Ellasbeth said curtly, her narrow nose in the air as if she smelled something rank as she looked them all over. "I was hoping I'd find you lazing about in the hall. Megan, Lucy is asleep, but do wake her up to give her a bottle. I want her to go down this afternoon after her mental stimulation period, and she simply won't if you don't wake her up now."

Mental stimulation? Is that her word for playtime? Trent thought, edging toward Megan.

"Yes, ma'am," Megan said politely. "Is Mrs. Withon here yet?"

Ellasbeth looked down the breezy hall. "No, but I'm sure you can handle it until she arrives. I'm going to be busy the rest of the day with my guest."

That would be me, Trent thought, thinking his ploy with the radio was paying off handsomely. They were probably still looking for them, then.

"I'm sure I can," Megan said sourly, half under her breath, and Ellasbeth turned, her motion to leave halted with a severe abruptness.

"Excuse me?"

The men surrounding them stiffened, and Megan smiled politely. "Of course, ma'am."

Ellasbeth eyed her, clearly having heard the first comment. Trent looked past her and the still-open door into the softly lit room, his pulse quickening and his feet itching to move. He was going to see his daughter.

"Go on, get in there," Ellasbeth said as she gestured. "Both of you. I'll be happy when I can get rid of all of you tomorrow. None of you are worth the salt that runs in your veins."

"Ma'am . . ." the man with the scanner said, his eyes flicking to Trent's, and Ellasbeth glared at Megan and Trent, still standing next to her.

"What are you waiting for? God to say go?" Ellasbeth barked. "Get in there! She's alone!"

"Yes, ma'am," Megan said, looking neither left or right as she smartly walked past Ellasbeth. Trent, too, made for the door, giving the scanner man a shrug as he entered. It was obvious that he wasn't happy about not seeing that scrap of paper that was still around Harold's neck, but he clearly didn't have the authority to countermand Ellasbeth's petulant demands.

Or perhaps he didn't care, Trent thought as he turned in the doorway to give Ellasbeth one last look. The man with the scanner was wearing an ugly expression. Ellasbeth was already twenty feet down the hallway, her feet silent in her silken wrappings and her nose in the air. Her rapid but shuffling pace hesitated as if feeling his eyes on him, and Trent slipped inside and shut the door before she could turn.

The soft sounds of the distant ocean and the wind rushing through the monastery were cut off with a shocking suddenness, replaced by a warm, moist air carrying the strains of classical guitar. After the chill breezes in the hallway, it felt stuffy, and Trent scanned the twenty-by-twenty featureless room without looking as if he was. It was clearly an outer chamber of some sorts, the whitewashed walls empty and the floors bare. Megan showed her ID again to an older, somewhat overweight man sitting on a folding chair next to an open archway. Beyond it was a darkened room.

Trent's pulse hammered, and Jenks stomped on his head until Trent looked away from the open doorway, putting his hungry gaze on the floor as he tried to hide his growing excitement. He hadn't been expecting a nursery guard, and he wanted to save his questionable sleep charms for getting out of here. Trent grimaced, remembering his promise to not respond with a fatal force unless necessary. Why was it always necessary?

"Hi, Harold," the old man in the chair said, casually gesturing him forward. "It's stupid, but I need to see your ID." His eyes rolled, going to the camera in the corner as he sighed.

Trent's jaw clenched. Even better. Someone was watching. There was no lock on the door, and even if there was, there was no other way out of here. The room had no windows, and his explosive gum wouldn't work on three-foot-thick walls. Even if he put this man down, someone would be alerted and be in here in seconds.

"I got this," Jenks whispered, and Trent blinked, remembering Rachel telling him that Jenks was a camera expert.

It took all his boardroom polish to keep a casual smile as he approached the man in the chair, trying not to shiver as Jenks tugged at Harold's hat and slipped out at the nape of Trent's neck, tickling him. "Yeah, ah, here," Trent said softly, trying to cover the sound of Jenks's wings in the empty, echoing room. Fortunately Megan had gone into the nursery, and the lights were slowly brightening as she woke Lucy up as naturally and as slowly as possible.

He didn't want to meet his daughter screaming in fear at the sound of another man dying. Perhaps he should use one of the sleep potions. The man was old and deserved his respect.

Digging in his pocket for one as if it was his badge, Trent watched the man's eyes dart over his shoulder, widening as they went to the camera in the corner. His gaze came back to Trent, alarm in them as he reached for his pistol. He'd seen Jenks.

Damn.

"We're good!" Jenks said, his voice muffled, and Trent moved.

The older man was rising, his hand fumbling at his holster, and Trent sprang forward to meet him, flipping the top to the sleep potion vial as he went. It splashed across his startled expression, and then the man's eyes rolled back.

"I'm sorry, old man," Trent said, easing him to the floor, his jaw clenched. He had one charm left. One. And he wasn't sure how long the one he'd used would even last.

"We're on a loop," Jenks said as he zipped down from the corner, clearly cheerful in that he'd been needed. "I'll check out the nursery before you go in." Hovering over Trent's shoulder, he put his hands on his hips and looked down. "That was fast."

"You had better not have killed Bob," Megan said, and Jenks swore, darting up to the ceiling.

Trent rose as well, backing up with his hands raised as he eyed her smart-looking pistol. It could be one of those splat guns that Rachel was so fond of, but he doubted it. "He's not dead."

Megan's harsh expression eased, and she motioned for Trent to move away from the downed guard. "I thought you were Kalamack," she said, then flicked her weapon again. "You should have come last night. The night nurse isn't as good as me. Ribbon off. Hat too. And if I feel you tap a line, I'm going to plug you. Move!"

Motions slow, he pulled the ribbon from his neck, and Megan's eyes ran him up and down in appreciation as the charm went with it and he looked like himself again. Her grip on her weapon tightened, and she lifted her chin to point at the hat. Disgusted, he took that off too, letting both ribbon and hat drop to the floor. It was official. He was without magic, such as it had been. Trent made fists of his hands, frustrated. "What gave me away?" he asked, seeing Jenks slip into the nursery. Lack of magic or not, this wasn't over.

"You stink like fireplace and strained peas, and I could hear your bare feet on the tile even though it looked like you were wearing boots. You didn't take a pan in with you into the pantry, but I heard someone get hit with one. Harold thinks I'm a foulmouthed harlot, and you opened the door for me and let me hold your arm. Did you kill him?"

Shaking his head, Trent realized why the woman had made him walk with her. She was still going to go down, but now it would be harder. One potion left. The trick would be how to get it out of his belt pouch. He wasn't going to kill her. Trent's heart thudded.

"You got me," Trent said, ears straining for any sound from Jenks. "Why did you wait?"

Megan knelt beside the old man, never taking her eyes from him or her aim wavering. "There's a five-million-dollar reward for the person who catches you," she said, motioning him to move to the other end of the room before she felt for a pulse. "I don't like to share."

Trent thought of the ten men in the hallway, probably down to six again. In here, though, there was only two, and she clearly cared for the old man. "Ah, I normally abhor people trying to hire my help from under me," he said, pitching his voice low, "but would you consider putting that pistol down and coming to work for me for a ten-million bonus?"

The woman smiled, her weapon's aim never shifting. "Tempting, but I wouldn't survive to spend it. The hands-off agreement you and Ms. Tight-ass have extends to Lucy, not people who you steal with her. Over there where I can see you. By the wall."

"I understand." Tension pulled him tight, making his motion smooth as he moved to the far wall away from the nursery. "If we were talking about anyone other than the Withons, I'd tell you I could offer adequate protection, but you understand I can't." Jenks was looking at his daughter. It was enough to drive him insane.

Finally the woman glanced down, her fingers touching the guard's jugular for a pulse.

Trent lunged, his eyes widening as the gun she was pointing at him went off with a soft puff. Twisting wildly, he tried to evade the potion pellet headed right for him, but he was too close. He wasn't going to make it. Grimacing, he tapped a line and tried to set a circle, but his bruised neural net sent a pulse of agony through him, and it flickered and died before it formed.

"Got it!" Jenks shouted gleefully, a bright streak of silver darting between them. His silver trail jerked sharply to the right as he snagged the splat ball in midair, turning the woman's five-million-dollar smile of satisfaction to one of shock.

Twisting, Trent landed wrong, his ankle giving way with a ping of pain as he fell on his side, his gut clenched so he wouldn't knock the air out of himself.

"Damn bug!" the woman hissed in anger, and Trent scrambled to his knees, lunging for her ankle, foot, anything to yank her off balance as she swatted at Jenks, merrily bating her at the ceiling.

"He is not a *bug*!" Trent said between clenched teeth, gaining a hand-hold on a shapely, long-muscled leg and giving a yank.

The woman made a muffled yelp, and fell backward, her arms flailing and gun going off again to make a wet splat on the ceiling. Jenks darted under her falling form and away, the unbroken splat ball rolling slowly from where he'd left it.

"Son of a bitch!" Megan said as she hit the floor and brought her hands together, aiming her gun at Trent.

Heart pounding, Trent knelt where he was, his hands in the air, then jumped when Jenks landed on his shoulder, smelling of wind and sunshine. "Wait for it . . ." the pixy said, clearly in a good mood as he pointed at Megan with his bared sword.

"If you made me wake up that baby . . ." she snarled, and then her face lost all expression and her arms fell, spell pistol hitting the tile with a knuckle-bruising *thunk*. With a sigh, the woman went unconscious, the splat ball she had fallen upon finally breaking and the potion touching her skin.

Jenks's laughter sounded like chimes as he darted off Trent's shoulder to make a victory dance on the woman's nose. Trent slowly got up and dusted off his biking tights. Slowly he put his weight on his ankle, wincing. He could walk on it, but running full out might be a problem.

"That was so sweet!" Jenks said as he stood on her nose and did the happy-pixy dance. "We downed her with her own splat ball. Zip bang! She's out. Rachel would laugh her ass off." He stopped moving, his expression going more serious as he saw Trent mincing over to pry the gun out of her fingers. "Thanks for drawing her fire."

Drawing her fire? Sure, that's what I'd been doing. "No problem." Trent opened the hopper. He didn't know how many splat balls were in there.

Enough, maybe. Aiming down, he shot her twice more in the gut. Then he turned to the downed guard and did the same again. Earth magic wouldn't last long in the salty air, but three charms each ought to give him at least five minutes.

Jenks had risen back up into the air at the first puff from the gun, and he hovered beside Trent as they both looked down at the sleeping people. "So get your kid and let's get out of here," the pixy said, and Trent's breath caught.

His head turned to the dark archway, and his knees became rubber.

"Well, go look!" Jenks prompted. "I've got the cameras all on loops, and I'll keep watch out here. I can tell when the sleeping beauties here are going to wake up, and by their auras, they're down for at least two minutes."

Two minutes, Trent thought, eager to see his daughter, but then the handle of the door turned. Every last iota of his cool vanished as if it never existed. Panicking, he lunged to the door, scooping up his ribbon and cap before putting his back to the wall. Jenks darted to the ceiling. The bodies of Megan and Bob lay askew on the floor. There was no help for it. His heart pounded, and he raised Megan's gun. There had to be a Goddess—only the divine would get entertainment from this, making him think he had a chance, then piling even more impossible odds before him.

The gun felt warm in his hands, and remembering the six guards outside, he held his breath as Mrs. Withon entered.

The woman stopped short at the bodies on the floor, and Trent grimaced, knowing it was over. Jenks chirped his wings softly, and her eyes went up, a mix of delighted recognition followed quickly by fear crossing her face as she saw and recognized the pixy—then Trent.

"Please come in and close the door," Trent whispered, cocking the gun. "Call them if you have to, but I want to talk to you alone first."

The woman stiffened, but she kicked the door shut with her foot, only turning to Trent when it latched shut. For a moment she was silent, and Trent's resolve stiffened as the older woman looked him up and down, unknown emotions flitting across her face. "Are they dead?" she asked, her voice tight and her eyes never shifting from his to the gun.

"No. There is a third in the pantry. I'm sorry about the man in the field. I was careless."

Ellie took a slow breath, her narrow shoulders easing slightly. Her back to the door, she could have them all in here in a second if she wanted to. Trent doubted she would, though. Most of the magic texts in his library originally came from here, and slowly he dropped the gun's aim. He would have to win this by guile, the one elven art he had practiced all his life.

The refined woman looked nothing like Ellasbeth, standing almost eight inches shorter, dressed in cool shades of gray and silver that matched her fair hair, wispy and thin, exactly like Trent's, exactly like his mother's. "Have you seen her?" she asked, afraid and proud.

"No." Again her shoulders dropped, but still she didn't move. "Ellie, I'm sorry it has come to this," Trent said, relieved that he hadn't killed anyone inside Ellie's home. He'd always thought of gaining Ellie as a mother-in-law the best part of the arranged marriage. "Ellasbeth brought this on herself. Refused any other way. You know I tried."

"You can't escape these rooms," she said firmly, a hint of fear in her, and Jenks snickered from the ceiling. "Even if you take me or Lucy hostage. The guards have been instructed . . ."

"To what?" Trent said bitterly. "Kill your grandchild rather than allow me to escape with her?" Frustration filled him, and he saw it mirrored in Ellie's eyes. Horror ebbed into him as he realized the depth of Ellasbeth's hatred. He had been counting on Lucy granting him a measure of immunity, but if they were instructed to kill him without regard to Lucy's safety . . .

"My God, Ellie, call them if you have to!" he said loudly as he tucked the gun away. "Put me in chains and let Ellasbeth take her spoiled-child revenge out on me if you must, but let me see her first! You owe me that!"

"Keep your voice down. Don't wake her!" the older woman said, actually reaching out to grab his arm, and Trent hesitated. She was afraid. Why?

"Please, promise me you won't wake her, and . . . I'll let you see her," the woman said again, and Trent's eyes squinted. There was a thread of mischief in her, a streak of deviltry. The woman might be older than him and more frail, but she was of pure blood, purer than her daughter. If she let him see Lucy before calling the guards, there was a reason for it.

"Go look," she said, her eyes flicking to the doorway, and Trent's unease increased. He glanced at Jenks, and the pixy shrugged.

"You first," he said, and the woman huffed, tugging her silken shawl over her narrow shoulders and stalking into the nursery, her back straight and proud.

Jenks dropped down as Trent looked at his hat and ribbon, then shoved them in the belt pack. "She's planning something," Jenks warned, and he nodded, looking into the room as it brightened.

"I can't shoot her," he said to Jenks. "The woman grew up with my mother! They loved each other like sisters. It's bad enough I'm stealing her grandchild."

The pixy rose up, his eyes on the door to the hall. "I'll keep watch out here. We're going to have one hell of a run if we can't use either of them as a hostage."

"I just need a west-facing window," Trent said, patting his belt pack. Time, time, he was running out of it.

From the nursery came Mrs. Withon's somewhat irate, "Do you want to see her or not?"

Jenks grinned, wings clattering a silver dust. "I always liked Mrs. Withon," he said, darting off to sit upon the doorknob.

"Me too," Trent whispered, his smile nervously fading as he turned to the nursery. He hesitated at the archway, looking in at the smaller room with soft lights, hidden speakers, and smooth walls—probably wallboard over the natural stone. A desk sat to one side, the cooling bottle sitting on an open journal of dates and amounts. A baby scale was next to a changing station, and it smelled faintly of lavender. It was stuffy and warm, and there was nothing to look at on the walls, everything painted a sterile white—a prison until her third month ended completely and his narrow window of opportunity to steal her was gone.

Mrs. Withon stood beside a white crib, Lucy hidden behind bumper pads with a print of horses on them. Ellie looked up, her expression a mix of fear and determination. She was up to something.

Feeling as if it was a trap, Trent edged in. He leaned over the crib, his lips parting as his eyes warmed and he smiled.

His daughter lay sleeping fitfully, her tiny fists shoving her blanket off her as her face screwed up in what looked like petulant anger. Wispy blond hair framed her angular face, her eyes tightly shut as she fussed in her sleep, making tiny noises of frustration.

"Don't touch her," Ellie whispered, her hands clamped possessively on the railing.

Trent's lips parted, and he remembered to breathe. "You didn't dock her ears," he said softly. He wanted to reach in, let her searching hand find his finger.

"It's tradition to wait until everyone who needs proof has the chance to see that she is an elf and not a changeling," the woman said distantly. "Her ears will be docked now."

Trent looked up, hearing a hint of bitterness. She didn't want Lucy's ears docked. Ellie wanted them to come out of the closet, but the birth of Lucy had taken Ellie's graceful political voice and granted it to her daughter because Ellasbeth could bear children and she could not. It was an old tradition created by a society obsessed with increasing their numbers, and it was no longer needed. He vowed to change it—if he had the chance.

He couldn't leave Lucy here, and with a new determination, he reached to pick her up.

"No!" Ellie pulled his hand away, and Jenks darted in, hovering in the doorway.

Angry, Trent grabbed the woman's hand, jerking her away from the crib. "That is my child," he said, holding both her wrists with one of his hands as the woman twisted within his grip, a faint warning of line energy rising between them as she glared fiercely. "I can take her now and what you want will be damned, but I want you to give her to me. *I want you to give her to me, Ellie.* That your voice be silenced simply because you can't bear children anymore is inane and no longer needed when our numbers are balanced to grow. I want you . . . *to give her to me.*"

Eyes wide, the woman hesitated, tense and thinking, worrying Trent more than if she had begun screaming for help or throwing curses. "She is my child, too," she said breathlessly. "What gives you any claim to her?"

Trent frowned, and anger filled him as he fought with his urge to look back in the crib, but he was afraid to glance away from Ellie. "Your daughter is a spoiled, belligerent brat who thinks of no one besides herself," he said bitterly. "I have sacrificed and risked my life to see that our species has a chance to survive, and I will again. Who do you want to raise this child? A self-centered woman who walks away from an agreement that will further our survival because it's disagreeable? A woman who will teach her that the self is more important than the whole? Ellasbeth walked away. She left me and the way to bring our people back. This child and everything we were to accomplish in our lifetimes is mine by right. I don't care what tradition says. Ellasbeth's word is dross. I want *you* to give her to me."

"But she's my granddaughter!" Ellie begged, tears swimming in her eyes.

His jaw tight, Trent shifted his grip on her wrists, the expression on her face prompting him to use both hands. "Ellasbeth can make more of her," he said bitterly. "Lucy is *mine!*" He hesitated, seeing that the older woman was nearly crying, even if she was angry. "We are still on the brink, Ellie. You know it. Lucy is worth dying for, but Ellasbeth doesn't understand that. I do. Give her to me. I will see her safely out of here. She is a child, not a bargaining chip that can be sacrificed for someone's pride!"

Ellie's tormented gaze went from Trent to the open door to Jenks, his head cocked as he hovered over the crib and looked down.

"If not for me, then for my mother," Trent said, his hands easing from around the older woman's wrists. "You know she hated hiding who she was as much as you do."

Ellie's eyes came back to his as he let go. "You fight dirty."

Trent couldn't help his nervous smile, but it faded fast. "And you could put me down with one spell—but you haven't. Why?"

The woman stood before him, smelling of wind and surf, of cinnamon and wine, her shoulders slumping in defeat enough to make Trent's breath catch in hope. "She has never smiled," she whispered, looking at the crib. "Her sleep is always restless," she added, her sorrowful eyes coming back to Trent's. "Wake her," she commanded, and that same uneasy feeling slid through him. She was up to something. "Go on, wake her!" she said loudly, and Trent winced, even as he moved to the crib. "I want to see what happens."

See what happens? he thought. Was he to win an empire by a child's laugh?

"Watch my back, okay?" he murmured to Jenks, and the pixy hummed an agreement. Trent gave one last look at the older woman standing against the wall, pensive and with her arms crossed before her, her jaw clenched and her eyes flashing in anger. But all his worry and fear slid from him as he looked into the crib, his own eyes warming as he smiled down at his daughter sleeping restlessly. He couldn't help it. Her skin looked so smooth, her sleep so distracted. His shoulders eased, and he found he couldn't bring himself to shake her awake.

"*Ta na shay, mi de cerrico*," he whispered, his voice cracking, and he took a deeper breath. "*Ta na shay, mi de cerrico day folena*," he sang, his voice becoming stronger as she frowned, her fitful arm movements hesitating. "*Rovolin de mero, de sono, de vine. Esta ta na shay, me de cerrico.*"

Jenks's wings clattered as he landed on Trent's shoulder, and together they watched as Lucy's eyes opened. They were green as an angry ocean as she fastened them upon him, and Trent smiled, delighted at her fierce rebellion. "Hi," he breathed, and his daughter kicked her legs and cooed as if saying "Where have you been?"

Only now did he reach in and pick her up, holding her high so her blanket slipped away and he could see all of her at once in her little pink dressing gown. "Lucy!" he said, feeling as if the world could end right now and he would be happy. "Look how perfect you are!"

The little girl laughed, kicking at him at delight of the sensation of air around her until she saw her bottle on the table. Expression clouding, she leaned to it, her happy-baby sounds turning desperate.

Alarmed, Trent pulled Lucy to him, his eyes down and avoiding Ellie's pensive quiet as he tucked Lucy against him, feeling awkward and uncomfortable as he managed the bottle. Lucy grabbed it with a fierce determination, sucking hard as she studied Trent's face, comparing it to Ellie, now standing next to them.

"I'm not leaving here without her," Trent said, not sure what was going to happen next.

Ellie's face hardened. "Then you will die here."

"Then so be it," he said, turning his back on the woman and heading for the outer chamber. Excitement tingled through him, and he thought of the sleeping potion gun in his pocket. It would be difficult to carry Lucy and fire it at the same time, but he'd manage. Jenks's wings clattered at his shoulder, the pixy clearly uncertain at Trent's calm.

"You cannot escape this room!" Ellie exclaimed in a hushed whisper, and Lucy sucked harder on her bottle, her hand clenching on the glass with a fierce determination. "Those butchers are instructed to cut you down on sight! Even if Lucy is with you!"

The woman sounded desperate, and a quiver of anticipation ran through him. She didn't want her granddaughter in danger. She wanted him to take her, but needed a little shove. "If we're to be shot on sight, I'll need your help, Jenks. Will you do me the honor of protecting my child while I take care of the guards?"

Jenks hovered close, and Lucy went cross-eyed, her sucking hesitating when he landed on the end of the bottle. "To my last breath," he said, his dust shifting to a deep black.

Nodding his agreement, Trent brushed past Ellie.

"Trenton, no!" she cried out as he reached for the handle. "They might kill her!"

"Then help me," Trent said, his back to her as he waited, counting to three. There was silence, and his grip tightened on the knob.

"Wait," she whispered, and Trent's heart pounded, his eyes closing in thanks to the Goddess. He'd been bluffing. There was no way he would walk out of this room with his child and risk her life. But it wasn't over yet, and he cradled Lucy in his arm as she finished her bottle, making his expression a hard mask for both her and Ellie to study as he turned.

The older woman glanced at the door behind him, fear in her eyes. "The guards won't listen to me. You can't go that way. Pixy dust is an explosive accelerant, yes?" she said softly.

"Hey!" Jenks said belligerently. "Who told you that?"

Ellie shrugged. "Trent isn't the only one with an old library. Most of his mother's books came from me." Her eyebrows high and saucy, she turned to Trent, making him wonder if this had been her intent all along and she'd only been seeing the length of his resolve. "The westernmost wall in the nursery is an outer wall. You can go through it."

"It's three feet thick!" Trent exclaimed, and Lucy kicked out, responding to his voice. "My explosives are designed to break locks, not masonry walls."

"There's a window." Ellie turned, striding into the nursery. "It's not three feet of rock. It's three feet of insulation," she said loudly from the second room, and Trent looked at Jenks. The pixy was hovering uncertainly.

"Why do I feel like I've been had?" Trent said softly.

Jenks snickered. "Because I think we have."

Holding Lucy close, Trent strode into the nursery, seeing Ellie tapping at the wall, her ear bent toward it. Lucy fussed, and he snatched up the blanket in the crib. "Why?" he almost barked at Ellie as he inexpertly tried to wrap the blanket around Lucy, who kept kicking it off.

Ellie turned, looking crafty as she leaned toward the wall, listening as she tapped it with a knuckle. "I liked what I saw when you woke her."

Trent came closer, lifting his hand in a gesture of disbelief. "She cried for her bottle."

The echo behind the wall changed, and she straightened. "I wasn't looking at Lucy. I was looking at you. Go. Before I change my mind." Her fond smile faltered, and she reached out, tucking Lucy's blanket in properly around her. "I'm going to miss you, sweet pea," she said, giving the fussing baby a kiss on the forehead. Lucy clamped a fist on her bangs, and blinking fast, Ellie disentangled her fingers, placed her tiny hand on her middle, and then turned away, her head low.

Guilt hit him, and he took out his tiny explosives he had to pick locks. Jenks *oooo*ed and *ahh*ed over them, taking his sword and punching through the wallboard to place them properly.

"Ellie, why?" he asked again.

"I've been following your progress," she said softly, still not turning around. "Not today, but since your father died. I thought that you were misguided, easily led. I was wrong—you were keeping your enemies close. I thought that you were too timid, unable to think flexibly—yet you got in here with very little effort and against changing odds. You have been too careless with life—but something in you has shifted and I'm willing to chance you raising my granddaughter better than I have raised my daughter." She turned, her tears obvious. "We need Lucy, but we need her with the strength that I know you can give her." She dropped her head, tears falling from her unremarked upon and untouched. "You have made sacrifices," she said, turning Trent's hand over and tracing a finger upon his palm and the twin life lines that had bothered his mother and made his father frown. "Not just in the past, but the future as well. Besides, Ellasbeth has lots of dolls already."

It was bitter, and Trent swallowed hard, her grief washing over him like a bright wave, sun sparkling on top, harsh and cold below. He took a breath to say something, anything, but nothing was to be said, nothing that he could give her. Ellie was making the largest sacrifice of them all. *Give me strength today, and I will strive to find within me the person that can be both.*

"Okay! We're set!" Jenks said brightly as he wiggled out of the hole in the wall that he had made, a string of ignition wires trailing behind him. "You want me to use what's left over to seal the door?"

Trent nodded, and Ellie set her shoulders resolutely, sniffing back her tears. "I'm a foolish old woman," she said softly, a determined fix to her jaw.

"Get your rappelling stuff out," Jenks said, clearly excited as he darted into the outer room ahead of them. "Don't you have a sling for her or something?"

Trent nodded, hesitating as he realized he was going to have to set Lucy down to put it on. Ellie held her arms out, and he reluctantly set her into her grandmother's arms. The little girl reached up, patting her damp cheeks, and Ellie make a choking gurgle of a laugh, smiling through the tears.

Jenks gave Trent a sick look, then went back to check the linkages. Head down, Trent prepped himself for the trip down, fastening the safety harness around himself, checking that the baby sling would not be pinched, coiling the wire-thin, strong filament that would hold them into a smooth bundle. Ellie was cooing at Lucy, and the little girl was cooing back. Trent's stomach churned.

"Nine months," he said, unable to take it anymore, and Ellie looked up, confusion in her expression. "Give me nine months alone with Lucy, and I will reconsider renegotiating a new settlement with Ellasbeth," he said, taking the baby from Ellie's unresisting arms. *Damn it, why did I do that?* he thought, but the woman had lit up, her tears making her beautiful. "I'm doing this for you, not Ellasbeth," he added, embarrassed.

"Thank you," she said, clutching at his arm and glancing at the door as if she couldn't wait for them to escape so she could tell someone. Seeing her joy, Trent became even more angry at Ellasbeth. This could have been avoided. The trip out here, the deaths, the turmoil, everything. Ellasbeth was a selfish fool.

But looking down at his feisty daughter, he found himself smiling again. "I hope you're rested, Lucy," he said, jiggling the baby as Jenks came back in. "We have a busy afternoon. Can you be quiet for me?"

Jenks hovered over his shoulder, eyeing the baby now reaching out for the little man with wings. "You do know she doesn't understand a word you're saying."

Trent shrugged. "You ready to do this?"

"Does a troll pee green piss?" The pixy laughed.

 FIVE

"A re you sure this isn't overkill?" Trent muttered to Jenks as he crouched between Ellie, Lucy, Bob the guard, Megan, and the open archway to the nursery. His explosive gum would only make a tiny pop, and Jenks was treating it as if it were a stick of C4.

Jenks eyed him, then darted to the door where Trent had pasted the last of the gum on the door that led to the hall. A curious sliver of green dust slipped down, and, arms over his chest, he dramatically snapped his fingers.

A tiny wave of force exploded out of the lock, making Trent duck and Ellie gasp. Jenks rode the bubble of air like a surfer, grinning as he spun to a stop in front of Trent's nose. From the hallway came muffled, alarmed voices. "You might want to duck," the pixy said saucily. "I put ten times that between the drywall and insulation over the window."

"Right." Glancing at Ellie, he shifted his weight to resettle Lucy in her baby sling. "Everyone cover their eyes." His hand went protectively under the little girl, and she gurgled happily. Trent couldn't help his proud look down at her. He'd known her for only five minutes, and he already liked what he saw: grit, determination, acceptance of excitement. He didn't have much experience with babies, but how could this be a bad thing?

"Here we go!" Jenks said as he tucked in under Ellie's ear, then made a chirp with his wings, the two-toned sound like tinfoil on Trent's teeth.

A flash of sound and light boomed through the open archway. Orange and green mixed like auras against his vision, blending with the memory of thunder. The floor shook, and Trent met Ellie's eyes, seeing the pain of Jenks's wing noise still in her expression. It turned to shock as they all stumbled, even crouched on the floor as they were, and Trent put a hasty hand on the stone to keep from falling.

"My God . . ." Trent breathed, absently patting Lucy as she stared horrified at him to see how she should react before finally giving up and beginning to wail. "Oh no, it's okay, Lucy," he said as he stood, his free hand extended to help Ellie rise. Bob and Megan were still unconscious, and Jenks took off from Ellie's shoulder, his passage making twin whirlwinds in the dust now spilling into the outer room along with the muted sounds of the ocean and a bright white light.

They'd done it. The amount of light coming through was substantial, and Trent tried to quell his growing excitement. Taking a huge breath, he shoved it deep under a thick layer of hard-won boardroom protocol. "Are you okay, Ellie?" he asked calmly, even as he stifled a tremor at the moist smell of ocean. Lucy's wailing had become loud, and the pounding from the door even more frantic.

"Fine," she said, letting go of his hand and bending to brush the dust from Megan's face. "I wanted to redecorate the baby's room anyway." Her brow pinched, and she looked away.

Guilt tugged at him, even as he clenched his jaw resolutely.

"We got a hole! Let's go!" Jenks shouted from the other room, and Trent leaned into motion, patting Lucy through the carry mesh when her furious, red-faced wailing cut off sharply as she coughed.

"That's a good girl, Lucy," Trent said, smiling down at her and giving her a jiggle. Distracted by her cough, she forgot what she was crying about and her complaints subsided into a tear-streaked pouting. "See at the sunlight on the ceiling!" he said as he looked into the demolished room, and even though she had no clue what he was saying, his tone soothed her.

"Wow." Trent blinked at the destruction, thinking he'd never used the word before, but Jenks was right. They had a hole. A bloody big hole with the sky and water beyond it, blue and sparkling. A fresh breeze eddied in to dispel the last of the powdered rock, replacing it with the scent of salt and seaweed. From her sling, Lucy squinted at the bright light, fussing when he shifted to put her in the shade.

Trent half turned as Ellie came in, exhaling in dismay. The desk was a mangled mess of rock and wallboard. The crib was broken. "Don't let Ellasbeth see this without knowing that Lucy is safe first," he said, and Ellie's feet scuffed.

"I won't," she breathed. "Trenton . . ."

It was time to go. He could hear a power tool whining at the door. One hand under Lucy, he peered down the drop-off. He was too practical to be afraid of heights, but his stomach clenched as he saw the perfect unmarred water and then looked at his watch. *Where's the boat?* Feeling his tension, Lucy kicked.

"You got a hot date or something?" Jenks asked, darting in and out of Lucy's reach to make the little girl squeal. "You keep looking at your watch."

"Something like that." The boat wasn't there, but it could be just around the spit of land, and they'd never see it until it was almost on them. "Let's go." Fingers fumbling, he brought out a mountaineer pin. If it worked in friable cliff rock, it would work here. Kneeling, he hammered it into the floor, his strikes mixing with the blows to the outer door in a harsh discord.

"Trent," Ellie tried once more when Lucy, frightened at the rough motion and sound, began to cry again, but he ignored the older woman. It was clear Ellie wanted to hold her one last time, but he was afraid to let her. Here, at the literal brink, she might change her mind. No wonder Ellie hadn't wanted him to touch Lucy. Something had shifted in him when he had. Without warning, he had become witness to something that stretched back through the eons, ties both elastic and enduring, surpassing death, surpassing life. She was his child. It was that simple and that complex.

Head down, he fastened the cord to lower himself to the pin, then the pulley on his harness. It looked too thin. His jaw tightened when Ellie came close, and then he looked up. The noise from the hall was furious, but words needed to be said.

"Thank you," he said simply, hoping she would understand. "If not for you, I would have had to . . ." His words faltered, and understanding broke over him. If Ellie hadn't come in, he might have had to storm the hallway. He would have done what was needed, killing not just the men in the hall, but his last hope of being something he wanted. *I think you saved me*, he thought, but he couldn't say it.

"You're welcome," she whispered, tears slipping from her as she smiled. Ellie gave them a hug, her breath catching as Lucy squealed happily at the contact. "It would have been messier, perhaps," she said, glancing to the hallway, "but you would have done it."

She didn't understand the narrowness of where he had been balanced, and he turned away, ashamed that he could have failed so easily. Perhaps he owed the Goddess a little more faith. "Thank you, Ellie. Knowing you accept this means more to me than you will ever know. Don't let Ellasbeth silence you. That tradition dies tomorrow."

The older woman, nodded, her sad smile becoming more intense as Lucy grabbed her finger and tried to stick it in her mouth. "I'm still going to hold you to our nine-month agreement. You'd better go. That door isn't going to last much longer." She leaned forward and gave Lucy a kiss on her forehead and disentangled her finger. "Bye, sweet pea. It was good to see you smile."

Jenks's wings were a harsh clatter as he darted back in, his dust edged in red. "Ah, I hate to break this up, but they've got a blowtorch . . ."

Nodding, Trent turned away. Feeling protective of Ellie, he picked his way through the rubble to the edge. Still no boat. Checking his gloves, he winced at his bare feet, and started to descend.

"Be careful!" Ellie said, and he looked up, unable to wave back.

Then the wind hit them, and he looked down to pay attention to what he was doing.

It was shockingly cool, the wind coming up from the water cutting right through his tattered biking tights. The hiss of the specially designed rope was a steady *shush-shush* as he bounced away from the rock face and found it again. Practice kicked in, and muscle memory took over. Lucy protested at the wind and brighter light, looking as if she was considering crying again.

"Jenks?" Trent called, his legs and arms aching. "How far down is it?"

The pixy dove from somewhere, the cheerful sound of his wings drawing Lucy's attention like a magnet and cutting her whimpering off. "You're about a third of the way," he said, bobbing up and down, his wings making music as he struggled to stay in one spot in the stiff wind.

Trent's brow furrowed. He had asked that the cord be made to the height of the cliff, but it did tend to shrink in the cold.

The sudden ping of shattered rock struck Trent, as he kept one hand on the wire, one on Lucy.

"They're shooting at us!" Jenks shrilled indignantly, looking up and darting sideways as Trent pushed out again, making his swing more erratic.

Angry, Trent pulled Lucy's blanket over her head, making the already fussy baby begin to wail. Faster now, he pushed the lowering mechanism to its limits, starting to shake as two more slugs shattered the rock where he had just been. If he fell, they would both be dead. Was Ellasbeth truly insane?

"Talk to me, Jenks!" he shouted, the cord beginning to hum in the wind. He knew it was because of the distance and how fast he was moving, but he couldn't help but wonder if they might cut the cord. Again he pushed out from the wall, his jaw clenched and his knees flexing to absorb the impact. He looked down, blanching. Almost there, but still too high for his liking. The rocks were wet with spray. There was no beach here, just jagged corners and pounding waves.

"Jenks!" he shouted again, wondering if the pixy had gotten himself killed. Lucy cried and kicked, and he tried to calm himself. *She is like a little barometer*, he mused as he pulled her blanket back enough so she could see him, and her cries ebbed into angry fussing. She saw Jenks before he heard his wings, and relief spilled into him even as he pushed off and descended another few feet.

"I really like Mrs. Withon," Jenks said as he landed on top of the pulley, a silver dust falling from him as they pushed out and down again.

The rope seemed to give way, and Trent panicked, reaching for it as it spun through the pulley and Jenks darted off. But it had only been Jenks's dust lubricating it, and he frowned when the pixy came back when they hit the wall again, having descended almost three times the usual amount. "How that nice woman ended up with a kid like Ellasbeth is beyond me," Jenks added as if nothing had happened.

"Yeah?" Trent panted, unable to make himself push off again.

Jenks grinned, his wings pinned to his back in the stiff wind. "She just threatened to throw the next man who shoots at you out the window. Megan is awake. She offered to help. God, Trent, what is it with you and women?"

Trent looked down again, smiling past Lucy. Her diaper had gone heavy against him. That drop had been scary. She hadn't cried, though, and he gave her a comforting pat as he pushed away in a series of short hops to reach the end. A wave of something passed through him, chased by panic. Lucy trusted him? She trusted him to keep her safe? God help him, he could not fail her.

Swallowing the emotion back, Trent slowly descended the last few feet. The sound of the surf was loud, and the smell of dead things strong. He exhaled loudly as his bare feet finally touched the spray-wet rock. Knees trembling, he put a hand to the rock face. It was not over, though, and he looked out past the crashing waves. Still no boat.

"Look out!" Jenks shouted, and Trent shied as a weird sort of swallowed sound *schluup*ed through the rising and falling water six feet out.

Scowling, Trent looked up the line. They were shooting at him again, and concerned, he put a hand to the cord to feel it humming from more than the wind. They were coming, not afraid to shoot him dead now that he was on the ground.

"I think you're okay," Jenks said, peering up as three more bullets cut through the water, the closest too far to be a worry. "The angle is wrong. But you got three minutes before they show up, rappelling down your rope." Jenks landed on an outcrop, his hair blowing wildly as he held his wings to his body. "I know you said there was a boat coming to pick us up, but how are you getting out to it? You elves got gills?"

"Something like that." Head down and fingers fumbling from the spray, Trent shimmied out of the harness, leaving only the one that kept Lucy snuggled close to him.

"Seriously!" Jenks said, hovering between him and the wall as he tried to keep out of the wind and away from Lucy's frustrated reach. "You can swim, but what about her?"

"Boat," Trent said shortly, glancing up briefly to see that it still wasn't here. It wasn't a holiday, was it? It would be just like the Goddess to decree that his entire plan, haphazardly implemented and disastrously flawed, would end here at the end with his goal in sight but just out of reach, devolved by a slipped timetable or obscure holiday. *A goat. I'll give you a Goddessblessed goat. Just get me out of here alive.*

"I don't see no boat," Jenks said, and Trent finally got his tiny knife and lighter from his belt pack. He'd brought it to blow the gum, but it would also burn the rope, and Jenks whistled in appreciation as Trent cut the cord, exposed the flammable core, lit it, and it smoked and burned like a fuse, shaking slightly as it burned upward.

"Nobody is going to make it down here on your rope now!" Jenks said in appreciation. "You just bought yourself ten minutes, you little cookie maker!" Jenks landed on his shoulder, his wings cold on his neck. "Ah, your boat going to be here by then?"

"Yes." *Two goats*, he thought as he kicked the harness into the water. Crouching with Lucy before him, he inflated the little cockleshell boat using the compressed air that he'd brought to inflate a blown bike tire. In two seconds, one ounce of specially designed plastic became a small boat for one.

"That takes care of Lucy," Jenks said, peering upward again. The bullets had stopped, but they'd start back up the instant they moved from the lee of the cliff. Trent doubted they would shoot at the little boat, so obviously carrying Lucy, but they'd try for him, even if it meant she might dash against the rocks. Maybe he had promised to revisit the custody arrangements too soon. This was insane. He'd gotten her, gotten out of their stronghold. Enough was enough.

"Here you go, sweet pea," he found himself saying as he inexpertly wiggled Lucy out from her sling, the little girl's eyes drooping. The stimulation of wind, water, and motion had begun to take their toll, and she frowned at the sudden cool breeze against her. "You can sleep in the boat," he whispered, tucking her blanket in around her and drawing the thin plastic top over her to protect her from spray.

He felt funny talking to her with Jenks listening, but the pixy only nodded at the care he took, seeming to be satisfied. Perhaps he'd done better than he ever dreamed, bringing Jenks along with him. The pixy was a seasoned parent, and if he deemed the precautions he took adequate, then perhaps he wasn't doing badly.

"I still don't see a boat," Jenks said as Trent carefully picked up the floating basket, wincing as the rocks cut into his feet.

Saying nothing, Trent waded out into the water. One bullet whizzed past him, then another, making Jenks swear and Trent's eyebrows rise. The cold was breathtaking, and the bike suit soaked it up, holding it to him. Six steps put him to his chest, the waves jostling him until he gave up and pushed off, holding Lucy before him. He should have had the engineers fashion a way to tie her to him, he mused as he began to swim, the *schluup*s of the bullets making his jaw clench. If not for the erratic bobbing of the waves, he'd likely be hit by now. It only made him angrier, and he kicked harder, falling into an awkward but effective rhythm. Shove the boat, stroke, stroke—shove the boat, stroke, stroke. *Where is the bloody pickup boat!*

"Boat?" Trent sputtered when they finally got far enough from the rocky edge so that he wasn't fighting waves coming from both directions.

"Sure! Got it!" Jenks's wings hummed, and Trent started when the smooth shape of the rocking cockleshell boat pulled away from him.

"No!" Trent said, his reaching hand smacking into it to make it rock violently. He panicked, thinking he had gotten Lucy wet, but she didn't make a sound, apparently asleep. "I meant, do you see the pickup boat yet?" he asked as he began to tread water.

Jenks darted off, flying a good five feet above the water to make Trent wonder about sharks. If they had fish that would snack on Jenks, then there would be sharks, eating the fish, right? The cold was beginning to get to him, and he began swimming to generate heat, pushing forward going nowhere. He'd once pulled Rachel out of the frozen Ohio River. She'd been suffering from hypothermia after only a few minutes. He hadn't had an issue with the cold, but he'd been in the water here for at least twice that. The bullets had stopped, and he was thankful. But maybe that only meant they had their own boat out here and didn't want to hit it.

Doubts tugged at him, and his thoughts began to slow. He'd been awake almost three days in a row getting out here, and he'd asked his body to perform far beyond what he had prepared for. Jenks was gone, maybe eaten. He'd brought his daughter out of her safe home and for what? To die a cold and frightening death in the middle of the ocean?

The sound of Jenks's wings brought his head up, and he leaned his body into treading water, the cold seeping into him. He peered up at him, squinting into the sun as the pixy landed on the edge of the cockleshell boat. "No boat," Jenks said, making Trent's heart sink. He'd been a fool. A fool to believe he could do this. The Goddess was laughing at him. He should have promised her more, but doing this without killing anyone had been his greatest sacrifice. Perhaps he should have tried harder not to kill the man with the knife. It had been instinct. Instinct had caused his downfall. He was not enough. He should turn around and take her back to them. He would die, but Lucy would live. Rachel would be furious with him. She was expecting his help, and a feeling of guilt swept through him. Just one more broken promise. He was no better than his father.

"Unless you're talking about that nasty-looking whale-watching boat," Jenks said, his expression pinched as he bobbed on the water and looked into the distance.

Trent's head slipped under as shock stilled his slowly moving legs. "That's the pickup boat!" he sputtered, kicking violently and steadying Lucy.

"That rat trap?" Jenks blinked, his wings turning an embarrassed red. "Oh man, I'm sorry," he said, rising up and looking to the north. "Damn, I'm sorry, Trent. I though you had some sort of fancy-ass speedboat arranged to pick us up. I'll go get them. They can't see you from here. Hang on. I didn't think you'd rely on something as chancy as a whale-watching tour boat!"

"Neither would the Withons," Trent said, his exasperation turning into a weary elation, but Jenks had already zipped off. He should have told Jenks what to look for. Why did he keep treating him like an accessory? The man was more efficient than Quen at thinking on his feet and had more endurance than one of his racehorses.

From inside the tiny boat, Lucy began to cry, scared upon waking up in a rocking, shifting world of color and sound after her bland sterile room at the Withons'. Treading water, Trent looked in the direction that Jenks had gone, hearing a boat but not seeing it. He carefully pulled back the protective cover, using his weight to lean it enough that he could see in.

"Hi," he whispered, and her eyes fastened on him, her momentary confusion at finding him with his hair plastered to his head passing at the sound of his voice. "We're going to be okay, Lucy," he said, and she kicked at him as if disagreeing. "You watch, Jenks is going to get them, and we'll be okay."

A marine horn tooted, and he looked up, waving at the row of people standing at the railing of the two-story whale-watching boat, binoculars all aimed at him. His heart pounded, and he felt a wash of protectiveness pass through him. Lucy's eyes drifted, finding Jenks as the pixy spiraled down, dusting heavily. "I told them you were waterskiing and the boat crashed," he said, darting off his first landing place that was within Lucy's reach.

"Excuse me?" Trent pushed the damp hair from his face.

"Seriously, I told them you misjudged the tides, and your boat drifted off while you were out walkies with your kid," he added, kicking at the air-filled cradle. "You're going to have to explain it from there. I don't know what you're going to tell them about her ears."

Trent frowned, thinking it was a bad story to begin with, but the chugging of the boat's engine was growing loud, and Jenks darted off as helping hands reached over the side of the boat. Some were brown from the sun, others white with age, but he smiled as he accepted them, feeling reborn as they took first Lucy, then himself, dripping from the water.

It was a confused babble of excitement as tourists cooed over Lucy, making her cry until he took her back. The men surrounded Trent, talking of tides and past fishing excursions, and he sniffed, saying as little as he could, accepting the blanket that someone offered him, and then the diaper and cleaning cloths from someone else, cheerfully given from a worn diaper bag. No one remarked upon Lucy's ears, no one asked what they were doing in the water. For the first time, he felt accepted as a person, and the new emotion soaked into him. The difference had to be Lucy.

Finally all the questions were answered, all the women pacified, all the men in a corner still talking of the dangers of being on the water, all the kids distracted by Jenks on the far side of the boat. The sun was warm, and he held his daughter in his arms, both of them in borrowed clothes, both swaddled in blankets against the stiff wind.

Finding no eyes on them, Trent slipped to the lee side of the wind next to the boathouse, settling into the patch of sun with a tired sigh. The soft thrum of the engine worked its way up into him, as he sat with his back to the wall, his feet propped up most ungentlemanly on the seat so he could hold Lucy more securely.

Smiling, he looked down at her sleeping, her soft frown easing as he touched her tiny hand with a single finger, watching the way the wind shifted her fair hair about her pointy ears. "I think we're going to be okay,

Lucy," he whispered, and he leaned his head back, eyes shutting against the bright sun, listening to the wind and water, peace and exhaustion working together to ease him into the first good sleep in days.

They would be okay. He believed it to the bottom of his soul. Rescuing Lucy was the easy part. Surviving the next twenty years was going to be a little more chancy. After today, he thought he could do it with help, and now he thought he had the courage to ask for it.

Lucy would give him strength.

BEYOND
THE HOLLOWS

PET SHOP BOYS

I originally wrote "Pet Shop Boys" as one of two possibilities for an anthology. I don't submit to many anthologies, but this group came to me through my agent, impressed with my Dawn Cook titles, and asked me to try my hand at writing about vampires. This was before the dual nature of Kim and Dawn had been revealed, and I was so tickled they asked that my automatic no turned into a yes. I worked up two shorts, trying to get as far away from the Hollows vampire mythology as I could. Under the advice of my agent that "Pet Shop Boys" had the potential to become a series, I retained it to sit in my cabinet until now.

I've long loved the idea of the fey living in a world twin to ours, passing through to snare the unwary when the veil was the thinnest. Bringing vampires into the mix was the icing on the cake.

 ONE

Good luck with the puppy," Cooper called as the boy leaned back against the glass door, the bells ringing as he tried to push it open. It wasn't until the boy's dad lent a hand that the night air slipped in with a dusting of snow and they got outside, their new bundle of yaps and wet spots on the carpet wiggling in the boy's arms.

"And have a merry Christmas," he muttered as the door jingled closed behind them. He didn't like selling dogs and cats when there were strays that needed homes, but the owner, Kay, insisted on always having dogs, and sometimes cats. The Lab pup was the last of the litter, and the shop now felt empty without the soft snuffing and hush of paws on newspaper.

Tired, Cooper rubbed the back of his neck, head bowed as he came around the counter to hang up the six collars the father and boy had been deciding between. Snatching a fold of newspapers, he knelt by the open-topped mesh corral to wad up the used paper and lay new for the next litter. The bubbling of the fish tanks and twittering of finches slowly returned the pet shop into the peaceful haven that had convinced him to work here at minimum wage instead of taking the professor's assistant job he'd turned down three years ago.

Kay might have had something to do with it, though. Sex in jeans with her own money, she seemed to enjoy his company but kept him totally at arm's length. He didn't get it. Every time he was tempted to bag it, she gave him just enough encouragement to stay. God, he was a chump. He didn't want to be thirty and still cleaning up someone else's dog crap.

Grimacing, he rose to throw the papers away, pushing through the sheets of milky plastic that separated the back room from the store. The storage room/office was cold—it had been snowing all day with only the dog people coming in since it had become dark. He was tempted to flick the Closed sign around early, but Kay would give him hell for closing before eight.

It'd give me an excuse to talk to her, he thought as he trashed the papers and grabbed the disinfectant spray. Kay spent most of her time in the back when she was in. Cooper was the one who actually ran the place—except for the dogs. Kay brought them in from some exclusive breeder. The cats were from a local shelter.

The warmth of the store was welcoming as he slipped back through the plastic curtain. A quick spray, and the round kennel was clean, all evidence of the dog erased under the scent of bleach. Cooper straightened with a sigh. Twenty-five and a pet shop geek. He'd swear Kay wasn't gay—the occasional flirting suggested otherwise. Maybe it was him.

The sudden whirling of the birds in their cages brought his head up, and the hair on the back of his neck pricked. Feeling like winter had slipped in under the door, Cooper turned to the big plate-glass windows dark with night and the peaceful falling snow in the streetlight. His eyes widened at the little girl, no more than nine, standing in the middle of the aisle: white tights, little black shoes, and a coat made of black fur. Her vividly red hair was straight under a matching fur hat, and her hands were hidden in a muff.

"Oh! Hi!" Cooper stammered, pitching his voice high as he looked for a parent. "You surprised me! How long have you been in here?" She must have come in while he was in the back, but he hadn't heard the bells ring.

The little girl beamed. "Did I?" she said cheerfully, seeming to think it funny to have scared a grown-up. "May I see the kittens?"

Cooper nodded as he set the spray bottle on a back counter, trying to hide his annoyance. He liked kids, but not when their parents dropped them off as if he was a babysitter—especially fifteen minutes to closing. "Sure, but don't let them out, okay?"

Huffing a sigh of preteen independence, she strode confidently to the multistory cat cage. Crouching, she made a tiny trill of sound, and two gray heads and one black one popped up from the sleeping pile. The kittens fell over themselves to reach her, pressing against the mesh and meowing. "They like me," she said shyly, endearing as she glanced at him with her green eyes.

Cooper stood with his arms over his chest and looked at his watch. He couldn't kick her out. It was cold outside. "Is your mom around, sweetheart?" he asked. There was a discount store across the street, but it was closed. Maybe the bar down the way. The girl seemed as if she was used to being alone.

"I want the black one." She looked up, her hair framing an almost triangular face and lips too red for such a little girl, fingers pushed into the cage as far as she could get them. "She looks like me."

Cooper dropped back a step and smiled. He didn't see the resemblance, but he wasn't nine years old. "You can have her if your mother says it's okay. Why don't you go get her? We close in five minutes."

The girl pulled her hand from the cage and stood, her eyes alight. "I'll trade you for her."

Oh, for crying out loud . . . Cooper glanced at the Open sign and sighed. He'd dealt with children before. "My boss won't let me trade. Is your mother at the bar, honey?" He was getting the oddest vibe from the kid, a weird mix of wealth and abandonment, like a child of privilege raised by a rich drunk, a child never lacking for anything except a constant source of love, forced to take it in overindulgent spurts when sobriety hit.

"I'll trade you." The little girl confidently got to her feet and reached into her muff. "His name is Leonard. He bites, the little brat. I wanted a cat so we could play, but Mama picked a dumb bat. See?"

Cooper's eyes widened when her thin fingers opened to show a mouse-size wad of fur coiled up and its eyes tightly closed. *She's got a bat!* he thought, images of rabies and needles racing through him. "Oh, sweetheart," he said, swooping to the nearby display stand for a rodent box. "Put it in here. You shouldn't ever play with a bat. Never, ever."

"See! That's what I told Mama!" she said triumphantly as her little white hand dropped the dead or unconscious animal into the box, and Cooper closed it, stifling a shiver as the animal's tiny nails scraped. "She thinks bats are safe 'cause they can fly, but I like cats. They can sneak around even in the day."

Oh my God, Cooper thought, wondering if he should take the little girl in the back to wash her hands. A bat that let you pick it up wasn't healthy. Who the hell was supposed to be watching her? "Honey, do you know your mom's phone number?"

"You want to trade?" she asked, innocent eyes wide.

A chill took him as he patted her head. "If your mother says it's okay. Do you have her cell number?"

From the front of the shop, a feminine clearing of a throat startled him. Snatching his hand from the little girl, he spun to the woman standing just inside the door, arms over her chest and her hip cocked as she looked severely at the little girl.

The bells didn't ring, he thought as the little girl scuffed her shiny party shoes, the black kitten settling in her arms and almost disappearing in the girl's fur coat. *How . . .* , he thought. *How did she get the cat out of the cage so fast?*

"Emily, I told you to wait for me," the woman said as she approached, her narrow hips swaying and pointy boots making a decisive tap on the oak flooring. But for all of Cooper's worry that she'd seen him touch her daughter, the woman was clearly amused, her angular face and small nose showing a delightful good humor. The family resemblance was obvious, from their red hair to the deep green of their eyes, skin so pale as to make their lips blood-red.

Cooper's face warmed, and he stepped away from the little girl. He shouldn't have touched her, but by God, a child shouldn't be running around with a dead bat in her pocket.

"I was careful, Mama," the little girl said defiantly. "I waited until the dog left."

"I'm not angry about the dog," the woman said as she laid a possessive hand on her daughter's shoulder. "You can't sell Leonard, no matter how you dislike him."

"He bites!" she protested. "I hate him! You always take his side, and it's not fair!"

"Ma'am, any bat that lets you pick it up is ill. I have to turn it over to Animal Control," Cooper started, wanting them out of his store but having a legal responsibility, too.

"The bat is a pet," the woman said. "It has never seen the night sky but for today." Her eyes narrowed in a staged severity as she glanced at her daughter. "You and I are going to have a chat, young lady."

Cooper hesitated, and the woman extended a long slim hand for the box. He couldn't help but notice there was no wedding ring, and her smile held a sly evaluation as his eyes rose from it to find she had seen him look.

"Please," she said, her voice softening. "The bat isn't ill. I wouldn't allow my daughter access to disease-ridden vermin. What do you take me for?" She laughed, throwing her head back to show her long, beautiful neck, and the birds fluttered, clinging to the mesh and twittering.

Uneasy, Cooper handed her the box. "A pet?" The woman obviously wasn't a drunk; she looked thin from aerobics and Pilates, not alcohol. "I think he's dead," Cooper added, and the woman's expression fell.

Jerking, she popped the box open, her eyes closing in relief as she brought the bat out and held it for a moment before carefully placing it in her coat pocket. "He's sleeping," the woman said in relief, shooting an angry look at her daughter, who was now holding the kitten like a baby, rocking back and forth and crooning.

"Please, Mama," she said, her loving gaze fixed on the kitten. "You never let me have anything."

The woman's eyebrows rose. "Don't I just? Well, how would you like me giving you a year's grounding?"

"Mama!"

"Put the cat back and wait for me outside, or I'll make it two!"

Emily puckered her lips, and Cooper thought he was going see a temper tantrum to end all tantrums, but when her mother cocked her head, the little girl lost her bluster. "I waited and waited," she whined, swaying petulantly to make the hem of her coat hit her legs. "I was patient, just like you said. You never let me have anything!" But it was soft in defeat, and Cooper took the kitten, feeling awkward as the little girl stomped to the door and pushed the heavy door open, the bells making only a dull thud against the glass as she went out.

Cooper shivered in the draft before turning back to the woman. Damn, she was striking, her cheekbones high and her eyes wide and full of a questioning depth as she waited for Cooper to stop watching her daughter skipping across the snowy parking lot to the late-model Jaguar.

"Sorry," he said, embarrassed for no reason he could fathom. He wasn't the one with the kid running around with a bat.

She smiled to show very white teeth. "Don't be," she said, reaching to touch his shoulder before turning to the window. Surprised, Cooper froze. "I know how this looks," she said softly, watching Emily dance in a puddle of light with her arms raised to catch the drifting snow, her chiming laughter somehow making it through the glass. "Emily is a precocious thing. I appreciate you not calling the authorities. The bat is part of a well-maintained colony. He isn't ill, just ill-tempered. Teething."

With a small sigh, she started for the door. Cooper touched his arm, feeling as if her hand was still there. He couldn't help but watch her legs in her black nylons, gaze rising to her round, very grabbable ass, and then to her thin waist, all shown off by an expensive-looking leather coat. He sighed as well, for an entirely different reason, flushing when the woman paused, clearly having heard him. Poised before the door, she turned. "The snow is beautiful tonight. Are you free?"

"Uh, no," he muttered, suddenly uneasy. Kitten still in his arms, he went behind the counter. The woman was gorgeous, sexy, and sophisticated. What would she want with him?

Hand on the door, she looked to her daughter, a wistful expression on her face. "She misses her father."

"Really." He didn't know what to say, and he perched himself on the worn stool. He couldn't help but look. But that was as far as it was going to ever go. Right?

"She's been watching your store for months," the woman said, her heels tapping a curious *tat-a-tat, tat-tat* beat as she came back to him. "Her heart has been set on a kitten, but I won't allow her to take a stray. Must not start bad habits. It's sweet, really. She thinks you're immeasurably brave for taking care of dogs. She calls you the dog master."

Cooper nodded, looking at a clipboard of fish inventory as he began cursing himself. A lonely, rich, beautiful woman was coming on to him, and he was looking at fish totals? But with a young child and a dead or divorced husband, she would have enough emotional baggage to ground a plane. He didn't want to become involved no matter how good the sex might be, even crazy good. "No harm, no foul," he said, jaw clenched.

"Well," the woman said as she stood before him, her hands spaced wide on the counter, "you're being extremely nice about it. I feel as if I owe you dinner at least."

Cooper glanced up, but his refusal hesitated at the look in her eyes: hesitant, hopeful . . . vulnerable. "No, really. It's okay," came out instead his intended, "Sorry, I'm busy."

"I insist," she said. "My name is Felicity. My employer is hosting a holiday party at Gateways tonight. That's where we're going . . . dressed like this."

Cooper nodded, his pulse quickening. He was cautious, but he wasn't dead. Gateways was one of the most exclusive dance clubs in the tristate area, having opened six years ago. And, judging by the number of times it made the front page, it had been a problem to the local cops since that time. He'd never been in there.

"He's got the entire place rented out. Arranged for a band. If I don't bring a man with me, I'm going to be fending off drunk coworkers all night," the woman said, dropping her elbows on the counter and cupping her chin in her hands, her green eyes daring him. "You'd be doing me a favor."

Her blouse was falling open, and with a herculean effort, he didn't look—much. But the rest of her bent over the counter like that was even sexier, and Cooper struggled to keep his thoughts on what she was saying. He wanted to go, but he hesitated. She was smart, beautiful, and she didn't care that he worked at a pet shop. *What's wrong with this picture, Cooper?*

"Emily will be there," she coaxed as she stood, and Cooper began to breathe again. "It's family oriented. We'd love to have you join us."

Cooper thought of his microwave dinner waiting for him at his two-room apartment. Frozen meals, sitcoms, and reality TV were dragging him down, killing his ambition. *I'm an ass if I let this slip away. Go get yourself a story to tell!*

"Okay, you convinced me."

The woman clapped once as her red hair flew everywhere and her black boots tapped on the old oak flooring. "The band starts at ten," she said, and Cooper was struck by how much her alive and excited eyes looked like her daughter's when she had held the kitten. "Why don't you come early so we can talk before it gets noisy?"

"Nine thirty," Cooper affirmed, and she smiled, extending her hands for the kitten.

"Wonderful! Emily is so perceptive. How much for the cat?"

"You're going to get it for her?" Cooper asked as he handed the squirming thing over.

"Absolutely!" Felicity snuggled the animal under her chin and smiled as whiskers tickled her neck. "I can't have her trying to trade Leonard again!"

Cooper raised his hand against her credit card, brought out from the same pocket the bat was still in. "No charge," he said, thinking of the germs that might be attached despite the woman's assurance that it was a pet. "We don't actually sell the cats, but we do ask that you make a donation to the Humane Society."

Felicity smiled as if confused and tucked her card away. "See you at nine thirty, Cooper. Tell them you're with me, and they'll let you in. Felicity. Remember it."

"I will," he said, then hesitated. "How did you know my name?"

"Emily told me," she said, eyes glinting. "I told you, she's been watching the store for months." And then she turned, steps clacking as she walked out the door with the kitten in hand.

Cooper watched appreciatively, thinking that he had the right seeing as they were going on a date. The bells didn't jingle for her either, and his smile fading, he followed her to turn the Open sign around. Bemused, he shook his head, thinking about how the rest of his evening might go if he played his hand right. "If nothing else, I'm finally going to see the inside of that place," he said to the remaining kittens, and they curled up in an uncaring little gray ball.

Smiling at the reminder of how good she looked, Cooper paused in his reach for the old-style, iron bolt as a familiar figure came running to the door, her shuffling gait looking almost pained. It was Kay, and standing sideways, he pushed the heavy door open for his boss as the sleek black car with Felicity and Emily in it pulled away.

"Oh God. It's cold tonight!" Kay exclaimed, coming in with a gust of snow. "I think I just froze my tail off!"

"Tell me about it," he said as she stomped her feet and brushed the snow off her short leather coat. "Where have you been? You're late. Uh, not that you can't be," he said as he threw the bolt.

Her expected laugh didn't come. Nose wrinkled, she looked over the store, slowly taking off her snug knit hat to reveal blond hair cut just below her ears. It framed her round face to give her a sweet look with her turned-up nose and blue eyes. "You sold the Lab?"

Cooper nodded, feeling tall beside her as he always did. He couldn't help but compare her to Felicity; the woman's long legs, pale skin, and obvious interest stood in stark contrast to Kay's petite stature, tan complexion, and companionable distance. Why had he wasted his time trying to get to know Kay when she so clearly wasn't interested? "Ah, a few minutes ago," he said when she turned to him, blue eyes questioning at his lack of an answer. "Nice man with a kid."

Silent, she looked him over, her small hands unwinding her long scarf. Nodding, Kay strode to the back trailing clumps of snow. "Can you come in early tomorrow?" she asked as she vanished behind the plastic curtain. "I've got a new litter I've been wanting to bring in, and you're so good with the paperwork."

More dogs? "Christmas is in four days!" he shouted so she'd hear.

"Yeah. I know!" she shouted back. Boot heels clacking, she strode back into the store, coat on but open, her nose still wrinkled and a disgusted look on her pretty face. "What is that smell? Did something die?"

In a pet shop? Probably. Cooper headed for the dog kennel. "I took the papers out already."

"No, it's not that," she said, hunting with her nose and pausing when she got to the cats. "You sold a cat, too?"

"Little black one, right after the dog. Weirdest thing—" he started, his words trailing off. Christ almighty, he couldn't tell her he gave it to a woman who had a bat. Kay would have a fit.

Kay's eyes narrowed. "Really? What did he look like?"

"She," Cooper said reluctantly, flushing as he remembered Felicity bending over the counter. "A little girl and her mom. Hey, I've got a date tonight. Would you mind if I did my close-out list in the morning? I should splash on some cologne or something." *And shave*, he thought as he touched his jaw.

Focus distant, Kay drifted to the register. "Take a bath. You smell funny."

"Gee, thanks, Kay."

"Anyone I know?" she asked, head down as she opened her breeder file.

"I doubt it. She looked like she was from the university." Distracted now, he vowed to ask Felicity tonight if only to prove he was interested in more than how she looked.

"I need you here tomorrow at eight, okay?" Kay said, hand on a folder as she looked out into the night like it meant something. "Where are you going?"

Cooper leaned over the counter for his coat, suddenly feeling as if the cotton fabric wasn't good enough. Gateways was totally out of his league. "Golly, Mom. It's just a date."

That brought a smile to her, but it faded fast. "Cooper . . ." she said, reaching out to touch his shoulder. Cooper stopped, surprised, and her hand dropped, her fingers closing into a little fist. Biting her lip, she looked up at him with her big blue eyes. The woman never seemed to lose her tan, even in the dead of winter. "You said your grandmother used to tell you stories. Fairy tales."

His arms halfway into his coat, Cooper stared at her. "You mean like crossing yourself when you see a ring around the full moon, never eat food left out because the fairies might have claimed it, or that you can see lost souls on Halloween when you look between the ears of a barking dog? Yeah. She was a weird old bird. She taught me how to play poker, too."

Not giving him the expected laugh, Kay took a breath. "Be careful tonight. It's slippery out there."

"You got it. Thanks, Kay. Have a good night."

"Godspeed, Cooper."

The bells jingled brightly as he went out, the snick of the lock behind him sounding as cold as the air now burning his lungs. Striding quickly to his beat-up Volvo, he mentally went through his closet, hoping he had something that wouldn't make him look like a total loser. Shower, shave, and some cologne to get rid of the dog smell. Tonight would be a date to remember.

TWO

The hint of warmth from his car vanished as Cooper's door thumped shut and his shoes squeaked on the snow. His face scrunched up and the cold pinched his newly shaven face as he looked over the full lot to the tall, somewhat ornate building with its theater marquee and unused ticket booth. In its beginnings, Gateways had been a burlesque theater sandwiched between a brothel and slaughterhouses until a fire in the late '50s burned down the entire block but for the theater. Housing remained several blocks away, but new fire codes and NIMBY neighbors had kept almost everything else out, chain-link fences and decades-long litigation over who owned the surrounding property making it a lonely place when the sun was up.

Squinting, Cooper sniffed, a hint of excitement quickening his pace as he wove through the cars. There was already a line at the door. He was going to be pissed if this was a joke.

Hands in his pockets, he walked with his head down, hunched and uncomfortable in his dress shoes that didn't do a thing to stop the cold. His ears were frozen since he hadn't wanted to put on a hat and risk putting a wave into his hair, still damp from his shower. He'd changed into slacks and a shirt and tie, but he knew he wasn't going to look like anything other than a poor grad student. "Which is what I am," he muttered, his head coming up as he settled in behind the laughing, excited pair who had run to get to the door ahead of him.

The doorman didn't look cold at all, standing with a short leather jacket covering his thin dancer's body. Expression bland, he checked his clipboard against the name the two people had given him, then pointed to the line snaking from the door where people dressed nicer than he stood and shuffled for warmth.

Crestfallen, they moved to the end of the line, and Cooper stepped forward, worried. The music was thumping already; he was late, but he'd wanted to shower and shave. What had he been thinking? The doorman hadn't let *them* in. This was going to be a disaster.

"Name?" the man asked, bored.

Cooper glanced at the beautiful people in line. "Uh, I'm Cooper. Felicity invited me."

Like magic, the man's almost too-pretty mouth curved up in a smile, and he stepped aside, not even looking at his clipboard. "She will be delighted. Welcome to Gateways."

The people huddled in line groaned, and Cooper's jaw dropped, even as the man pulled open the door for him. "Go right on in."

With an unexpected feeling of importance, Cooper brushed by him, having to get closer than he liked. The music thumped, and the sound of laughter drew him in. An obvious sniff from the man turned him around as the door began to shut, and he saw the doorman wrinkling his nose right before the heavy oak slab shut out the night.

Eyes on the moving people on the dance floor, Cooper stood to the side to take off his coat and hand it to the small woman reaching for it, slipping his bulky car keys and cell phone into his jeans pocket at the last moment. Starting to smile, he looked over the spacious, noisy room still holding on to the faded grace of another time. Red velvet on the walls tried to soak up the noise, failing. What looked like the original chandeliers still hung, the crystal catching the darting lights to send flashes everywhere, but the sloping floor one would expect in a theater had been leveled off, bringing the ceiling down somewhat. Before him, the large stage was full of movement as three men pounded out a heavy beat with bobbing heads. A good three feet below it was the dance floor, thick with gyrating bodies and waving arms. Apparently Felicity worked with party animals. Around the edges were tall tables where people stood, laughing and talking in excitement. Closer to the door, there were more private booths with black leather and paintings that were almost more frame than picture. The bar was a gigantic wood and glass edifice that took up one entire side. There had to be at least five bartenders, all moving with a quick, certain efficiency. Everyone was dressed better than he was.

Except them, he thought, finding two men his age standing before it, clearly working out their chances of going home with the striking woman they were talking with. They weren't alone. The entire length of the bar were clusters of two or three average people being wined and dined by red-haired beauties of both sexes.

The warmth of the place was stealing into him, and the scent of wine and . . . frosting? Head starting to move to the beat, Cooper looked closer, his smile fading as he noticed a clear division between the haves in leather and expensive-looking jewelry, and then the have-nots, dressed like him in shoes that hurt and knockoffs. Maybe not have-nots, he decided as he dove into the mass and headed for the extravagant bar, but people trying to make it in a class a couple of rungs higher than they could easily afford. There were beautiful people here—Hollywood beautiful—and it made everyone else look common.

Beginning to feel unsure, Cooper looked from the band rocking on the stage to the dance floor and the weird mix of mosh pit jumping and . . . clogging? Frowning, he scanned for Felicity. He'd say hi, then leave. This had all the earmarks of a recruit drive for a pyramid cleaning-supply scheme. And what was with all the red hair?

"Hors d'oeuvre?" a soft voice breathed beside his ear, and Cooper spun. Two steps back, a smiling woman in a short skirt and a pageboy haircut raised a tray of white petits fours in invitation.

That explained the sweet smell of frosting, he mused, his wish for a beer vanishing upon seeing the little square cakes on the white napkins. "Thanks," he said, trying not to be obvious as he looked the woman over in her skintight uniform.

"Have two. You're a big one," she said, and Cooper's eyes shot to hers, wondering if she was coming on to him. He hesitated, and in that instant, he was jostled, his reach overshooting and almost hitting the woman in her chest.

"Cooper!" Felicity called breathlessly, laughing as she caught her balance against him, and he wondered if she was drunk. "I thought you'd stood me up, you lovely man." Before he could think to answer, she linked her arm in his possessively, her free hand coyly playing with a long silver chain about her neck. "Amber, go bother someone else," she said as she began dragging him away. "Cooper is *my* invite."

"Nice to meet you." Cooper grinned as he looked over his shoulder, but the woman had already turned away, frowning in annoyance.

"You don't want anything Amber has," Felicity said as she led him to an empty table, and Cooper's eyebrows rose at the thinly veiled insinuation. "She sneezes a lot."

"Sorry I'm late." Cooper eyed the people eating off little white napkins, twice as hungry now that he'd almost gotten something to eat. "I wanted to clean up."

"I'm so glad you came." Felicity stopped at a tall round table with two empty and abandoned drinks on it. "You had me worried."

"Wouldn't miss this for anything," Cooper said as he moved the cups to a passing tray, marveling at them. They were made of wood instead of glass, worked so thin he could see the shadow of his fingers through it. "I didn't want to come in here smelling like dog," he said, and then remembering the sniff from the doorman, he tugged at his collar.

"Silly man." Felicity snuggled up to him, her warmth pressing into his side. "I like the way you smell." Leaning in, she whispered, "Dogs scare me."

He was here, and she was here, and it was going great. Cooper tugged her closer, smiling, but then he cocked his head. "What did you do to your hair? It looks different."

Felicity touched the tips playfully. "It must be the light. Do you want to sit down?"

What he wanted was a drink, but no one with a tray of those wooden champagne flutes was anywhere near them. "Your hair looks darker in this light. Your eyes, too."

"I thought you weren't coming," she said, explaining nothing. "But now that you're here, I'm all yours, Cooper."

Her smile dove to the bottom of his gut and set his thoughts wandering. Confidence seemed to flow into him with her beside him, and he leaned back against the table with Felicity, his worries that it had been a joke gone. She looked fabulous in her calf-length, shiny dress that clung to her like Saran wrap. That she was jealous of the waitress had made him feel good, and the thumping music had him wanting to get out there and move. He should've given up on Kay a long time ago.

"Come on, I want to see how you dance," Felicity coaxed, eyes sparkling as her hands took his and she stepped to the dance floor, backing up right into a dignified man in a suit. He had appeared as if from nowhere, and she spun, hand to her mouth and charmingly surprised.

"Papa!" she exclaimed, and Cooper spied Emily beside the man, the new kitten in her arms making her look sweeter than the petits fours.

"Hi, Mama," the little girl said, swinging to and fro to make her dress swirl. The older man, however, wasn't happy, one hand holding Emily's, the other gripping a wooden flute of champagne, his rings sparkling in the reflected light.

"Your dad?" Cooper whispered even as he tried to look more respectable under the man's hawklike stare.

Felicity grimaced. "It's a family-owned business," she said, leaning in to make him shiver as she whispered it in his ear.

That explains all the redheads, he thought, though the man before him had jet-black hair.

Looking even more severe, the older man gave Emily a gentle push. "Take your kitten to the back rooms, Emily," he said, his voice deeper than his narrow shoulders would suggest. "There's a good girl. And share her with your brother."

Cooper flicked his gaze from Emily to Felicity. "I didn't know you had another child," he said conversationally, hoping Felicity would introduce him before he had to do it himself.

"Grandpa," Emily whined, and the man gave her a harder shove to the stairs. Cooper's smile vanished as the little girl caught her balance with a skipping of shiny black shoes, and Felicity grabbed her arm, tugging her to stand behind her instead.

"Stay with me, Emily," Felicity said, her narrow face beginning to show her anger.

Cooper, too, felt a surge of protectiveness, and he extended his hand, intending to grip the older man's hand with a shade too much pressure. "Hello, I'm Cooper."

But the man in the gray suit ignored him and his hand. "All yours, Felicity?" he said, not a glance at Cooper. "We've talked about this. You shame yourself. Again."

Felicity flicked her eyes from Cooper to her father. "It's just an expression."

"One would hope." Only now did he look at Cooper, his lips pressed tight and his dark brown eyes narrowed in a tired, old frustration.

"This is Cooper," Felicity said with a sudden meekness, as if only now after he'd looked at Cooper could she introduce him. "He takes care of dogs and was kind to Emily."

"It's good to meet you, sir," Cooper said, but he didn't hold his hand out again.

With a single glance, Felicity's father dismissed him. "I forbid it. Everyone to his place, and a place for everyone. What you want goes against tradition."

"The hell with traditions!" Felicity said loudly, shocking Cooper when she dramatically flung a hand into the air, and he wondered again if she was a little drunk. "If it was wrong, then it wouldn't be possible!"

Wincing, Cooper looked around, but no one was even watching them. What the blue blazes had he been thinking, coming here? Of course crazy girlfriend would have a lunatic psycho dad. Lunatic, psycho, rich dad.

Felicity's father made a rumble of discontent. "I have two men I want you to meet. Now. It's growing late, and I have things to attend to."

"You know what?" Cooper said as he glanced at Emily rocking her kitten and crooning to it as she ignored their argument as if from long practice. "Maybe I should just go."

"No!" Felicity clutched his arm, and another surge of protectiveness shocked through him. She was so beautiful, vulnerable. "I want to talk to you." She glanced at her father, who was smiling in an ugly way. "Please stay with Emily. This won't take long."

It was her tremulous smile that did it. That and the shove her father had given Emily. If the man pushed children at a Christmas party, then he probably did a lot worse in private.

"I'll stay," he said, and she exhaled happily. Cooper's pride swelled. For all her money, she needed him.

"Thank you," she said, letting go and sliding closer to her father to look small.

Immediately the older man's mood shifted. "Good to meet you, Cooper," he said distantly as if he was already somewhere else. "Have some wine. I've not started on this one."

He extended the glass, and Felicity bumped him. "Whoops!" she said even before the cup hit the floor, and Cooper edged back to avoid the splash when the thin wood broke like glass. "Papa, I'll be right with you. Let me get Cooper a new drink," she said, kicking the pieces under the table. "Emily, come with us."

Her father's eyes narrowed, but Felicity had taken Cooper's arm and was leading him through the crowded floor. Cooper looked back once as they were jostled, then leaned close, shouting, "Why do I have the feeling that your dad thinks you're too good for me?"

She was smiling when she looked back at him, her grip on his arm tightening. "Because he does," she said, clearly angry though her voice was barely audible over the pounding music. "He thinks you're a stray."

Rich bastard. "Felicity, you're a beautiful woman, but I should leave," he said when they got through the crush.

Immediately Felicity stopped, Emily beside her as she tried to get her kitten to eat one of those little cakes. Her troubled gaze flicked over his shoulder, then back to him. "Please, stay," she pleaded, pulling him closer again. "This will only take a minute. He has my best interests at heart, but he's a pain in the ass. Don't eat anything while I'm gone, okay? Promise? Wait for me."

Cooper jerked his gaze from Emily still coaxing the kitten into eating that sweet. "I'm starved," he admitted.

"Me too. I'll bring something back. Something special. Please?"

Felicity looked truly distressed. Behind her on the other side of the club in one of the private booths, her father waited with two men, giving them each a wineglass and toasting until they drank. Cooper thought it interesting that they were younger than him, dressed even more casually. It wasn't his wallet that alienated her father; it was something else. "Okay," he finally said, and she smiled, making everything right.

"Emily?" she called, and the little girl swayed closer.

"Yes, Mama?" She'd gotten the kitten to eat a bite, and Emily was wiping her whiskers with a white napkin.

Felicity dropped gracefully down to crouch before Emily and, using a finger, lifted her chin up. "Would you be a big girl and entertain Mr. Cooper for me?"

"But I'm already watching Leonard," the little girl complained.

What was it with the bat? Maybe the thing really was a pet.

"Grandpa wants me to meet someone," Felicity was saying firmly to Emily. "I don't want anyone thinking Cooper is a stray while I'm gone."

Emily peered around Cooper. "One has nice hair," she offered, surprising Cooper.

Felicity smiled. "We'll see." The crumb of cake dropped to the floor, and the kitten struggled to get it, settling back when Felicity plucked it from the floor and fed it to her. Tiny little canines lunged for it, grazing Felicity's finger. "Where's Leonard?"

"Under the pool table," Emily said, and Felicity stood, touching her shoulder.

"Then take Mr. Cooper over there so he doesn't get lonely."

"But Mama," she began to whine, and Cooper smiled.

"Just do it, Emily," her mother said sharply, and the little girl deflated. "The sooner I finish with Grandpa, the sooner I can take you on the dance floor. You, me, and Mr. Cooper."

"Promise?" she begged, deep green eyes wide as she looked up at them both.

Felicity nodded even as Cooper wondered how that was going to play out. "If it's okay with Mr. Cooper."

He smiled as Felicity squeezed his hand in parting. No amount of crazy-woman sex was worth getting involved with a woman with two kids, a bat, and an abusive father. He should leave and give the next in line a chance. But as Felicity angled her way around the dance floor, he crossed his arms over his chest and settled back with Emily. He couldn't leave her unattended.

"So your cat can eat cake, but I can't," he said sourly, and Emily beamed at him, nodding. "What did you name her?" he asked, curious, and Emily turned to a quiet corner where a soft glow lit a span of green felt.

"I didn't," she said, surprising him. But she was walking away, and he scrambled to keep up. She was surprisingly fast, and with sudden quickness, he found himself in a back corner of the bar, feeling as if he'd stepped through a curtain. The music still beat into him, but it was muted. The air was cooler, and the smell of food less, which was a relief. He was starving.

Emily had crawled under the pool table and was talking to Leonard, probably, and Cooper shook his head, finding a nearby chair to fall into. Sighing, he looked at the ceiling, glad he had a moment to gather himself. Felicity's family was just too weird.

"Isn't she soft?" Emily said right in front of him, and he pulled his head down to find her standing between his knees, far too close. She had shoved her sleepy cat right into his face, and he straightened, taking her shoulders and moving her to stand beside him instead. "She smells so good!" Emily added, pushing the sleepy cat into his face again.

Taking the kitten in self-defense, Cooper buried his nose into the long fur, breathing in a scent that smelled vaguely like rabbit. "She smells perfect," he said, and Emily's green eyes narrowed.

"Mine!" she demanded, hands reaching.

"You shouldn't feed her cake," Cooper said as he handed the kitten back. "She's a carnivore. You know what that is?"

The kitten once more in her arms, Emily gave Cooper a big sloppy kiss, the cat pressed between them. "It means she likes blood," the little girl said in her high, innocent voice.

Surprised, Cooper wiped his lips, wondering at the slight bitter taste Emily had left behind. "I suppose. Cake might give her a tummy ache."

Emily dropped to her knees and crawled back under the table with her cat. Cooper settled back in relief. She was a sweet girl, but he wasn't comfortable around kids. There were a few children on the outskirts like Emily. None of them were playing with each other but were alone, talking with grown-ups. Talking with beautiful, lyrical people with black hair.

Frowning, Cooper wiped the bitterness from his mouth again and sat up. *Where had all the redheads gone?*

Leaning, he looked at Emily under the table, playing with her kitten. *What is taking Felicity so long?* "Are you excited to be able to stay up late?"

"No," came her sweet voice, and she crawled out to climb into the chair beside him, swinging her feet and cuddling her kitten. "Are you sure you don't want to dance?"

"Pretty sure," he said, looking for Felicity's red hair among the brunettes. He finally spotted her clear across the bar, arguing with her father. Slowly he frowned. "That's odd."

"What?" Emily asked as she buried her nose in her kitten's fur.

Cooper ran a finger between his collar and his neck. "I could have sworn there were more people here with red hair."

Emily laughed. "You're funny, Mr. Cooper," she said, cuddling her cat.

"And you need to name your kitten, young lady."

He'd meant it as a joke, but the little girl looked at the cat seriously, purring in her arms with her eyes closed. "I'll name her Happy," she said, and Cooper nodded, satisfied.

"That's a good name." Sucking on his teeth, he watched the people around him, counting the red to brunette ratio. Everyone on the dance floor had black hair now, moving fast in a complicated line dance, feet hitting the floor simultaneously to make the chandeliers shake.

His gaze drifted over the shadowed booths, landing on a particularly amorous couple, arms wrapped around each other and heads locked together as the rest of the table ignored them, one blond woman with her head on the table next to her wineglass, and the other staring vacantly into the dancing mob.

Chuckling, he started to look away, but a glint of teeth yanked his attention back.

Jaw dropping, he stared as the man pulled from the woman for a breath of air, then slowly bent back to her, shifting her head slightly to show her bleeding, torn flesh. *Holy shit!* he thought, going cold as a wash of fear hit him. He'd bitten her! The woman was bleeding!

Cooper looked from the woman passed out on the table to the one staring vacantly at nothing. *Sweet Jesus*, he thought in a panic. Was he in a bestial bar? He'd heard about these, places where bored, wealthy people went to abuse poor slobs . . . like himself.

His blood pounded, and he forced himself not to move, freezing like a cornered animal. The food he'd been warned not to eat . . . Was it drugged?

Why else would someone sit there and let another person take a chunk out of them!

"Emily . . ." he whispered, and she looked at him, sweet and innocent as she played with her kitten, little feet swinging in those white stockings and shiny black shoes.

"Your eyes are brown," he stammered. And her hair was black. Her hair was black. He knew it had been red, like autumn leaves. *Sweet Jesus, save me, I'm going crazy.*

The little girl beamed at him. "They're only green when I'm hungry, silly."

Swallowing, Cooper looked at the kitten, unmoving in her arms, at the spot of blood on her fur. In a rush of motion, he stood. Emily had bitten her. The little cat had let her, drugged when it ate that piece of cake. Felicity had helped her.

"My God," he whispered, not knowing what to do. Emily hadn't been smelling the cat's fur, she had been biting it!

"Oh my God . . ." he breathed again as the band hammered out a pulse-pounding beat and people howled like savages praying to their gods. "I have . . . to go."

He scanned the bar, counting more than a dozen people unconscious, some being carried out the back to who knew what. There were too many people between the door and himself. Terrified, he took a step.

"Cooper."

Felicity's voice cut through the noise, diving to his middle and igniting his panic. He spun, knowing his fear was obvious when she held up a hand. Her hair was darker, and her eyes were now a deep brown. Cooper's gaze flicked behind her to the doorman hoisting one of the men she had been talking to over his shoulder and carrying him away.

"Y-You . . ." he stammered, his stomach twisting. "My God . . ." He couldn't say it. She was a beast. She'd bitten that man. Like a vampire. He'd known the woman had problems, but this was unreal!

Felicity wiped the corner of her mouth with a pinky before saying, "How else am I supposed to know which one tasted the best?"

Flip, but still true. Reeling, he staggered back, hand reaching for the support of the chair. "Oh my God!" he said louder. "This is not happening! You. All of you! This isn't happening!"

Emily had crawled back under the pool table, and Felicity came close, making Cooper retreat until he couldn't move any farther. "Keep your voice down!" she almost hissed, and Cooper could smell a weird, musky smell on her breath.

Not one of the beautiful people in the bar had red hair anymore. They were all black haired now, their faces pale and their lips red as they danced, their motions becoming wilder as they left their "invites" at the tables for others to remove so they could join the dance. The music had become bestial—arms flinging, feet stomping, chanting in unison.

"Oh my God," he breathed. Feeling as if he might pass out, he fell into a chair and put his head in his hands. Things like this weren't real! This wasn't happening!

"Shit," Felicity said, and she stood between him and the rest of the bar. "Emily, did you let him eat anything?"

"No, Mama," came from under the pool table.

Cooper jerked when someone touched him, and he looked at the two in horror, Felicity peering at him in concern and Emily petting her kitten, passed out in her arms. "I gotta go," he said thinly, and Felicity pushed him back into his chair.

She was stronger than she looked, and Cooper flopped back, feeling his chest where she'd touched him as she moved a chair to block everyone's view of him and sat. "If you want to die, get up and run to a door you can't open," she said, her expression hard. "If you want to live, really live, sit down, shut up, and do what I tell you."

This is not happening.

"You can't get out," Felicity said, her musty breath mingling with his as she leaned close. "The veil is on the cusp of turning, and we're in the gateway."

He tried to stand again, and she put a hand on his chest, holding him down. "It's sealed!" she whispered as she saw his panic. "There's only one way to go, and that's through the veil. You can either pass through with me as my consort or as part of my father's larder. Listen to me!"

Panting, he looked up, seeing her dark eyes, her ebony hair—her red, red lips. Seeing his attention, she moved her hand from his chest to his fingers, holding them lightly. Behind Felicity, people danced, and he nodded, humoring her. He had to get out of here.

"I'm immortal, Cooper," she said, a curious lilt to her voice as if she delighted in it. "I've been raising Emily and Leonard alone after my fool husband died when a hunter thought a bearskin rug would be a fine thing to have. I love my children, but they grow so slowly, and I'm tired of doing this alone. I can't trust anyone else."

Cooper tried to stand, halting when she squeezed his hand and his knees threatened to give out. "You drink blood!" he whispered, cold as he saw Emily sitting cross-legged under the pool table with the kitten. "Oh God, she's killing that cat," he moaned.

"Don't be silly," Felicity snapped. "That cat has to last Emily for at least a year. She's not about to kill it." She turned, smiling. "Are you, lovey?"

"No, Mama," the little girl said, hugging the unmoving animal.

Nausea bubbled up, and Cooper forced it down. "I don't feel good," he said, unable to keep his head up. He shivered when Felicity touched his hair, petting him. Shoving her hand off him, he stared at the lyrical figures wildly dancing, the food he had been told not to eat, and the unconscious people being carried away. "You're fairies," he said, and Felicity blinked. "My grandmother told me never to eat with fairies or I'd be spirited away for a hundred years."

"Fairies?" Felicity said, laughing. "Fairies are facets of us given their own identity by ignorant humans who see only half of it. A wispy daydream of us at our green-eyed least. Vampire is more the truth, and even then you get it wrong. We can break through the veil at any time, but only when it's at its thinnest can we bring anyone back. Immortal doesn't mean invincible, and beyond the veil, we are safe from you."

It's the solstice, he remembered, feeling haggard. "Don't touch me," he demanded as she tried to pet him again, and this time, she backed off as if he'd slapped her, a hurt expression on her face. "You drugged me," he accused.

"No, it's the veil," she said, leaning to look under the pool table. "Emily, bring Leonard out to meet Mr. Cooper properly," she said, then smiled at him. "You're in the gateway. Until you land to one side or the other, it feels as if you're holding your breath."

Gateway? Cooper watched a little boy crawl out behind Emily, his chubby fingers holding tight to her hand. He had to be about four, shy as he snuck glances at Cooper from behind his mother. *Leonard? They named the bat after him?*

In a sudden surge of fear, he figured it out. *Leonard* is *the bat.* Emily had tried to sell her brother. What older sister hadn't wanted to do that at some point? She'd tried to trade her little brother for a pet she hadn't bothered to name. "I'm in hell," he whispered, and Felicity huffed.

"Don't be silly," she said as she pulled Leonard onto her lap. "Hell smells better than the swill you breathe."

Cooper sat up, adrenaline giving him strength. He wanted to stand but wasn't sure his legs would hold him. "You're a demon," he said. "You are *eating people!*"

Anger flickered over her face, and she jiggled Leonard a little too hard. "We are *not* demons," she said hotly. "Filthy little . . . stinky-tailed vermin." Her expression became coaxing. "Please, Cooper. We're running out of time. If I had wanted to poison you, I could have done it. I want to take you home—not as food, but as an equal. I need help, and Emily likes you. So do I. I can't trust anyone else."

Emily was nodding, clearly having been in on the decision.

"One kiss," Felicity soothed him, her hand on his arm to make him shudder. "With that, the veil will part for you as it does for all of us. I don't want another cow. My father keeps me well set. I've been careful. I've enough for two. Enough for all of us until the veil thins again in a year."

Enough? Enough what? Enough bodies suspended between life and death to feed upon?

"Oh my God!" he whispered, panic rising anew. He had to get out of here!

"Please," Felicity begged, looking as beautiful with her black hair and her dark eyes as she had with her red hair and green eyes. "I'm offering you everything a man wants. A beautiful wife, loving, obedient children. Power, status, people moving aside as you walk by. I'm from a wealthy house, Cooper. Old blood. And Cooper? We dance. We dance *forever*," she said, her eyes glowing with possibility. "You could have every earthly pleasure before you're too old to enjoy it, because it comes with everlasting life. I promise!"

Fingers trembling, he looked at his hand, seeing in his thoughts as if it was worn and aged already. The music beat like a second, communal heart. Guttural groans from the dance floor were like the passion that she promised him. His head came up, and he stared at little Leonard, the boy grinning to show red teeth before he slid from his mother and ducked behind his sister.

"You're animals," he breathed.

"As if you are not," Felicity said indignantly.

Yeah, but we don't generally eat each other. He groaned, leaning away from her, from immortality, from savagery beyond belief. This was a nightmare. A freaking nightmare.

"Cooper. Listen to me," Felicity said, a new urgency in her voice. "The veil is thickening. If we wait much longer, you can't come through. I know this is a lot, but I promise I will love you, and you will learn to love me. I just don't have time right now!"

She laughed, shaking her head ruefully. "I'm going to live forever, and I don't have the time. Cooper, let me mark you so the veil will let you through. Just one kiss, and you'll see everything as it truly is, not the faded wisps that the sun bleaches everything into. Be my husband. Be Emily's and Leonard's father. Please."

Behind Felicity, the dance floor was going empty. People were being carried away, slung over shoulders with their arms dangling. Food? "No!" he said forcefully, and her eyes went round with surprise. "You are a blood-sucking monster!" he shouted as he found the strength to rise to his feet.

The music died, and pale faces turned. "All of you," he panted into the sudden silence, weaving on his feet.

Everyone was looking at them, and Felicity bowed her head. "Why can't I find just one decent man? Just one?"

From across the room, her father stood. "Damn you, Felicity. I said no," he said, pointing directly at two young men. "Take him. Dump enough wine down his throat to get him across. I want this one as an object lesson."

"No!" Felicity stood in a panic, and Cooper blinked up at her, heart pounding. "If you won't allow me a new husband from the families, I'll make one!"

"I won't allow you a new husband because I decided your line should die out, you stupid cow!" her father exclaimed, and the remaining dancers began to leave the dance floor and gather their things, skulking to stay out of his sight. "You and the ill-gotten spawn that ignorant sidestepper engendered. Who do you think closed the veil to him?"

"Papa!" she shrieked, her eyes shifting to a pale green. "You? You killed my husband?"

Cooper tensed, eyeing the door. It looked too far away with too many people between him and it. But no one was looking at him. Sweat broke out. They were animals, feeding on people. Feeding on him. Feeding on his cat!

In sudden impulse, he grabbed the animal. Emily shrieked and Felicity turned, tears slipping from her eyes. Grunting, Cooper shoved them both at the two men coming for him. Amid yells and screams, they all went down. Heart pounding, he ran for the polished bar.

The kitten tucked under his arm didn't move. He hoped it was still alive as he shoved a woman of incredible beauty out of his way. A cry of outrage followed by a laugh went up, and his tired legs found strength. Hands grasped him, but he slipped them all, jumping onto the bar and running down it, scrambling to avoid the reaching hands.

"Someone catch him!" the old man demanded. Felicity was crying at his feet and Emily was curled into a ball, sobbing for her kitten.

Cooper jumped from the end of the bar, fumbling for his car keys knowing he'd have precious few seconds to get in and get it started. Feeling like he might make it, Cooper hit the door at a run, slamming into the lever, but the door didn't move. Panic hit him. The thick wood took his pounding, giving nothing. The lever rattled up and down, but nothing happened. Through the smoked glass, the moon shown through the trees—tall, huge pine trees green in the snow and moonlight. It wasn't the parking lot.

He stared, jerked out of his shock when someone touched him. "No!" he shouted as he was yanked backward into the room, grunting as he hit the floor and curled up to avoid crushing the kitten. His keys went flying, the Harley bell that his grandmother had given him ringing clear and sharp as it pinged across the floor.

As one, every single vampire cowered, howling in pain. He froze, seeing the little bell roll in a circle to become silent. First one, then another black head rose to look at him, pain still etched on their faces.

Cooper surged after his keys, scrambling on the floor until the little key chain with the Florida emblem and the Harley biker bell that his grandmother said would keep him from hitting potholes was back in his grasp. "You're animals!" he shouted, shaking it to make it ring, and they all fell back in pain. Only Felicity's father stood tall at the far end of the room. Blood trickled from the man's ear, and Cooper remembered the bells on the shop door hadn't rung when Emily and Felicity crossed the threshold.

With a renewed hope, he ran for the door. "Let me out! Let me through!" he screamed, pounding on it.

A crack split the air, throwing him back into the bar. The lights went out as he hit the floor, landing awkwardly so he wouldn't hurt the kitten still in his arms. The door swung out and open, and the cold night smelling of exhaust spilled in: gray snow, frozen slush, leafless trees, and the lights from the gas station across the street illuminating the parking lot that held a scattering of cars.

Standing beside his snow-covered Volvo, staring at the bar with her feet spread wide and her hands on her hips, was Kay.

Scrambling, Cooper lunged for the door as it began to close.

"Cooper!" Kay cried, her red scarf flying as she ran forward. "Don't let the door shut! For God's sake, keep it open! Keep it open!"

Cooper scrambled out onto the threshold, breathing in the smell of exhaust and cold snow. The people in line waiting to get in were gone. Behind him, the bar was filled with angry howls and screams. The moon was down. It had to be almost dawn. Felicity's cry of pain jerked him straight and he looked behind him into the darkness. She was a monster.

Why should he care? She wanted to turn him into a goddamned dancing fey, bloodsucking vampire!

"Cooper, don't let the door shut!"

He flung out his free hand at the last moment, the heavy wood pinching his fingers before he pushed it open again. Inside, someone was screaming his name. "Kay?" he stammered as she slid to a breathless halt beside him, her eyes bright and her red scarf falling off her neck. Her fur-tufted boots were leaving clumps of snow on the swept front, and she looked alive, thrilled. "What are you doing here?" he asked, then yanked her back when she tried to go in. "Stop!" he shouted. "It's a flesh club! I saw one take a chunk out of someone!"

Kay jerked her attention from the dark opening, grinning. A strong scent of pine wafted over him, clearing his head, and the kitten in his arms stirred. "Yeah, I know," she said. "Don't let go of the door," she added as she put his hand on the door. "Promise me you'll keep the door open for me. Please, Cooper. I don't know how, but you got the door open. You can hold it. Just give me five minutes. That's all I want. Five minutes."

"You can't go in there!" he exclaimed.

"I can now," she said, flashing him a savage smile. And then she ran, screaming as she dove through the opening and vanished in the darkness of the bar.

A second later, a flash of red light lit the room, glittering scarlet in the chandeliers and turning the gold on the bar to a burgundy sheen. Shocked, he stared at the cowering forms and savage snarls. His hand slipped from the door, but he caught the edge before it shut again, grunting when he needed to put all his weight behind it to pull it back open. He almost let it go again in surprise when two cats raced over the threshold, their coats smoking as they ran into the snow. When he looked back, the stage was on fire.

No one was trying to get out. Figures slumped across tables or on the floor. The people still moving were screaming in outrage—snarling as they circled the stage and tried to get into an inky black spot at the back of it. It hung behind a smoky gray figure wielding a bright sword. Whenever someone would try for the fog, the apparition would attack, cutting them down with three swipes and a horrific, satisfied scream. That others would slip in behind it and escape while their brethren died was not going unnoticed, but the sword wielder didn't seem to care as long as someone was dying.

"It's on fire," he whispered as he realized the sword wasn't glowing red from reflecting flame. The sword was really on fire.

Blood slicked the stage and dripped to the floor with each new sweep of the blade and falling body kicked off the sword. Feeling ill, Cooper slumped, almost letting the door slip shut as a wave of nausea hit him. "Kay?" he warbled, finally sitting down on the cold cement to prop the door open. It felt as if his energy, his stamina, was being sucked into the bar. "Kay? I can't hold it . . ." he whispered, his hands still cradling the kitten, now a shivering ball. His fingers were so cold he couldn't feel the softness of fur, and he hunched into himself, holding the door open with his deadweight as the screams grew fewer, more distinct, and finally, ended.

"Kay," he whispered, not altogether conscious when someone smelling like a pine tree wedged a shoulder under him and lifted.

"God save you, Cooper," he heard Kay whisper, and he felt them start to move. "I told you it was slippery tonight."

"The people," he muttered, unable to lift his head as he shuffled over frozen ruts, kitten cradled in his arms.

"I couldn't save them," she said, her voice lacking her usual warmth. "I don't even know how you got out."

"Didn't eat the food," he said, shambling forward. "Grandma told me not to eat food with dancing . . . fairies."

A boom of sound shoved them forward as the bar exploded, and by the light of it burning, Kay got his passenger-side door open. She practically shoved him in and slammed the door shut. It seemed like forever before the driver's-side door opened, and he blearily watched her grunt at his key ring, giving the bell a little tap. "That might explain it," she said. "Cooper, you are one lucky bastard," she added as she revved the engine and left Gateways to burn to ash behind them.

THREE

S hivering violently, Cooper waited in Kay's office for her to come back, a feminine shawl that smelled like flowers draped over his shoulders as he practically sat on the space heater. It roared as it kicked out the heat, but he still shook with cold and shock. His shiny shoes squished with snow melt, and his slacks were soaked from it. A soft bundle of fur cowered in his lap, and he curved a hand about the little black kitten as if it was a talisman. *What the hell happened?* he thought, flexing his free hand to see his strength returning. He'd say he had gotten some weird drug into him and had hallucinated the entire thing if not for the changes in Kay's appearance—changes she didn't seem to know he saw.

The familiar soft sounds of her feet filled him with new foreboding, and he managed an uneasy smile as she pushed past the hanging sheets of milky plastic to hand him a cup of coffee. "Better?" she asked as she sat on the edge of her flower-decaled desk and sipped her own hot chocolate.

Cooper set the cup down, the heat from it seeming to burn his cold-soaked fingers. Kay was sitting almost as close as he was to the heater, not wearing her coat but still having her scarf around her neck to make her look kind of trendy—in a petite, preppy, sword-wielding-warrior, pet-shop-owner kind of way. "Yeah," he croaked out, feeling his throat. "Tell me that didn't happen."

The woman gave him a toothy smile. "What, you getting drunk and me having to spend your Christmas bonus on bail money? You owe me, Cooper. You owe me a week of Sundays in the store, and don't think I'm not going to take advantage of it."

Cooper's lips parted. "Jail?" he said, one hand around the kitten, the other circling the hot coffee. "I was at a dance club. They were vampires, and you broke down the door and slaughtered them." He didn't believe it, but that's what he'd seen, and he risked a glance at her, her eyes crinkled up in laughter as she sat on the desk like she was a normal person—a little closed and reserved perhaps, but normal.

Her laughter dying away, Kay brought a knee to her chin and wrapped her arms around it. "Vampires," she said as she rested her head on her knee. "That's what the cop said you were raving about. Drink your coffee," she said, glancing at it. "It will make everything all better."

A quiver went through Cooper at her words even as he lifted the mug, his grandmother's words echoing in his thoughts again. Feeling Kay's eyes on him, he dutifully brought the hot coffee to his lips, letting it touch his lips and nothing more—faking it. Sure enough, a hint of bitterness blossomed, reminding him of that sloppy, little-girl kiss that Emily had left on his lips. He hadn't eaten anything, but what if that kiss had changed him? It might explain how he got the door open and could see the changes he now saw in Kay, things that had been under his nose for three years, but he hadn't seen until now.

"Better?" she asked, all innocence and light, and he pretended to take another drink, sneaking looks at her and wanting to be sure what he was seeing was real. "You take the cake, Cooper," she said as she slid from the desk and stretched to make Cooper look away fast. "It's not every boss who will come down at two in the morning to bail out an employee. It's a good thing you got drunk enough to be hauled out, though. The place burned down an hour later. You were lucky. No one made it out. They'd bolted all the doors to keep out the riffraff, and everyone inside died. Terrible. Just terrible."

"Yeah, lucky." Looking past the clear plastic curtain, Cooper had a view of the bus stop on the opposite side of the street. Under the slatted bench was a straggly black cat with a bedraggled kitten. They'd been there for the last fifteen minutes. Felicity and Emily? Cooper had been waiting for them to do something, but all they did was stare malevolently at the store. He was not going out until they left—or had a dog with him.

He shivered, and Kay touched his shoulder. The warmth of her hand came through the blanket to feel like the sun itself. "You okay?" she asked in concern, but he couldn't look at her, afraid she might notice where his eyes were drawn to.

"Fine," he said, his gaze on the old oak floorboards. "I need to warm up before I go home."

She turned away and reached for some paperwork. "Sure, go ahead. I can take you home when I pick up the puppies."

"Mind if I pick one out?" he said, and Kay hesitated in her reach for a pencil. "I've been wanting to get a dog for a long time," he said, carefully not looking at her. "I can keep it here at the store with me in the day, and take it home at night. Besides, it will give Ember here someone to grow up with," he added, petting the kitten still curled up in a frightened ball against him. He couldn't call her Happy—that was a name of a snack cake.

"That's a great idea." Kay stuck the pencil behind her ear and headed to the front of the store with a clipboard to do the year-end inventory.

He watched her walk away, free to stare now that she wasn't looking. *Next to that long pointy ear of hers is probably a really good place to wedge things*, he thought as he watched her floor-length, dexterous tail push aside the grimy plastic curtain so she could go through without touching it with her hands. It wasn't that her pointy ears were especially big. Actually, they were kind of small and cute, but the little horns poking out right next to them cinched it. The pencil tucked between her ear and that cute little wedge of bone wasn't going anywhere.

And neither was he, he decided, holding Ember close and breathing her fur smelling of pine and iron.

TEMSON
ESTATES

I wrote "Temson Estates" about the same time that I began working on the short that eventually became the first chapter of Dead Witch Walking. *I wanted to know what a dryad might be like if the Greek and Roman visions of tree spirits were real, possibly giving a scientific reason for both their absence and possible resurgence. I played with a few ideas here that I went on to use very loosely when developing the Bis/Jenks short, "Ley Line Drifter," but I liked my dryads here better, which might be why I never took the Hollows dryads any further.*

That two of the characters have the same names as my to-be editor and her assistant was just plain weird, especially since it would be another year or two until I actually knew of their existence. I thought about changing them, but sometimes you just have to let the weird things stay.

Will shifted uncomfortably in the hard-backed chair, hot in the wool suit that he'd bought yesterday in a doomed attempt to try to make a good impression. It was itchy, but he wasn't going to run a finger between it and his neck a second time. He had a feeling the man who had sold it to him had taken advantage of him, but that only proved yet again that he was totally out of place here among the rich carpets, tooled mahogany, and good manners. The young woman across from him already thought he was a crass Yank. Maybe she was right. It wasn't his fault he was here—not that she'd ever see it that way—summoned across how many time zones to sit in a foreign law office and face down these two women over something he had no control over.

"I'm sorry, Ms. Temson," the lawyer said, his voice sympathetic but firm. "Your father's wish is quite clear. In the presence of a male heir, Temson Estate cannot fall to you. You retain the house, grounds, and your brother's considerable offshore investments, but the woods themselves belong to Mr. William Temson."

Ms. Temson, his grandfather's sister apparently, pressed her lips together in quiet thought. Though clearly shaken, she was thinking hard, and that worried Will more than the fire and sparks coming from the young woman at her elbow. She'd been introduced as Diana and was Ms. Temson's caregiver. Though to be honest, Will didn't think the old woman needed any help. She looked too crafty to die from anything but a curse, as his father would have said.

Diana was about his age, dressed so smartly in her shape-fitting, pale cream linen suit that he felt like a used-car salesman. Seeing Will eyeing her, she squinted at him, her short nails clicking as she drummed her fingers once. "You drew that will up yourself!" she finally said, her accent charming even while furious. "How could you lose the Temson Estate to some—some—Yank!" she exclaimed.

"Diana," the old woman murmured, and the young woman gave her a look both contrite and defiant. Will winced. It wasn't his fault. All he wanted to do was sign the papers and go home. The money from the sale of the forest would be a godsend, enabling him to finish his master's with enough left over he could really make a difference.

"There is nothing I can do," the lawyer said as he stood in the thin light seeping past the wooden blinds. "The title and everything with it goes to him."

Diana stood, angry and abrupt. "Let's go, Grandmum." She turned to him, fuming. "We are contesting this. If Arthur had known that entitlement had been in there, he would have changed it!"

Concerned, Will met the lawyer's eyes, and the stiff man subtly shook his head, a sublime confidence in the way he opened the folder and began leafing through the legal papers.

The old woman ignored Diana's anger, her hands in their stark-white gloves sitting on the table. "You know I can't let the axes in there, Ryan. It would be murder."

Uneasy, the lawyer glanced from the papers to Will, an apologetic crinkle in his eyes.

"Murder?" Will said, interested as papers were slid before him.

"Grandmum, please," Diana murmured, her entire demeanor shifting to one of embarrassment as she touched the older woman's shoulder as if to prod her into motion. The old woman pursed her lips, then finally giving in to Diana's gentle tugging, she got to her feet. Will hastily rose, his chair scraping.

"She's a bit creaky in the attic," the lawyer said a shade too loudly as he handed Will a pen and pointed where to sign. "She and her brother, God rest his soul, never let anyone in that woods, but it's yours now. You'll be selling it . . . I presume? We don't handle property transfers, but here is my brother's card. He can get you a good price on it."

Diana's urgent, hushed, and utterly one-sided conversation with Ms. Temson was an uneasy backdrop as Will signed the last place and handed the pen back. "Thank you," he said, tucking the card in his pocket. "I'd like to take care of this as soon as possible." He wanted to go home. It was too cold and rainy here—too many people.

"You cannot log those woods," Diana said bitterly as the lawyer closed the file and gestured for them all to leave. "We have worked too long. You don't understand."

At her words, the woman dug her heels in at the threshold, Diana's arm slipping from her. Alarmed, the young woman turned as Ms. Temson faced Will, her gloved hands holding her tiny purse before her and her stance upright and ramrod straight. "Diana," the older woman said firmly. "You are absolutely right. I would speak with Mr. Temson before we leave."

Diana's face went white. "Grandmum. No," she said, and inclining his head, the lawyer snapped his folder on the table and left. Will was tempted to mutter some excuse and bolt after him, but Diana's sudden shift of mood from angry frustration to one of . . . hidden secrets caught his interest. She didn't want him logging out the woods, but she didn't want him talking to Ms. Temson, either.

Diana's eyes flicked between them. "Grandmum . . . He's not going to sell it back to you. He wants the *money*."

Will cringed at the emphasis she'd put on the last word, as if it was dirty. Yes, he wanted the money. He had a lot of things he wanted to do, and being a realist, he knew it took money to make a difference—lots of money. But Ms. Temson's deep look of concentration worried him. He'd found old ladies were the most devious creatures on earth.

"Call me Will, please," he said as he took the woman's fragile-looking hand, startled at her firm grip in her white gloves. "I'd like to extend my deepest sympathy—"

She waved a hand, interrupting him. "Arthur's passing was a blessing," she said, shocking him when she smiled and touched his arm familiarly. "Your grandfather died from a heart attack five years ago. It just took his body until now to realize it." Commandeering his arm, she led him out. To the casual observer, it might seem he was helping her, but she was in complete control of the situation and both of them knew it. Diana lurked behind, walking far too close and making him feel awkward as he held the door for her. She was still scared, too, concerned at what might come out of Ms. Temson's mouth. Which was exactly why he hadn't left yet.

Both women went out before him to stand on the wide stoop, hesitating as if for a few last words. The thin sun struck him, and he relaxed, glad to be out of the gloom and circumstance of another country's law. "Thank you, love," his grandmother said with a sigh, seeming to be glad to have the sun about her again as well. "You will picnic with us."

"Grandmum!" Diana gasped, her pale cheeks blushing.

"Tomorrow. It will be a lovely stomp through the woods," the older woman said, holding up a hand in gentle, silent rebuke.

"I—uh—wouldn't dream of imposing." Will's eyes flicked to Diana. She was all but baring her teeth at him, thinly disguising it as a smile.

"Nonsense." Ms. Temson shifted into his line of sight, smiling as if they were lifelong friends. "You will be logging out the woods. Don't deny it. The offers undoubtedly began before you arrived, and you will find three more at the hotel when you return there. They've been hounding me for decades. Promise me you won't allow one marker, not one clawed boot into my . . . your woods until after tomorrow."

He nodded hesitantly—mistrusting this but curious—and the old woman straightened as if a load had fallen from her, the deep lines about her eyes easing.

"I will teach you of trees, young man," she said in a low voice. "If you let the axes into your woods before you see, the loggers will rob you blind. They will say it's hedge maple and pay you accordingly when what they take is oak and larch and beech as big around as a bathtub. I can't allow a Temson to get cheated," she said dryly. "It makes me look like a fool by association."

He flushed, feeling hot in his new, uncomfortable suit. "Really, Ms. Temson," he said. "I was going to do a survey myself before I leave. I went to school to be a forester."

"They have a school to learn about trees?" she said, her eyes bright and a knowing smile quirking her lips. "Hear that, Diana? He went to school to learn about trees. Tomorrow then. Diana will bring the tea, I will bring the tree, and you"—she gave him a wicked smile, cornflower blue eyes smiling—"will bring the wine. Two bottles. Domestic. Make sure it's domestic."

Confused, Will shifted his gaze between the two women. Ms. Temson seemed pleased, but Diana still looked scared. Maybe they were going to take him out back and hit him on the head with a shovel. "Wine, Ms. Temson?" he questioned.

"I'll show you the oldest groves, the thickest stands," the woman said, her bird-light voice an odd singsong.

Will's curiosity was piqued as Diana became white. "I'd like that," he heard himself say, and the old woman took his hand and gave it a motherly squeeze.

"Fine," she said. "Two o'clock. Good day, Mr. Temson." She gave him a sharp nod, then sailed regally down the bright walk to the lane where an ancient Rolls waited in the shade, her heels clicking smartly on the cobbled walk, Diana hunched and worried at her elbow.

"That will never do, love. You won't even get through the meadow in those."

Standing at the stone wall separating the manicured smoothness from the wilds, Will looked sheepishly at his dress shoes poking out from under his jeans. His boots were two thousand miles away, drying on his back porch. He hated to fly, hated the damp weather this country was afflicted with, and hated his forgotten history for making someone else's problem his. But the chance to go stomping about the old-growth forest he had heard about as a boy from his father was stronger than his belief that the two women were going to hit him over the head and bury him—even if there was a shovel propped against the wall beside a slim beech, its roots carefully wrapped in burlap.

He shifted uneasily as Ms. Temson ran her eyes over his faded flannel shirt and worn backpack, nodding as if their disrepair pleased her. Blinking in surprise, he found himself pulled down, and she adjusted the new red cap he had picked up in the gift shop. "Oh-h-h-h," she murmured, the weak sun dappled by her wide-brimmed hat. "They'll like that."

"They? They who?"

"The dryads, love. The dryads."

Will froze. The sound of boots on the gravel path interrupted his confusion, and he slowly straightened as Diana approached from the nearby manor house. Jeans tucked into heavy boots and a worn green sweater had replaced the stiff lace of the lawyer's office. Her hair was back in a ponytail, and he thought she looked better this way, even if worry pinched the edges of her eyes.

"Diana?" Ms. Temson's thin voice, sounding like bees, carried well in the hazy sunshine. "Be a dear and show William the stables. I believe Arthur left a pair of boots there. We won't see any dryads if he turns his ankle."

"Yes, Grandmum."

Dryads? he thought. The lawyer was right. The old woman was off her rocker.

The slant of her eyes dared him to say anything as Diana set her pack down by the fence and gestured belligerently for him to follow. The abandoned stables were a good step away, and she appeared determined to ignore him the entire distance.

"You don't look anything like your grandmother," he said, trying to break the silence in as inoffensive a manner as possible.

"She isn't. I just call her that."

Okay, he thought. It was cold and stiff, but it was a start. "This wasn't my idea."

Pace fast and arms swinging, she eyed him. "Logging out the woods is."

Angry, she was angry again—not afraid. "I'm not going to clear-cut it," he said. "My God, you must think I'm a total barbarian."

"Yes, I do."

He admired her loyalty to Ms. Temson, but this was getting him nowhere. "She was joking. Wasn't she?"

Diana turned sharply to the barn, and Will's eyebrows rose at her sudden, almost hidden alarm. "About what?"

Feeling he was close to it, he picked up his pace to stay even with her, the dark silence of the barn looming over them. "The dryads."

Her jaw clenched and a flush rose. Reaching for a frayed rope, she gave it a tug and the barn door swung open in a majestic silence. The smell of old hay and dry rot eddied about his feet. Without hesitation, she vanished into the darkness. Will stepped to follow, jerking back when Diana almost ran into him coming back out. There was a worn pair of leather boots in her hand, old but serviceable, and she shoved them at him as if wanting to bean him over the head instead.

He grabbed them by instinct, silent as he took in her pressed lips and evasive eyes. "You think there're dryads in those woods too, don't you."

Chin lifted, she finally met his eyes. *Her eyes are blue,* he thought, liking the way she could go from pressed and perfect to capable and athletic.

"I don't believe in anything I can't see except for God," she said as she pointed to an overturned bucket by the door. "Let's get one thing crystal. You here was not my idea, and the sooner you leave, the happier I will be. Understand?"

Feeling as if he'd won a point, he sat down. "Ms. Temson wants me out here," he said, and she turned away, arms over her middle, fuming. *I'll be damned if I'm not starting to like her,* he thought as he tugged on the boots, the leather cool on his toes in the thick haze of the day. It wasn't until he was rocking experimentally back and forth in them that he realized she hadn't answered him.

Leaving his dress shoes on the bucket, he followed a belligerent Diana back to the gate, accepting Ms. Temson's delighted hug in that his feet were the same size as his grandfather's. The wide field beyond ending in trees had probably once been a manicured green by machine or sheep, but it was now yellow and brown, tall grasses rising up to his knees. Diana stewed as Ms. Temson clucked and fussed, her sour mood not unnoticed by either of them. It was obvious that Ms. Temson was honey to Diana's vinegar, but curiosity kept him there. *Dryads?*

Will wedged the sapling and a surprisingly modern folding shovel into his pack, earning a peck on the cheek. He was spared the task of making conversation as they crossed the damp meadow. Ms. Temson kept up a nonstop chatter, covering everything from world politics to the life cycle of a sheep tick. She was the sharpest insane woman he had ever met.

Once under the trees, though, she went silent. Together she and Diana stood listening. As one, they turned to the east. He shivered and couldn't say why. Ms. Temson gripped his arm for a moment, her fingers like cords of steel. "That way."

It was a very quiet stomp through the woods. For the first time in his life, Will felt awkward under the trees. Ms. Temson's hunched stature, which made her look old in the sun, now served her well, letting her glide around snags and deadfalls with the sureness of a dance. There was no path among last year's leaves, but he was confident the two of them knew exactly where they were.

The trees became taller, their shade grew deeper, and the silence more profound until it seemed as if they were the only people who had ever walked the earth. Not a gum wrapper or cigarette butt broke the illusion. Will looked up and frowned.

The forest had changed while he had been focusing on the little things at his feet. Circles of bare dirt were scattered among the leaf litter. Within the sharply defined borders there was no scrub, no twigs, no leaves, nothing. It was mystifying, but he was determined not to ask. Diana's eyes as she looked back at him were mocking, daring him to speak. Her worry was gone, replaced by . . . anticipation?

The circles of cleared ground became more frequent, turning into patches of moss ringing a tree here, one there. He knew some trees could extrude a toxin, stunting or killing anything growing under them. But these were beech, and elm, and oak. And what about the leaves? No. The ground had been purposely cleared—right to the root line.

They topped a small rise, and by an unspoken agreement they stopped to marvel at the past glory of a long-dead tree. It was a tremendous beech, still standing straight and gray, its thicker branches yet holding up the sky. Beneath it, its own castoff twigs and leaves littered the ground, looking disorderly after the pristine green about the other trees.

"Here," Ms. Temson said, seeming pleased with herself. "We'll rest here.

"No, love." She caught Will's arm as he stepped to a nearby cleared circle. "Here."

Will's eyebrows rose. Diana was kneeling beneath the dead tree, unpacking amid the scrub and sticks when a perfectly good mat of moss was a stone's throw away.

"Sit," Ms. Temson called, patting the checkered cloth. "It's your grandmother's tree."

Will sighed as his backside hit the dirt, and he eyed the sapling they had brought out. If they thought he was going to go soft and sloppy and not log the woods because he had planted a tree with them, they were sorely mistaken. "She planted it?"

"Not exactly."

Tea came with light conversation and terrible, dry crackers. Diana slowly lost her tension as Will told her about his life and classes—though he didn't appreciate Ms. Temson's nods and insinuating nudges. Even so, it meant more than it should to him when the young woman laughed at the face he made after trying the marmalade. He reached for the wine to wash it down, and Ms. Temson halted him with a brown, wrinkled hand.

"Don't drink it," she said. "I'll put it on the new tree."

Will stared at her, then at the label. "I bought what the man said," he protested. "It can't be that bad."

Diana made a rude sound, and Ms. Temson frowned at her. "It's fine," she reassured him, "but it's for the tree. We'll plant it far enough away from the others, but you never can tell. Wicked little things, they are."

He glanced from Diana to the old lady. "Um—Ms. Temson?"

"Grandmum always plants a tree when she comes out." Diana glared at him, daring him to say a word. "The wine keeps the dryads from pulling it up."

Oh yeah, he thought sarcastically as it began to make a deranged sense. The dryads. Not wanting to break the truce they seemed to have found, he simply nodded.

"Come, Diana." Struggling slightly, Ms. Temson rose and reached for the sapling in the pack. "I want your help putting this one to bed. No, you stay," she admonished Will as he grabbed the shovel and levered himself up. "This isn't your work."

Diana's eyes were worried as she took the shovel from him, but it was a new worry, one of the heart. Not knowing what to make of it, Will sank back down, resting his head upon his empty pack and listening to the small sounds of the ladies drifting away: Ms. Temson's high-pitched warble, Diana's concerned response, the clank of his wine bottles. He liked both of them, but one afternoon was not going to change his mind. The forest was going to be thinned out at the very least. If his grandfather hadn't wanted him to have it, he wouldn't have given it to him.

Still, guilt pricked at him as he leaned back and closed his eyes. He loved the woods. He'd grown up surrounded by trees in the mountains out west, studied them at the university, and found a poor-paying job working with them. He didn't care. It was what he was good at, and if he allowed an acre or two of these stately trees to go to the ax, he could manage better. Much better.

The wind in the trees and the long walk shifted him close to sleep, only to jerk awake at the giggle and a tug on his hat.

"Hey!" he shouted, snatching a thin arm and sitting up. Shrieks and squeals erupted, and the brown-skinned women scattered. Only the one who had tried to take his hat was left, crouched as far from him as she could as he still had her wrist.

Gasping, Will dropped her arm. She was like no one—like nothing—he'd ever seen. Looking at her was like trying to track the moon through a mist. His eyes kept drifting, unable to fix upon her. She was a black, frog-rimmed pool smelling of loam and wind, the hushed still point of winter and the quiet growth of summer. Brown as the earth, just as fragile, just as enduring. Eyes like the bottoms of clouds before a summer storm. Innocence. Feral innocence. But wise beyond knowing what wisdom was.

"Who are you?" he breathed.

She turned and pointed. From behind the nearby trunks came urgent whispers and frightened, envious eyes. The girl licked her lips and glanced eagerly at his hat among the leaves.

Will shifted closer. "You want that?"

She nodded, making no move to it.

A twig snapped, and her head came up like a startled deer's.

"No!" he cried. "Wait!" But she was gone, and he was left staring at the earth where she had been.

"Diana," he heard Ms. Temson admonish from behind him. "You did that on purpose."

"Dryads?" he mouthed, unable to say it aloud. There was a rustling, and Diana sat down in his line of sight. She smirked at his bewildered expression, seeming relieved to see it.

Ms. Temson carefully lowered her frailty beside her and poured a cup of tea from the insulated bottle. His fingers gripped the plastic cup numbly as she placed it into his hand. "Tree spirits, love. Your grandmother was one, as was mine. I'm a quarter dryad, but all human." She sighed.

Diana spooned a glop of marmalade onto a cracker and popped it into her mouth. "She gets moody on cloudy days, though."

"Diana," she rebuffed gently, then turned to him. "You, William, are nearly a third dryad. That's why they came, to see if your grandmother had returned to her tree. That, and to steal your hat." Ms. Temson smiled. "They adore clothes. Risk almost anything to get them. I dare say they used to be the cause for many an embarrassed skinny-dipper." The sound of her laughter rose like butterflies up into the canopy.

It took Will three tries before he found his voice. "My grandmother? But from—how?" Then his resolve grew. "No. I don't know who those women were, but they weren't—tree spirits!"

"I told Arthur it was a bad idea," Ms. Temson was saying. "But he was young and of the belief that love could change the nature of things. And he did love her, I'll grant you that. He knew it was possible. It was family knowledge that our grandfather had. . . ." She colored, hiding her embarrassment behind her cup of tea. "My grandfather wasn't a polished man."

Diana snatched his hat from the ground and picked the twigs from it in agitation. "They're wickedly gullible, believing anything you tell them. If they become with child they can't return to their tree, seeing as they carry something completely foreign to their nature. By the time the baby is born they can't return to their tree at all, having grown too far apart from it to accomplish it." She threw his hat at him in disgust. "They don't live very long after that."

He'd heard enough. Will stood, and Diana looked up at him in anger. "You saw them!" she shouted, pointing. "What color was her hair? What was she wearing? You don't remember, do you! And you won't, except for the fleeting breath between wake and sleep! Why can't you believe!" Her voice softened. "It's not hard—to believe."

Slowly, he sank down. She was right. He couldn't remember. All he was left with was the way the woman had felt. She was the will to survive given substance, ruthlessly uncaring, an essence, nothing more. She had been too unreal to not *be* real.

Will's eyes flicked among the silent, gray trunks. What the devil was he thinking? He was a biologist, for God's sake! He wouldn't believe in fairy tales!

"Where's the myth that doesn't have a grain of truth at its center?" Ms. Temson said, seeming to read his mind as she sipped her tea. "Dryads just happen. Saplings sprouted from the seeds of a dryad tree seem to show them sooner, but not always. They're jealous little mites, pulling up anything within reach of their roots once they're strong enough to leave their tree."

"The circles of cleared earth." He gave himself a little shake. It wasn't rational. But her eyes. He remembered her eyes. "They're beautiful," he breathed.

"They're vicious." Diana glanced up from her crackers and jam. "If the roots of two dryads mesh, they'll try to kill each other's tree." Making a face, she closed the jar and packed it away. "They usually both die."

Ms. Temson drew herself up. "Now you understand why I let everyone think I'm daft for never allowing an ax into my woods."

Will looked up. It was a joke. It had to be an elaborate plot. The cleared circles, the women themselves.

"Oh, you can tell by looking which trees have come into dryad and avoid cutting them," she said. "But the reverberations of a tree being cut resounds from root to root until the entire wood feels it." She frowned. "My grandfather tried selective logging. It sent them into hiding for nearly ten years. Trees have a dreadfully long memory, you know. We have since learned to keep the meadow as a buffer, making my—ah . . . the woods into an island of sorts. But you need acres and acres of trees." Her eyes went distant in memory. "Arthur and I have been planting trees for ages. We added twenty acres on the fringes and they began talking in sentences. Twenty more and they began to sing, dance, invent nursery rhymes."

Diana had a pinky in her tea, trying to rescue a bug. "How clever they are doesn't depend upon how old the tree is but how close to the center of the woods it sits. When one dies, the rest regard the ground as hallowed and won't disturb anything under it." Frowning, she gave up and threw her tea away. "Rather superstitious, but it does give the chance for a new tree to take root."

Will gave a start, shaking the tea from his hand as it spilled. "It's a secondary survival mechanism," he breathed, his schooling taking hold. "I see it now! When the density of trees in a closed population passes a critical threshold, space becomes such a limiting factor that the tree needs to find a new way to preserve its territory. It's forced to evolve a way to step out of itself, to directly influence, to physically defend its domain. Hence the dryads!" Will leaned forward, his fingers tingling. "The more trees in the system, the smarter they have to be. And when there's the threat of logging, they disappear, able to compete using their more mundane defenses. It's fantastic!" he gushed. His eyes focused upon Diana. She was smiling, relief making her beautiful.

"So you'll stay? You won't log the woods?"

Will's smile faded as reality rushed back. His gaze went distant into the gray, fog-laced trees. It would be easy to stay, to take the place that others had made, but he couldn't. The thought that he had done nothing to earn it would rob him of any pleasure he might find here. "I came to sell the woods," he said slowly, hating his father for instilling in him so strongly the belief he must make his own way in the world. "I don't see any reason to change my plans."

Ms. Temson's cup hit the ground.

"But the dryads!" Diana cried. "You can't!"

Will's gaze dropped. "Ms. Temson can't inherit it," he said slowly. "So I'll sell it to her."

Diana's eyes grew wide in understanding. "But you're a Temson! You belong here! Especially now that you know."

"No, I don't." He gestured weakly to the woods. "Like Ms. Temson said, this isn't my work. This woods isn't mine. I was raised surrounded by trees, always knowing there was more, something just out of reach. You can't imagine what it's like to suddenly find out . . ." Will looked beseechingly up at the dead branches, searching for words.

"Listen!" he said abruptly, desperate for them to understand. "Now that I can see, I can't help but wonder, what would the spirit of an ash or a wild hickory of the forests *I* grew up in look like. The spirit of a stately hemlock, an entire hillside of birch, the scattering of wild cherries, lighting the understory with flashes of white in the spring . . . do their spirits even exist anymore? Is it too late? I want to know. Now that I can see, I want to know! Can you understand?"

The two women gazed at him with the infinite wonder of youth and the eternal hope of the old. "How much do you have in your pocket?" he asked his grandfather's sister numbly.

With trembling fingers, Ms. Temson brought forth a faded coin purse and extended two coins. Feeling his chest tighten in what might be grief, Will accepted them. The thin weight of them rested in his hand a moment, and then he threw them into the woods. The sound of their fall never reached him. Instead, a delighted cry and a giggle came drifting upon the heavy air, hazy and golden with the unseen sun. "Your lawyer can draw the papers up on Monday," he said, knowing he had given Ms. Temson her life back, even as he felt something indistinct and indefinable slipping from him.

Sitting ramrod straight before him, Ms. Temson silently started to cry. He said nothing, knowing she'd be embarrassed. Diana begin to fuss over her, sneaking glances at him. "I beg your pardon," the old woman warbled. "The cold is seeping into me. I think it best we go."

Helping her up, Diana looked at him with a new light in her eyes, as if seeing him free of the shadow of her fear for the first time. He held himself back as they moved to leave. Standing apart, he took a shuddering breath. His hat felt rough in his fingers. With a last look, he hung it forlornly on a dead branch and turned to follow them out.

"Plenty of good timber in there, Billy."

"It's William. William Temson." Will scuffed the dry, waist-high grass, looking for the rich loam he knew would be there, smiling as he found it. Sunlight pressed down like a physical sensation, maddening the cicadas into a shrill protest and driving the last of England's chill from him. From beside him came Diana's almost imperceptible sigh as she took in the gently rolling hills of his homeland. It had surprised him when she insisted on coming back with him, and even though it was only to help him pick out his land, he hoped she would stay.

The farmer sucked his teeth, and shrugged. "You want it then?"

Will wrote a figure and passed it to him. The money had come from Ms. Temson. "A loan," she had said as she had pressed the check into his hand and strode quickly away into the crush of airport traffic. The iron-hard look in her eye had forbidden any protest; her stiffly held back demanded they not make a scene.

The man stared at the paper for a quiet moment. "More 'n what I'm askin'," he said, the scrap clutched in his thick hand.

"I want it all. The entire valley."

"We-e-e-ell, I was gonna give my Peggy the lake as a weddin' present. Build her a house."

Will shifted impatiently. "That's why the extra."

The man scratched his stubble. "I want to keep the huntin' rights."

Beside him, Diana shook her head and pulled him down to whisper in his ear. Will wrote a new figure.

"You sure you got that much, son?"

Will nodded.

"It's yours." The man's eyes glazed, and he turned to the rusting pickup. The door creaked open, and he looked back. "You coming? It's a long walk into town."

"No, go ahead." The wine bottles were heavy in his pack, and the seeds were light in his pocket, sifting through his fingers like dry rain. "I think we will just stomp about for a bit."

Diana's hand slipped into his, and the man grinned knowingly. "Suit yourself. Watch out for the snakes, miss." He laughed uproariously, revved the engine, and was gone.

Together, he and Diana stood and listened. Slowly the humming silence of insects, wind, and grass reasserted itself. As one their heads lifted to the lake. "That way, I think," he whispered, and they began to walk.

SPIDER SILK

"Spider Silk" is another one of my ventures into exploring dryads where the tree is a prison not a sanctuary. I'm not sure I like this bloodthirsty, devilish, sentient version that might be real or might be a mental delusion passed from mother to daughter. Though the story is told from first the grandmother's, and then the mother's point of view, Meg is the character that I'm most interested in, the one that I'd follow if I ever took the next step, curious to see how she handles twenty when the curse falls upon her fully. But seeing the beginnings of a dysfunctional family has its own appeal, and I hope you enjoy it.

 ## PROLOGUE

The half-heard singing of her granddaughter Meg was as cheerful as the sparkling creek, low enough to safely play in now that drought had taken more than half of it. Even the water spiders braved its reduced flow, and they danced around Meg's calves as she turned over rocks in her search for crayfish. Sitting on the simple car bridge that spanned it, Emily dangled her feet over the water, weighing the trouble of taking off her shoes and tying up her skirts to join the nine-year-old. Days like this were rare. Something in the wind spilling from the surrounding wooded hills reminded her of her own youth—holding the promise of something new—something all her own she would never have to share.

"Little copper penny, stuck in a tree," Meg sang, head down and her feet finding purchase on the cool stones below. "Tree falls down, and you can't catch me. Little copper penny, as lonely as can be. Nothing lives for-ever but my penny and me!"

Emily's smile faded, her gaze rising to look past the farmhouse she shared with her daughter and granddaughters to the woods beyond. *No. God, no.* It had to be a mistake. Leaning forward, Emily clasped her arms around herself, cold. "Meg, where did you hear that?"

Oblivious to the warning in her voice, the little girl straightened, water drops sparkling on her arms. "Penny," she said, beaming a squinting smile up at her with one eye open, one shut. "I can hear him singing right through my toes. Gram, can I ple-e-e-ase go for a walk in the woods? It's too hot in the pasture. I'll stay on the path. I promise."

Fear caught her breath, memory folding time as if the last five de-cades hadn't happened and she was fourteen, balanced on womanhood and fighting for her life. Penn. Penny. How long had Meg been singing that song? Days?

"Ple-e-e-ase?" Meg begged, her creek-cold hands making a spot of ice on her knees.

Emily's breath came in with a gasp. Reaching down, she yanked Meg from the water, her back all but giving way as the little girl protested when they fell together onto the dry, sun-baked wood. Emily blinked fast as Meg regained her feet, complaining.

"Meg, go in the house."

Looking at the water, the little girl protested, and Emily reached up, pinching her arm. "Go in the house! I'll get your shoes," she said again, and, looking sullen, the little girl went, rubbing the grit from her arms.

Heart pounding, Emily looked past the farmhouse. The sun still spar-kled on the water, enticing her to come and bathe in its coolness. The wind in the woods promised sweet release if she would slip under its soothing umbrella—it was a lie.

Her snare hadn't held. He was loose. He was singing. He was free.

ONE

Hands clenched, Lilly stood outside of Meg and Em's door, listening to her mother's age-lightened voice rising and falling as she told the girls their bedtime story. Leaning forward as if to knock, she frowned. Part of her desperately wanted to interrupt, to stop what she thought might be the first signs of a slow decline in her mom. Part of her listened with a rapt attention, remembering hearing the story herself as a girl when the sunset-cooled air breathed its first relief into her room, the very room her own children now called their own. The wide window edged in white lace looked out onto the woods, and she recalled all too well the times she'd kept herself awake listening for the wolves that no longer lived there, wishing that her mother's fairy tales of a beautiful, mischievous boy with red hair were real. She had wanted an adventure so badly, but he had never come whispering under her window to lure her into dancing in the moonlight.

Feeling ill, she rocked back, hand going to her side. Penn, her mother had called him, her gaze distant and eerie as she told her stories, stories where the guardian of the woods could appear as a clever wolf or take on the face of a trusted friend to lull you to an untimely death in his unremorseful search for a soul—a beautiful boy with laughing eyes and a wont for mischief that no one could see unless lured into sight with the promise of honey. Crossing running water could save you from him, or trapping him in a tree. Dangerous, yes, but he would be your friend if you were daring enough to impress him. Then you'd be safe.

Her mother always had stories to tell. Her parents had been among the first settlers to the valley, attracted to the fertile farmland in the lowlands, the tall trees in the hills, and the cool waters coming from them. But her mother had scared her this afternoon with a frantic story of a monster in the woods, one that would kill unless it was stopped.

Resolute, she reached for the knob, hesitating when Meg asked, "Wasn't the little girl scared?"

"More scared than anything in the world," her mother said confidently, "but she knew that to believe him would let him destroy everything she loved in the world, so the brave girl shoved him into the tree and said the magic words to make the tree swallow him up forever."

"And he couldn't get out?" Meg asked, her voice earnest with admiration.

"Not for years and years, love. And everyone lived happily for a time, driving the wolves away and not fearing the woods anymore. But trees grow old, rocks fall apart, and waters shift their course. Even so, you don't have to worry. Stay out of the woods, and you'll be safe. Promise me that you'll stay out of the woods, Meg. You too, Em. Quickly now."

Lilly let her hand drop and she took a step back into the dark hall as the two little girls earnestly promised. Maybe it wasn't that bad. Her mother's stories were harmless. And they did help keep Meg out of the woods. Vengeful tree spirits weren't real, but hunters often overlooked the Keep Out signs. Not to mention the holes that opened up into unknown caves beneath your feet. The woods were dangerous. Perhaps this was her mother's way of keeping the ever-wandering Meg close to home. Her younger sister, Em, wasn't so venturesome, but Meg . . .

Head down, Lilly turned to go downstairs, shoes silent on the thin green runner as she left them to their bedtime ritual. Her worry trailed behind her like perfume, coloring her mood as she made her way down the narrow, steep stairs, working around the creaking boards so her mom wouldn't know she'd been listening. Behind her, three voices—one old and featherly, two young and off-key—rose in a familiar, singsong chant.

"Wraith by moonlight, hunter by day; Bond is sundered by sun's first ray.

"Blood is binding, blood is lure; Flesh is fragile, to blade's sweet cure.

"Sunder wraith from flesh ill-taken; And bind fey spirit to wood awakened."

Brow furrowing, Lilly looked up the dark stairway as her mother told Meg and Em that they were good girls and Meg giggled at the praise. She hadn't realized her mother had taught them the fanciful, morbid rhyme. It was how her mother had once tucked her in, sandwiched in between her bedtime story and her prayers.

Her mood worsened as the poem echoed in her mind and memories.

Pace fast, she went into the brightly lit kitchen, snatching up a cloth to move the dishes from the drying rack to shelves. Pepper, their yellow lab, stood waiting at the door, her tail waving fitfully, and Lilly let her out. The dog's nails scraped as she took the porch steps, and she was lost to the night, leaving only the jingling of the dog collar to show she was there.

Still in the threshold, Lilly's eyes went to the car bridge shimmering in the moonlight. Distressed, she let the screen door slam, agitated as she remembered Meg coming in this afternoon, hand on her arm and unhappy that her grandmother had pulled her out of the creek. Her mother had come in a few moments later, white-faced and distracted with her wild claim, going to her room for hours under the pretense of taking a nap brought on by too much sun, but she had heard her rummaging in her closet. Her room had looked unchanged when Lilly peeked in later.

The creak of the three bottom stairs made her eyes narrow, and she slid the four plates away as her mother came in. Her fiery resolve vanishing, Lilly put her hand on the counter and dropped her head, trying to find a way to begin.

"It's my turn to put the dishes away," her mother said, and the hint of challenge brought Lilly's head up.

"Mom." Lilly blinked, taking in the change in her mother. She was still wearing the cotton sundress with the blue flowers and honeybees, her hair done up in a gray and black braid at the base of her neck. Suntanned, wiry arms were crossed over her chest, and her pale blue eyes looked defiant. She stood in the threshold of her kitchen, almost as old as the house itself, almost as much a part of the land as the creek and woods beyond it. Her incredible stories of danger, death, and temptation had always balanced her no-nonsense, vine-tight grip on the here and now that had kept her family intact through the sorrow and heartache that came with farming alone at the outskirts of nothing. But now, taken to this extreme . . . Lilly was scared.

"I don't care if you believe or not," her mother said, coming to the point with a painful bluntness. "The girls need to be able to protect themselves. Especially Meg. She's too close to becoming a woman."

Arguing was comfortable in its familiarity, and Lilly slumped. "Mom,

I love that you tuck the girls in, but I'm the one they come piling into bed with when they get scared. Can't you just read them Snow White?"

Snatching the towel from her, her mother brushed past her to go to the sink. "Yes, a story of a murdering stepmother is so much better than a warning to not believe an attractive man who promises you can have him forever if you do him one small favor, no matter that it will damn your soul and set him free to wreak havoc on a world ill prepared to fight him anymore. No one believes. *That's* why he will survive. *That's* why he will kill again. He's loose, Lilly. I couldn't hold him."

"Mom . . . 'Blood is binding, blood is lure'? You're scaring the girls."

"I am not."

It was sullen, and Lilly came forward, hand out, pleading. "You're scaring me."

Her mother pressed her lips together, determination etched in her every move. "I need to go see. Maybe the tree died. I should have kept a better watch, but I didn't think he'd ever remain awake this long."

Fear slid through Lilly, fear that her mother was starting to lose her grip. "There is no tree spirit murdering men who chop down trees!"

"He is out there!" Her mother pointed at the moonlight beyond the window, her loud voice shocking Lilly. "Meg heard him sing. Today in the creek. He can't cross running water, but he can speak through it, and if the tree he was in has died . . . He could be out there right now, watching us, learning what we most want in the world."

Lilly watched her mother go pale. "Bittersweet," the older woman whispered. "He didn't like bittersweet. Do you remember what fencepost we saw it growing on last fall? I can tie some over the girls' window. Maybe it will keep him out."

"That is enough!" Lilly exclaimed, then glanced at the stairs, worried Meg might hear and come down.

"He's out there!" her mother said virulently, eyes wild. "Meg is vulnerable. He hates men, but he is charmed by women and he *knows* what little girls want to believe. If we don't find him and bind him, he's going to hurt her. People are going to die! People you know and love!"

Lilly jumped when her mother's grip pinched her wrist. "Blood will

424   **KIM HARRISON**

bind him, but he needs it to become strong enough to be seen, so he'll risk it," she hissed, and Lilly recoiled. "I don't want my grandchildren having to go through that hell! He's so cruel, so beautiful."

Lilly watched her mother's tired eyes fill, and she pulled her arm to herself when she let go.

"My grandbaby," her mother said, head down as she turned away. "He's singing to her. She can hear him. I should have done better. I should have told you the truth, but I didn't *want* you to have to believe!"

"Mom?" Damn it, now she was crying. Frightened by the mood swings, she put a hand on her mom's shoulder. "Mom, it's just a story," she said as the older woman took a tissue from a tiny pocket and hid her eyes. "It's going to be okay. If you wouldn't fill Meg's head with stories of unicorns and evil witches, she wouldn't make stuff like this up! Nothing is going to happen. Meg is fine! Em, too."

Still she cried, and Lilly's thoughts spun full circle. "Where's your medicine?" she said suddenly. "Do you still have it?" Her mother hadn't had a spell like this in twenty years. Not since Emily's husband had died when clearing a windblown tree from a fence. The weight shifted when a limb was cut free, and the entire tree fell on him, killing him instantly.

"It's poison. I threw it out," the older woman said, grasping her sleeve and drawing her to a halt. "I'm okay. You're right. Meg is making the voices up." Color high, her mother touched her face, smiling even through the last of her tears. "It's just a story. You're right. I'm a foolish old woman who's had too much sun."

Hearing the lie, Lilly's stomach clenched as she watched her mother set the drying cloth on the table and turn her back on her. "I'm tired," her mother whispered, not meeting her eyes as she headed for the hallway. "I'm going to lie down."

"Mom?"

Emily smiled tremulously again, hesitating in the threshold, one hand on the wood, the other clenched in a tight fist. "You have a good night, Lilly. I'll see you in the morning. You're right. It's just a fanciful story of an old woman. I'll gather the eggs in the morning. No need for you to get up early."

Lilly's eyes narrowed, and for the second time that night, she crossed her arms over her chest, angry with her mother. She didn't believe the sudden change of heart for a second. But still, worry lingered as she draped the cloth over the drying rack and turned out the light to better find Pepper ranging in the moonlight.

Beyond the window, the creek shone, a moving, living ribbon of silver. Maybe she should call Kevin despite wanting to gouge his eyes out with a ice pick. Kevin was a prick, but his dad had grown up with her mother. Something had happened when her mother was fourteen, something that no one talked about and had never made the papers. It wasn't a tree spirit, but maybe someone she trusted had raped her and she invented the drama to make it more bearable. Meg's silly rhyme today might have brought it all back. Aging people remembered things from the past better than the present sometimes.

Kevin's dad would know. He'd been her mother's best friend.

TWO

Though the rising sun was bright in the girls' room, little Em was still asleep, and Lilly eased the door shut, smiling at the pout the four-year-old was wearing. Her smile faded quickly as she went downstairs, the air becoming cooler, but no less humid. It was going to be a scorcher of a day, and she was glad the hay had come in already, filling the barn where her art studio was with the scent of summer.

The chance to lose herself in her work pulled at her, her restless sleep filled with images of honey-eyed wolves. She blamed her mother, and she slipped into the kitchen, seeing the basket of newly washed eggs next to the sink.

It was quiet, even for a lonely farmhouse at the edge of nothing. The come-and-go squeak of the porch swing mixed with the ever-present crickets and bubbling creek, and she leaned on tiptoe over the sink to look out onto the porch. Meg was in the long swing, a half-melted Popsicle in her grip, Pepper sprawled out beneath her. The sun bathed her in its glow, and the nine-year-old girl in her shorts and straight brown hair looked wisely innocent—a small spot of quiet intelligence calmly swinging as if waiting for something to come up the road, something she wouldn't share with her mother.

"Good morning, Meg," she said softly out the open window, holding the faded curtain aside so she could see her daughter's blue-stained smile. "You're up early. Where's Gram? Still in the barn?"

The creak of the long swing slowed, but didn't stop. "She went for a walk in the woods." Meg pulled her attention from the car bridge, twisting to pull her legs up under her as blue dripped from a bent knuckle.

Meg's words tightened through Lilly. She drew back in, her hand looking like her mother's for the first time as it let go of the curtain. Her mother had said she was going to go into the woods to see if her dryad's tree had decayed. This fantasy had gone on long enough.

Brow furrowed, Lilly headed for the porch, her sneakers silent on the faded linoleum. The squeak and slam of the screen door shocked through her, and she forced a smile so as not to worry Meg. "She went into the woods?" she asked, coming to sit beside Meg and keep the swing moving. "What for?"

Meg tilted her head, tongue reaching to get the threatening drop of blue. "She made me promise not to tell, but it's okay. She knows Penny is a liar."

Damn it. Damn it all to hell. Lilly took a slow breath, feeling the heavy air settle deep into her lungs, making her thoughts scattered and her muscles unwilling to react. "How long ago was that, sweetheart?" she asked, trying to hide her anger.

Meg shrugged, tilting her head to bite off one side of the last inch of blue ice.

"Meghan Ann!" she snapped, and the little girl blinked, her cheeks bunched out against the spot of cold in her mouth. "How long!"

Eyes wide, she crunched through the Popsicle. "The sun wasn't over the trees yet," she volunteered, her gaze never leaving her mom's face as she ate the last chunk of sweet ice.

Agitation drew her to her feet, the swing bumping the back of her legs and settling as she looked at the woods. "Less than half an hour," she muttered, headed for the kitchen. Enough was enough. She was going to go find her, and then they were going to have a talk about fantasy and reality. Her mother was not crazy, and she was not losing touch with reality. But if she couldn't be trusted to not run off to the woods chasing a fairy tale, then maybe things were worse than Lilly wanted to admit.

A new fear joined her old ones as she grabbed her cell phone from her purse by the front door. She snatched her work boots from beside the back door, and her sun hat from the pegs. Em's and Meg's hats were hanging there beside hers, but her mother's was gone.

"Meg, watch Em for me, okay?" she said as she came out and sat on the rocker to kick her sneakers off. "I have to find Gram."

Her Popsicle gone, Meg slipped off the swing, the stick between her teeth. "Gram told me you were going to go after her. Can I watch TV?"

Head down, Lilly shoved her feet into her boots. "Yes, but let Em pick the channel when she wakes up."

"She always picks baby shows," Meg complained, leaning heavily on the armrest of the rocking chair as she bent in far enough to lift her toes from the old wood floor.

"Make her a peanut butter sandwich for breakfast, okay?" Lilly said, fighting to keep her impatience in check. "And don't leave the house. Lock the door when I leave, and don't open it except for Mrs. Elliot. She'll be here in an hour to pick up the bread for the church social. I should be back before then."

"Okay. She smells funny, though."

She smells like stale whisky, Lilly thought, then froze in the idea that she was making a mistake, like the mother in the fairy tales who leaves her children to go to town, telling them not to let the wolf in only to return to find them gone. *Oh, for God's sake, Lilly, it's the twenty-first century.* "Pick up the phone if it's me." She looked up from tying her boots, seeing Meg not listening to her. "Meg?"

"Okay." With a worrisome confidence, the girl leaned back to set her feet on the porch.

Lilly stood, motions slowing as she put on her hat. A glance back at the kitchen tightened her anger. She was *not* going to take a jar of honey with her. She gave Meg a quick hug, then stomped determinedly down the four stairs, angry with her mom for making her do this.

Heat rose like a wave from the dormant, burnt grass, her steps all but silent on the puffs of fine dirt as she took the path to the barn. Ticked, she powered up her cell phone, scrolling until she found Kevin's number.

But then she hesitated, pace slowing as the shade of the barn took her. The snap of her phone closing was loud, and she looked up as she tucked it away, the call unplaced as she remembered their last conversation. There was no need to get him involved. She knew where her mother was.

Squinting, Lilly slowed to a stop at the edge of the woods, her shadow running long behind her. The sharp dividing line between farm and woods was kept true by the yearly mowers, and seeing the understory laid bare and clean in the morning sun was eerie. The cooler air wafted out, shifting her hair like a lover, and she tucked a stray strand under her hat.

The image of a beautiful, devious boy she'd never actually seen rose up unbidden. It was followed by the memory of countless hot summer nights when she would kneel at her bedroom window, arms on the sill as she gazed into the black woods, heart hammering as she imagined the fireflies were winking for her, telling her to come dance with them in a magical glen.

Staring at the woods, Lilly's breath came and went in a slow sound. She turned back once to reassure herself that Meg had gone inside with Pepper. The porch was empty. Woods lay on one side, the grassland and cultivated field on the other, the house that three generations of women shared in between—and the sun rose over it all like an angry god bent on restitution. "It's just a story," she whispered, but a niggling doubt tingled down to her clenched hands as she strode forward into the coolness.

A single strand of spider silk brushed her, and she waved her hand, having forgotten that particular hazard of walking in the woods. There was no path, but she knew where she was going. It would be a simple task to walk a straight line until she found the creek and then following it upstream to the thicket-enclosed glen where her mother had told her never to go but of course she had.

Almost without realizing it, she fell into a familiar rocking pace that both made good time and allowed for unexpected shifts of balance. The poem ran in her mind, her steps beating it deeper into her thoughts.

Sunder wraith from flesh ill-taken; And bind fey spirit to wood awakened, over and over it came, again and again. She'd loved the magic of it when she was a child, but now it only made her mother sound crazy, that much closer to an unwilling move to a sterile, cold home with her most precious things arranged on a stark white counter, mementoes whose only purpose was to give well-meaning visitors something to coo and reminisce over.

Sunder wraith from flesh ill-taken. What the hell did that mean? But there was no meaning to be found, and Lilly forced herself out of step, trying to get rid of it.

But slowly her pace slipped back as the peace of the woods crept into her bones. The memory of being here as a child suffocated her anger: looking for mushrooms with her mother, the excitement of finding the forest lilies that she was named for, the dark depths of moss-rimmed pools of water that might vanish unexpectedly when a hole opened up and drained the water away through the caverns that riddled the hills. The woods had been a playground, potentially threatening, but feeling safe.

From almost under her feet, a grouse exploded into flight, shrieking its fear and making Lilly stop short with a gasp. Barely she caught her cry. She wanted to laugh, but the sound never came. The sound of water running came from up ahead. And chanting.

Lilly frowned as she recognized her mother's voice. She walked faster, anger making her misstep and almost twist her ankle when her foot rolled on a log. The creek gave her no cheerful chatter to warn her, and she found it with a shocking abruptness, almost walking right off the edge. Pulling up short, she blinked. If the creek looked drained at the house, it looked positively minuscule here, the once full-force flow now reduced until the tops of rocks that might never touch the bottom of a boat showed dry. The tall edges of the watercourse looked like raw wounds, and the once-loud chatter of the water was a bare hint. Fish as long as her arm lay in deeper puddles, their gills pumping as they struggled to survive another day in the hopes of rain.

A huge, glacier-dropped rock sat in the middle of the stream. The water had gouged a deeper hole before it, but rocks with dry tops showed to either side of the huge monolith her mother used to jump from, skinny-dipping before her fourteenth birthday when everything had changed. A tree grew at the center of the rock, finding enough soil over the ages to somehow survive.

"I know you can hear me, Penn. I've given you enough blood for a week. Show yourself!" her mother's voice rang out, and Lilly's attention jerked to the right.

Frowning, she ran from the stream, dodging around trees that bent over the creek as if to hide it from the sun. The ground slowly began to rise, the soil became dryer, and the trees were spaced farther apart, looking almost twisted. Who was her mother talking to? The squirrels? Almost she hoped so, for if she was shouting at a tree, Lilly was going to check her into the retirement home just outside of town.

"Mom," she whispered as she hauled herself up a rill and looked down into a shallow glen. The soil here was broken rock, not giving enough purchase for anything but grass and brambles apart from the very center where a pine tree eked out a living, its branches dead or dying as it stretched out its limbs as if desperately trying to touch its neighbors for help. Thorny berry bushes made an almost impenetrable fence, but her mother had gotten through somehow, and the old woman knelt at the base of the pine tree, her sun hat askew on the ground and her hair undone.

Lilly's brow furrowed. Pissed, she pushed forward to find a way through the bushes. She took a breath to shout at her mom, wincing and drawing back when she walked through an entire spiderweb, backpedaling and brushing at her face.

Shuddering, she stopped, her lips parting when she looked up and she saw her mother wasn't alone. The muscles in her face went slack, and she squinted, taking a step forward and snapping another web. The bright sun made it hard to see, but there was a long-limbed boy standing over her mother, his hands on his hips and the sun turning his shoulder-length, tousled hair to a flaming copper.

A thousand stories over a thousand summer nights passed through her mind. Her heart pounded, and she took another step, anger filling her as her mother began to cry, kneeling at his feet. "You!" she shouted, unwilling to believe. "Get the hell away from my mother!"

The boy looked up, his astonishment becoming a devilish smile. "Your daughter can see me, Em. How delightful," he said, and the sound of his whispery voice shocked Lilly to a halt. Something in her fluttered. Something older screamed out a warning. He was perfect, but only death was that beautiful. "I don't love you anymore," he said, bending close over her mother. "But you knew that. Perhaps your daughter? Your . . . granddaughters?"

Lilly jerked from her stupor as her mother surged to her feet, rocking like a drunken ship. "You stay away from my girls!" she shouted. "I swear I will scorch every tree on the hill to ash if you so much as whisper in Meg's ear again! Stay out of her mind, you hear me!"

Frantic, Lilly paced the edge, looking for the way in.

"No. I don't." The beautiful boy touched her mother's face, and Lilly burned at the sound of heartache her mother made. "You were so beautiful, Em. Now you're dried up and withered. Beauty gone. You're not good for anything now."

"Mom!" Lilly cried as her mother tried to slap him and the boy darted back, laughing.

"Wraith by moonlight, hunter by day; Bond is sundered by sun's first ray!" her mother shouted, and the boy lightly danced forward, gleefully kissing her on her withered cheek.

"Blood is binding, blood is lure; Flesh is fragile, to blade's sweet cure!"

"The tree no longer holds me, Em," he said, reaching up to pull himself into the broken, needleless branches. "The wood is dead, and you can't bind me to it. I am free. And I will have the blood of your blood as my own for your penance."

"Sunder wraith from flesh ill-taken; And bind fey spirit to wood awakened!" Lilly's mother cried out, and the boy dropped to the rocky earth. Lilly watched, the thorns pressing into her as he looked at her mother in disdain and then reached out and slapped her.

Lilly sucked in her breath as the sound of his hand meeting her cheek cracked through her. "Get away from my mother, you son of a bitch!"

"Oh, if only," the boy said. Without thought, Lilly pushed into the brambles, tiny thorns biting her as the canes locked as if to bar her. Fire pricked from a hundred wounds, and she cried out in impatience as she stomped forward, trying to crush the thorns under her feet and make a way.

"Leave my mother alone!" she cried out as she shoved her way through, only to get her foot snared and fall forward. The ground slammed into her, and she struggled for air, the breath knocked out of her. But then she froze as the boy was suddenly right in front of her, his feet even with her eyes. They were a rich brown with pale white nails, and she gasped when he fell to the earth before her to stare at her. Amber eyes flecked with gold arrested her attention, and everything in the world vanished. Behind him, she could hear her mother crying.

"You're Lilly," the boy said, and Lilly could say nothing. His hair was like spun copper, glinting in the sun, and she sucked in her breath when he reached to touch her hair.

"Did your mother ever tell you that we picked out your name together? Ten years before you were even born. It was my idea. I do so like the forest flowers."

Lilly wedged an arm under her to get up. Thorns drove into her, and she looked down, hissing at the sudden pain. "Mom!" she called out as she finally got up, but the boy was gone. "Mom, are you okay?"

Brushing pieces of cane and leaves off her, she stumbled onto the rocky circle. "Mom?"

The questionable shade of the dying tree chilled her, and Lilly put a hand to her mother's shoulder as she knelt, feeling it shake. Still her mother didn't look up.

"Yeah, you'd better run!" Lilly shouted at the surrounding trees. "You hit my mom; I'm going to pound you, you little thug!"

"He got away..." her mother lamented. "The tree died. The spell broke. And he got away!"

Lilly brought her gaze back from the empty trees, the heat in the air turning to steam in her lungs. It was hard to breathe, and she recoiled at the dead, decapitated chicken at the base of the tree. Horror took her, becoming shock when her mother slowly rose, wiping the blood and feathers stuck to her hand on a corner of her tied-up dress. Askew in the dirt and scree was one of her butcher knives. *Blood is binding, blood is lure; Flesh is fragile, to blade's sweet cure.*

What by sweet Jesus was her mother doing?

"Mom?" The imprint of a hand shown bright red on her mom's face, and Lilly wavered, the blood rushing out of her head. There was a dead chicken on the ground. There was a knife in the dirt. Blood stained her mother's hands. "What are you doing? My God, did you butcher a chicken out here?"

Tears still slipping down her wrinkled face, her mother turned her lips in, biting them as if to keep from sobbing. "I can't make it stick a second time," she said, her eyes on the woods as if they still held the wolves of her childhood. "He doesn't trust me, and even if I could, the tree has died. Nothing can hold him in dead wood. Nothing."

Scared, Lilly shook her mom's shoulder. "Do you know that boy? Mom, who was that?"

But her mother just stood there, tears spilling over one by one, turning her beautiful. "You saw him? Lilly, I'm so sorry. I never should have told you about him, but I thought he was gone forever. That you knew his name made it easier for him to force his way in, to make you see him."

Her mother's eyes suddenly rose in a new thought, and she gripped Lilly's arm tightly. "Where's Meg?"

Her fear struck Lilly, and she shoved aside and buried it under logic. But still the fear seeped up like water. "She's at home. You think I'm going to bring her out here? Why did you kill one of our chickens?" *Blood is binding, blood is lure. My mother is crazy.*

"You left her alone?" Snatching up the knife, her mother strode to a large rock embedded into the soil. Using it as a stepping-stone, she laboriously lifted herself up onto it, and hopped a tentative, uneasy path through the briars. "He will twist her with one smile, and that's assuming he's not already gotten her outside in the moonlight! How could you leave her alone? I told you he was free. I told you—"

"Shut up! Just shut up!" Lilly shouted, the heat of the sun pounding on her. The echo of her anger and frustration came back to her from the surrounding trees as she stood in the rocky ground beside the dead pine tree and watched her mother jump from rock to rock as if she was ten. "There is no forest ghost. You are sick, Mom. Give me that knife!"

Like a wild thing, she crossed the three stones that separated them and wrestled the knife from her mother and threw it beside the dead chicken, the blood already soaked into the ground. "We are going home, and you are *never* going to talk about this again unless it is with a psychologist. You understand me?"

"Take your hand off me this instant, Lilly Ann."

Her mother's voice was cold, and Lilly found her grip empty as her mother yanked away. The older woman stood straight and unbowed upon the next rock, her hair waving about her and her lips pressed tight. "I am not crazy," she said, clearly angry. "You saw him. Don't deny it. You saw him and he spoke to you. What did he say?"

Lilly hesitated, scared at the change. "You didn't hear him? He was right there."

Eyes squinting mistrustfully, Emily shook her head. "Penn is the protector of the woods, born from the first tree's cry of pain from the woodsman's ax. He appears as a mirage to those who believe in him, as real as you allow him to be, as beautiful as you imagine, in the form of your choosing. He is everything, he is death. He can take over the bodies of wolves and men, though the blood needed to do so is enough to kill a man. He survives the ages by taking refuge in the trees he protects. It is his saving grace. It is his downfall. His greatest desire is to have a soul again, and he will lie to get it. I was able to protect you from him, Lilly, but he no longer believes in me." Her jaw clenched, and she lifted her head proudly. "I'm old. He doesn't love me anymore." Her mother shivered, becoming scared again. "We need to get home."

Lilly's heart pounded as she followed her mother to the edge of the brambles, catching every thorn, every briar that her mother avoided. Threads from spiders brushed against her, shimmering in the sun as they ballooned on the still, stagnant air. Lilly brushed them aside as she walked, but her mother accepted them in grace, whispering thanks as if each one was a benediction.

Getting home sounded like a good idea.

THREE

The porch swing squeaked in time with the waving of her make-shift fan, and realizing it, Lilly set the magazine touting fall bulbs aside. The evening was stifling, and even the slight motion to make the rocker move seemed extraordinary. Her mother on the larger porch swing seemed unaffected in her sundress, but Lilly pulled at her shirt, trying to cool off.

Out on the grass, Meg and Em jumped and ran in erratic spurts, catching fireflies and imprisoning them in a jar for a nightlight. Their shouts echoed against the black woods, and Lilly shivered. Okay, so she had seen a honey-eyed boy with brown, dirt-smeared feet. There was an explanation. Entire families lived in the hills like aborigines, never coming down. Maybe that's where the boy had come from. That he had slapped her mother made her angry, but the dead chicken had her scared, scared enough to keep her silent.

"You stay out of that creek!" her mother shouted, and Lilly glanced at her, angry that she couldn't be like everyone else's mom. Why did everything have to be twice as hard for her?

"Trapping him in a tree again will be difficult," the old woman said, rocking, still rocking, her old woman hands quiet in her lap. "I dared him to show me how he did it the last time, and I sealed him in place, but he's wise to it now. He won't believe me a second time. He can't cross moving water, and he can't move through rock, but I doubt I can trick him into an open sarcophagus. We might have to burn the woods if I can't think of something."

Lilly was silent, her anger growing as she thought of the phone in her pocket. She was going to make an appointment with the doctor tomorrow as soon as they opened. She wanted to know what her options were. Fortunately the house was already in her name. If it was only her, she wouldn't be as concerned, but Em and Meg shouldn't have to deal with this.

"A chicken has enough blood to make him visible for a week," her mother said, and Lilly ignored her, watching the girls jumping for the insects. "Too bad the river is so low. I'd be tempted to have David bring his bobcat over and cut a trench around the house. Take down the car bridge. It would put us on an island so he can't reach them. Not with no tree roots to make a bridge for him."

Lilly's jaw clenched, and she forced herself to take a sip of her tea, the ice long melted and the glass dripping from the bottom. Her mother was delusional. And yet . . . the color of Penn's eyes wouldn't leave her, amber and gold like honey dripping from the comb. There was no way she could have imagined it, but the idea that he was real was even more unlikely.

"He could still cross the water if he took possession of a wolf, but what are the chances of any wolves still being in the forest?" her mother said, shocking Lilly from her thoughts.

"I'm sure they're gone," Lilly said lightly, humoring her. "I've not seen a wolf in ages."

The creaking of the swing stopped, and her mother's brow furrowed. "You've never seen a wolf, ever. I don't care if you believe me or not, Lilly, but I will not be humored."

Lilly warmed, jaw clenched to keep herself from saying something she'd regret later.

"You were there," the woman said, her voice holding anger. "And still you don't believe? You saw him in your mind, and still you turn a blind eye?"

Lilly glanced at the girls, their dark shadows halfway to the barn. "I saw you kill a chicken under a tree, Mom. I want you to come with me and talk to Doctor Sarson. We can get this sorted out. Get you back on your meds."

Her mother's eyes narrowed, and she started the swing into motion. "Perhaps it's my fault. I made you safe, but in doing so, I put the girls at risk. Meg will be his target. She's young, but she's the one who will listen, believe. Your daughter will believe everything he tells her, and it will destroy her, you, me, the town. People will die."

Anger flared. "Stop it!" Lilly hissed, resentment tightening her gut. "Stop it now. Not another word, or I take you into emergency tonight!"

Huffing, her mother turned away. "I knew you were timid, Lilly, but I didn't raise you to be a fool."

Lilly stood, knowing her mother would call her bluff. "Meg! Emily! Time to come in!"

From the cooling field, Meg groaned dramatically. "Just one more firefly?" she shouted, and seeing it would tick her mother off, Lilly nodded. "One more, then upstairs to take your baths."

Delighted, Meg high-fived her sister, and the two ran to a beckoning green light.

"The woods are still mine," the old woman grumbled. "I'm going to log it out and burn it."

Sighing, Lilly put her arms over her chest as she watched Meg and Em huddle together over their latest catch.

"You can lock me in the old ladies home after that," her mom finished. "I won't care then."

"Mom . . ."

But her mother stood, her expression stubborn and her motions jerky as she strode to the screen door. "I'll see to the girls' baths."

"No stories," Lilly demanded, frowning when her mother let the screen door slam. From inside, lights turned on one by one as she made her way upstairs. Her shoulders slumping, Lilly sat down where her mother had been, feeling the weight of the last few days heavy on her. From the porch steps, Pepper raised her head, not knowing who to follow.

The girls had gone quiet, knowing that they were up until she noticed them. At a loss for what to do, Lilly took her cell phone from a pocket, weighing it in her hand as if it might hold the answer. Eying the whispering girls, she punched in a familiar number. Anger crept up her spine as it rang, and she took a quick breath as the line clicked open.

But it was only his voice mail, and she fidgeted as Kevin's deep, expressive voice rolled into her. Where once it was soothing, now it just pissed her off. The entire town knew what had happened. The embarrassment had been mortifying, even if she wasn't the one who'd been a dick.

"Hi, you've reached Kevin. If you're trying to reach me in an official capacity, call 911. Jennifer will route you to me. If you're looking for a date, leave a message, I'll get back to you. If you're looking for alimony, call me at—"

The message was interrupted by a beep, the old joke falling flat. Kevin had never been married. Her smile at her girls was gone. She was still angry with him. Not so mad at Deana, despite what she had screamed loud enough that half the town heard her. But she needed to talk to someone, and everyone else was too old or too young. Besides, she wanted to know what had happened to her mother when she had been fourteen, and her mother wasn't talking.

"Hi, Kevin. It's me, Lilly," she said, hearing the anger in her voice despite her attempt to hide it. "I need your official opinion on something that's been going on for a few days. You're still a bastard, but I don't know anyone else who can look at this impartially. Give me a call when you can."

Her mouth stopped moving, but her thoughts continued, circling around and around. *How could you be such a jerk? Did you think I wouldn't find out? Did you think it wouldn't matter?*

She ended the call, her silence intact and her face burning. She was thirty-nine and feeling stupid, angry. How did she get here, a single mom with two kids, living on an artist's income in her mother's house?

Gripping the phone tightly, she looked out over the slowly undulating fields, dark and orderly in the rising moon. She could feel the woods behind her, a threatening presence. Heat lightning flashed in the distance over the fields. "I suppose it could be worse," she said, seeing her girls jumping at fireflies, their smooth limbs and excitement making them beautiful, wild, ephemeral, almost. She had one good thing in her life, and she wasn't going to mess it up.

From the window overhead, her mother called for Meg and Em, and like flowers to the sun, they turned, happy with the world and at peace with the universe as they raced to a cool bath and a soft bed. *When did I lose that joy?* she thought as they flowed past her, Lilly's hand barely managing to touch their hair in passing. Pepper stood, tags jingling as she followed them in.

The lingering heat of the day rising from the earth seemed to vanish as the memory of amber eyes flashed before her, trailing like dust in the wake of her children. The heartache of her mother crying, and the fear that that boy—that clever, devious, uncaring boy—could hurt her little girls swallowed everything, taking her last thread of solace.

"What is wrong with me?" Lilly whispered, still standing at the railing as the sounds of her daughters arguing filtered down from an open window.

The chatter of the water under the car bridge seemed to grow louder in the silence, and depressed, Lilly watched the glint of moonlight around the rocks. Meg had said she could hear voices in the water. The fanciful girl was always talking to herself, having one-sided conversations that Lilly never gave any mind to. But what if her imaginary friends were really Penn? What if her mother wasn't crazy? What if . . . what if what she saw today was real?

Lilly started for the bridge, her heart pounding. The darkness slipped around behind her, the glow from the upstairs window vanishing as she entered the night. The heat rose, shifting her hair until her sandals clumped on the thick wood, and the chatter of the water muffled the crickets. The air over the water was cooler, and she leaned on the railing to see the fireflies above her to look like fairy stars.

The sudden need to take off her sandals and put her feet in was almost unbearable. The water sounded so inviting, and the hot earth was full of her past, a chain weighing her down and preventing her from moving. She had to be free of it if only for a moment. If there were voices to be heard in the water, then she'd hear them. She'd know once and for all.

"I can't believe I'm doing this," she muttered as she sat down on the edge of the bridge and slipped her sandals off. Below her, the water moved, a silken sheet of silver looking like heaven's breath flowing among the living, unseen but not unfelt. A moment, and it would be over. Either her mother was crazy, or she was.

Lilly held her breath and leaned over the edge, wishing for something, anything to tell her what was real. It lay below her, just beyond the skin of shimmering silver.

But then the familiar sound of Kevin's SUV rose over the crickets. Still sitting on the bridge, she turned to see a pair of lights bouncing over the ruts, coming in from the outskirts and back into town.

Lilly drew her feet up and stood. Her pulse quickened, and she shoved her anger down. She was a grown woman. She could talk to him and not let their past get in the way—even if the past was all anyone had.

Her motion slow and somewhat antagonistic, she left her sandals on the bridge and walked through the powdery dust and grit to the main road, not wanting him to drive into the yard as he usually did. She had called him, but she was not going to go back to the way things had been. Arms crossed, she waited by the mailbox, trying to decide what she was going to say.

The squeak of the brakes was familiar, and Kevin—good-looking, football hero, gone-away-to-college-and-come-home, good-old-boy Kevin—swung his head as he brought the police SUV to a halt, parking on the wrong side of the road and turning the engine off. She frowned as the hot engine ticked as it cooled, remembering how his hands had felt on her, the feelings he drew through her, the plans they had made that he had ruined. She'd thought he might be someone she could spend the rest of her life with. Now nothing was left but bitter betrayal and a frustration for four wasted years.

"Lilly," he said in greeting, almost taking his hat off. "You look good barefoot."

She swallowed back six different ugly words. "You got my message?"

He had the decency to look embarrassed, ducking his head as he turned down the police radio. "I saw it was you and I was afraid to pick up."

The crickets sang as her toes dug into the soft, warm dust. "Kevin."

"I deserved everything you said." Kevin's face was red. She could see it even in the dark. "I can't argue with it. You were right. It stings a little, though."

Suck it up, little man. But she was silent as she remembered the shock on his face when she had walked in, Deana's nervous laugh as she scrambled for her clothes. *I should have torched your car*, she thought, hearing the crickets chirp faster. *That would really sting.*

Nervous, Kevin leaned back in his seat, his hands still on the wheel. "We can still talk though, right? Go to the same picnics? Avoiding you is hard in a small town."

His smile pissed her off. "Sure."

Thinking everything was okay, he leaned forward again with a relieved smile. "So what's up? Is it Pepper? I've had a string of calls this week about missing pets. Dogs and cats, mostly, but Perrot found a gutted yearling at the edge of his pasture. I'm thinking coyotes, but the track looked bigger. Pack of wild dogs, maybe. You might want to keep Meg and Em close to home until we're sure."

Nice of you to think of them. "I'll do that. Kevin, it's about my mom."

Relaxing, he put an arm on the window between them, his eyes going to the house and the lights shining onto the sun-baked grass. "Emily? What's the matter?"

"She's been acting odd. Wandering." Lily was glad the night hid her flush.

He pulled his arm in, concerned. "She's not that old."

Lilly nodded, quashing the grateful feeling that he—that anyone—cared. "I know. That's what worries me. She's been talking about the past a lot. I think it's because Meg is getting older, reminding her of something she's tried to forget." She took a deep breath, resolving to be out with it. This was why she called him, not just anyone.

"Kevin, did your dad ever tell you what happened when she was fourteen? My mom won't tell me anything." There was no way she was going to admit to him that her mother was having delusions of a beautiful boy in the wood and killing chickens to try to turn him into a tree.

Kevin's brow furrowed as he ran a hand across his stubbly chin. "No. He won't talk about it either, but I've heard things. One of the perks of working with people who remember you in diapers is that they think you're either an idiot or deaf."

Lilly's heart pounded, and she moved closer to the truck. "Was she raped?"

Her relief when he shook his head was almost enough to make her knees wobble. "No. Thank God. She and my dad found the body of a murdered vagrant while they were picking blackberries."

Dead vagrant . . . That explained a few things. And yet, it makes Mom's story more believable, too.

"There was some talk for a while that whoever had done it was going to come after them, and the two of them pulled a Huck Finn, vanishing for a few days before showing up for dinner muddy and scratched. Everything was shelved when the state couldn't find out who the man was and no one ever claimed him. He's still at the old potters' field in case someone comes asking. I can show you the gravestone if you want. There's no file. Least not one I could find."

"No, thanks anyway." A curious mix of relief and dread was making it hard to think. Distracted, she pulled at her shirt to get the air moving. It was stifling.

"You want me to look around? Check out your barn? Wild dogs are dangerous when they pack up. I should check the caves you have on your property."

"No." It had come out too fast, and she smiled a fake smile. The last thing she wanted was him on her farm, her land. "We haven't seen any dogs. Pepper would tell us if there were any. Thanks for telling me about what happened."

He nodded, clearly not ready to leave, wanting to say something. Lilly didn't want to hear it, and she backed up, hands in her pockets. Kevin's smile faltered, and Lilly didn't give a damn if he was unhappy. She wasn't the one sleeping with the woman who cut her hair.

"Okay then," he said, his gaze going down the road to the unseen town. "If you ever just want to talk . . ."

As if. "You drive safe, Kevin. Watch out for the armadillos."

He hesitated, his hand falling from the ignition. "Lilly, I'm sorry. I was a grade-A ass. I know it won't change anything, but I'm sorry I hurt you. It was a mistake. A big fucking mistake."

Teeth clenched, she looked over the roof of the SUV to the heat-faded stars, cursing that he could sound so reasonable. Even when she'd found them, he'd been calm, her screaming and his silence making her seem irrational. *I don't want to be alone.*

Probably thinking her silence was a wavering resolve, he shifted closer to the door, hanging an arm over the window. "What can I do to prove it to you? I know you don't want to hear that it won't ever happen again, but it won't. It was just a one-night stand!"

Her eyes came down and her resolve strengthened. "That's just it,

Kevin. If I had lied to you, or pushed you away, or slept around I could understand what you did. If you actually loved the little bitch, I could understand and even maybe forgive you. But you were bored and wanted a quick piece of ass. And you want me to believe that it won't happen again?"

Kevin slowly pulled himself back into the cab.

"Now that I think about it, I think I understand it, after all," Lilly said bitterly.

Looking at his hands, Kevin sighed. "We can get through this." His head slowly came up. "I know we can. Just tell me what you want me to do, and I'll do it."

The band around her chest tightened. Behind her, her home lay silent, an island in the sea of crickets. She had let him become important to her, and now she was paying the price. "I want you to leave. I want you to leave town and never come back."

Kevin's brow furrowed. "This is my home, too. Lilly, I'm trying to make this better. I love you."

Not enough, apparently. She let his last words hang until he had the decency to drop his eyes. "I'm going to say thank you for talking to me, Officer Lowel. But if you put one foot on my land outside of your official capacity, I'll set Pepper on you. You understand me?"

His motions stiff, Kevin sighed and started his truck.

Lilly backed up as he drove his truck away, gravel and dust spurting. The wood of the bridge under her feet was like textured heat, and she scooped up her sandals, reluctant to put them on with grit between her toes. She was shaking, hating the confrontation, hating him all the more. Without thought, she sat on the edge then slipped into the water.

Her breath came in with a gasp as the chill of the water hit her feet, the growing ache at her ankles rising up her calves. The cold shocked her from her anger, and feeling vulnerable, she lifted her head to the stars faded from the humidity and the charge of heat lightning. Her mother's warning to stay out of the water rose, and her shoulders hunched. Her mother was a old woman, touched by her past and fighting to hide it. Finding a murder victim at fourteen would leave a mark on just about everyone.

The shock of the water dulled, and she moved a few paces, feeling the current push against her even as it cooled her flush, calming her emotions and making it easier to think. From the house, the lights went off in the girls' room and flicked on in her mom's.

"I'm listening, Penn," she whispered, still angry at the world, angry that her mother was doing this to her. "I'm here, you son of a bitch. Show yourself. If you're real, show yourself!"

But there was nothing, no singsong voice in her head, no sun-browned vision of youth and deviltry come to mock her. Nothing.

Relief slipped into her, quickly followed by worry. What was she going to do about her mother?

A lump filled her throat, and she looked past the house to the woods beyond. It was hard to raise two girls alone. Fortunately the farm was paid for and Paul's alimony went a long way. Because of her mother, she'd been able to do what she loved. That the girls were spending time with her mother had been great—until now.

Calf deep in water, she shifted her toes among the smaller rocks to find the silty grit below. She didn't want to become one of those ungrateful daughters who only went to visit on Sunday after church, the girls getting a skewed vision of their grandmother, not the strong, proud, capable woman she knew her to be. Guilt pushed out the fear and she looked to the heavens, the weight of the atmosphere pressing down and making her feel small. "Why are you doing this, Mom?" she whispered.

But there was no answer, and she turned back to the steep bank, hesitating before she stepped out to enjoy the feel of the water coursing over her feet. Like cool silk, it brushed her, and she closed her eyes, one hand on the bridge as she felt the warm breath of the night touch her with the first night breeze. Despite everything, she missed Kevin. Or rather, she missed the way he had made her feel. Why had she ever believed him? Why had she ever believed any man?

"Because you are a goddess, my sad little wood lily. It's how you're made, just as I'm made to love you for it."

Lilly gasped, her eyes snapping open as she felt something skate over her skin, rising from the water to touch her in a wave. *Penn.* He wasn't a delusion. He was real.

"I'm here," he said, and she turned, finding him sitting cross-legged at the very center of the bridge at its highest point.

"You can't cross running water," she breathed, then thought that was a foolish thing to say. He wasn't real, but he was.

He smiled, his head cocking slyly to look at her from under his shaggy bangs. He looked about nineteen, far older than the image bending over her mother in the sun. His shoulders had a lean strength, his limbs still showing a lanky growth that had yet to be grown into. "I'm not touching the water. I'm sitting on a bridge." His chin lifted, and his smile became benevolent. "You're broken. Let me fix you. I can do it. I promise."

Lilly swallowed, glancing up at her mother's lit window. "You're not real."

Penn's eyebrows went up, and he shifted where he sat as if the statement bothered him. Moonlight puddled around him to make him into a dangerous shadow. "I am, though I admittedly have no flesh. Your mind perceives me and gives me an image that you can see . . . and feel. Little girls know this for a fact. How is it you've forgotten?"

Oh God. Insanity runs in families. "I'm crazy, just like my mother."

In a motion of grace, Penn stood. She froze as he moved to her, his feet placed on the hard wood toe first, silent. The wind gusted, and he sat before her, close enough to touch. "Crazy?" he whispered, and she could feel the cool of the woods in his breath. "Lilly, you are too old to believe without knowing first. You are too wise, too beaten by ugly-minded men to draw me to your innocence long lost. But you ache like a newborn woman wanting the perfection she deserves. I heard you. I came."

His hand rose, and she backed away, her feet numb in the cold. "Don't touch me."

"Too scared to run in the field, too timid to swim in the river."

"Shut up!"

"Too old to learn how to love a man beyond his faults." Unbothered, Penn did slow handsprings to the end of the bridge, eyes sparkling as he met her gaze. "And men are all flawed, aren't they? I warn them. I warn all young women, but they never believe. I don't need to warn you. You know it twice over. I see it in you. Betrayed. I'd never have done that to you. I'd never betray Meg."

Oh God. Meg. Em. Why hadn't she listened? But it had sounded . . . delusional. "Leave my girls alone."

Penn lay down on the bridge, his arms behind his head as he stared at the sky. "Then you *do* believe in me." His smile was chilling. His build had changed, his shoulders widening and his jaw carrying the first hints of maturity, and a hint of a gold stubble glinted in the moonlight. "Your mother was beautiful. I can see echoes of it in you, and waves of it in Meg."

His voice was deeper. Fear moved Lilly, and she splashed closer. "You will not touch my daughters!" Penn said nothing, and flustered, she added, "Why are you here?"

Penn sat up, his clothes catching the moonlight like still water as he spread his arms wide as if to take in the world. "Everyone has to be somewhere." Stretching out again on his side, he leveled his amber eyes with hers, glinting with challenge. "Run with me. I know a tree where fireflies gather every year. They'll shine like stars for you. I can show you. You will run without tiring, Lilly, if you run with me. Remember running without tiring? The moonlight a river in your lungs, your bare feet hardly touching the ground as the darkness opens and closes behind you? Run with me." He reached to touch her face, and she pulled back.

Oh God. A young girl could never resist this. "You are cruel."

Penn smiled all the wider, his teeth white and catching the light. "I am life at its strongest, and life is cruel." Shifting his body, he leaned in as if to tell her a secret. "It is exhilarating—if you live it right. It's not too late. You are beautiful, Lilly, your scars becoming. Exciting. I like them. You're not like anyone else who can see me. You . . . might understand."

The masculine scent of him was rising between them, familiar but promising something new. A shiver ran though her, and Penn's smile widened upon seeing it.

"Oh, you long to find out. It glows from you like an ache. Come with me. Live."

She shook her head but didn't pull away. She felt so young with him. It was a false feeling, the only one that was keeping her sane. "What do you want?" she asked, and he blinked.

Slowly he sat up, and moonlight fell between them. "I live as a spirit, though I feel the ache of having had flesh once," he said, and Lilly levered herself up onto the bridge. "The gods took my soul from me when I disobeyed them, giving me the power to feel the world only when I existed within a tree, hoping that I'd stay in one. It's a sad thing, to feel only what comes your way. I want to be whole again, not just for a night, but forever. I need a soul."

"That's why you like women, not men," she guessed, and Penn blinked, clearly surprised.

"Oh, I like you best," he said, his voice deepening even more as he looked her up and down in an entirely new way. "Yes. Women have the power of creation; they are lesser goddesses, though they know it not, believing the lies that men tell. A soul is pure creation energy, and only a woman, even one just born, can divide a million times and never be less, only more. I want a soul, Lilly. I want freedom. Is that wrong?"

She drew back into herself as he put a hand between them and leaned in, the heat of him giving her goose bumps. His copper hair was a thick wave and his muscles had taken on the weight of maturity, of strength. He was becoming what she wanted, and she couldn't help her fascination.

"I want the freedom to go anywhere, do anything," he whispered. "You have everything, and you do nothing with it! My penance is to be without a soul until a woman gives me one anew. But only the young ever see me. *Until you.*"

"What would you do?" she asked, and his artless guile fell from him.

Putting a finger to his lips, he drew away, pulling himself up to crouch on the balls of his feet before her. "Such a question. Let's run to the middle of the field and stop for a time. There are ways to make the moon move slowly. I will share them with you."

Fear slid through her as he extended a hand for her to rise. She had sacrificed so much, and for what? *It would be so easy . . .* This was no angel, but a demon. "Did you kill the man my mother found?" she asked, and Penn slowly stood, his hand dropping to his side.

"No." He looked older, thirty perhaps, but a lean, confident thirty, and her lips parted when she recognized Kevin's youth in him. "The boy with her did."

Stunned, Lilly blinked up at him. *Kevin's dad?*

Penn shrugged, moving with a dancer's grace and looking more and more like Kevin with every step. "He thought it was me talking to Em, and the boy killed the man as your mother watched." Lean and slim, he turned sideways, the light catching the glint in his eye. "He meant to save her, but the guilt pinned her to the earth to die. She grew old, just as I warned her. But it's not too late for you."

Horrified, Lilly touched her mouth, turning where she stood to look at the silent farmhouse behind her. She jumped, startled when Penn sat down beside her, the scent of a frog-rimmed pool flowing over her.

"Why do you sully yourselves with unfaithful men? This is why you mourn, Lilly—no man can be true to a goddess. But I'm not a man. I know the patience of the winter, the glory of the spring. I will be true where mere mortals cannot. You ask too much of them, then weep when they fail you."

His breath on her cheek made her close her eyes. The unsaid promise was there, and something in her responded, wanted it even as she knew it was a lie.

"Run with me," he whispered. "That's all I ask tonight. No more than that. It will bring you alive. Remember being alive? Aching for something you know is there and willing to give all to have it?"

Frightened, she pulled from him, shivering as his hand hung a breath from her jawline, almost touching. Eyes widening, she rose, backing up until she found the earth again. Penn stood in the middle of the bridge, waiting for her.

"Run with me," he asked again, a hand outstretched.

"No." It was a harsh croak of denial, and her breath came fast as he looked past her to Meg's dark window. "No!" Lilly cried out again, this time in fear for her daughter, and from inside, Pepper began to bark.

When Lilly looked back, the bridge was empty.

Parental instinct turned her back to the house. Within three steps, she spun and took five more to the bridge. She had to stop him. She had to save her daughter. Meg would run with him. She would go with a sun-brown boy who smiled and dared her to climb to the top of a tree to see the butterflies beyond. She would give him everything he asked to keep him with her. She would believe. And she would be tossed aside when he got what he wanted.

All but crying in her frustration, Lilly stopped at the foot of the bridge, her arms wrapped around her middle, not knowing what to do.

Perhaps it was time for her to believe as well.

FOUR

The sun wasn't up yet, but the air had grown transparently gray, hinting at it. Lilly lay in her bed, listening for the bedsprings in the room next to her. The palest blue slipped in around her curtains, and only the crickets marred the silence. Soft and easy, her breath slipped in and out of her as she waited, her mind calm and at peace. Her mother had risked her life for her. Once was enough. She would not allow her to do so again. If Penn was real, then she'd trap him. It wouldn't be with a dead chicken and a fairy-tale poem, either. There was dynamite in the barn, and caves in the hills. But first she had to slip her mother's apron strings.

The click of Pepper's nails on the hardwood floor jolted through her, and Lilly jerked at her mother's soft admonishment in the hall downstairs. Cursing, she flung the covers aside and rolled out of bed. Somehow her mother had gotten up without shifting the bedsprings, and as she flung on her clothes, she watched out the window for her mother's hunched shadow headed for the barn.

Rugged pants, thick socks, and a short-sleeve button-down shirt would keep her safe from the cave's jagged edges, and if all went well, she'd be back before it got hot. Opening her door, she listened, hearing nothing from downstairs. Lilly felt like a teenager as she snuck to the top of the stairway, touching her daughters' door in passing. They would be safe after today, one way or the other. Lilly eased down the stairway, avoiding the creaky steps and freezing when the squeak of the front porch's screen door split the silence. Pepper's soft whine followed.

Moving faster, Lilly paced into the kitchen, giving the golden lab a pat as she looked out over the sink, through the window and to the barn. He mother was striding to the barn, another big knife in her hand and a canvas sack. "Either she's crazy, or I am," Lilly whispered, but the memory of Penn reclining on the bridge, staring up at the stars was too real, the breath of his words on her cheek too heavy, and the scent of his wild spirit too thick in her. *How could any girl see his snare?*

Lilly snatched up a biscuit from last night's dinner, and taking her floppy hat at the last moment, she gave Pepper a pat, telling her to stay. Then she dropped another biscuit into the dog's bowl to distract her as she eased the porch door open and slipped outside.

The sky was a perfect pale blue, shading to orange and pink at the horizon over the fields and the unrisen sun. Cool and humid, the morning breeze brushed against her as Lilly crept down the porch steps. Her mother was almost to the barn. Heart pounding, Lilly waited until her mother tugged the tall door open, then she jogged after her, breaking a spiderweb as she ran under the apple trees.

Her pace slowed as she got closer and heard her mother inside. Breath held, she halted at the door, ear to it as her mother muttered over which hen hadn't been laying properly. Fingers trembling, Lilly eased the barn door open and went in.

The darker gray of the barn smelled like hay, familiar and welcoming. Looking up at the cupola as her eyes adjusted, Lilly squinted at the soft cooing. Her mother was already in the converted chicken coop, and Lilly pushed herself into motion. The door to it was a thick heavy pine, the latch old iron.

The snick of the simple lock sliding into place was hardly audible, and Lilly backed up at the sudden sliding sound behind the door.

"Lilly?"

Mouth dry, Lilly clasped her hands before her like a scolded child. "I'll be back in an hour to let you out, Mom."

"Lilly!" It was stronger this time, and Lilly edged to the big barn door and the scrap of gray morning showing. "Lilly, let me out of here right now! I am not crazy. The girls are in danger!"

Lilly's breath caught as her mother rattled the door. She might get out by crawling through the chicken door, but it wasn't likely. "I believe you." Her mother swore, and Lilly backed up even farther. "Mom, I don't want you to be hurt anymore. I'll take care of Penn. It's my turn. You protected me, and I'm going to protect Meg and Em. Take care of the girls if I don't make it back." Oh God, she was going to blow up the mountain.

"Lilly, let me out of here!" her mother cried, pounding on the door to make the latch rattle. "You don't know how evil he is. I don't want you to have to pay that cost! Lilly? Lilly!"

But she was walking away as if in a dream. The two sticks of dynamite were right where she'd seen her grandpa leave them, wrapped in a cloth and tucked up in a hole in the barn. They'd been left over from when her great-grandpa had shifted the stream that now ran around Rock Island to bring water closer to the house and dry out a neighbor's field.

"Lilly!"

The banging on the door was almost unheard as she left the barn. In the yard, chickens darted out of the coop with a flustered agitation. She wasn't going to take a chicken, and she wasn't going to take a knife. She was going to lure Penn into a cave and blow up the opening. Her mother said he couldn't move through solid rock, so it should hold him. *What if it didn't?*

Thoughts of her daughters alone in the house kept returning again and again as she trudged into the woods, following a path she'd often taken to meet Kevin. Bitter memories of Kevin mixed with worry for her children, pounding up through her in time with her feet on the earth. How could she have just left them? Wraith by moonlight, hunter by day, the singsong went. He could lure them away from their beds, or attack them as a wolf. What was she doing out here?

Fear pushed her into a faster pace until she was almost running, weaving through the woods as if she were a deer, taking small fallen trees with a jump and using her momentum to swing around trees. The explosives bumped her with each step, smelling of barn dust and reminding her of her risk. The wind of her passage whispered in her, tugging her hair and caressing her cheek. Angry, she pushed aside her thoughts of Penn. He was a lie, like all the rest.

The sky was bright with a false dawn as she found the steep climb to the opening of the cave that she and Paul had found while marking out the lines of the farm. It was a dry cave. Even the bats didn't use it.

Squinting at the top, Lilly shifted the sticks of explosive and started up the rude path. There were poles rammed into the earth to provide hand-holds, remnants of her innocent, trusting past. She and Paul might have found the caves, but it had been she and Kevin who had used them as a romantic hideaway.

"Son of a bitch," Lilly muttered, her anger giving her the strength to reach the top. Her heart pounded as she found the last step and turned on the narrow ledge to face the valley below.

Trees obscured her near view, but fields rolled in the distance. The freshening breeze lifted through her hair, cooling her. She could see the barn and house, a glint of light in the kitchen strengthening her resolve. Her mother had gotten out of the coop. By the time she realized where she'd gone, it would be over.

Her arms ached as she turned to the cliff face and lifted the vine curtain to reveal the opening. Cool air sifted out, the smell of dry dirt barely discernible. Numb, Lilly went inside, finding the lighter where she had left it, using it to ignite the lantern. Two bottles of unopened wine, a corkscrew, two glasses, and a wool horse blanket was all that was left of a broken romance, and flushing, Lilly looked away.

Moving quickly, Lilly wedged a stick of dynamite where it would bring the roof down about ten feet into the cave. Men were not all pigs. She knew this. And she wasn't looking for Mr. Perfect. Just a nice guy who wouldn't hit her kids or have sex with the town's hairdresser.

Pissed, Lilly jammed the last stick right by the opening. Her hand slipped, and a sharp pain lanced through the fleshy part of her thumb. Biting back a cry, Lilly clutched her hand, giving the half-hidden stick a glance before moving to the opening to see what she'd done. It wasn't bad, and she sucked at the small cut.

Blood is binding, Blood is lure. . . .

Lilly slowly took her hand from her mouth. Feeling daring, she wiped the blood on the edge of the opening with an abrupt defiance. The air was fresher at the opening, and she lingered, standing in the hole in the mountain, watching the air become clear as the sun neared rising. Inside, the lantern hissed.

Frowning, she stepped out onto the ledge, letting the vines fall to hide the opening. Her mother had tricked him once. She could do the same. "Penn?" she called, feeling foolish, then louder, "I was thinking all night about what you said. Can we talk?"

She listened, leaning to the edge. Three birds flew up from the forest below, but there was no whisper in her mind, no breath of wind on her cheek. No honey-eyed spirit to lie and lure her. Nothing.

"Lilly . . ."

The maybe-whisper came from behind her, and she spun, heart pounding. But there was nothing there, just the stark stone face with its trailing vines.

A crack of rock from below jerked through her, and she leaned over the edge. "Penn?"

The tops of a bush shook, and her breath came faster as she saw a masculine silhouette working its way up the switchback path. One hand on her hat, the other on the rock face, she leaned, her expression going sour as Kevin looked up at her, unmistakable in heavy denim pants, plaid shirt, work boots, and a hat and sunglasses.

Kevin? Damn it, what is he doing here? Frustrated, Lilly leaned back into the rock, jerking forward when it felt as if something gave behind her. "I told you to stay off my land!"

"Leave? But I heard you call me," Kevin said, the cadence of his words having the sound of the wind.

Lilly started, her expression going slack as she turned back to the drop-off. It wasn't Kevin, it was Penn. Even his stance was different, poised to move effortlessly, graceful as he took the last switchback, the new sun shining on his stubbled cheeks. He looked even better in the sun than the moonlight. "Y-you," she stammered, backing up almost into the cave as he lifted himself up the last bit and rolled gracefully to a stand.

Penn held his hands out to the rising sun, fingers spread and smiling. "It feels different up here. Sharp. It almost hurts, the sun rises so fast." Head tilting, he eyed her. "I had almost forgotten how stunning sunrises can be—with the right woman beside you."

"But . . ."

He took a step toward her, and she recoiled, holding a hand out in warning. "Don't touch me."

Penn stopped short, his gaze going to her hand. "You're bleeding."

Lilly froze. His hand slipped into hers, both familiar and new, sending a shiver through her. Was this Kevin, or was it Penn? Maybe she was going crazy after all. "You can touch me," she said in awe, feeling a cool sensation that seeped under her skin to cool the heat of the day.

His smile dove deep into her, kindling a spark. "I can touch you. Thank you, Lilly, for believing me."

Her eyes closed as he gently took her in his arms, and they slid backward into the dark, the vines rustling until they were surrounded by the earth. She let him move her, praying that he wouldn't look up and see the stick of dynamite. His lips touched her neck under her ear, and she exhaled softly. It felt so good to be desired. His touch was gentle, reverent, and she wished it wasn't a lie.

"I thought about you all night," he said, and she remembered his eyes, glowing in the dark on her bridge like a wild thing come to seduce her with the promise of life. "Did you think of me?"

She couldn't stop her shiver as his hand dropped to the small of her back and gently pulled her closer. "I thought about what you said," she murmured, turning her head to draw away from his lips, but he only traced a line of sensation down her neck.

"You are amazing," he breathed.

She looked up at him, knowing she was playing with the devil. "I want to believe," she lied. This was for her children. This was for her mother. She would not allow her mother's pain to be for nothing.

Still, he smiled, the faint light coming past the vines tinged with red as it struck them. "Believing is the easiest thing in the world. Just ask any child singing in the dusk at the edge of the forest. You, Lilly, will be my everything. I promise. It will be different this time."

Oh God, he was touching her again, his hands slipping under her shirt to grip her waist, his thumbs pushing at her midriff, massaging, hinting at what he might do.

"You will be my world," he whispered, his words moving her hair, and she wanted to believe. "I will love you forever, and we will do everything, go everywhere."

She pushed back, blinking when she saw Kevin's brown eyes, not

Penn's golden ones, but the confident smile and heat of passion were there, and she knew it was the spirit. "Show me," she demanded, and his smile widened as he bent to her, lips parted.

She gave in to her desires, meeting his passion with her own, standing in the shadowed sun between earth and sky as he met her mouth, hungry for all, for everything. *To live,* she thought, feeling everything as sharp and new as if she'd never felt the kiss of the sun or caress of the wind. Each touch was a shock through her, each soft sound drove her to more daring, more freedom. His hands were a demanding pressure, and she pressed into him, feeling a rising desire.

His hands rose, a thumb running under the curve of her breast, and she pulled away as a thrill of adrenaline ran though her. Wild, his eyes met hers, enticing, daring, promising more as his hands moved unceasing, and she panted, wanting it to never end. But it would. They all screwed it up in the end. "Do you promise?" she breathed, a trembling hand shifting a lock of hair from his eyes. "I want to hear it."

"Everything," he whispered, and she ran her hands down his body to feel him, to see his response, shuddering his delight at her touch.

It was enough, and she hooked a finger in the top of his jeans, pulling him deeper into the cave. Only now did she allow a wicked smile to play about her lips, and seeing it, he held her tighter as they moved, his hands always shifting, changing pressure and demand like the pulse of the world across her. "Tell me you're not a ghost," she said as they found the comforting dark of the back, and her shoulders pressed into rock. "That you'll never leave me."

The heat of him covered her, and he kissed her neck, his teeth sending jolts through her. "Give me this, and I'll be beside you every morning. I promise."

It was what she wanted to hear. His hand tugged at the hem of her shirt, and she moved sinuously, raising her arms and letting him take it from her. The darkness brushed her, raising tingles, and then his lips as he found her. Her head flung back, and she gripped his hair, encouraging him as her leg twined about him.

"You are everything to me, Lilly," he said, her breast going cool where his lips had been. "Everything. I promise you everything."

His lips found her again, and she arched her back as his hand ran lower, finding the curve of her back, and then lower yet, tugging her into him. All but oblivious with desire, she found his zipper and lowered it tantalizingly slowly as he pulled upon her, mirroring her tease. She was gasping when the zipper would move no more, and almost she was willing to abandon herself to the lie of Penn to have this . . . forever.

And with that thought, her resolve came rushing back. It was a lie. Nothing was forever.

"Wait. Wait!" she gasped, and he made a growl of frustration, pinning her shoulder to the wall.

"I have waited forever," he said, his eyes inches from hers, the glow of her passion reflected in them.

"Then you can wait thirty seconds more," she said, reaching past his zipper to find him. "Wait."

Eyes shut, he trembled as she touched him. Slowly they opened as she reluctantly left him, and he moved aside and let go of her shoulder to make it clear he was indeed . . . waiting. "I have watched you grow up, Lilly. I have seen your tears, and I have dried them. I will wait," he said as she pushed herself in motion, her pace unsteady and her pulse fast as she moved from him. Every step was hard, every motion cried out that she was a fool. Yes, men lied. Yes, they were stupid. But the way he had made her feel, the power she had over him . . . The power he had over her . . .

She turned, seeing his eyes glowing gold at the back of the cave. Her thoughts turned to Meg and Em, to her mother a tender fourteen. He was a monster. It would end here.

"But I will not wait forever," he said, and staggering, she picked her shirt up.

"You won't have to." Feet stumbling on the uneven floor, she fumbled for a candle, lighting it from the lantern still glowing by the door.

"Lilly?"

Shaking, she lit the fuse, the sparks as it ignited making her resolute fear easy to see.

"Lilly."

He was unsure but clueless, and she steadily paced to the front of the cave, her blood cooling and her ardor already ash. "Good-bye, Penn."

"Lilly!" he shouted, but she ducked outside, putting her back to the wall as the earth shook and a billow of cool dust and rock-chip cloud exploded from the opening.

"Lilly!" he screamed, but she wasn't sure if it was real or in her mind.

The second explosion was stronger, and she fell, arms grasping for anything, finding nothing to hold as she was thrown down the steep incline. Her breath came out in a cry as she slammed into a tree, and she looked up in awe as the rock face high above cracked and slid down, covering the opening that the first explosion had sealed.

Lilly!

The rumble of earth was only in her memory, and the waving trees stilled. In the near distance, a jay screamed. She stared at the raw cut of stone, seeing the shimmering line of a spider ballooning on the early rising air. The perfect fragility of it was shocking against the raw destruction. It glinted blood red in the sun, going invisible as it touched the stone now covering the opening and seemed to vanish. Another joined it, and then a third.

Lilly turned away. Her shirt was in her hand, and she looked at it numbly. Slowly, arms aching and thigh bruised, she put her shirt back on and turned her face away from the woods and to the sun. Her children waited. Her mother would be worried.

Blinking, Lilly picked her way back to the open meadow. Before her the sun rose like a goddess, powerful, uncaring, and blood-red.

 FIVE

The creek's chatter was absent as Lilly emerged from the forest, trudging past the barn to the house. Damp rocks glistened in the bright sun, the bridge spanning an empty gully. The water was gone.

Her mother had not been in the henhouse when she had gone by, and there was a clatter of silverware and cheerful, high-pitched voices coming through the kitchen window. Numb and depressed, Lilly wearily walked up the porch steps, hesitating at the top a moment before going in. The scent of fresh biscuits and eggs drifted out, making her stomach clench.

Pepper whined at the screen door, and her mother looked up from the counter, a damp cloth in her hand and an apron around her waist. Her hair was in an unusual disarray, and she glared at Lilly, understandably angry. Behind her, the kitchen table was empty of all but one place setting. Lilly pulled the screen door open, not responding when the girls at the sink splashed each other. Em was on a stool but still almost chest high with the counter as she studiously washed their breakfast plates.

"I'm sorry," Lilly said, her eyes rising from the unused plate on the table, and her mother went to the girls, her lips pressed tight as her old hands lightly touched their backs in an expression of security.

"I'll get the rest, loves. You go on out to the barn. Make a fort out of the straw bales or something. Your mother and I will finish cleaning up."

In a happy chatter and dropping suds, they flowed out of the kitchen, long hair and cries of "Hi, Mom!" streaming behind them.

The screen door slammed shut, and still Lilly stood, just inside the door of her mother's house, her arms around her middle. Penn was trapped, doomed to die maybe if he stayed out of a tree long enough. So why did she feel like a little girl who had hidden the broken cookie jar? *He had been so beautiful, so dangerous.*

"I can't believe you locked me in the chicken coop." Motions abrupt, her mother went to the sink to finish the dishes.

"I said I was sorry." Coming in, she tried to wash her hands to help, only to find herself rebuffed. "I didn't want you to hurt yourself."

"Like crawling through that chicken hole was easy? I could have used your help this morning out at Rock Island."

Lilly's head came up. "Doing what?"

Her mother huffed, setting the last rinsed plate to drip. "What do you think? I managed okay, but we're going to need to let a nest or two of eggs go to hatching. I was up all night thinking of how we could snare Penn without having to burn the woods." Her gaze went distant as she looked out at the fields, seeing nothing. "I love that woods."

She turned as the dishwater gurgled out. "Running water will hold him as much as stone, so I forced him into that tree on Rock Island, and once he was there, I shifted the water course back where it was when your grandparents moved here. The dam was almost rotted anyway. We lost the creek running by the house, but that's a small price to pay. Even in drought, Rock Island is going to be surrounded." Her expression softened. "The girls are safe. We all are."

Then who did I trap in the cave?

Seeing her horror and not understanding, her mother reached out and touched her shoulder. "Honey, it's okay. It's not the first time I've been locked in a henhouse."

Lilly reached for the table, her balance leaving her. Kevin. She hadn't killed him, had she? "You couldn't have trapped him in a tree. I trapped him in a cave," she said, feeling nauseated and sinking down on her chair at the table.

Her mother turned from putting the plates away, her confident smile fading. "What?"

What if she'd been wrong? She looked up, blinking. "He was with me this morning. At the caves by the north pasture. I trapped Penn in it behind a rock slide."

"You couldn't have," her mother said, her face pale. "I trapped him on Rock Island."

Lilly looked at the table, her fingers spanning the little red apples the plastic and felt tablecloth was decorated with, horror making it hard to breathe.

"Lilly . . ."

Had she killed Kevin by mistake? Oh God, what if she had!

Her mother's hand was shaking as it touched her shoulder, the older woman looking out through the kitchen window when a dusty police car eased into the yard. "It's Aaron," she said, her voice quavering.

Kevin's dad? Oh God.

Her mother gave her shoulder a warning squeeze. "We don't know that wasn't Penn in the cave. He might have escaped before I got the water to rise. You did good, Lilly. I'm proud of you."

Lilly stood, her chair scraping. "But it might have been Kevin! Mom, he might still be trapped. Alive!"

"What does Kevin have to do with this?"

A car door slammed, and Lilly scooted closer to her mother, almost frantic. "Penn looked like Kevin. Mom, what if it really was him?"

Lips a thin line, her mother flicked her attention to the porch. "It wasn't. Hush up!"

"Mom!"

"I said hush up!" It was an angry hiss of a sound, and Lilly jerked as her mother pinched her shoulder painfully. "What are the chances that I could trap him a second time? I'm an old woman, and he doesn't love me. Penn was with you. That was *Penn* with you before sunrise. If we open that cave up now, Penn will escape and he will be on Meg and Em before the moon rises. Now stop looking guilty!"

The last was accompanied by a savage squeeze, and then her mother let go, beaming a welcoming smile at the heavy steps on the porch and a soft knock at the screen door.

"Aaron, come on in!" her mother almost crowed, wiping her hands off on her apron and going to the door. "Let me get you a cup of coffee. What brings you out here this morning?"

The man looked tired as he pushed open the screen door, his officer uniform hanging wrinkled and a little loose on him. He was her mother's age, and working mostly because he knew everyone and he couldn't bring himself to retire. Pepper had gone to him, and he absently fondled the dog's ears as he nodded first at her mother, then Lilly. "Morning, Em. Lilly. You haven't seen Kevin this morning, have you?" he drawled, his cigarette-rough voice holding a hint of worry as he glanced at the unused place setting.

Fear struck Lilly, and she froze. They would take her children. Lock her away. "Last night, why?" she managed as she gathered the silverware, her fingers shaking. Behind her, her mother went to the coffeepot.

Aaron shifted from foot to foot, looking nothing like a police officer and everything like a worried father. "We found his truck this morning over at Perrot's pasture, his thermos of coffee still warm. You saw him last night?"

Oh God. She'd killed him. What if she had invented Penn all along, a delusion fueled by her anger and her mother's dementia, striking out at Kevin instead. Maybe she had *wanted* to kill him. What if she was crazy herself? "About nine," she heard herself say as she carefully put the knife and fork away, marveling at the even tone of her voice. "The girls were going to bed. I wanted to talk to him about . . ." She hesitated, not wanting to mention her earlier worries about her mother being crazy. ". . . something," she finished as she turned and went back for the pale white plate. "But he left. He didn't make it home last night?"

"By the looks of it, yes. You know anything about the explosion I heard this morning?" he said, and fear shifted through her.

"That was us, I'm afraid," her mother said, setting a steaming cup of coffee at table and putting a warning hand upon her shoulder. "I know I should have gotten a permit, but I was hoping that if we blew the dam early enough, no one would notice."

Lilly marveled at her mother's calm lie, wondering if she had ever known her at all.

"We shifted the creek back to its original bed this morning," she said as she gave Lilly's shoulder one last squeeze and returned to the coffeepot. "The girls are getting older, and I want to try beans in the lower field next year. We have enough to get by, but Meg is going to need tuition in a few years, and the creek isn't making us any money running in front of our house."

"You were both at Rock Island?"

Aaron didn't sound convinced, and Lilly turned to him, somehow managing a smile as she leaned back against the counter, the dust and dirt of the explosion covering her like the lies she was saying. "All morning. You're not going to turn us in, are you? That was the last of the dynamite."

Aaron's gaze shifted to her mother, then back to her. "Lilly, I know you and he had words."

Fear flashed through her. They would take her, lock her up. She'd never see her girls again. "He wanted to know how he could make it better. I told him to leave," she said evenly.

"I would hope so!" her mother said as she forced a steaming cup of coffee into Lilly's grip and putting a hand upon her shoulder. "I love your son as if he were my own, Aaron, but he's a fool who doesn't know how to keep his pants zipped. If he's not hightailed it out of Greenwood out of pure embarrassment, I'm sure he'll show up before long. I poured you a cup. You want to sit a spell?"

Aaron took a long look at her mother standing beside her. From outside, the sound of the girls playing in the drying creek came in, and Pepper whined, wanting to join them. "Thank you, Em. Don't mind if I do," he finally said, his eyes narrowing in mistrust as he sat down.

"I've got some biscuits," Lilly said, heart thudding. "Fresh out of the oven, Officer Aaron. Let me get you a plate."

And smiling, Lilly held it out to him, proud that her hand didn't tremble at all.

GRACE

The character of Grace has a curious history. She began before the Hollows found publication in a preindustrial setting that had far more scope than I gave her here. Her world was originally smaller and the narration of her story was split between the protagonist and antagonist. I had intended to leave those first hundred pages of text forgotten in the back of my closet after I fell in love with the faster pace and more modern feel of urban fantasy, but the characters of Grace, her lover, and the protagonist refused to be forgotten and Grace successfully made the jump from medieval to modern, proving to me at least that the character is all and the setting is just the framework of the tale. Originally Grace came to me as an older character, but I give you a glimpse of her now when she is young and full of hope so you can understand her better when she falls.

 ONE

Ears down, Hoc hung back as Grace and Boyd got out of the shiny black sedan with its one-way-locking back doors and secondary restraints masquerading as seat belts. Most times they didn't need the extra precautions, but the dog's behavior as he reluctantly jumped from the front seat and padded alongside Grace told her that this was not going to be an easy acquisition. Not that any of them were.

"Hoc's edgy."

Grace gave Boyd a wry smile. The thin, older man was almost a head taller than she was, a bad cop to her more youthful good cop—at least that was the appearance they usually went with. Sun glinted in his silvering hair, and his long legs easily took up the distance as he came around the car to meet her on the sidewalk. They weren't cops, but the thought was there, especially since they were both in dark navy suits, the stark white of Boyd's cuffs and collar matching her blouse in an almost uniform consistency.

"I noticed." Grace waited, her hand on Hoc's head, soothing her canine partner with a gentle warming flow of energy. He was agitated at something in the house. It wasn't the same excitement he showed when they visited kindergartners looking for unregistered throws among the kids, oblivious that their lives might change if Hoc loved them too much. Like a drug dog, he would go into doggy delight when finding an unbalanced throw, attracted to the tiny surges of electricity most gave off. No, this was something else, and Grace squinted up at the two-story, four-bedroom, two-car garage house.

Suburbia at its best, and she felt a brief pang. She'd grown up somewhere very close to this—until it had all fallen apart.

Hoc's ears pricked as three kids on skateboards rumbled down the shady road with loud voices and not having a care in the world. It was nice, peaceful. *Well, we can change that*, Grace thought as she pushed off the black car and fell into step beside Boyd.

The walk was cobblestone, matching the drive in a show of wealth as it gently sloped upward to a large porch decorated for Halloween. Frowning, Boyd checked his watch. The innocuous-looking instrument actually functioned as an informal erg meter as well as a timepiece. If the watch was running, he had control of his balance, if it was stopped, he knew he'd lost it somewhere.

Grace glanced at her own watch, seeing the second hand sweeping the face smoothly, but she knew things could change fast—especially when they were escorting an unregistered throw. That's what humans who could shift the balance of energy existing naturally in the human body were called. Throws, or throwbacks. That Grace and Boyd were throwbacks themselves never seemed to mean anything to those they tried to bring in.

Head down, she hit a button to tag the time for the medics as one where her watch's time might be impacted by the kid they were after. The medics checked it weekly, and if her time was off by more than thirty seconds without a reason, she had to go in for a refresher course on control. It hadn't happened in six years. Hoc had her on edge. The boy was older than usual. It made things tricky.

They mounted the stairs together, Boyd's steps in perfect time with hers and the border collie's nails scraping. *It's for his own good*, she thought as they left the tidy green yard, the absence of toys and bikes saying as much as the report in the car that there were no other children. Most parents stopped having kids when one showed signs of being a throw. But then, most parents brought their kids to a Strand "party" to be assessed after they shorted out the TV one too many times, charting their life for service in the Strand if they had enough control and/or aptitude, or quietly adjusted to remove the ability if they didn't.

Still, there would always be misguided parents who managed to hide their children's abilities until a mistake was made and an anonymous call brought Grace or any one of the Strand's envoys to collect, instruct, and administer to—in that order and not always with the parents' or child's approval.

Grace and Boyd were collectors. She was good at it, though it chafed that she was still doing the same thing after four years. Her knack in evaluating potential initiates was to blame. "Attention to Duty" her yearly evaluation said, but the honest truth as to why she was so good at bringing in the difficult cases was because she had run herself and she knew what scared the shit out of them.

"You okay?" Boyd asked as he tagged his own watch for possible disruption and knocked at the door. On the knocker was a smiling pumpkin with Happy Halloween stenciled on it. Grace's brow furrowed. It was too perfect here, like a Hollywood set.

"Fine," she said, hearing the dull echo of fiberglass. Hoc's ears pricked as he stared expectantly at the door.

"I just don't want you messing with my times," Boyd said distantly. Again he knocked, then rang the doorbell. "I'm having enough trouble staying in norms as it is."

Grace turned, seeing his avoidance. "You're having balance issues? Why didn't you tell me?"

He glanced at her and away, his wrinkles making him look old to her for the first time. "I just did," he said, then cleared his throat at the sound of approaching footsteps.

Sure, but only when I can't say anything, she thought, as the door opened and a tall woman in jeans and a baggy sweater looked out at them. Her haircut was short, styled and highlighted in the latest middle-aged fashion. Expression questioning, she took in their suits, paling as she saw the car behind them. Hand gripping the door, she ducked behind it, almost hiding. "Can I help you?"

Can I help you, Grace thought. Not *no thank you,* or *not interested.* She knew who they were and what they wanted, and Grace's skin tingled. At her heel, Hoc wagged his tail, and she suppressed her excitement. Excitement didn't unbalance her erg strength, but it didn't help maintain it, either.

"Mrs. Thomson?" Boyd said, his deep voice rumbling.

"Yes?" She was scared, and Hoc's tail slowed as it brushed the porch. "What do you want?"

Grace dropped a hand onto Hoc's head to ease the animal's stress. "Mrs. Thomson. I'm Grace Evans, and this is my partner, Boyd. It has come to the Strand's attention that—"

The woman ducked behind the door, slamming it hard enough that the pumpkin on the knocker flopped against the fiberglass with a little thump. At her feet, Hoc whined.

Boyd and Grace didn't even look at each other. It was obvious the woman was just behind the door; they hadn't heard her walk away. A moment of pity washed through Grace, and then it was gone, forced out by common sense. The woman's son could throw energy. He needed to be assessed and trained so he wouldn't be a menace to himself or anyone else.

"My God," Grace complained loud enough for the woman to hear. "It's not as if we're going to give him a lobotomy."

Standing straighter, Boyd knocked lightly on the door again. "Mrs. Thomson? Your son has been documented throwing in vivo energy.

We're not going to harm or change him. But for his and your own safety, he needs to be evaluated for control and depth of ability."

You don't want him to accidentally burn your house down after he's had one too many lattes because you asked him to take out the garbage. Staring at the door, Grace grimaced. It had been more than that. Lots more.

"Can we please talk to you for a moment?" Boyd tried again.

Grace held up a hand, and Boyd went silent. Together they leaned to the door, listening.

"They're going to brainwash and castrate me, Mom!" a young, understandably frightened voice said. That was another well-touted fallacy. Unless you were in one of the more energy-rich jobs, having children was encouraged. The Strand didn't brainwash anyone either. True, most throws worked for the Strand, but once you retired, you could work for any number of industries—if you were careful.

"He's going to run . . ." Boyd said, and Grace nodded.

"Either that, or blow up the house," she muttered as a tingle went through her. Together she and Boyd looked at their watches. They had stopped. The boy had lots of power, with just a shade less control. This was going to be nasty.

"You brought the sedative, right?" Boyd's tone was joking, but the question was real enough.

Grace cocked her hip, watching Hoc's pricked ears for any sign of the seventeen-year-old sneaking out the back door. "Mrs. Thomson, if you refuse to talk to us, a second team will be here in thirty minutes to break down your door and forcibly take your son." It was a lie, and as Boyd looked at Grace, she shrugged. "I'm in a hurry." He cracked a smile to show his long teeth.

"You can't do this! It's against the law!" the woman shouted from behind the door.

"Yes we can." Grace checked her watch. "Knowingly harboring an unregistered throw is punishable by fines that will take your house and leave you penniless." That part was true.

A whisper of pity went through her, and she lowered her voice, knowing there was a hushed argument going on by Hoc's cocked head. "I know it's hard, Mrs. Thomson. I've been on the other side of the door myself. If Zach sees you cooperating, he won't be scared. We're here to help both of you."

This too, she believed. She had to. Putting on a suit didn't divorce you from your humanity, even though she wondered about some of her superiors. But even in the best of acquisitions there was anxiety and fear.

At her feet, Hoc whined. The door cracked open, and a frightened half-face showed. "He's my only son. I can't lose him."

Relief swept through her, and Grace smiled. "I'm my grandmother's only living grandchild. We had lunch yesterday. We're not here to take Zach from you, Mrs. Thomson. You're encouraged to come with us, to be there to help him make this decision. It's a chance for him to have a say in his future. Please don't start his new life with unnecessary fear."

Hoc waved his tail, and Mrs. Thomson opened the door wider. Outside on the street, a van drove by, slowing when the driver saw the black car. "You can both do what he can?"

"Yes, ma'am." Boyd ran a hand over his silvering hair. "The Strand taught me what to avoid and how to control the rest, and I went on to get a free ride at the college of my choice and a steady paycheck after that."

It had been a bit different for her, but he was right about the steady pay—not that she ever had much use for it.

Hoc's ears pricked, and he stood, tail waving as he trotted off the porch. Tension slammed into Grace, and Boyd stiffened. Zach had left the house.

Seeing their expression shift, the woman's eyes widened. "Please come in," she said, flinging the door open. "I'll go get him."

From behind the garage, a motorcycle engine revved and roared.

Shoes scraping, Boyd ran for the car. Grace followed, while Hoc tore after the scooter that skidded out from behind the garage, almost spinning out of control when it jumped the curb and fishtailed down the street.

Belying his age, Boyd slid across the top of the hood. He was in the car and starting it before Grace had even lifted the latch to the door. "I hate it when they run," she muttered as she fastened her seat belt, knowing Boyd wasn't going to slow down for anything. He liked a good chase as much as she did.

Hoc was vanishing down the avenue after Zach. The boy was hunched on his bike, no helmet, sneakers and a white T-shirt making him look vulnerable. Impressed his cycle was still running, Grace reached for the radio, her hand dropping in disgust. Damn, he had fried it.

"No, wait! Come back!" his mother was crying as she ran down the cobbled walk, her hands waving. Boyd hit the gas, and Grace rechecked her belt.

"I don't know if I should be impressed or worried as all hell that he didn't stall his bike," Boyd said, and Grace reached out the open window to put a flashing light on the roof as they raced through an empty four-way stop.

They weren't gaining, and knowing that she could find Hoc anywhere given enough time, Grace braced herself against a turn and tried to open the map. The GPS was gone, too. It wasn't hard to insulate a vehicle, but all the little gadgets were harder. That Zach had enough power to unconsciously short out their watches yet enough control to save his bike said a lot. Successfully bringing him in might get her enough kudos to demand a transfer to the elite. It wasn't that she didn't like collecting, but she wanted more—so much so that it hurt.

"Steak dinner says he's heading for the expressway," Grace said as they careened around the corner. Zach was taking them through a small cluster of light commercial buildings, and people scrambled back onto the sidewalk as cars beeped at them. "He's going to have to go through an industrial park. Take the next main right. We can cut him off."

Hand gripping the car frame, Grace braced her feet as Boyd jostled over a railroad track. Just that fast, they were free of people, and Boyd stepped on the gas. The wind pushed through her hair, and she leaned forward, enjoying it. Grace squinted past the waving strands as Boyd raced down a dusty industrial road, lights flashing but no siren.

Zach had fried their watches, so anything that happened from here on out could be justified as necessary force, but no one would thank them if this ended with the local power grid collapsing. Blaming the power outage on a squirrel caught in a transformer only worked once. All she cared about though was finding Zach before he learned enough to become a real threat—if it wasn't too late already. There were ways to increase the amount of ergs you could throw, and figuring out that cup of coffee in the morning was why you could now toast your bread with a finger was not hard.

She could feel him . . . a spot of energy sizzing like a worn tension wire, and she pulled her windblown hair out of her mouth. "I think we're in front of him," she said, and Boyd nodded.

"I can hear his bike. How do you want to do this?"

Grace thought of the blast of polarity that had exploded from Zach when he had run, frying their car's gadgets and stopping their watches. He had enough aptitude and guts to know how to use it, and probably enough caffeine in him to accidentally kill someone. "I'm open to suggestions . . ."

Taking a slow breath, Boyd reached into an inner jacket pocket and pulled out a candy bar.

Seeing it, Grace felt herself go cold. "Boyd . . ." she warned, turning where she sat as he slowed the car and parked in the shade of a quiet building. Caffeine could boost their power, but it made their abilities unpredictable. It wasn't illegal for them to eat it, but like a drug, it was easy to get hooked, lured into believing you could handle the increased power until they found you dead of an overdose, your heart fried by your own brain. *Shit. He said he'd been having balance issues . . .*

"You're not going to tell on me, are you?" he said, smiling sickly as he fumbled unfamiliarly at the plastic wrapper.

"Boyd, how long have you been . . . Stop!" she yelled when he crammed half of it in his mouth. "Are you crazy?"

"No, I'm scared," he said around his full mouth. "Grace, I'm losing it. This is the only thing keeping me on the street working."

He got out. Grace sat where she was, stunned. Her partner was a booster. He wasn't able to keep his levels up, and he was relying on self-dosing caffeine to find it. There was an unregistered throw coming at them at forty-five miles per hour on a bike, and her partner was going to do something incredibly stupid.

She looked at her watch, having forgotten Zach had fried it. Outside the car, Boyd crouched to look in the window. Guilt pinched his aged eyes.

"He's insulated his bike. I need to give it one hell of a pull. I can't do it without the boost. I'll stop the bike, you stop him."

"Then you'd better drop him, because I'm not chasing after him if you're high on caffeine," she said, and the sound of the bike grew closer. *Damn it, her partner was boosting. How long? How long had he been doing this?*

"I only ate half," he grumped as she got out. "I know what I'm doing!"

Boyd gestured for her to cross the street to get out of his blast radius. Nervous, she jogged across the broken cement, not liking this but not knowing what else to do. Boyd had been throwing energy longer than she'd been alive. She remembered eating her Halloween candy as a little girl, and then exploding pumpkins afterward to get rid of the extra energy. It hadn't been the pumpkins that had given her away to the authorities.

The *brum, brum* of the bike grew louder, and Boyd ambled out into the middle of the street, adjusting his suit to look like a gunslinger. "Zach! Stop your bike!" he shouted when the scared kid turned a corner and slowed, taking in the new situation. Grace tensed when he gunned it.

"Bad choice," she said, checking her motion to run into the street when the kid angled his bike right at her partner.

Boyd calmly scooped up a bent pipe, swinging it dramatically in a loop over his head, gathering the energy his cells could burn in a day into one microsecond pulse. With a yell that echoed as loud as the bike, he threw the pipe at the bike.

Zach swerved and the pipe hit the ground in front of him. Hitting him wasn't Boyd's intention, and Grace's brow pinched in fear when a visible line of blue energy arched from Boyd to the pipe, stretching between them as a bridge of power.

A sparkle of black raced from Boyd's outstretched hand following the trace. It hit the pipe and jumped to Zach. Grace cowered, hiding her head when a boom of force exploded from it, knocking Zach from his bike and shattering windows. In the distance, a car alarm went off. Even farther away, an industrial klaxon began honking. *Now we've done it*, she thought as Hoc limped into view at the end of the street. Seeing her, he loped forward.

Zach's bike slid twenty feet, without Zach on it. The kid slowly sat up, his jeans torn and his arm bleeding. Her eyes darted to her partner. He was down on one knee, and as she watched, Boyd clutched at his left arm and fell to both his knees.

"Boyd!" she screamed, running to him.

Zach staggered to his feet. "I'm not *ever* going to be one of you!" he cried out, shambling into a shaky run.

She slid to a stop beside Boyd. He was ashen faced, his expression drawn and in pain. "Boyd, are you breathing? Is your heart okay?" she exclaimed, holding his shoulders and keeping him upright.

"I'm okay," he wheezed, clearly not. "Get the . . . little bastard."

She hesitated in indecision, and he pushed her to go as Hoc limped up to them, his ears down and his tail tucked.

"Get him!" Boyd shouted, shoving her again. "I'm okay!"

Breathless, she stood. Feeling she was making a mistake, she looked at the silent buildings. "Hoc. Who do you love?" she said, using the words for him to find throws among innocent children.

Hoc brightened at the clear order, and he ran to a closed machinist shop across the street. Heart despairing, she followed, thinking of the chocolate bar Boyd had eaten. She couldn't hide what he'd done, but by the looks of it, he'd been boosting for some time. God! Her partner was playing with fire. How was she going to explain this?

The tip of Hoc's tail flashed white as he slipped into the building ahead of her, and she followed. The three-story echoing building was dark, the windows boarded up, and she listened as she tried to slow her breathing as her eyes adjusted. Hoc was deep in the building somewhere, and a sharp, angry bark brought her head up to the old offices that ringed the upper floor.

"Upstairs. Why can't it ever be down?" she panted as she grabbed the cold iron pipe banister and started up. A wave of force passed through her, and she yelped, letting go of the metal. Outside came the pop of a transformer blowing. Shit.

But when Hoc yipped in pain, her heart thumped.

"Hoc!" Scared, she thumped up the stairs, two at a time. The sun made a dirty smear of light through the dirt-caked skylights ten feet above her head. Dusty beams almost a foot wide made a long aisle of empty space where work desks once stood. The sound of breaking glass drew her attention to Zach kicking out a window at the far end of the room. He looked at her, flipping her off before he angled a foot through the new opening and slipped onto the roof of the adjacent building.

Hoc was down on the dusty floor, and she ran to him, sliding to a kneel and gathering his head up into her hands. His gums were pale when she pulled his lips back, and there was no breath coming from his nose.

"You son of a bitch!" she screamed after Zach as she dug her hands into Hoc's fur, finding his skin with hers. Her dog. He had tried to kill her dog!

Pushed by her grief, she sent her thoughts deep into the core of her body. Frantic, she exhaled, willing the energy in her body to shift, to flow in an ever-growing wave from her feet to her hands buried in Hoc's ruff. A blast such as Boyd's lacked finesse, and the control for this was exacting. Too much, and she would kill Hoc outright. Too little, and she would fail to restart his heart and he would die. She could have gone into the medical field if she hadn't had her sights set on the elite.

Between the space of one heartbeat and the next, Grace gathered all the free energy in her, then spun her thoughts around again and again until she had drawn an entire day's worth of energy into her hands. It had to be perfect, and the strain of holding it back ached through her.

"Hoc!" she cried, releasing her hold. With a tiny pop, the energy dove from her, struggling to equalize. It arced through the dog, jolting him.

Sobbing, Grace felt her hands slip from Hoc as the room dim with the light eking in the dirty windows began to spin. She couldn't get enough air, but to take a deep breath seemed like too hard a task. Her body was depleted. It had been too much. It hadn't been enough.

Cold, she fell over.

A wet nose nudged her, wiggling under her arm and snuggling against her. Relief penetrated the thick haze, making it hard to think. Hoc was alive, his back nails digging painfully into her as he tried to get closer. Mumbling, her eyes closed and she shushed him.

It would be okay, she thought, smiling as she slowly lost consciousness, her body struggling to recover. It would be okay.

 TWO

T
he greasy smell of fat-slap layered itself over the scents of anti-septic and latex in a familiar, yet totally unappetizing smell that reminded her of her early days in the Strand, a young girl struggling to find her place and her balance, both in her body and with those around her.

Not much has changed, Grace thought sourly as she adjusted the collar of her borrowed sweat suit and continued down the hospital's hall in a slow, steady pace to hide her fatigue. She hated sweats, but the gown she'd left in the nurse's gym was even worse. She couldn't sneak out wearing a gown. Sweats would be hard enough. Hoc at her heel didn't help, either, but the dog had refused to leave her side and was known enough in the compound to be allowed to stay. As the only border collie on base, Hoc stood out.

Grace tried to give off an air of health and efficiency as she nodded smartly to the orderly standing at the elevator. Suspicious, he angled to watch her as she passed the nurses' desk, Hoc's nails clicking on the tile. The hair on the back of her neck prickled, but she was still on hospital grounds. She could be down here if she wanted.

The commissary was on this level, and the smell of fat-slap was making her feel nauseated, even as she found her stomach rumbling. The protein-rich slop was full of complex carbs and slow-digesting proteins that would help regulate her body chemistry, but it tasted worse than its name sounded. That she would devour it ravenously when her reserves were depleted as they were now was just disgusting.

Grace breathed a sigh of relief as the elevator dinged, and she snapped her fingers for Hoc's attention and continued down the hall as the orderly forgot about her. She was looking for Boyd, not having much luck since the nurses on her floor were taciturn and uncooperative, and word got around.

She didn't need coddling; she needed to be moving. It wasn't the first time she'd depleted herself into exhaustion. It wouldn't be the last.

Hoc in tow, Grace passed an informal living room with wide windows looking out onto the parking lot and the sun-drenched park beyond. The sterile furniture looked hardly comfortable enough for a quick sit-down to catch your breath before hobbling back to your room. The room was empty, but Hoc's ears had pricked, his pace expectant as he trotted ahead of her a few doors and nosed one open.

A welcoming hail drifted into the hall, and Grace's slight frown eased. Recognizing Boyd's voice, she knocked with one knuckle on the thick, overly large door, smiling as the almost-baby-talk of her partner to Hoc turned into a more confident "Come in, Grace."

Still smiling, she eased in past the door. The low morning sun spilled into the private room. Boyd was up, sitting at the tiny table, his robe showing his hairy legs and bony feet in his bland slippers as he gave Hoc an expert ear rub, the dog happily standing with his front paws on the man's knees. It was probably the first time she'd ever seen Boyd out of a suit, and he looked vulnerable and tired with his gray hair untidy and uncombed. But that was not why her smile froze and faded.

Jason.

The tall, slim man had pushed himself up from the low dresser he'd been sitting against as she had entered, the sun catching his blond hair and the metallic thread woven into his uniform. His expression was confident, his eyes calmly watching her from under his bangs as he waited to see how she was going to react before he reacted in turn. He was like that, and it irritated her how good he was at putting his emotions aside to get the better of an argument.

They'd entered the Strand on the same day, both of them on the same track of study, both aiming for the elite. They'd come from different paths, hers one of shame and fear, his from the joy of discovery and proud parents. Determined to outdo each other when they realized they had the same goals, they bound their fates together. His love had taken the place of the anger in her soul, but he'd been promoted when she had not, and when he won a place in the elite and she was passed over one too many times, they parted ways. Jason wasn't her boss, but as a member of the elite, he outranked her, able to give her orders she was required to follow. The fact that he was here chatting with her partner was not good.

"Jason," she said evenly in greeting, and the two men exchanged an unreadable look. "Good to see you," she lied, forcing her jaw to unclench. My God, it had been four years.

Hoc whined, dropping from Boyd's knees to come to her. Grace snuck a look at her hospital wrist monitor as she ruffled his mane, and he lay down almost on her feet. It wasn't her usual watch hanging about her wrist, the hospital-grade monitor recording milliseconds of erg imbalances. She hadn't been able to take it off like she had the peekaboo gown, and it was irksome. She wasn't an invalid, and it probably had an insulated, building-wide GPS in it.

"I was wondering when you were going to show up," Boyd said, breaking the uncomfortable silence. "Sit. You want some fat-slap? They gave me enough for six people."

He'd turned back to his breakfast, and Grace unwedged her feet from under Hoc. "No thanks," she said as she came forward to give Boyd a hug. He never put his fork down as he gave her a sideways embrace, gesturing again for her to sit. The smell of the fat-slap made her stomach growl, but she wasn't going to eat it even if she was starving. She'd had three portions already this morning. "You're looking good."

Boyd smiled, saluting her with his fork before shoveling in some more. He looked wan, pale with more than the expected drain, especially when his efforts yesterday had been caffeine assisted. The sun coming in made gaunt shadows on his face, accentuating his wrinkles. Sure, he was in his late fifties, but he was sharp as a tack. Three days, and they'd be back on the street looking for Zach.

So why is Jason here?

"Why are you here?" she said bluntly as the man knelt to pet Hoc. The dog had always liked him. He'd been with her when she'd rescued him from the pound.

Jason looked up, making her breath catch with the memories that came back when their eyes met. "Looking for you," he said simply, and her jaw clenched at his voice rolling through her, pulling even more memories into existence. "I figured this would be the best place to start, seeing as the women's nurse desk said you'd left against their orders."

"Not yet, but I'm working on it." She knew he'd smell like gun oil and leather if she got closer, and she forced her jaw to unclench. Again. "How you doing?" she asked Boyd.

The older man eyed them both, fork never slowing. "Fine. I'm not the one they found passed out."

Grace reached a hand down to draw the dog away from Jason. "Hoc is my buddy. I'd do the same for you."

"Almost needed to, from what I heard," Jason said softly, his eyes averted.

Lips pressed, she crossed her arms over her chest and sat on the edge of the untidy bed, one leg drawn up under her so she could face Jason. "They have you behind a desk yet?"

"No, but they're trying."

Damn it, he was smiling at her, and she tried not to fume. It wasn't his fault he'd been promoted. It was her fault for not keeping up. She enjoyed working with Boyd, wouldn't have changed anything. And yet . . .

Both men went silent, and a stab of uncertainty went through her. "What," she said flatly, and Boyd set his fork down.

"Grace," the older man started, and she stiffened, looking from Boyd to Jason's unhappy expression and back to Boyd's resignation.

Shit. "You're fine," she said quickly. "Look at you. That unregistered throw was pulling power like he'd been in the Strand for three years, and you used exactly the right force to stop him, no more. It's only going to take a day or two for you to get balanced."

"Grace."

"Hell, it's going to take me that long just to equalize *my* balance."

"Grace, I'm transferring to the Island."

Her breath went out and didn't come back in again. Cold, she sat back on the edge of the bed, feeling as if she'd been kicked in the gut. "You're not that bad . . ." she whispered, hating that Jason was standing there, a pitying expression on his face.

"Short term. For evaluation," her partner said, but he wouldn't look at her as he pushed his tray away. He was lying.

"But you look great!" she said again. The Island was where they sent half the kids they brought in. It was part hospital, part mental ward, part butcher where they burned out your abilities if you proved to be a danger to society and wouldn't work within the system.

Boyd shifted his chair, looking old in his white robe. "I'm great here," he said, taking her fingers and touching his head with his free hand. "But here is another story," he added, bringing her cold fingers to his heart.

Jason cleared his throat, clearly uncomfortable as he shuffled to the door. "Excuse me, I have to take a call," he said, closing the door softly behind him.

Coward, she thought, her confusion and dismay turning to anger. "They're making you do this, aren't they?" she said hotly, seeing Jason's presence in a new way. "Boyd—"

"Listen to me," he interrupted, but she shook her head, pulse racing as Hoc whined. Boyd had been her partner since day one, her surrogate family when she'd lost all but her grandmother. He couldn't just leave!

"Everyone uses caffeine once in a while. You know when to stop. You're not a addict!"

"Will you shut up!" he said loudly. "I'm trying to tell you something!"

Grace closed her mouth, wide-eyed and panicking. Her world was shifting, and she could do nothing about it.

"Grace, I'm losing it," he said softly, his hands taking hers. "I've been boosting on and off for the last three years just to keep up. I thought I could handle it. I'm sorry. I should have told you sooner. I know you're scared."

"I'm not scared," she said, mouth dry.

"I've talked my options over with Jason. I'm going to the Island to get detoxed and reevaluated."

"Liar," she whispered, and his eye twitched. There was only one reason anyone went to the Island this late in their career. He was leaving her. He was going to get himself burned out and be normal. "You're my partner," she pleaded, sitting down in the chair across from him, still holding his hands in hers. "I don't want another."

He smiled, looking like the father she wished she had had as he took one of his hands from her and tucked a strand of hair behind her ear. "I'm ready to be done," he said, his eyes pinched. "And you are ready for a new partner. You're not too old to train up a new throw. Maybe the same kid who slipped us. Zach has a knack. Lots of power. Just needs some guidance. Like you did not so long ago."

"Boyd," she protested, her chest hurting, but he was shaking his head. He was going to burn himself out. "Don't do this. Please."

Eyes pained, he took a breath to say something, hesitating then at the soft knock on the door. They both looked as Jason came back in, and Grace wiped the back of her hand under her eye and stood. She was not crying, damn it.

"Ah, can I talk to Grace for a moment?" he asked uncertainly. "Business . . ."

Business. As if he wasn't part of it anymore. But Boyd was gesturing for her to go, that same sad smile on him he was wearing when she'd walked in.

"Go on, go," he prompted, pulling his hand from hers and gesturing at the door. "Do good things. I'm proud of you, Grace. You'll go farther than me. That's why I took this job. I should have retired a long time ago, but I wanted to have a few years with you, to be able to say I was there when you learned how to be the best operative the Strand has been graced with."

"Boyd, this is a crock—"

Jason cleared his throat from the door, and Boyd flicked his eyes past her. "Your control is slipping." He ruffled Hoc's collar. "Bye, Sport. Keep Grace from being alone, okay, boy?"

Hoc turned and trotted out as Jason snapped his fingers, and Grace warmed, looking at her monitor. "My control is fine," she said, but Boyd had reached up and pulled her down into a hug. "This is shitty, you know?" She felt as if she was never going to see him again. "If there's anything I can do . . ."

"You just did it," he said, smiling, still smiling as he looked past her. "You'd better go. I'll e-mail you next week and tell you what a double espresso tastes like."

Gut tense, she began to turn away. "I'll get him for both of us."

"I know. Shut the door on your way out, will you?"

She felt sick. Numb, she turned to the door and left, shutting the door softly. Leaning against it, she closed her eyes and tried not to cry. Seeing him like this was hard. He wasn't a caffeine addict. He wasn't! What was she going to do? She didn't want another partner, and to work alone was not accepted.

"I'm sorry."

Her eyes opened, finding Jason waiting for her across the hall with Hoc. Frustrated, she pushed herself up. "He is not a booster," she said, keeping her voice down lest Boyd hear her. "Everyone does caffeine once in a while."

"You don't."

No, she didn't. Not since burning her family's house down when she was sixteen.

Memories of double funerals, of her grandmother steadfastly holding her hand, never blaming and always defending her, hiding her for another year as she rebuilt her life on the framework of guilt and duty.

"Grace, we've been monitoring him for the last eleven months. It was his decision to do this. He turned himself in."

"After you told him you already knew, right?" she snapped, clicking her tongue against her teeth for Hoc as she strode back down the hall.

Jason's feet were loud in his insulating boots as he stomped to catch up. "Why are you mad at me? This wasn't *my* idea."

"I don't have anyone else to be mad at. God, I'm hungry."

"Good." She jerked as he took her arm, but he didn't let go. "I'm ready for a second breakfast myself."

Sick at heart, she couldn't find it in her to keep tugging away from him. Jason hadn't left her. She had left him. "Since when do you eat a second breakfast?"

Sensing a shift, he smiled. "Since I've been brushing up on my joint-operative techniques."

He had something to tell her. She could tell. Hoc, too, knew something was up, and he padded along, waving his tail happily with his two favorite people beside him as the hall became busy.

"You've been working on joint-operative techniques?" she said, looking askance at him as they walked down the hallway, seeing more people the closer they got to the commissary. "Are you taking a demotion?"

"Not exactly, no," he hedged. "It's no secret that you're our best collector in a six-state area, maybe the entire US. The Strand is very interested in you bringing Zach in, especially now. They're impressed with his ability and rudimentary control, and they're not willing to let him go free and you to sit idle for the time it takes to become comfortable working with another operative. As Boyd said, we've worked together before. I've been given leave to help you collect him."

Her eyebrows rose as he opened the big plate-glass doors to the commissary for her and the smell of starch, fat-slap, and fresh bread rolled out, making her even more hungry. It was noisy with the chatter of people, both professionals who worked at the hospital, patients like herself up and around, and even a few uniforms matching Jason's from upstairs where the elite's bosses had their offices. Throws were a close-knit group, and the room was warm and bright with humanity, but she couldn't help the tiny feeling of warning trickling through her.

She might be the Strand's top collector in the field, but Jason was one of their best covert agents. Why would they let him go to help her bring in an unregistered throw, powerful or otherwise? True, she'd worked with him before, but there had been complications. That's why she'd requested a new partner, one old enough to be her father.

Jason handed her a tray, his hand on the small of her back as he guided her to the line. "Well, don't get so excited, Grace," he said sourly. "You might set your balance off."

She licked her lips, remembering the two years they had shared an apartment, a life. "Jason, I appreciate the offer, but us working together might not be such a good idea. I can get Zach on my own. We understand each other."

"Yes, I see that," Jason muttered as he reached in front of her, setting a bowl of onion soup on her tray, following it up with four pieces of bread. "I thought we did good together. Here. You're going to need this."

She flushed. "I can't burn through that many calories in one day," she said, even as her stomach growled.

"You will today," he said cryptically, and then, as if unable to contain himself any longer, he blurted, "Grace, Zach is the oldest unregistered throw found since you were collected at seventeen. We know throws who mature naturally like you and Zach are substantially stronger, but their control usually sucks and we have to deadhead them to remove their abilities. Zach is the exception, like you, and if you can successfully bring him in and convince him to work within the Strand's framework, I think you might get that promotion to the elite you've been looking for."

She turned, her heart pounding. The elite? It was what she wanted. What she had aimed for since entering the Strand, welcoming the peace and order it represented.

Seeing her understanding, he nodded, beaming as he put an extra large orange juice on her tray. "Move down, will you? I can't reach those meat tarts. It's high time you joined the elite. Overdue if you ask me. Your skills are top-notch, and control unquestioned. If you wouldn't do stupid stunts like almost killing yourself to save a dog, you'd probably be my superior by now."

Grace stopped, her feet becoming one with the floor. *Stupid stunts? Saving my dog is a stupid stunt?*

"We've got a busy day, you and me," he was saying as he filled his own tray. "I've already been over Zach's paperwork, but I think it would be prudent to do a few team-building exercises to be sure we can modulate easily before we go out. Since you've been in contact with him before, I might be the better choice for going in vanguard, but it's your call."

Her call? Her eyes narrowed. "Saving my dog was not a stupid stunt," she said, conscious that the conversations at the nearby tables had gone silent. "Hoc is my partner as much as Boyd was. Is."

The lights over the food flickered. Jason noted it, frowning. "This is your last chance at getting into the elite, Grace. I'm doing you a favor."

Ticked, she shoved the tray at him, and he took it, stumbling. "I don't need your favors. See you around."

There was a clatter as he put her tray next to his on the counter. "I don't understand you," he said loudly. "I'm giving you a chance to prove yourself. You're not young anymore, Grace. No one over twenty-five has ever been admitted to the elite. Don't you want to do something important with your life?"

Grace stopped. Hoc stood at her heel, the dog cowering as if she'd yelled him. She wanted a chance to prove herself so bad that she could taste it, but she wanted to earn it on her own merits, not buy it with a lie. Part of her job as a collector was evaluating a throw's moral makeup, her words counting heavily on the question of whether an older, unregistered throw should be trained or have his or her abilities burned out of him or her for the safety of society. Zach was powerful, yes, and control could be learned, but she feared he had no sense of duty to himself or those he loved, that he would take what they taught him and use it for his own gain.

If she collected Zach and passed him into the Strand at the will of the elite, it would assure her place among them. If she decided he was unrecoverable and advised him to be deadheaded, she would lose her last chance to become what she most wanted.

"I *am* doing something important," she said, every eye in the room on her. "Working with Boyd was not a *mistake*. Saving Hoc was not a *mistake*. That dog is my partner, more than you'll ever be."

The lights flickered overhead. Still standing where she'd left him, he crossed his arms over his chest. People were fidgeting, their own balances being pulled out of whack. "Your emotions are betraying you."

Not even looking at her monitor, she stomped back over to him. His face lost all expression and he loosened his arms, but all she did was push her sleeve up and shove her wrist under his nose. "My balance is perfect," she said softly. "Maybe you should try wearing one of these yourself."

Her tone was bitter, and his face softened, even as he glanced at it. "Don't walk away from me. If you don't do this, you'll be bringing in unregistered throws the rest of your life."

"It's what I'm good at," she said bitterly, seeing the awful choice he had given her. "You can take your elitist job and shove it," she said, trembling. "I'd rather work alone with dogs than with your pack of overgrown boys who think the rules don't apply to them."

He reached for her, and she backed away at the anger in his expression. Spinning on a heel, she walked out, pace fast and Hoc at her side.

"Grace!" he shouted as she pulled the door open, feeling the weight of it all the way to her bones.

She let the door slam, reaching out and snapping the electricity flow like a rubber band. A startled cry rose up from a handful of people, and the lights went out.

She'd done it intentionally, and her balance, she noted bitterly, was perfect—even if her insides were churning like storm waters.

She could lie and be rewarded, or be truthful and remain where she was, and it pissed her off that she was even tempted.

 THREE

Grace found herself listening for Boyd's footsteps as she reluctantly walked up the cobbled walk to the peaceful slice of suburbia hiding its shame and misery behind lush green lawns and environmentally friendly recycle bins. Behind her, Hoc whined through the open window, the obedient dog staying where she told him. He was not coming in until she knew Zach wasn't there. It felt odd without her partner, and her arms swung stiffly. She wished that Boyd would be coming back from the Island, but once you started to boost, you came to depend on it—making it a hundred times harder to maintain your balance. That Zach wasn't an addict already was a miracle. But then again, if he had been, they would have found him a lot sooner.

Grace pushed the doorbell, hearing it ring. She was angry at Boyd for being weak, angry at Jason for his choice that wasn't one, but most of all she was disillusioned by the Strand's policies. If by some miracle Zach was morally suited for great power, her choice would be easy, but after nearly half a decade of bringing in older unregistered throws, she knew the chances were almost nil. There was a reason the Strand worked hard to find throws in kindergarten. Morality was best taught early.

Brainwashed? she wondered as she listened to the footsteps approach. Perhaps, but the alternative was allowing a small but powerful demographic of people to abuse the rest until the majority rebelled, killing them all, the good along with the bad.

Hearing the steps behind the door falter, Grace rang the bell again, tired.

"I told you he's not here. Go away!" Mrs. Thomson shouted through the door, and Grace pulled herself straight.

She had to try. Maybe Zach was the exception. "Mrs. Thomson? Please, I just want to talk."

"I said go away!" the frustrated woman all but screamed, making Grace even more tired.

"Zach put my partner in the hospital. He's okay. I thought you might want to know." She hesitated, motioning Hoc to stay where he was, and the dog's ears drooped. "I know Zach's a good boy," she said, hoping it was true. "He reminds me of me when I was found. It was hell."

Uneasy, she tugged her uniform straight as she turned to face the street. "I want to help Zach," she said, feeling a twinge of doubt and guilt. "I'm sorry, Mrs. Thomson. It's going to go harder on him if I can't bring him in today. The next people coming out here will . . . not be understanding."

Depressed, she took a step down, Hoc's tail waving as the door cracked open behind her. Grace didn't smile. She'd come out here hoping to find that Zach was morally sound, but a part of her wanted the boy to rot in hell for trying to kill her dog.

"Someone was here already this morning," Mrs. Thomson said, her voice trembling, and Grace turned.

"Here? Already?" she said, and the scared woman opened the door a little more.

"A sandy-haired man. Your age, your height. Thin, like my Zach. He was alone, but I knew it was one of you. His coat had silver in it and his hat had a triton on it."

"Jason?"

Hoc whined at hearing the man's name, and the woman came halfway out onto the shady porch. "He said his name was Stanton."

Grace turned all the way around. Jason. She glanced back at her car, a hundred options going through her mind. "Can I come in?" she asked, and the woman withdrew, her head down. "Mrs. Thomson, you don't want Jason to bring your son in. He's a lying bastard." Not to mention he would pass him into the Strand for the promotion.

"There is nothing wrong with my son!" the woman said, then dropped her eyes again.

Nodding her agreement, Grace crossed her arms over her chest and leaned back against the post holding up the porch's roof. "My grandmother realized what I could do when I was three," Grace said softly, her voice distant in memory. "Ten years after the poles flipped and everything fell apart. She said there was nothing wrong with me, too. She gave me a big girl's watch for my birthday that year. It was a secret between us. Even my mom and dad didn't know. I broke it the first fifteen minutes I had it on, and she gave me another just like it to hide what I'd done."

Grace looked down at her far more complicated timepiece, smiling as she remembered. Her grandmother was one smart woman. "That second watch lasted three days, and she gave me another. By the end of the month, I wasn't breaking them anymore, just slowing them down. It helped, finding that control. Having a secret. I loved my grandma. Still do."

Guilt tightened her jaw, and she shoved the memory of casseroles and well-meaning neighbors away. "I watched three kids make a lightbulb glow the following year in prekindergarten," she said. "The teachers made it into a game. Made the kids who could do it feel special. They couldn't make the bulb glow the next year after summer vacation."

She turned back to the house, seeing that the woman was listening. They didn't use the lightbulb test anymore. Too many kids like her had been coached to feign ignorance. "My mom might have guessed. My dad, probably not. I don't know. They died when I was sixteen." Her hands fisted, and she forced them to open. It was the year before she'd been collected.

"Mrs. Thomson," she pleaded, shoving her guilt aside, "Zach needs professional instruction. If he wants to go through the rigors of training, he can, and there will always be a job for him. If not, they will safely burn the ability from him and he can return to you otherwise unchanged. He can't be allowed to remain as he is. It's not safe for him *or* anyone else."

Damn the Strand. She was going to do her job. *Wasn't I?*

"They'll chip him," the woman said sullenly, as if anyone really had any freedom.

Grace lifted a shoulder and let it fall. "Any form of ungrounded GPS wouldn't last thirty seconds. It's easier to find us with our cell phones."

"Brainwash him," the woman said, still hiding behind the door.

"Why?" Of all the urban legends, this was the hardest one to dispel, the easiest to believe, probably because it was somewhat true with those under the age of five. They didn't bother trying with anyone older, just deadheaded them if they were unsuitable and let them go home. "If he doesn't want to develop his abilities and control, he's free to go without them."

"They will butcher him!" she almost hissed, as if Grace was betraying her own kind. "Strip him of what he can do if he refuses to work for the Strand. There is nothing wrong with my son!"

Grace nodded. "I agree. But you don't give a man who shows no restraint a gun full of bullets. It's a sucky system, but it's the only one we have." Coming up a step, Grace blinked as she found the shade. "Without control and regulation, throws like Zach and me would be hunted and killed like witches in the 1800s." There'd been a class at the Strand promoting the theory that witchcraft scares had been caused by natural dips in the earth's magnetic field, brief instabilities that triggered an aberration in the human genome that wouldn't fully express itself until the poles flipped.

"Zach has control," Mrs. Thomson said, but Grace heard her voice softening. She wanted the best for her son; she was just afraid.

"He attacked my partner, Mrs. Thomson. It wasn't an accident, but we forgive a lot in the name of fear and ignorance. He's not beyond acceptance. Let me help him. He's scared. He doesn't need to be." No need to bring up that her son had stopped her dog's heart. Killing a dog wasn't a punishable crime, even if it was reprehensible. It would, however, enter into her own private deliberations, and she clenched her jaw. *Damn Jason, anyway...*

The woman before her dropped her gaze, her brow furrowed and her feet shifting in agitation. Her head came up, a dangerous light in her eyes. "Promise me."

Grace's expression blanked. "Promise you what?"

The woman came out, still holding the door as if she might dart back

inside. "Promise me you won't let anyone hurt him. You said you understand him. He's only seventeen. He's just a boy!"

She had been seventeen when they'd found her, backed into a corner
like a wild thing spewing threats. It had taken three of them to bring her
down. That she hadn't hurt anyone had been a miracle—and the only
reason they gave her a chance—the only reason they wanted Zach now.
"I'll do my best. It's up to him."

Oh God. The best for him, the best for her, the best for the Strand. It
was not going to add up to an easy sum. Someone was going to lose, and
Grace's pulse hammered when the woman edged out, her tired, weary gaze
on the stacks of the distant industrial field. "He's with his friends," she
said. "Over at the gravel pit. It's about five minutes—"

Grace was already moving. "I know where it is. Thank you." A brief
thought flitted through her that she should give the scared woman a hug—
or at the very least, a handshake—but she was already down the stairs, her
insulated boots hitting the cobbled walk.

"Wait! Ms. Evans?" Grace turned, impatient to be away, and the
woman came out onto the porch. "Is your mother proud of you?"

Grace stiffened as she turned. "My mother is dead," she said, forcing
her breathing to remain even. "But she would be. I think."

Her head down, she walked back to the car, her first flush of excitement
of possibly bringing Zach in and gaining entry into the elite tarnished. Hoc
was in the front seat, and she halted, tension slamming into her when she
noticed Jason sitting behind the wheel.

"What are you doing here?" she said tightly, conscious of Zach's mom
watching from the porch. "This is still my collection."

"I'm trying to help you," he said, shoving Hoc to get the dog to jump
into the back so he could lean across the seat and peer up at her. The silver
on his uniform glinted, and his cap was on the dash. "I knew you could get
her to tell you where he is. Get in."

She frowned, not reaching for the handle. There was a simple pair
of mitten-like mufflers on the front seat and a bang-go, a crass name for
the complex techno device that interfered with the ability to organize the
energy in your body once imbedded into your skin where you couldn't

easily reach it. "Those aren't legal on unregistered throws," she said, and he shrugged and started the car.

"They are for me." He looked up at her, his eyes tired. "He tried to kill your dog, Grace. Going after him alone is a bad idea. I can make a call and shut you down in three seconds, but no. I'm sitting in your car trying to help you. Get in before she calls her son and he runs."

Gut tight, Grace reached for the handle. She slid in, feeling his presence. "Gravel pit," she said shortly, and Jason snorted.

"Figures." He put the car in motion, making a slow U-turn. The woman was gone when they turned around, and Hoc settled himself in the backseat, mournfully watching her.

Grace stared at nothing, putting her elbow on the open window to feel the air in her hair and on her hand. It brushed against her, and she relaxed as the balance in her shifted as the wind pulled electrons from her. "When we get there, I want you to stay in the car."

"Okay."

Astonished, Grace pulled her elbow in and stared at him. "Okay? You're not going to argue with me?"

Jason was silent. He squinted at the red light down the road, and a car coming from the right jerked to a noisy halt when the light changed unexpectedly. Grace's eyes narrowed at the questionable use of power. His chin was higher than usual, and his finger twitched.

"I'm not going to pass him into the Strand if he's not suitable," she said, wondering if she could force Jason to leave. If he was there at the collection, his words would be heard at the hearing and what she said might not matter. Besides, there was a reason Jason had moved into the elite and she'd gone into the more delicate task of bringing in older, unregistered throws. He was far more willing to shoot first, shoot second, and forget there was a question at all.

"The Strand wants more powerful throws in its elite, Grace," he offered cryptically, going through the intersection at a cool sixty miles per hour, the sleek black car looking enough like a cop's to avoid complications. "They're going to get them one way or another." He glanced from the road and tossed her his cover. "Here, try it on."

He wasn't talking about just the hat, and she caught it with one hand. The metal in the band felt like tinfoil on her teeth, and she set it on the dash, angry at the decision she faced. "No thanks. I'm good."

Jason said nothing, his grip on the wheel tightening and letting go. Feeling ugly inside, Grace glanced at the bang-go between them, remembering the feeling of it, the disorientation, the headache. It had been hell—and it hadn't done a thing in convincing her that the Strand hadn't been lying bastards. Maybe her seventeen-year-old self had been right all along. But Zach was coming in one way or another. If the Strand wanted him, they would have him. Why not help herself out in the process?

Just the thought made her lips turn down, a sick feeling cramping her gut. She'd spent the first half of her life hiding, the second glorying in her freedom. She wanted more, not less.

Jason made a slow turn, his silence familiar. It had bugged her when they were dating, and it bugged her now. "I'll stay in the car if you want," he said, perfectly in control, perfectly reasonable. "But it's stupid to go out alone. Hoc can't call 911."

Her fingers drummed once on the roof of the car. She had a fool's hope that Zach would be cooperative, make both of their lives easier. So far, she'd managed to convince his mom everything would end happy. Zach would probably not go along with it. A fairy-tale hope had her out here. A fairy-tale hero was what she needed.

"You'll wait in the car?" she said, and he stared at her, his expression giving nothing away. "Let my voice be the only one raised at his placement trial?"

"If that's what you want me to do."

A quiver ran through her. A part of her wanted him to be there. He'd speak favorably for Zach, freeing her to say the truth and still allow the Strand to have their way. Grace stared out the window, the heat rushing over her as she quietly panicked.

Suburbia had given away to a dusty, hard-packed road running straight through a young-sapling forest out to the gravel pit. The sound of insects rushed over her as the memory of working with Jason rose through her. There had been twenty of them in the high-needs class, doing mostly team-trust exercises to develop the skills to meld one's energies with some-one else's. She and Jason had melded easily. It had taken two weeks of prac-tice to harmonize her erg wavelengths to Boyd's. You could have a partner that you never melded with, but being able to was a huge advantage.

They bumped over a rut, and Grace caught the edge of the window.

"You got quiet," Jason prompted, driving with one hand, and she shrugged. He looked different even if he was still wearing his uniform—casual, relaxed. She knew he wasn't. He was tighter than a piano string, the faint energy lifting from him making her skin prickle and her watch tick a shade too fast. His control had always sucked.

"I was remembering coming into the Strand scared and full of the lies they tell about us."

Jason chuckled. "I was terrified they were going to cut my balls off."

That got her to smile. "That most throws have families didn't mean anything to you?" she said, and he put both hands on the wheel.

"It's easier to believe the scary stuff."

Grace's smile faded. "He reminds me too much of me," she said with a sigh. The gravel pit swung into view, abandoned and holding green water.

"I know. What are you going to do, Grace?"

Grace tightened her watchband. "My job."

"Fine, throw your career away," he said, jaw tight as he turned to the silent cutting building. There were three dented, late-model cars already there. Tall grass grew up next to the three-story building, broken mortar and graffiti marring its surface. "Still want me to stay in the car?" he asked as he swung around and parked so that he had a clear shot out the only entrance.

Grace listened to the car's engine tick as it cooled. Hoc sat up on the seat, his ears pricked. The wind brushed her face to bring a clay smell to her. Saying nothing, she got out, slapping her thigh to bring Hoc to her. Three cars could hold a lot of angry friends. "No."

"Good."

She jumped when Jason slammed his door, and she pushed her own door shut hard in a show of bravado. A face showed and vanished at a dusty second-story window, and her pulse thudded. Jason was looking up at it, squinting before he reached back in the car and put his cap on. It turned him from a good old boy to a cop. Doubt slithered through her. She was not going to kid herself that the Strand chose their collectors solely on ability. She was good at her job because she and Boyd looked harmless. Jason had attitude, and it wouldn't mix with whatever was in that building.

"Jason . . ."

He jerked, and they both turned at the sound of grit scraping. Zach was standing at the door, three young men his age behind him. Frowning, Grace pushed Jason out of her mind. Forcing her shoulders down, she tossed her hair behind her shoulder and told Hoc to stay.

"Your mom told me where you were," she said as she came forward, hoping Jason didn't move from beside the car's front door. "I just want to talk."

Jason snorted. "That ought to do it, Grace."

Scowling, and she remembered why she'd requested not to work with him. "She's worried about you, Zach," she said, stopping ten feet before him. "She has every right to be. I've been exactly where you are right now. I know you're scared."

It was the wrong thing to say, and the electrical balance in the air shifted as Zach's expression turned ugly. "Get the hell out of here!" he shouted, gesturing, and Jason jerked his hand off the roof of the car. The smell of burning rubber rose up, and Hoc whined, feeling the large disturbance. "I'm not scared of you!" Zach exclaimed.

Grace stifled a jerk when the headlamps exploded in a superheated burst. It was hard to learn how to throw energy, but the car was a big sink, and she wasn't as impressed as his friends, hooting and giving each other high fives behind him. The outflow had the sharp feel of caffeine, and her doubt grew.

"Then come out and talk to me, big man," she taunted, drawing on four years of dealing with scared adolescents who thought they knew everything.

Behind her, Jason leaned against the car to ground it through the metal in his trousers and the metallic toe clip on his shoes. "Okay," he said as he squinted up at the sun. "I take it back. You're pretty good at this."

Grace's smile lasted all of three seconds as Zach pushed his way into the parking lot, the three guys swaggering out behind him. One had a pipe, the other a pool stick, the third, a length of chain that he dramatically wrapped around his fist. Zach's hands looked stiff—not good.

"Ah . . ." Jason pushed up from the car, immediately becoming a threat.

Grace motioned Hoc to stand down. Four against three. Not bad odds. Part of her job was to scare a potential initiate into a last desperate act to evaluate them at their worst. Zach wasn't there yet, but he was close. She had to get him alone. "You and Hoc get the norms, I'll get the throw."

"Okay." His voice was unsure, and she smiled. He was worried about her. Perhaps working with him—just this last time—might be just the thing to get him to grow up.

Focusing on Zach, Grace pushed the sight of the three angry men behind him out of her thoughts. Zach was looking at Hoc, a whisper of doubt marring his teenage superiority complex. "I started his heart back up," she said, dropping her hand onto the dog's head. "He never even knew he was down. My partner is okay, too. Just taking a few days off. It's okay, Zach. All the best operatives run. There's a place for you, if you'd relax and listen."

As she expected, Jason edged away from her, mirroring the three guys looking eager for a fight. Zach was left alone, and he cocked his hip. "You ran?" he said in disbelief, shaking his too-long hair out of his eyes.

"Across four state lines," Jason offered, shifting his weight to find his balance. He was itching for a fight, and Grace wondered if she should have told him to take it easy on the three guys. "Taking her down shut off six square miles of grid."

Grace flushed. "It was three state lines," she muttered. "Zach, give me a chance."

The kid flicked his eyes over the dusty car, then his buddies. "It's just the two of you?" he said, discounting Hoc completely.

A tingle of adrenaline went through her. He wasn't going to make this easy. She would have to play this all the way to the end.

"Mistake," the guy with the pipe said, smiling stupidly, and his buddies laughed.

The thin tracing of energy from Zach prickled along her soul. Deflecting it into the car, she leisurely came forward as Jason dramatically gestured for the norms to come at him. Unaware that she'd shifted his focus, Zach sent a blast of heat through his trace. Behind her, the car's electrical system shorted out in a flash of sparks. Used to it, Hoc still cowered. Zach froze, shocked, and Grace shook her head.

"You're good," she said, focused on him. "Got a lot to learn, though."

Jason grunted. Just within her peripheral sight, she saw the three go at Jason in a seemingly unfair fight. Pipe high over his head, one came at him, screaming. Jason sidestepped him, touching the back of his neck in passing. Grace's field shivered, and the man dropped, out cold. Seeing him down, the guy with the chain yelled and came forward, only to get Jason's shoe in his gut—the Strand's martial arts training standing him in good stead. The third man with the pool stick was harder, and Jason spun in an elegant turn, blocking the man's first strike and downing him with an electric-supported jab to the kidneys.

"Get him!" Zach exclaimed, and the guy with the chain staggered to his feet. Head hanging, he came at Jason, the chain whirling. Grace winced when Jason reached for it, the chain wrapping his hand and probably bruising if not breaking a knuckle or two. Thinking he had him, the man grinned and yanked Jason forward into what would be a bear hug.

His face grim, Jason went, but the man was falling even as his arms reached for him, his mind shocked into a temporary state of nonfunctioning through the chain itself. "Damn, that hurt!" Jason said half to himself as he was almost pulled down by the man, shaking his hand to disentangle the chain from himself.

All through this, Grace kept moving forward, Hoc at her heel. Zach stared as the last of his buddies fell. She shrugged and held out her hand as his eyes came to her. "It's up to you, Zach. Ready to grow up and find out how powerful you are, or do you want to stay here and impress your friends with making the lights glow and warming up their beer?"

Zach took one gasping breath of air. Hoc jerked when he turned and ran back into the building, and Grace grabbed his ruff, stopping him. Fine. She could use a little stretching of her legs.

"Stay," she said, letting go. "You too, Jason!" she shouted, her adrenaline pounding through her as she jolted into motion, following the panicking kid.

"Are you serious?" Jason shouted from outside, but she had halted just inside the door. It was dark and chilly, the thick walls keeping out the heat. There was more graffiti, and the place smelled like urine. Sun spilled in the far side where huge bays gaped open to where the granite had been brought in to be cut, and a scuff pulled her eyes to the stairway snaking up to the roof.

"Run from me, you little ant piss," she muttered, angry now as she took off after him. She thundered up the metal staircase, blowing into a heated fog Zach had made from the water spilled through the ceiling.

"Nice!" she shouted at him, listening to his running steps as she gently warmed the mist until it rose. "I'm telling you, Zach, you're a natural at this, probably get yourself into the elite. What I'm wondering is why you're still running from six months of flirting with girls just like you. You aren't alone. It's an entirely new world. Damn it, will you stop for a minute?" She hesitated at the top of the stairs, not wanting to run into a nasty surprise in the next room.

"I like my old one!" he shouted, and she nodded. Third office on the left.

"Then you can come back to it," she said, catching her breath as she inched down the hall.

"After you burn me!" he screamed. Zach was trapped with nowhere to go, and he knew it. His subconscious was fighting against him, putting him somewhere he couldn't run from. She'd done the same thing after two weeks of hiding. She liked her life, but something in her still wondered what might have happened if she had just kept running.

"I can't argue with you," she said softly, knowing he could hear her when his feet scuffed from the third room. "If you aren't honest with them, they're going to burn every last nanometer of brain that can throw energy. Why would you want to do that? We're not the enemy."

Senses alert, she peeked into the next room. It was empty. She stared at the wide window and the drop beyond. *Had he jumped?*

A soft pad of feet behind her was too small a warning, and she cried out when he hit her from behind, instinct shifting her erg balance until his blast of energy faltered and died. She managed to turn as she fell, and she hit the floor hard, her breath knocked out of her as Zach landed, pinning her there.

"I'm going to kill you," he snarled, his eyes wide, panic making him face drawn and ugly. "I'm going to kill you and anyone else they send after me. You'll never find me!"

Her breath finally came in. Eyes narrowed, she wiggled, finding he had pinned her securely. She couldn't move. She wouldn't have to. "Wrong on all three counts," she said, her back hurting. "I'm sorry, Zach. I did try."

Teeth clenched, he flooded her with energy, trying to stop her heart.

Expecting it, Grace nevertheless gasped, her heart pounding and her head exploding in pain. Lungs on fire, she felt the waves of his energy coursing through her, going askance to her own rhythm. The discordant flow crested, worsened, and she struggled to match it, feeling her body start to warm and the tiny capillaries in her lungs begin to explode.

The pain of that galvanized her, and aching, she began to shift the balance of her body to match his, equal the pressure he was applying and match his energy flow, resonating to his own pulse. Changing hers to match his snuffed the threat and filled her with a sense of well-being, almost euphoric. As if like magic, the pain vanished. The heat in her fell to nothing, and she exhaled it in a breath of steam. Her eyes opened to find Zach's.

He stared, wide-eyed, knowing something had shifted.

If he had been schooled, he could kill her still, but he wasn't, and something in her raged as she decided she couldn't allow him entrance to the Strand, the elite be damned. She could forgive a lot in the fear collectors engendered, but he wasn't suited to the rigorous morals of the Strand. He could not be allowed to keep his talents. Damn Jason and his offer.

"Get the hell off me," she snapped, angry at herself and smacking him smartly on the cheek as she shoved him away.

"Wha-a-a?" Zach stammered as he slid three feet, shocked that he hadn't downed her.

Grace stood up, pissed. Yes, she'd promised his mother she would take care of him, but screening possible recruits was her job, damn it. It wasn't a collector's responsibility to simply bring in throws, but to scare them into the worst place they'd ever been to see the way their moral compass pointed. Now she knew. Zach would misuse his gifts, give them all a black name. She didn't care if the Strand was willing to overlook his moral faults. She wasn't.

"Trying to kill me was rude," she said as she felt her middle. Nothing felt ruptured, and the blood she spit out was probably only from broken capillaries. "You really thought you would be better than me?" Zach stared up at her, still on his ass with his legs askew. "I know everything about you, you little ant piss."

The jingle of Hoc's collar grew louder, and she shifted from the door, knowing that Jason wouldn't be far behind. He'd given her room to work—to flush her own career down the can—and now that her evaluation was done and her decision had been made, he could interfere all he wanted. It would be her testimony at his hearing, and no one else's.

Zach scooted back, his gaze darting behind her. "How did you do that?"

"Balancing your resonance to someone else's is first-year stuff," she said, edging farther into the room, knowing if he tried to flee, he'd run right into Jason. She almost hoped he would.

Zach's eyes went to the door when Hoc and Jason entered, Hoc's nails snapping on the dusty wood. Grace didn't look at either of them, shaking not from fear, but anger. She wasn't going to lie to gain entrance into the elite. Jason could suck eggs and die. They all could.

"You are a limp-dick, rude little boy," she said, hands on her hips. "I could have taken you in standing up, walking beside me free and unfettered to learn how to control the gifts that the universe gave you, but no. You have to go and try to kill me." She leaned over him. "I'm going to personally see that you get every last erg-sensitive synapse burned out of your thick skull."

White faced, Zach scrambled up and put his back to the wall. His eyes darted to the three-story drop out the window, then to Jason standing at the door. Jason sighed, making her face burn. Telling an unregistered throw what his or her fate was before the formal trial was a mistake, but she wanted Jason to know she thought he was scum. She would not lie for them.

"Grace . . ." Jason pleaded.

"Go screw yourself," she snarled. "Both of you." Hoc slunk to hide behind Grace, knowing she was unhappy. Ticked, Grace felt the small of her back, thinking a massage might be in order after she visited Boyd and told him how scummy the elite were, drowning their joined sorrows in pretending both their worlds weren't collapsing. She had thought the Strand was beautiful, pure. But it was as corrupt as everything else in the world.

"You. Out," she demanded, her head pounding when she spun a wad of energy out of her cells and shoved it into her hand to make the air around it glow like St. Elmo's fire.

Zach's eyes widened. His shoulders slumping, he edged past Jason. Jason reached out to grab his arm, and Zach spun, making Hoc yip and skitter sideways. There was a flash of silver, and Jason grabbed Zach's hand now pressed into his side, the knife in his fist already deep in Jason's ribs. "You'll have to kill me to take me in!" the kid shouted. "You're all brainwashed bastards!"

Shocked, Grace reached out, and Jason screamed as Zach flooded him with another burst of energy, the knife sunk deep into him and bypassing his grounding cloth.

"No!" Grace cried, yanking Zach off Jason. Her hands burned as she flung him across the room, hearing him hit the floor as she struggled under Jason's weight, trying to get him to the floor. The clatter of the knife was loud, and Hoc's nails scraped as he ran to stand over it, snarling.

"Jason!" she shouted, cradling his head. "Oh my God, Jason!"

Wincing up at her, Jason pressed his hand into his side. "The little bastard stabbed me to get past my grounding. It's okay. He cauterized it trying to burn me." His brows furrowed. "Ow."

He was okay! The thought sang in her, and she looked at him, not caring if he knew how afraid she'd been. "Are you sure?" she asked, her first thought spinning into the hundred other ways you could die from a knife wound.

Jason sat up, shifting his hand until the flow gushed. His face went white, and he pressed it back, Grace's hand atop his. "Uhhh . . . It's not as cauterized as I thought." His eyes went behind her, and worry bunched his eyebrows.

Hand still on his, Grace turned. Hoc was standing over the knife, but he wasn't growling anymore. Zach was slumped against the wall, his legs twisted at an unusual angle, his chest utterly unmoving.

"Oh shit." She hesitated, not wanting to leave Jason, and the soldier sat up, wincing as he pushed her to go to him. Cold, Grace almost crawled across the dirty floor. In a calm panic, she felt for a pulse, pulling Zach onto his back when she found none. Her hand sticky and red with Jason's blood, she hammered at his chest, one, two, three times. Felt for a pulse. Listened for a breath than never came.

"Damn it, I didn't give him enough to stop his heart!" she cried, her own doubt keeping her head down as she searched for a pulse. "Did I?" Eyes wide, she looked across the dirty room to Jason.

Expression pained, he stared at her. Panicking, she looked back at Zach, the color already draining from his face "Shit, shit, shit!" she whispered as she looked to make sure that she wasn't touching him, and pushed her sleeves up, preparing to shock him back to life as she had Hoc.

"Grace, wait!" Jason said, and she jumped when his hand hit her shoulder and she spun to see him standing over her, listing somewhat with his hand pressed to his side. "It's too late. Grace, it's too late!"

"No, it isn't!" She hadn't meant to kill him. Had she? The brat had killed her dog, ruined her partner's career. Tried to kill her. Stabbed the one man she had thought she could love . . .

"Stop!"

Hand pressed into his side, Jason stood across from Zach, pity in his eyes. "Listen to his ergs. He's gone. I think I did it, Grace. It was me, not you. He was dead before you pulled him off me."

Grace fell back on her heels, staring up at him, wanting to believe but knowing Zach had been alive when she'd pulled him off Jason.

"I killed him." Jason couldn't look at her. "It's my job, fighting hand to hand. It was instinct. I'm sorry."

His head came up, and she felt like he had kicked her in the gut. *Was he lying?*

"This was my fault." He shifted his bloody hand to gauge the bleeding, pressed it back, and leaned against the wall. "Can you call me an ambulance? I don't feel so good and I think the car's shorted out for good."

Numb, Grace felt for her phone, having to make the call three times before the link would hold long enough. Her balance was off. They wouldn't let her ride in the ambulance if she couldn't master it between now and then.

"It wasn't your fault," he whispered as he sank to the floor, propped up against the wall. "It was mine. You saved my life. Please come and work with me so I have the chance to save your life in return, huh? I'll never live this down. Stabbed by a damn kid."

She closed the phone, her fingers shaking. Zach was dead on the floor, his face going as pale as Jason's. "I can't," she said, but not for the reason he thought.

"Why?" he whispered, wincing as his fingers moved, and she looked away, going to the window to look for the ambulance.

Because I love you, and I will kill for you. I don't want to be that person.

But she couldn't say it aloud.

 FOUR

The sun was bright, and Grace squinted as she strode toward the Strand's tower. She felt alone without Hoc, but taking him back into the hospital to visit Boyd would make her stand out, and standing out was the last thing she wanted today. She was depressed, her failure with Zach weighing heavily on her. They hadn't allowed her into the room when they told his mother what had happened, but she'd been down the hall and heard her anguish. Every word the woman had said was true. It was a shitty place to be.

Squaring her shoulders, Grace paused at the crosswalk for a slow-moving van. When it passed, she started across, her pace bobbling when she saw Jason waiting for her just outside the twin glass doors. He was dressed in full military blues, the light sending glimmers of shine from the silver threads in his cap and the metallic toe points as he slowly pushed up from the planter he had been leaning against. There was a plastic-covered coat with a feminine cut lying beside him, a matching cover with the elite's triton lying atop it.

"You look great," she said as she stepped up onto the curb, and he smiled, taking off his sunglasses and tucking them away. "They have you back on duty already?"

He shrugged, touching his side and wincing. "Limited duty."

Her gaze touched on the jacket and cap, then came back to him. "I'm here to see Boyd. He's gone, isn't he," she said, making it into a statement. Why else would Jason be here?

Sure enough, the man's smile faded. Behind her, Grace listened to little-girl complaints as a harried mother ushered her child inside. *To get her tested, or to visit their injured father?*

"Grace, I'm sorry. I'm the only one who knows you were going to deadhead him. You can still enter the elite. Just tell them you were going to pass him."

Arms around her middle, Grace looked up at the blue sky, squinting at the light. "No." She'd rather stay where she was than work with people she couldn't trust. She wasn't sure what she was going to do now. Balance. She had no balance. Boyd was gone, her job in doubt. Nothing made sense anymore. She was at a crossroads, and she couldn't see through the fog.

"Is that your last word then?" Jason asked tightly, and she nodded.

He sighed, seeming to relax as he looked at his watch. "Do you have the right time?" he asked, seemingly out of the blue.

Her teeth clenched, and she forced them apart as she thought of her day, stretching long and alone. "Yes, of course," she said, knowing that her erg balance, at least, was spot on.

"And what time would that be?"

The hint of eagerness in his voice pulled her attention down.

Mistrusting this, she glanced at her watch. "Nine twenty-eight." Visiting hours started at nine-thirty. She had known Boyd was leaving today, just not when. To be early had seemed prudent. Now it looked like a desperate attempt to grasp at the edges as her world was jerked out from under her.

Jason's eyes were smiling. "That's what I have, too." Carefully picking up the jacket and cap, he looped his arm in hers, turning them both back to the double glass doors. "Come on, I don't want to be late."

Grace went with him, not caring. "Late for what?"

He let go of her long enough to open the door. "You'll see," he said cryptically.

The plastic-scented air of the Strand's tower took her, shocking her out of her funk. "Jason . . ." she said, eyeing the cap.

Still smiling, he shoved the cap and jacket at her. "Hold this, will you?" he said as they halted at the elevators. She watched, her alarm growing as he ran a card through a reader, and the executive elevators at the end of the elevator bank dinged.

"The upper levels?" she said, alarmed. "I said *no*."

But he pushed her forward into it. It was only his good mood that kept her moving, kept her pliant. "Don't ruin it," he cajoled as her sneakers sank into the rich red pile.

The doors closed, and Jason scanned the bank of buttons as if unfamiliar with them, making a positive grunt when he found the one he wanted and pushed it. The lift rose, and Grace looked at him in his dress blues, perfect from his trimmed hair to his metal-tipped shoes—ribbons in between. Licking her lips, she glanced at her tatty sneakers, then the jacket she was still carrying.

Was he humming?

Her ears popped, and the doors slid open to a white-and-silver reception office. The woman behind the desk looked up, then back down at her work. "Have you ever been up here?" Jason asked as he strode confidently forward, and she obediently followed.

"Once." Her shoes were silent on the whitewashed wooden floor. The furniture was sparse, all wood, no metal. The air felt rich with ozone, soothing her jangled nerves. Windows spread along one entire side, letting the light in with an odd gray feel. They were at the top of the tower, and she felt a wash of nervousness.

Jason waved to the secretary and she nodded as if expecting them. Leaning across her desk, she buzzed them through a glass door. "Officers Stanton and Evans are here, sir," she said as Jason opened it for her, and Grace's worry grew. They were expected.

The hallway beyond was dark where the reception room was bright. Rich mahogany and lavish furniture that no one ever sat in decorated the long hallway. The electrical interference was almost nil. It should have been like wrapping herself in a fur, but instead, she grew more uncomfortable. It was nothing compared to her dismay when Jason stopped at a wide oak door. The name on it widened her eyes. *Rath Walters?* He was the head of the elite, Jason's boss and sort of hers, seeing as he could pull strings from the hospital to the Strand's elementary school.

Again she looked at Jason, comparing his sharp military bearing to her casual clothes. "Did you bring this for me?" she asked, holding up the jacket in explanation, and Jason nodded, beaming.

"I thought you'd never ask."

Her heart pounded as she ripped the plastic off and threw it into a posh-looking can that had never seen trash before. Mouth dry, she turned her back to him, and he helped her put it on, arranging her hair over the collar. The silk lining whispered over her shoulders, the silver tracings in the fabric iced over her like snowflakes. She shifted her shoulders to test the fit, then zipped it up all the way to cover her neck as Jason's jacket was. It was a perfect fit, but then they had shared a closet for years.

"And your cover," he said, frowning as he looked at her shoes. "I can't help you there, but at least the black pants don't clash."

She adjusted the cap, then took it off as Jason faced the door and knocked. She'd never met Walters but had seen him once at graduation. The man was huge, almost obese. Her thoughts darted to her decision to deadhead Zach and her refusal to pass him in to them, then his accidental death. "I'm not changing my mind," she said, frightened that Jason might try to lie for her. But it was too late. Either they were pissed that she'd thumbed her nose at them and deadheaded him, or pissed that she had killed him to avoid the conflict of morals.

"I know. That's why we're here." Jason took off his own cap when Walter's robust "Come in!" filtered out through the heavy door.

"You want to try making some sense next?" she whispered, and Jason opened the door, gesturing for her to go in first.

"You going in or not?" he prompted.

It was his eager, proud smile that convinced her, and squaring her shoulders, she exhaled and tugged her jacket down and went inside.

Walter's office continued the dark wood theme, as sophisticated and rich as the man she remembered chatting over champagne and cheese with the rest of the elites. Windows encompassed one entire side of his office, and the light coming in turned the mahogany into a rich, almost glowing red. The rather rotund man was standing before the windows, turned slightly to see them come in. Hoc was sitting at his heel.

"Hoc!" Grace exclaimed, wondering how the dog got here, then flushed. "Excuse me, sir," she said, telling Hoc to stay down with a small finger motion as the excited dog *click-clacked* his merry way to her.

"Not at all." Walter's rich voice rolled out to fill the office, as warm and dark as the wood he surrounded himself with him. "That's what I like about dogs. They don't give a fig about ribbons and bank accounts. Thank you, Jason. I appreciate you bringing Grace up. And Hoc. He's a part of this, too."

Grace's awe at where she was vanished. "I am not changing my mind," she said, wishing she was brave enough to throw the cap in her hand away.

Jason fidgeted. His smile was the only thing keeping her from storming out of here. That, and Hoc now lying on her feet, his tail thumping happily. "Hurry up, Walter," he demanded, making Grace's eyes widen at his familiarity. "I can't stand it."

The older man smiled as he came forward to sit on the edge of his desk. "So tell her! That's why you're here. Apart from the fact that you're the only one Hoc would go with—and I wanted him here for this."

Here for what?

Nodding sharply, Jason took her cold hands in his as if he was going to ask her to marry him. "Grace, the elite have their own collectors. It's not a formal position, one that we occasionally take from time to time—"

"You want me to be a collector for the elite?" she interrupted, flushing in anger. "I told you no! I am *not* going to compromise myself just so you can break and twist things to your satisfaction! Allowing Zach in would have been a grave error." She glanced at Walter, her jaw clenched. "Sir."

Hoc's waving tail slowed, and Jason's brow furrowed as he tightened his grip on her hands until she yanked away. "Will you let me finish?"

Walter shifted his bulk. "No wonder the woman refuses to work with you," he grumbled. "You're making a mess of this. Grace, Jason was evaluating you for entrance into the elite. Refusing to pass your latest, unsuitable catch into the Strand won your place with us, not the other way around."

Grace's held breath left her in a rush. Understanding crashed over her, and her knees threatened to buckle. "You lied to me?" she accused Jason, but the man was beaming at her, taking her hands again. "You told me they wanted a high-ability thrower at all costs."

"And they got one," he said, grinning. "Congratulations, Grace."

Shocked, she could do nothing. *He'd been testing me? Son of a bitch!*

"You've not been scrutinized as most of the elite's members," Walters said as he moved back behind his desk. "Most of them we've known since grade school. The idea of making you part of the elite—a young, untested woman of great power and control . . . No, we had to be sure."

Shocked, she sank down onto a chair, then bounced back up again. The elite? The chance was real? "But . . ." she said, looking frantically at Walter to see if it was a bad joke. The man was smiling, and he gestured to Jason.

"I told Walter how well you and Hoc work in a small force team, even if you did almost kill yourself starting his heart. The Strand wants to see what you and Hoc can do, so I'm taking you into my team, work you in, let you freelance Hoc as you see best. If human/dog teams have an advantage, you'll eventually head up a new group of your own." His smile widened and sparkles of familiar energy prickled through her palms though he wasn't touching her. "That is, if you want to."

Walter turned from where he had been pouring thimble-sized drafts of a dark liquid. "Welcome to the elite, Grace," he rumbled as he handed her one, then another to Jason.

She looked down at it, blinking as she realized it was coffee—the amount of which would give her a mild buzz, nothing more. The memory of Zach dead on the floor of the abandoned granite pit rose up, swamping her. "I can't," she whispered, gently setting the cap with its elite emblem down on the nearby chair. "Sir, this is an honor, but with all respect, I decline."

"Decline!" Jason exclaimed, and Walter rumbled as he backed toward the window as if wanting a better view of the two of them. "Why! It wasn't your fault that Zach died!"

At her feet, Hoc thumped his tail apologetically. Grace set her drink on the desk. "May I be excused, sir?" she barked out, her chest feeling as if it was caving in. She wanted this, and yet she had to say no.

Jason took a breath to protest, and Walter cleared his throat. "Jason, will you excuse us?" the heavy man interrupted smoothly.

Clearly frustrated, Jason eyed Grace's stiff stance and Walter's easy assurance. Ears red, he crisply set his untasted coffee on the desk beside Grace's. "Sir," he said respectfully. "Grace," he added, his tone accusing. Without another word, he spun on a heel, strode to the door, and left, shutting it softly behind him.

Grace stood stiffly, her dog miserable at her feet as she stared past Walter at the empty sky. She was in hell. What else could you call being handed everything you ever wanted and knowing you didn't deserve it?

Walter sighed heavily as he poured himself a second drink. "I love my coffee," he said idly as he took a careful sip. "Do you have any idea how hard it is to steel yourself against the very thing you want the most in the name of balance?"

"Sir," she started.

"I bet you do," he interrupted her, his tone drawing her eyes to his. Her next protest died at the deep expression of thought.

Walter sat behind his desk, the move lacking utterly in any hint of finding a dominate position. He was tired, that was all. She felt a pang of guilt that her failings yesterday had something to do with it.

"I know you want this," he said, touching the single sheet of paper on his desk, and her chest hurt when she realized it was her transfer papers. "What I don't know is why you are refusing it. Is it Boyd?" he questioned, and she shifted her shoulders. "His long-running caffeine addiction is not your failing. We knew about it. We also know that he kept it from you, quite well, actually."

Unable to stop herself, her eyes met his in a flash of guilt. He was her *partner*. She should have been able to tell. "No sir," she said truthfully. She regretted it, but it was not reason to decline a promotion.

"The death of the unregistered throw?" he asked next, and she stiffened. "I am sorry about that. Unfortunately it happens," Walter said, not pleading but with a hard tone of fact. "That you avoided it for so long is a testament to your abilities, not your failings. That you were able to make that hard decision is the reason you're being offered a position in the elite now."

Her head turned to him, and anger pushed out the guilt. As much as she regretted what happened to Zach, his death was the result of her failing, not the cause. "I want this, sir," she said, trembling as she tried to explain. "I've wanted it ever since setting a foot on the cobbles of the Strand. I want it so bad that when I walk out of this office, I am going to hate myself for a long time. It isn't because I killed Zach, sir. It's *why* I killed him."

Walter leaned back in his chair, gesturing for her to continue.

Her gut twisted. Grace closed her eyes as she took a slow breath. "I found my breaking point, sir," she said softly as they opened.

"Ahhh." She stared straight ahead, but she could see him lean even farther back, his hands laced across his ample middle. He knew what she was talking about. It was her job to find the breaking point of possible recruits, to push them to the end of their moral resources, either by fear or anger, to see if they would use their abilities to kill someone who had not struck out at them first. Jason had found hers.

"It's Jason," she said, the lump in her throat somehow not coloring her words. "Zach tried to kill him, and I overreacted." She turned to him, meeting his eyes so he would understand her failure. "Jason didn't kill him, I did. I burned out his entire brain because I love Jason. I may have passed the elite's test, but I failed in doing so."

Walter cocked his head, seemingly unconvinced. "Jason . . ."

She nodded, swallowing hard as her life crashed down around her. "I should be on the Island being evaluated, not Boyd. Rewarding me with a promotion is a travesty. With proper monitoring, I feel I can continue in perhaps a teaching capacity, but I'd ask that I be removed from my current position of collector immediately."

It was more than she deserved, but she couldn't bear to leave the Strand. It had been peace when she had been in turmoil, sanctuary when she had been lost.

"And I can't change your mind?" Walter said, his tone empty of emotion.

"No sir." Her jaw was clenched. Hoc was lying on her feet, his eyes giving her distress away. Maybe they would still let her do the preschool runs. It was unlikely she'd be provoked by four-year-olds.

Walter exhaled loudly as he leaned forward. The sound of her papers crumpling up was loud, and she stared when they flashed into flame halfway to his trashcan. He was already pulling a new form out, handwriting her new assignment. Grace's shoulders bowed in her grief as she abandoned her dream of doing anything important, of making something unique of her talent, of making a difference in the world.

"Very well then," the man said as he scratched and scrawled, using his left hand. "They say the practitioner knows his or her limits. There will be a lot of people sorry to see you go."

"Thank you, sir," she said, her heart breaking. She'd wanted to work in the elite ever since walking through the arches and into the peace of the Strand, had envied Jason when he reached the elite's halls before her, and for one brief moment, had felt the joy of having a chance to do what she wanted. She'd still be a part of what the Strand stood for. She could teach and not be a threat to those around her. It wasn't what she wanted, but it would be something. Her grandmother would be pleased—she'd be free now to start a family.

Grace's gut clenched as she wondered if that was what she wanted. It didn't feel like it.

The sound of the paper sliding across the desk brought her eyes down, and Grace took it automatically as Walter stood. "You have three days until you are required to take on your new duties. Is that enough to get your and Hoc's affairs in order?"

"Yes, sir. And thank you, sir," she said, not looking at it, ashamed for her demotion even as she had asked for it.

And still, he did not release her. "Did you know that you are the oldest recruit the Strand has ever allowed to remain unburned?" he said, turning to the window with his tiny thimble of coffee. "You entire career has been scrutinized, your actions weighed more carefully than anyone else's. You were very nearly burned out twice, once when we found you, once in the middle of your training. But wiser heads held off because with all the anger, all the fear you have worked through, you never tried to hurt anyone."

"Thank you, sir. I appreciate that. But perhaps I should have been."

Walter turned, not a hint of a smile on him. "The elite kill, Grace. Jason kills. I killed." His expression hardened. "We are soldiers. Soldiers kill."

"You don't kill innocents," she whispered.

"Was Zach innocent?" he barked, and she jumped, making Hoc cower. "I say no. Don't confuse youth with innocence. You have balance. You have control. You will not be *allowed* to quit."

"Sir?"

"Look at your orders. Look at it!"

Nervous, Grace looked, her clenched jaw loosening. It still held the elite's stamp.

"Bright and early, Grace." Walter came forward from around the desk, his mood shifting completely. "Testing of the Strand's own never ends. Ever," he said as he put a hand on her shoulder. "And bring that dog with you. I still want to know how far you and he can go together."

"But I failed!" she exclaimed, not understanding.

He was smiling as he handed her that same tiny cup. "I don't see it that way. You know why you broke. You have determined that it should never happen again, taken steps to prevent it. That is a sign of maturity, not wanton disregard of life."

The paper in her hand drooped. "This is entry into the elite's fighting force. I'm a risk."

Walter took the paper before it fell, folding it in thirds. "We all are, Grace. The Strand is an illusion of fences and security so that those who can't throw may feel safe. We do the best we can by removing the ability from those who would clearly use it for ill gain. We shift the fate of those we reach with early education. But we are people, and people make choices. Make mistakes. Besides . . ." He handed the folded paper to her, and she took it. "Jason's team isn't the only one on the cobbles. If you curtail your relationship to one entirely outside of work, I don't know why your control should be suspect. As I recall, your balance was never compromised during the entire acquisition."

Grace blinked, remembering. No, her balance had never bobbled for even a microsecond. She had been in complete control, even as she had killed Zach.

Hope flashed through her. "Don't tell him why," she blurted, then flushed.

"Don't tell Jason that you love him?" Walter chuckled as he picked up her cap. "You don't think he already knows?"

Grace lifted her chin. "Don't tell him that I broke because of him. I can't . . ."

Her words cut off as Walter put a hand on her shoulder and led her to the door. "Love is strength, Grace. Don't come away from this learning the wrong lesson."

He handed her cover to her and opened the door. She went through it, desperate to make him understand. Jason waited for her at the end of the hall. She could see him in the sun, standing on the whitewashed boards, his dejection and anger clear in his stance. "Please," she begged Walter as Hoc trotted to the end of the hall to meet Jason. "Make something up—for both of us. His career and mine. I can either have a family or a career in the Strand. Not both. And I want this, sir. I want it bad enough to give everything."

Standing in the doorway to his office, Walter puffed and blew, thinking about it. "I'll tell him that Casten pulled strings and got you into his flight. You can go as far as you want under him."

Relief spilled into her, and she shook his hand, flushing in that she probably shouldn't have initiated the contact. "Thank you, sir. Thank you, very much."

The large man smiled, touching her shoulder as he gestured for her to go. "Thank you, Grace. But drop the sir. Call me Walter. It makes slogging through the muck easier."

"Yes, sir, I mean, Walter," she said, exuberant as she turned and strode down the hall. She was an elite. She was an elite, and the world was now clear. Her path chosen. She'd been given a gift and the chance to make a difference. If she let it fall to the side, everything she believed in, Boyd's sacrifice and Zach's death would be a lie.

Hoc bounced through the glass door as she opened it up. Jason waited beyond, mystified at her smile.

"What happened?" he said, and she gave him a hug, not caring that Walter was still standing at the end of the hall.

"I said yes," she breathed, then added, "But I'm not going to work with you. We're under Casten, and you watch. Hoc and I are going to head up our own division in three years." Smiling, she spun to the elevator, turning to look at him over her shoulder.

"Catch me if you can!"

My grateful thanks to Erika Thompson who helped
me keep my story straight.

Shorter chapters appearing in this collection were previously published. Copyright information is as follows:

The text called *Love* by Kim Barnes... first published in *Fourth Genre*... *Northwest*...

Bits and essays by Kathleen Dean Moore and Marilyn... first published in various...

Students'...... *Love* by David... first published in *Sojourn...*... *Inland...*... *Voice from the* 2009.

Henry Gray... by Kim Barnes... first published in *Fourth Genre*... *...* 2009.

The essay *A Bird... Part I...* by Kim Barnes... first published in... *Sojourn... Words to...* (2007).

Gathering... by Kim Barnes... first published... *Columbia University...*... *...* by Kathleen Dean Moore... first published by... *Walk...* Minneapolis 2011.